The Honey Bride

by Diana Lesire Brandmeyer

Dedication

Dedicated to Mike and Lisa Hoppe, my bee friends.

12 Historical Brides Find
Love in the
Good Old Summertime

The 12 Brides
of Summer
Collection

Mary Connealy, Margaret Brownley
Diana Lesire Brandmeyer, Amanda Cabot, Susan Page Davis,
Miralee Ferrell, Pam Hillman, Maureen Lang,
Amy Lillard, Vickie McDonough, Davalynn Spencer, Michelle Ule

BARBOUR BOOKS
An Imprint of Barbour Publishing, Inc.

Print ISBN 978-1-63409-029-2

eBook Editions:
Adobe Digital Edition (.epub) 978-1-63409-030-8
Kindle and MobiPocket Edition (.prc) 978-1-63409-028-5

Published by Barbour Books, an imprint of Barbour Publishing, Inc., P.O. Box 719, Uhrichsville, OH 44683, www.barbourbooks.com

Our mission is to publish and distribute inspirational products offering exceptional value and biblical encouragement to the masses.

Member of the
Evangelical Christian
Publishers Association

Printed in the United States of America.

Contents

Chapter 1

May 1887, Trenton, Illinois

Wind-whipped water plopped, splattered, and then moistened Katie Tucker's forehead, rousing her. Something wasn't right. She'd fallen asleep with open windows, hoping for a breeze to relieve the early summer heat. Now the wind was wicked, pulsating against the bedroom panes and blowing in rain. She sat, reached for the window, and closed it with a bang. The sky lit up once, twice. The hair on her arms stretched for heaven. *Crack.* The second story sizzled and popped. Lightning. She shivered. Was it a tornado, like the one she'd read about last month? Five people in Wabash County had died.

Papa would be yelling to go to the cellar any minute. *Please, God, not down there.* Chill-bumps raced up her arms.

Henry, her younger brother, banged against her door and called out, jarring her from the nightmare of spider webs stuck in her hair.

Had he said *fire*? In the house? The barn? Shaking, she fumbled for her wrapper, found it, then rushed her arms through the sleeves. Her shoes were by the back door. Henry waited at the bottom of the stairs.

"The barn's on fire. Papa's out there."

"Get a bucket! I'll get the stew pan. Where's Oma?"

"Sleeping."

"I'll wake her. Get as many things filled with water as you can." Henry's boots pounded sharply against the wood floor in time to her heartbeat. She needed to wake her grandmother.

Oma met her at the doorway.

"What's the yelling about?"

"Lightning started a fire in the barn. Papa is getting out the animals. I was coming to wake you."

"I'm up. Go help. I'll be there as soon as possible."

Katie hesitated. Should she insist her grandmother stay inside?

"Go, *Schatzi*. Now."

7

Her grandmother's strong words urged her feet forward and she hightailed it down the stairs for her shoes. She trembled on the bench, trying to get her shaking fingers to work her laces into place. The unnatural noises from the animals made her want to run back to bed. No matter how fearful she was she couldn't. There was work to be done.

Outside, the smoke lay heavy in the air. They needed help. The farmhand Papa hired hadn't shown up. If only they could get word to the fire department, but they were too far from town. She'd send Henry to the Gibbons'. They were the closest.

Henry worked the pump, water pouring, splashing against the bucket sides. "Where's Papa?"

"Still in there. He got Starlight out first."

"Good. Get on her, ride to the Gibbons', and tell them we need help."

"I can help."

"We need more than the three of us. Hurry. You're faster than me."

Henry ran for the horse. Katie picked up the bucket of water Henry had filled. The handles bit into her hands as she carried it to the barn. "Papa! I have water!"

"I'm here." He grabbed the bucket and ran inside. Seconds later he was back. "Fill it again. Hurry." He coughed. "Where's Henry?"

"I sent him for help." Flames licked the inside of the dry barn wood.

"They won't make it before it's burned to the ground." Her father bent over coughing. When he was able to catch his breath he handed her his kerchief. "Wet that and bring it with the next bucket. Lady Jane is still in there."

She shuddered. Lady Jane was difficult on a good day. In a fire, who knew what the horse was capable of doing.

☯

Unable to sleep, Pete Dent paced the Gibbons' barn, where he slept. The rhythm of the rain didn't bring its usual soothing. Storms didn't bother him, but this one did. Too soon, too dangerous, after the one last month. He stood in the open door and noticed Roy standing on the porch. He jogged across the yard and up the steps. "Thunder keeping you awake?"

"Scared Frances. Alma's taking care of her." Roy said.

Crack. The lightening startled both men.

"That was close. Sounded like it hit something." Roy ran to the edge of the porch.

Pete looked the other way, toward the Tucker place; Katie on his mind, again. He'd like to get to know her better. It had taken him a few months, but he'd managed to get her to smile at him at church anyway. Shy little thing. He'd been ready to pull up stakes and find another place to work when she'd caught his eye. Katie might be the one person to tip the scale and keep him in Trenton.

"Do you see that?" Roy pointed in the direction Pete stared.

"That's a bright light. Too bright. Think they got hit with that last bolt?" Pete's heart pounded. "I'm riding out. They might need help if it hit the house or barn."

"Go. I'll let Alma know and meet you."

Pete wasted no time saddling Biscuit and urging him to a gallop. As he grew closer to the Tucker's, he knew something was burning. Probably the barn with the way the flames were flicking the sky. Someone rode toward him. Katie coming for help? He slowed his horse.

"Hey, our barn's on fire. Can you help?"

"Henry, is that you?"

"Yeah, Pete. Katie told me to get you. Hurry! Papa's getting the animals out and. . . ." Henry stopped to catch his breath.

"I heard you. That's where I'm headed. Roy's behind me."

Henry turned Starlight around.

Both horses stretched into a neck and neck race for the Tucker barn.

When they arrived, the smoke was thick, but the bright flames licked through, illuminating the night, revealing Katie lugging a bucket. Pete dismounted and tied Biscuit to the porch railing. He ran to Katie and pried her fingers from the handle. "Fill another one and keep filling. I'll get them to the barn. Roy's on his way."

"Papa's in there! I can't get to him."

Cold sweat tickled down his back. If Mr. Tucker was still in that barn, the odds were he wasn't coming out. *Please, God, let her father be alive.* He ran inside, keeping low. "Mr. Tucker! Holler your position!" The roaring flames sucked his words into silence. He tossed the water on a bale of hay and ran out, gasping for air.

Katie waited with a pot of water. He took it and rushed back inside. He had to find her father.

∞

Katie sat on the back steps, hugging Henry close to her. Waiting. Most of their church congregation either stood in the yard or were in the house. Katie and Henry sat alone. She couldn't talk to anyone, not even Alma.

Pete Dent had been kind, explaining how her father probably inhaled too much smoke and couldn't breathe. He'd seen it before, serving on the volunteer fire department. He told her to take Henry inside, but she couldn't. If she left these steps, it would be real. So she clung to Henry and waited.

Tears rolled down her cheeks, bringing some relief to the sting from the smoke.

Chapter 2

A few weeks later, Katie walked head down to avoid speaking with anyone on the street. She only had to collect the mail and return home, nothing more. She'd fussed about coming into town at all, but Oma insisted, saying it was time for a letter from Katie's sister.

The warm yeasty fragrance of fried dough and sugar drifted through the bakery door. The pleasurable scent slowed her steps. Those doughnuts sure smelled good. But were they enough to risk a conversation about that awful night? Her mouth watered, and she pictured the joy on Henry's face when she gave him one. Even Oma might perk up.

Guilt squeezed her heart. Would people think it wrong of her to buy something so enjoyable so soon after the fire and her father's death? Her desire burned and then settled into ash in her mouth. Maybe next time.

She took one last deep breath and then headed for the post office. She glanced at the bakery. It was almost as if Papa were with her. She could hear him laughing about her worrying about being judged by others again. She shook him away. He might be right, but he didn't have to live with the upturned noses.

Settled with her decision, she made her way into the post office.

"Miss Tucker, it's nice to see you in town again." Mr. Rutherford, the postmaster, turned to the row of wooden boxes where mail was filed. He pulled out a few envelopes and handed them to her.

"*Danke*. Thank you, sir." She glanced at the top letter. It was from Kentucky. Oma would be pleased to hear news from her other granddaughter. She wanted to rip open the envelope, but it wasn't addressed to her. Oma would share any news with her and Henry.

The other came from a bank in Lebanon, addressed to Papa. Why would they be sending him mail? This one she could open. Maybe Papa had an account there? That would be a blessing. They needed to rebuild the barn. She scooted through the door and smacked into Pete Dent.

"Whoa! Where's the fire?"

Her breath caught, and in a flash, she was back there at the barn the night of the storm, listening to him say those awful words about Papa. Her lips moved but no sound came forth.

11

Pete's face turned the color of rhubarb. "I'm sorry, Miss Tucker, that was—"

Not waiting for the rest of his apology, Katie brushed past him, stiff and broken as the charred beams that had collapsed in on themselves in her yard.

She headed for the bakery. People may talk, but her hope was that the sweet heaviness of a doughnut would fill the crater in her heart caused from Papa's death and Pete Dent's careless words. Shoulders straight, she marched inside and asked for three doughnuts.

The bank letter lay heavy on her mind. Last fall Papa said the farm was paid for, but what if he'd borrowed money? And why did he go to Lebanon when they had a bank here? Something wasn't right. She could feel it. *Weibliche* intuition, Oma would say, a woman always knows. She'd stop at Alma's on the way home. Then if the news were truly bad, she'd have someone to pray with her. Oma wasn't strong enough to handle any more formidable news. "Please, could you wrap another half dozen?" She didn't want to arrive empty handed at the Gibbons'.

∽

Pete was an idiot. He had been waiting to speak to Katie, and his first chance he'd reminded her of the one thing she wanted to forget. As it was, the memory of her sitting on the porch, hugging Henry that night, wouldn't leave him. He knew the shape of her heart, felt it in his own. The freshness of being alone returned, almost bringing him to his knees and would've, too, if he weren't a grown man. His mind told him it wasn't the same as what had happened to him. Yes, both her parents were now dead, but she had a home and family. That had to make a difference, didn't it?

"You here for the Gibbons' mail?" Mr. Rutherford had already turned to the boxes behind him. "Just one, this time."

"Thank you, sir." Pete took the letter, a little sad there wasn't one for him. Why would there be? He had no one. Even if he did, they didn't know how to find him, since he'd shortened his name from Dentice. A clean break from the past. He'd given up finding his brother, sure by now he'd have a home and family of his own. Probably didn't even remember his old last name.

Outside, he walked to the Ginzel Mercantile, where his loaded wagon waited. Did he need anything else? The doughnuts smelled good but Alma had promised a rhubarb pie for dessert. He'd hang on to his money. Someday he'd have enough for a farm of his own. In Trenton, he hoped, if he could find someone willing to sell.

He climbed up on the wagon seat and set the horse to moving. The feeling that it was time to move on, that he didn't belong here, snuck up on him last week. It wasn't Roy's fault he'd found a wife and now had time to work on his own farm. If Pete left this town, he'd sure miss those little girls, Elsibet and Frances. They had him thinking of settling down and having children, made him feel like this town could be his home.

Pete hadn't gone far when he spotted Katie, walking. Her shoulders were rounded as if she literally carried the death of her father on them.

She moved closer to the side of the road for him to pass. Instead, he slowed the horse, and then stopped beside her. "Miss Tucker, would you care for a ride?"

Her hat barely tipped up far enough for him to see her eyes before she looked away. "Yes, I'd—"

Pete climbed out of the wagon ready to help her board before she finished her sentence.

"Thank you. You won't have to take me far. I plan to visit Alma."

"I'll be happy to see you home, after." He glanced at her. She was studying a letter.

"Good news?"

She startled, grabbing the edge of the bench seat.

"I'm sorry. I didn't know you were lost in thought."

Katie looked at him for a second. Her blue eyes were watery. What should did he do about that? Should he ask if she was crying or offer a hanky? Maybe it was dust in her eyes? There was enough of that floating in the air.

"No. It's not."

"Not what?"

"Good news. My father took out a loan and it's due in August. I—I need to see Alma." She sniffled.

Tears then. He guessed she didn't want him to know how bad things were because she said nothing and kept her head turned.

How much had her father borrowed? Did that mean the Tuckers would have to sell the farm? It would be good for him. He could buy it and be close to the Gibbons. But where would Katie and her family live? She had a sister in Kentucky. Maybe she'd move there. And why did the thought of Katie living in another state bother him?

∞

Katie couldn't clamber off the wagon fast enough. She was out before Pete could help her down. She wouldn't let him see her crying. If she didn't hurry into Alma's happy kitchen right now, he wouldn't see just a few tears but sobs.

She managed a quick "thank you for the ride" and bolted up the stairs and into Alma's arms. "I have to sell the farm. How am I going to tell Henry and Oma?"

Chapter 3

Katie slumped in the oak chair at Papa's desk. His scent clung to the room she'd rarely entered. It seemed he'd walk through the door any moment and catch her snooping through the drawers.

The information had to be here somewhere. Papa was meticulous about what needed to be done. He must have been the same about his financial records. So far she hadn't discovered this year's ledger. She opened a drawer and took out a stack of papers. There had to be a reason he'd borrowed money. She and Oma had discussed it last night, and they couldn't figure it out. Nothing new had been purchased, no livestock had arrived. Even the workman she thought was supposed to come hadn't appeared.

"What are you looking for?" Henry climbed into the chair in front of the desk, as if he were at home in this room where children weren't allowed.

"Papa's ledger. I need to find out how much is in the bank and what bills are due."

"The green book?"

"How do you know it's green?"

"Because it's like mine."

"Uh huh." She'd spent a lot of time teaching her brother and reading to him since he was small. She'd never taught him how to keep accounts. Probably Papa had given him an old book to play with. She pulled more papers from the drawer and set them aside.

Henry stood. "I know where it is."

The authority in his voice made him sound older. She stopped pulling papers from the drawer and gave him her full attention. "I'm listening."

"Papa kept our books together." Henry opened the glass-fronted bookcase and removed several books. Behind them were the ledgers.

"Why did he hide them?"

"Papa said valuable information shouldn't be left where it is easily found. He was teaching me how to write down expenses so I'd know how when the farm is mine."

Which it was now. That's what Papa always said, never intending Henry to

14

be in charge at ten.

"Could I see Papa's ledger, please?"

He held it tight against his chest then handed it to her. "Katie, I'm supposed to be the man of the house, but I don't feel like one. There's so much I don't know how to do."

She saw him fighting to keep from breaking into a sob. She had been his age when he was born, and their mother died. Over time she'd become more of his mother than a sister. She set the book on the desk and pulled him into a hug. "You have some growing to do. One day you will be in charge of this house, but for now, would you let me and Oma take care of the finances?"

Breaking away, he gave her a smile. "Does that mean I can quit school?"

"No, it means you get to work hard on the farm and come inside and do your lessons at night."

"Why? All the learning I need is outside."

"No it's not. You have to know how to figure out how much grain we need to keep for the winter, how much to sell, and what to do with the money made."

Henry's lips twisted then his forehead wrinkled. "Do I have to start today? I wanted to go fishing."

Too soon, responsibilities would weigh on his shoulders. "Bring back something for supper."

He left so fast it was as if she'd imagined him. But she hadn't. The answers to the loan sat between green covers on Papa's desk.

∞

Pete brushed Biscuit while waiting for Roy in the barn. He needed to pull away from this family before the pain of leaving created a scar that wouldn't heal. What would it be like if he'd been adopted with his younger brother? Would they have a place of their own? Wives? Would he be an uncle? Maybe he was already. "What do you think, Biscuit? Could I be some little one's Uncle Pete?"

The curry comb moved faster, followed by the brush. He'd tried to locate Billy after he'd run away from the home he had been placed in. Some home. They gave him a room in the barn, and he ate his meals on the porch. Not much different than the way Pete lived now—except for here. He was invited in to eat with a family; two little girls followed him, always talking; even Alma had been kind, showing him how to sketch. She'd bought him a book and some special pencils to practice last winter.

He'd found himself trying to capture Katie Tucker on the paper. She was a hard subject. That's what Alma called the kittens, even though they were soft as dandelion puff. They were precious but difficult to put on paper because they

15

wouldn't stop moving. Katie didn't move a lot, but she wouldn't look at him long enough for him to study her face.

"That horse ain't going to have any hair left if you don't stop." Roy held out a piece of pie. "Alma sent this out for you. You hurt her feelings not wanting to eat with us."

Pete closed the stall door. He set the grooming tools on a shelf and then took the pie. "I'm sorry. I'll apologize later."

"Yes, you will. Can't have my Snow Angel with tears in her eyes."

"I think it's time for me to move on."

"Why would you think that? Your home is here. My girls love you, and I need you." Roy's face turned red. "Did you get a better offer? If it's a property you want or a house, I'll sell you a piece of land and help you build."

"Hear me out before you get a pitchfork." He took a bite of the pie. He considered his words with care. "I've been wanting to talk to you about leaving, but until this week I hadn't come up with the where to go."

"Why don't you start with explaining your need to leave?" Roy settled against the barn wall.

"You know it. I told you when I came to work for you that I never settle anywhere for long. I stayed as long as I have because of the girls."

"You'll break their hearts if you leave."

"Just wait, here's my idea. When I dropped Katie off at her farm last week, it wasn't hard to tell nothing's been done since the fire. The barn smoldered and died with her father, not a board has been moved. She said her father had hired someone, but he hasn't shown up."

"So you want to buy her place?" Roy straightened. "That don't seem like you, Pete, taking advantage of two women and a boy."

Pete shook his head. "No. I don't think that's what she wants. We know her father took out a loan, so she might lose the place if we—I—don't help her."

"What's your plan? She won't accept charity."

"Thought I'd tell her you sent me to get the barn built."

"How's that not charity?"

"If Alma helps, we can do this. Katie will listen to her. Tell her you two want to loan her the money to buy the lumber and you'll pay my wages—not that I'd expect that. I've got enough saved that I can work there for a while." He kicked at some loose straw. "Besides, I think Henry needs a man around the place. Help him figure out how to run it."

Roy laughed. "And his sister? Perhaps you think I haven't seen you working up the nerve to talk to her all spring."

"I wouldn't be opposed, but I don't think she approves of me, being a drifter with no family."

"I found it's best not to put thoughts into the minds of others." Roy scratched his chin. "Let me talk to Alma. See what she thinks. She won't want you staying over there at night."

"Why would that be different than the farmhand that hasn't shown up?"

"No barn. Where do you think you'd be sleeping?"

"There, that's the reason to get Alma to get Katie to accept my help. If she hires someone else, no telling what might happen to her."

∞

Katie's trembling hand held the screen door closed as if it could protect her from the tobacco chewing, slovenly, smelly man on her porch. "When did my father hire you?"

"Don't much matter to you, missy. He's the one I need to see." The man spat a wad of tobacco on the porch.

Katie tried to summon her voice to tell him to leave. She couldn't let this man know Papa was dead. But if Papa hired him, how would she fire him? *Please, God, don't let Henry come up from the creek*. He'd for sure spill the news.

Taking a breath, she called on God to give her courage she knew she didn't have. "What's your name?"

"W.D. Where's your papa, missy?" His gaze traveled from her feet back to her face. "You're a right pretty gal, when you look at a man."

Her legs quivered and her stomach roiled.

Chapter 4

Still full from dinner or rather Alma's gooseberry pie, Pete rode down the lane to the Tuckers' place. He'd come with Alma's blessing and the note she'd written to Katie.

His thoughts wandered to what a future would look like with her if he had something to offer. Lost in a world that seemed more of a fairy tale, he didn't notice the man on the front porch until Katie's voice broke through.

"I said you must leave."

A man Pete hadn't seen before stood close to the door, close enough that he could've been kissing Katie through the screen.

He kicked Biscuit in the side, moving him on a little faster, not enough to alarm Katie but quick enough to help if needed.

"You're late, and Father said he wouldn't take you, seein' as you didn't even let him know you weren't coming on time."

Her voice shook. Was she mad or scared?

"I don't think your pa is even here. Why don't you let me inside to wait for him?"

"You, there. What's your business here?" Pete halted Biscuit at the bottom porch step. "Miss Tucker? Are you all right?"

"I was telling W.D. that Papa didn't want him here."

Was she okay? Had she slipped into some kind of place where people don't remember things that happened in the past? He dismounted, looped Biscuit's reins around the spindle, and climbed the stairs. He saw Katie through the screen, her hands tight on the door handle. Her eyes were wide, beautiful, and pleading. He stood taller, much taller, than she.

"Sir, I'm sorry you've come so far out of your way. Mr. Tucker hired me on last week. He couldn't wait any longer. You understand how that could be." He pointed to the barn. "With the fire, he needed help."

"Looks like you haven't started." The man backed away from the door.

"The lumber hasn't arrived. Why don't you head back to town and ask around? Might find work at the mine."

"I ain't working underground." He shuffled closer to the steps. "Guess I ain't wanted here. I'll wait in town a few days." He left the porch and mounted his horse. "You send word when that lumber comes as Mr. Tucker might need an extra hand."

"Papa won't be needing help." Katie said.

She'd found her voice. Pete almost smiled. Her hands dropped from the handle. That small sign of trust brought a feeling he couldn't name, but he knew he liked it.

The man tipped his hat. "Like I said, I'll be around." He rode off at a slow pace.

Pete moved toward the steps. He should go after him, make sure he understood not to come back.

He noticed the wet lump of tobacco on the porch and almost called the man back to clean it, but he smelled like he'd been soaking in beer. No. He'd take care of the porch. No need to give the stranger time to figure out there was no Mr. Tucker.

∞

Katie wasn't sure what to do about Pete standing on the porch. He'd saved her, but if she invited him inside, she'd have to talk to him, because Oma was napping. She forced a smile, pushed open the door, and stared at his boots. "Thank you. I didn't know how to make him leave."

"It was smart of you not to tell him your father passed."

She risked a look to see if he meant it. Their eyes met. Heat rushed through her, like she'd never felt before. What did that mean? She felt safe and warm, very warm.

"He made a mess of your porch." He slipped a handkerchief from his back pocket and wiped his brow. "I'll clean it."

"I'll do it. You've done enough saving me from that man. If you hadn't come—" She laced her fingers together and squeezed her palms. "Why are you here?"

"Alma sent you a letter." He reached into his shirt pocket and withdrew a piece of paper. "Why don't you sit on the swing and read it? I'm to wait for a reply."

She grasped the note. Her fingers froze against his; they were rough and calloused, a hardworking man's hand, Oma would say. The kind you want in a husband. She swallowed. "Can I get you lemonade?"

"No. Go, sit. I'll take care of this mess."

She puzzled at his kindness but accepted his offer. "There's a bucket by the pump."

"Back by the porch. I remember."

Of course he'd know that. He'd been here that night. She composed herself. "That's right. I haven't forgotten what you've done for us." She spun quickly so he wouldn't see her nose turning red as tears swelled. "I'll have an answer when you're done."

She heard him sigh, followed by his boots thumping against the porch. Only then did she risk watching him walk away. He had fine broad shoulders. His dark hair needed a trim, but she had to admit Pete Dent was the first man she'd ever wanted to look at.

Settled in the swing, the motion soothed her confusion. A letter from Alma was unusual, but a delight to the eyes. At the top, Alma had sketched a cardinal. As Katie read the sentences, her feet, fueled by agitation, pushed the swing back harder. Did her friends truly think it was a good idea to loan her money to rebuild the barn? And what about Pete being here every day? Bumping into him at the noon meal, maybe even dinner? The swing struck the house, taking her by surprise.

Water splashed across the wood. "Guess the way you're sending that swing to the moon, you aren't liking what the Gibbons are suggesting?"

She slowed the swing and smoothed the paper on her lap. "The Tuckers don't accept charity."

"I believe it's a loan."

"What if I can't pay them back?"

"Your crops are in. After the harvest you'll have what you need."

Would she? Maybe, but there was the matter of the other loan. A bee flew up from the roses and buzzed by Katie. Screaming, she shot out of the swing and crashed into Pete.

He caught her and held her tight. "Don't move. It's when you move they sting."

Katie held her breath, her worst fear and deepest shame bound in one little body. How she'd begged Papa to have hives, only to turn her back on the idea when a sting brought welts on her arm.

"It's gone." His arms dropped to his sides.

She stepped back. The sudden release from the sweet security of his arms felt worse than the sting would've. Crossing her arms over her chest, she made a decision. "Tell the Gibbons I'll accept their kind offer."

"I'll also inform them about the stranger. I think they'll agree I need to stay here, because once he gets into town, he'll find out about your father's death."

☙

"It has to be this way. If not, how will I protect you?" Pete held his hat and rubbed the brim with his thumb.

"No. Absolutely not. You can't stay here, not in the house. Oma won't allow that, nor would I." Katie spat the words at him. "Besides, I can shoot. I'm not in danger."

The screen door squeaked. "What's this commotion? Are you all right, Katie? Where's Henry?" Oma's questions shot as fast as a rapid-repeating rifle.

"We had a man asking about work. He said Papa hired him."

"If your father hired him, why would you send him away? We need help."

"He spat on your porch, ma'am, and was talking rough to Katie. I didn't care for him."

Oma squinted toward the field. "Where's Henry?"

"Down at the creek, catching dinner." Katie moved closer to her grandmother and patted her shoulder. "I'm sure he's fine. He'll come back, wet and muddy, carrying a fish or two."

"Can't lose another person. I won't survive it." Her grandmother's face faded like a summer blossom in early fall.

"That won't happen. Mrs. Tucker, I'm coming to stay. I was telling Katie that because the barn is destroyed, I'll have to sleep in the house."

Her head jerked up. "No. I'll not have Katie's reputation soiled."

Pete's jaw tightened. Once again cast as a man without a stellar reputation, one he'd never deserved. Traveling city to city looking for his brother and a place to settle hadn't done anything for how he was viewed by others.

"What would you suggest?"

"Get that barn done so you have a place to lay your head. Until then, you'll ride back to the Gibbons'. Katie, take me inside. I feel another headache itching to make me miserable."

Katie took her grandmother's arm. "Mr. Dent, thank you for helping me. I'll put Papa's rifle by the door. I won't be unprepared next time. And please, thank Alma. We'll see you tomorrow. I'm sure Henry will be excited to have you around."

Before Katie reached the door, Pete had it open. "Do you need help getting her settled?"

She gave him a sad smile. "We'll be fine. We're three-cord strong around here. Just like the Bible says, it's harder to break when there are three bound together."

A lump formed in his throat. He wanted too much to be one of the strands. "I'll see you in the morning."

Pete rode back to the Gibbons' to pack a kit, because he was staying over, no matter what Katie and her grandmother thought. He'd seen men, worked with some, like the one on Katie's porch. They weren't to be trusted. Protecting her from a bee was a small thing, from the stranger, much bigger, but the bee had sent her into his arms. He pushed his hat back.

"Biscuit, the woman was more afraid of that little honeybee than the man. It doesn't make sense."

Chapter 5

Still trying to cool off from the weather and Mr. Dent's assertion that she'd let him stay in her house, Katie downed a glass of lemonade. She poured another for her grandmother, who had settled in the porch rocker.

"That was a lot of excitement this morning." She handed her the cold glass. "Do you think we made the right decision? What if that man comes back?"

"Then we'll scare him off." The rocker slowed. "You aren't afraid, are you? If so, we can let Mr. Dent sleep in the room next to mine. Henry can fetch him whenever he gets back."

"No. I'm fine." She still shook, but having Mr. Dent in the house caused more alarm than the stranger returning. "I'm going to look over Papa's ledger. Are you all right?"

Oma drank the last of her drink and handed Katie the empty glass. "I'm all right. I believe I'll rest here." She settled into the chair and closed her eyes.

Katie gave Oma a long look. Had Papa's death been too much for her? Not knowing what else to do, she stepped inside Papa's office.

She began going through the pages of numbers and what they were assigned to. Nothing seemed out of place. Grain, the mercantile, even fabric purchased for aprons was listed. Flipping the page, she ran her finger down the side, more of the same, except—

Twelve dollars each for ten Italian queen bees. Heartsick, she knew what the loan had been for. She'd begged Papa to let her start a colony of bees, thinking they could sell the honey and wax for a nice profit. A few days later, she'd been stung on her face. The welt was so huge and painful that Oma had slapped mud from the garden on her face. She shuddered, remembering its slimy feel.

Had the bees come and Papa started the hives? She wasn't going searching for them, even if she did feel bad about the money spent.

That night Katie lay awake. The full moon brightened her room with its kiss of light. What if the bees were still here, making honey? How did one get it from the hives without being stung? Giving up on sleep, she slid from bed and paced the floor. Her bare feet against the waxed wood barely made a sound.

The house, built by her grandfather, was exceptional. He'd put a lot of time into making sure the yellow pine floors didn't squeak. And the woodwork had taken several winters. Downstairs he'd carved roses into the newels, and ivy vines up the stair balusters and on the sides of the banister. Even the bedrooms, usually plain, were created with care; the rosettes in the doorframes were all made by her grandfather.

What else had Papa bought? How could he have put them in danger of losing their home, their heritage that was to go to Henry someday? And to her. Papa had said she could live here forever if she never married.

Had he known then, when she was fifteen, that no one would want a timid wife? One subject to tears when her nerves frayed? Papa called her his delicate rose.

She hated it. She wasn't delicate, and she wasn't fancy like a rose. No, she was more like those fuzzy bees that frightened people.

When Henry married, would she still have this room? Or would a new wife want her to move to the attic? Maybe even out of the house?

She sat on the bed, her hand tracing the quilted line in her coverlet, while she looked through the open window at the rows of corn swaying with the touch of a slight breeze. The stalks weren't quite knee high but it looked like they would be by the Fourth of July.

There had to be something she could do to make sure they kept their home. She had to figure out how much money they'd need and how to get it. Her heart seized. What if it meant working in town? She fell back on the bed. "Father, please help us. I can't go near bees. I'm too scared. And I can't work in town." Her whispered plea floated through the window.

⁂

Pete adjusted his head on the bedroll. He'd rode in late and expected to be greeted at the door with a gun barrel pointed at his belly, but no one noticed his horse or him. Not even a light flickered. That was good, because he wasn't going back to the Gibbons'. Alma had argued with him, saying Katie was right, that he couldn't stay there. Roy had stood there nodding his head in agreement. He'd gone to his room, but the more he thought about the stranger, the more determined he became. Something strong pushed him to his feet. He'd found himself riding Biscuit with a bedroll tied to the back.

He'd sleep on the porch every night until he knew the stranger had moved on.

"...work in town." Soft words floated through the night air. Katie's voice. Who was she talking to? He sat up and considered walking into the yard to see if there were shadows or light. She hadn't sounded scared but would be if she looked out the window and saw him. No, better stay where he was. It wasn't any of his business.

He'd almost fallen asleep when he heard a sneeze, followed by two more. He perched on his elbows and looked around. He was sure it came from Katie's room but if it hadn't. . .that was enough for him to pull his boots on, grab his shotgun, and take a walk. The moonlight made seeing easy. Nothing seemed out of place. Relieved, he headed back to the front of the house.

Someone stood by the door.

And it wasn't one of the Tuckers.

∞

"Miss Tucker!"

A pounding on the door sent Katie flying from her bed. She met Henry and Oma in the hallway.

"What time is it?" Henry rubbed his eyes.

"Late. Stay here. I'm getting Papa's gun—"

"You there!"

Katie jumped at a voice different from the first. There were two of them. Her heart palpitated against her chest so hard she was sure there would be bruises. What could she do against two men?

Thump. Bump. Crash. The sounds and grunts went on forever, yet she stood rooted to the landing. The men were fighting.

Henry whipped around her and charged down the stairs.

"Stop! Don't go out there!"

"I have to. I'm the man of the house."

Oma held out her wrapper. "Take this and go after him. That boy don't have any sense. Get your papa's gun. Don't be afraid to use it."

Katie nodded, yanking the wrapper around her, and ran after Henry. *God, this isn't right. Why did you take Papa from us?*

She found Henry on the front porch. The fight had ended. No need for the gun. The moonlight lit their rescuer's face. Pete held on to the man who had come earlier.

She chewed her bottom lip, trying to understand what she was seeing. She pulled Henry close. "Mr. Dent, what are you doing?"

"Protecting you."

"You lied. Said your pa didn't need me. That ain't true. He's dead." The man's lip was bleeding. He wavered on his feet and slumped to the floor.

Pete jerked him up. "You aren't staying. You're drunk. Get on your horse and ride out."

"Don't got one. Lost him in a poker game. Just want the job that was promised to me. And I mean to get it."

Chapter 6

K atie shivered. What did he mean by "he'd get the job?" She'd already told him no.

"You won't work here or anywhere in this town, the way you're acting." Pete held on to the man's arm. "Henry, get the wagon. We're taking him in to the sheriff."

"No, please. Not there. I won't come back, at least not like this."

"Not like anything. Miss Tucker said you aren't needed, so there isn't a reason to return."

Katie stiffened. She should be the one giving the orders, or at least Henry. "Mr. Dent, what if you let him sober up and get clean? If he can do that and come back acting civilized, perhaps we can have him help?"

"Doing what?"

"Fixing the barn. Maybe he's fallen on hard times and needs the help of Christians." Had she said that? She had no money for wages.

"How will you pay him?"

"I—I was thinking about that. I won't." Not only wouldn't she pay him, she couldn't, and Pete knew it. Still something nudged her to offer this man a place. Oma always said to listen to the voice in your heart because it was probably God nudging you.

"I ain't workin' for free." The words were slurred, but the message clear.

"Mister, the only pay you'll receive is a place to lay your head, and meals. When Mr. Dent feels you're sober and worth paying, he'll help you find a job." Katie licked her lips. She'd never been so nervous speaking words that made sense. Maybe she needed a second chance to prove herself, too.

"Don't take orders from a woman either." The man spat on the porch.

Pete let go of him. He tumbled, landing on the glob of tobacco he'd just spat. "First thing you'll do is clean up this mess. Then a bath. We'll work on manners while you're here."

"Where do you think he's going to be sleeping, Miss Tucker?" Pete glanced down at the man then back to her. "I don't imagine you want him in the house any more than you wanted me."

"Why, he can sleep on the porch, next to you, as you seem to find that a reasonable place to lay your head at night."

"They can sleep in my room." Henry stood on the bottom step, making him taller than his sister. "That way I can keep an eye on both of them, protecting you and Oma."

Katie's heart fluttered. She wanted Henry to feel like the man of the house, but his suggestion that both of those men—one of them drunk—should sleep down the hall from her. . .

"Nonsense." Oma had come up behind her. "Henry, if you want to sleep with them, you can sleep out here, too. Mr. Dent, I'd get that man scrubbed clean before morning. He'll need some clean clothes. Don't suppose he's brought any with him?"

"I've no idea. We'll ask him later." Pete scratched his head. "Looks about my size. Guess it would be the Christian thing to loan him something to wear while his get washed."

Katie looked back at the man on the porch. His eyes were closed and he snored. He didn't seem quite so scary. "Oma, it is almost morning."

"Then there's no time to waste. Let's get water on the stove. Henry, you and Pete drag the washtub out close to the pump and start filling it. Once that's done, drag him over. Doesn't matter to me if he goes in with his clothes. Might as well wash everything at once." She took Katie's arm. "We'll get ready for the day. After breakfast, we'll decide if we need to send him on his way or give him another chance."

∞

"Time to wake up." Pete roused W.D. enough to stand, but not for long from the way he wobbled. Pete draped an arm around his neck to support him and half dragged, half carried him to the waiting tub. He would enjoy watching W.D.'s face when his body hit the water. "Stand back, Henry. He's going to wake up mad."

Standing W.D. at the end of the tub, Pete let go. The man fell backward into the cold water.

"What in the—"

Pete plunged his hands into the water and grabbed W.D. by his shoulders, pulling his face close to his. "Watch your mouth, or you'll be walking back to town in soggy britches."

W.D. relaxed.

Figuring the fight had left him, Pete let go and stepped back. "Humph. You've landed in a soft place for sure. Anyone else would've sent you to jail."

The screen slammed behind Henry. "Katie sent soap. Sorry, mister, it isn't Saturday but she said you had to scrub like it was." He handed him a small sliver instead of a bar. "She said to keep this. If you need more, I'm to get it."

W.D. grimaced and took it. "I didn't want to put anyone out, just wanted a job."

"And you've got one, but first you have to prove your worth." Pete didn't like the idea of this man hanging around Katie, but right now she called the shots. "Soon as you're clean and scrubbed, we'll get started building a lean-to, where we'll both sleep."

"I have clothes in my pack. I had it last night. Did you see it?" W.D. unbuttoned the top of his shirt. "Wouldn't feel too good to walk around in wet clothes. As hot as it is already, by noon, I'll be steaming like a kettle."

"Didn't see one. Henry, you mind running down the lane? Take a look. See if he dropped it."

"Yes sir. I'll be quick." Henry took off.

Pete glared at W.D. "I'd rather not, but I'll loan you clothes if yours can't be found."

W.D. nodded. "Appreciate that."

"Now that you're sobering up, you and me are going to converse." Pete straightened, rubbed his hand through his hair, missing his hat. Without it, he didn't feel dressed. He stared at W.D. Something about him seemed familiar, but he couldn't place the man.

"You mind if I wash up without you gawking at me?" W.D. had stopped undressing.

"Just want to make sure you're fit for the job and you don't leave until we've had our chat."

"I ain't going anywhere. That's the point of me being here, remember? I came to get the job I was offered."

"And it's up to me if you stay."

⚭

In the kitchen, Katie hovered near the doorway, trying to listen. Her fingernails found their place between her front teeth.

"Katie, stop worrying those fingers. You'll have them bleeding again." Oma tied an apron around her waist. "Let's get breakfast made. The coffee's about ready. When Henry comes in, we'll send him out with some. That will help that man clear his head."

"I'm not sure one cup will be enough. I've never seen anything like that. A man fallen down, so drunk, he goes to sleep with his face in a wad of chewed tobacco." Katie slipped her apron over her head. "Did I do the right thing? What if he is more than a drunk? What if he's dangerous and will murder us while we sleep?"

Oma patted her cheek. "Schatzi, Mr. Dent is here. If he thinks the man needs to leave, he'll tell us. I think God put those earlier words in your mouth."

"Why?"

"Because usually such things make you chew your fingers. Instead, God opened your mouth and you offered Christian charity." She spun Katie around and tied her apron strings.

"I never would've thought of it that way." Her hand went back to her mouth, but she forced it away. She needed to change. She could no longer allow the things that scared her to keep her from being who God meant her to be. "Oma, would you pray God will make me more courageous, like Rahab?"

"The harlot? It's an odd thing to ask for, but yes, I will ask God, as I have many times, to give you calm nerves." Her wiry eyebrows scrunched together. "Make no mistake, that's the only thing I'm praying for. Rahab turned out to be a blessing, but we don't need to have you imitating her early ways."

"Oma! I'd never!"

"See that you don't. I believe once W.D. gets cleaned up, he and Mr. Dent are going to be fighting to see who wins your hand. And you'll see W.D. is going to be every bit as good looking as Mr. Dent."

Katie felt the warmth rising in her cheeks. "What a thing to say! They won't have any interest in me, you'll see." But what if they did? She wanted Mr. Dent to be the winner. Dare she hope to imagine what it would feel like to be a bride? She twisted a loose curl in her hand. No. She'd buried that desire. No use lighting the fire of hope now. She stuck the wayward tress back into the bun where it belonged.

Chapter 7

S he'd wrestled all night, asking God to help her make a choice between searching trees for beehives and being a waitress. No heavenly directions came. She had to choose. The fear of one had to be less than the other. *God, please, there has to be another way.* Again she was met with silence. Looking for work at the diner won. Katie made it to town, her shoes coated in dust, but she hoped that wouldn't keep her from getting hired. With the weight equal to an anvil on each of her shoulders, she pushed through the door.

The smells, smoke, and sudden silence of forks no longer clanking against plates greeted her, turning her stomach. Every eye was directed her way. Her hands shook at her sides. She clasped them together, holding them close to her chin—then realized she must look as if she were getting ready to lead everyone in prayer. Slowly she relaxed her grip and let her hands slide against her skirt, where they had been.

"Miss Tucker? Are you here for breakfast?"

Penny Otto. They had gone to school together. The heaviness on Katie's shoulders slid away as she walked to the counter where her friend stood. "No." Her gaze fell from Penny to the pine plank floor. "I'm looking for work."

"Are you sure? The only need we have is for the breakfast shift. You'd have to take orders and serve food to a rough group of hard-to-work-with men. You'll have to talk to a lot of men that like to flirt with pretty girls."

Katie searched her friend's face and saw concern. Or was it doubt that she could do the job? "Will you be here?"

"Every day but Sunday."

"I'd like to try."

"It doesn't pay much, and the work is harder than you're used to." Penny's face flushed. "I don't mean you can't do it. It's like harvest time every morning, and I know you've done that."

"Harvest is only one time a year."

"Yes, and this comes every day. And on each one, there is someone who will take a likin' to you and make you miserable, and there won't be anything you can do but smile, rebuff them, and refill their coffee cup."

"Why do you do it then?"

"When I told Papa I'm picking my own husband, he said I had to work here, because sitting around the house cost him money." Penny wiped at the counter with a rag. "I'll be leaving as soon as I find the right man. So do you think you can be here before the sun rises?"

"You don't have to ask your father first?"

"No. But don't think Papa will let you stay if you can't do the work." Penny frowned. "He'll make you leave, in front of everyone, if you don't get the orders right. Papa's a bit," she leaned in and whispered, "difficult to work for sometimes."

∞

Pete had worked on the barn all morning with W.D. and Henry. Katie had left early, looking like she'd drunk a pint of sour milk.

"Henry, where'd Katie go?"

"She's looking for a job at the diner." Henry wiped the sweat from his forehead and then handed some nails to Pete. "You know why, right?" He kept his voice low, as if he didn't want W.D. to hear.

"Because she needs money. She ought to do well waiting tables." Pete pounded a nail into the board that sided the barn.

"Doubt it. She doesn't like to be around people. That's why Papa bought the bees, so she wouldn't have to talk to anyone."

"Bees? He paid for the bees buzzing around the rose bushes?"

"Yes sir. That and a bunch of stuff that goes with making them stay on our farm. He was going to show me how to take care of them this summer." Henry's eyes filled with tears. "Guess that ain't going to happen."

Pete looked away to allow Henry time to clear his eyes without embarrassment. He put in a few more nails. The barn was coming together, but he still wasn't happy about W.D. being here. So far they'd worked fine together, as long as they worked on opposite sides of the barn, but at some point they were going to meet in the middle.

"I don't get it. What do the bees have to do with Katie? And with her not liking bein' around people?"

"Papa bought them for Katie because she'd told him about how making honey and selling it could bring in good money, and he knew she wouldn't ever get married because, well—you know."

"No, I don't. Explain it to me. What's wrong with her?" Pete's heart cracked a little for Katie's pain. It must hurt her something fierce to know her family thought she wouldn't get married.

"She can't talk to anyone without getting all shaky inside, especially anyone who's come to court her. She gets all red in the face, bursts into tears, and gets a headache." Henry shook his head.

Pete almost laughed. Katie was shy, but that didn't mean she'd never get married. She hadn't met the man who could get her talking. Though she'd talked to him and W.D. this past week. Could it be she didn't see either of them as being the marrying kind? He'd have to change her mind.

"Katie is a sensitive creature, Papa said, and we had to help her find a way to take care of herself. Guess it's up to me now to figure out how to do that."

"She doesn't like bees." Pete's memory had him back with her in his arms, the day she ran from one.

"No. She's scared of them. She got stung, before any of the bees and equipment came to raise them. Papa never told her about them, afraid she wouldn't leave the house if she knew they were living by the creek."

"Doesn't she ever go there?"

"Nope, I told her that's my special place, and I don't want no girls there." Henry frowned. "Papa said I might want to take a girl there someday. But he was wrong."

"I think your papa knew what he was talking about. It's all about the right time for things to happen."

But Mr. Tucker was wrong about Katie. Pete had an even stronger desire to reach out, protect, and love her, as soon as he broke through her turtle-tough shell.

⚭

Pete and Henry stood at the edge of the clearing, near Sugar Creek. Pete counted twelve hives. "Your pa must have thought this bee business would work."

"He said it would make us a lot of money once the honey gets out of those hives." Henry tugged Pete's arm. "I ain't afraid of a bee like Katie is, but I figure there's hundreds of them in those boxes."

"Might be. Did you say there is a hat?"

"Papa bought all kinds of stuff."

"It wasn't in the barn, was it?" If it were then getting what they needed would cost. How much, he didn't know.

"I thought it was, but I found it in the woodshed. Katie never goes in there, so I'm guessing that's why Papa put it there. There's a book in Papa's office on how to get the honey out of those hives." Henry frowned. "It probably has big words that I don't know. You know how to read?"

Though taken aback by the question, Pete had a feeling he shouldn't laugh. He'd been taught to read at the orphanage. In fact, he liked reading. "Sure do.

Think you can get that book for me?"

"Yes sir. I'll get it now, while Katie is gone. I don't want her to see it. We don't want to upset her—that's what Papa always said."

Pete couldn't understand why Henry and his father thought Katie was so weak. He'd seen her during the fire, and then again, telling W.D. to go away. She hadn't seemed sensitive then. But Henry was in charge, so he wouldn't insist on telling Katie. Yet.

"Have you figured out what we'll do with the honey? We can't hide that from her."

"Nope. Guess I'll need to do some thinking on it." Henry grinned. "I know she'll be happy when we show her the bees. She thinks Papa let them go."

Chapter 8

Heavy knives scraped against china plates, and male voices rumbled around Katie. Her hair slid out of its pins. This morning she'd left before sunrise. Oma agreed to handle breakfast while Katie worked, though she had to listen to another lecture about trusting God and not rushing before answers were clear.

So far she had backed away from a man who said she smelled nice and asked her to come closer so he could get a good whiff of her, and another who winked and mentioned the better the service, the bigger his tip. Both encounters made her skin itch. Why hadn't she waited for God's answer? Because she was in charge of taking care of the family, that's why. God had only brought two extra mouths to feed. Shame filled her. She was grateful to Alma for sending Pete. It was the other one she'd like to send away.

"Missy. My coffee's cold." The man she'd nicknamed Mr. Cold Cup pounded the table, making the silverware jump.

It was the third time she'd refilled that man's cup since he'd come in. She gave him a half grin. "I'll be right there." Several plates waited on the ledge behind the counter—her orders were up. Every time she turned, more platters waited. Penny was right. This was harder than harvest. There hadn't been one woman come in this morning.

"Hard time keeping up?" Penny handed her two plates, filled with eggs, potatoes, and bacon.

"The man in the corner seems to need a lot of coffee." The smell of the bacon toyed with the hunger in her stomach. She hadn't had time for breakfast before leaving home.

"He's trying to make you cry. He's done that with everyone we've hired." Penny snatched the coffee urn. "I'll take care of him. Get those platters where they belong, then hang back and watch."

"You bothering my waitress, Robert?" Penny strolled over to his table.

"She's not fast enough. My coffee's cold." He held up his cup.

Penny tipped the pot. "Drink faster and leave the help alone. I can't afford to lose anyone, so be nice like your mother taught you."

Robert smirked. "I'd be plenty nice for you, Penny." He tugged the side of her apron.

Penny grazed the hot pot against his arm.

He yanked away his hand. "Careful, missy."

"That goes both ways. I'm not here for you to be touching. I'm not your wife, and no, before you ask, I have no interest in marrying you."

Katie watched with horror. She'd never be able to act or speak like that to anyone.

"I heard Dent's buying the Tucker place. I guess that's why Katie's working here."

Hearing her name, she stilled. Not wanting to take part in the whispered conversation, she tried to move on, but couldn't. She didn't know the raspy-voiced man and wanted to know why he had said that.

"He's moved in already and rebuilding the barn. I know he's been looking for a place. Guess he found one. Probably for the best. Nobody there to work it anyway." The heavyset man dropped his knife against the plate edge.

Her legs trembled. Pete was trying to steal the farm. Her nervous stomach tumbled. The air thinned.

While she struggled to take a breath, Penny pushed past her. "What's burning?"

Smoke billowed from the kitchen. A fire. Not again. The room spun. She grasped and found nothing to keep her from hitting the floor.

∞

The rumble of wheels came down the lane. It didn't sound like Roy's wagon. The wheels weren't squeaking. Too light for a delivery wagon. Pete stepped away from the barn to look.

Dr. Pickens pulled up with Katie on the bench next to him, her face the color of ash.

Pete ran to the carriage. "What happened? Is she all right?"

"Too much excitement at the diner. There was a fire and Katie passed out. Stew Rutherford caught her before she hit the floor."

With great care, Pete lifted Katie from the carriage and held her in his arms.

"You smell nice." She rested her head on his shoulder.

"I don't think so, but thank you anyways."

"Take her inside and put her to bed. I gave her a dose of laudanum to calm her down," Dr. Pickens said. "She was crying and shrieking. I don't think she ought to be working there. It's too much for her. I admire her for trying, but there's always a chance of a fire in the kitchen. Her father wouldn't approve."

"Maybe not, but she's trying hard to make the farm work. I'm proud of her, given she has trouble talking to people. Yet she hasn't once complained." He shifted her in his arms, causing her eyes to open wide. "Shh. It's okay. I'm taking you inside, and your grandmother will take care of you."

She reached up and stroked his cheek.

Dr. Pickens coughed. "Best get her inside to her grandmother before she does something you'll both regret."

"Thank you for bringing her home. You'd be welcome, if you care to stay."

"I'm on my way to Alma's, but maybe next time."

Pete propped pillows around Katie's head and stepped back from the couch. "Time for you to take a nap. I bet you'll have some sweet dreams."

"I'm dreaming of what it would be like to have you kiss me." Her head fell back. Her eyes closed. A tiny snore escaped from her nose, making him smile. Someday he was going to kiss the tip of that perfect nose.

∞

"Oma, what am I to do? I don't want to sell the farm." Katie held her head between her hands. The stabbing pain didn't want to let up.

"Drink tea. The more you do, the better you'll feel. About this other matter, I do not know." Oma patted Katie's arm. "God does and He has a plan. You'll see."

A knock on the door sent lightening through her head. "Come in, but quietly, please."

"I'm sorry. I wanted to see how you were feeling this morning." Pete held his hat in his hand.

He was so tall, and she remembered thinking how comforting it was to lay her head on his shoulder. She felt her face flush. Was he thinking about that, too? "I'll be fine. Though I don't know what I'll do to pay you." She stood, her chair screeching against the pine floor. "Are you planning on buying this farm? I heard that yesterday, and I want to know now if you're here to help or hurt us."

Pete looked at the floor then back at her, with the softest brown eyes she'd ever seen. "No. I'm looking for a place of my own, that's true, but this is Henry's farm."

"So you're leaving as soon as we get the barn built and the crops harvested?"

Henry popped through the door. "You can't leave. You promised to help me with the—"

"And I will, Henry. I can't stay here. You're the—"

"Help him with what?" Katie crossed the kitchen floor and poked Pete in the chest. "What are you teaching him that you don't want me to know about?"

"Uhm, nothing. Girls, maybe." Pete's face turned red. He tugged on his ear. "I promised I'd show him how to ask a girl out. Henry, are you watching?"

"Yes sir."

"Miss Tucker, would you please go with me to the Fourth of July fireworks?"

"That's it? You just say her name? What if she says no?"

"Ah, but Henry, what if she says—"

"Yes, Mr. Dent. I'd enjoy being escorted to the big doings at the park."

Pete winked at Henry. "That's how it's done. Now let's get back to putting the barn together."

Katie had a feeling she'd been left out of something else. But she didn't care. Her headache had flown away. She had a fellow. A mighty fine one at that.

Chapter 9

Sweaty and hot, Katie pushed her sleeves to her elbows and walked through a grove of trees, trying to follow a bee. At a distance. She'd seen one fly this way and knew from reading they often built hives in trunk hollows. If she could locate at least one hive, maybe with Henry's help they could harvest and sell the honey. It was going for a good price, and like she'd told Papa, it was a good investment.

Still, they were bees and they stung. She slowed her search. If she wasn't willing to be stung, why did she want her brother to be? She sniffled. Something about this time of year made her head hurt and nose twitch. She sneezed. Fearing a headache, she turned back to the house. She'd search another day. This afternoon she'd rather be deciding what to wear to the Fourth of July celebration than looking for bees.

She wanted to wear the blue taffeta dress. Papa bought it for her when he'd traveled to St. Louis to visit Doc Pickens in April, when he was there studying. She'd yet to wear it, not finding an occasion worthy of the way it made her feel. Beautiful, tall, and almost courageous.

Silly. Courage comes from God, not a dress. But maybe He used it to show her? Sometimes when she tried to figure out what God was all about, she came away more confused than when she started. But Papa always said, *"Go back to the beginning and what you know."*

She knew God loved her, that He sent His Son to die for her sins, and He wanted His children to be happy. Well the dress made her happy, so it must have come from God. Pete made her happy, too—she wanted to stretch her arms wide and turn like a five year old until she could no longer stand up. But she was much too old for that behavior and, besides, her head was beginning to hurt.

☙

Bassler Park dressed with kerosene lamps made the night feel like a fairy tale, and she a princess. The wavy light highlighted the golden tones in Pete's brown eyes. Would he be her first kiss? Katie didn't know what to do with the feelings piling up inside, like logs in a dam. Pete held on to her elbow as if it were treasure. The night air was soft, not too sticky. The fireworks popped, cracked, and sizzled; lighting up the sky with their sparks. At first the smoky smell and bright light twisted her stomach enough to make her feel faint. Then the beauty of it struck Katie. Papa would want her to enjoy this, and to enjoy Pete. He'd be happy she'd caught someone's eye. Probably relieved that she might not end up alone after all.

Soon the sky exploded with the bright zigzagging streams of fireworks and then grew dark.

"Did you like it?" Pete squeezed her hand. "The smoke didn't bother you, did it? I should have considered that it might."

"I enjoyed it, very much." His consideration of her feelings increased her desire to love him.

"Katie, we need to find Henry and get back."

And then she turned back into the farm girl who lived in Trenton. "Isn't he supposed to meet us at the buggy when the fireworks ended?"

"He might not think it's over until he and his friends inspect for those that didn't go off."

"Henry's not like that. You'll see. He'll be there." He'd better be there. She'd hate for Pete to think Henry would be disrespectful.

They strolled up the sparsely lit path, passing the brewery. From the shadows, a man stepped in front of them.

Katie gasped then settled when she recognized W.D.

"Miss Tucker, when am I gettin' paid?" W.D. stood, arms crossed, blocking the path.

Katie sought Pete's arm.

"You know the deal, W.D. You get money later. Right now you get a place to sleep and food to eat."

"Says you, Dent. I bet you're getting paid in other ways. How's those lips of hers? Soft as a—"

Pete lunged forward. "Don't talk about her like that. Have you been drinking?"

"What if I am?"

"I'm not fighting a drunk." He stepped away. "Find somewhere else to sleep tonight. Tomorrow come and get your things. You're done at the Tucker place."

∽

"I'm sorry, Katie. I shouldn't have fought with him at all." Pete helped her into the carriage.

Henry came panting up to them. "I heard there was a fight and Pete walloped W.D. Why'd you do that? Sure wish I hadn't of missed that. That's more exciting than looking for dead fireworks."

"You were supposed to come here after they ended." Katie glanced at Pete. "It seems tonight no one is who I thought they were."

She pulled the hem of her dress close to her feet. "Get in, Henry, and be careful not to step—"

"On your most beautiful dress ever—that you've been saving for the perfect time. I know." Henry climbed in.

Pete let that information sink in. She'd worn her best for him. Something loosened in his heart. Was God really listening to his prayers?

Chapter 10

After Pete had seen Katie and Henry home, and taken care of the horse and buggy, he couldn't help but stare at the empty bunk where W.D. should be. Anger surged through him as he remembered the hateful words the man had shouted at Katie. He had better not show up here tonight, or Pete would finish what was started.

He yanked off his boots and tossed them on the floor at the foot of his bed. God had judged people when they were wrong, so why feel bad about his own indignation? Feeling righteous, he picked up his Bible and scooted close to the lamp.

Reading Judges would prove him right. He opened the book, intending to head straight there. Instead his hand stilled at Ephesians, chapter four. He wanted to keep turning but feeling a push to read, he did so. *"Be ye angry, and sin not: let not the sun go down upon your wrath."* The sun wasn't even out when he ran into W.D. Did it mean he could go to sleep without worry?

He read further: *"Let all bitterness, and wrath, and anger, and clamour and evil speaking, be put away from you, with all malice: And be ye kind one to another, tenderhearted, forgiving one another, even as God for Christ's sake hath forgiven you."*

No way he was going to sleep easy with those holy words running through his brain. He set the Bible on his bunk. Unease poked his shoulder. A walk and a talk with God was in order. He put on his shoes and grabbed the lamp. He might as well check on the bees while he was conversing.

∞

Katie sat on Oma's bed, tracking the tiny stitching of the Dresden Plate quilt with her finger while her grandmother brushed her hair. Something she hadn't done in a long time. Tonight she longed for a mother, but grandmother was the closest she'd ever have. Did she experience the same kind of fluttery feelings when grandfather courted her? She wanted to ask but didn't know if that would make Oma sad.

The brush pulled against Katie's tangled, wavy locks. Maybe she shouldn't have pinned it so well, but it was the only way she could get it under her hat.

"The singing was nice enough at the picnic, but nothing like the time they put on the opera."

"The *Pinafore*? I can only imagine what that must have been like. I wish I could've seen it, Oma." The performance had been given by locals talented enough that the older people still talked about it with great enthusiasm every time a concert was held at the park.

"The Trenton Brass Band was as good." Oma stopped brushing. "What's the matter, Schatzi? You not have a good time tonight?"

Katie whipped around and faced her grandmother. "It was—I can't find the words! The lights in the park were like jewels, and being with Pete made me..."

"Lit a fire in you, did he?" Sparkles danced in Oma's eyes. "I knew he was a good man. Patient with you, not worried about your nervousness. I've been praying for God to send a man like him for you. I knew your father wasn't right."

"What are you saying?"

"He loved you, remember that. But he didn't think you'd ever find a husband, with your condition. That's why he wanted to make sure the bees were a success. If you could make the honey business work, he knew you'd be able to do anything you set your mind on. It was hard on him when you were so afraid. He was praying for God to send a man who could see past the skittishness."

"And you think that's Pete?"

"Would he make you happy?"

Katie wanted to say no, but the way her lips were stretching past the normal corners of her mouth would give her away.

"Good. Then we will pray Mr. Dent asks you to be his wife." Oma wasted no time. Her head bent, hands folded, she began her plea to her Lord.

☙

Should he have brought the smoker with him? Pete considered going back, but he didn't plan on getting close to the hives. It was a destination, more than anything. He'd not go close. Besides, he had a nudge or a shove between his shoulder blades urging him to turn back and head to town. It had to be from God because the last thing he wanted to do was talk with W.D., especially if he had continued drinking.

Sticks broke underfoot. Something skittered off the path in front of him. He hadn't brought his gun. Foolish mistake to come out after dark without it. Coyotes and other night critters—what was that?

He stood stone still. Buzzing. Loud buzzing. Buzzing that shouldn't be coming his way this time of night. From the sound there had to be more than one bee headed right at him.

He turned to run.

The bees followed.

He held the light to his face, hoping the flame would scare them. It heightened their anger. As he ran he twisted the knob, extinguishing the light. But he couldn't put out the fire on his skin.

He dropped the lantern and ran for the creek while slapping at his shirt trying to kill the bees that found a way into it. He bit back a yell as another one found his skin. It came out as a whimper. Wading into the water, the mud sucked at his feet and determined bees came at his head. He flopped forward, submerging his head, over and over, until the last bee had either died or returned to the hive.

Soaking and shaking from the experience, he now understood Katie's very real fear. He also got God's message. Once he changed clothes, he'd be headed to town to find W.D.

Chapter 11

Pete turned Biscuit down Railroad Street and headed toward White's Saloon, figuring it to be the most likely place to find W.D. Every movement on the horse made his chest ache. He wanted to be back on his cot, soaking the painful areas with baking soda, but he wasn't about to argue with God. At least, he wasn't taking a chance that God wasn't the one sending him on the hunt for W.D.

He liked riding through town at night. Sometimes a curtain hadn't been closed and the light inside gave him a peek of what he wanted his life to look like. A father hugging a little child, or a head bowed in prayer. He had quite a bit saved and wanted to ask Katie to marry him; but what would they do about the farm? It was Henry's of course, but he was too young to leave alone with it.

The noise coming from inside White's Saloon meant the celebration continued. He slowed Biscuit and whispered a prayer that he wouldn't find W.D. inside and, if he did, the man would be reasonable about coming outside for a conversation. What that would be about, he wasn't sure. He'd depend on God for those words. He tied Biscuit to the hitching post and went inside.

The kerosene lights turned the smoke-filled room into a thick yellow cloud. Glass mugs clinked against the bar top, laughter thundered from the corner. Pete walked past tables until he found W.D. alone, hat resting next to an empty mug and spilled beer.

Pete slid the heavy wooden chair out and sat in front of W.D. "I came to talk."

"Not interested." He didn't look up.

If only it were easy and he could say, "Me either." But his heart felt heavy, and he couldn't up and leave. "Truce? Let's go outside and watch for the train, maybe talk instead of using fists?"

W.D. cocked his head. "Watch for the train? That brings back an old memory. Why not?" He picked up his hat and shoved it on.

The two of them stepped outside and found a quieter spot on the porch. Both of them leaned over and anchored their hands to the banister. Pete knew he held on, unsure of what he'd say. W.D. probably held on to steady himself or keep from swinging at him.

"Why'd you come looking for me? You don't seem like someone to search out a fight."

"I'm not. Just something I felt I needed to do. Let's start over, you and me. Why don't you tell me what W.D. stands for?" Somewhat relieved at coming up with an easy question, he let go of the banister.

"William Dentice. Dentice was my last name before I was adopted."

Pete no longer noticed the bee stings. He couldn't feel anything. He'd been searching for his brother for years, and now he was standing next to him.

∞

In bed, Katie rolled one way, then the other. Her nightdress crawled past her hip and cinched her waist. She tugged it back in place.

The loan date circled in red was fast approaching, and the only money coming in came from the chickens. If they had another cow they could sell the milk. But they didn't.

Maybe she could nail up a notice, offering to take in ironing. But then she'd be taking money away from the widow with seven kids.

If she could find a hive, there had to be honey. She could sell it and the wax quick enough to make a payment to the bank. But she had to face her fears. Did she know enough about beekeeping? She knew a lot from reading the book, like the bee that came after her on the porch the day Pete saved her was a worker bee. She sat up and scratched at a mosquito bite. The crickets sang outside her window. Had Papa bought the smoker and netted hat, too? Maybe even enough hives to build an apiary?

What if all of those things that could save the farm were in the barn when it burned? She fell back on the bed. Her eyes stung. *It's too much, God. I can't do this alone.* She hoped for a calming verse to pop into her mind but it didn't. If her mind would settle, she could sleep, but how could that happen, when all she could hear was Papa died thinking she'd failed?

She tossed the blankets aside and lay on her stomach, letting her pillow contain the weight of her worry and tears. In the light of day, she knew Papa was in heaven and probably knew how her story was going to turn out. But she was still here, and life was, well, unsettling.

She fell asleep and dreamed of watching the farm being auctioned. Pete couldn't be found and W.D. bought her memories.

∞

"Billy?" Pete pushed the name through his lips, still not believing this drunken man could be his brother.

"Nobody calls me that." W.D. growled and let go of the banister, his hand balled into a fist. "That's a child's name. I stopped being one of those a long time ago."

Pete dropped his gaze and studied his broken thumbnail. He had to tell him. He took a deep breath. "I think you might be my younger brother."

"Naw, your name's Dent. I had a big brother, but I can't remember his first name. I've been searching for another Dentice but came up empty."

"I changed it." Pete's voice cracked. "I looked for you. I went to the farm where you were supposed to be."

"Wasn't there. That family moved to Kansas and used me for labor. Took out on my own when I was fifteen. Came back this way about a year ago."

About the time Pete quit searching.

"Why'd you change your name?"

"No one could say it."

"That's some truth. I'm sorry about saying what I did about Miss Tucker. You care for her, easy enough to see that. Don't know why that bothered me so much."

"Maybe you're looking for a home as much as me?" How would he explain all of this to Katie? Would she want to be associated with him once she knew W.D. was his brother? If she didn't accept him, could he walk away from her? He knew he wasn't going to let W.D. slip out of his life again. The pain of losing him twice might erase his desire for living.

"Guess this is where we say good-bye again." W.D.'s voice thickened. "Sure wish I'd have shown up at the Tucker's better behaved."

"No. We're not being separated again. You're coming back with me, and we'll figure out how this is going to work in the morning."

"I don't want to come between the two of you."

"Things will work out. Let's get you on your horse and get back to the farm."

"I want you to know I haven't always been this way." He trailed behind Pete. "The last few years aren't something I'm proud of. I've done things that—"

"Everyone has, Billy." The old name rolled off his tongue with ease. He stopped and turned back. Under all that facial hair was a face he might've recognized. "Make no mistake, there's no one alive that hasn't sinned. That's why we're thankful for God's grace."

"Don't think He has grace enough for me, but I'm sure glad I found you."

"We'll talk about it tomorrow when you can think clearer. Let's go home, brother." He turned his head to hide his tears of thankfulness. God had answered his prayer. Not the way he'd hoped, but it was an answer.

Chapter 12

Pete found Katie fighting a breeze while hanging sheets on the line. "Let me help you with that." He took one corner, stretched it, and waited for her to pin it.

"What's got you helping me with laundry?" She cocked her head. "Not that I don't appreciate it. Hanging sheets is hard enough without the wind whipping them around."

A gust blew the sheet, sticking it to both of them. Laughing, they untangled themselves.

"See what I mean?" Katie fiddled with her hair, fixing a loose pin.

He found her beyond adorable. Sliding a finger under a flyaway strand, he tucked it into place. Then without thought, his lips found hers. The connection could've been lightning forging them forever in that moment. He pulled away and felt a canyon-deep emptiness. "Katie. I'm sorry—"

She reached for him, and settled his lips against hers. Just as quick she broke away. "I'm not. But now I think I shouldn't have done that."

Pete swallowed, took a breath, and willed the fire between them to simmer. "Let's finish this chore. We need to talk."

Katie grabbed another sheet. She didn't look at him. "I know what you are going to say. You aren't interested in having a skittish wife. That's why I kissed you back. I'll never get another one."

He groaned. "You're wrong. I've been wanting to kiss you for a year. But after you hear what I have to say, you may want to send me away." He took the sheet from her hand and put it in the basket. He held her hands in his. "Last night I went looking for W.D. I found him at the saloon."

"I hope you left that dreadful man there."

He let go of her hands. She'd reject him as soon as she knew. He hated choosing, but he couldn't let his brother leave without trying to help him.

"Katie, I know how you feel about W.D., but he's my brother. I thought I'd lost him forever. I can't let that happen again. I'll leave, and Roy will help you find someone to work the farm." He leaned over and kissed the top of her head, hoping she'd say something. When she didn't, he backed away. "I hoped you would be able to forgive him."

He wanted so much to stay. If only she'd say something. Anything that would let him hope there was a chance for them that would include W.D. With great sorrow, he turned and walked away.

∞

He'd kissed her. Topsy-turvyed her world and then tore it apart with his words. Leaving. That's what she heard. The only man who'd ever shown an interest in her, that she'd been brave enough to kiss back, hadn't even given her a chance to tell him he could stay.

She didn't know he had a brother.

Henry came running through the sheets. "Katie, have you seen Pete?"

"Stop that! You'll get them dirty! He's in the barn. Pete's leaving. It's the two of us against the bank, Henry." She reached for a clothespin and tipped the bucket, spilling them on the ground. Pete had kissed her. Her first kiss, and now he was running away. If Henry weren't standing there, she'd kick the bucket across the yard.

"Why's he going?" Henry's lip trembled.

Crushed at Henry's pain, Katie pulled him close. "We have each other, Oma, and God. We're going to be okay." But would they? Katie wanted to kneel on the grass and yell at God.

"Henry, Katie." Pete stood behind them.

Katie's heart fluttered. Maybe it wasn't too late. She held on to Henry but turned to Pete. "We don't want you to leave."

"I came back because I thought about our. . ." He blushed and brushed his fingers over his lips.

Surely he wouldn't say anything about the kiss in front of Henry! Katie jumped in. "If W.D. can change, then we'd like him to stay. Wouldn't we, Henry? Pete, he's your family and you have to try."

"Yeah, besides our project needs finishing." Henry strode in front of Pete. "I can't do it by myself." He straightened his body and wore a serious look. "Besides, I saw you kiss my sister, and I think we've some talking to do. Man to man."

"You're right, Mr. Tucker. If I could speak with you privately, we could discuss the situation while working on the project."

"What are you two up to? And why speak with Henry? You aren't Papa."

Henry's shoulders drooped. "No, but I'm doing the best I can. Come on, Pete. Follow me."

∞

Pete stopped on his way to the house, struck by Katie's beauty. Her blond hair glimmered in the evening sun, where she sat on the back steps, snapping green

49

beans. Soon he'd ask her to be his wife, but first he had to show her the bees. "Come with me. There's something Henry and I have been working on. He wants me to show you."

"What is it?" She snapped the ends off a bean and tossed them into a pan at her feet.

"Always curious, aren't you?" And beautiful. He'd asked Henry if he could marry his sister. Henry said yes, with great enthusiasm. They'd discussed what that meant for the farm, and the two of them came to an agreement. He and Katie would live in the house until Henry married, then build another house.

"Papa said I was worrisome and nervous." She set the beans aside and stood, brushed off her apron, removed it, and draped it over the porch banister.

"I think you are a wise woman, not ready to jump in until you know the facts. That's why Henry and I haven't told you about any of this." He held his hand out and, when she took it once again, felt God answering another prayer.

"You haven't said a word about the big secret."

"Will you trust me enough to follow me to Sugar Creek?" All afternoon he'd been thinking of a romantic way to ask her to marry him. He should have proposed during the fireworks. Henry suggested he buy her doughnuts, but Pete thought that was what Henry would want. He'd ask W.D. if he had any ideas when he turned in tonight.

"That's Henry's place. Don't you know girls aren't allowed?"

"He said it was okay."

"Is it safe?"

"Please, Katie. You need to see this." Pete held out his hand. "I'd like to show you before it gets dark."

"Should I get a lantern?"

"No!" His chest hurt thinking about the night he'd taken one with him.

"Then we'd better hurry so we can get back before the June bugs come out." They walked in silence to the field by the creek.

Pete stopped just out of sight of the hives. "Remember, you're safe with me. Don't run. Are you ready?"

She nodded but her eyebrows let him know she was worried, along with her strong grip on his hand.

As they grew closer, she gasped. "There's an apiary! Did Papa do this?"

"Yes, and Henry and I have been taking care of them. We have jars of honey stacked in the woodshed."

"Wax, too?" She beamed. "You saved us and the farm. How did you know what to do?" Her eyes widened. "Did you get stung a lot? How much honey did you harvest? Are those all the queen bees Papa bought?"

"God saved you. I read a book." And fought off a swarm of bees. "Yes, I got stung. I forgot how much honey, you can count the jars and yes, those are the Italian queens your father purchased." He smiled down at her. "Anything else?"

"I want to go closer." She stepped forward then turned. "Not by myself!"

No one would call her nervous and skittish now. "I'll be right by your side." He felt her hand tremble in his. "We can go now. Henry wants you to know that he and I will take care of the bees. All we ask of you is to get the honey into jars."

"I can make hand creams, too." Her nose wrinkled.

Pete had a bad feeling, but before he could do anything, Katie sneezed. Loud. Bees came flying out of their hives, wings sounding like a train. "Run! We've got to get in the creek!"

Katie screamed once, twice, and then they were in the water.

"Put your head under!"

A few minutes later, the bees left, no longer considering them a threat. Katie's hair had come undone and was plastered to her face. Already there were welts forming on her cheeks.

"I'm so sorry! I didn't know they'd come after us if you sneezed."

"Guess we do now. I must look awful with all these stings."

"I love you, Katie Tucker. Honey, will you be my bride?" He plucked the hair from her cheek. "I could call you my honey bride because the bees brought us together."

"Yes! Yes! I'll marry you, Pete Dent."

∞

August came in hot and humid, but Katie didn't care. She and Oma had spent days fixing honey cakes for the wedding today. She wore her mother's wedding gown. It was a perfect fit. Oma said that was a sign she'd found the right man to marry. And that man was waiting for her at the altar.

Henry threaded his arm through hers. "Ready, Katie? Cause I sure am."

Katie swallowed; she couldn't speak. She nodded at her brother and took her first step down the aisle, where Pete waited. Soon she'd be Mrs. Pete Dent.

Dog Days of
Summer Bride

by Margaret Brownley

Chapter 1

Bee Flat, Kansas
1883

Seven-year-old Timmy Crawford looked up from the piano. "I don't have enough fingers to play eighty-eight keys," he complained.

Marilee Davis smiled down at her young student and straightened the sheet music. "But you have more than enough to play these three notes." She demonstrated, calling the notes out loud. "C...D...E....Now your turn."

Timmy poked each piano key with his forefinger as if squashing ants at a picnic.

"That's better," she said, not wanting to discourage the boy. "Now try again using *three* fingers."

This time Timmy got the fingering right but not the notes. Marilee was just about to correct him when her dog beat her to the punch. Shooting across the parlor in a black-and-white streak, his front paws landed on the ivory keys with a clash of dissonant chords.

Startled, Timmy cried out and almost fell off the piano stool.

Marilee pulled the dog away. "That's enough," she scolded. Naming him Mozart had been a mistake, though she called him Mo for short. All it did was put ideas in his furry head and make him think *he* was the music teacher instead of her.

"I'll take it from here." Her stern voice clearly showed she meant business. "Lie down!"

The dog's black tail drooped like a wilted flower. With a soft whimper he circled three times and flopped on the rug with an audible sigh. Muzzle lowered onto crossed paws, he gazed up at her with woeful brown eyes.

Mo didn't fool her a bit. Every doleful look and sorrowful gesture was an attempt to win her over, and nine times out of ten, it worked. But today her sympathy was with her young student, who stared at the dog with big round eyes.

"What's wrong with him?" Timmy asked. "How come he jumped up like that?" This was only Timmy's second lesson with Marilee, and he wasn't used to Mo's strange ways.

"Nothing's wrong with him," she said. *Much.* It was just her luck to get saddled with an eccentric, know-it-all cow dog. "He was just pointing out your wrong notes."

Mo usually let out a couple of warning barks before attacking the piano, allowing her to grab him before he did any harm. Today he sprang without warning.

"How does he know I played the wrong notes?"

"He can hear them. I think it hurts his ears." A tendril of blond hair escaped her tightly wound bun, and she brushed it away from her face. "So where were we?"

Timmy had taken lessons previously, but his original instructor had retired. The boy could barely play a scale let alone a simple melody, but that didn't keep his mother from insisting he was a gifted musician. Her opinion was based on him cutting his first tooth on a banjo case.

"Start from the beginning."

Timmy pulled his gaze away from the prone dog, swiped a strand of red hair out of his eyes, and scooted around to face the piano.

He really was a sweet boy, but with all his energy he would be better off playing ball with the other boys or cooling off in the nearby water hole.

Timmy hit another wrong note. Before Marilee could correct him, Mozart whimpered and covered his eyes with a paw. They were all three saved by the musical chimes of the grandfather clock. Mo rose on all fours, ears alert, tail wagging.

Marilee swore the animal could tell time. "That's enough for today, Timmy."

The boy didn't have to be told twice. He slipped off the piano stool and cautiously circled the dog.

"He won't hurt you," she said. Mo really was all bark and no bite. Usually, she put him outside during lessons, but this was Friday, and that was always the day the dog ran off to parts unknown.

She handed Timmy his music book along with a little bag of penny candy. "See you next week. Don't forget to practice."

"I won't."

"And don't let the dog out—"

Her caution came too late. No sooner had Timmy opened the door than Mo took a flying leap outside.

By the time Marilee stormed after him, Mo was halfway down the road. "Mozart!" she called, hands at her waist. "Come back this minute. Do you hear me? Now."

Calling the dog back did no good. It never did.

"Sorry, Miss Davis."

"It's not your fault, Timmy." Nothing could keep that dog from running off to God knows where every blasted Friday. Not even the high fence in back which he tunneled under with the ease of a child crawling under a bed.

Shading her eyes against the late-afternoon sun, Marilee watched until Mo was but a speck in the distance. For the love of Betsy, what was wrong with that crazy dog? She gave it a good home with lots of attention. So why the disappearing act?

Where he went was anyone's guess. All Marilee knew was that when he came back he reeked like last week's fish dinner.

If the unpleasant odor wasn't bad enough, he also conveniently forgot everything she'd taught him and returned home with the manners of a hog. He jumped on her good furniture, begged at meals, and drank from unsavory places. Well, enough was enough!

Mo didn't know it yet, but his wandering days were about to end. Marilee meant to see that he stayed put even if she had to keep him under lock and key every weekend from here to doomsday.

After watching Timmy race down the road to his house, she stepped back inside and closed the door. He was the last student of the day. Her work was over, and she was free to do. . .what? She sighed. She had two students on Saturday, but the only bright spot in the weekend was Sunday worship.

Without Mo the house seemed empty, and she sat down at the piano to fill the loneliness the only way she knew how. Closing her eyes, she let her fingers fly up and down the keyboard with the ease of rippling water. She lost herself to Chopin, Mozart, and Beethoven. She loved what the music helped her remember.

She loved even more what it helped her forget.

Chapter 2

B lacksmith Jed Colbert pounded the heated horseshoe into shape. Sparks flew with each clank of steel. He couldn't remember a July so hot, and he paused for a moment to brush the perspiration from his forehead with his arm.

He held up the U-shaped metal piece with a pair of tongs. Satisfied, he tossed it onto a growing pile just as his friend Curly Madison walked in.

"Got any hub rings?" he asked.

"Over there." Jed slanted his head toward a wooden box. "Sure is hot."

"Yep, sure is," Curly said, pawing through the metal parts. "It's the dog days of summer all right." Anyone meeting Curly for the first time might think his name a joke, for he was bald as a newly shorn sheep, the unruly curls of his youth nothing but a fond memory.

Curly set two metal rings on the counter and dug into his trouser pocket for a handful of coins. "Where's Dynamite?" he asked. Dynamite was Jed's black-and-white cow dog. "Still taking off on you?"

"Yep, every Monday like clockwork." Jed shook his head. "It's the craziest thing. I can't figure out where in the name of Sam Hill the fool dog goes. Who ever heard of a dog disappearing four out of seven days a week?"

Curly shrugged. "A dog gets something in his head and there's no changing it. Take Barney, for example." Barney was Curly's terrier. "It's been three years since I got him from his Catholic owner, and the dumb dog still refuses to eat on Fridays."

"Is that so?"

"Crazy, uh? Have you tried keeping the dog tied up?"

Jed picked up a piece of rope from his workbench. "Chewed right through it."

Curly shook his head. "It sure does look like he lives up to his name."

Jed tossed the rope back on the bench. "It wouldn't be so bad if he didn't come back smelling of perfume." Not that it was an unpleasant smell; not by any means. But it sure had caused him a wagonload of trouble.

The dog never failed to stink up the place, and the lavender-rose fragrance led Maizie Denton to jump to all the wrong conclusions. Now half the town considers him a womanizer and the other half wants to know his secret.

"Maizie still won't have anything to do with me. She's convinced I'm seeing other women."

Curly commiserated with a shake of his head. "Maybe you don't spend enough time with the dog. Maybe he seeks female companionship because he's lonely."

Jed hadn't considered that possibility. "I take him fishing every week. What more could he want?"

"Beats me." Curly palmed two coins on the counter and pocketed the rest. "I have enough trouble understandin' me own dog."

Just then a bark ripped through the air, and both men turned to the open double doors of the blacksmith shop.

"Speak of you-know-who," Curly said.

Dynamite rushed into the shop and greeted Jed with wagging tail. "It's about time you got here, boy." Jed scratched the dog behind both ears.

Woof!

"Whoo-eeee." Curly waved a hand in front of his nose. "It smells like a bordello in here."

"What did I tell you?" Jed said. "I've asked around town and no one, including Madam Bubbles, knows anything."

"All I can say is you better find out where Dyna spends his time or your love life will go to the dogs." Laughing at his own joke, Curly picked up the two metal hub rings and hobbled out of the shop. "See you at church," he called over his shoulder.

"See you." Jed stared down at Dyna. The dog had caused him nothing but trouble of late. It all started around four months ago. One day Dyna was a perfectly contented and normal dog. Then without warning, he started his disappearing act, and it had been one thing after another ever since.

Thanks to Maizie, his undeserved reputation as a philanderer had resulted in a decline of business. Some customers even went so far as to take their smithy needs to the next town.

The way things were going he'd soon be bankrupt, and all because of one dumb dog.

∞

By the time Marilee arrived at church that hot Sunday morning, the only place left to sit was next to that awful womanizing blacksmith, Mr. Colbert.

Mrs. Pickwick, president of the women's auxiliary, had warned her and every other woman in town to stay away from him. To hear her tell it, the man was quite the lady-killer and no woman was safe from his roaming eye.

None of this particularly worried Marilee. She was quite capable of taking care of herself. At least where men were concerned. Still, sitting next to him in church could put a dent in her reputation. People tended to expect the highest moral standards from teachers, even those who taught music.

Bee Flat wasn't an unfriendly town, but neither did it greet strangers with open arms. Some matrons seemed especially wary of single, independent women.

Until Marilee was fully established as a music teacher and had proven herself trustworthy, she would have to watch her step where men were concerned.

Mr. Colbert turned to look at her as she slid onto the pew next to him. A crooked smile followed a quick nod of his head.

Up close, the man was quite the looker, and it was all she could do not to stare. Eyes the color of cornflowers looked out from a rugged square face. A brown swag of hair dipped from a side part, partially covering his brow. Dazzlingly white teeth showed from beneath parted lips, and for some odd reason, her cheeks grew warm beneath his steady gaze.

Since it would be rude not to acknowledge him, she nodded likewise but refused to favor him with even a polite smile. A woman couldn't be too careful around a man with his reputation. Looking away, she pulled off her kid gloves and accidently nudged his arm with her elbow.

"Sorry," she mumbled and focused her gaze on the organist to the right of the altar. Her trained ear picked out a popular ditty amid the more somber notes.

Mr. Colbert leaned sideways and whispered in her ear. "'My Irish Molly-O,'" he said, naming the drinking song.

As if sharing a private joke, she met his smile with one of her own, and a moment of rapport sprang between them. She doubted that anyone else in the congregation had picked out the wayward tune. Not only did the organist have a sense of humor, but Mr. Colbert obviously had an ear for music. The clearing of a voice startled her into pulling her gaze away.

From the pew in front, Mrs. Pickwick shot her a disapproving look. Her boat-like hat would have looked more at home sailing across the deep blue sea. It made Marilee's modest straw hat look almost too sedate in comparison.

No sooner had the last of the organ's chords faded away than Reverend Hampton took his place behind the pulpit. An older man with gray hair and sideburns, he wore a black robe with winglike sleeves. "Let us pray."

Closing her eyes, Marilee clasped her hands in her lap. During the silent prayer, she tried to concentrate on her blessings and not dwell on the lost dreams of her past.

"Amen," the minister said and promptly began to preach on the dog days of summer. "Tempers flare as the mercury rises," he expounded. "But what if we think of it as the inverted *God* days of summer? How would that affect our ways?"

It was an interesting concept, and Marilee was eager to hear more, but she was soon distracted. Next to her Mr. Colbert was sniffing like a bloodhound. Or was he sniffling?

She certainly hoped he wasn't coming down with something. The last thing she needed was to catch a summer cold. She tried scooting closer to the aisle but was already as close to the edge as possible.

Mr. Colbert leaned sideways and his shoulder touched hers. "Your perfume reminds me of my dog," he whispered.

Thinking she'd not heard right, she glanced at him. "I beg your pardon?" she whispered back.

"My dog," he said. "You smell like my dog."

Her mouth dropped open. Had she really heard what she thought she heard? She'd been warned about his womanizing ways, but nobody mentioned his lack of good manners.

He remained silent for the rest of the sermon except for an occasional sniffing sound. Whenever she thought it safe to do so, she stole a glance at him. Invariably, she found him looking back. At such times she quickly turned her head and continued to seethe. Like his dog, indeed!

The congregation stood for the closing hymn. As the last organ chord faded away, she jumped to her feet and scurried up the aisle.

Outside, she was stopped by the mother of one of her students who anxiously inquired about her daughter's progress. Since it was neither the time nor place to discuss such matters, Marilee responded in general terms.

"Yes, Charlene is"—*a sweet girl but musically impaired*—"coming along quite nicely," she said. "Be sure to have her practice."

If it wasn't for mothers seeing genius where none existed, most music teachers would be out of business. Of course, the word *genius* was never used in describing female children. *Domesticated* was the best a girl could expect. The ability to play the piano was considered almost as important in landing a future husband as learning to cook and sew.

Not that it had helped Marilee. If anything, her ambition to play in an orchestra had proven to be a detriment in matters of the heart. No man was interested in a woman with such lofty ambitions. At the age of twenty-four she'd reached a dead end in both a marriage prospect and her dream of playing in a symphony orchestra.

While calming the anxieties of yet another student's mother, she saw Mr. Colbert step outside the church and head her way. Since he stood taller than most of the other men, it was hard not to notice his commanding presence.

He caught up to her just as she reached her springboard wagon. "Your glove," he said.

"Oh." She took the offered glove from him. Perhaps he wasn't completely without manners. Since he towered over her by a good six inches she was forced to look up. "Thank you."

"I fear we may have gotten off on the wrong foot," he said.

She drew on her glove and wriggled her fingers into the silky depths. "The wrong foot?"

"In church." He hesitated a moment. "I didn't mean to offend you."

"You mean by telling me I smelled like your dog?" she said, her voice cool.

He lowered his head and rubbed the back of his neck. "I meant it in a good way," he said and grinned.

She wasn't sure if it was the sheepish look or the crooked smile, but her irritation melted away like wax from a candle. "In that case, I guess there was no harm done," she said.

A look of relief crossed his face. "I don't think we've ever been formally introduced." He doffed his wide-brim hat. "I'm Jed Colbert."

Behind him Mrs. Pickwick stopped to stare, her pointed face dark with disapproval.

Marilee drew in her breath. "Miss Davis," she said, careful to keep her expression neutral for the auxiliary president's sake. "Now if you'll excuse me. . ."

"Sorry. Didn't mean to keep you."

Scrambling up to the driver's seat as quickly as decorum would allow, she gathered the reins in hand. "Good day, Mr. Colbert."

He raked her over with bold regard. Tipping his broad-brimmed hat, he flashed a smile. "I like it," he called up to her.

"Like what?"

"Why, your perfume, of course. My dog likes it, too."

She snapped her mouth shut. *Impertinent man!* Such a personal comment was bad enough, but to say it out loud so anyone could hear was beyond the pale.

With an indignant toss of her head, she shook the reins hard and drove off.

Chapter 3

Jed stood on the bank of the Bee Flat River. Bamboo fishing rod held over his shoulder, he brought it forward with a snap of the wrist. The line sailed overhead and hook and sinker hit the water with a splash.

Rod in hand, he settled onto a grassy spot. Nearby, Dyna sniffed the bucket of fish.

He came back Friday doused in perfume, but today only the faintest aroma of lavender-rose remained. Still, it was enough to trigger the memory of a pretty round face, big blue eyes, and hair that looked as light and soft as corn silk.

The perfume smelled a whole lot better on the music teacher than it did on Dyna, that's for certain and sure. It crossed his mind that she might know something about Dyna's disappearing act, but he soon discounted that idea. A fine lady like her wouldn't look twice at a big clumsy cow dog like Dyna.

He'd noticed her in church before, but this morning was the first he'd seen her up close. She was one of those uptight women from the east and obviously didn't think much of him.

He just wished she hadn't looked at him like he had rabies or something. Not that he blamed her.

There was probably a better way to say *"You smell like my dog."* The memory made him wince. Since being on the outs with the ladies, his manners had grown as rusty as an old water pump. It was scary to think he was better able to talk to an animal than a member of the opposite sex.

As if to guess his thoughts, Dyna let out a short, sharp bark.

"Shh. You'll scare away the fish." He picked up a stick and tossed it. Dyna bounded after it, ears back. Instead of retrieving it he stopped to sniff around a huge cottonwood. The stick forgotten, Dyna began to dig, dirt flying from beneath his front paws.

A clod of dirt landed in Jed's lap, and the smell of damp earth absorbed the last of the lavender-rose fragrance. "Watch it," he said, but the dog paid him no heed. He just kept digging.

Jed reeled his line in slowly and gave his bait a jerk. He didn't even know why Miss Davis was on his mind. She obviously wanted nothing to do with him. Nor he with her. He'd had his fill of female troubles in recent months. So what did he need a stuck-up music teacher for?

Dyna nudged his arm. When he failed to respond, the dog dropped something into his lap and barked.

"Shh. I told you—"

Thinking Dyna had dug up a bone, Jed lifted the soil-caked object between thumb and forefinger. Nope. Not a bone. He shook off the dirt, blinked, and shook some more. "What in blazes?"

He reeled in his line and set his pole on the ground. He then reexamined the packet. This time there was no question. Dyna had dug up a stack of money bound by a paper band.

Dyna ran to the hole he'd dug underneath the tree and looked back as if to say *what are you waiting for?* Jed jumped to his feet and followed. Dropping down on his knees, he reached into a rotted gunnysack and pulled out a second packet.

Hauling the sack out of the hole, he ripped it all the way open and his jaw dropped. There had to be at least fifty grand staring him in the face. He pushed back his hat and shook his head. Holy mackerel!

Chapter 4

Marilee bumped into Mrs. Pickwick at Henderson's Dry Goods early that Monday morning.

"How lovely to see you," Marilee said with a smile. With all her faults, the woman had been kind enough to take Marilee under her wing when she first arrived in town. It was Mrs. Pickwick's brother-in-law who rented her the house.

"You, too." Mrs. Pickwick ran a jeweled hand across a bolt of calico. "You are coming to the Tuesday Afternoon Club meeting, aren't you? I thought we would discuss what book we want to read next."

"I'll be there," Marilee said.

Mrs. Pickwick lowered her voice. "Was that Mr. Colbert I saw you talking to?"

"Mr. Colbert?" Just saying his name put her in a state of confusion. One moment he had insulted her and the next... "Oh, you mean in church?"

"Yes, and after."

"I left my glove behind, and he kindly returned it."

The woman stared down her pointed nose. "Well, you better watch your step. As you know, he broke Maizie Denton's heart with his womanizing ways."

Oh yes, Marilee did know that. Maizie and her broken heart had been the main topic of conversation for weeks and had taken up most of the Tuesday Afternoon Club meetings.

Thanking the woman for her concern, Marilee paid for her goods and walked out of the store with her basket of purchases flung over her arm.

At the end of the street a crowd of people was gathered by the windmill. A man stood on a soapbox talking through a megaphone. The bulk of his body told her it was Mayor Blackmon. Thinking it was a political rally, she set her basket into the wagon, anxious to get home before the heat of the day.

Just as she started to climb up to the driver's seat she heard an all-too-familiar bark. The sound came from the direction of the crowd. Shading her eyes against the sun she scanned the area. Was that Mozart sitting next to the soapbox? She couldn't be certain, but it sure did look like him. Of course most cow dogs looked alike. Still. . .

Only one way to find out. Reaching for her parasol, she popped it open and hurried toward the knot of people.

Standing on tiptoes, she craned her neck to see over the crowd. Next to the mayor stood none other than the blacksmith—Mr. Colbert, looking tall and handsome and very much in command. At his feet sat a black-and-white dog with exactly the same markings as Mo. If it wasn't him then it had to be his twin.

Closing her parasol, she inched her way through the crowd to get a better look. Marilee never thought to have something in common with the likes of Mr. Colbert, but it seemed they both owned similar dogs.

The mayor patted Mr. Colbert on the back. He barely reached the blacksmith's shoulders, but what he lacked in height he made up for in width.

"If it wasn't for Jed, here, and his dog, we might never have found the money," he said, and the crowd applauded.

Marilee waited for the clapping to stop before turning to the man next to her. "What's this about money?" she asked.

"The bank was robbed two years ago, and they just now found the stolen loot," he replied.

"Oh, I see." Marilee shouldered her way to the front of the crowd.

"As a token of our appreciation," the mayor was saying, "It's my pleasure to present this check for—"

Just then the dog looked up, spotted Marilee, and barked. He leaped toward the crowd in a streak of flying fur and practically knocked her down, his dirty paws all over her skirt.

She rubbed his head. "Mo, is that you?" Phew. What a dreadful odor. A wagonload of fish on a hot day couldn't smell worse. "What are you doing here?"

She looked up to find the mayor and Mr. Colbert staring at her. "Excuse me, ma'am, but I'm trying to make a presentation here," the mayor said. "The dog is a hero."

A hero? Mo?

"There must be some sort of mistake," she said. "This is my dog and—"

The mayor reared back and looked at Colbert. "What is she talking about?"

"That's what I want to know," Colbert said. "Dyna, come here, boy."

Much to Marilee's chagrin, her dog turned and ran to the soapbox. He plopped his behind next to Colbert, and his tail swept the ground like the broom of a fastidious housewife.

"Excuse me, sir," she called politely, not wishing to make a scene. She walked up to the soapbox. "But I do believe that's my dog."

As if to concur, Mo rose on all fours and moved to her side.

The mayor looked from Colbert to Marilee and back to Colbert. "Is that true?"

"Of course it's not true," Colbert said. "Dyna, come here, boy." The dog obeyed.

The mayor scratched his head. "The reward is supposed to go to the dog's owner."

"That would be me," Colbert and Marilee said in unison. They locked gazes.

"The dog is mine," she said. "His name is Mozart, but I call him Mo."

A look of annoyance crossed Colbert's face. "I'm afraid you're mistaken, Miss Davis. His name is Dynamite—Dyna for short."

Just then Marilee's student, Timmy Crawford, stepped forward. "That's Miss Davis's dog."

"Nonsense," yelled a baldheaded man. "That's Jed's dog."

Others jumped into the fray, taking sides. Soon it seemed as if the whole town was up in arms.

"That dog belongs to Miss Davis," a student's mother exclaimed. "And that's that!"

"Are you out of your cotton-pickin' mind? That's Jed's hound."

"Jed's hound my—"

"Hold it," the mayor pleaded. He held his hands up, palms out. "I'm sure we can settle this matter in an amicable fashion."

"I'll show you amicable," a thin man with a bushy beard yelled. "It's Jed's dog, and that's all there is to it. He owes me money and promised to pay me out of the reward."

The man next to him refused to back down. "I'm telling you that's Miss Davis's dog."

With that he punched the other man in the jaw.

No sooner had his knuckles made contact when fists began to fly. A baby let out a wail in high C, and his mother ran for cover. Thinking it was playtime, Mo barked joyfully as he pranced around two men rolling on the ground.

Marilee winced at the sound of pounding flesh. "Stop," she cried. "Please stop!" But her pleas fell on deaf ears. She glanced around for Mr. Colbert, but he was busy pulling two battling men apart.

The skirmish brought the sheriff on the run. He yelled for everyone to hold their horses and when that failed to get the desired results, he pulled out his pistol, pointed the muzzle upward, and fired three shots.

That did the trick. Men rolled off each other groaning and rubbing sore jaws.

The sheriff holstered his gun and his horseshoe mustache twitched. "What's going on here?"

Everyone started talking at once.

"She—"

"He—"

"One at a time!" the sheriff yelled. He pointed to Marilee. "What's this about you trying to steal Jed's dog?"

"I am *not* stealing his dog." Her voice shook with indignation, as did her parasol. "He's *my* dog. He was a stray, and I took him in and—"

"That dog ain't no stray. He's Jed's dog!" yelled someone from the crowd.

"Quiet!" the sheriff barked. This time he turned to Colbert. "Is this your dog or ain't it?"

"It's my dog, all right," Colbert said. "You know it is. Raised him from a puppy."

The sheriff circled the dog. "Well, it sure does look like Dynamite."

"Only it's not," Marilee said, fearing the tide had turned against her.

The sheriff pushed his hat to the back of his head and looked at her with narrowed eyes. "Okay, I'll give you two choices. One, we can split the dog in two and you'll each get half—"

Marilee gasped. "That. . .that's a horrid idea!"

The sheriff shrugged. "Worked for King Solomon."

Colbert glared at him, obviously in no mood for jokes. "What's the second choice?"

"The second choice is to put the dog in jail until we figure out his rightful owner."

Marilee shuddered at the thought of her dear sweet dog behind bars. "That would be downright cruel."

"And it still doesn't tell us who gets the reward money," someone yelled.

The sheriff took Mo by the collar. "I guess that will have to wait till these two figure out who owns what."

"Wait." Marilee moistened her lips. "You can give Mr. Colbert the reward. I'll take the dog."

"I don't care a fiddle about the money," Mr. Colbert snapped. "All I care about is Dyna."

"His name is Mozart."

Mr. Colbert leaned forward until his nose practically touched hers. "What kind of dumb name is that for a—"

The sheriff stepped between them. "All right, you two, that's enough. We're

68

gonna handle this in a democratic way. We'll let Dyna—Mozart—whatever his name, decide who he wants to go home with."

Mr. Colbert folded his arms across his chest. "Fine by me."

"Fine by me, too," she said, glaring up at him. *Harrumph.* The man looked so sure Mo would choose him. He would soon find out otherwise. Oh yes, indeed he would!

"All right then," the sheriff said. "Take ten paces back, both of you." He spread his arms to demonstrate.

Marilee counted her steps and turned; Colbert did likewise. They faced each other on the dusty road like two unflinching gunfighters about to draw their weapons. Their gazes clashed like swords.

"A silver dollar says the lady wins," the owner of the livery stables shouted.

No sooner were the words out of his mouth than bets flew back and forth like swarming bees.

Marilee tapped her foot. She didn't have time for this nonsense. It was hot, and she just wanted to take Mo home. She raised her parasol over her head and waited.

"Quiet!" the sheriff yelled at last with a wave of his arms. He waited for the crowd to fall silent. "This is how it's gonna work. You'll each call the dog by name. You have thirty seconds to get him to come to you and no more." He pulled his watch out of his vest pocket and held up a hand. "We'll let the lady go first."

Marilee patted her leg. "Come here, Mo. Come on, boy. Let's go home."

Mo wagged his tail and barked, but didn't move, not even when she promised to give him a nice juicy bone.

The sheriff dropped his hand to indicate her time was up and swung his attention to Colbert. "Your turn."

Colbert touched the brim of his hat as if to say this is how it's done. He then turned to the dog. "Come, Dyna. Let's go home." He promised to take the dog fishing and play ball.

The dog cocked his head and his ears perked up, but he stubbornly remained in place.

The sheriff shrugged. "It looks like the dog goes to the jailhouse with me."

Alarmed, Marilee tossed Mr. Colbert a beseeching glance. Her voice was shaking so much she could hardly get the words out. "Please, there must be another way."

Colbert's eyes were as dark as the night sky, and for several long moments no one spoke. "Dyna can go home with the lady," he said at last. "Least till we have time to figure this out."

"What about the money?" the mayor asked.

"Hold on to it for now," Colbert said. He then stalked away, and the crowd quickly dispersed.

Marilee walked over to Mo, who didn't look the least bit guilty for all the trouble he'd caused. "Let's get you home. You need a bath."

Waving the fishy smell away, she grabbed the dog by the collar and led him to her buckboard.

Chapter 5

By noon the next day it seemed as if half the women in town had beaten a path to Marilee's door. Mrs. Pickwick arrived a little after one in the afternoon.

Mo looked up from where he was napping. He gave a halfhearted wag of his tail and laid his head down again.

"I swear, every summer is hotter than the last," Mrs. Pickwick said, cooling herself off with a vigorous wave of her fan.

Marilee commiserated with a nod. "Do sit, and I'll get you a glass of lemonade."

Instead of sitting, Mrs. Pickwick followed Marilee into the kitchen, shaking her feathered head like a clucking hen. "Everyone in town is talking about the confusion with the dog. Who ever heard of such a thing?"

"It's crazy, I know." Marilee filled two glasses with lemonade and set them on the table. She then followed this with a plate of freshly baked macaroons.

"What are you going to do?" Mrs. Pickwick asked as she sat at the kitchen table and helped herself to a cookie.

Marilee took a seat opposite her. "I've been praying about it, and I've decided it's only right that I return Mo to Mr. Colbert."

Mrs. Pickwick practically choked. "Right? How could that be right?" She daintily wiped crumbs away from the corner of her mouth. "Why, you love that dog. And you take such good care of him."

"Yes, but I've only had him for a few months, whereas Mr. Colbert raised him from a puppy." Now that she knew where Mo went every week, she couldn't in good conscience claim Mo as hers. Through no fault of their own, she and the blacksmith had both been duped.

Mrs. Pickwick reached for another cookie. "If you ask me, it's a crying shame that you have to give him up."

"Yes, it is," Marilee said and took a sip of lemonade. She set her glass down, her mind made up. "But I've been thinking about what Reverend Hampton said about the *God* days of summer, and I know it's the right thing to do." If only it didn't hurt so much.

~

A familiar bark drew Jed's gaze from his workbench just as Dynamite bounced into the shop. A smile spreading across his face, Jed set his hammer down and stooped to give his dog a proper welcome.

"What are you doing here?" he asked. On a weekday no less.

For answer, Dynamite licked his hand, his tail whipping back and forth like a trainman's lantern.

A shadow blocked the open door and Jed looked up. He suddenly found himself drowning in the music teacher's pretty blue eyes.

Flustered, he stood. It wasn't often that such a lady set foot in his shop. "Miss Davis."

It was hotter than blazes, but she looked as cool as a cucumber in a blue skirt and lace shirtwaist that showed off her feminine curves to full advantage. Her outfit was topped by a straw hat tilted at a perky angle.

"Mr. Colbert," she said, matching his wary demeanor.

He reached for a rag on his workbench and mopped his forehead. "What brings you here?"

"I've been. . .thinking."

"Go on."

"It seems we've been sharing the same dog. I believe Mo. . .uh. . .has been taking advantage of us."

He'd been thinking along those same lines himself. It was the only thing that made sense.

"Seems that way."

"Since I've only had him for a few months and you've raised him from a puppy, it seems only right that you claim ownership."

He rubbed the back of his neck. "Well, now." Praise the Lord, his troubles were about to end. He could now claim the reward money and maybe even repair his undeserved reputation. Who knows? Once the whole story came out, maybe even Maizie would give him a second chance.

"That's mighty thoughtful of you, Miss Davis. Sure do appreciate it." He just wished he didn't feel so doggone awful. It was obvious she cared deeply for Dyna, just as he did.

She moistened her lips. "Do you mind if I say good-bye to him?"

"No, no, of course not. Go right ahead."

She stooped next to Dyna and rubbed his head. "I'm going to miss you, Mo, but this is where you belong."

Her voice broke, and much to Jed's dismay, her eyes filled with tears. He felt in his pockets. Blast it all. Of all the times not to have a clean handkerchief on him.

He moved toward her meaning to comfort her. Take her in his arms even. Make her tears vanish. But before he had a chance to do any of those things, she rose to her feet, lifted her chin as if trying to control her emotions, and backed toward the door.

"I—I better go," she stammered. Without another word, she turned and dashed out of the shop.

"Wait!" He chased after her, catching up to her just as she settled in the seat of her buckboard.

"Feel free to visit him," he called up to her. *Every day if you want.*

She blinked as if trying to clear her vision. "What?"

"Dyna. . .Mo." Whatever his name. "You can visit him any time."

She shook her head, and he could see her struggling for control. "I don't think that's a good idea. It would only prolong the pain. But. . .but thank you anyway. It was very kind of you to offer. Just. . .just take good care of him." She reached for the reins and drove off.

Watching her he felt awful. The worst. Lower than dirt. He didn't do anything wrong, but he sure did feel like a heel.

He blew out his breath. That crazy dog would be the death of him yet. He spun around and stalked into his shop.

"Now look what you've gone and done, you dumb dog." He stopped and looked around. "Dyna?" When that got no response, he called, "Mo?"

He looked under his workbench and behind the forge, but the dog was nowhere to be found.

Chapter 6

Arriving home, Marilee hardly had time to remove her gloves and hat when she heard the bark.

"Oh, no. God, please don't let that be—"

But it was. No sooner had she opened the door than Mo bounced inside and took up residence on her green velvet sofa.

"Mo. Down, now."

Mo hopped off the sofa and pranced around barking. Marilee dropped down to her knees and ran her hands through the dog's soft, fragrant fur. He still smelled pleasant from his earlier bath.

"You've got to go back, Mo. You can't stay here." The longer he stayed, the harder it would be to let him go. The problem was she didn't have time to take him back. A student was due to arrive at any minute. "As soon as I'm finished here, I'm taking you back to Mr. Colbert. Is that clear?"

A knock on the door announced her student's arrival, and she hurried to let the child in.

∞

Jed locked the door to his shop. His horse, Marshal, greeted him with a wicker. He ran his hand along the bay's neck. Thoughts of Miss Davis continued to plague him. If only she hadn't looked so devastated when saying good-bye to her. . .his. . .dog.

"Jed. Yoo-hoo!"

Much to his surprise, it was Maizie Denton, who hadn't talked to him since the day Dyna first came home reeking of perfume. He waited for her to cross the street. She was a tall, slender woman with blazing red hair and lively green eyes. She stopped and gazed at him over the saddle of his horse.

"I heard all about the fight over Dyna," she said. "It seems I jumped to all the wrong conclusions."

He tightened the cinch on the saddle. "Oh?" He frowned. "What conclusions were those?"

"I accused you of seeing other women." She did her fluttering eyelash thing. "All the time it was your dog carrying on."

He frowned. "I tried to tell you."

"Yes, you did, and I'm really sorry." Lips pouted, she gave him a beseeching look. "Will you ever forgive me?" she asked in a high-pitched voice usually saved for babies and puppies. When he didn't answer, she persisted. "Well? Do you or don't you?"

"Do I or don't I what?"

She looked at him all funny-like. "Forgive me."

"Sure. Why not?" he said. He wasn't one to hold a grudge, but he was still irritated at her for spreading rumors and ruining his reputation.

It was obvious she wanted him to say more, and when he didn't, uncertainty crossed her face. "You don't look like you forgive me."

"We'll talk about this later, Maizie." He splayed his hands in apology. "I've got to go and find Mo."

"Who's Mo?"

"What?"

"You said you had to find Mo?"

"I meant. . .Dyna. I have to find Dyna."

Her forehead creased. "I have to say you're acting very strange," she said, looking hurt.

For the second time that day he felt like a heel. None of this was Maizie's fault. Anyone smelling perfume would naturally assume he was seeing other women. If only she'd trusted him enough to believe him. Or at least trusted his faith in God enough to know he wouldn't lie to her.

"I just have a lot on my mind, is all. We'll talk later."

"When later?" she persisted.

"Tomorrow."

Satisfied that he had placated her, he untied his horse from the hitching post and mounted. He avoided her eyes as he turned his horse and galloped out of town.

∞

No sooner had her student left when Marilee heard a rap at the door. Mo jumped up with wagging tail.

"Sit, Mo."

Mo sat, but only long enough for her to open the door. He then sprang past her and greeted the visitor like a long-lost friend.

"Mr. Colbert!" she uttered. "You shouldn't have come all the way out here. I would have brought him back."

He looked up from petting the dog. "Jed."

"What?"

"My name's Jed."

"Marilee," she said without thinking, and he immediately repeated her name as if committing it to memory.

Normally she would object to such familiarity. But she liked the way her name sounded when he said it—like a rolled piano chord.

"Please come in," she said, a bit more primly than she intended. No sense keeping him standing on the porch for all the neighbors to see.

He straightened and stepped inside, his long lean form seeming to fill her parlor. The room suddenly seemed too small. He knocked against the kerosene lamp, catching it before it fell to the floor. Turning, he almost sent a music box flying off the low table.

"Sorry," he said, catching the music box just in time, only to knock against a porcelain figurine. Straightening, he glanced around as if checking for other obstacles. Clearing his throat, he ran a finger around his collar. "About the dog. . ."

"I had nothing to do with his return," she said. "He just showed up on my doorstep."

"Yes, well it seems we have a problem. But I think I've come up with a solution."

"A solution?"

His gaze locked with hers. He really did have nice eyes. Kind eyes. "We could go on just like before. He's yours from Monday to Friday. The rest of the time he's mine."

She bit her lower lip. "That doesn't seem fair. You only get him for the weekends."

He shrugged. "Not much I can do about that. He made the schedule, not me."

She tucked a strand of hair behind her ear. "It does seem like a rather strange arrangement, don't you think?"

"It's no different than what we've been putting up with for the last few months."

"I suppose. But I do want you to have the reward money. You had Mo first."

"Dyna," he said. "His name is Dynamite."

She gave her head a slight shake. "Such an unpleasant name for such a sweet and gentle dog, don't you think?"

"Sweet and gentle? He's a herding dog. Nothing sweet and gentle about that. Put him with a herd of cattle and we're talking Dyna the Terrible."

She glanced at Mo and gasped. He knew better than to sit on the sofa. "Mo, down. Now."

Jed frowned. "Is there something wrong with the sofa, ma'am?"

"What?"

"The sofa. You were worried about the dog sitting on it. Thought maybe a leg was loose or something. I'll be glad to fix it if you like."

"There's nothing wrong with the sofa. I just don't want him getting his fur and muddy paws all over the cushions."

Jed frowned. "I guess that means he doesn't get to sleep on your bed either," he said.

"Certainly not. No one gets to sleep—"

He raised a brow, waiting for her to continue. A moment of awkward silence passed between them before she cleared her throat. "Dogs don't belong on the furniture," she said.

"And Dyna agrees to your rules?" he asked, clearly astonished.

"Dyna doesn't, but Mo does," she said.

He surprised her by laughing. He really was a handsome man when he wasn't scowling. "That's all we need, a dog with a dual personality."

She laughed, too. She couldn't help herself.

He stared at her for a moment before seeming to catch himself. "I won't keep you any longer." As he backed toward the door, he bumped into the hat tree, catching it before it toppled over.

Suddenly she didn't want him to go. Or maybe she didn't want to face yet another night alone. "I was just about to have supper. Would you care to join me? I have plenty."

He looked surprised by the offer, but no more surprised than she was for making it. "That's mighty generous of you, ma'am. If it's not too much trouble."

"N–no trouble at all." Now look what she'd gone and done. Mrs. Pickwick would have a fit if she knew she'd invited the womanizing Mr. Colbert to supper.

"Make yourself at home," she said.

She left him alone with Mo while she escaped to the kitchen. It had been a long time since she'd entertained a gentleman guest. Not that he was a gentleman guest, of course. At least not in the full sense of the word, so there really was no reason for her heart to bounce around like a rubber ball.

Hands on her chest to still the thumps, she chided herself for behaving like a silly schoolgirl. Now where was she? Oh, yes. The stew. . .

Chapter 7

After nearly knocking the lamp over for a second time, Jed looked for a place to sit. Not brave enough to risk his bulk to the spindly chairs, he sat on the only sincere if not altogether stable piece of furniture in the room: the sofa.

He wasn't usually so clumsy, but the furniture seemed to crowd in like animals at a water hole. About the only thing he hadn't knocked against was the bookshelf, which contained at least half as many books as the lending library across town.

Pulling off his hat, he set it on the cushion next to him and raked his fingers through his hair. Confound it. He needed a haircut. Why hadn't he thought about that before?

The delicious smell wafting from the kitchen made him forget his hair. Whatever she was cooking sure did smell good, and his stomach rumbled. Should he join her in the kitchen or wait to be called? The lady seemed to be a stickler for rules, so he better wait.

Leaning forward, he rubbed his hands between his knees. That's when he noticed his dusty boots against the pristine red carpet. He lifted one foot and then another, wiping each toe box in turn on the back of his trouser legs.

"I'm lucky the lady didn't toss *me* in the bathtub," he muttered. He should never have come here straight from the shop.

As if to commiserate, Dyna sat up, ears perked. *Ruff!*

"You got that right. Dealing with women is rough all right." Especially one who was such a lady.

"Supper's ready," Marilee called.

Standing, he straightened his vest. He walked into the kitchen just as she set the second plate of stew on the table—and what a table it was. Candles and fresh flowers shared space with gold-trimmed china dishes and sparkling glassware.

Dyna padded after him and sniffed at the dish on the floor before gulping down his food.

"It sure does smell good," he said. "Real good." He hadn't had any honest-to-goodness home cooking since Maizie stopped talking to him.

He held her chair for her before taking a seat opposite. Dyna licked his plate clean and flopped down on the floor between them, resting his head on crossed paws.

Jed stared down at the confusing amount of silverware. Why anyone needed three forks and two spoons he couldn't imagine.

"Would you care to say the blessing?" she asked.

"Sure thing, ma'am." He might not know which spoon was which, but he knew how to talk to the Lord. He lowered his head and thanked God for the company, the food, and all that was good in the world. "Amen."

"Amen," she said. She picked up her napkin and, giving it a dainty little shake, spread it across her lap.

Following her lead, he picked up his own napkin and, forgoing the dainty part, set it on his lap still folded.

"If you don't mind my asking," he said, helping himself to a roll, "what brought you to Bee Flat?"

"Actually I ended up here by accident." She buttered her roll like an artist painting on a canvas. "I was on my way to San Francisco. When I came to the end of the train line, I couldn't find a stage or wagon train willing to haul my piano the rest of the way."

He stabbed a piece of meat with his fork. "So you decided to stay."

She shrugged. "At the time, it seemed like God's will. What better place for a music teacher than a town named Bee Flat?"

His fork stilled between the plate and his mouth. "I'm afraid I don't see the connection."

"B flat. It's a musical note."

"Don't know much about music," he admitted. "Don't know a B flat from a bullhorn."

"But you have an ear for it," she said. "You did pick out that ditty in church."

She sounded impressed and that surprised him. Surely it didn't take any special talent to recognize a tune. "I always wanted to play an instrument but never got around to it." He took a bite of his meat and chewed. Something occurred to him and he chuckled.

"What's so funny?" she asked.

"Actually, Bee Flat has nothing to do with music. It was named after a real person. Her name was Beatrice Flat. Bee for short. Story is that her covered wagon broke down on the way to Oregon. She refused to lighten the load by parting with her books, so she and her husband abandoned their plans to travel west and stayed here. They lived in a soddy and founded the town. Thanks to

Bee Flat the lending library was built first and the rest of the town sprang up around it." Not that he was a book person, himself, but judging by the number of books in the parlor, Marilee was an avid reader.

Her eyes shone bright in the soft yellow light. "I can understand someone not wanting to give up her books," she said.

"I reckon you can." He tried to think if anything he owned meant that much to him. Maybe his horse. And of course, Dyna. He buttered his roll with the same broad movements it took to feed the hogs.

"What's in San Francisco?" he asked.

"Music. Concert halls," she said. "I thought it would be a good place for a music teacher to live."

"Doesn't Boston have concert halls?"

"How do you know I'm from Boston?" she asked.

If the way she pronounced her As didn't give her away, her dress and manners surely did. "Lucky guess," he said.

"My mother was British, and my father was a military man stationed at Fort Warren."

"Is that right?" That explained a lot. The British were as rigid in deportment as the military. No wonder the dog wasn't allowed to sit on the furniture. "So why'd you leave?"

She hesitated as if she wasn't certain she wanted to answer the question. "I won a blind contest and the prize was an audition for the Boston Symphony Orchestra. It was a dream come true."

The closest Jed had ever come to hearing an orchestra was when Bruce Miller played his mouth organ along with Jake Randall's fiddle and Bob Henshaw's washboard. "What's a blind contest?"

"Contestants were required to play behind a curtain so the judges couldn't show favoritism to friends or relatives. No one knew I was a woman until the winner was announced. When my name was called it caused quite a stir."

He grinned. "I can imagine. But they let you audition, right?"

She shook her head. "Women aren't allowed to play in the orchestra no matter how well they play. I was accused of duping the judges, and it made the front page of the *Boston Globe*."

"That's. . .that's terrible."

"The worst part is, I was betrothed to a man running for his second term as senator. He lost the election because of me."

He blinked. A senator? She was engaged to a senator? "Surely he didn't blame you."

She shrugged. "Wouldn't you?"

He shook his head and covered her hand with his own. "I'm sorry."

Her cheeks turned pink as she glanced down at his hand, and he quickly removed it. An awkward silence passed between them before she asked, "What about you? How long have you lived in Bee Flat?"

Grateful for the change of subject, he reached for another roll. "Moved here from Austin, Texas, when I was seventeen. I was a wild one, and my pa sent me here to live with my uncle and learn the blacksmithing trade. When my uncle died, I took over the shop." He mopped up his plate with his roll.

"A wild one, huh?" she said. She flashed him the prettiest smile, but there was something in her manner that alerted him, a sudden reserve perhaps. Maybe she regretted being so candid about her past. His cousin accused him of being insensitive. In reality he simply didn't pick up on nuances. He needed things stated flat out, plain and simple. But oddly enough, tonight he was aware of every smile, every voice inflection, and every expression that crossed her pretty round face.

They chatted for the rest of the meal. She talked about growing up in Boston and how a German immigrant had taught her to play the piano in exchange for free room and board in her parents' home.

"The problem with living with your piano teacher is you couldn't get away with not practicing," she said.

He talked about growing up in Texas. He was only nine when his mother died, and that's when he started playing truant and getting into mischief.

"You must have missed her very much," she said.

"Yeah, I did."

Somehow the talk turned to Dyna. "When he came back smelling of perfume, everyone thought I'd been with other women," he explained. "Even though I hadn't."

"I'm so sorry." This time it was her hand that sought his. He stared down at the lily-white hand with the long tapered fingers, and his looked like a big clumsy paw in comparison.

He offered to help clean up afterward, but she refused to let him. So there really was nothing left to do but take his leave. But he didn't want the evening to end. He couldn't remember having such a good time.

"Thank you for the grub," he said. Since the word hardly did the meal justice he quickly corrected himself. "Eh. . .stew. You're a fine cook."

She smiled again and glints of golden light replaced the earlier sadness in her eyes.

"Don't worry," she said. "I'll take good care of him."

His mind drew a blank. "Him?"

"Mo...uh."

"Dyna," he said.

The dog stood between them looking from one to the other as if waiting for them to make up their minds what to call him.

She followed him out of the kitchen. Careful not to knock anything over, he plucked his hat from the sofa and set it on his head.

"Did you bring all this stuff with you on the train?" he asked, glancing around the room.

She shook her head. "My mother arranged for it to be shipped here. She insists that no one can be a proper lady without a properly furnished parlor."

"Well, then..." His gaze drifted to the piano. Would it be rude to ask her to play? Probably.

She opened the door and a whoosh of air teased the draperies and ruffled Dyna's fur.

He stooped to pet him. "See you on Friday, buddy," he said. "Don't forget."

"I'll see that he doesn't," she said.

He stood and touched a finger to the brim of his hat. "Mighty obliged."

No sooner had he stepped outside than she whispered a good-night and closed the door. The soft prairie breeze had cooled the air, and the sky was a mass of twinkling stars.

Overhead, Orion arched his arrow. Nearby was the constellation Canis Major—Orion's hunting dog. Jed didn't know much about music, but he knew about the stars. There wasn't a whole lot to do on a lonely night but gaze at the sky.

Just as he reached his horse, the sound of music wafted from the house. Marilee was playing the piano. The piece was unfamiliar but it wrapped around him like satin ribbons—or maybe a woman's loving arms.

Startled by the image that came to mind, he stood in the dark listening until the music stopped and there was nothing more to do but go back to his own lonely abode.

Chapter 8

During the week that followed, everything worked out according to plan. On Friday, Marilee opened the door and Mo took off like a streak of lightning.

She felt a certain obligation to follow through with her part of the bargain, but there really was no way of knowing if Mo reached his destination. Unless, of course, she drove into town to check.

Telling herself that she had only the most noble of motives in mind, she harnessed her horse to the wagon the moment Timmy's lesson was over.

Mo barked in greeting as she walked into the blacksmith shop. Jed looked up from his workbench, and she was momentarily distracted by the blue depth of his eyes.

Catching herself staring, she pulled her gaze away to pet Mo. "I—I just wanted to make sure he got here okay," she stammered, feeling foolish. She shouldn't have come.

Jed wiped his hands on a rag. "Just as we planned," he said and smiled.

She smiled, too. "I—I won't keep you then." She glanced at his workbench.

He followed her gaze to the haphazard accumulation of motor parts and tools. "Thank you for taking care of him."

"It was my pleasure," she said. Mission accomplished, she turned and walked out of the shop, the hem of her skirt flapping against her ankles.

∞

On Sunday, Jed sat next to Maizie in church, and Marilee didn't get a chance to talk to him and find out how Mo was faring.

Late that Monday afternoon, Mo showed up on her doorstep. As usual, the dog smelled like he was pickled in tuna, and his fur was matted with dirt. A good scrubbing took care of both problems in quick order. She towel-dried him and brushed him till his fur was soft and shiny, and then she changed into her prettiest blue frock.

A knock came at the door. Pinching her cheeks and moistening her lips, she hastened to answer it. It was Jed, just as she'd hoped.

"Wanted to make sure Dyna got here all right," he said, pulling off his hat and holding it to his chest. He looked particularly handsome this day. He'd gotten a haircut, and his shirt and trousers were clean and pressed, and boots polished to a high shine. Obviously, he was on his way someplace special.

"Yes, Mo got here with no trouble."

"That's good," he said. They stood staring at each other. "Something sure does smell good," he said.

"Roast beef." She hesitated. "I'd invite you to stay, but I know you have other plans."

He looked puzzled. "I don't have any plans, except to go home."

"Oh, I thought. . ." She glanced at his shiny boots. "Then perhaps you would care to join me for supper? There's plenty." She'd made certain of that.

He stood on the walkway in front of her house, a crescent-moon grin on his face. "Well, now. Since you put it that way. . ."

∞

The following Monday when Jed showed up on her doorstep to check that Mo had safely arrived at her house, he stayed for both supper and a piano lesson.

They sat side by side on the piano bench, elbows and shoulders touching, and she took him through the basics. He was a fast learner and seemed to enjoy the lesson. Mo enjoyed it, too. Not once did the dog growl or bark, not even when Jed hit a wrong note.

Jed didn't have a piano to practice on, so Marilee invited him to come back the following night. Taking her up on the offer, he appeared on her doorstep with a huge bouquet of sunflowers, a bone for Mo, and a candy dish to replace the one he'd broken.

On Wednesday night he showed up with a bowl of fresh strawberries from his aunt's garden, a piece of rawhide for Mo, and a tool kit to fix the broken leg on the chair he'd sat on.

On Thursday he surprised her with a box of striped candy—her favorite—a rubber ball for Mo, and a new lamp to replace the one he'd knocked over the last time he came.

"You don't have to bring me gifts," she said, though secretly she was flattered.

"You won't let me pay for my piano lessons," he said. "This is the least I can do."

Mo barked in agreement, and she and Jed shared a laugh.

∞

The Tuesday Afternoon Club met in the social hall of the Bee Flat Congregational Church. A dozen women belonged to the group, including the perpetually heartbroken Maizie Denton.

Only today she didn't look all that forlorn. For once she was all smiles as she took her place next to Marilee.

Mrs. Pickwick called the meeting to order. "Ladies," she said. "I have some exciting news. The best. . .Maizie, do you want to tell it or should I?"

Maizie grinned like a new bride. "You can tell," she said with a giggle, her curls bouncing off her shoulders. Dressed all in yellow, she looked and sounded like a canary.

"Very well," Mrs. Pickwick said. "Maizie and Jed Colbert are back together."

Marilee's mouth fell open. Jed was at her house every night for the last two weeks and hadn't said a word about Maizie. Not once during all that time had he so much as mentioned her name.

Applause followed the announcement and Marilee clapped along with everyone else, but her heart wasn't in it. Not that she wasn't happy for Maizie. Jed, too. But she would miss the long leisurely evenings she and Jed spent together. The lessons. The laughs.

"When's the wedding?" Mrs. Harper asked, and the question was like a knife in Marilee's heart.

"We haven't talked about that yet," Maizie said. "But he's taking me to the Dog Days of Summer Dance on Saturday. Who knows? Maybe he'll propose to me then."

Mrs. Pickwick pressed her hand against her forehead. "Speaking of the dance, that reminds me." Her gaze shot to Marilee. "Reverend Hampton asked if you would play that night. Our usual fiddle player will be out of town."

"Well, I—"

"Oh, please say yes," Mrs. Thompson pleaded. A recent newlywed, she was a pretty soft-spoken woman with a slight lisp. "I've heard you're a talented pianist."

Mrs. Pickwick interpreted Marilee's silence as consent. "Ah, good. It's settled then."

It was far from settled, but there really was no polite way to decline.

Maizie leaned sideways. "I bet you'll be glad when the dog situation is resolved."

"Resolved?" Marilee raised an eyebrow. "What do you mean?"

"Once I make a proper home for Jed, I'm sure Dyna won't want to wander anymore."

"I'm sure you're right," Marilee said, and added beneath her breath, "But Mo will."

⤸

That night Jed knocked on her door just like always. He looked and acted as if nothing had changed. He held flowers and candy but for once no replacements for broken furniture or knickknacks. That's because she had been quietly packing stuff away to make room for his large physique and broad movements.

"Well, aren't you going to invite me in?" he asked.

She stared at him dumbfounded. "How—how could you?"

He frowned. "How could I what?"

His innocent act floored her. More than that it infuriated her.

Since he continued to stare at her as if she'd taken leave of her senses, she decided to spell it out. "I'm sure Maizie would not approve."

A baffled look crossed his face. "Why would she mind? She understands the situation."

Marilee blinked. Was that all she was? A situation. "Maybe *she* does. But *I* don't. Good night!"

With that she slammed the door in his startled face. The nerve of him! What kind of woman did he think she was? Entertaining a single man in her home was shocking enough, but bucking convention with a betrothed man went against all common decency.

Jed pounded on the door. "Marilee, open up!"

"Go away."

"We need to talk."

"We're done talking, Jed Colbert. Now leave me alone!"

Maybe it was her tone of voice. Or maybe he just got tired of standing on the doorstep, but he finally left. She moved a curtain aside and watched through the window as he rode away on his horse.

Flopping down on the sofa she squeezed her hands tight on her lap, determined to hold her emotions in check. She wasn't even aware that Mo had joined her on the sofa until he laid his head on her lap. The dog was not allowed on the furniture, but Marilee no longer cared. Nothing mattered anymore. Not her music and certainly not the blasted sofa.

And that's when the tears came.

Chapter 9

The Dog Days of Summer Dance was held each year on the second Saturday in August.

Marilee crossed the still-empty dance floor and sat on the bench in front of the piano. Fortunately the instrument stood next to the window and a slight breeze cooled her heated brow. The dog days of summer traditionally lasted for forty days, and she hoped that held true for this year. So far it had been a hot and sultry summer, and she was anxious for it to end.

After smoothing her blue satin skirt and adjusting the sleeves of her white lace shirtwaist, she rubbed her hands together and stretched her fingers. She then played an arpeggio to test the keys.

The piano was so old that the F sharp sounded more like a G. If that wasn't bad enough, the foot pedals groaned beneath her feet like an arthritic old man.

Nevertheless, she sat primly upon the mahogany piano stool and gamely coaxed with nimble fingers whatever melody the yellowed ivories were willing to release.

Chatter mingled with the music as couples began arriving. Matronly chaperones sat on either side of the dance floor determined to nip an inappropriate touch or whispered proposition in the bud. Soon the party was in full swing.

Somberly dressed men whirled their partners around the dance floor. Next to the dark trousers and plain shirts, the women's frocks looked as bright and colorful as flowers in a summer garden.

Jed and Maizie walked in, and Marilee felt a squeezing pain in her chest. She didn't mean to stare, and when he looked her way, her fingers fumbled and she hit several wrong notes. Mortified, she pulled her gaze away from the couple and focused on the sheet of music with unseeing eyes.

Irritated at the way Jed affected her, she brought her hands down hard on the keys. Jed meant nothing to her. They were at the most friends—and new ones at that. She had no right to feel—what?

Abandoned? Betrayed? They shared a few meals together, had a few laughs. Oh yes, and they owned the same dog. But that was no reason to feel like she'd lost something dear and precious—like pieces of her heart.

Maybe she was just lonely. She'd made friends galore since arriving in town but none were really close. Only Jed. She'd confided in him, told him why she'd left Boston. Trusted him. Funny how two people can hit it off right away and others took a lifetime to know.

That was behind her now. She did what had to be done, and no matter how many times he'd returned to her doorstep—and there were many—she hadn't wavered.

Setting her thoughts aside, she pounded out waltzes, polkas, and, for the older folks, quadrilles. Music. That's the only thing she could rely on. That and her dear heavenly Father. As for the hurt, eventually she'd get over it. She always did.

∞

Jed knew the instant that Marilee left the dance hall. It wasn't just that the music had stopped, but the room had grown notably dimmer, as if she'd taken some of the light with her.

Fortunately, Maizie was busy talking to the new doctor in town, so she didn't notice him slip away. He hadn't even wanted to go to the dance, but Maizie had insisted "for old time's sake." By the time he realized he had feelings for Marilee, it was too late to back out.

Outside it was a warm and balmy night. A shiny gold moon glittered against a velvet jewel box sky. He found Marilee at the rear of the dance hall gazing upward.

The laughter of partygoers filtered through the slatted sides of the building, but not loud enough to drown out his pounding heart. Most certainly it was wrong of him to follow her. She obviously wanted to be alone, and she had made it clear—more than clear—that she wanted nothing more to do with him.

Still, he couldn't help himself. He wanted—needed—an explanation as to why she had suddenly turned against him. Was that too much to ask?

He hadn't known how much the evenings spent together had meant until they were no more.

He cleared his throat. "That's Sirius, the dog star," he said. "It's the brightest star in the sky." When she failed to respond he continued. "Since it was so bright, the ancients thought it contributed to the heat of the day. That's where the term 'the dog days of summer' originated."

This time she looked at him and he promptly forgot all about the night sky. Instead he wondered how her dewy lips would taste. What her hair would look like flowing down her back. How it would feel to take her in his arms and twirl her around the dance floor.

"Where's Maizie?" she asked.

He leaned against the trunk of a tree and hung his thumbs from his belt.

"Inside talking to friends."

"I better go back in." She started to leave, but he stopped her with a hand to her wrist. "Wait."

Her eyes widened and her lips parted slightly.

He forced himself to speak. "About Maizie—"

She shook her head. "Don't try to explain."

"She means nothing to me."

"Don't," she whispered. "Please don't."

Desperate to reach her, he tried another tactic. "Dyna arrived home all right." It's not what he'd wanted to say, but obviously it's what she wanted to hear for she relaxed beneath his touch. "Tomorrow I'm taking him fishing."

"I'm sure Mo will like that," she said, and the slightest smile touched the corners of her mouth.

"I miss you," he said.

The smile died, and a look of panic took its place. She pulled her hand from his and backed away. "Don't say that!"

He took a step forward. "Why not? It's true."

He heard her intake of breath. "I—I better go back inside."

He nodded but then something strange happened. It was as if his hands had a mind of their own. For suddenly he reached out and pulled her into his arms. Before either of them had a chance to recover, his lips claimed hers. And, just like that, she kissed him back.

Holy mackerel. It felt like he was floating on a cloud. Jumping Jupiter. The kiss was every bit as wondrous as he'd imagined—every bit as sweet and gentle. Every bit as tender and warm.

All too soon it ended. With a look of dismay she pushed him away. That's when the full impact of what he'd done hit him.

"I'm sorry. I had no right—"

"Go," she whispered. "Just go!"

He spun around and stopped in his tracks. Maizie stood a short distance away. Judging by the look on her face, she'd been there awhile. Eyes rounded, she let out an ear-piercing scream—just before attacking him with pounding fists.

Chapter 10

Marilee didn't dare show her face at church on Sunday. Ashamed by what had happened, she was even afraid to step foot out of the house. The gossipmongers were probably having a field day. It was like living through the Boston scandal all over again.

Why, oh why, did she let Jed kiss her? What made matters worse, she had kissed him back. Of all the stupid things to do. But all she could think about at the time were the delicious sensations his lips unleashed. His kiss had touched a part of her that only music had been able to reach. Nothing—not even the thought of playing in a full symphony orchestra—had made her feel the way Jed made her feel.

She clutched her hands together and closed her eyes. "God, forgive me. But if I had it to do all over again I would still kiss him back."

∞

On Monday Mo returned just like he always did. He barked and scratched and barked some more, wanting to be let in.

Marilee pressed her head against the door but didn't open it. "Go away, Mo. Go home."

Having Mo under her roof was just too painful. He only reminded her of Jed and how much she missed him.

She should never have gotten involved with him. Mrs. Pickwick had warned her about his womanizing ways. But did she listen? No, she didn't! The nerve of him, using her to cheat on poor Maizie.

She palmed her forehead. Now her name was mud. Already she'd lost several students because of one unguarded moment of ecstasy.

Mo whined and barked and scratched some more, but then all was quiet. She cracked the door open. Mo was nowhere to be seen.

Closing the door, she leaned against it before sliding to the floor and promptly bursting into tears.

∞

Curly shook his head and leaned against the doorframe of the blacksmith shop. "Tell me again how you happened to take one woman to the dance and ended up kissing another."

"I'm not really sure myself," Jed said. He wasn't proud of what he'd done. He had no right to even think about another woman until the issue with Maizie had been resolved. He thought it *had* been resolved.

Curly's forehead crumbled. "I never thought you could hurt Maizie like that."

"I didn't mean to." Jed raked his fingers through his hair. When did things get so out of control? "It was the last thing I wanted. I told her plain out that the two of us had no future together. The only reason I took her to the dance was for old time's sake. That's what she called it. How was I to know she told everyone we were a couple again, hoping that would make me change my mind?"

Curly rolled his eyes. "Sounds like you have no better luck handling women than you do your dog."

"Yeah, well, don't forget it was Dyna who got me into this mess in the first place."

"One thing is obvious," Curly said. "You have it bad for the piano teacher."

Curly didn't tell him anything he didn't already know. "Yes, but it would never work out," he said, though it pained him to admit it. "Marriage would be a disaster." He pointed to the pile of tools on his workbench. "I'm a slob. I like to go fishing and hunting and. . ." He shook his head. "I can't even sit on her furniture without causing mayhem. And her bed. . ."

Curly's eyebrows shot up and would have reached his hairline if he had one. "What about her bed?"

"She won't even let Dyna on it. What chance would I have?"

"It seems to me that you're concentrating too much on your differences and not enough on your similarities."

"What similarities? What are you talking about?"

"You both like music."

Jed shook his head. "I'm not even in the same country as she is, music-wise." He'd never even heard of Mozart and Chopping—or whatever his name was—before he met her.

Ignoring the comment, Curly continued. "You share the same dog, and most important of all, you're both Christians. Sounds like the perfect match to me."

"Try telling that to Marilee. She won't even talk to me. Said she refused to be a party to breaking Maizie's heart."

Curly shook his head. "You sure are in the doghouse."

Jed blew out his breath. He was in the doghouse all right, in more ways than one. Already he'd noticed a drop in business because of what happened at the dance. Since Marilee was part owner of the dog, he hadn't felt right about claiming the reward money. But the way things were going, he might have to collect it just to stay afloat.

∞

A knock sounded on Marilee's door early that Saturday morning. Upon finding Jed on her doorstep, she tried closing the door but he jammed his foot in the threshold.

"I have nothing to say to you," she said through the crack.

"I just want to know if there's a problem with Dyna."

She frowned. "What do you mean?"

"He didn't show up at the shop yesterday."

She yanked the door open all the way. "Yesterday? He should have returned home on Monday."

Jed's eyes widened. "What?"

"I sent him home on Monday." She covered her mouth with her hand. "Oh no! You don't suppose—"

He stepped inside the house. "Let's not jump to conclusions."

"But what if he's injured?" She clutched her hands to her chest. "Or was run over by a wagon. What if—"

"We'll find him," he said. "Someone must have seen him."

She gazed up at him, her eyes burning. "It's all my fault."

"It's nobody's fault," he said, his voice low. He wrapped an arm around her and murmured in her hair. "Dyna has a mind of his own. You know that."

She ducked from beneath his arm. His very nearness confused her, and right now all she could think about was Mo. *Oh God, please let him be all right.*

Jed shuffled his feet, tugged his hat down low, and almost knocked over the lamp again. "I'll go find him."

"Wait." She grabbed her gloves and hat. "I'm going with you."

Chapter 11

Jed drove the horse and wagon up and down the streets of Bee Flat with Marilee by his side.

"Mo!" she called, cupping her hands around her mouth.

"Dyna," he shouted.

He drove clear out to the Webber farm to the west and the Anderson flour mill to the east. They rode past fields of newly harvested wheat and acres of mile-high corn. Sunflowers grew in wild abundance alongside the road, the dark bonneted faces turned toward the sun. Sheep grazed next to a woolen mill, and cows lounged beneath a grove of cottonwood trees.

Neither of them mentioned Maizie or the dance. Today was about finding their dog.

No one had seen either Mo or Dyna and, as the day wore on, Marilee grew more distraught. Jed reached over to squeeze her hand.

"We better get something to eat," he said. Already the sun was playing footsies with the horizon, and neither of them had had a bite since morning.

She moistened her lips and nodded before pulling her hand away. A squeezing pain filled his chest as he drove back to town.

They stopped at Aunt Lula's Café, but neither he nor Marilee felt much like eating. Since it was too dark to continue the search, he drove her home and walked her to her front porch.

In the soft glow of moonlight, she looked even more beautiful than usual. "Better get some sleep," he said, his voice husky.

"You, too."

He lifted his hand to her cheek, and her skin felt cool beneath his touch. "Marilee—"

She backed away, warding him off with a shake of her head. "You'd best go."

⌒

Jed had unharnessed his horse from the wagon and started toward the wooden staircase in back of his shop leading up to his living quarters when he heard a familiar bark.

Heart leaping with joy, he spun around just as Dyna came shooting out of the dark. The dog jumped up on him, tail wagging so hard his entire body swayed from side to side.

Jed ran his hands through the dog's fur. "Where you been, boy, eh? I've searched high and low for you."

"He's been with me."

Jed lifted his gaze just as Curly stepped out of the shadows and into the yellow haze of the street lamp.

"Where'd you find him?"

"I didn't. He found me."

Jed straightened. "What's that supposed to mean?"

"He showed up on my doorstep last Monday."

"Monday!" Jed pushed Dyna down. "You had him all this time and never said a word?" He stared at his friend, incredulous. "You knew Marilee and I would be out of our minds with worry. What were you thinking?"

Instead of looking apologetic or regretful, Curly shrugged. "Don't blame me. Blame Dyna. He's a cow dog. He has herding instincts."

Jed's temper snapped. "What's that supposed to mean?"

"Bringin' critters together is what he does best, and I'd say he's done a good job of bringin' you and that pretty music teacher together. If you didn't take advantage of his disappearin' act then you're a bigger fool than I thought."

"What are you talking about? Take advantage. Why would I do such a thing?"

"Because that fella with a bow and arrow sure buggered you up. I mean we're talking big time."

Jed opened his mouth but denial stuck in his throat. "I don't want to hear this." He didn't need Curly or anyone else telling him what he already knew. He took the stairs two at a time with Dyna at his heel. He opened the door to his place and struck a match to light the lamp.

Curly walked in uninvited. "You might not want to hear it, but it's true. I can see it in your face. Nothin' makes a man look more miserable than love."

Jed wasn't sure that's how he looked, but it sure in blazes was how he felt. "It doesn't matter. It would never work out."

"You keep saying that."

"That's because it's true. She has a whole lot of book learning. Me? I didn't even finish sixth grade."

"So? Stay away from topics that require five-dollar words."

Jed grimaced. Vocabulary was the least of his problems. "Do you know who she was engaged to marry, back in Boston? A US Senator." God knows, even her scandals were high class. Most scandals involved money or sex, but not Marilee's; hers concerned no less than a symphony orchestra and a member of congress.

Curly shrugged. "She didn't marry him, did she?"

"No, but she would have had he not lost the election."

"If that's what's bothering you, then run for office. I hear tell that they're looking for someone to run for dogcatcher—too many dogs running around loose," he said with a pointed look at Dyna. "You'd be a shoo-in."

"I'm not running for dogcatcher."

"Well, you gotta do something. Otherwise you're gonna lose her fur good."

Jed sighed. "I've already lost her for good. She made it perfectly clear that she did not want to hurt Maizie more than she already was."

Curly made a derisive sound with his mouth. "You can forget about Maizie. After the fiasco at the dance, the new doctor took her home, and they've been cozying up ever since."

Jed's eyebrows rose. "Are you saying that Maizie and the doctor—?"

"Yep. It sure didn't take her long to get over you, did it? What is it they say about out of sight out of—?"

Jed's mind whirled. With Maizie out of the picture, he was free to. . .what? Mope around? Follow his heart? Continue his lonely life? The last thought moved him across the room. "Stop yakking and help me with this." Jed scooted the well-worn couch away from the wall.

Curly frowned, but he grabbed hold of the other side of the couch. "Why in tarnation are we moving furniture? And watch my back—"

"Quit complaining. You told me to do something and that's what I'm doing."

∞

Early Monday morning, a rap sounded at Marilee's door. She glanced at the tall clock. Normally this was time for Lucy Dillon's piano lesson, but her parents fired Marilee following the Dog Days of Summer Dance scandal.

She opened the door and blinked. Was that a couch? On her front lawn? She leaned forward for a closer look. It was a couch all right, but what was that awful piece of junk doing there?

She stepped onto the porch. Seeing Jed, she froze, as did her heart. "What is the meaning of this?" she managed to squeak out. "Why is this. . .this thing in front of my house?"

"This. . ." Jed began, "is a solid piece of furniture." He plopped on it and bounced up and down. "A man can sit on it without fearing for his life. Best of all, it will hold two people and even a dog all at the same time."

"Mo?" she whispered.

He slanted a nod toward the horse and wagon parked in front of her house.

She craned her neck for a better view, and her heart leaped with joy. "You found him!"

"Actually, he found me."

Her hands flew to her chest. "Thank God!" Drawing her gaze back to Jed she frowned. "But that still doesn't explain what this sofa is doing in my front yard."

"Oh, this." He rubbed the back of his neck and gave her a sheepish look. "I have something important to say. When I talk I tend to need a lot of elbow room, and if I have to replace any more broken stuff I'll end up in the poorhouse." He patted a sagging cushion. "I was hoping that the second person it would hold would be you."

Her breath caught in her lungs. Why was he doing this to her? "I told you I can't." She swallowed hard. "Maizie—"

He shook his head. "I just came away from seeing Maizie. She's now being courted by the new doctor and gave us her blessing." He waited for her to say something, and when she didn't he added, "Maizie has known for weeks that it was over between her and me. She just didn't want to believe it."

Marilee didn't move; she couldn't, for fear of waking up and discovering that none of this was real.

"No matter what you might have heard, I don't lie, and I don't cheat. I also have no right to be here." A muscle quivered at his jaw as he continued. "I don't have much school learning, and I'm never gonna run for dogcatcher. I'll probably tramp dirt on your rugs and forget to use a napkin. There'll also be times I'll come home smelling like a kettle of fish, and we'll probably have to keep replacing lamps." He drew his eyebrows together. "I'm not doing a very good job of selling myself, am I?"

"You're. . .you're doing just fine," she whispered.

Eyes burning with intensity, he continued. "What I'm trying to say is that I love you. Don't know how those Chopping or Baytoven fellows would have said it. All I can tell you is that I love you to the Dog Star and back."

She stared at him, unable to find her voice. Did he say *love*?

He rubbed his chin. "Do. . . Do you think you can make room in your life for a big oaf like me?"

Her heart pounded, and she inhaled sharply. She'd avoided naming her feelings for Jed for fear it would only lead to another broken dream. But now the word *love* played across her heartstrings and reached into the deepest part of her soul. The music rose to such a crescendo that she had to run to keep up with the rhythm.

And run she did, down the porch steps and into his arms. "Oh Jed!" He fell back with a startled look, but that didn't keep him from pulling her close and showering her with kisses. Or maybe she was the one showering him.

"I love you," she said when they stopped for air. "I love you more than Chopin and Schubert and Beethoven and—"

Jed matched her declarations with a few of his own—all to the tune of Mo's incessant barks.

Reluctantly, Marilee pulled her mouth away from his. "Do you think Mo planned for us to be together?" she asked. It sounded crazy, but after everything that happened, not that implausible.

Jed thought for a moment before shaking his head. "He might have brought us together, but I'd say that God was pulling the whiskers."

She laughed. "The *God* days of summer," she murmured between kisses.

She then drew her head back and called, "Come on, Mo."

The dog barked but remained in the wagon.

Jed whistled. "Dyna! Come on, boy." Still the dog refused to budge.

She met Jed's gaze. "What do you suppose is wrong? Why won't he come?"

"I don't know. Unless. . ." Jed lifted his voice. "Dyna-Mo. Come."

This time the dog jumped out of the wagon, cut across the yard, and jumped on the couch, all wagging tail and slobbering tongue.

Jed laughed. "So what do you say? Will you take this sorrowful looking piece of furniture to be your lawfully wedded couch?"

She pretended to give the matter some thought. "Only if you and DynaMo come with it."

Jed turned to their dog. "What do you say, boy? Is it a deal?"

Awf.

Jed grinned. "You heard it from the boss."

Joy bubbled out of her as she pulled from his arms. She then grabbed his hand and coaxed him to his feet. Laughing like a schoolgirl, she led him up the porch and into the house with Dyna-Mo at their heels.

"What are we doing?" Jed asked, knocking against the lamp.

Releasing his hand, she moved to the side of her sofa and pointed to the other end. "Grab hold," she said. "We're moving this one out and the other one in." The stilted furnishings were better suited for Boston's formal lifestyle and not for the new life ahead of her as Mrs. Jed Colbert.

Jed grinned from ear to ear. "Well, now. I'd say that's a doggone good idea.

What do you say, boy?"

For answer Dyna-Mo wagged his tail and flopped down on the floor as if he meant to stay.

The Fourth of July Bride

by Amanda Cabot

Chapter 1

Cheyenne, Wyoming Territory
June 1, 1886

I'm sorry, Miss Towson. I know you'd hoped for a different outcome. So did I." Though Dr. Winston was discussing her mother, he directed his comments to Naomi as he said, "Your mother's condition is deteriorating more quickly than I had hoped. I imagine you've noticed that."

Naomi nodded. No one could deny that Ma had been bumping into more things recently. The new spectacles that had cost far too much didn't seem to be making any difference, and the brown eyes that had once been the same shade as Naomi's seemed cloudier each day.

"How long do we have?" she asked. Ma was being uncharacteristically reticent and had said nothing since the doctor had completed his examination.

Doc's frown seemed at odds with his boyish face. Though many in the city believed him too young to be capable, Naomi had as much confidence in him as she did in Gideon Carlisle's ability to raise the best cattle in the territory. She shook herself mentally. Now was not the time to be thinking about Gideon.

"I hope I'm wrong," the doctor said, "but if the disease continues to progress at its current rate, your mother will be totally blind before Christmas."

Christmas! Naomi gripped the edge of the battered desk, struggling not to cry out. Every other time she'd brought her mother here, she'd found reassurance in the slightly shabby office. Not today. If Doc Winston was right, she and Ma had less than seven months before their lives reached another crossroads.

Naomi had believed they had far longer than that. It was true that Ma's eyesight had failed so much that she'd been unable to sew since last November, leaving Naomi as the family's sole support, but neither of them had expected total darkness to be so close.

As Ma nodded in apparent resignation, Naomi wrapped an arm around her shoulders. Her mother might have accepted her future, but she had not.

"Isn't there something we can do? Stronger spectacles? Different eye drops?" Though Naomi hated sounding desperate, she couldn't bear the thought that the woman who looked far younger than her forty-five years might lose what little vision remained. Naomi would do anything she could to save her mother's sight, and if that involved another pair of spectacles, somehow she'd find the money to pay for them.

The doctor shook his head. "Neither spectacles nor eyedrops will slow or stop the disease. There's only one possibility, and it's risky."

For the first time since they'd entered the office, Ma straightened her spine and looked directly at the physician. "Tell us more," she said, her voice as determined as ever.

Doc leaned across his desk, his expression radiating excitement. "I've read about surgery to remove the growths. If it's successful, patients experience a restoration of sight." His smile faded. "I must warn you, though, that there are many dangers. If infection sets in, death may occur."

The way he refused to meet her gaze when he pronounced the last sentence told Naomi he was worried. "What are the chances of that?"

"About half."

Terrible odds. Feeling her mother shudder, Naomi looked at the doctor. "Would you give us a few minutes alone?"

"Certainly."

When he left the room, Naomi turned so she was facing her mother. "What do you think?" Ma might not see clearly, but Naomi did, and she wanted to read her mother's expression.

"I don't want to be a burden to you." Ma's words were firm. "You've been the best of daughters. Not once have I heard you complain, even when you've had to shoulder more responsibility. By now you should have a husband and children of your own. Instead you're spending your life caring for me."

Naomi shook her head vehemently. It was true that she dreamed of marriage and cradling a baby in her arms, but until recently, there had been no man with whom she could picture sharing the rest of her life. And now, even though one man fired her imagination, she knew he was not the one God intended for her.

"There was no one I wanted to marry. I didn't love any of the men who came to call, not the way I love you." She gripped Ma's hand, needing the physical contact with the woman she loved so dearly. "The surgery frightens me, but it's your decision. I want to do whatever will make you happiest."

Her mother was silent for a moment, her eyes focusing on something in the distance. Then she spoke with no hesitation. "I don't want to be blind. I'm not afraid to face death, but I am a coward where blindness is concerned."

"Then we'll have the surgery." Naomi rose and opened the door, welcoming the doctor back to his office. "We've made our decision," she told him.

"It's a wise choice," he said when Naomi explained her mother's wishes. "I'd like to do it immediately, but that's not possible. I want to have a more experienced physician assist me." He pulled out a telegram. "Dr. Hibbard is the best in the country. I took the liberty of consulting him. He's willing to come out here, but he's not available until the middle of September."

"I can wait." Though they were only three short words, Naomi heard the enthusiasm in her mother's voice. After months of steadily declining vision, Ma finally had a reason to hope.

"There's one other thing," Doc said, "and that's Dr. Hibbard's fee."

Naomi tried not to flinch. Somehow she'd find the money. Perhaps Esther would let her work more hours. But when Doc named the amount, Naomi felt as if she were drowning and someone had just pulled the life preserver away from her. The other doctor's fee was more than she could earn in a year.

"So much?" Ma's voice rose with disbelief.

"He's the best," Doc explained, "and he's agreed to travel all the way from Boston to help you."

"I see." But the truth was, Naomi didn't see how she'd be able to pay for the operation her mother so desperately needed.

As if he understood her dilemma, Doc steepled his fingers and nodded. "You don't need to make the decision today. I told my colleague I'd have an answer for him next week."

"Thank you for everything you've done, Doc. I won't mislead you. It'll take a miracle to find that much money." Naomi rose and helped her mother to her feet. "Let's go home, Ma. It's time to pray for a miracle."

∞

He missed her. Gideon Carlisle tried not to frown. That would only make things more difficult for the artist, and that was not Gideon's intention. Jeremy Snyder had rearranged his schedule and was working extra hours to accommodate Gideon. The least Gideon could do was keep a pleasant expression on his face while his portrait was being painted. But he couldn't deny that he missed Naomi.

Though her beauty had caught his eye the first time he'd come here, he'd soon discovered there was much more to Naomi Towson than glossy brown hair, eyes the color of chocolate, and perfect features. Her wit and sense of humor were the reason he looked forward to his portrait sessions. Of course, he wouldn't tell Jeremy that.

"When can I see what you've done?" Gideon asked, trying to keep his thoughts from the lovely young woman who should be standing behind the counter helping customers decide whether to buy white or pumpernickel.

Though a bakery was an unusual place for an artist's studio, no one in Cheyenne seemed to care that Jeremy Snyder painted in a corner of his wife's bakery rather than in a studio of his own. His talent had made him one of the city's premier artists, and that was all that mattered.

Jeremy nodded as if he'd expected the question. "Another week. I promised it would be finished by June 10, and it will be. Don't worry, Gideon. Your mother will have it before the Fourth of July."

"Thanks." Gideon realized he'd never told Jeremy the reason he had commissioned his portrait at this particular time. "Mother's been pestering me to go back East to celebrate our nation's birthday ever since I arrived here. For some reason she won't believe me when I tell her Cheyenne has its own celebration and that it's a fine one. The painting is my attempt to placate her. I figured if she couldn't have me, she could have my likeness."

As he mixed paints on his palette, Jeremy nodded again. "If she's like many of the women I know, she'll want her friends to see both her son's likeness and the house he's built." It had been Jeremy's suggestion to include Gideon's home as part of the background, and he'd spent hours sketching the three-story mansion on what was being called Millionaires' Row.

Gideon still marveled at how he'd parlayed a small investment and a lot of hard work into a sizable fortune. There was no doubt about it. The grasslands of eastern Wyoming were the ideal spot to raise cattle. His had thrived to the point where he was now considered a cattle baron.

Gideon wrinkled his nose. He wasn't certain he liked that term, but he did like knowing that his mother could no longer claim that he was wasting his life. As the oldest of four sons, Gideon had been expected to follow his father's example and join the family law firm, but the law had never appealed to him. For as long as Gideon could recall, he'd wanted to spend his days outside. And now he did.

"Would you like some coffee and a piece of cake?" Esther Snyder asked as she approached her husband's studio. Though it consisted of nothing more than two stools and space for Jeremy's easel, the studio's location next to the tables where customers enjoyed cakes and cookies gave them the opportunity to see an artist working and had led to both additional commissions for Jeremy and more sales for Esther.

Esther laid the tray on the closest table and removed two plates of cake and a pair of coffee mugs. "It looks like Jeremy's ready for a break, and I suspect you are, too."

It was true that Gideon looked forward to the breaks, but the reason had little to do with the food. It was Naomi's company that made them special. "Did Naomi make the cake?" Perhaps she was merely running errands for Esther and would soon return. Though decorum dictated that he not mention her increasing girth, Gideon knew that Esther and Jeremy were expecting their first child before summer ended and that Naomi had been hired so that Esther could rest occasionally.

Esther shook her head. "Not today. She had to take her mother to the doctor this morning and asked for the whole day off." Esther gave Gideon an appraising look, as if she realized his question had been more than casual. "She'll be back tomorrow."

"Good." He wouldn't insult Esther by telling her that Naomi was a better baker. It might not even be true. After all, it was possible that the stories Naomi told while she shared cake and coffee with him were what made the baked goods taste so delicious. All Gideon knew was that he had no appetite this afternoon.

He rose and stretched, then looked at Jeremy, who had wrapped his brush in a cloth. "If you're finished with me today, I've got some business to attend to." It wasn't a lie, but the simple truth was that Gideon wanted to be anywhere but here where Naomi's absence weighed on him.

Once outside, he headed north to Twentieth Street, then walked two blocks west to Ferguson. He'd built his house on the corner next to Barrett Landry, the man some said would be one of Wyoming's first senators once the territory gained statehood. Gideon didn't care about that today. Today he didn't care about much, and that wasn't normal. Ever since he'd discovered Naomi wasn't at the bakery, Gideon had been disgruntled. Surely that would improve once he was home.

"Good afternoon, sir," Preble said as he opened the door. In his midforties, Preble was tall, thin, and distinguished, the perfect butler. "I put the mail in your office."

The small frown that accompanied his statement made Gideon ask if anything was wrong.

"I'm not certain, sir. You have a letter from Mrs. Carlisle."

No wonder Preble was concerned. Gideon's mother was as reliable as the Union Pacific, writing one letter each week, and that letter always arrived on Friday. Today was Tuesday.

Gideon nodded and handed his hat to Preble. "I'd better see what she has to say." Seconds later, he stood behind his desk and slid the single sheet of paper from the envelope. His eyes widened as he read the few words she'd inscribed. No! Not that!

Chapter 2

Gideon stared at the paper, unable to believe the words now engraved on his brain.

"Bad news, sir?" Preble stood stiffly in the doorway. Even though Gideon had told him there was no need for formality when they were alone, Preble had firm ideas of a butler's role and was not inclined to bend them.

"I suppose that depends on your definition," Gideon said. "My mother is planning to pay me a visit. It appears she doesn't believe my tales of Cheyenne's Independence Day celebration and wants to see it for herself." When Preble nodded, Gideon continued. "She's arriving on June 18 and will be here for two weeks." Or longer, if Gideon failed to meet the condition she'd outlined.

"I don't understand, sir. That sounds like good news to me. Surely she will be impressed with the city."

"If only that were all." Though Preble was privy to most of Gideon's business dealings, he would not tell his trusted butler some things, including his mother's determination to see him married.

It's time for you to wed, Gideon. If you can't find a bride in Cheyenne,
I'll order one for you. Gladys Fowler's son sent for one by mail, and she's
already a grandmother three times over.

"My mother is a stubborn woman. Once she makes up her mind, there's no way to change it." As distasteful as the prospect was, Mother would be here in less than three weeks, fully intending to set her last living son on the road to matrimony.

Preble inclined his head slightly. "I can assure you the house will be spotless and the meals excellent."

"I hope that will be enough." But it wouldn't. The sole thing that would satisfy Mother would be a bride or at least a fiancée.

There had to be a way out of this predicament, Gideon told himself as he paced the floor, ignoring the pot of coffee and plate of sandwiches Preble had brought him. Mother might be stubborn, but so was Gideon. No matter what she said, no matter what she threatened, he would not marry simply because she believed it was time. There had to be another way.

∽

"What's wrong, dear?" Esther asked as she measured a spoonful of peppermint leaves into the teapot. Though the bakery's owner was normally in the kitchen hours before Naomi, today she'd gone to Fort Russell to visit her niece and had left Naomi in charge. Within minutes of her return, Esther had turned her attention from the cakes Naomi had made to Naomi herself.

"Nothing's wrong." It was a lie, but Naomi didn't want to distress the woman who'd been so kind to her. Not only had Esther given her a job when she needed one, but she'd become more friend than employer, sharing both her kitchen and her clothes with Naomi until Naomi had saved enough to buy the simple skirts and waists that Esther deemed appropriate garb for the showroom part of the bakery.

Esther shook her head again and pulled two cups and saucers from the cabinet. "Your face tells a different story." She touched her expanding waistline. "You needn't coddle me, you know. Having a baby is perfectly natural, even at my advanced age."

Though Esther's lips quirked into a wry smile, Naomi knew she worried about being too old to be having her first child. She'd confided that both she and Jeremy had believed themselves beyond the age for marriage and had felt blessed to have discovered love. Learning that Esther was with child soon after their wedding had brought them both unexpected happiness and worries. Perhaps that was the reason Esther felt the need for the soothing comfort of mint tea.

"You and Jeremy aren't old," Naomi said firmly. Jeremy was just over forty, and Esther had yet to reach that age. "You're going to be the best parents any child would want."

"With God's help." The way Esther touched her stomach told Naomi the baby was kicking. "And with God's help and a cup of my peppermint tea, whatever is bothering you will lessen. Now, sit down, drink the tea, and tell me what's wrong."

Naomi blinked back the tears that had been so close to the surface ever since she'd heard the doctor's diagnosis, knowing she might as well tell Esther what had happened. One way or another, the older woman would get the truth from her. "It's Ma. Doc Winston says she'll be blind before Christmas unless she has surgery."

"Is she afraid of it?"

108

Naomi shook her head and took a sip of the steaming tea. Esther was right. Both the aroma and the flavor of the tea were soothing. Unfortunately, tea would not resolve Naomi's problem. "No. She's willing to take the risk, but we can't afford the doctor's fee."

"Don't worry." Leaning across the table, Esther put her hand on top of Naomi's, her touch as reassuring as her words. "Jeremy and I will help you."

If only it were so simple. Naomi's eyes filled with tears again as she told Esther the amount and watched the blood drain from her friend's face.

"Oh my dear. We don't have that kind of money."

"I know. No one does." At least no one she could ask for a loan.

If rumors were true, Gideon Carlisle had more than enough money to pay for ten surgeries, but though Naomi spent half an hour with the man on the days when he came for his portrait sitting, listening to tales of his adventures as a cattle baron and sharing stories of her decidedly more prosaic life, she could not possibly ask him for money. A lady simply did not do that, no matter how kind the man appeared to be, no matter how often the lady's thoughts turned to him. Naomi couldn't ask Gideon any more than she could approach a banker for a loan, not when she had no way of repaying it.

Esther was silent for a moment, her expression so peaceful Naomi knew she was praying. Then as the sound of men's laughter drifted into the kitchen, Esther rose and put her arm around Naomi's shoulders, giving them a quick squeeze. "God will provide," she said. "He always does." Moving to the other side of the room, she pulled a tray from one of the cabinets.

"Right now you need to provide for Gideon Carlisle. I never saw the man as disgruntled as he was yesterday. I offered him spice cake, but he wouldn't eat it because you hadn't baked it."

The thought gave Naomi her first smile of the day. "That's silly. You're a better baker than I am."

"Not according to him. Now, pour his coffee and take him a piece of that chocolate cake you made with the lemon filling. You know how he likes that."

"Of course." Naomi brushed the tears from her eyes before patting her hair to ensure that no strands had come loose. It might be foolish to be primping like this, but she wanted to look her best. Gideon Carlisle wasn't simply a customer; he was. . . She paused, trying but failing to find the correct word. All she could say about Gideon was that he was special.

When she entered the bakery's main room, he was in his normal spot, his back to the room as he posed for Jeremy. His blond hair was as unruly as ever, the curls refusing to be subdued even by macassar oil. Though she couldn't see them, Naomi knew that his eyes were the deep blue of a summer sky and that his nose tipped ever so slightly to the right. Gideon Carlisle wasn't the most handsome man she'd ever seen, but his face was one she could not forget.

Normally he waited until she had placed the tray on the table before he moved, but today he turned at the sound of her footsteps and rose from his stool.

"I'm glad you're here," he said. Surely she only imagined the strain in Gideon's voice. He gestured to a chair. "Please sit down. I have a proposition for you."

Chapter 3

"A proposition?" Naomi couldn't imagine what Gideon meant, but this was neither the time nor the place for a serious discussion. Over the course of the weeks Gideon had been sitting for his portrait, he and Naomi had discussed many things, but with the exception of God—a subject on which they had a decided difference of opinion—they normally focused on lighter topics. Judging from Gideon's expression, this proposal—whatever it was—was serious.

As if he recognized their need for privacy, Jeremy laid down his brush and headed for the kitchen, leaving Naomi and Gideon alone in an unexpectedly empty bakery. At least now no one would overhear whatever it was Gideon planned to propose.

He took the chair on the opposite side of the table, ignoring the coffee and cake she'd laid at his place. That simple action confirmed Naomi's belief that today was not an ordinary day. Normally Gideon assuaged his thirst with a slug of coffee before he spoke.

"I find myself in a bit of a dilemma," he said. "My mother is coming to Cheyenne."

Naomi didn't bother to mask her confusion. She wasn't certain what she'd expected, but it wasn't that. "That's good, isn't it? I remember you saying you hadn't seen her since you moved here." And that had been more than three years ago. Naomi couldn't imagine going three years without talking to her mother. Letters were all fine and good, but they could not compare to hearing Ma's voice and feeling her arms around her.

Gideon started to reach for the coffee, then drew his hand back. Something must be seriously wrong if he still wasn't drinking.

"It would be fine if her only reason for coming was to visit," he said. "Unfortunately, she has another motive. Mother plans to find me a wife."

When the doorbell tinkled and a customer entered the bakery, Esther hurried out to serve her. It was an ordinary day for most of Cheyenne's residents, but clearly not for Gideon.

Faced with his astonishing statement, Naomi found herself at a loss for words. "A wife, but. . ." Though her thoughts were whirling faster than a tumbleweed in a winter wind, she couldn't form them into coherent sentences.

A small smile crossed Gideon's face. "That was my first reaction. If I didn't love my mother, I would simply tell her I'm twenty-eight years old and the decision of who and when to marry is mine, but I can't do that. She'd be hurt. Besides, Mother's a determined woman—some would call her stubborn—and she won't give up. She really will send for a mail-order bride if I don't find one on my own."

From the first day she'd met him, one of the things Naomi had admired about Gideon was his determination. Though she'd assumed he owed that to his father, who'd been a prominent attorney in Philadelphia, now she realized that it had been inherited from his mother. Today Gideon needed more than determination. He needed a wife.

"I wish there were something I could do to help you."

His smile grew, and a twinkle filled those deep blue eyes. "There is. You can be my wife."

Naomi felt the blood drain from her face, and her heart began to pound as she stared at the man she thought she knew. Surely he hadn't said what she thought she'd heard.

He nodded as if he'd read her mind. "That's my proposition." As if pronouncing the words had returned him to his normal routine, Gideon reached for the coffee and took a sip. "I realized I don't actually need a wife. All I need is a fiancée for the two weeks Mother will be here. I'd like you to pretend to be my fiancée until the Fourth of July."

While Gideon spoke as calmly as if they were discussing the possibility of a late spring snowfall, Naomi's pulse continued to race. She heard the words, but their full meaning had yet to register. *Wife. Fiancée. Pretend.* Those simple words had never before been applied to her.

"It wouldn't demand too much of your time," Gideon continued, "though I would expect you to attend the celebrations and a few other events with Mother and me."

Naomi hadn't imagined it. He was serious. "I'm not the woman you want. Your mother will expect someone like Miriam Taggert." Not only was Miss Taggert beautiful, but as the daughter of one of Cheyenne's premier newspapermen, she frequented the same social circles as Gideon.

The corners of his mouth curved up as if he were amused. "I've met Miriam Taggert," he said. "She may have more expensive clothing than you, but she's only half the woman you are."

Gideon's compliment sent blood rushing to her cheeks. "Clothes matter," Naomi said, then laid her fingers on her lips. That sounded as if she were considering his proposal. Surely she wasn't.

"I agree. I'm also certain Madame Charlotte will be happy to create an entire wardrobe for you. At my expense of course."

"That wouldn't be proper." A well-bred lady did not accept personal items like clothing from a man who was not her husband.

Gideon disagreed. "The rules are less stringent for affianced couples. Besides, Madame Charlotte has a reputation for discretion."

Naomi took a deep breath, trying to imagine herself in one of the famous modiste's gowns. Though Naomi had never set foot inside the shop, she knew that Élan was where all the best-dressed younger women in Cheyenne bought their clothes. She'd heard several of them complimenting each other on their exquisite gowns when they stopped at the bakery for a pastry and a cup of tea.

Gideon reached across the table and laid his hand on top of one of Naomi's. "Please say yes. I need your help." His blue eyes darkened, leaving her no doubt of his sincerity. "I'm not asking you to do this out of the goodness of your heart. I can offer you more than the clothes you'll need for this charade."

He lowered his gaze for a second, then looked at Naomi again. "I didn't mean to eavesdrop, but I couldn't help overhearing your conversation with Esther. If you'll pretend to be my fiancée, I'll pay for your mother's surgery."

Naomi's breath caught as hope surged through her. Was this the miracle she'd prayed for? It felt like it, and yet she wasn't certain. "I'd be living a lie. That would be dishonest."

Gideon shook his head. "I won't deny that there would be some deception, but no one would be hurt by it. My mother will be happy, and your mother will have a chance to have her sight restored." He squeezed Naomi's hand. "Say yes, Naomi. Please."

She was tempted. Oh yes, she was. There was no denying the appeal of attending the opera, perhaps even dining at the InterOcean with Gideon. The clothing that he promised would be beautiful, but what attracted her most was the idea of spending more time with Gideon. Naomi enjoyed his company more than any man she'd ever met, and even when they were apart, Gideon was never far from her thoughts. Though she'd told no one, she'd dreamed of strolling through the park, her hand on his arm. If she accepted his proposal, that could happen.

Naomi closed her eyes for a second, trying to marshal her thoughts. Was

Gideon right in saying that no one would be hurt? If so, she owed it to her mother to agree. Hadn't she said she'd do anything within her power to save Ma's eyesight? Besides, the pretense would last only a few weeks, for as much as Naomi enjoyed Gideon's company, she could never marry him, even if he asked her.

From early childhood on, Naomi had known that the man she married must have a strong faith. Gideon did not. Their one serious disagreement had come the day Gideon had said that he hadn't attended church services in years and had no intention of ever doing so again.

"Why should I worship a God who doesn't love me?" he'd asked, and nothing Naomi had said had changed his mind.

As the memory of Gideon's declaration echoed through her brain, an idea began to take root. Perhaps this was the miracle she'd prayed for, a way to pay for Ma's surgery, but perhaps it was more than that. Perhaps Naomi was being given the opportunity to make a difference in Gideon's life.

She nodded slowly. "All right, Gideon. I'll do it. I'll be your pretend fiancée on one condition: I expect you to go to church with me."

∽

Gideon strode down Seventeenth Street, scarcely glancing at the opera house and the other buildings that dominated this section of the city. He had far more important things to worry about than what Arp and Hammond had displayed in their front windows. Relief that Naomi had agreed to his plan mingled with regret. He hadn't expected her to add a stipulation to their agreement, especially not that one. For the briefest of moments, Gideon had considered rescinding his proposal, but he did not, for he knew of no other woman in Cheyenne who could play the role he needed.

Gideon had met a number of single women whose mothers considered him a good catch, but they'd bored him. Even if one of them would agree to a pretend engagement, Mother would never believe he planned to marry her. Miriam Taggert was the exception. She was intelligent and entertaining, but unless he was mistaken, Barrett Landry intended to court her. Gideon wouldn't interfere with that. Besides, Naomi was a better choice. She was fun, she was feisty, and Mother would like her. If only she hadn't insisted on attending church.

He pushed open the door to Mullen's Fine Jewelry and blinked to adjust his eyes to the relative darkness.

"It's good to see you again, Mr. Carlisle." The proprietor whose massive handlebar mustache was as famous as the quality of his merchandise greeted Gideon. "I trust your mother liked her brooch."

"She did indeed, but today I want something different. I need a ring for my fiancée." Though it felt odd saying the word, Gideon knew he had to get used to it if the charade was going to be a success.

Mr. Mullen nodded as he led the way to one of the back counters. "Do I know the lucky lady?"

"I doubt it, but she's special." Even if Sunday mornings were painful, the rest of their short betrothal would be enjoyable, because—as he'd told Mr. Mullen—Naomi was a special woman. "I want something special for her."

The jeweler reached beneath the glass and pulled out a tray of rings. Though most were diamonds in various shapes and sizes, there was also an assortment of pearls and colored stones. And, as had been the case when he'd chosen his mother's brooch, each piece was beautifully made.

"These are my finest pieces," Mr. Mullen said, "but if none of them suit you, I can make something different."

Gideon had no time for custom jewelry. He planned to slip a ring on Naomi's finger tomorrow before she had a chance to reconsider their agreement. He glanced at the tray, smiling as one caught his eye. "That's the one. It's perfect."

Ten minutes later, Gideon was headed home, the square ring box tucked inside his pocket. As he walked north on Ferguson, his pace decidedly slower than when he'd left the bakery, he paused at the corner of Eighteenth Street. It wasn't difficult to understand why this location had gained the nickname of Church Corner, since it boasted churches on three of the corners.

Looking at the buildings, he wondered which one Naomi expected him to attend. Though his muscles tensed as he clenched his fists, Gideon tried to dismiss the sinking feeling that filled him at the thought of entering the house of God. That was far more dishonest than his pretend engagement.

Gideon hadn't set foot inside a church since the day God refused to answer his prayer. How could he praise a God who let his father and three brothers die of typhoid? Gideon couldn't, and he refused to be a hypocrite by attending weekly services as if he were a true believer. But now, thanks to Naomi, he had to do exactly that. He could only hope there would be no lightning bolts when he walked through the doors.

Chapter 4

Naomi was humming as she entered the small apartment she shared with her mother. It might consist of only two rooms and a tiny kitchen, but that had always been enough for them. She had heard others speak of feeling as if a great weight had been lifted from their shoulders, but she hadn't experienced that until this afternoon. For the past year, her worries about Ma had overshadowed everything, even the beauty of spring. Now those worries were greatly reduced, all because of Gideon.

"You sound happy," Ma said, raising her cheek for a kiss as she stirred the beef stew whose delicious aroma was filling the apartment. "I haven't heard you hum in weeks."

"I am happy." Rather than setting the table for supper as she normally would, Naomi grabbed her mother's hand and led her to a chair. She wanted Ma to be sitting when she heard her news.

"Our prayers have been answered," she said. "I found a way to pay for your surgery."

Though the growths had clouded Ma's eyes, there was no hiding the excitement that shone from them. "So soon? What happened?"

"I'm going to be an actress."

The excitement faded, replaced by confusion and disappointment. "I don't understand. You're a baker. How can you be an actress? You don't know anything about the stage."

Naomi realized the term she'd used so casually had created a problem when that hadn't been her intention. "Not on the stage. This is more of a private performance. Do you remember me telling you about Gideon Carlisle?"

Though she still seemed perplexed, Ma nodded. "The handsome young man who's having his portrait painted."

He was that and more. Much more. But Naomi had no intention of admitting how often her thoughts turned to Gideon. Instead, she patted her mother's hand as she said, "Gideon's faced with a dilemma." After she explained about Mrs. Carlisle's visit and edict, Naomi concluded, "So I agreed to pretend to be his fiancée while his mother is here."

Once again doubt colored Ma's expression. "Are you sure that's the right thing to do?"

"I am. I believe God gave me this opportunity to help you, but I need you to help, too. No one must know that it's a temporary engagement. We'll break it off quickly once Mrs. Carlisle leaves, but in the meantime it has to seem real. That means you'll have to be an actress, too." It was true that Ma didn't leave the apartment very often, but once word of Naomi's supposed betrothal spread, it was likely that friends and acquaintances would visit.

"I'll try." Ma removed her spectacles and rubbed her eyes, then opened them wide as if trying to imagine what it would be like to see clearly. "You're right, Naomi. This opportunity seems like a miracle, but I wish it was a real engagement. More than anything, I want to see you settled with children of your own."

"I know, Ma. I know." But that wasn't going to happen. Not with Gideon.

∽

"Good morning, Naomi." Though Gideon smiled, the smile didn't reach his eyes when he knocked on the door early the next morning. "I hope you haven't changed your mind."

It was an unusual greeting, but Naomi couldn't blame him. She'd wakened this morning wondering if their engagement had been nothing more than a dream. "I haven't changed my mind," she said, watching relief wash over him as she shook her head. "Come inside and meet my mother."

As she led him toward the table where Ma was still seated, Naomi could only imagine how the apartment appeared to a man who lived in a mansion. The main room, which served as dining room and parlor, was small, its furnishings shabby, but at least it was clean.

If the modest surroundings bothered him, Gideon gave no sign. He smiled at Ma as he said, "I'm pleased to meet you, Mrs. Towson. Although our arrangement is unusual, I can assure you that I will do everything in my power to ensure that Naomi is not hurt by it."

Ma peered through her thick spectacles for what felt like an eternity before she nodded. "I trust you." The approval surprised Naomi. In the past it had taken her mother weeks to pass judgment on the men who wanted to court her daughter.

Rising from her chair, Ma looked at Gideon. "If you would like some time alone with Naomi, I'll be in the kitchen."

Gideon nodded. "There is one thing I want to do before we go to Madame Charlotte's. Perhaps you'd like to sit down."

Naomi flushed, realizing she'd been remiss in not offering him a seat. But when she settled on one of the chairs in the parlor area, Gideon remained standing. A second later he descended to one knee in front of her, looking so much like a genuine suitor that Naomi's breath caught.

"I would be honored if you would wear my ring," he said, pulling a square box from his pocket.

Though she hadn't thought of a ring, it made sense that she would need one as a tangible sign of the engagement. As Gideon lifted the lid, Naomi gasped. Not even in her dreams had she imagined such a magnificent piece of jewelry. "I've never seen anything so beautiful." Three perfectly matched stones, a ruby, a diamond, and a sapphire, were set in a simple gold band.

Gideon's relief was evident. "I hoped you'd like it. When I saw the red, white, and blue stones, I thought they'd be a nice reminder of this particular Fourth of July. It seems my timing was perfect, because Mr. Mullen had just finished the ring an hour or so before I came into the store."

Naomi stared at the ring as Gideon slid it onto her finger. "I don't know what to say. It's magnificent." Looking at it she could almost believe the engagement was real.

"Let's see if we can find some gowns to go with it."

They walked the three blocks to Élan, Madame Charlotte's dress shop, and Naomi felt as if she were living a dream. Here she was, simple Naomi Towson, strolling with her hand on cattle baron Gideon Carlisle's arm, his ring on her finger. Only in her dreams would that have happened.

Gideon rapped on the door to Élan, and one of the most striking women Naomi had ever met opened it. Though Madame Charlotte was about the same height as Naomi and had the same dark brown hair and eyes, the similarities ended there. Madame Charlotte's almost regal posture and the perfectly fitted gown made her look like a creature from a different world.

"Good morning, Mr. Carlisle." Though it bore no hint of a French accent, Madame Charlotte's voice was low and cultured. She smiled as she greeted Naomi, and while her eyes assessed her, Naomi saw no disdain for her clothing. "It will be a pleasure to dress you, Miss Towson. I have a few garments I think will suit you."

The dressmaker motioned Gideon to one of the chairs in the main room before leading Naomi into a dressing room where she'd hung three gowns. Though she called them simple day dresses, the intricate detailing of the seams and the addition of double box pleats around the hem made them anything but ordinary.

An hour later Naomi's head was spinning when she left the shop. As

Madame Charlotte had predicted, two of the dresses needed only minor alterations, and one was a perfect fit. She'd insisted that Naomi wear that one. With its beautifully draped skirt edged in what the modiste told her was French lace, its small bustle, and the signature pleats, it was the most beautiful garment Naomi had ever owned. And the fancy gowns Madame Charlotte was planning to make for her were beyond anything she'd ever dreamed of.

"I feel like Cinderella getting ready for the ball," Naomi told Gideon as they strolled slowly down Ferguson Street.

"Don't worry," he said, his blue eyes sparkling with mirth. "My coach won't turn into a pumpkin."

But the engagement would end. That was how it had to be.

∞

Gideon smiled as he handed Naomi into the carriage. The past two weeks had been more enjoyable than any he could recall. Though Naomi still worked in the bakery, Esther had agreed that she was only needed in the morning. That gave them afternoons to spend together.

Believing it was important that his colleagues saw him with Naomi before Mother arrived, he and Naomi had done the things any courting couple would. They'd taken walks through the parks and drives through town, and of course, they'd attended church services together.

Those hadn't been as bad as Gideon had feared. Instead of thunderbolts the sermons had touched on God's love. The way the parishioners had nodded had made Gideon wonder if he was the only one who didn't believe in God's love, but he wouldn't think about that today. Today would be the first true test of his and Naomi's acting abilities, for today was the day his mother arrived.

Though Naomi smiled when they arrived at the depot, she was unable to hide the faint trembling of her hand. Gideon gave her a reassuring smile, hoping to allay her concerns. "It'll be fine," he said.

She nodded and gestured toward the construction site. "I'm glad we're getting a new depot." It was an obvious attempt to change the subject from her nervousness.

Gideon agreed, both with her sentiment and the diversion. "It'll be more suited to a city of Cheyenne's stature." The old depot was a simple wooden structure, whereas the new one would be an impressive red sandstone edifice. "I'm surprised it took the Union Pacific so long to agree to build it, but there's no doubt that it will be beautiful when it's finished. Who knows? We may even have statehood by then."

A whistle announced the approaching train, and Naomi turned her attention to the passengers emerging from the iron horse. She wouldn't recognize Mother, but Gideon did. His smile broadened when he saw the familiar figure descend the steps. Mother looked no older than she had when he'd left home, but it appeared that she'd gained a few pounds and was now decidedly plump. Though her clothing was covered with dust from the long journey, she showed no sign of fatigue.

"Gideon!" Mother cried, opening her arms to greet him.

He suffered the hug and the cloud of perfume that surrounded him when she wrapped her arms around him, then turned toward Naomi.

"Mother, I'd like you to meet Miss Towson. Naomi has done me the honor of accepting my ring." He remembered Naomi's concerns about dishonesty and chose his words carefully.

For a second, Gideon thought his mother had misunderstood him, but as a grin spread across her face, he realized it had simply taken her awhile to believe him.

"Is it true? You're really getting married?"

Rather than lie, he said, "That's the normal end of an engagement." Perhaps he was prevaricating, but Gideon didn't want to contribute to Naomi's discomfort. She gave him a quick smile as his mother approached her.

"Oh my dear, let me look at you." Ignoring the other passengers who were still disembarking, Mother tipped her head to one side and gave Naomi a thorough appraisal. To his fiancée's credit, she did not flinch but simply smiled as if this were a common occurrence.

"You're a lucky man, Gideon, to have found yourself a girl as pretty as Naomi," Mother said when she'd completed her inspection. She turned back to Naomi. "You will let me call you that, won't you?"

"Certainly, Mrs. Carlisle."

Unsure what his mother would do or say next, Gideon gestured toward the baggage being unloaded from the back of the train. "Let's get your trunks into the carriage. I imagine you're tired from your journey and would like a chance to rest."

"Nonsense! I want to get to know my future daughter-in-law. Take us somewhere we can have a cup of coffee while we get acquainted."

Though the logical destination would have been Esther's bakery, Gideon didn't want to run the risk of other customers recognizing Naomi as the woman who used to serve them. Gideon wasn't ashamed of Naomi's work—how could anyone be ashamed of the delicious cakes she baked?—but he didn't want Mother to realize how sudden their engagement was. And so he took them to

Mr. Ellis's Bakery and Confectionary.

Once inside, Gideon sat back, watching the two women. He no longer harbored any doubts about Naomi's ability to carry off the charade. She kept Mother entertained with anecdotes of how Cheyenne had grown and changed over the past few years, while Mother interjected her own stories of life in the East, leaving Gideon no need to do more than murmur an occasional assent. The day was turning out even better than he'd hoped.

"You've done well for yourself," his mother said at supper that evening. "Naomi is exactly the kind of woman I hoped you'd marry. I'm proud of you, Gideon."

He swallowed in a vain attempt to dislodge the lump that had taken residence in his throat. He'd wanted Mother's approval, but oh, how he wished it were not based on a sham.

Chapter 5

"Let me feel the fabric."

Naomi bit the inside of her cheek, trying not to cry. Here she was, dressing for dinner with Gideon and his mother at Cheyenne's most prestigious hotel, wearing the most beautiful gown she'd ever owned, and her mother could barely see it. Though neither of them discussed it, Naomi knew that Ma's eyesight was worsening. That was why she wanted to touch the fabric.

"Madame Charlotte told me it's dupioni silk that came all the way from China," Naomi said as she placed a fold of the sumptuous material in her mother's hands. By some small miracle, her voice bore no hint of the worry that weighed so heavily over her. If she'd had any doubt that her agreement with Gideon was the right thing to do, watching Ma's vision fail would have erased it. Naomi had to do whatever she could to restore her mother's sight.

Ma gave her a bittersweet smile as she stroked the sapphire-blue silk. "It must be wonderful to sew with fabric like this. Of course," she said with a chuckle, "my customers had nowhere to wear anything so fine. Now turn around so I can see that demi-train you've been telling me about."

When Ma had admired the drape of the gown, she sighed softly. "I wish I could see Madame Charlotte's store. All those beautiful fabrics and the dresses..."

That wish was easy to grant. "I'll take you there on Monday. I'm sure she'd be happy to show you around."

But Ma shook her head. "I can't do that. It wouldn't be right to take her time when I have no intention of buying anything from her." Ma's expression brightened at the sound of a knock on the door. "You just enjoy your evening. I expect you to tell me every detail."

As Naomi ushered Gideon into the apartment, he gave her an appreciative look and grinned. "I'll be the envy of every man in Cheyenne when I walk into the InterOcean with the most beautiful woman in all of Wyoming Territory on my arm."

Though his compliment made her flush with pleasure, Naomi couldn't accept it. "It's the gown. Madame Charlotte's creations flatter everyone."

122

"It's not the gown," Gideon said firmly. "Remember, I've seen you in your work clothes. You were just as fetching then."

The light flush turned into a full-fledged blush. "Are you trying to turn my head?"

He shook his head. "I'm simply telling the truth. Now, if you're ready..." He led her outside and helped her into the carriage where his mother was waiting.

"That's a lovely gown, Naomi. Did you order it from Paris?"

Naomi smiled at Mrs. Carlisle. Though they hadn't discussed what they'd be wearing tonight, Gideon's mother had donned a light blue silk gown that complimented Naomi's sapphire blue. "It's not from Paris. There's a wonderful dressmaker right here."

"I'm surprised."

Gideon chuckled as he flicked the reins. "Admit it, Mother. Almost everything about Cheyenne surprises you." He turned and gave Naomi a rueful smile. "Despite the letters I've written her, until she arrived here my mother believed everyone lived in tents and had a steady diet of pork and beans."

"I don't imagine that's on the menu at the InterOcean."

It wasn't. With its linen tablecloths, fine china, and silverware, the Inter-Ocean's dining room lived up to its reputation as Cheyenne's most elegant eating establishment. The food was equally good, the menu featuring elk, venison, and trout in addition to a wide selection of beef dishes. Succulent vegetables and breads almost as delicious as Esther's made it an unforgettable meal, while the array of desserts surpassed anything Naomi had seen.

"You were right, Gideon," Mrs. Carlisle said as they savored the delicate crème brûlée they'd chosen to end the meal. "Cheyenne is not what I expected. It appears to be a fine place to raise a family."

She turned to Naomi. "Won't you tell me about your family? Do your parents live in Cheyenne? How many siblings do you have? Just call me a nosy old woman, but I want to know more about the woman who's going to marry my son."

Though the questions were far from intrusive, Naomi was uncomfortable with them, simply because she and Gideon hadn't discussed how to address the issue of her mother. Deciding that her only recourse was honesty, she said, "My father died five years ago, and I'm an only child."

Mrs. Carlisle took another sip of her tea. "That sounds as if your mother is still alive. Does she live in Cheyenne?" When Naomi nodded, Gideon's mother's face brightened. "Wonderful! I'd like to meet her."

They hadn't planned for this. Naomi shot Gideon a look, but his expression was inscrutable. She was on her own here. "My mother's eyesight is failing, and she rarely leaves our home."

"Surely she'll make an exception for me." Mrs. Carlisle turned to Gideon, the firm line of her lips confirming Gideon's statement that his mother was a determined woman. "Do your best, son, to persuade Mrs. Towson. I'd like the four of us to celebrate the Fourth of July together."

Gideon nodded. "I'll do what I can."

Though Naomi saw regret in her mother's eyes, her voice was firm as she said, "I'm sorry, Mr. Carlisle, but I don't believe that would be a good idea. I bump into things in unfamiliar places. I wouldn't want to embarrass you."

"I assure you, you wouldn't embarrass anyone. My mother is genuine in her wish to spend time with you."

Naomi bit back a smile at the evidence of Gideon's determination. If she were a betting woman, she would wager that Ma would capitulate.

Ma was not smiling as she plucked at her skirt. "It shames me to admit this, but I have nothing appropriate to wear to the Cheyenne Club."

Gideon had explained that the plans for the Fourth of July celebration included attending the parade and then dining at the private club where he and many of Cheyenne's wealthiest businessmen were members.

"Madame Charlotte can remedy that," he said smoothly.

Ma shook her head. "You know our situation." Though she didn't say "financial situation," the implication was clear.

Gideon would not be dissuaded. "I shall, of course, pay for your clothing as I did for Naomi's."

"That would not be proper." Ma had questioned the propriety of Gideon's buying Naomi's fancy clothing but had ultimately agreed that as long as no one other than Gideon and Madame Charlotte knew, it would not compromise Naomi's reputation.

"Surely a man is permitted to give his future mother-in-law a gift."

"But she's not your future mother-in-law." Though she'd been silent during the exchange, believing it was between Gideon and her mother, Naomi couldn't help interjecting her protest.

His eyes were serious as he said, "In the eyes of the world, she is." Turning to Ma, he continued his argument. "If you agree, you'd be making my mother very happy and giving Madame Charlotte additional income. Are you willing to deprive them?"

Though Ma hesitated, Naomi knew her mother was on the verge of agreeing. "All right, Mr. Carlisle."

"Gideon," he said firmly. "I insist you call me Gideon."

"All right, Gideon. I accept."

After she'd escorted Gideon to the door, Naomi turned to her mother. "Do you know what just happened?" Without giving Ma a chance to reply, she said, "Gideon made your wish come true. Now you have a reason to visit Élan."

⟶

"They're thick as thieves." Gideon gestured toward the two mothers who'd been talking practically nonstop since they emerged from church. This was the first time the women had met, and though Gideon had had fewer concerns than Naomi, he was still grateful that Mother had taken an immediate liking to Mrs. Carlisle. Despite the concerns she'd voiced about her vision, he had not noticed any hesitation when Naomi's mother walked into church, nor had she bumped into anything—or anyone—when they'd been at the parade.

Since the Fourth of July fell on a Sunday this year, the schedule had been altered slightly, with the parade delayed until noon to ensure that it did not conflict with worship. When the church service had ended, Gideon had taken the three women back to his house for what Preble termed a light repast, and from then on, his mother and Naomi's had acted more like long-lost friends than new acquaintances.

Gideon wasn't complaining. Far from it, for the older women's absorption in their own conversation meant that he could devote all of his attention to Naomi.

She was more beautiful than ever today, with that lovely dark hair arranged in some kind of intricate style. He wasn't sure how a woman would describe the dress she was wearing; all he knew was that it showcased her beauty. His heart had swelled with pride as he'd stood at her side during the parade, watching the marching bands, the school children, and the politicians make their way through the city streets. And now they were seated on the porch of the Cheyenne Club, waiting for dinner to be served.

"I haven't seen Ma this excited in years." Naomi kept her voice low, though Gideon doubted that either of their mothers would have overheard her.

"I could say the same thing about my mother." She'd been content before, but today she was almost radiant with happiness. "Her visit is working out even better than I'd expected, and it's all because of you." Gideon leaned over and placed his hand on top of Naomi's. "Thank you, Naomi. This is turning into the best summer I can remember."

How he hated the thought that it would end.

125

Chapter 6

The aroma of bacon greeted Gideon as he descended the stairs, leading him into the dining room where he found his mother seated with a plate of bacon, eggs, and toast in front of her.

"Good morning, Mother," he said, wondering why she was downstairs half an hour earlier than normal. His mother was a creature of habit, and once she established a schedule, she rarely deviated from it.

She smiled and gestured toward his chair at the head of the table. "Indeed, it is a good morning." When he was seated and had poured himself a cup of coffee, she spoke again. "You were right when you told me I'd like Cheyenne. I do. So much, in fact, that I've decided to spend the whole summer here." She glanced at the door leading to the butler's pantry, as if expecting it to open. "Preble told me it's unusual to have snow before October, so I shall plan to leave on October 1."

Mother was staying? Gideon stared at her, realizing he hadn't been this shocked since the day he'd received her letter announcing her plans to come to Cheyenne to meet his bride-to-be. What was he going to do now? Mother was supposed to be here for two weeks, not more than three months.

Count your blessings. Gideon could practically hear his mother's admonition, and so he followed it. At least she hadn't decided to remain until the wedding. He'd be in a real pickle if she did that.

"Aren't you going to say something, son?" Mother wielded her knife and fork, cutting a slice of bacon into precise bite-sized pieces. As she slid one into her mouth, she lifted an eyebrow in a gesture Gideon knew meant that her patience was fading.

"I'm surprised." He wouldn't admit that he was shocked. "I thought you couldn't leave the Ladies Aid Society for more than a few weeks."

Mother's hand fluttered in a dismissive wave. "Nonsense. Gertrude Menger will do an excellent job leading them. She's been hoping for an opportunity to make some changes. This will be her chance." When she'd stirred a teaspoon of sugar into her tea, Mother nodded. "I'll send her a telegram today."

Gideon tried not to groan at the realization that this wasn't a passing fancy and that he would never dissuade her.

"What's the matter, Gideon? Don't you want me to stay?"

"Of course I do." It wasn't a lie. He enjoyed having Mother here. It was simply that the pretend engagement complicated everything. "I'm concerned that I won't be able to entertain you properly. I have to go out to the range this week. My foreman does a good job, but I need to check on him and the hands occasionally."

Mother's smile brightened. "That won't be a problem. I can spend the time helping Naomi and her mother plan the wedding." As she spread jam on a piece of toast, Mother gave Gideon one of those "mother knows best" looks that he remembered from his youth. "I do wish you'd reconsider and have the wedding before I leave. Christmas Eve may seem romantic now, but there's nothing like being a summer bride."

Unbidden, Gideon pictured Naomi carrying a bouquet of wildflowers, smiling as she walked down the aisle toward him. He caught his breath, startled by the intense longing that rushed through him. Though the idea was more appealing than any he could recall, now was not the time to regard marriage the way a drowning man did a life preserver. When he married—if he married—it would not be merely to placate his mother. But though he tried his best, Gideon was unable to dismiss the image of a wedding—a real one.

∽

"Gideon." Naomi was startled by the sight of him entering the bakery kitchen. Ever since she'd begun the pretend engagement, though she no longer served customers in the front room, she spent her mornings in the kitchen, helping Esther mix and knead the breads and pastries that were the bakery's mainstays. Never before had Gideon interrupted her.

Naomi washed her hands and turned toward him. "Is something wrong?" she asked, unable to read his expression.

When she'd seated herself, Gideon took a chair across from her at the table that served as both a work surface and a dining table for Esther and Jeremy. "I'm not sure. I hope not. How is your mother?"

Something was definitely wrong, because Gideon didn't normally dither. Naomi blinked at the non sequitur. "Ma's fine. This morning she told me again how much she enjoyed yesterday."

"So did mine." Gideon nodded, the corners of his mouth descending into a frown. "She enjoyed it so much that she's decided to extend her visit."

While Gideon was visibly uneasy with the idea, the jolt of happiness that spread its warmth throughout her shocked Naomi. Her heart sang at the realization that if Mrs. Carlisle remained in Cheyenne, Naomi would have a reason to continue spending time with Gideon. It was foolish—oh so foolish—to care, and yet she did.

"How long does she plan to be here?" Naomi asked as calmly as she could.

"Until October first." Gideon's increasing discomfort told Naomi she was the only one who rejoiced in the prospect of more time together.

He leaned forward slightly, placing his forearms on the table. "I hope you'll agree to extend our arrangement. I know October is far later than we'd agreed, so I'll do more than pay for your mother's surgery. I'll set up a bank account for you and will deposit the same amount as the surgeon's fee into it now and then again in October when Mother leaves." His tone was as flat as if this were a business arrangement. But, of course, that was exactly what it was.

"No!" The word came out more forcefully than Naomi had intended. It hurt—oh, how it hurt—to be reminded that she was nothing more than an employee, even though that's what she was. Naomi bit the inside of her cheek, trying not to cry out in frustration. Their agreement had been clear. It was only she who'd thought she and Gideon were friends, or maybe even something more.

Gideon's eyes darkened with shock, and his face registered disappointment. "I know it's a lot to ask, but I need you, Naomi. Tell me what it'll take for you to agree."

"Nothing." He'd misunderstood her protest and had no way of knowing that she'd been insulted by his offer of money. "You don't owe me anything more. I agreed to be your pretend fiancée while your mother was here, and I will do that for however long she stays."

Unable to hide his relief, Gideon nodded then shook his head. "That doesn't seem fair. I feel as if I owe—"

"You don't owe me anything." Naomi cut him off. "You've already gone beyond our original arrangement by paying for my mother's clothes. She and I will probably need a few more dresses if we're to continue the charade until October. That will be enough."

But it wasn't. Naomi wanted a real engagement followed by a real wedding followed by life with Gideon. Unfortunately, what she wanted could never be.

Chapter 7

Gideon tried not to fidget. These minutes before the service began were always difficult for him. He knew he was supposed to focus on God, but instead his thoughts were whirling in a dozen different directions, reminding him of tumbleweeds in a storm. When they landed, it was often on the woman at his side.

Lowering his eyes, Gideon stared at the floor, trying to corral his thoughts. It had been more than a month since Mother had announced her extended stay. Though Gideon had been concerned by her insistence on helping with wedding plans, Naomi had managed to sidestep the issue, citing a reluctance to make any arrangements until after her mother's surgery. That was a valid-sounding reason, and Mother had accepted it.

She and Mrs. Towson had tea together every afternoon, talking endlessly. Gideon had no idea what they discussed and suspected he was better off not knowing. He wasn't complaining though, for the time the two mothers spent sipping tea was time he had with Naomi.

The woman was amazing. His suppositions from before they'd begun their charade of an engagement had proven to be true. Each day found Gideon more fascinated by the woman who was pretending to be his fiancée. Naomi had a lively sense of humor and an open curiosity. She even seemed genuinely interested in his cattle. That made her the only woman he knew who could listen to stories about roundups and orphaned calves for more than a minute without her eyes glazing over.

When they were together, Gideon felt complete, as if Naomi filled the emptiness deep inside him. Perhaps that was the reason he thought of her so often and even dreamed of her. Perhaps that was the reason the time he'd spent on the range had seemed endless. Perhaps that was the reason he wanted to be with her, not just for the duration of his mother's visit but forever.

He closed his eyes and bit back a groan. It didn't matter how much he wanted Naomi as his wife. Gideon knew that would never happen, for there was an insurmountable obstacle between them: God.

An hour later, he tucked Naomi's hand into the crook of his elbow and escorted her down the church steps. "Why do you think God loves you?" he asked as they headed north on Ferguson, trailing the two mothers on their way back to Gideon's home. His question was more than an idle one. If he had any hope of breaking down the barrier to their life together, he needed to understand why Naomi was assured of God's love. Though Gideon felt peace steal over him during the services, he still had no evidence that God loved him.

Naomi looked up at him, her eyes so filled with joy that envy speared him. What must it be like to have such comfort? "I don't *think* God loves me," she said. "I *know* it."

"How? What happened to make you so sure?" This was a strange conversation to be having as they walked along one of Cheyenne's most elegant streets, nodding at passersby as they traveled the two blocks to Gideon's home, but an urgency he could not explain compelled him to keep probing.

Naomi paused and turned so she was facing him. This time her expression was solemn, as if she realized how important the discussion was. "I've seen the evidence. Whenever I most needed something, God provided."

Did she know how fortunate she was? Gideon hoped so, because his experiences had been far different. "Can you give me an example?"

"I'll give you two. You know my mother used to be a seamstress. Late last year her eyesight became so bad that she could no longer sew. At the same time, I lost my position as cook at the boardinghouse down the street. No matter how hard I tried, I couldn't find other work. Sooner than I thought possible, our savings were depleted. I didn't know what to do other than pray for help. That same day I saw a sign in the bakery window, saying that Esther was looking for an assistant. The money I made there kept Ma and me from being evicted."

It was no wonder Naomi's faith was so strong. Her prayers had been answered. Gideon's had not. "You said you had two examples."

She smiled, the sweetness of her smile setting his pulse to racing. "You were the second answer to prayer. I knew it would take a miracle to find the money to save Ma's sight, so I prayed for a miracle. The next day you proposed our engagement. That wasn't coincidence, Gideon. That was God's hand. He brought you into that bakery at exactly the right time to hear about my problem and then solve it."

Gideon had been told that God had a sense of humor. Perhaps this was an example of it, making a man like Gideon, a man who didn't believe in God's love, His instrument. "I can see why you believe that God was at work," he told Naomi. "The problem is, He's never once answered my prayers."

"Are you certain of that?"

Remembering his father's and brothers' graves, Gideon nodded. "I am."

∽

"I can't believe I'm here." Though she'd admired the building that was one of Cheyenne's landmarks from the exterior, this was Naomi's first time inside the Opera House. The grand staircase, the chandelier with its fifty-two electric lights, and the skylights that loomed overhead were even more magnificent than she'd heard. "I feel like Cinderella again."

Gideon laid his hand over hers and squeezed it as he smiled. "You're more beautiful than Cinderella ever dreamed of being."

Though her pulse raced as much from the touch of his hand as his effusive words, Naomi pretended to be unaffected. "I keep telling you it's due to Madame Charlotte." Tonight's gown was a ruby-red creation with deceptively simple lines and intricate beading on the bodice. The combination was more than eye-catching. It was stunning.

Knowing this was probably the only chance she'd have to wear the gown and her sole opportunity to visit the Opera House, Naomi was determined to enjoy every minute of the evening. In little more than a month, Mrs. Carlisle would be on her way home, and the engagement would be over.

Naomi tried not to frown. She wished—oh, how she wished—that the engagement didn't have to end. Though she wasn't certain how or when it had happened, Naomi could not deny that her feelings for Gideon were deeper than she'd thought possible. Everything she did, every thought she had centered on him. When she was spreading filling on the cinnamon buns this morning, she thought of how Gideon would make a show of sniffing the air when he smelled their distinctive aroma. When she was dressing her hair tonight, she remembered how a lock had come loose one day and he'd touched it, telling her it was softer than the finest silk.

She'd even begun to dream of Gideon. The dreams were always the same, with Naomi walking down the church aisle toward him, the smile on her face matching the joy she saw shining from his eyes. But the dreams invariably ended before she reached him.

Even though she woke with tears staining her cheeks, Naomi knew that was as it had to be. No matter how deeply she cared for him, she could not marry Gideon, just as she could not marry any man who dismissed God's love. She'd hoped and prayed that the time they spent in church and their discussions of God's grace would open Gideon's heart and that he would recognize all the gifts he'd been given, but so far it hadn't happened.

"Let's agree to disagree."

Naomi stared at Gideon in confusion. Had he read her thoughts? Of course he hadn't, she realized a second later. He was talking about her gown, not God's love.

"All right," she said with a forced smile. "I hope we don't disagree about the opera."

They did not. When it ended, they admitted that while they'd enjoyed the music, they both wished they'd been able to understand the lyrics.

"It's too nice a night to spend inside," Gideon said as they moved slowly down the staircase toward the exit. "Would you like to walk in the park?"

Naomi nodded. "City Park is one of my favorite places." Though it had been only four years since the city had planted trees, the cottonwoods had grown quickly. Combined with the curving paths and beds of flowers, they made it a lovely place to visit.

A few minutes later, Naomi and Gideon were strolling with her hand on his arm, admiring the flowers, talking about everything and nothing until they reached the center of the park. As if this was his destination, Gideon paused next to the fountain, then turned toward her. Though the night was moonless, the park's lights illuminated his face, revealing the uncertainty in his eyes. Whatever he was about to say worried him. Naomi wanted to reassure him, but she could not, for she was unable to read his thoughts.

"I told myself I would wait, but I can't wait another day." Reaching forward, Gideon took both of her hands in his. With one finger, he touched the ring on her left hand. "I know this was supposed to be a business arrangement, but it's become far more than that for me."

For her, too. Naomi's pulse began to leap at the thought that Gideon shared her feelings.

He took a shallow breath, exhaling as he said, "The way I feel about you has nothing to do with business. My heart races when I see you, and when we're apart, I can't think of anything but you. I love you, Naomi."

She had told him she felt like Cinderella, and she did—now more than ever. Naomi stared at the man she loved so dearly. Gideon was her very own Prince Charming, and here he was in one of the most romantic spots in Cheyenne, declaring his love.

"I don't want to live without you," he said, raising her hand to his lips and pressing a kiss on her gloved fingertips. "Will you make this a real engagement? Will you marry me?"

The happiness that swept through her shocked Naomi with its intensity. She'd never felt like this, never even dreamed that such happiness was possible. But, like Cinderella's night at the ball, it could not last. A second later, reality crashed through the fragile bubble of happiness.

"Oh Gideon, I wish I could. I love you." She tugged one hand free and cupped his cheek, wanting him to know how deep that love was. "I want nothing more than to be your wife, but I can't." What separated them was far more important than a fairy tale carriage being turned back into a pumpkin. What separated them was the matter of life and death, eternal life or never-ending death.

Tears welled in her eyes as she gazed at Gideon. "You know how important my faith is to me. No matter how much I love you—and I do love you—I cannot marry someone who does not share that faith. I'm sorry, Gideon. So sorry."

Chapter 8

Naomi's rejection hurt more than anything he could remember, more even than the time a bully had punched him in the stomach, knocking the breath from him. Gideon tried not to wince, but the pain was so deep it was physical. He shouldn't have asked her. Before tonight he'd had hope, but now that was gone, replaced by the bittersweet knowledge that she loved him as deeply as he did her but that they had no future.

That hurt. Oh, how it hurt! And yet Gideon was filled with admiration for her. Once again Naomi had proven to be a woman of unflinching integrity. No matter how it pained her, and he could see that it did, she would not compromise her principles.

"I'd give almost anything to change your mind," he told her, "but I won't lie to you."

The light from the street lamp cast shadows over her face, yet he could see the anguish in her eyes. "I know."

Gideon took Naomi's arm, suddenly eager to leave what he had thought would be a romantic spot. "I'm not sure what to tell my mother," he said as they walked toward the park's entrance.

"There's nothing to tell her. We'll continue as before until she leaves."

And they did. It must have been a convincing performance, because Mother had given no sign that she realized anything was different. It was only Gideon who knew that everything had changed. He'd had a glimpse of love and happily-ever-after, and it had been snatched from him. He wouldn't dwell on that. Not today. Today he had a call to make.

"This is most irregular." The white-haired doctor whom Doc Winston had introduced as Dr. Hibbard frowned. "I cannot discuss a patient's condition with someone outside the family."

Doc intervened, taking advantage of the fact that they were in his office and Naomi's mother was his patient. "Mr. Carlisle is soon to wed Mrs. Towson's daughter."

Though that wasn't true, Gideon had no intention of admitting that, especially not now. He needed to know what Naomi and her mother would be facing tomorrow. "Perhaps you could describe a hypothetical case, one with similar surgery, for a woman of Mrs. Towson's age. How long would such an operation take?"

Dr. Hibbard relaxed. "That's a perfectly valid question, and one I'm happy to answer. If all goes well, such an operation should require no more than an hour. If there are complications, which sometimes occur, it could be up to two hours. Anything longer than that and the prognosis is dubious. Surgery of that length would indicate serious problems."

"And what might those problems be?" Gideon wanted to learn everything he could before he brought Naomi's mother here.

The older doctor listed a mind-numbing number of possible complications, all of which made Gideon's skin crawl. As if he'd seen Gideon's reaction, Doc Winston spoke. "We've both examined Mrs. Towson and have no reason to believe there will be complications."

"Have you explained everything to Naomi?"

Doc shook his head. "We don't want to worry her unnecessarily. I would suggest you follow our example."

Gideon did, even though it meant he'd passed a sleepless night. Today, despite Naomi's protests, he'd brought his carriage to their house and had escorted both her and her mother to the doctor's office. Now he was seated next to Naomi in the small waiting room while the two doctors attempted to save her mother's vision.

"You don't need to stay with me." Though she was unable to hide the fear in her eyes, Naomi's voice was calm. "I hate to think of your mother being alone."

"She's fine. As a matter of fact, she's having a fitting at Madame Charlotte's today. I couldn't convince her that she has more than enough dresses at home, so she visited Élan yesterday and arranged an appointment."

Gideon didn't care how many gowns his mother bought, and he knew Naomi didn't either. He was simply talking to avoid looking at his watch. The first hour had passed, and though he didn't want to know how long it had been since he'd last checked, he couldn't stop himself. Reaching into his watch pocket, he pulled out the fancy gold timepiece that had once been his father's and opened the case. As he had feared, it had been more than two hours since the surgery had begun. The doctors had found complications— serious complications.

Gideon looked at Naomi, his heart aching at the thought of what this could mean to her. Dr. Hibbard had been frank in saying that death was a very real possibility if the surgery extended too long. This had been much too long.

Gideon clenched his fists. He couldn't just sit here doing nothing. There had to be some way to help. But how? He knew nothing about medicine, and even if he did, Dr. Hibbard was the expert on this type of surgery. That was why Doc Winston had summoned him. If Dr. Hibbard couldn't help Mrs. Towson, no one could.

As his gaze rested on Naomi, Gideon knew that wasn't true. There was One with infinitely more power than Dr. Hibbard. According to Naomi, He answered her prayers. Though He'd ignored Gideon in the past, Gideon had to try. He had to do everything he could to help Naomi's mother.

"Is something wrong?" For the first time since they'd entered the waiting room, Naomi's voice registered concern.

"Why did you ask?" Gideon didn't want to answer directly for fear of frightening her.

"You look so solemn."

It was no wonder he looked solemn. He was more worried than he'd been in many years. "I want to pray," he admitted, "but I'm not certain how to begin."

Surprise flitted across Naomi's face, followed by unmistakable happiness. "You don't need fancy words. Just tell God what's in your heart."

Would He listen? Would He answer Gideon's prayers today? There was only one way to know. Gideon slid to his knees and bowed his head.

"I'm not sure You're listening," he said softly. "I wouldn't blame You if You weren't. What kind of child am I if I only talk to You when I need help?" There was no answer, but Gideon hadn't expected one. He continued. "I hope You're listening today, because Naomi's mother needs You. I ask that You guide the doctors. Show them what to do to restore her sight." He paused for a moment, searching for the words to express all that he felt. Swallowing deeply, he said, "I know You have the power to do this."

As he murmured an amen, Gideon felt peace settle over him like a warm blanket on a cold night. He didn't know how long he knelt there, feeling lighter and freer than ever before, but gradually the feeling changed as images floated through his brain.

He remembered the morning he'd broken his arm and heard the doctor say it might not heal properly, but it had. Then there was the afternoon he'd found Mother weeping after Father and his brothers died. Gideon hadn't known how to comfort her, but the next day a stray dog appeared on their doorstep. That dog became Mother's companion and brought her the comfort her son hadn't been able to express. And then there'd been the day Gideon had worried about how to satisfy Mother's demand that he find a bride and how Naomi's inability to pay for her mother's surgery had occurred at exactly the same time.

A smile crossed Gideon's face as he realized how wrong he'd been. God had answered his prayers all along. He simply hadn't recognized it. Gideon might never understand why God had let Father and his brothers die, but he knew as surely as the September sun was shining outside that there had been a reason. A good reason. And he knew that God had heard his prayer for Naomi's mother and that He would answer it. . .in His way.

Though she didn't want to intrude on what was obviously a private moment, Naomi couldn't help watching Gideon. He knelt there, a broken and battered man, but when he raised his head, the tension that had marked his face was gone, replaced by what she could describe only as peace. Gideon's prayers had been answered, and so had hers: the man she loved had opened his heart and let God in. Closing her eyes, Naomi uttered a silent prayer of thanksgiving.

It was perhaps five minutes later that Gideon rose and reached for Naomi's hands, drawing her to her feet. "You were right," he said, his voice so filled with joy that she wanted to weep from sheer relief and happiness. "God does answer prayer. Not only yours, but mine, too. I was just too blind to see that."

Tears of joy welled in her eyes, and Naomi felt her throat thicken. Somehow she managed to speak. "Oh Gideon. I'm so happy."

"And you haven't even heard my news."

They both turned at the sound of Doc Winston's voice. His smile and the relaxed lines of his face left no doubt of the outcome.

"The surgery was successful." Naomi made it a statement rather than a question.

"Yes. I won't deny that it was challenging. The disease had progressed further than either of us had realized, but Dr. Hibbard is confident that your mother will make a complete recovery. It will take several weeks before she can resume all her normal activities, but she should notice improvement every day."

"Thank you, Doc." Gideon extended his hand to the doctor.

As the doctor shook Gideon's hand, he nodded. "Mrs. Towson will be asleep for some time. There's no need for you and Naomi to remain here. Why don't you come back in three or four hours? I imagine you have other things to do."

"We do."

Gideon stared at Naomi, his surprise evident. "We do?"

"I thought we'd take a walk in the park," she said as they left the doctor's office. The moment she'd seen Gideon's face when his prayer ended, Naomi had known what she needed to say. Now she was being given the opportunity to do it in the perfect setting.

Though Gideon appeared bemused by the request, he handed her into the carriage and drove to City Park's perimeter, seemingly unfazed when she promised to explain only when they reached their destination.

Once they entered the park, Gideon let Naomi lead the way. Though he said nothing, she wondered if he realized they were retracing the steps they'd taken the night he'd asked her to marry him and if he had an inkling of what she planned to say.

It had been weeks since that night, weeks of pretending that nothing was wrong when her heart had been breaking. Had Gideon felt the same way, or had he changed his mind? She'd soon know.

When they reached the center of the park, Naomi stopped and looked up at Gideon. Though her heart was racing, to her amazement, her voice did not quaver when she spoke. Keeping her gaze fixed on him, she said, "The last time we were here, you asked me a question and I gave you an answer neither one of us liked. If you ask me again, my answer will be different."

A light breeze fluttered the cottonwood leaves while a ground squirrel scampered at their feet. Though it was an ordinary day in the park for others, Naomi could scarcely breathe while she waited for Gideon's response. Her future happiness hung in the balance.

The wait wasn't long—perhaps no more than a second or two—but Naomi felt as if an eternity passed before he spoke. "I'm not the same person I was then," Gideon said solemnly. "Many things have changed, but one thing has not, and that's my love for you. I love you with all my heart."

Gideon paused and laid one hand on Naomi's cheek, mirroring the gesture she'd used the last time they'd stood here. This was what she'd hoped for. Gideon loved her as much as she loved him.

The sweetest of smiles curved his lips as he said, "I love you, Naomi, and I always will. Will you make me the happiest man alive? Will you marry me?"

Yes! Yes! Yes! Though the words wanted to tumble out, Naomi found herself asking, "When?"

She couldn't blame Gideon when he blinked in surprise. That was not the answer he'd been expecting. "What do you mean?"

"When would you like us to be married?" As they'd entered the park and the summer sun had warmed her back, Naomi had realized that she did not want a long engagement. Though they'd been pretending to court, she and Gideon had spent more than three months doing the things an affianced couple would. They knew each other, and now that the final obstacle had been removed, there was no reason to delay the wedding.

A mischievous grin crossed Gideon's face. "How about today?"

As appealing as the idea was, Naomi did not want to marry without her mother at her side. It would be a few days before Ma would be ready for that.

"I was thinking about next week," she said. "While you were out on the range, your mother did her best to convince me that I should be a summer bride. We still have seven more days of summer, so if we married next week, both of our mothers could be with us, and I could be a summertime bride."

Gideon's eyes shone with happiness and so much love that Naomi caught her breath. "Sweetheart, I'll marry you whenever and wherever you want." As a mischievous smile crossed his face, he wrinkled his nose. "There is one problem, though. You still haven't answered my question. Will you marry me?"

Naomi's giggle turned into a laugh. "Of course I will. I love you, Gideon— now and forever." And then, though it might scandalize anyone passing by, she raised her face for his kiss. This was Gideon, the man she loved, the man God had brought into her life to make her dreams come true. Together they would share a life of love and happiness, a life that would begin the day she became a bride of summer.

A Bride Rides Herd

by Mary Connealy

Chapter 1

Montana
July 23, 1894

Matt heard the scream and whirled in his saddle.

A fast-moving creek barreled down the mountainside, and the scream came from that direction. Another scream, louder, higher up, from someone else.

Matt vaulted from his gelding and sprinted toward that water.

He cleared the heavy stand of ponderosa pines in time to hear another scream and see someone drowning, swept along by the current at breathtaking speed.

The creek was narrow, but it plunged down a mountainside. So did whoever was drowning.

Matt saw a spot just ahead littered with stones. Branches snarled up, damming the creek and making it deeper without slowing it down.

Whoever had fallen in would be smashed to bits on this barrier, and if they somehow got swept past it, there was a waterfall a few dozen yards ahead.

He leaped up on the boulder closest to the bank and slipped. His boots weren't made for rock climbing.

There was no time to shed them.

"Grab my hand!"

The youngster, because Matt saw now it was a child careening down the rapids, turned to look at him then went under. Matt assumed this wasn't deep water, how could it be when it was rushing downhill, but it was deep enough for a child to submerge. He caught himself holding his own breath as if he'd gone under. He stepped across the stones, picking his way.

Ready.

He'd have one chance to grab this child, a girl, he saw long blond braids, and then he'd never see her again.

Heart pounding, Matt dropped to his knees and extended his arms to the limit. The child raced toward him. A tree just upstream of the rocks bent low enough…Matt was going to lose sight of the little one for a few crucial seconds right before he had to make his grab.

Then the child vanished behind the branches.

Matt braced himself to not let go and not get swept off the rocks.

The tree suddenly bowed until the branch looked ready to snap. Then it whipped up and the child went flying into the air, kicked her legs hard, and swung to the shore, landing neatly.

Another scream. A second child.

Now Matt barely had time to gather his thoughts and get ready when the tree bowed again, snapped up, and another little girl went sailing upward, swung, and landed right where the first had.

Matt sprang to his feet as the two laughed hysterically.

One, slightly smaller than the other, said, "Let's go again!"

His knees almost buckled, and he jumped across the rocks to get out of the water. He didn't want to finish this off by falling in.

Then he really saw them.

White-blond hair, skinny, wild—Matt had a gut-wrenching suspicion. "Are you by any chance named Reeves?"

The two spun to look at him, ready to run, he thought. Good self-preservation instincts. To stop them he said, "I'm your Uncle Matt. Mark Reeves is my brother."

The older child edged back, but her eyes were full of fascination. "We've got lots of uncles. You aren't one of them."

Imagining them running upstream and casting themselves into the water again, Matt said, "I haven't ever been to visit before. Can you take me to your pa and ma?"

"Nope." The older one seemed to do the talking for both. Matt had heard about Mark's three daughters.

"You're Annie, right?" Matt said. That earned their full attention. He then turned to the littler girl. "And you're Susie."

Both girls' eyes went round with amazement. "You know our names?"

"Sure I do. Mark, your pa, writes home about you a lot." Well, about once per child and those letters came from his wife, Emma. "And I know you've got a little baby sister named Lilly. Let's go home."

He had to get them away from this wild stretch of water and tell Mark what he'd caught his children doing. Even as he trembled in fear he thought of all the crazy stunts he and his brothers, including Mark—especially Mark—had gotten up to over the years.

But that was different, they were boys.

Little girls were supposed to stay to the house and be quiet and sweet. Like his ma.

"We'll take you to our house, but we can't take you to Pa." Annie reached out and took his hand. She looked to be about six, though Matt knew nothing of girls and could only guess. Susie took Matt's other hand. The sweetest, softest hands he's ever felt. Matt realized right then that he loved his little nieces with his whole heart.

"I have to bring my horse." He tugged on their hands, and they came along happily. Susie even skipped a few steps. Matt couldn't stop himself from smiling.

They were beautiful little girls. He'd never met Mark's wife, Emma, but she must be a pretty thing.

They found Matt's horse, grazing where he'd ground hitched it, and Annie ran forward to grab the reins, then led the horse back to Matt and took his hand again.

They headed off in the direction Matt had planned to ride.

"What do you mean you can't take me to your pa?" It hit him that maybe something had happened. Matt had been roving for a long time. For all he knew his brother could be long dead and buried.

"He's on a cattle drive."

Matt's panic ended before it had fully begun. "So we'll go see your ma then."

"Nope." Annie gave him a look like he was stupid, but if her ma and pa were both gone then—

"Annie! Susie, where are you?" A voice that sounded like a woman being gnawed on by wolves cut through the clear mountain air.

"That's Aunt Betsy. She screams a lot." Annie shrugged one shoulder as if to say her aunt's ways were a complete mystery.

"It sounds like she's worried about you." As well she should be. "I'd better answer her," Matt said quietly then he shouted, "They're over here."

Pounding footsteps came at him through the dense woods. Aunt Betsy sounded like she weighed three hundred pounds.

Then a beautiful woman with hair and eyes so dark she couldn't possibly be related to these girls, charged into view. Not three hundred pounds. Not. Even. Close. She had a white-haired baby on her slender hip, and the tyke was clinging for dear life.

She skidded to a stop when she saw Matt, and, faster than a man could blink, she drew a gun, cocked it, and said in a dark, dangerous voice, "Get away from those children."

Matt raised his hands, stunned at the dead serious look in Aunt Betsy's sparking black eyes. Trouble was, the girls had a firm grip. When he raised his hands, they clung and he lifted them right off the ground. They started squealing, and the fire in Aunt Betsy's eyes seemed to take their glee for alarm.

Quick before she pulled the trigger, he said, "I'm Mark's brother, come to visit. I found the girls, and they were showing me the way home. You must be Aunt Betsy."

Betsy kept her gun level and cocked. "You have the look of your brother, I'll give you that."

Matt had the impression that Betsy was inclined to shoot first and sort things out later—which Matt conceded spoke well of her protective instincts. But that didn't mean he wanted to be full of bullet holes out of respect for her vigilance.

"He knew our names, Aunt Betsy," Annie-the-Talker said. "Even Lilly's."

Then Matt remembered the tone of pure panic in Aunt Betsy's voice and the speed at which she'd come running. He knew something that would distract her. "I found them riding the creek down the mountainside. Looks like they're old hands at it."

Those black eyes went so wide with fear, Matt could see white all the way around her dark pupils.

"Girls, I told you to stay out of that creek." Her eyes, formerly trained on him, now looked at the soaking-wet girls. "Your ma and pa told you clear as day it was dangerous." Betsy lowered the gun, looking mighty defeated.

Matt suspected that if she was in charge of these two, and with a baby on her hip besides, well. . .after knowing his nieces for around ten minutes, he felt some sympathy for pretty Aunt Betsy.

"Let's go back to the house, girls." It looked like his life was out of jeopardy from poor Aunt Betsy, but he wanted to be farther from that rushing, rocky creek.

Betsy's lip quivered and she nodded, shoving her gun into a pocket in her skirt that looked like it'd been sewn for just that purpose, as the gun fit perfectly. She came toward him, her shoulders slumped.

Lilly, who looked too young to walk, bounced on Betsy's hip and giggled then reached out her arms to Matt and said, "Papa."

Matt had been holding babies since before he was even close to old enough. He saw the launch coming, and Betsy must be an old hand, too, because she didn't let Lilly hurl herself to the ground.

Matt took the baby without dropping his horse's reins, and earned a grin with four teeth. Nine months old at the most. "Howdy, Lilly. I'm your Uncle Matt." He tickled her under her chin.

Betsy took Susie's hand and tried to take Annie's. The older girl dodged and caught hold of Matt's arm. He quit tickling and let himself be guided through woods so dense no sunlight reached the ground. There was no trail Matt could see, but the girls seemed familiar with the woods, pretty surprising when this was an area forbidden to them.

Well, Ma had done her share of "forbidding" with Matt and his brothers. And she'd had poor luck earning their obedience—though he wasn't sure she ever realized it.

The woods thinned out and Matt saw the house and was surprised by his pang of envy.

Chapter 2

Betsy saw the house and was all too familiar with the pang of terror. Emma was going to kill her if she came home and found both girls had died or run off or been kidnapped by roving outlaws. Oh, there were a hundred ways to come to grief in the West. And that was if you were careful. These girls didn't show one speck of caution. . .which meant there were a thousand ways to die.

"Nice house," Matt said, sounding almost reverent. Polite, too, and smart enough. His horse looked like it was well cared for. He wore a gun as if he knew how to use it.

Betsy decided then and there to do some kidnapping herself. Matt Reeves wasn't going anywhere until his brother came home.

"I'll have the noon meal ready in an hour, Matt. Turn your horse into the corral and come on in."

She wondered if she should pick her moment and hide his horse or depend on her feminine wiles to get him to stay.

Not that she had any feminine wiles. Ma hadn't been of much use when it came to teaching such things. Belle Harden was more the type to advise her daughters on how to run men off. Betsy was a hand at it, and she had Pa and Ma to help. . .even when she didn't want help.

And that's how she'd ended up a near spinster. Eighteen years old and not a beau to be found.

She was too busy most of the time to care, but a girl had a few daydreams.

"I'll be right in." Matt, the gullible fool, handed Lilly over. The baby screamed and cried and threw herself at Matt.

Well, Betsy had been handling babies from her first memory, so Lilly didn't manage to cast herself onto the ground, but it was a near thing.

Susie escaped while Betsy wrestled Lilly. Then Matt plucked the baby out of her arms, Susie took Annie's hand, and the four of them. . .five counting the horse, left Betsy behind.

She started to yell warnings to Matt but figured anything she warned him of would just give the girls inspiration.

She was abandoning those girls to a stranger, and she dreaded it. Not because of danger to the girls. Nope. She was purely afraid Matt was going to come to his senses and run off.

Heading for the house to make the best meal she could manage, she wondered just what the man was made of. Those girls would soon reveal his every weakness.

∞

Matt snatched Annie out from under the restless hooves of his horse just as Susie climbed to the top of the pen that held a snorting, pawing mama longhorn.

Faster than he ever had in his life, Matt stripped the leather from his horse, with a baby in his arms, then went to turn his gelding loose in a stall that stank of dirty straw.

What was going on here? Who was tending this barn?

He shooed the horse out into the corral, while juggling all three girls. Doing the minimum while saving the girls' lives at every turn, he was an hour getting to the most basic chores.

More attention should be paid to the barn, and the stalls needed forking and his horse needed hay. Then he thought of pitching some of the lush hay filling the mow in Mark's barn down for his horse, and imagined taking all three girls up there. He ran for the house with them before he lost one permanently. Betsy could watch them while he did chores.

He shoved them inside, thinking to slam the door and run. Then he smelled sizzling steaks.

His favorite.

"Dinner's ready." Betsy was just about the most beautiful girl Matt had ever seen. Not that he'd seen many girls. Not that many wandering in the mountains, and that's where Matt had been for the last few years.

But she was the prettiest, bar none. And while he was at it, staring at that thick curling black hair and those big shining eyes and her tempting pink lips, he decided she was the most beautiful woman ever, including all the ones he'd never seen.

There couldn't be one more beautiful.

Maybe her lips were tempting because she was talking about food and he was just plain starving. Especially starving for a meal cooked by a woman's hand.

He'd eaten a lot of roasted rabbit, quail, and trout. It was tasty, but some variety was tempting indeed.

He should go back out and clean out that stall and turn his horse into it and water and hay him, then hit the trail and give Mark a week or two to come home.

She pulled lightly browned biscuits out of a cast-iron oven and moved a halfway-to-done pie to the center.

Pie and biscuits.

Matt wasn't going anywhere. He was as surely caught as one of those trout he'd eaten.

It was every man for himself. His gelding was going to have to survive on its own.

∽

He'd brought the girls back alive.

She admitted to being surprised.

Well, that wasn't exactly true. She'd expected the man to keep the girls alive or she'd have never let him leave with them. That he'd stayed away so long and managed to get the saddle and bridle off his horse and get the critter turned out to pasture *and* kept the girls alive.

That was the impressive part.

No notion if the man was any good with ranch chores beyond turning his horse loose, but the barn wasn't on fire and that was good enough for Betsy. She had to admit her standards had dropped through the floor since about four days ago when Mark's last hired man had quit and left her to run the place alone. The nasty, selfish varmint.

Mark had left four behind. One had quit because Susie dropped his boots in the water trough. A second had taken to the trail after Annie accidentally let the bull loose, which knocked over the outhouse while he was in it, wearing nothing but long red underwear and those, down around his ankles.

Betsy hadn't seen it, but the final hired man had told her, laughing until he cried.

Then Lilly had wet clean through her diaper while toddling a bit too close to the last cowpoke's lunch pail. He'd grabbed a handful of mane and lit out for California.

Wimps.

Now she had another man in her clutches. She smiled and fluttered her eyelashes. She'd seen her ma give her pa a similar look, and usually Belle got what she wanted when she did it. Of course Ma wasn't pretending, she really did look at Silas in a way that warmed Betsy's heart and made her curious about love.

Now, Betsy had to fake it, but she tried to make it look natural and Matt came on in, sniffing the air. Paying the fluttering lashes no mind but apparently fascinated by the smell of a baking pie.

Fine enough. Betsy would use anything that worked.

"The steaks are ready to take off the fire. I've got fried potatoes ready, and the pie will come out of the oven about the time we're done eating." She fluttered again, just for practice. It was the first meal she'd cooked since she'd taken over. They'd been living on biscuits and milk, and sometimes jerky and water. The family on the trail drive were eating better than she was.

Matt happened to look at her right at that moment. He quit sniffing. He gave her a smile that was like the August sun coming out after a January blizzard. The man must love pie.

Annie picked that moment to jump on a chair and climb onto the table. Matt snatched her just as she prepared to fall face-first onto the platter of hot biscuits.

He made a quick move that settled Lilly in a high chair, then grabbed Susie as she stumbled and tripped right toward the burning-hot stove.

"Emma is going to be so sorry she left these little imps with me when she comes home and finds them all maimed." Betsy's lower lip trembled. She hadn't cried a tear in her life until this week.

"Where are the hands?" Matt sat Susie at the table, and as the four-year-old started to stand, Matt slapped a biscuit in her hands and said, "Sit still, or I'm taking that back."

Susie stayed in place.

Hah! As if that would last.

"I want a biscuit, too!" Annie yowled. Both girls tallied unequal treatment more closely than a miner watches his gold.

"Sit up to the table, then." Matt set a biscuit in front of another chair, broke a third one up and put it in front of Lilly as Annie clambered into her chair, and the room went silent.

He looked back at Betsy, who felt her lashes flutter without giving it one thought.

"The hands? It looks like they're behind on the chores."

"The last one quit on Monday."

Matt flinched. "It's Saturday. How long has Mark been gone?"

"Two weeks, and they'll probably be at least three more before they get back."

"Strange time of year for a cattle drive. We drive in October in Texas."

"Fall comes early here and Emma doesn't like cutting it close. She's mindful of the high mountain gaps filling in with an early snow. They normally go later than July, but this is the first one she's gone on for years. She's either been round with a baby or had one mighty young. She loves a cattle drive though. I convinced her to go and let me watch the girls."

Betsy's lashes fluttered again, completely of their own accord. Matt had come closer, and the girls were feasting. Betsy dropped her voice to a whisper and added, "The stupidest thing I've ever done. I'm not taking good care of the girls. And I'm not taking any care at all of the ranch."

"And the hands all quit?"

Nodding, Betsy said, "Mark left a skeleton crew, four men, plenty to watch what's left of the herd and do daily chores, but two days after he left the steadiest hand broke his arm diving to save Annie when she fell out of the haymow. I'd let her get out of my sight and she'd climbed up there, and Hank saw her in time to catch her."

"Is he here, just laid up?"

Shaking her head, Betsy said, "He saved Annie, but he rammed his head into the barn wall, besides breaking his arm. He was knocked out cold as a mountain peak. They had to take him to Divide to the doctor, and when they got back they said the doctor wants him to stay in bed until he stops seeing two of everything. I don't know when he'll be back.

"Then the other three quit one at a time. I think if any of them but Travis had been last, they'd have stuck it out rather than abandon me. But Travis was always the least useful of Mark's cowpokes. He gloated when he told me he quit. Then when he rode off and left me he looked back and laughed. The man works with cattle and horses all day. A leaky diaper makes him quit?"

"Betsy, you need help."

She waited for him to say the obvious. He was silent.

Stupid, useless, fluttering lashes.

Not wanting to beg unless she absolutely had to, she rested one open hand on his chest and leaned close so the girls wouldn't start talking and scare him off.

"I need you." She spoke barely above a whisper.

His eyes focused on her words. Or rather her lips, but that was the same thing. He said nothing.

Inching closer, because the situation was dire, she whispered, "So will you help me, Matt? Will you stay? You're going to want to see your brother, aren't you?"

Matt was nodding, watching her. He seemed dazed.

Betsy smiled, and his eyes almost crossed. She gave him a friendly pat on the chest then stepped back, just as his hand whipped out and pulled her close.

She bumped right into his chest.

Then as if the impact woke him up, he let her go and took a step back.

Betsy reconsidered the power of fluttering lashes as she whirled to the stove and started scooping up food.

A chair scraped and she glanced back to see Matt sink into it. He looked stunned. She could well imagine. What had happened? She felt like time had stopped and the world had turned soft and beautiful and very private.

∽

Matt felt like he'd been hit with an ax handle.

It took a bit to gather his thoughts, and by then he was eating and no speech was required. When the meal was finished all three girls looked as if their eyelids were drooping. Nap time. Matt knew all about nap time. How he'd hated it for himself.

How he'd loved it for all his whirlwind little brothers.

"For the next two hours we will have peace," Betsy said. "Then it all begins again until night."

"Will you be all right then, in here, while I go fork out the stalls and do a few other chores?"

Betsy, who had ignored him completely while they ate, suddenly looked at him again. Her eyes, so dark brown he could barely see where the pupils began, gleamed with relief and pleasure. "You're really staying then?"

He couldn't do much else. "Yep. Uh. . .you won't let the girls in the creek again, will you?"

Betsy's smile flashed as bright as her eyes. "I handle them fairly well except when I try and do the chores. I just don't have enough hands and eyes. And apparently not enough sense. If you'll do the chores, I can take care of the girls."

Matt nodded and pushed back his chair. "I'll get to it, then."

He took his Stetson off an antler used as a hook and clamped it on his head and pretty much ran outside.

He'd be fine. . .unless he wanted to eat again. Then things could get confusing.

Chapter 3

S omeone pounded the door with the side of their fist. Betsy rose from the chair, the first time she'd been off her feet all day. But whoever was here sounded urgent.

She rushed to the door, flung it open to find Matt, water dripping off his head, right onto Annie, who grinned and revealed a missing tooth.

Betsy was pretty sure the child had all her teeth just an hour ago when she went up to bed.

"How did you get outside?"

Annie jerked one shoulder. Betsy had sounded ferocious, and yet Annie didn't even quit smiling.

"I went out. It's easy." Then she pointed to her mouth. "I lost a tooth, Aunt Betsy."

"And you lost one of your children." Matt looked furious. His face was red enough the water drenching him might turn to steam at any time.

"I sat with them until they fell asleep. I promise you, I did."

"I believe you." Matt spoke between clenched teeth. He clearly wasn't happy with how this week was going.

Betsy was cooking the best food she could manage, and that was pretty good. Anything to keep from running him off.

"What happened?" Betsy knew that was a stupid question.

"Escaped child. Water trough. Nearly died." Matt growled more than spoke. "Same as every day."

"That's just so true it's almost heartbreaking," Betsy said. "Come in and get changed."

"I'll change in the barn."

"You're freezing. That trough is fed with water from a mountain spring. Run and fetch a change of clothes while I heat up some coffee."

Matt closed his eyes and dragged a deep breath in through blue lips. Betsy appreciated that he was fighting for calm. He'd been sleeping in the bunkhouse all week, and he was doing a fine job of running the ranch. . .for a man without help. She'd tried to help a few times with all three girls at her side. What else could she do but bring them?

"No! Don't even think about helping me." He seemed to rein himself in when he realized he was shouting. More calmly, he said, "I would appreciate something warm. I'll be right back."

He stood Annie on the floor rather than shove her into Betsy's arms. Which Betsy appreciated. She would have gotten soaked.

Matt stomped away dripping.

Betsy thought she showed great restraint by not snickering. . .until after he was out of earshot.

"Bye-bye, Aunt Betsy." Annie had shed her dress and was on her way out the back door, stark naked. Betsy quit laughing and made a dash to catch the little imp.

Chapter 4

"Another fine meal, Betsy." Matt leaned back from the supper table and patted his stomach—which Betsy couldn't help but notice was flat and hard as a board—even though he put an alarming amount of food away every time she fed him.

All three girls were either asleep or the next thing to it. Matt had moved the baby's tin plate, or she'd be snoring with her face resting in gravy.

"I'll help you get them settled."

"I'm not tired!" Annie wailed. Then her head nodded, jerked up. Susie gave up, crossed her arms on the table, and laid down her weary head.

"Thank you, I'd appreciate it."

Betsy and Matt had learned to work as a decent team. Matt changed diapers with easy skill. Betsy had the two older girls in their pajamas and tucked in bed by the time Matt had pulled the sleeping gown on Lilly and brought her in. All three girls slept in one room. Mark and Emma shared another. There was a large kitchen with space for a stove and table and sink and some cupboards on one side and a fireplace with a pair of rocking chairs on the other.

It was a tightly built, well-tended home, and when all three girls fell asleep instantly after they laid down, Betsy followed Matt out to those rockers and sank down beside him.

It had become their habit to talk for a few minutes at the end of the day, while they waited to make sure the girls wouldn't stage a prison break.

Matt had nailed the window shut in their bedroom as well as the front door and every other window in the house. The back door was the only way out, so to get out, the girls had to come past Betsy.

The summer nights were cool up here in the mountains, and Matt always laid a fire and started it burning before they ate the evening meal.

By the time the girls were tucked in, it felt good to sit before it for a few minutes. Both of them sighed, such an identical sound that they looked up, and Betsy smiled, then Matt laughed.

She said, "I don't know how Emma does it. I'm sure it helps to have practice, but I spend all day either cooking for them or chasing after them. Lilly can't walk yet, but she crawls so fast and pulls herself up on everything. She scaled a chair and then the kitchen table this morning. She was sitting right on top of the butter dish playing with a butcher knife by the time I got to her."

Betsy shuddered to think of the danger.

Matt shook his head. He took a look at the butcher knife, now hanging from a nail high on the wall, and grinned. "Good spot for it."

"The nail was there. And there's a hole in the knife handle. I suspect that's where Emma keeps it. I just forget all the ways these wily children can find to harm themselves." They shared a look of terror, then both of them laughed.

"How are things outside? Have you cleaned up the mess I made?"

"You couldn't possibly do the outside chores and tend those girls. It wasn't a mess you made, it was you making the right choice and caring for those girls. That's a job that takes all day every day."

Betsy's heart swelled a bit at the kind words. "I think we've almost found everything they can use to kill themselves."

There was an extended silence, broken only by the creak of the rockers. Finally, Matt said, "You're an optimist, aren't you, Betsy?"

They both broke down and laughed hard. It was the closest to a sane adult moment they'd had since they'd met.

"So you've got a herd of little brothers, is that right?" Betsy asked.

"Yep, and one little sister. She's seven years old and that's the last baby Ma had, but Ma is getting up into her forties now. Time for her to slow down with the babies."

Smiling, Betsy said, "I remember all those years I was growing up, Mark telling tales of his family full of boys. Then when your ma had a baby girl, he was so stunned, we thought he'd ride all the way to Texas just to check and make sure they were right."

"I did it."

"What?" Betsy turned away from gazing in the flames to stare at him.

"I went to check. I was in Oregon when I got word, and I rode all the way home. It was just such a shock. I was slow getting there, and Hope was near a year old. And Ma had taken control of the family."

Betsy felt her brow wrinkle. "Taken control how?"

"She made everyone settle down so her baby girl wouldn't be raised in a madhouse. It was a great home to be a growing boy in. A lot of the things we got up to remind me of how Mark's girls act. But the unruly ways of my brothers drove us all away from home at a young age, looking for some peace. Now, well, I thought long and hard about staying down there. My older brothers Abe and Ike are both living near my folks, and I've got several nieces and nephews growing up there. I may wander back down thataway in the end. I've just never quite got the wanderlust out of my blood."

"Where all have you been?" Betsy sounded wistful to her own ears. "I've never been beyond the state of Montana. In fact, I've barely traveled from here to Divide and Helena. Ma likes to keep us close to home. She doesn't even think her daughters should show themselves in town."

"Why not?"

Betsy shrugged. "Just a habit. The trails are better, and there's a train spur from Divide to Helena now. We can get there in half a day. But when we first settled here we were mighty cut off, and there were a lot of wild men around. Ma didn't like them knowing she had a passel of girls living out in this remote area."

"Well, I've been to near every state in the Union west of the Mississippi. I've never gone back East—except once. I don't know much about city living, but I can survive in the wilderness with a knife and a rifle, don't need any money nor a job. But it's a lonely life. I grew up surrounded by a crowd. I don't last too long on my own before I start longing to hear another voice. I've turned my hand to most every job a man can do. Mining in New Mexico. Lumberjacking in Idaho. I've scouted for the cavalry in Arizona and driven a stagecoach in Colorado. I went to sea in California and sailed all the way around the southern tip of South America. I even landed in New York City, but it was so huge and dirty, I stepped onshore and signed on to a boat sailing back only an hour later. I've seen the Grand Canyon and worked a dozen ranches from Texas to North Dakota. I was even a sheriff in Kansas for a while. I've loved my wandering ways. I reckon I need to settle down one of these days, but it's never stopped being fun to live such a free life."

They talked and rocked late into the night. Betsy knew the morning would come early, with hungry livestock and hungrier girls. But she found herself almost desperate for the quiet adult conversation. It was too sweet to end.

A log split and sent a wash of sparks out of the fireplace. They both jumped up, and Betsy realized how low the fire had burned.

"How long have we been sitting here?" She felt as if the outside world had intruded on something very personal.

Neither of them had a pocket watch, nor was there a clock in the house, but it had to have been more than an hour.

"I reckon I've talked until your ears are aching." Matt gave her his friendly smile, so like the brother-in-law Emma loved so dearly.

They stood, and Matt stepped to the fireplace. "It's a cool night. I'll build up the fire before I go."

"No, it's a tight house. We'll be fine. Thank you." Betsy stood just as Matt turned from the hearth and nearly bumped into her. Matt caught her by the arms to keep from stumbling then was still. His eyes wandered around her face. She felt it like a caress.

He asked, "How did you end up with such shining black curls? Mark told me Emma's hair is whiter than his, and the girls are all so blond."

"Ma married and was widowed. We have different fathers, and Ma says I take after him in looks. My real name at birth was Betsy Santoni; my pa was Italian. But he died when I was a baby, and Ma married Silas. He's the only man I've ever known as my father, and he's a good one and I'm proud to carry his name. My ma said my own pa was pretty worthless."

Matt smiled. "I don't know what kind of man he was, but he must have been good looking to have a daughter as beautiful as you."

Betsy felt something awaken deep in her chest. Something she hadn't known was sleeping. Something she hadn't known was there.

"Thank you." She wondered if she was blushing. She had skin that tanned deeply, and she wasn't given to blushes.

Matt lifted a hand and drew one finger across her cheeks. They must've turned red. . . Why else would he touch her?

"Don't tell me you haven't heard that before. The men in Montana aren't all blind."

Betsy shrugged. "Ma and Pa don't let men come around much."

Matt grinned. "How'd Mark ever get past them?"

"There was trouble and Mark was the right man to help, and somehow, when the trouble passed, he and Emma were planning a wedding. It was fun watching Ma and Pa try'n run him off. And your cousin Charlie was with him, and he ended up married to my sister Sarah."

"I'll have to see Charlie while I'm here, too." Matt's hand opened and rested on her cheek. Quietly, he said, "I don't want to talk about my family anymore."

He leaned down and kissed her.

Her first kiss.

∞

It was his first kiss.

Matt wasn't sure how in the world Betsy Harden had ended up in his arms, but he wasn't going to waste time wondering because it was the best thing that had ever happened to him.

He slid his arms around her waist, his only thought to get closer. He drew her hard against him.

"Matt." She turned her head to break the kiss. Her hands came up to press against his chest. "Wait. Stop."

Her words shocked him into using his head for the first time in a while. He dropped her, only realizing as she slid away that he'd lifted her off her feet.

He stepped back and slammed into the fireplace, which sent him stumbling forward, and somehow, she was right back in his arms. His lips descended, and hers rose to meet him.

The next time they stopped his hands were sunk deep in the dark silk of her hair. He carefully unwound all those lush curls, lingering, kissing her eyes and her blushing cheeks.

She hadn't said "wait" the second time. In fact, her arms were wound tight around his neck. It all added up to her liking this kiss just as much as he did.

This time she stepped back then turned away and breathed deep. "Um. . . you'd better go."

"I want to talk about what just happened here, Betsy. I want it to happen again. I want to have the right to kiss you."

She looked over her shoulder. Her lips were swollen from their kiss. Her hair had tumbled from its bun and flowed wild around her shoulders. She had a little dimple in her chin and her cheekbones were high, her nose strong in a feminine way. He wanted to get to know every bit of her as well as he knew her face.

"What are you saying, Matt? Are you saying you want to court me?"

That wasn't what he was saying. He wanted to marry her and carry her to the bedroom right this minute. And as a man who knew almost nothing about women, he thought he had a great idea of how to proceed.

But courting?

That cleared his thoughts. "Uh, courting. How does a man even court a woman when he's living with her, eating with her, and raising three children with her? That sounds more like two people who have been married for years." Except of course in one very important way.

His thoughts honestly shocked him a bit because he'd always kept to manly places like the mountaintops and the sea, mining camps and remote ranches. He'd never so much as spent time alone with a woman, not once. Never long enough to consider rounding her up and claiming her.

"Well, nothing like this can happen again as long as we're here alone. It's sinful."

Matt thought it might well be sinful except his intentions, passionate though they were, were completely honorable.

"So you go on now, and when Mark and Emma get back we can talk more about such things as"—kissing, holding, loving? Which would she say?—"courting. Until then, this is improper and a bad example to the girls."

Who were fast asleep and wouldn't know a thing about it.

Matt figured he'd had the only run of luck he was going to get tonight, so he nodded, not agreeing one whit that he needed his big brother around to tell him how to behave, and headed for the door. "I'll see you in the morning for breakfast then, Betsy."

He plucked his Stetson off the hook then turned back to see her watching him, one hand gently touching her lips. Only a will of iron kept him from crossing the room and gathering her right back into his arms.

"Good night." He clamped his hat on his head to keep his hands busy.

"Good night, Matt. I'll see you at breakfast."

Chapter 5

Matt might've just gone whole hog pursuing Betsy Harden if it weren't for those girls, and about a thousand head of cows.

The thunder and lightning in the night had kept Matt from sleep, along with thoughts of beautiful Betsy. As the storm came, Matt felt like he was in the middle of it. Up this high, the clouds sometimes went across the lower slopes of the mountains, below a man. But not this time. The storm was all around him, and sleeping in the bunkhouse, he felt like he was in the middle of a plunging lifeboat at sea.

When the worst passed, he made a dash for the house, worried about Betsy handling the girls. He'd just slammed the door open when the thunder started again. Only it sounded wrong enough that he turned to see hundreds of cattle charging right for him.

He swung the door shut just as a thousand-pound bull leaped up on the porch and ripped the railing away. The animal hit the house so hard it rocked.

A scream behind Matt turned him around to see Annie running for a window, as if she needed to escape. The window was nailed shut and shuttered, but Matt dashed forward and nabbed the little lunatic just as a longhorn rammed its head through, shattering glass and sending shards of wood blasting through the room.

Matt jumped to the side and dropped to the floor, ducking under those horns as fast as he could without crushing Annie. He felt a few sharp slashes, but he missed the worst of it. Then a bellow whipped his head around, and he saw the animal that had busted the window get bunted so hard he came right through, into the room.

Betsy rushed out with a shrieking Susie in her arms. She yelled and grabbed for the broom by the fireplace. She brandished it as the panicked yearling skidded on the split-log floor then fell, jumped to its feet, whirled, and leaped out the same window it'd come in.

The door shuddered under an impact. Matt, still holding Annie, threw his back flat against it. He didn't think he could hold back a charging bull, but if the animal hit the door a glancing blow and Matt kept the door in place, the cattle might not storm inside.

The thundering hooves were deafening.

A wail from the bedroom had a nearly stunned Betsy turning around and rushing in to get Lilly. "Annie, come here to me," Betsy called.

Matt lowered the little girl to the floor. Matt's arms must have seemed like a haven because she turned and jumped back at him.

He hoisted her up, hoping a cow didn't run through the door and crush them both.

Betsy came back, Susie on one hip, Lilly on the other. The noise went on and on.

"The lightning must have spooked them." Betsy spoke loud enough to be heard.

Nodding, Matt started thinking beyond survival moment by moment. "How am I going to round them all up?"

"You can't do it alone. We'll have to ride after them."

"We?" Matt looked at how full her hands were. His, too. "We can't take three babies out to herd cattle."

"We can and we will. I don't see as we have much choice. Hopefully they'll calm down and stay mostly together. But if not we'll be combing them out of the trees for ten miles. You can't do that alone."

Matt tried his best to think of something else, but, "You're right. I can't do it by myself. We'll have to let the girls ride with us."

"Emma has a pack she wears so she can strap the baby on her back."

"So one of us wears Lilly?"

"Sure, didn't your ma have something like that?"

"Nope, when we took the wagon to town, the baby sat on her lap until a new one came along, then he joined the brothers in the wagon box."

"Well, we can't hope to herd cattle with a wagon, so we have to ride."

"Listen."

Betsy's eyes lit up. "It's over."

"Almost. They'll tear along for a while, but they'll tire out and calm down."

With a comically arched brow, Betsy said, "That sounds a little like the children."

"A little." Matt grinned as he patted Annie on the back. "The girls never do seem to quite calm down."

They shared a smile, their arms full of children until the last of the thundering hooves faded in the distance.

Betsy realized what else had faded. "The rain and thunder are over."

Nodding, Matt said, "We can't wait until sunrise; who knows how far they'll wander by then. Let's get saddled up."

Chapter 6

When Emma asked me to watch her children while she went on the drive I was just plain tickled." The leather of the saddles creaked as they rode along the trail left by the rampaging herd.

Betsy kept up easily, though Matt set a fast pace. They were hoping to catch the cattle before they'd spread far and wide.

Matt had Annie riding in front of him. The little girl's head lolled over Matt's supporting arm. She was deep asleep, as were her sisters.

"I wanted to spend time with my sweet nieces." Betsy gave Susie's tummy a gentle pat. She rode in front and Lilly was on her back.

Matt had wrangled with her, wanting the heavier load, but Betsy had persuaded him that if there was any hard riding—and there would be—he'd have to do it. Betsy let him think he was the better rider, and maybe he was, but she'd done her share in the saddle and could carry her share of the load.

"And of course the chores would all be done by the hands."

"Those men oughta be horsewhipped for abandoning you."

Nodding, Betsy went on as they rode in the dark. The storm had passed, and the trail, churned up by the cattle, was muddy enough they rode off to the side to avoid the mud as best they could. When the trees got too thick, they were forced to wade through the only existing trail, but when they found open meadows, they could get away from the deep mud. And in those openings, they could see the sky awash in starlight.

If they hadn't been facing hours of grueling work, it might've been nice.

If they hadn't been toting three children, it might've been romantic.

If letting all of Emma's cattle run off wasn't financially ruinous, it might've been fun.

"I thought of it as an adventure. And an honor, honestly. Emma never leaves the girls. She's a fierce, protective mama. So I knew it was a high compliment. Also the cattle drive to Helena is a long, treacherous journey. Even though someone from my family drives cattle every year it's never easy. So Emma must have wanted to get away, have a break from the ranch. I was determined to prove to her she'd done right by trusting me."

"You've kept them alive; no one could dare hope for more."

"So far I've kept them alive. She's not home yet."

Matt smiled, and Betsy realized she could see his face. The gray light of encroaching dawn was pushing back the night. "It was a different kind of adventure than I expected."

"Yep, less like fun and more like a constant battle for survival for all five of us."

Betsy smiled back and spoke the simple truth. "I don't know what I'd have done without you, Matt. I'd have had to abandon all care for the cattle. Which is bad enough without this stampede."

"I'm glad I got here when I did. Betsy, I think, um. . .that is. . .don't you think. . ." The bellow just ahead turned them to face a longhorn bull as he stepped out of a clump of aspen trees, pawing the earth, its ten-foot spread of horns lowered.

"Whoa!" Matt pulled his horse to a stop so suddenly, his gelding reared.

"Go right." Betsy issued the order with a snap then wheeled her horse to the left and raced into the trees. She glanced back to see Matt vanish into the woods on the opposite side of the trail, giving only a moment's thought to the fact that he'd obeyed her so quickly. She'd probably ordered him to do something he was already doing and about to shout at her.

They made a pretty good team.

Betsy put distance between her and that wiry white-and-tan beast, giving the old mossy horn time to calm down as she picked her way through a forest so dense she had no business in it. No trail anywhere. Underbrush between the trees grew until it was almost impenetrable. Bending low to duck branches, letting her horse pick his way through, she headed forward, hoping to get behind the bull and maybe drive him back toward Emma's ranch.

If they could get him moving in the right direction, he would probably just follow his instincts for home. The other cattle might even realize the bull, their natural leader, was gone and follow him.

The practical ranch woman in her doubted it would be that easy.

She thought she'd gone far enough when she heard the lash of a whip. Matt had carried one he'd found in the barn, so he must be working the bull. She headed back for the trail to find the longhorn headed for home, trotting.

Matt heard her emerge from the woods and turned, his alert look telling her that bull had given him all he wanted to handle.

As he rode up, he smiled. "Let's see if we can turn a few more back without getting gored."

"How many cattle were in the herd closest to the house?" Mark and Emma had the cattle spread into several grassy stretches of the high mountains.

"Probably two hundred. I looked before we rode out, and about half are still there. They probably ran a bit to the west and let the thick woods stop them and turn them back. I'd say we're looking for at least a hundred head of cattle."

"So one down, ninety-nine to go?" Betsy sighed. "It's going to be a long day."

The sun peaked over the horizon now, though they were in thick shade. It was finally full light.

"It seemed like a lot more than that when they were crashing around the house last night," Betsy said as they rode on in the direction the cattle had run.

"Well, one bull jumping into the house is a lot." Matt shook his head. "I can't believe there was a longhorn in Mark's house."

Betsy smiled then chuckled. "Emma is going to want us to do some explaining about that."

A small clearing in the woods opened to a couple dozen of the runaway cows. These were docile and their bellies full, so they cooperated nicely and headed down the trail the way they'd come.

"I hope they keep moving, because I'm not going to follow them all the way home." Matt and Betsy sat side by side to watch them disappear down the trail for home.

"You know what else I hope?" Betsy asked.

"What?" Matt reined his horse around and they moved on, following a clear trail that led farther into the woods.

"I hope we catch up with these cows pretty quickly, because I want to get everything in neat order before Emma gets home, or she'll never let me babysit again."

"You mean you want to?" Matt sounded horrified, and Betsy turned, annoyed. He was smiling, laughing at her, and she couldn't help laughing at herself.

The laughter and the sunlight helped wake Susie and Annie up. Lilly slept on as they chased cattle. They got another dozen straggling along the forest path headed back. Then another dozen, then another.

"Another thing I hope…" Betsy said when they'd finished with that clearing. Probably seventy-five cows now bound for home.

"What's that?" Matt asked as the woods surrounded them again. Tracks went on even farther from home.

"I hope we find the rest of the cows soon, because if I want to keep this secret we're running out of time." The woods thinned sooner this time, and Betsy saw a few cows ahead. Most likely not all of them, but Betsy decided they'd call this good and give up. They needed to gather what they had and count them, then they could comb the woods for the rest of them over the next few days.

Lilly cried from the pack on Betsy's back.

"We've got to stop. She needs a dry diaper, and I have some food for all the girls. We're all due to stretch our legs for a bit." Betsy swung down and Matt was just a second slower. Then he stood Annie up on legs that wobbled from riding so long. He led the horses a safe distance away and staked the critters out to graze.

When he came back, he said, "What do you mean by running out of time? We've got as long as it takes."

"I mean we're getting too close to Ma's place."

"Your ma? I thought she went on the cattle drive." Mark led Annie to where Betsy had set out apples and jerky and biscuits. She'd packed well. He could see she'd figured to be all day with this. She changed Lilly's diaper with quick, well-practiced skill.

He doled out the food, and Annie and Susie ate like they were starving, which they most certainly were not.

Betsy sat on the rock with a small cup of milk she'd poured from a canteen and began giving Lilly sips. Matt broke up a biscuit and gave Lilly bites between drinks. He sat beside Betsy, mighty close, since the rock wasn't overly large. He liked the feel of her pressed up to his side.

"Where'd you get an idea like that?"

"I reckon I got it because you were over at Mark's alone. When the last hand ran off, why didn't you load the girls in the wagon and take them to your ma's house to get help?"

Betsy shrugged one shoulder. "It's because my ma raised me and my sisters mostly alone and ran the ranch, too, after the husbands died."

"The husbands? You mean Emma's pa and yours?"

"And one more. Your cousin Charlie is married to my sister Sarah, and she's got a different pa than Emma and I do. She'd buried three husbands before Silas. They were all a worthless lot when they were alive. So she did it all herself.

"I felt like I should be able to handle the girls and the cattle for a few weeks at least. I wanted to prove I could handle whatever trouble I faced. It's because I didn't want to go home, crying for help. And it's worse now than then."

Matt frowned as he slid one arm around Betsy. He was a little hurt. He'd been helping her. "Why's it worse now?"

"Because Ma's not going to like it one bit when she finds out you've been at

Emma's with me without an adult chaperone. In fact, she might consider that you've been dishonorable."

"She won't be harsh with you, will she?" Matt was angry at the thought of Belle Harden being wrathful with her daughter. He felt protective. He pulled her closer, the baby still between them but not keeping them far apart.

"I won't let you come to any harm, Betsy." He leaned down and kissed her.

"I'm not worried about me coming to harm, for heaven's sake." She went to push him away and darned if her arm—that wasn't holding Lilly—didn't circle his neck instead and pull him closer.

"You're not? Then what's the matter?" He didn't really care, not right now. He was too busy kissing this beautiful woman. And enjoying just how enthusiastically she kissed him back.

Betsy broke the kiss but only held herself away a fraction of an inch. "I'm afraid Ma might shoot you on sight."

A chill rushed down his spine at her dead-serious tone. Before he could ask her if she was as serious as she seemed, a crash from the far end of the trail turned his attention. Longhorns plunged out of the woods. The noise was so sudden and startling, that the girls all rushed to Matt's side, and he pulled Betsy close and put an arm around both girls.

Cows kept coming and coming. Probably nearly every one of the unaccounted-for cattle lost in the stampede.

Smiling he looked down and said, "They're all back! We're done with our roundup." He leaned down and kissed her deeply and joyfully.

The sharp crack of a rifle cocking broke the kiss, and he turned to look right down the barrel of a Winchester.

"Get your hands off my daughter."

Chapter 7

A woman rode straight toward him, her rifle drawn and leveled.

The woman's eyes flashed with golden streaks that a man might mistake for lightning.

Right behind her a man rode, also armed. He was as mad as the bull that'd almost taken them.

Belle and Silas Harden. They didn't look one speck like Betsy, and yet there wasn't a doubt in his mind.

Matt let go of Betsy fast and stepped well away from her. He hoped he lived to tell Mark about how he'd met his in-laws.

The woman's eyes shifted between him and Betsy. Matt figured she didn't miss a thing.

Then he only saw Betsy's back. "Ma, you can't shoot him, he's Mark's brother."

"That ain't enough to save a man who's got his hands on my daughter."

Betsy's head tilted a bit. "It is if he's got my permission."

The pistol sagged, and Belle Harden didn't look like the kind of woman who ever got careless with a weapon. Then with abrupt, angry motions, she reholstered it. He noticed Silas still had his in hand but pointed in the air.

"He came to visit Mark right after the last hand quit. He saved the girls' lives when they got away from me."

"And why didn't you come to me when that happened?" Belle swung off her horse and ground hitched it. Matt noticed the horse stayed right there, a well-trained critter.

Betsy suddenly broke from where she stood, guarding Matt. . .which had been humiliating, but at the same time he really appreciated it. Leaving Annie and Susie behind, Betsy, with Lilly on her hip, threw an arm around her mother and started crying.

Matt started praying.

He spent a few moments recommitting his soul to the Lord and making sure his spiritual affairs were in order. Because one wrong word from Betsy and he'd be standing at the pearly gates.

Belle didn't shoot, but Silas dismounted and stalked straight for Matt, who scooped both girls up in his arms and said, "Grandpa's here, girls. Let's give Grandpa a hug, shall we?"

Both girls yelled with glee. Silas looked frustrated as the girls flung themselves out of Matt's arms and into his. Hard to beat up a man while little girls are hugging you. The look Silas gave him told Matt he was well aware of what Matt was up to. But Silas couldn't resist the little girls and quit trying to burn a hole through Matt with his eyes.

Finally believing he might survive, Matt realized more people were flooding into the canyon. It looked like Belle had found the stray cows and sent up an alarm.

Betsy was babbling something to Belle. It sounded like she was just telling about the cowhands and the trouble. He definitely heard the words, "girls drown" and "Matt came and saved them both."

Which probably wasn't true. The cute little monsters had been fine.

A beautiful redhead rode in, and right behind her was Matt's cousin, Charlie. Charlie would save him. Or Matt would get Charlie killed.

Whichever happened, it was nice to see a familiar face.

A little redheaded boy on Charlie's lap, who looked a lot like the pretty redhead, gave Matt hope. Belle wouldn't shoot her son-in-law's brother, would she?

Matt kept up his praying just to be on the safe side.

Charlie saw him and rode straight over. He dismounted and almost ran, not that easy while wearing cowboy boots, carrying a toddler, and threw his free arm around Matt and pounded him hard on the back, laughing.

He pulled away not knowing he was now a human shield.

"Which one are you?"

Matt had heard that question hundreds of times in his life. It was a fact, he and his many older and younger brothers bore a mighty strong resemblance to one another.

"I'm Matt."

Nodding, Charlie said, "You look so much like Mark I was trying to figure out how he could be here and in Helena at the same time."

"I'm so much better looking than Mark it ain't even funny."

Charlie started laughing. "And is it true that your ma had a girl?"

"Yep. Pa's thirteenth child was finally a girl."

"Twelve sons?" Belle exclaimed. "And your ma didn't lose her mind or take after your pa with a skillet?"

Betsy turned to Matt. "Ma's always been fond of her girls."

Belle was now holding Lilly, which made her seem far less dangerous.

Silas came up beside Belle. "You're fond of your sons, too, aren't you, honey?"

"That I am, Silas. Right fond of the sons we've made." Belle gave Silas such a warm look Matt was almost dazed.

A young man caught up with Belle and stood beside her, grinning. "I've taught you how good it can be to have a boy, haven't I, Ma? Me and my four brothers?"

"This is my little brother, Tanner." Betsy pointed to another barely grown boy. "And that's Si. The rest of the boys went on the cattle drive with Mark."

Tanner was as tall as Silas and had his ma's hazel eyes, and skin that was as tan as an Indian. Si was probably Silas Jr. He took after his pa, though both the parents were brown haired, so the resemblance between them was strong in general coloring.

Charlie shook his head. "It was all we could do to stop Mark from riding for Texas when he got word about a baby sister. He figured a terrible mistake had been made, and if it hadn't, he was scared for his little brothers."

"Most of us got home to see if it was true. Ike's moved home permanently and married Laura McClellen."

"I hadn't heard that." Charlie's eyes lit up. He looked at Belle. "Laura McClellen is Mandy Linscott's baby sister."

"Sophie McClellen ended up with a Reeves in her family, too?" Belle looked glum.

The pretty redhead plucked her little boy out of Charlie's arms.

"Why is my sister crying? Betsy never cries." Less friendly than Charlie by a country mile. Matt remembered her name was Sarah. Betsy had mentioned her plenty of times since he'd gotten here.

Charlie looked from Matt to Sarah to Betsy. His brow lowered with worry, and he rested a hand affectionately on Sarah's back. "We found Mark's cattle coming onto our property. Figured the storm stampeded them. I sent word there was trouble, which brought Belle and Silas and a passel of others. How long have you been living with Betsy?" Charlie choked over that and cleared his throat and said, "I mean, uh. . .how long have you been sleeping together at Mark's place. . .no, I mean—"

Matt kicked Charlie in the ankle, and he didn't even care that everyone saw it. "Stop talking before you get me killed."

There was a long silence. Charlie looked to be thinking of what to say and discarding many possible choices. Finally, he raised his hands as if surrendering and said rather weakly, "Welcome to Montana, Matt."

If this was how a man got welcomed to Montana, it was no wonder the state was mostly empty.

"Let's get these cattle home, then we'll settle this." Silas took charge, which seemed mighty brave for some reason. It stood to reason the man of the family would take charge, and yet there was something about Belle that said no one took charge of her, ever. Matt would bet she wasn't a tractable kind of wife. Love and honor, sure, if she deemed a man worthy.

Obey. . .most likely she'd only do that if she was ordered to do something she planned to do anyway.

But Silas looked like a man who knew ranching, which Belle most likely respected, so her going along with him, well, if a body wanted to call that obedient they were welcome to do so.

A couple of the hands went on ahead. The rest of the hands, along with Betsy's two little brothers, hazed the critters in the clearing toward the trail and fell in behind them.

The cattle were tired from a long run, and their bellies were full of lush grass. It had turned them into purely docile critters.

The Harden family—and Matt—brought up the rear. They were on the way to Mark's in a matter of minutes.

But the trail was barely wide enough to ride two abreast, and Belle led the family group with Betsy at her side and Lilly strapped on her back. Betsy had Susie in front of her.

Silas was next, riding side by side with Sarah. Silas had Annie.

Matt found himself at the end of the line with Charlie, and Charlie's son riding on his pa's lap. The riding arrangements didn't suit Matt at all. He needed to talk to Betsy, and he knew about decent behavior, so he needed to set things right by having a talk with Betsy's pa about his intentions. . .even though he hadn't exactly had time to figure out what his intentions were.

As they rode, Matt thought that no two girls ever looked less like their ma than black-haired, black-eyed Betsy and green-eyed redheaded Sarah.

Matt leaned close to Charlie and whispered, "Do you have any control over your wife?"

Charlie grinned. "Not mostly."

"Can you get her back here so I can have a talk with Betsy's pa?"

Charlie's eyes went wide. Fear, plain and simple. "I've done that before. It ain't an easy talk." Then Charlie, who'd always been Matt's favorite cousin, said, "Welcome to the family."

Much like his welcome to Montana. Charlie was just full of interesting ways to greet a man. And then he proved to have another one. He looked down at his boy, whose name Matt hadn't even asked yet, and patted the tyke affectionately on the tummy.

"Sarah," he spoke so his voice carried to his wife, "I haven't fed the baby in a while. You have some biscuits we could feed him, don't you?"

Sarah went from ignoring Matt and talking quietly with her pa to looking down at her son with concerned maternal eyes.

She dropped back, and Matt didn't waste a moment urging his horse ahead to take Sarah's place. He saw Charlie grab his wife's reins when she tried to block Matt. Then Matt was there and Silas turned the coldest blue eyes on Matt he'd ever seen.

Well, Matt was no boy, nor was he a coward. He'd spent time kissing Betsy, and as an honorable man, who wanted leave to kiss Betsy any time he wanted, he didn't hesitate to do what was right.

Chapter 8

Elizabeth Harden, what were you thinking?" Belle set a brisk pace, and Betsy had the sense her ma was trying to leave Matt in the dust.

Since Matt was riding along with Charlie, who knew the way, Betsy didn't figure they'd lose him.

Every time her ma called her Elizabeth, it sent a chill down Betsy's spine, because trouble always followed.

Well, Betsy was past the age of getting a hiding, and Ma had never been one to hand out her punishments in that harsh way.

But on the other hand, there was never any doubt that making Ma mad was going to be followed with long, deep regrets.

"Why didn't you just load up the girls and come home? We'd have helped." Then Ma's expression changed from anger to something else. Something soft and sad, as if she was hurt. Her pain was a lot harder to take than anger.

"Have I ever acted as if you can't come to me for help, Betsy? You know I'll always come a-runnin' if you need me. I haven't acted as if you can't, have I?"

"No, Ma." Betsy reached across and gave her ma's arm a squeeze. "It's because I knew you'd come that I didn't ask. I wanted to prove I was up to handling everything. I've heard the stories of you taking care of our whole ranch with no man. I felt like a failure because I wasn't up to it. I kept meaning to just come for you, but then I'd think I could just get through one more day, prove to myself. . .and you and Pa, that you'd raised me right."

"Betsy, you're as smart and hardworking as the day is long. You don't have to prove a single thing to me because I've seen plenty of proof over the years."

Letting go of her ma's arm, Betsy smiled, but inside she couldn't help feeling the twist of failure. "But you did it, Ma. Why couldn't I? Because I was sure enough failing at it. And if Matt hadn't come. . ." She thought of that fast-moving creek, and a cold chill raised goose bumps on her arms. "Matt saved the girls' lives, Ma. They'd slipped away while I did chores, thinking they were napping. If he hadn't been there. . ." Shaking her head she couldn't control a shudder.

"But you shouldn't have been kissing a man you'd only met days ago."

A long silence followed. Betsy glanced back and saw that Matt was now riding alongside Pa and Sarah had dropped back and was fussing with her baby. Betsy said a quick prayer to God to protect Matt from Pa.

Leaning close to Ma, she spoke so her voice wouldn't be heard. "How long did you know Pa before you kissed him the first time?"

Another long silence. Then Ma said, "Don't try and change the subject. I've told you before that a man can't be trusted. You know better'n to—"

"How long, Ma?" Betsy knew her ma real well, and she knew when a question was being dodged.

"Anthony, your pa, came around for weeks before I—"

"I'm talking about Silas, and what's more, you know it. He's the only man I call Pa."

Ma glared at Betsy, who'd been raised to be tough, even with her own mother.

Betsy arched her brows and stared right back, maybe not so ferociously as Ma, but then Betsy wasn't half trying.

Finally Ma looked away. "When we first kissed isn't the point. We'd known each other through a long, hard cattle drive. I knew the kind of man he was. I respected—"

"That fast, huh?" Betsy smiled then snickered. "Why, Belle Tanner Harden, you scamp. I think the two of us need to compare our history and just see which of us is better behaved around men."

Ma's eyes narrowed, then after a few seconds she rolled them toward heaven and said, "Our first kiss came too fast."

"I'm sure mine and Matt's did, too. But it was only a kiss. He treated me with honor; he worked hard outside, slept in the bunkhouse every night, and helped with the girls as well. He's got a passel of little brothers, and he's as good with children as I am, maybe better because by his own admission he was as much of a scamp as Mark growing up."

"No one can be as much of a scamp as Mark." Ma didn't admit it often, but Betsy knew she was right fond of her son-in-law, and Emma was still very much in love with her husband.

"That's true. But Matt seemed to keep ahead of the girls as if he'd seen it all before."

Ma glanced back then looked quickly away. "You're sounding like you're pretty serious about this young man. Just because he's Mark's brother doesn't mean you really know him. You need time to learn if he's an honest, God-fearing man who will be dependable over the years."

"I agree. I like him real well, but I'm going to spend time getting to know him better. I can promise you I'm not going to be rushed into anything with a near stranger."

"Belle." Pa had closed the distance between himself and Ma.

"Yes, Silas?" Ma looked as if she wanted to keep pestering Betsy.

"Matt just asked for Betsy's hand in marriage. He wants to ride straight into Divide and have the wedding today."

Chapter 9

Betsy started coughing.

They emerged from the woods with only a wide pasture ahead of them before they reached Mark's house.

Matt rode past Silas and brought his horse right up beside Betsy—on the side away from Belle. He patted her on the back until she recovered.

"I wanted to talk with you about it first, honey." He gave Silas a narrow-eyed look for being so blunt. His soon-to-be father-in-law. . .if Matt handled all this right. . .looked completely unrepentant.

Now here he was with Silas and Belle watching his every move, and Charlie and Sarah close enough to have heard everything—and riding in closer. And Betsy looking like she wanted to make a run for it.

"Give your horse to your pa and let's walk together the rest of the way."

"You're not going anywhere alone with my daughter," Belle snapped.

Matt knew good and well that before this was over he was going everywhere with Betsy Harden. He let that thought keep him from growling.

Instead he dismounted and plucked Betsy off her horse. "Watch us. Listen to me talk then, Belle. But Betsy deserves to hear some nice words about how wonderful I think she is. And she needs to hear. . ." Matt looked away from Belle and talked to pretty Betsy.

". . .you need to hear that I want the right to kiss you anytime I choose. I want to spend my life with you, Betsy. You're the prettiest woman I've ever seen. The prettiest I've ever imagined."

Matt realized that the crowd was gone. They were probably disgusted, but maybe they also had a little shame. For whatever reason, the family had ridden on for the ranch house, Charlie leading both Matt's and Betsy's horses.

"But that's not why I want to join my life with you. I can see your goodness, and I respect your toughness and your fine heart and sharp mind. I would be the luckiest man in the world to have you marry me. You're the kind of woman a man would want to have by his side to weather life's storms like last night, and to enjoy during the good times."

Betsy honestly wanted to say yes, but he'd yet to say the one thing that would matter, and what's more, he couldn't say it. They'd been through a hard spell together. She'd seen how he handled trouble. But that wasn't enough for her. She wanted what she saw pass between Ma and Pa. Between Mark and Emma, Charlie and Sarah.

"I know you're a practical woman, Betsy. So I've given you practical reasons why you should marry me. But the real reason I'm asking is, I've fallen in love with you. Now, I don't reckon—"

Betsy threw herself into his arms and kissed him before he could say something that would make a hash out of the beautiful words. Matt's arms came around her waist; he lifted her straight off her feet. Then he whirled her in a circle and broke the kiss to laugh out loud with joy.

When the celebration ended, Matt eased her away from him. "I'm taking that for a yes, but I'd like to hear the words."

"Yes, I'll marry you, Matt. And I'll consider myself the luckiest woman on earth."

They were awhile speaking again, then Betsy pulled away and said, "Let's go on and catch up with the others."

Her family had to have settled the cattle in by now. So they'd be waiting at Emma's house.

Nodding, Matt looked at her for too long, and Betsy had never felt so wanted, so loved. Not in a man and woman kind of way.

"Let's go." He slid his arm around her waist and they walked toward the ranch house, a hundred yards away.

Chapter 10

Five riders approached the cabin as Matt neared it. His spirits rose—and that was sayin' something because they were already sky-high. One of those riders was his brother.

"Mark's home. That must be Emma at his side."

"Yep, we made it. We kept all three girls alive."

Matt chuckled, then he laughed, and Betsy laughed along with him until the two were nearly limp.

They were calming down when they reached the house. Mark had gone inside, but he came running out looking around. His eyes landed on Matt.

"Matt!" His big brother rushed to him, and they grabbed each other. Matt was shocked at how nice it was to see someone from his own family. He had one terrible moment when a burn of tears washed over his eyes. He fought them off and hung on to Mark, pounding his back and laughing.

Mark finally backed up and dashed his wrist across his eyes, but Matt saw what just might have been tears. He'd have tormented Mark about it if that wouldn't have made him a hypocrite.

"It is good to see someone from home, little brother." Then Mark turned to Betsy. "And I was inside long enough to hear my brother was asking you to marry him."

The smile that broke out on Mark's face helped Matt to make some decisions on the spot. The main one being he'd find a way to stay in this area, because he'd been considering taking Betsy on his wandering with him while they hunted for a place to settle. Maybe taking her home to Texas. But having Betsy's family nearby, and Matt having his brother and cousin, was too tempting to resist.

Betsy's smile was as wide as Mark's. "Yep, we're getting married."

"We didn't talk about when." Matt took Betsy's hand. "But I'd like to see to it right away."

He met Betsy's eyes, and she nodded. "As soon as we can hunt up a parson."

Matt took her hand and threaded his fingers between hers. "That suits me just fine."

∞

"I now pronounce you man and wife." Parson Red Dawson smiled as he closed his prayer book. "You may kiss the bride."

Matt turned to Betsy, humbled and thrilled to have gotten such a treasure for a wife. The kiss was quick and sweet, a completely appropriate kiss for two people standing before a throng of family and friends.

They faced the gathering, then Matt took Betsy's hand and hooked it through his elbow and they marched down the aisle formed by their wedding guests.

He was outside and surrounded by well-wishers when he saw a familiar face. "Mandy McClellen?"

"Matt!" Mandy took both his hands, smiling so big it was blinding. "Have you been home lately? Have you seen Laura since she married Ike?"

The two chattered together a long while. Matt loved seeing another face from home. Since Matt had been home recently, Mandy was full of questions about her sister Beth, not to mention her other sister Laura who'd married Matt and Mark's brother Ike. Mandy quizzed him until he'd told everything he knew.

Then a tall blond man dragged Mandy's hands away from Matt.

"Oh Matt. My husband, Tom Linscott. Tom, this is Mark Reeves's brother. He's got another brother, Ike, married to my little sister Laura. You remember when I got word Laura was married?"

Matt saw clear as day that Tom Linscott hadn't liked another man holding his wife's hands. But he must have trusted his wife—he'd have been a fool not to. Mandy was the most upright fussbudget Matt had ever known. Mark especially had lived to torment her when they were kids—and Matt had helped all he could.

Belle joined them, her hazel eyes serious, stern, worried. Well, Matt would ease her worries by being the best husband a woman ever had. But it would take time to prove all that to Belle.

"We've all brought potluck," Belle said. "We can have a feast."

Silas was behind his wife. "I've got a stretch of land for you, Matt. It's a nice high valley that will be close to Charlie and Mark and close up the distance between us and our Lindsay. I've a mind to own every inch of the trail to Helena before I'm done. And with all our boys," Silas slid his arm behind Belle's waist and smiled down at her, "I think we can do it, don't you, honey?"

Since Matt was determined to make his wife happy and living next to Mark suited him, he nodded as Silas Harden arranged his life.

Charlie came up as soon as there was a break in the hand shaking and back slapping. "I've got a line shack near my place. I sent my men out there to make sure it's clean and stocked with food and to set it up so you can have privacy."

A wave of dizziness came over Matt to think of the wedding night ahead.

Mark was right behind Charlie. "Trust me, Matt, you don't want to stay overnight at your in-laws' house on your wedding night."

Matt had himself a wife, and he wanted to be with her, as a man was with a wife.

"I'll tell Betsy. I didn't figure I was ever gonna be alone with her." Frowning, he added, "It sounds like Silas is going to tell me where to live and build me a house and give me some cattle. He doesn't have to do that. I have some money saved up, and I'm not afraid of hard work."

"He did that for me," Mark said. "It was like standing in front of an avalanche. I tried to tell him I could take care of my own wife, but he wouldn't hear of not helping me get set up. The whole Harden clan is crazy to protect their daughters. Belle's first husband left her to do everything on her own. I guess this is their way of not letting that happen to their girls. And it made Emma happy, as well as making our first years together much more comfortable."

Matt looked at Charlie. "You and Sarah, too?"

Charlie nodded, "Yep, 'tweren't no stopping him. And when I protested I was a little bit afraid Belle was going to shoot me, so I just gave them what they wanted."

"Anyway, the land he's speaking of is a beautiful place. And not too far from here."

They'd gotten married at Mark's place.

Mark slapped Matt's shoulder. "I'm glad to have some more family close by. Charlie and I have been treated real well by the Hardens, but to watch them all be a close family makes me lonely for more of my own brothers. I'd love to see Ma and Pa, too. I might do it now that you're close. Emma and I could ride to Texas, catch a train part of the way, and leave the girls here with you and Betsy."

"That's not going to happen, Mark." Betsy's horrified voice turned them to face her. "You take them with you if you want to go to Texas."

"I can't. Ma and Pa are snowed in during the winter, and there's too much work during the summer."

"They're not snowed in anymore. Ma made Pa dynamite the opening so it's wider. They come and go all winter long now."

Mark gasped. "How'd she get him to do that?"

"There've been a lot of changes since that baby girl was born."

"I'd heard there were, but I never dreamed they'd blasted the canyon entrance."

"Yep, the little brothers never miss school either."

"They must hate that."

"Not really. Ma brought order to the whole house, and the boys behave well at school, too. It's shocking at first, but you get used to it. But even if you couldn't go in the winter, we wouldn't watch your young'uns." Matt went to his wife and slid his arm around her waist. "Your daughters are more than we can handle, Mark. You take 'em with you, or you don't go."

Emma said quietly, "I noticed the bars on the windows." She glanced at Mark and smiled. "Why didn't we think of that?"

"Besides," Matt went on, "Ma will want to see her grandchildren." Matt looked down at Betsy, who was smiling at him, probably grateful that he was saving her from Mark's daughters.

Nope, he sure as shootin' didn't want to spend his wedding night with his in-laws.

"Let's go saddle up, wife. Charlie has cleaned up a line shack for us. We can commence to having our honeymoon as soon as we get there." Just saying it out loud made Matt's head spin. He urged Betsy toward the horses.

"Pa wants to help build us a house, but he'll wait until tomorrow." Betsy smiled and leaned against him then she lifted her right hand to show him the satchel she carried. "Tonight we're on our own, and I'm ready to go."

Epilogue

The peace of a new beginning washed over him as they said their good-byes and walked toward their horses together.

The line shack wasn't far, but far enough. When they came to the front door, Matt dropped the satchel and swept Betsy up into his arms.

"I've heard of a tradition, Mrs. Reeves. It's supposed to bring good luck to a marriage if the groom carries the bride over the threshold of their first home."

Betsy gave him a teasing smile and reached down to open the door of the tiny one room cabin. "Good luck brought by such means smacks of superstition, Mr. Reeves. And I don't hold with such things."

"Neither do I, Betsy darlin'. But your ma gave me such an evil look when I told her we were leaving the party, I think I can use all the luck I can get. And the protecting hand of God, too."

Betsy laughed. "Carry me in, then, and you can carry me into our home, too, when Pa gets it built."

"That will be my pleasure. Any excuse to hold you close." Matt walked inside, and Betsy gasped.

"Did Charlie do this?" The room was filled with wildflowers, and the scent of them made the little cabin homey and welcoming. A pot of stew simmered on the stove, adding to the pleasant aroma.

"He said he sent some of his hired men over to bring bedding and food. I'm betting your sister thought of the flowers. That ain't Charlie's style."

Betsy laughed.

Matt stood Betsy on her feet and closed the door, shutting out the world.

"I have myself a wife who is tough and smart and sweet and kind. The prettiest woman I've ever imagined. I can't wait to get on with being a husband who is worthy of you."

"You know, Matt, even though I spent most of the last week inside, I really am used to helping outside. I know horses and cattle. I understand mountain grazing and treacherous trails. I'm going to be a partner to you in this ranch."

"So I've got me a bride who rides herd, huh?"

"You do, indeed."

Matt kissed her soundly and got on with being a husband in the most wonderful way of all.

Blue Moon Bride

by Susan Page Davis

Chapter 1

Ava Neal's younger sister burst into her bed-chamber.

"Ava!" Sarah hurried across the room as quickly as her long rose-colored taffeta dress and her fashionable shoes would allow. "Conrad has proposed. We're getting married."

Ava pulled her into a fierce hug. "Oh my dear! I'm so happy for you."

"Really?" Sarah drew away and eyed her critically. "Are you sure?"

"Of course. Why wouldn't I be? Conrad is a fine young man, and he obviously adores you. He'll make you a wonderful husband."

"Well, we always thought you'd be the first down the aisle."

"True, but we Neal sisters are unconventional, aren't we? We've never set much store by what people think."

"You're not crying, are you?" Sarah asked.

"No! Well, perhaps." Ava chuckled and swiped at a tear escaping down her cheek. "But these are happy tears, I assure you."

"They're not"—Sarah studied her with an anxious frown—"not because of Will Sandford?"

"Of course not! That was long ago."

"Yes."

Ava grasped her sister's hand. "You've told Mama and Pa of course."

"We did, and they seem quite pleased about it. They asked me to run up and get you. You'll join us, won't you?"

"I certainly will."

Ava steered Sarah out to the landing and down the stairs to the parlor. The more people the merrier just now, and if anyone else alluded to her state of singleness at the age of twenty-two, or to her heart being broken when Will Sandford died, she would ignore them.

At the parlor door, she allowed Sarah to draw her in and over to Conrad's chair. He stood, blushing a little, as Ava laid her hand on his sleeve.

"Conrad, Sarah has told me the good news. I am so pleased."

"Thank you." He let her draw him down for a kiss on his cheek, which made him flush even deeper.

"Sit down, girls," her mother said. "I've made fresh tea."

Mama had also brought out the macaroons and ginger gems they had baked that afternoon. Mama always had some confection on hand when her daughters received gentleman callers.

"Let me help you." As usual, Ava served while her mother poured the tea. They had developed the routine years ago, without discussing it. She gave Conrad the first cup, then Sarah, and then her father. While Mama poured for Ava and herself, Ava passed the pressed-glass plate of cookies.

At last, she settled on a chair near her father.

"Have you discussed a date between you?" Mama asked Sarah.

"A little." Sarah glanced at Conrad. "We thought we'd like to have it in June if we can, though time is short."

"Of course, a June bride." Mama's smile belied any difficulty in organizing a wedding in less than six weeks.

Ava sipped her tea and let the talk flow around her. Conrad must have approached her father sometime during the day, probably at Pa's office in town. He had obviously received permission to offer Sarah his hand, as Pa now seemed perfectly contented with the way things were going.

Ava tried not to imagine how different things would be now if she were the one being courted, or if she were now a married woman and could host a party for Sarah in her own home.

She was only fifteen when Will went off to war, and sixteen when they'd heard he'd been killed. Some had supposed she was too young to truly know love, but her family understood how the news shattered her. Ava often thought that, because she was so young, those feelings had faded more slowly than they would have in an older woman.

"And you'll need a new gown, Ava," her mother said, jerking her back into the present.

"Wh— Oh, for the wedding?"

"Of course, darling," Sarah said. "You will stand up with me, won't you?"

"If you wish it."

"I wouldn't have anyone else." Sarah reached over to squeeze her hand. "I was thinking pale blue watered silk. Or would you prefer green?"

"Whatever you decide on," Ava said. No one would ever suggest she wear pink or burgundy, with her auburn hair. She could trust Sarah's judgment there.

"Perhaps you ladies should go to the shops tomorrow and see what they have laid in," her father suggested.

Ava looked at him in surprise. Pa was in a generous mood this evening. He must truly be happy with Sarah's choice. Perhaps he was relieved that he would have one less eligible daughter to worry about.

"What a splendid idea," Mama said. "We'll make a day of it and eat luncheon in town. Now, Conrad, do your parents know?"

The corners of Conrad's mouth quirked, and he glanced at Sarah. "Well, I did drop a hint to them before I left the house. They seemed quite agreeable. My mother told me to ask if Sarah may join us for dinner Sunday."

"Of course," Mama said. "And we'll want to have your whole family over soon. Maybe next week."

Ava realized her father was watching her, not the prospective bride. He gave her a gentle smile.

"Ava, would you mind refreshing that tea? I think we need another pot."

"Of course, Pa." Ava rose and took the nearly empty teapot off the serving table.

A moment later, her father followed her into the kitchen.

"All right, kitten?"

"I'm fine, Pa." She measured the dried tea leaves into the infuser and placed it in the teapot.

"Right." He stood there watching her work.

"What?" Ava asked.

"Memories waylay us at the most inconvenient times."

She grimaced. "I hoped it wasn't obvious."

"Not too badly."

"I'm truly happy for Sarah and Conrad."

"I'm sure," her father said. "That doesn't make it easier though."

Ava sighed and turned to the stove for the teakettle. "I thought maybe I'd do some traveling this summer, Pa. After the wedding of course. I wouldn't leave before then."

"Travel where?"

"I'd just like to get away. Maybe have a little adventure of my own." A thought came to her, and she glanced up at him. "I could go out and visit Polly Tierney."

Her father blinked, frowning a little. "Polly? Kitten, she lives clear out in the Wyoming Territory."

"Well, yes, but it's civilized now, or nearly so. And travel is so much easier out there, now that they have railroads clear across. I could take a train to Cheyenne. Polly and Jacob could fetch me there."

"I don't know. . ."

Ava poured the boiling water into the teapot. "Please, Pa? It would give me something to look forward to after the wedding."

"Maybe so. I'll mention it to your mother tonight. Start her thinking about it a little."

Ava laughed. "I doubt you can get her to think about much besides wedding plans right now, but it wouldn't hurt to plant the idea in her mind."

ᗡ

Joe Logan sat in the waiting room at Becker and Fixx, Attorneys at Law, and doodled on the edge of the newspaper he'd picked up. He hated waiting, and his fingers always reached for a pencil when he had to sit for a while.

The front page of the paper had a story about the devastating effects of a recent hurricane on Labrador, and another on outlaw Jesse James's latest escapades out west. Joe sketched a man on horseback, his face obscured by a knotted handkerchief, riding with a pistol in his outstretched hand. Not bad. Joe still thought he might be able to find a place as an illustrator, but he'd probably have to go to New York for that, and rumors said the price of food and lodging there was outrageous.

A bell sounded briefly from the next room, and the secretary who sat at a desk across the room looked at him. "Mr. Becker will see you now."

Joe brushed a bit of dust from his jacket and fingered the tie knotted around his neck before entering the inner office. Mr. Becker was particular about his employees' appearances.

"There you are, Logan. I have a job for you if you want it. It's a bit more involved than the jobs I've given you before."

Mr. Becker nodded toward an empty chair, and Joe sat down.

"That's fine, sir." Joe would like having more regular income, but he hadn't been able to secure a steady position since his old employer had died in November, leaving him at loose ends. The courier jobs and errands he performed for Hartford businessmen barely paid his living expenses.

The attorney sat back and studied him for a moment. "I've a client who doesn't trust the postal service, and he wants a packet hand-delivered."

Joe nodded, glad it wasn't a summons to serve a court witness. He always found that task distasteful. "Is it documents, sir?"

"Er, no. The gentleman was recently widowed, and he wants to send a few of his wife's bits to their daughter. She's married and living in San Francisco."

Joe tried not to let his excitement show in his face. He had never set foot west of the Appalachians. San Francisco, and all expenses paid. Those "bits" must be valuable.

"You'll need to get some signatures, too. I sent some papers in January, and the daughter claims she signed them and sent them back, but they never arrived here." Becker shook his head. "You just can't rely on the mail west of the Mississippi, I'm afraid. So you'll take the papers out and have her sign them when you give her the jewelry, and then you'll bring the documents back."

It sounded simple enough. "When do you want me to leave, sir?"

"Soon. I'll have Mr. Franklin see to your railroad ticket. Next week, I suppose. End of the month. You'll have a berth on the train, but you'll have to find a hotel once you arrive. I don't expect it will take you more than a day or two to take care of your errand, and then you must head right back."

Joe nodded. Surely somewhere in there he could squeeze out a few hours to enjoy seeing San Francisco. It might as well be Paris—distant, exotic. He could hardly wait.

"You will wire me when you have completed the delivery," Mr. Becker went on.

"Yes sir." That would, of course, be his first order of business when he got to San Francisco.

"We will advance you money for your expenses and pay you fifty dollars upon your return. Is that acceptable?"

To Joe, it was very acceptable. The trip would take him less than a month—perhaps much less, and he fully expected to enjoy himself.

"Perfectly," he said.

"All right. See Mr. Franklin at the front desk. Come 'round to get your ticket the morning before your departure, and we'll give you the client's packet."

"Very good, sir."

"And Logan, if this goes well—that is, if you successfully deliver this parcel—why, we might have regular daily employment for you on your return. Are you interested?"

"Oh yes, sir. Thank you." Joe left the office whistling and went back to his boardinghouse. Unfortunately, he would probably have to pay for his room in advance, or the landlady would let it out to someone else in his absence, but overall, he felt good about the prospect of this new venture.

After dinner, he went down to the parlor to save burning his own lamp oil. He found a quiet corner where the other boarders would hardly notice him and opened his drawing tablet. He had splurged on it a couple of months ago, but it was full now, and he had to flip through it before he found a page with enough empty space for him to draw a locomotive spurting smoke. San Francisco! He would most definitely have to buy a new sketchbook before he embarked.

Chapter 2

Safely across Mississippi

Ava reread her brief message. Mama would fuss about the unnecessary expense if she added much more. She would save her descriptions of the journey until she had a chance to write a full letter. Still, her parents would be waiting fretfully for news, especially Mama.

So far, the railroad journey had been interesting, especially after they left New England and passed through vast tracts of forest and farmland. As yet there was no bridge across the river at St. Louis, though one apparently was planned, and Ava had joined her fellow passengers on a ferry ride over the roiling waters of the Mississippi. Seeing the mighty river, the barges of coal and wheat, and the steamboats plying up and down the channel had thrilled her. Thanks to the modern wonder of the submerged telegraph cable, her parents would receive her message before suppertime.

While the porters transferred the baggage from the ferry to a wagon, the passengers drifted toward the eateries near the waterfront. They had an hour before their next train would board, and most of the travelers hoped to find a decent meal in the interval. Ava found a lunch counter that served soup and sandwiches. When she gave her order, she asked for a packet of extra sandwiches to take with her.

She entered the railroad car before most of the other passengers and found a window seat two rows back from the vestibule. Last week, she and her father had engaged in quite a discussion on the merits of window seats versus aisle seats. Her mother, on the other hand, seemed only to be fretting about the impression a young woman traveling alone would give. As the others entered and claimed places, Ava tucked her handbag and sandwiches between herself and the wall and peered out the window at the flurry of activity on the platform.

"Pardon me. Is this seat taken?"

She looked up into the keen blue eyes of a young man, clean shaven and of respectable dress, who stood in the aisle, his derby hat in one hand and a small leather valise in the other.

"Not at all." Ava's lips curved—not too encouraging, she hoped. Mama had been quite expansive about the encouragement young men might take from a winsome smile.

She tried not to look at him as he settled in, but she noted that after placing his hat on the rack overhead, he slid his leather case beneath the seat and kept the heel of his shoe nestled against it when he sat down, as though he didn't want to lose track of that case for a second.

The car filled rapidly, and the conductor passed through. Two gentlemen arrived separately and claimed the seats opposite them, offering the perfunctory greetings of strangers. The train started with a lurch and then a steadily increasing rumble. Ava was getting used to the sounds and rhythms of the rails, and she felt like quite a seasoned traveler now. One of the men across from her opened a newspaper, and the other leaned back and closed his eyes. Ava studiously gazed at the shifting landscape outside.

When the conductor came to check their tickets, the young man leaned back and allowed her to present hers first.

"We'll reach Cheyenne late tomorrow morning, miss." The conductor tore off a portion and handed her the stub.

The young man gave him his ticket, and the conductor nodded. "And you've got quite a trip still ahead of you, sir. You should arrive Wednesday morning, 11:15. Independence Day."

"So it is," the young man said. "I expect they'll have some doings in San Francisco?"

"I shouldn't wonder." The conductor gave him his ticket stub. "Let me know if you folks need anything."

When he had moved on, the young man turned to Ava. "I'm Joseph Logan, by the way."

"How do you do? Ava Neal." She held out her gloved hand, and he grasped it briefly.

"I admit I'm curious," he said. "What draws you to Cheyenne?"

"I'm going out to visit an old friend. She married a Westerner, you see. Polly's father ran a stagecoach stop, and she wed one of their drivers."

"How romantic!"

Ava smiled. "Yes, it was, really. I admit I was a bit jealous when she wrote me. I envy her life now. I haven't seen her for four years, and she's got a husband and two babies."

"It will be quite a reunion for you," Mr. Logan said.

"She's my dearest childhood friend. I can't wait to see her again." Ava hoped she wasn't chattering too much, or revealing too much about herself. Time to turn the conversation. "And what about you, Mr. Logan? I believe the conductor said you are going to San Francisco?"

"That's right. It's business. I shan't stay there more than a day or two, then it's back to Hartford."

They talked quite freely through the afternoon and shared their pleasure at the scenery their window afforded, which was new to both of them. As they rolled across the state of Missouri and headed northward for St. Joseph and the Nebraska border, Ava was grateful for congenial company. Mr. Logan's conversation was far from boring. He told her a bit about his sporadic work for a firm of lawyers in Hartford, and his hopes for steady employment if he succeeded in his mission to California. What that errand was, he did not divulge, but he certainly held her interest. The personable and handsome—yes, by now she admitted inwardly that he was very good looking—young man was an unexpected dividend for this trip.

After tomorrow, Mr. Logan would continue on his journey without her, while Ava began her visit with Polly and Jacob Tierney, but she was satisfied that her adventure had already begun. If nothing else out of the ordinary happened during her excursion, these hours spent in conversation with Mr. Logan were worth the time and expense of the trip.

∽

"Oh, look! The moon is rising." Miss Neal leaned eagerly toward the window then sat back again. "I'm sorry, I'm blocking your view. Can you see it?"

"I can." Joe leaned forward to get a better look, being careful not to get too close to her. Their train was running northward for a ways, and so they looked out toward the east, where their view of the sky was unobstructed for several miles.

"Isn't it lovely?" she asked, so close that her breath tickled his ear. "It's full tonight, isn't it?"

"Yes." He relaxed against the seat and studied her expression. His fingers itched for his drawing pencil, not to sketch the moon, but to capture her eager innocence.

"It looks huge, just on the horizon like that." She peered out again at the big, yellowish orb that hung like a glowing lantern over the hills in the distance.

"There'll be two full moons this month," Joe said. "A blue moon, they say, on the thirty-first."

"I hadn't realized. That's rare, isn't it?" She chuckled. "Of course. That's why they have the saying."

He nodded. "'Once in a blue moon.' I don't suppose it comes even once a year, but I'm not certain. Perhaps an almanac would tell."

"I'll have to look it up sometime."

"Next stop, St. Joe," the conductor called, coming down the aisle with a swinging gait. "Thirty minutes on the platform."

"Thirty minutes," Joe said. "That's hardly time for dinner, and we don't have a dining room on this train."

Ava hesitated. "Please don't think me forward, but I have some sandwiches that I bought in St. Louis. If you'd like, we could share them."

Joe grinned. "That sounds marvelous. Perhaps I can step off and get us some sarsaparilla or lemonade on the platform."

As soon as they stopped, he retrieved his hat and stepped out into the sultry evening air. Dusk had fallen, and the moon was higher now and more normal looking, but still gorgeous in its plump roundness. What a beautiful evening—and his dinner companion would be a very charming young lady. He liked Miss Neal very much, especially her confidence. She didn't exhibit the timidity most women would if traveling alone, and she was making this solitary trip because she wanted to. She had made no apologies for her lack of a chaperone.

The memory of her auburn hair and glittering green eyes in the moonlight that shone through the window was firmly fixed in Joe's mind. He would definitely draw her portrait when they had parted company. A few minutes later, he made good on his word, returning to the car with not only bottled sarsaparilla but two apples and a half-dozen raisin cookies wrapped in brown paper.

Miss Neal surveyed the bounty. "Oh my, we're having a feast."

"Only the best for you, madam." Joe kept a straight face as he shook out his clean handkerchief and spread it on the seat between them. He put the apples and cookies on it, and Miss Neal added her sandwiches, which looked to be good, hearty sliced beef and cheese.

The two gentlemen who had sat opposite had both left the train. Joe sat down and eyed Miss Neal across the picnic supper. "Shall we ask the blessing?"

She seemed to accept that as normal and bowed her head without signs of embarrassment, which was a relief to Joe.

"Dear Lord, we thank You for this and all Your gifts to us, and we ask Your care over the travelers on this train. Amen."

"Amen," Miss Neal said and reached for half a sandwich with a smile. "Thank you, Mr. Logan. This is so much nicer than bustling about the platform

197

trying to find a bite."

"It is indeed."

They had fifteen minutes of comparative privacy, of which Joe made the most, plying his charming companion with questions about her life back home. He learned that her younger sister had been married only the week before.

"Conrad is a nice young man, and I'm sure they'll be happy," she said. "He has a position as headmaster at a secondary school, which is a recent advance from just plain schoolmaster. I'm sure that is why he was emboldened to speak to Sarah."

"Well, yes," Joe said, thinking of his own spotty income. "A man would have to be sure he was able to provide for his bride."

"Exactly. Last winter, when he was just a poor teacher, Sarah despaired of them ever being able to set up a household. This new opportunity for Conrad was a great blessing for them."

Joe nodded, watching Miss Neal's expressive green eyes. How long would it take for him to be able to present himself to some young lady's exacting father as an eligible suitor for the daughter? He hadn't been too troubled by the question until now, but the longer he conversed with Miss Neal, and the more he drank in her understated beauty and sweet features, the more he felt worthiness to be a desirable quality.

His mission on behalf of Mr. Becker's client grew in importance. If he had a regular job with the law firm in Hartford, he could begin to think about the possibility of courting a respectable young woman. Someone, if he were lucky, like Ava Neal. It wasn't just the full moon or the romance of meeting someone attractive on a journey to a strange place. Joe saw beyond that to the substance that lay beneath her captivating appearance.

These pleasant thoughts still flitted about Joe's mind in the morning, when the sleeper berths were folded away. He located Miss Neal during the first stop and once again took a seat beside her. He bought coffee and biscuits for both of them from a vendor who came through the train.

"Did you sleep well?" he asked her.

"Well enough. I don't suppose anyone sleeps quite perfectly on a train, and knowing I'll see Polly and her family today kept me a little on edge."

"Excited to see your friend?"

"Oh yes!"

Joe nodded. Watching her face was a treat, but he would soon be denied this pleasure. "We're less than a hundred miles from Cheyenne."

"I'm all aflutter." She crumpled the paper that had wrapped her biscuit. "I suppose it's not for another three hours or so, but I'm already nervous."

Joe consulted his watch. "More like four. We have a couple more stops to make along the way."

Miss Neal glanced out the window. "We seem to be in quite desolate country now. Are there towns out here?"

"Not very big ones, I don't think. Cheyenne and Fort Laramie would be the largest in Wyoming, I'm guessing."

They ate their meager breakfast and continued to talk. It seemed fewer passengers boarded than left the train now. Joe and his companion marveled at the treeless expanse of plains they were crossing, but they also began to see hills, some of them thrusting up from the ground in unexpected places.

"If we could see out the front, perhaps we'd see mountains." Joe pushed himself up a little so he could better see forward. His finger slid into a break on the edge of the seat's upholstery. He smoothed the fabric down quickly, but he couldn't see anything from the windows ahead of them.

Miss Neal gave him a rueful smile. "I regret I won't be going far enough to see the Rocky Mountains. Maybe someday."

"This friend of yours," Joe said. "Surely her husband can't be driving a stagecoach now—not since they've taken the railway through?"

"He owns a short line of his own now, Polly tells me, from Cheyenne to a few smaller towns off the rail lines."

"I see."

The conductor came through, checking new passengers' tickets.

"Excuse me," Joe asked when he came even with their seats. "What's the next stop?"

"Pine Bluffs, but there's not much there. No restaurants or anything. There's a shack where the wagon trains used to trade a bit, and a few tents. One's a saloon. I expect it will draw more people now, since we stop there regular. There's some new stock pens, and a couple of ranchers put some cattle on the train this spring. Probably in the fall, we'll get more. Have to start hauling more cattle cars." He nodded at Ava. "Not far to Cheyenne after that, miss."

"Oh, thank you." Ava had foregone wearing her hat that morning, and she looked charming, but as soon as the conductor ambled on down the aisle, she began rummaging in her handbag. "I'm sorry, Mr. Logan, but I must find my gloves and put my hat on before we reach Cheyenne. Perhaps I can step into the lavatory while we're at Pine Bluffs and use the mirror in there."

"I'm sure you can. I'll get your hat down for you when we stop."

This preparation for leaving him unsettled Joe, as if she had cut the painter on a rowboat and would let him drift away. He took a deep breath. "Miss Neal, I shall miss your company on the rest of my trip."

Her fluttering hands stilled now that a plan for tending to her appearance was in place. "It's been good having someone congenial to talk to. I shall miss you, too."

Joe took courage. "Thank you. I wondered if you might consent to. . .to allowing me to write to you. I believe you said you'll be staying with your friend for several weeks?"

"We've planned on a month's stay." Her cheeks flushed a becoming pink. "I don't suppose it would be improper to receive a postal card from a fellow traveler."

"Thank you so much. You'll have to give me the address. It seems odd that I shall be back in New England before you, even though I'm journeying farther."

"Doesn't it?" She sobered. "I don't suppose we shall meet again after today, but yes, I'd like to stay in touch."

"I can—"Joe broke off as the train began to brake much more abruptly than when easing in at a station platform, throwing them both forward so hard he nearly fell. Instinctively, he put out an arm to break Miss Neal's flight. Even so, she plummeted to the floor between the facing pair of seats.

The train skidded to a halt with much squealing and grinding of metal on metal.

Joe braced himself until they stopped completely. He reached out to her. "Are you all right?"

"I think so." She brushed at her skirt and allowed him to help her up onto the seat. "Why have we stopped so suddenly?"

"I don't know." Joe looked around the car. Other passengers were righting themselves and taking stock of their bruises and wayward possessions.

Miss Neal peered out the window. "I can't see anything on this side."

"Perhaps I can—"Joe started to rise but sank back into his seat as two men entered the front of the car with pistols in their hands.

Chapter 3

A woman on the other side of the aisle gave a little shriek.

"Easy now, folks," the closer gunman said. A grimy bandanna covered the lower part of his face, and his felt hat was pulled low on his brow. "Everybody stay calm and keep your hands where I can see 'em."

Ava tried to breathe, but she couldn't get enough air. All around her, the passengers gaped at the two men. Many of the travelers' faces had blanched, and the woman across the aisle clung to her companion's arm as though she would swoon at any second.

Ava glanced at Joe Logan. Like most of the other passengers, he held his hands at shoulder height and stared at the two robbers.

"If any of you have weapons, don't even think about using them," the robber said. "I guarantee I'm faster'n you, and keep in mind there's a lot of innocent bystanders in this car."

The second masked man stepped past his partner, holding out a gunnysack. "You can put the goods in this." He holstered his sidearm, but the first man continued to point his weapon at the passengers, sweeping the barrel slowly from side to side and letting his gaze focus on one after another.

The man with the sack stopped in front of the two men in the first seats. "All right, gents, let's have it. Wallets, watches, and anything else that might come in useful to me and my pals. If you've got pistols, knives, or derringers, might as well toss them in, too."

The two men scowled and began emptying their pockets.

Ava put a hand to her throat. *Polly's grandmother's brooch.* Could she possibly hide it before the robbers got this far down the aisle? It wasn't worth much, but she was determined to deliver it to Polly. Oh, why hadn't she left it in her bag? She had been foolish to think it would be safer pinned to her dress.

She fumbled with it. If she could undo the clasp and slide the pin free of fabric before the robbers noticed, she might have a chance of keeping it. Mr. Logan looked her way, and she froze. His gaze traveled to her hand then back to her eyes. Cautiously, he lowered one hand while watching the robbers and held it toward her.

Ava's heart thrummed as she slipped the cameo brooch off her bodice and slowly lowered her hand.

The vestibule door thudded open, and a third outlaw entered the car. Ava could barely hear the words he spoke to his companions.

"We got the engineer and fireman trussed up. Hurry up though."

So there were more of them. While everyone else was distracted by the third robber's entrance, she slid the brooch into Mr. Logan's warm hand. His fingers closed over it. What would he do with it? He was closer to the aisle than she was.

As the robbers collected loot across the aisle, Mr. Logan bent his knees and stooped. He stuffed the brooch into an opening in the seam of the seat's upholstery and slowly straightened again, raising his hand to his former position.

"You!" The robbers faced them, one with his pistol pointed in Logan's face while the other held the open sack before him. "Let's have it. Wallet, watch, and anything else you've got."

Logan obediently reached inside his coat and pulled out his wallet. He hesitated, and the gunman waved the barrel at him.

"Drop it in, mister! Now!"

Logan let it fall into the sack.

"Empty your pockets," the man holding the sack snarled.

Logan pulled out a watch on a chain, a pocketknife, and a few coins and dropped them in the sack.

"That all?"

Mr. Logan nodded.

"What's that?" The gunman nodded toward the leather valise beneath the seat.

"Just, uh, papers and such," Mr. Logan said.

"Open it."

With a resigned expression, he bent and retrieved the case and unbuckled it. The robber with the sack peered inside. "What have we here?" He took out a small parcel wrapped in brown paper.

"It's nothing," Mr. Logan said.

"Hmm."

"Step lively, Bert," the robber's companion growled.

Bert dropped the package into his sack and looked at Ava.

"Now you, lady."

Ava's heart lurched. She opened her handbag and took out her small leather change purse. She stared into the gunman's steely gray eyes as she held it over the sack and let go.

"You got any more?"

"No sir."

"Maybe better put the whole thing in there," he said, eyeing her handbag.

"Oh, must I? There's nothing else of value to you."

A lump ached in Ava's throat. Her purse wouldn't matter that much—it now held only her comb, a few hairpins, a small container of pomade, and a fan. But why should these thugs take it?

"Come on, we ain't got all day." The man holding the gun seemed rather impatient. Bert grunted and moved on to the next set of seats. Ava looked sidelong at Mr. Logan. His gaze followed the gunnysack, and his mouth was set in a grim line.

∽

As soon as the robbers had left the car, Joe raced to the front door. The train rested in the middle of nowhere, with uneven plains stretching away for miles around them. He heard a commotion of hoofbeats, and a moment later a band of six horsemen appeared ahead of the locomotive, galloping off and veering away from the rail lines toward the southwest.

The conductor appeared at the main door of the car ahead. Joe waved to him. "Anyone hurt?"

The conductor hopped down and walked toward him. Satisfied he wouldn't do that if the train were about to move, Joe climbed down the steps and met him halfway.

"Apparently two of their men boarded the train at the last stop," the conductor said. "Their friends laid a pile of rocks and brush on the tracks and forced us to stop. We'll have to clear it."

Joe looked around. "They must have hauled it a long way."

"There's hills and ravines on the other side. They probably came out here and got it ready long in advance."

"I thought there were railroad police traveling on the trains now," Joe said.

"We've got one. He was in the next car, but they spotted him first thing and got the drop on him as soon as we started braking. They roughed him up a little and tied him up. There wasn't a thing he could do."

"Is he all right?"

The conductor nodded. "Mostly. I imagine he'll be back soon to talk to the folks in your car. It'll be hard for them to identify the robbers, though, with their faces covered."

They walked together to the entrance of the car in which Joe had been riding. The conductor entered first and called out, "Everybody all right?"

"If you call losing a hundred and twenty dollars all right," a man replied.

"I'm sorry, sir, but as your ticket stated, the railroad is not responsible for losses in robberies. Unfortunately, the gangs are getting bolder and, it seems, a little smarter. We've got a detective up ahead in the next car. The robbers beat him up a little, but he's starting to talk to the people up there and get their stories. He'll be back here in a few minutes. Be ready to tell him what you lost and also any details you recall about the robbers. Once you've done that, gentlemen, we could use your help in clearing the tracks so we can get under way again as soon as possible."

Joe slid into the seat next to Miss Neal. "I hope you're not too shaken by this unfortunate incident."

"It could have been so much worse," she said. "Are you all right?"

"I'm fine, but. . ."

"They stole something from your valise," she said. "Was it important?"

"Yes."

"I'm sorry."

He gazed into her sympathetic eyes for a moment. "Thank you. I shall have to disembark at Cheyenne and send a telegram to my employer."

"Oh dear."

"Yes."

He felt along the edge of the seat and located the break in the seam. After a moment's probing, he retrieved her brooch and held it out to her.

"Oh, thank you!" Miss Neal took it and gazed at it. "I can't tell you how much this means to me. My friend Polly's grandmother asked me to take it to Polly, and I was afraid I would lose it to those bandits. I don't suppose it's worth much, but Polly will be so happy to get it." Her eyes flickered. "You lost your watch, too, and all your funds, I suppose."

He leaned toward her and lowered his voice. "Not so bad as all that. It was a cheap watch, and I've got twenty dollars hidden on my person, so I'll be all right."

Her face flushed, and she whispered, "I have a bit of cash sewn into a seam myself. My mother insisted, and she was wiser than I gave her credit for."

"Good." He picked up the valise from where he had let it fall after the robbers took his parcel. From it he took out a tablet and pencil. He flipped open to a blank white page and began to draw with swift, sure lines.

"Oh! You didn't tell me you are an artist," Miss Neal said.

"Of sorts." He glanced at her apologetically. "If you'll forgive me, this may be important."

"Of course."

She watched him sketch the face of the robber who had held the sack. Joe hadn't been able to see his entire face, but he had taken note of the shape of his nose, eyes, and brow, and the full growth of beard that showed on the sides, where the bandanna didn't cover it all.

The detective entered the car with a small notepad in hand. The lines at the corners of his mouth bespoke fatigue and maybe some embarrassment at his inability to stop the robbery. He went down the aisle fairly quickly, taking each passenger's list of stolen items and descriptions of the robbers. When he reached their seats, Joe nodded toward his companion.

"Miss Neal."

While she told the detective about the change purse and small amount of cash she had lost, Joe put the finishing touches on his second drawing. This one wasn't as good—he hadn't managed to catch as many details of the gunman's face. He didn't even attempt to draw the third man. He had concentrated instead on memorizing enough to make an accurate drawing of one man and a passable likeness of the second.

"What's this?" The detective leaned over him.

"That's one of the robbers, sir." Joe flipped back to the previous page. "This is the one who held the bag of loot. His companion called him Bert. If you'd like to come back here after you've spoken to the others, I can also draw the gunman's pistol for you."

"That one looks just like the man with the sack," Miss Neal said, pointing to the drawing of Bert.

"Hmm, these could be helpful," the detective said. "What's your name, sir?"

"Joseph Logan. I lost some very valuable property, which I was employed to deliver to San Francisco, as well as my wallet and my watch."

Joe went to join the other men who were clearing the tracks, and soon the train was once more moving toward Cheyenne. He kept up a conversation with the charming Miss Neal, but his mind kept going over the robbery. If he had put the parcel in his coat pocket, the robbers might not have gotten it. . . or perhaps if he'd stuffed it inside his hat on the overhead rack. Ah, well. Too late to change anything now.

When they pulled in at the station, Miss Neal gazed out the window anxiously and seized his wrist when the train was nearly halted.

"There's Polly, and that must be Jacob with her! They've brought the children. Oh, I'm so thrilled to be here."

Joe wished he had time now to draw her portrait, with her features so animated. Maybe later—he knew he wouldn't forget her soon.

"I hope you have a wonderful visit with them."

"Thank you. And again, thank you so much for your help during the robbery. I wish it had turned out better for you."

"I'll be all right." He said the words blithely, but his heart was heavy. Mr. Becker would certainly not be pleased with his performance.

"Will you come and meet them?"

He almost declined, citing the need to get his telegram off quickly. But what difference would a few minutes make? He would not be taking the train on to San Francisco, he was sure.

He gave Miss Neal his hand down the steps, and Polly Tierney dashed up and swept her friend into her arms.

"Ava! Your train was so late, and we heard the station master say something about a holdup. What happened?"

"It's true," Miss Neal said, smiling as though the whole thing had been a picnic. "We were robbed. But we're fine."

"Oh dear! You'll have to tell us the whole story later." Mrs. Tierney pulled her husband forward. He was cradling the baby in one arm and held a two-year-old's hand firmly with the other. "This is Jacob, and Harry Clyde, and the baby is Amelia."

"How lovely! And I'd like you all to meet Mr. Logan, who was of greatest assistance on the journey since St. Louis, especially during the robbery."

Joe greeted them all and turned down an invitation to join them for supper.

"I'm sorry. It sounds delightful, but I need to send a wire to my employer right away and get his instructions."

"Well, thank you for looking after Ava," Polly said, appraising him with her china blue eyes. "If you're in town any length of time, please call on us."

"Thank you, ma'am." Joe shook hands with Jacob Tierney and turned to Miss Neal. "It's been delightful. I hope we meet again."

She held out her gloved hand. As Joe took it and studied her sweet face, he realized how much he meant those words. But the next moment, Miss Neal took the baby in her arms and Polly led her friend and young Harry Clyde toward the family's wagon, while Jacob went in search of their guest's luggage.

Joe turned away, squared his shoulders, and asked for directions to the telegraph office.

He kicked around town while waiting for a reply to his brief message.

TRAIN ROBBED PACKET AND PAPERS LOST SEND INSTRUCTIONS

There seemed no need to go into detail. Becker and Fixx would see that the telegram came from Cheyenne and would decide what they wanted him to do. The stationmaster informed him that the next eastbound train wouldn't go through until the next morning, so Joe set out walking, suitcase in hand.

The city was young and raw, but full-blown in its offering of commerce. Cattle pens spread out beyond the railroad depot. Hundreds of businesses lined the streets, from small shacks with signs declaring them to be gun shops, saddle makers, or grocers, to substantially built hotels and emporiums. Joe hadn't expected to see a sturdy hardware store flanked by a barbershop and a lawyer's office. There seemed any number of places where a man could risk his money in a card game or buy a glass of beer. He found a restaurant that offered fresh beefsteak and rhubarb pie. Suddenly ravenous, he entered and sat down on one side of a long table where a dozen men were already eating.

The tasty meal fortified him, but Joe was still uneasy and knew he would be until he heard from Mr. Becker. He asked the restaurant's owner for the name of a quiet hotel. After he'd registered, he checked the view from his second-floor window and decided that if this was a quiet hotel, the ones nearer the railroad and stockyards must be noisy indeed. He could count four saloon signs without leaning out the window. The desk clerk had mentioned that Cheyenne was known as "the gambling capital of the world." Joe decided to stay in that evening. He couldn't chance losing the small amount of money he had left.

But first he must check to see if his employer had replied to his telegram. He wandered back to the train station by a different path and discovered more saloons, dance halls, and gambling dens, as well as a trader who bought buffalo hides and a group of Indian women sitting beneath a canvas roof not far from the depot, selling moccasins, baskets, and other handmade items.

His telegram came in just minutes before the office was scheduled to close for the night. Joe stared down at the words, his stomach churning.

HALF PAY ON RETURN EMPLOYMENT TERMINATED

He shoved the slip of paper into his pocket and trudged toward his hotel.

Chapter 4

The next day, Ava slept late and then joined Polly in the kitchen of the snug little frame house on the outskirts of Cheyenne. She ate a hearty breakfast and then held the baby while Polly coaxed young Harry Clyde to finish his oatmeal.

"Jacob's taking a stage to Horse Creek," Polly said. "He won't be back until this evening. Would you like to go shopping or just rest today?"

"Let's take it easy, unless you need something in town," Ava said. "I'd like to get used to not jostling along and have a chance to get acquainted with your adorable children."

Polly got up and went to the stove for the coffeepot. "All right. You must tell me all the news from home, and every detail about the wedding."

"It was lovely," Polly replied. "Sarah was the most beautiful bride I've ever seen. And they've gone to New York for their honeymoon. Conrad promised to show her all the sights."

Polly sighed. "New York. I'm sure she'll enjoy it, but I'm afraid I would feel claustrophobic now. Cheyenne is bad enough. Those years I spent on the prairie with Ma and Pa at the stagecoach stop, I learned to appreciate the open land."

"Where are your parents now?" Ava asked.

Polly laughed. "Three streets over. Pa's got a position with the railroad. He weighs the freight and makes out the invoices."

"Sounds like good, steady work."

"It is, and I think Pa likes not having to worry about the stock and the Indians and all of that."

Ava frowned. "You told me you never had any trouble with the Indians."

"We didn't, where we were. Some of the stations were attacked, but on Pa's section of the line, we had more trouble with robbers." She chuckled. "Now they've moved on to train holdups."

"Yes." Ava pushed aside the memory of the robbery. "It will be good to see your folks again."

"We'll take the kids over to see Ma tomorrow, if you like. Though it wouldn't surprise me if Ma showed up here today to check on you. She's as anxious to see a face from home as I was."

"Oh, that reminds me. I have some things from your grandmother." Ava stood and handed Amelia to Polly. "Here, take her for a minute, and I'll go fetch them."

A moment later she was back in the kitchen with the two books and jar of chokecherry jelly Grandma Winfield had pressed her to carry to Polly. Harry Clyde had been excused and was now playing on the floor with a half-grown puppy they called Spot.

"Here are your goodies." Ava laid the gifts on the table.

"Oh, how sweet of her." Polly picked up the jar of clear red preserves. "She knows I've always loved her jelly, and I can't find the chokecherries out here." She opened the covers of the books. "Dickens and poetry. I shall have to write Grandma a nice long letter. There's talk of starting a public library in town, but I can never lay hands on enough books to suit me."

"There's more." Ava held out her closed hand. She opened it, revealing the cameo brooch in her palm.

Polly gasped. "Grandma sent me her cameo?"

"Yes. She told me she had especially wanted you to have it, but she didn't dare send it by post. I guess she was wise in that, though I nearly lost it in the train robbery."

"So, they didn't look in the baggage?" Polly asked.

"It wasn't in the baggage. I was actually wearing it, to make sure it wouldn't get lost."

Polly gazed at her with wide eyes. "Did they not think it was valuable, then? Grandma always told me this was her most precious piece of jewelry, though I don't suppose it's worth an awful lot."

Ava felt the heat rise in her cheeks, all the way to her hairline. "Do you remember the young man I introduced you to on the platform? Joe Logan?"

"Oh sure." Polly eyed her carefully. "What about him?"

"You only have that brooch now thanks to Mr. Logan."

"Really?"

"Mm-hmm." Ava plunked down in the chair where she had sat for breakfast. There was no getting out of telling the whole tale now. "He rescued it from the robbers. Otherwise I'd have had to toss it in their vile gunnysack." She shuddered. "I felt so bad about it. I mean, he lost his watch and his wallet, and even the things his employer had given him to deliver."

"That's a shame." Polly shifted the baby to her other shoulder. "What's he going to do?"

"I don't know. I think he was afraid he would lose his job over it. But even in the middle of that, he helped me save your grandma's brooch. And afterward, he drew pictures of the robbers for the police." She smiled wanly at Polly. "He's quite an artist."

"I see he made quite an impression on you."

"Well. . ." Ava laughed and waved a hand through the air. "He was nice, and I admit I enjoyed his company, but I'll probably never see him again."

"I'll try to take your mind off that," Polly said.

"By showing me the West?"

"Yes, but besides that, Jacob and I have several unmarried friends."

Ava shook her head. "I came out here to visit you, dear, not to marry a stagecoach driver as you did."

"We haven't got so many drivers now, and the best of those are married, but I'm serious. There's a fellow at the feed store you might find interesting. I'm sure he'd be interested in you."

"Oh, really, I don't—"

"Then there are the Crawford brothers. They have a ranch west of here. They're a little shy, but they're good men, both of them, and they go to our church. We could invite them over for dinner on Sunday."

"Please don't. I'd feel like merchandise on display."

"Well, it's no secret there's a shortage of decent, eligible women out here. And you can't avoid meeting several bachelors at the Independence Day celebration tomorrow."

"Tomorrow? You're right—tomorrow's the Fourth. I fear I'd lost track on my trip."

"There are going to be speeches and displays and races and a shooting match, all over near the stockyards. There's a big field where they hold livestock auctions, with benches and—"

The puppy yipped in the next room, and a clang sounded, followed by a thud. Polly jumped up, holding Amelia out to Ava.

"Harry Clyde, what was that?"

"Nothin'."

"It's never nothing." Polly hurried into the small parlor, and Ava followed. In the middle of the modestly furnished room, Harry Clyde wriggled on the floor, with Spot licking his face. One of the toddler's shoes lay a couple feet away, beside the fireplace poker. Polly sighed and stooped to pick it up. "At least there's no fire today. Come on, young man. Let's get your shoe back on. I think it's time we took Spot outside and showed Aunt Ava the garden."

"And the chickens?" Harry's eyes lit with excitement.

"Yes, and the chickens."

Ava sat down on the rug beside them. She would rather concentrate on Polly and her family, especially since Joe Logan had no doubt left Cheyenne already. "Will you show them to me, Harry Clyde?" she said. "I adore chickens."

∞

Joe packed his few belongings in his suitcase and picked up the leather valise that had held the package. Heading home in defeat did not sit well with him. The one bright spot on this entire journey was Ava Neal, and now he would board a train taking him away from her.

He ate breakfast in the hotel dining room and walked slowly to the depot, but he was still an hour early for the train. A few yards from the ticket window was the railroad police's cubbyhole of an office, and on a whim, he stopped in.

The man behind the desk wore a suit as nice as those the lawyers wore back in Connecticut. Joe pulled his hat off and nodded.

"Good morning. I'm Joseph Logan. I was on the train yesterday when it was robbed. I wondered if there had been any progress in catching the thieves."

The man jumped up and came around the desk. "I'm Dan Colson. So you're the fellow who drew the sketches."

Joe nodded with a tight smile.

"As a matter of fact, there has been some progress," Colson said. "The local sheriff recognized the bagman from your drawing as Ed Robbins. They'd had him up before, for theft and disorderly conduct. They nabbed him late last night at his own house. He's not talking, though, and we haven't caught the rest of them yet."

"Well, that's something," Joe said.

"Yes. And they've recovered some money and things from Robbins that they're sure came off the train—including four pocket watches. I don't suppose you lost your watch to them?"

"Yes, I did. But I'd much rather hear they've found the packet I was carrying for my employer."

"Hmm. Don't know about that, but Detective Simms might be able to tell you."

"Him being the one who was on the train yesterday?" Joe asked.

"One and the same."

"Where could I find him?"

"He's set to travel on the eastbound today, and he'll probably stop in here in—oh, twenty minutes or so." The man glanced at the clock hanging on the

211

wall near the door. "You can wait for him if you'd like. They've got the recovered valuables in the vault over at the bank, until they can sort out what belongs to whom. If there's time, Simms might let you take a look for your package."

With renewed hope, Joe took a seat on a bench just outside the office and waited for Detective Simms.

A few minutes later, Simms came around, wearing a suit and bowler hat and carrying a small leather bag. He spotted Joe and stopped on the boardwalk. "Hello, Logan. Heading east today?"

"Yes. That is, unless you've recovered my parcel."

"Hmm, I don't recall anything like what you described yesterday, but we can go over to the bank and take a look if you wish." Simms pulled out his watch and opened it. "There's time if we don't dawdle." He poked his head into Colson's office. "Dan, I'm taking Mr. Logan round to the bank. I'll be back."

"Right," Colson said.

The banker obliged them by bringing out the box of items the lawmen had recovered from Ed Robbins's house, minus the cash.

"The railroad's orders are to return cash claimed on a prorated basis. You'll have to file a claim for that at the office."

"I did that, thanks." Joe poked through the box. "I don't see my wallet, or the parcel."

"How about those watches? Is one of them yours?"

Simms and Joe pulled four pocket watches from the hoard, but none of them was right. All were of distinctive designs, and three bore engraved names or initials.

"Those are all better than the cheap one I was carrying." Joe placed the last one back in Simms's hand.

"Well, they may have emptied all the wallets and purses into a general fund and then divided it," Simms said. "I didn't see your Miss Neal's coin purse either. Do you know if she filed a form for the cash she lost?"

"Yes, I'm sure she did."

"What was in this parcel you're so keen on?" Simms asked.

Joe huffed out a breath. "It's a little embarrassing, but I don't know, exactly."

"How's that?"

"I was delivering it for an attorney. He didn't tell me what it was, but it was some sort of inheritance for the recipient—a woman. I had the idea it was jewelry."

"There's a few pieces in there, but we know this isn't nearly all of the loot." Simms fished a bracelet and several rings from the box.

Joe shook his head. "I wish I knew for sure what I was carrying. I was just the messenger, you see."

"Might be worth stopping over a day and asking the lawyer to wire a description. And who knows? The marshal might catch the rest of the gang and get back some more of the stuff."

"That's a thought," Joe said. Either way, it wouldn't hurt him to spend another day in Cheyenne, and he admitted to himself that the possibility of looking up Ava and her friends appealed strongly to him. "I'll do it."

Simms nodded and signaled to the banker that they were finished with the box. "As for me, I've got to get on the train in a few minutes. We'll be more vigilant than ever since this latest holdup. There'll be two of us on the out-going train, in addition to the express agent in the express car—though I don't expect the robbers to hit us again so soon."

"They might," Joe said. "If they're smart, they'll hit you when you least expect it."

"True." Simms smiled grimly as they stepped out onto the sidewalk. "Dan Colson, over at the railroad office, was impressed by your drawings. They were instrumental in identifying Robbins, you know."

"I'm glad."

"They'll probably place them in evidence for when he goes to trial." As they talked, they walked toward the train station. Colson's door was open, and when they reached it, Simms paused and looked in.

"I'll be boarding as soon as the train pulls in, Dan."

Mr. Colson looked up from his desk. "All right. Logan, did you find what you were looking for?"

"No sir, but Simms suggested I wire the sender and ask for a description of the contents of his parcel, in case the outlaws opened the parcel and dumped it in with the rest of the stuff."

"Good idea." Colson rose and came to the doorway. "Say, Logan, you've got a good eye. We can use observant men like you. Not looking for work, are you?"

"With the railroad?"

"Sure. The pay's good, and the work's steady. Right, Simms?"

The detective chuckled. "Oh, it's steady, all right. There's the train. See you later, Dan." He strode off toward the ticket window as a locomotive's whistle cut the air.

Joe watched him walk away and turned to face Mr. Colson. "I'm interested, sir."

Colson nodded. "Terrific. Have you ever been arrested, son?"

"No sir."

"Good. I suppose you were too young to serve during the war."

"I joined up the last year, as soon as I turned eighteen. First Connecticut Infantry."

"Can you give me a couple of references for general character?"

Joe did some quick thinking. He wouldn't dare put down Mr. Becker after his recent failure for Becker and Fixx, but there was a Hartford accountant he had done several small jobs for, and he was in good standing with his landlady. He could approximate an address for his old sergeant, too. "Yes, I can."

"Better and better. You go send your wire and come back here. We'll talk. If things work out, maybe I can send you on the westbound first thing in the morning, with one of our detectives. You'd be gone overnight. It would let you get a feel for the job. What do you say? One of our most experienced men will be on that train."

"It sounds good."

Colson handed him a pencil and a sheet of paper. "Write down your references, so I can send a couple of wires. What town did you say you're from?"

"Hartford, Connecticut, sir."

"Right. I'll contact their police department, too. Standard part of the hiring process." He watched Joe keenly.

"I wouldn't expect any less, sir."

Colson smiled. "Good. Now, do you have a sidearm?"

"No sir."

"Hmm, I'll ask Detective Allen if he can lend you one." Colson took the paper on which Joe had written the names of the people he thought would vouch for him. "Come back here in a couple of hours, and maybe we can talk some more."

Joe headed for the telegraph office feeling better about his prospects than he had in a long time. And to be able to stay out here in the West—he'd never expected anything like this to happen. He was sorry he'd lost Becker's package, but maybe some good would come of it.

And there was Miss Neal. He didn't dare hope the railroad would allow him to stay in Cheyenne long, but there was always a chance he would meet up with her again.

Chapter 5

Ava tried not to stare, but wherever she turned some colorful new sight met her gaze. Men were leading sleek horses to the stock pens while soldiers set up targets for the shooting contest. Vendors called out to the passersby in hopes of selling everything from glasses of switchel to firecrackers.

"Not like back home, is it?" Polly asked with a laugh.

"No, not at all." Back in Massachusetts, Independence Day was celebrated with enthusiasm, too, but it had a certain serenity and dignity about it. Ladies strolled about on the arms of their beaux or husbands, showing off their summer bonnets and sipping lemonade. The speeches were applauded calmly, and the fireworks were saved for evening. Boys who broke that rule by setting off firecrackers and scaring the horses were reprimanded severely. Here, everyone seemed to expect a small explosion at least every minute, and the livestock didn't seem too upset by it.

Jacob, like most business owners except the saloonkeepers, had closed his office for the day. No freight runs on the Fourth of July. The entire town seemed to have put business aside and thronged the celebration area. Jacob carried the baby, while Polly and Ava took turns holding on to Harry Clyde's hand.

"There's the pastor," Jacob said, nodding to where several men stood talking.

"Let's introduce Ava." The warmth in Polly's voice made Ava suspicious.

Jacob was agreeable, and so they ambled toward the group.

"Well hello, Tierneys," called a man of about forty. He wore a conservative suit and a ribbon tie.

"Morning, Pastor." Jacob led them over. "This young lady is Polly's friend from Massachusetts, Miss Neal. She took the train out here to visit us. Ava, this is Pastor Worth."

"Welcome," the minister said, smiling at Ava. "That's quite a journey you undertook."

"It was interesting," Ava said. "I'm glad you have the railroad now. It really wasn't too arduous, compared to the trip Polly made when she first came out here with her parents."

The two men Pastor Worth had been conversing with were younger than he was, and both watched Ava with interest while she spoke.

"Allow me to introduce two of our church members," the pastor said, nodding toward them. "Hap Leland works at one of the local ranches, and Bill Ingram is employed at the mercantile on Central Avenue."

"How do you do, gentlemen?" Both returned her greeting heartily. Ava felt her face flush. Was this the reason for Polly's eagerness to show her around?

"Glad you had a safe journey, ma'am." Bill ducked his head and glanced at her then swiftly away.

"Well, it's not like she wasn't on the train when that outlaw gang held it up," Jacob said.

"You wasn't!" Hap's eyebrows rose.

Bill muttered, "Good gracious."

"I see you came through the ordeal unscathed," the pastor said.

"Yes. No one was hurt so far as I know," Ava said. "We passengers are all a little lighter in our purses, I'm afraid."

Jacob shifted little Amelia to his other arm. "I heard last night they'd caught one of the robbers."

"Perhaps some of the stolen goods will be recovered," the pastor said.

"I got held up once," Hap put in. "Was on the stage from Salt Lake. You ever get held up, Jacob?"

"Once or twice, a few years back, when I was working for the Overland," Jacob said. "But that's not a very pleasant topic for the ladies. What's on the agenda for today?"

"Governor Campbell will speak at noon, over at the Methodist Church," Pastor Worth said.

Ava glanced at Polly. "How exciting! Will we get to meet the governor?"

"I expect so," Polly said. "He's generally quite sociable at events like this."

"My father will be so impressed." Ava smiled at the minister. "You see, he told my mother this trip would be educational for me—and he was right, in so many ways."

"Did you tell 'em about the train robbery?" Bill asked.

Jacob glared at him, but Ava didn't mind the question.

"It's all right, Jacob. And the answer is, not yet. I wrote them a nice long letter yesterday, telling them I'd arrived safely and all about Polly and her family and their home, but I left out a few things, you might say. I'll probably tell them when I go home. I don't really want to keep it from them, but I know my mother would worry about me if she heard it now, and I'm not close enough for her to prod all over and make sure I'm still in one piece."

All the adults laughed, but by this time Harry Clyde was getting quite fidgety and pulling against Polly's firm grip.

"We'd better take this little fellow to see the horses," Polly said.

"Horses," Harry Clyde shouted.

"All right, young man." Jacob looked at the others. "See you later."

"If any of you gentlemen wish to join us at noon, you're welcome," Polly said.

"Thank you," Pastor Worth replied. "My wife is about here somewhere. She packed us a lunch, but if she hasn't promised anyone else, we'll be happy to eat with you."

"I might catch up to you," Hap said.

"I told the boss I'd eat with him and the missus." Bill was clearly unhappy to make the pronouncement, his gaze resting on Ava.

"Well, it was nice meeting you," she said and walked away with Polly and Jacob.

"They're both nice young men," Polly assured her. "Especially Bill, but he's on the shy side."

"Hap's all right, too," Jacob added. "I suppose he'd seem a little wild if you set him down in Boston, but ranch life does that to a man."

"You two know I didn't come out here looking for a husband, don't you?" Ava asked sternly.

Jacob laughed. "Is that right? From what Polly's been saying these last few weeks, I had the opposite impression."

"Hush, you!" Polly glared at him and then chuckled. "I'm sorry, Ava. I'll try not to foist too many young men on you, especially not ones who aren't of the first water. But there is one fellow I want you to meet—"

"Not Neil Conyers," Jacob said.

Polly stopped walking. "Yes, Neil Conyers. What's wrong with him?" To Ava she said quickly, "He's a blacksmith."

"He's from Alabama."

"So?"

Jacob shrugged. "I don't know. I didn't suppose she'd want to attach herself to someone from the South."

Polly turned to Ava with eyebrows raised. "My dear, you recall the late unpleasantness between the North and South?"

"Uh. . .yes," Ava replied, not sure whether to laugh or not.

"Well, it makes no difference to me—or to Jacob"—she shot her husband a meaningful look—"where a man hails from. But if you don't fancy a southern accent. . ."

"Mr. Conyers can't be too prejudiced toward the South if he's voluntarily left it for Wyoming Territory," Ava said.

"My thinking exactly." Polly nodded in triumph.

Jacob raised his free hand in surrender. "Fine. And Neil is a nice fellow. But I can't always understand what he's saying, his accent's so thick."

"We'll let Ava be the judge of that." Polly took her friend's arm and began walking toward the stock pens. "If you see him, Jacob, be sure to invite him to eat with us."

"The way things are going, we'll have an army to feed out of your lunch basket," Jacob said with a tolerant smile. "But then, you always pack enough to feed a regiment."

Ava said nothing, but in her mind, she knew none of the young men on Polly's list could quite match her standard. And what was that standard? To her surprise, it wasn't Will Sandford who came to mind, but a certain blue-eyed man she had met on the train from St. Louis.

∞

Joe walked with Jacob Tierney down the board sidewalk until it ended and they stepped down to street level.

"I walk to the stage stop every day, because it's so close," Jacob said, "but I suppose it's a mile from your hotel."

"That's all right," Joe assured him. Two days had passed since he had been hired by the railroad, and much of the intervening time had been spent sitting in either a passenger car or an express car, which carried freight as well as safes for valuables.

"We'll have to make sure we don't keep you too late." Jacob gestured toward a small frame house set back from the street. "There it is, home sweet home."

"It looks comfortable."

"It is, though it wasn't much more than a shack when we first bought it. Polly's pa helped me fix it up."

Joe followed him around to the back stoop. His host didn't knock, but opened the door and entered the warm, lamp-lit kitchen.

"Hey Polly, what's to eat?" he called.

Polly came to him, laughing. "I told Ava you'd say that."

"Papa!" Harry Clyde ran toward them and launched himself into Jacob's arms.

"Well, hello yourself, kid." Jacob tossed the little boy in the air and then set him down and gave Polly a quick kiss. He looked at Ava, who stood near the cookstove. "Ava." He stepped aside so the ladies could see his guest. "Look who

I found at the station when I got back from Horse Creek. He was kicking his heels and looking hungry, so I dragged him on home for supper."

"We've got plenty." Polly wiped her hands on her apron and stepped forward. "Mr. Logan, isn't it?"

"Yes ma'am. Good to see you again." Joe took her outstretched hand for a moment. "I hope it's no bother."

"Not a bit," Polly said.

Joe looked beyond her, and his gaze settled on Ava. She stood with a wooden spoon in her hand, a patchwork apron tied about her waist. Her auburn hair was pulled back with a green satin ribbon, and she stared at him but lowered her eyes when she caught his gaze. His pulse surged, and he realized he'd been anticipating this moment all day.

"Miss Neal," he managed to say smoothly.

"Mr. Logan, I'm so glad you came. We had no idea you were still in town. Or have you been to San Francisco and back already?" She set down the spoon and came toward him, her eyes bright.

"I've been partway there and back again. Changed my mind about heading east the other day."

"I've wondered how your business turned out," Ava said. "Perhaps you can tell us over supper."

"I'd be happy to."

Jacob showed him where he could wash up. When they had settled at the table a few minutes later, Joe enjoyed Polly and Ava's cooking.

"That's the best meatloaf I've had since I left Hartford," he said.

"Thank you," Polly said. "And Mr. Logan, I understand I owe you my thanks."

"What for?"

"Ava said that without your help, I wouldn't have received Grandma Winfield's brooch."

"Oh, that. I was happy I could do it and that we succeeded in thwarting the outlaws on a small scale. But won't you call me Joe? I wish you all would." His gaze lingered on Ava, and her cheeks seemed to go a shade pinker, but she was smiling.

"And you've no word on the items you lost?" she asked.

"Not yet, but my former employer did send a description of the articles in the parcel, so that I'll be able to identify them positively if they're found."

"What was it?" Polly put a hand to her mouth. "I'm sorry. I shouldn't ask."

"It's all right. Turns out it was jewelry, which I had suspected. Family pieces, worth a few hundred dollars, but of greater sentimental value to the one who would have received them."

"Like my brooch."

"Yes, sort of. But this was a pendant and a matching set of earrings. Garnets and marcasite."

"Oh, it sounds lovely," Polly said.

In the next room the baby cried, and Ava jumped up.

"Let Aunt Ava get her."

She brought Amelia to the table and held her on her lap while she continued to eat, even giving her tiny bites of mashed potato off her plate. Joe marveled at how Ava took to the children. She seemed to outright adore young Harry Clyde, but without telling the little lad as much.

When they had finished eating and lingered over more coffee, Joe revealed that he would be moving the next day from his hotel to a boardinghouse.

Jacob leaned back in his chair and said, "So, does that mean you're staying?"

Joe smiled. "I am. I've been hired by the railroad police."

Ava gasped. "Your drawings. I knew they would be impressed."

"Yes, that was what led to the offer. I'll need some training though. For the next couple of weeks I'll be learning about firearms and studying maps and how safes are constructed—and demolished. Things like that."

"That's marvelous," Ava said. "I know you were uncertain about your other job."

"Yes. They fired me, first thing when they heard I'd lost the package. Two words on a telegram—it cost them sixty cents to tell me." Joe shook his head. "Ah well, the Lord knew, didn't He?"

"That's right," Ava said. "Some good has come out of this."

Polly chuckled. "Next thing, you'll be saying you're glad you were robbed."

"I won't go that far."

Polly turned to Joe. "Do put cotton wool in your ears if you're going to be doing a lot of shooting practice. Bob Dexter, the gunsmith, is deaf as a post from test firing all those guns he fixes."

"I'll keep that in mind," Joe said, but he was watching Ava. He hesitated to produce his gift but decided to go ahead. "Speaking of the robbery, though, reminds me of something I brought you." He reached inside his jacket pocket and brought out a sheet of paper from his sketchbook and unfolded it. He passed it to Ava, observing her face anxiously.

"Why—it's me!" She smiled and held the drawing out to her friend. "See, Polly? I'm wearing your cameo, just as I did on the train."

"It's not a very good likeness," Joe said. "I can see that, now that I have you right here before me. But I was drawing from memory, and—"

"It's excellent," Polly declared, glancing from Ava to the drawing and back again.

"Next time, I shall do better." *Tonight when I get to my room.* He hadn't caught the shimmer of her glossy hair, or the exact tilt of her chin. But the next portrait would capture both.

"I'm immensely flattered," Ava said. "Am I meant to keep this?"

"If you like."

"I do. Very much."

At the end of an evening of pleasant conversation, Ava walked with him to the door. Joe didn't hesitate to put in a request.

"I wonder if I might call on you next week."

Her lashes swept down, shielding her green eyes for a moment.

"Why, yes. I'd like that. And I don't think Polly and Jacob would mind."

They settled on the details of the meeting, and Joe set out for his hotel, whistling as he walked.

Chapter 6

Jacob came through the back door two nights later and scooped Harry Clyde up into his arms. "They're saying in town that the marshal and the railroad detectives have gone out after the gang of train robbers," he told Polly and Ava.

"Not another robbery, I hope," Polly said, frowning.

"I don't think so. Maybe they got a tip on where to find them."

Polly sighed. "I hope they don't start robbing the stagecoaches."

"We don't carry the really valuable stuff anymore," Jacob said. "At least not often. But those outlaws were all my drivers could talk about today."

"Well, I hope they catch the men who hit the train I came on," Ava said.

Polly nodded emphatically. "So do I."

Jacob carried Harry Clyde over to the rack near the back door. "Maybe Joe Logan can tell us more when he comes around on Saturday night."

Ava said nothing, but her heart felt torn. Every time she thought about Joe's impending call, she wanted to sing, but the thought of him chasing around the wilderness trying to catch a band of ruthless outlaws made her shudder. Did she really want a strong attachment to a lawman who was constantly in danger?

Jacob took Harry Clyde's little hat from the rack and settled it on his head. "Going to help Papa with the chores tonight?"

Harry Clyde nodded so hard his whole body jiggled.

Jacob laughed and said to Polly, "We'll be back." He carried his son out the back door.

Polly came to Ava's side and slipped an arm around her waist. "Don't worry, dear."

"I try not to," Ava said, "but whenever I think about those bandits, it scares me."

"That's how I used to be. Now it seems you're worrying about Joe the same way I used to about Jacob whenever he was out of sight."

Ava gazed at Polly, who always seemed joyful, even when her husband was on the road driving a stagecoach. "How do you do it, when Jacob's away?"

Polly gave her a little squeeze. "I've come to where I've stopped fretting. It's not as dangerous as it used to be for stage drivers, and if anything is going to happen to him, I certainly can't stop it. I have to trust God for his safety."

"That's true," Ava said, "and Jacob is a quick thinker. I'm sure if he has trouble, he finds a way out of it."

"Yes, like the time his stage was stranded in a blizzard and some of the passengers were injured."

"You wrote me about that."

"Your Joe is no slouch in that department either."

Ava opened her mouth to protest at her designation of "your Joe," but she snapped her jaws shut. Maybe she was starting to think of him that way. Hard to believe she had met him less than a fortnight ago, and yet he meant so much to her.

Polly went to the cupboard for a stack of plates. "It's hard not to worry, but I can't think about it all the time. I don't know how to say this without sounding pious, but—"

"You, pious?" Ava chuckled. "A woman as jolly as you would never be thought pious."

"All right, then take this in the spirit it's meant: I give thanks for every day I've had Jacob, and I hope we get many more, but if not, we've had a wonderful time together. It's men like him and Joe who have made this country safe for families."

"I suppose you're right—men like your father, too, and all the railroad men and wagon masters before them, and lawmen and ranchers. . ."

"This territory is full of brave men." Polly began to set the table.

Ava couldn't help wondering if Joe was with the lawmen trying to catch the robbers. Rather than voice her thoughts, she decided to follow Polly's example. She sent up a prayer for Joe and the men he worked with and then tried to put it out of her mind.

A knock sent her to the front door. She opened it and stared in surprise at Joe.

"Come in," Ava cried. "I'm so glad to see you. We thought you might be off with the marshal, chasing robbers."

"Not me this time," Joe said. "I just came in on the train from Salt Lake City. I understand the outlaws have gotten away again though."

Polly stood in the kitchen doorway, wiping her hands on her apron. "That's a shame."

"Yes," Joe said. "Every time a posse trails them into the hills, they lose them. I'm afraid we've got to catch them red-handed."

Ava wasn't sure she liked the sound of that. The desperados would be more likely to shed blood if they were cornered.

"Well come on in," Polly said cheerfully. "You're just in time for supper."

∞

A week later, Joe set out on what might be his most dangerous assignment yet. The lawmen's earlier attempts to catch up with the band of robbers had come to nothing. He had managed two visits to Ava in between his stints for the railroad, but depending on how things went today, he might not see her for several days.

He mounted his horse and rode after Detective Simms. He was joining a posse of eight railroad policemen determined to catch the train robbers. To-night's westbound train was carrying a load of silver to a bank in Salt Lake City. Concealing that knowledge had proved impossible, and any number of people seemed to have been on hand when the specie was loaded in St. Louis. Mr. Colson, Joe's boss in Cheyenne, had received a telegram asking for extra men to be on guard when the train came through.

The train itself carried a dozen officers, riding with the treasure all the way from St. Louis, and several men had switched out at stops in the larger towns along the way. But west of Cheyenne, the open plains offered many miles of track through unpopulated country, where a robbery could be pulled off with impunity—and thousands of square miles of wilderness into which a gang of outlaws could disappear and never be found.

Colson had sent out posses before, but they had not been successful so far. They'd had eight robberies in various places since the beginning of the year. The increased losses to the railroad as well as the passengers' fears spurred the railroad's management to get rid of the outlaw gangs.

Still anticipating his first month's pay, Joe was riding a borrowed horse and carrying weapons loaned to him by his boss and Simms. He patted the bay gelding's neck and urged him to keep pace with the others.

They rode westward from Cheyenne, leaving the station thirty minutes before the train was due there. Several officers would be on hand while the train was stopped at the Cheyenne depot. Joe and the others with him would be waiting in case the robbers tried to stop the locomotive west of town. He and his fellow policemen knew the robbers could have planted confederates on the train, but no matter where the robbery took place, they would have to have cohorts waiting with horses to make their escape. The mounted officers rode beside the tracks for ten miles, when Simms signaled for them all to stop.

"Rest your horses, men. That train should have left Cheyenne by now. It will catch up to us soon."

"I haven't seen any signs of the outlaws," one of the other men said.

Simms nodded. "I doubt that gang would hold up the train so close to Cheyenne, but you never know." He pulled out his watch and looked at it. "If it passes us on schedule, we'll follow along."

"Should we scout the tracks ahead?" the man named Farris asked, gazing down the tracks westward.

"Yes, you and Logan go," Simms said.

Joe was glad to keep moving, instead of doing nothing while they waited for the train. He and Farris loped their horses a half mile, gaining the top of a rise from which they could see down into a slight dip in the prairie.

"What's that?" Joe pointed ahead at a dark blur on the tracks.

Farris's jaw dropped. "They've blocked the tracks. Put some logs on them."

"Logs?" Joe looked around at the treeless grassland.

"They must have hauled them out here in a wagon. Come on, we've got to tell Simms!"

They raced back along their path and began waving their hats when the posse came into view. Simms and the others loped their horses toward Joe and Farris.

"Obstruction on the tracks," Farris yelled.

Simms hauled back on his reins and fumbled to take a red flag from the cantle of his saddle. He handed it to Farris just as they heard the eerie whistle of the locomotive in the distance.

"Flag the train," Simms told Farris. "We'll try to clear it."

Joe didn't wait but turned his horse and galloped back toward the knoll. As they began to ride down into the depression, Simms's horse pounded up beside him.

"Hold on, Logan! The robbers are probably waiting nearby. I don't want to get you killed."

Joe slowed his mount to a trot and watched the skyline. Any fold in the open land could hide a dozen horsemen.

One of the posse members yelled and pointed. Half a dozen riders appeared on the next hill, streaking away across the prairie.

"It's the gang," one of the detectives shouted.

"Go," Simms called to him, waving him and four other men on. "Logan, you're with me. Quick, now!"

Joe followed Simms, whose horse cannoned down the hill to where three sizable logs lay across the steel rails. Both jumped from the saddle and ran to the logs. The smallest was about eight feet long and six inches thick. Each seized one end and carried it off the tracks. The train's whistle blew, closer.

"Think they saw Farris in time?" Joe asked, panting, as they went back to try to move the next log. It was a couple of inches thicker.

"I don't know," Simms said. "Come on, put your back into it."

The squeal and screech of the train's brakes seemed almost on top of them as they rolled the second log off. Their horses snorted and galloped away from the tracks. Joe looked back the way they had come. The locomotive had crested the knoll and was rolling toward them amid a thunderous noise and the release of a big cloud of steam.

"We can do it," he yelled to Simms, and they both heaved the last log from the tracks as the engine reached them. It had slowed considerably but did not completely halt until the cowcatcher on the front was a hundred feet past them. Farris's horse galloped toward them, with Farris holding the red flag beneath one arm.

Joe and Simms stood panting beside the logs while two men climbed down from the second passenger car and walked toward them. Farris reined in his horse and waited with them.

"Detective Simms, is that you? What's going on?" one of the men called when they were close.

Simms waved. "Hello, Peters. The outlaws had blocked the tracks. We weren't sure we could clear it in time, so we had Farris flag you down. Good thing, too. If the engineer hadn't started to brake when he did, we wouldn't have made it, and you'd have derailed."

"Takes a long time to stop these things," Detective Peters agreed.

The train's conductor came toward them from the first passenger car. "Everything all right?"

Simms nodded. "Now it is. A posse's gone after the gang that was hiding out here waiting for you. Tell the engineer you can proceed. No one should bother you for the rest of this run. Sorry we had to stop you."

"It's better than the alternative," the conductor said. He waved and turned toward the locomotive.

"We'd better get back on board," Detective Peters said. "You'll wire on down the line and let us know if you catch them?"

"I expect Mr. Colson will spread the word, whatever happens," Simms said.

Peters and his companion climbed the steps to the passenger car's platform and waved. Joe, Farris, and Simms waited until the engineer got the train moving again.

"I'll go see if I can catch your horses now." Farris jogged his bay over the nearest rise.

"I hope we can catch up with the posse," Joe said. "I'd sure like to be there when they catch that bunch of robbers."

Chapter 7

A va sat down to write to her parents. Her heart was in turmoil, in spite of her determination to remain calm like Polly. She mustn't let her agitation show through in her letter.

> *Dear Pa and Mama,*
>
> *I am having the most wonderful time with Polly and Jacob and the children. The Independence Day celebration was done up in grand style, and if not quite as elaborate as yours, I guarantee it was more enthusiastic. The horse races and shooting matches drew out the entire city, I'm sure.*

She hesitated and dipped her pen in the ink again.

> *Do you remember the man I told you about from the train? Mr. Logan? Well, he has stopped here in Cheyenne. When outlaws stole the parcel he was to deliver, he had no need to go on, and he has taken a job with the railroad police. He drew sketches of two train robbers for them, and that was instrumental in the capture of one of the thieves. Apparently the railroad officials were impressed by Mr. Logan's observation skills, and he is training to be a detective. He went to Jacob's stagecoach depot one evening and came home with him for supper and has been to visit since. He is coming by again tomorrow.*

Ava reread what she had written. Had she shown too much partiality for Mr. Logan—or Joe, as he had bid her call him? Her parents would surely read between the lines and see that she admired the man. She decided that was better than waiting to see if the acquaintance blossomed into more and then springing it on them. She let the paragraph stand but moved on to more mundane topics.

She had barely finished her letter when Harry Clyde entered the parlor, rubbing his eyes.

"Well hello, young sir," Ava said, rising. "Did you have a good nap?"

228

Harry Clyde shook his head but came to her and allowed her to take him up into her arms.

"Shall we go find your mama?" Ava asked. "I think she's out back, hanging clothes."

The little boy nodded and buried his head in her shoulder.

In the backyard, Polly grinned as she pinned one of Amelia's diapers to the clothesline.

"Hello! Is Amelia up, too?"

"Still sleeping," Ava said. She walked over with Harry Clyde and looked in the clothes basket. Half a load of wet laundry still awaited attention. "Why don't you take Harry in for his snack, and I'll finish this."

"I can do it," Polly replied, reaching for another diaper.

"Of course you can, but I want to."

After a little more persuasion on Ava's part, Polly and her son headed inside. The sunshine felt good on Ava's shoulders as she hung up the rest of the wash. A soft wind blew from the west, and when her basket was empty, she walked along the line feeling the clean clothes. At the far end, she found quite a few items from an earlier washing that were dry, and she took them down and folded them into the basket.

When she stepped into the kitchen, Polly and Harry Clyde were sitting at the kitchen table with a plate of cookies between them. Harry's glass of milk was half empty, and Polly had a cup of hot tea at her place.

"My, you're industrious," Polly said when she saw the clean laundry. "I poured you some tea. Hope it's not too cool."

"That looks lovely." Ava set down the basket and took her place at the table. She reached for one of the cookies she and Polly had baked the day before.

"Those are so good," Polly said, taking another. "I'm glad you remembered your mother's recipe."

"She always made the best sugar cookies," Ava agreed.

"Well, I held some back for you and Joe to have when he calls tomorrow evening, and I expect there will be some pie left from dinner, too."

Ava smiled and took a sip of her tea. If only she could be as optimistic as Polly. Instead, she had mentally added, "*If* he calls tomorrow evening."

"What?" Polly asked.

"Nothing."

"Now, Ava, are you still fretting about Joe?"

"I can't forget what Jacob said about the trains."

"That last robbery wasn't anywhere near here."

229

"I know, but. . ." Ava shook her head.

Polly frowned. "If you're going to marry a policeman—"

"Whoa," Ava cried. "Who said anything about marrying him?"

Her friend laughed. "I've seen the way you look at each other. Marriage is the logical conclusion."

"But. . .I'm only here for a month." Ava realized how quickly July was fleeing. "On August third, I'm to board the train back to Massachusetts."

"Are you?" Polly asked, as if it were the furthest thing from her mind.

"Yes, and it's coming right up."

Amelia's cry sounded from the bedroom. Polly took a quick sip of her tea and set the cup down. "I must get your sister now, Harry Clyde. You can entertain Aunt Ava for a few minutes."

⚭

Joe followed instructions when he reached the site of the standoff. Simms had picked up tips from a rancher and a freighter along the way as to where the outlaws had headed, with the posse in hot pursuit. When they found the other railroad police outside an old sod house, they dismounted and secured their horses with the rest. The men fanned out to surround the hideout and waited for a signal from their leader.

Joe's mouth went dry. He glanced to his left. He could see Farris crouched in the tall grass, and beyond him, Joe caught a glimpse of another railroad man's hat.

In the distance, Simms yelled, "You're surrounded by police. Come on out."

In answer, a volley of gunshots came from the soddy. A rapid exchange of fire followed, after which smoke hung in the air and the prairie seemed oddly quiet.

"You listen to me now," Simms yelled. "We've got you surrounded, and we're not leaving. In fact, we've got more men on the way. If you want to sit it out, by nightfall we'll have a hundred men here. You're not getting away. Ever. So, you think about that. Any time you want to come out peacefully, you let us know, and we'll hold our fire."

Joe wasn't really sure how it happened, but thirty minutes later Simms convinced the men inside to throw down their guns and come out. While the others bound the prisoners and prepared to take them back to Cheyenne, Joe helped Simms search the soddy. Under a couple of the mattresses they found small pouches of money.

"Well, what do you know?" Simms was poking beneath one of the bunks, and he brought out a small cracker tin.

"Anything in it?" Joe asked.

"Let's see." Simms lifted the lid. "Ha. Jewelry. Must be stuff they haven't had a chance to sell yet." He carried the tin to the doorway so he could examine the contents in the sunlight.

"May I see?" Joe went to stand beside him. A jumble of rings, brooches, and pendants lay in the tin, along with two pocket watches and a military medal. Joe lifted one of the watches and opened it. "I think this is mine. They stole it off me the day I came to Cheyenne."

"Take it," Simms said.

"Don't I have to make a report or something?"

"Tell Colson when we get back to town, and he can mark it off his list."

"All right." Joe pocketed the watch and picked out a necklace. "Are these garnets?"

"I'd say so," Simms replied.

"Then this could be the necklace my employer wanted me to take to San Francisco. He said garnet and marcasite."

"Those things that look like tiny little diamonds are probably the marcasite," Simms said. "There's an earring like it." He pointed.

Joe plucked the earring from the trove. "Is there another one? He said there were earrings that matched the pendant."

"Here, you paw through it." Simms thrust the tin into his hands. "I'll make sure everyone's ready to head out."

Joe followed Simms slowly, poking through the glittering jewelry with one finger. He was rewarded by the sight of the second earring turning face upward to wink at him. With a sigh he took it out and wrapped it in his handkerchief with the necklace and second earring. A little more exploration revealed a diamond bracelet. He wasn't positive about this one, but it might be the other item with which Mr. Becker had entrusted him. He folded it up with the other items and slipped the handkerchief into the inner pocket of his jacket then closed the tin and hurried after Simms.

Two hours later, when the robbers were locked up and the men were writing their reports, he showed the items to Mr. Colson.

"So you think that's what was in the package they took from you last week?"

"I do, sir," Joe said. "I've checked it against the message the attorney, Mr. Becker, sent me, and they fit the description. With your permission, I could wire him and ask for a few more details."

"Go ahead, but if it's his we'll send him a bill for the telegrams."

Joe nodded. "If this is the right stuff, I don't think he'll mind. What will they do with all these other things if no one claims them?"

Colson shrugged. "We keep recovered loot for a year or so, and then, if we can't find the owners, we sell it. There's a bunch in the safe now that's due to be sold."

When Joe returned later with Becker's assurance that he had found the right jewelry, Mr. Colson opened the safe to get it out for Joe.

"He wondered if I could go on and deliver it for him," Joe told his boss. "I wasn't sure, since I just took this job. I'd come right back though."

"San Francisco?" Mr. Colson said. "I guess so. You'd only be gone a few days, and you could work the trains going and coming."

Joe smiled. "That would be great."

Colson laughed. "Not every day you get paid by two employers at once, eh, Logan?"

He picked up another box that had been in the safe. "Here's the stuff we've collected that's never been claimed. Want to see it?"

"Sure."

When Colson opened the box, Joe caught his breath. One gem twinkled at him as though crying out for him to pick it up. Carefully, he took out the ring and gazed at the lovely blue stone. The round-cut sapphire was encircled by small diamond chips—or maybe more of the marcasite he'd seen on the garnet set, but these looked brighter.

"Pretty, isn't?" Colson said.

"It makes me think of the blue moon," Joe confessed. He hoped Colson wouldn't notice the flush heating his cheeks. "How much do you think it will sell for?"

"I don't know. I guess I can ask the jeweler down the street. You fancy it?"

"Well…" Joe chuckled. "There is someone I had in mind who might like it."

∞

Ava opened the door at the Tierneys' house to find Joe on the doorstep. She didn't try to hide her relief or her pleasure at seeing him.

"You're back! I hope the other men are safe."

"Nobody was hurt, and we caught the robber gang."

"Wonderful!" She drew him inside and closed the door. "Won't you come into the kitchen and tell Polly and Jacob? I know they'll want to hear all about it."

"Certainly, but first, there's something I'd like to say to you, Ava."

"Oh?" She turned to face him. Joe was watching her intently, and she felt her cheeks warm under the scrutiny of his clear blue eyes. "What is it?"

"We found the things that were stolen from me on the trip out here."

Ava clutched his hand for a moment then drew back, embarrassed by her own enthusiasm. "I'm so glad."

"Me, too. I'll be making a quick trip to San Francisco, to deliver them for Mr. Becker, but I'll be back in just a few days. And before I go. . ." He hesitated and gazed into her eyes.

Ava felt her heart quicken.

"The moon is full tonight," Joe said. "It's the blue moon."

"So it is. I'd forgotten."

He drew in a deep breath. "Would you like to step outside and see it? It's rising over the prairie, and it's a fine sight."

"I. . .all right." Ava took Polly's blue knitted shawl from the back of a chair and slipped it around her shoulders. They walked out into the front yard, and Joe pointed. The moon, plump and full, was peeking from behind the edge of a fluffy cloud near the bell tower on the church down the street.

Ava gazed at it for a long moment and sighed. "You're right, it's beautiful."

"I suppose it would be prettier if we had a big old maple tree and we could stare at it through the branches."

"Do you think you'll miss the trees?" Ava asked. "That's what Polly said she missed most when she moved out here."

"I probably will. But I've been living in town the last few years, so it won't be as if I've come right from the middle of a forest." Joe chuckled. "It doesn't look particularly blue, does it?"

"Not especially."

"Ava, I—"

"Yes?" She turned to face him.

Joe reached into his pocket and took out something that gleamed in the moonlight. "I had an opportunity to buy this today, and I couldn't bear to think of it going to anyone but you."

He placed it in her hand, and she held it up. A ring. She caught her breath. What could he mean by it?

"If the light were better, you could see it's a sapphire. It made me think of the blue moon, which made me think of you. Ava, I know we haven't known each other long, and—and I'm not very good at this, but I love you, and well. . .out here it seems a little foolish to wait a long time, so I'm asking you now. Will you marry me?"

Ava realized she was staring at him and lowered her gaze to the ring again.

"If you'd like time to think about it," he began after a short pause.

"No, I don't need time. I think we shall get along splendidly."

"Really?"

"Yes." She looked up at him and smiled. "I wouldn't make you wait for another blue moon, Joe."

He leaned down and kissed her lightly then with more purpose.

Ava leaned against him for a moment. "Perhaps we should go inside and show Polly and Jacob," she whispered.

"I'm sure we should. Would you like to put it on first?"

"Yes." She let him slide the band over her finger and laughed. "I can't wait to see it in good light. Come on."

Later that evening, when Joe had gone, Ava was too wound up to sleep. She sat down to write a letter to her parents. The moonlight shone through the window, so bright she didn't even need to light the lamp.

Dear Pa and Mama,

I have some news for you, and I hope it makes you happy. On this rare blue moon, an even rarer thing happened to me. You remember Mr. Logan, the man from the train? Well, he wishes to become your son-in-law.

Ava reread the paragraph and smiled. She spread her hand and gazed at the sapphire ring and then dipped her pen in the inkwell.

We wondered if you would like to come out here for the wedding. If not, Joe and I will save until we have enough to travel back there. He said the railroad will discount our tickets. I shall write more soon, but I couldn't wait for you to hear.
Your loving daughter,
Ava

The Dogwood Blossom Bride

Miralee Ferrell

Chapter 1

Gracie Addison bit her lip to keep it from trembling—from anger rather than a desire to cry. Of all the tomfool things she'd ever heard of, this had to be the worst. She gave a light stamp of her foot, hoping her father would take her seriously for a change. "I have no interest whatsoever in Jerold Carnegie. I'm not cut out to be a high-and-mighty society lady, married to a politician." She flicked a finger at her trousers and dusty boots, peeking out from under the rolled cuffs.

Her father snorted his disapproval and leaned his arm against the mantel in the drawing room of their spacious home. "Exactly my point. You need to cease wearing those ridiculous costumes and utilize the manners your mother taught you before her death. If she had lived past your ninth birthday, she would be horrified at some of the choices you've made."

"Oh posh, Father. Of all the people in my life, she understood my tomboy tendencies better than anyone. I'd think by now you'd be used to how I dress and the things I do."

He straightened, and a frown pulled at the corners of his normally cheerful mouth. "She understood when you were nine, but she would not have approved at nineteen. It is high time you act like a lady. Climbing trees and riding astride, not to mention wading into the creek to set traps for fish and any of the other numerous things you do, aren't becoming. I want you to marry well, and Jerold Carnegie will succeed in this world. He's a good man with an excellent reputation. What could you possibly have against him?"

Gracie rolled her eyes. "He's boring. B-O-R-I-N-G. He doesn't have a particle of humor in his dry bones, and his mustache twitches at the slightest provocation. Besides, you're doing a fine job caring for me. So whatever do I need with Mr. Carnegie?"

His shoulders slumped. "Has it ever occurred to you that you are my only child, and as such, I would appreciate you carrying on our family line?"

Gracie forced herself to relax her tense posture and stepped forward to give her father a hug. "I'm sorry for arguing. But I truly have no interest in Mr. Carnegie, and I see no need to rush into marriage."

His eyes closed for a brief moment then opened, and the corner of his lips tipped up. "All I ask is that you try, Gracie. To please me, if for no other reason. I have invited Mr. Carnegie to supper tonight, and I will expect you to dress and act the lady I know you can be. He is new enough in town not to have gotten wind of your antics yet—please, give yourself a chance to get acquainted."

She pressed her lips together and tried not to smile. Only last week the man in question had come upon her on the outskirts of town while she was riding her horse astride and wearing trousers. In spite of that start, she'd still glimpsed a flicker of interest in the man's eyes. Somehow she'd have to find a way to quell that.

Mr. Carnegie wasn't altogether horrid. He was simply unappetizing—like a bowl of day-old bread soaked in milk when she hungered for steak. But she did hate to disappoint her father. "All right. I'll be here for supper, but don't expect anything more."

He grinned and started to reply, but she shook her head. "I mean it. I'll be polite, but that's all. And now I'm going to go for a walk." Gracie pivoted and waltzed out of the room, humming a tune. Maybe she could position herself in a tree that Mr. Carnegie would ride beneath on his way to their home and discourage his attentions.

She hid a smirk. The sight would shock him so much he wouldn't return.

⚭

Will Montgomery slumped in the saddle, weary and glad to have finally reached the outskirts of Goldendale. He glanced behind him to check on his eight-year-old niece, Laura. She had withstood the journey better than he had. The three-day-long winding climb up the Columbia Hills from The Dalles was enough to tire man and horse alike, but it wouldn't have been so bad if he'd slept last night. A cougar screaming in the distance had kept him patrolling the area in front of the fire.

It hadn't awakened Laura, but he couldn't take a chance the big cat would spot the little girl and decide she was an easy meal. The only things he wanted now were to get to Curt Warren's home, see the child settled, and roll into bed. He twisted in his saddle and watched the bright-eyed girl riding her horse like she'd stepped into the saddle only an hour before. "Are you all right, Laura?"

She nodded and grinned. "I'm getting kind of sore, but I don't mind. I just wish I could wear trousers like you."

"We'll be there soon, and you can rest." He smiled to himself. Laura was so like her mother, Karen. Pain shot through his chest at the memory of his sister who had died an unnecessary death.

He pushed the thought away. His new boss didn't expect him to start work right away, so he'd have a few days to settle in before tackling his new profession. He was thankful for the job, but it was a far cry from the life of a cowboy he'd lived for the better part of his adult years. He hated giving up his life on the range, but it was time to find something that would provide a decent living—especially if he ever hoped to find a wife and settle down.

He scowled. Not that he'd had much luck in that direction. Lucinda, the last girl he'd thought he cared for enough to marry had been nothing but a flirt. Something he hadn't discovered until she'd dropped him for a newspaperman with aspirations of bigger and better things than a cowboy could ever attain.

He wanted a woman like his mother had been—feminine and faithful to her man and her home. Looking back, Will felt as though he'd been saved from a bad marriage. Lucinda had sworn she'd never look at another man when they'd met, and he'd believed her.

Until Reed Jenkins waltzed into town. No, a solid girl with her head on her shoulders was what he needed, and he wouldn't settle for anything less.

Will came to a fork in the road and reined his horse to a stop under a flowering dogwood. If he remembered correctly, the Warren home and woodworking shop were to the right, but he'd better reread the directions in Curt's letter.

Will kept one hand on the reins and reached around with the other to his saddlebag. He fumbled with the buckle but finally got it open. As he searched inside, something overhead in the widespread branches of the dogwood tree rustled the leaves, and a shower of pink blossoms cascaded onto his shoulders. Dusty, his dapple-gray gelding, snorted but didn't move.

The branches close above his head shifted and swayed, and two trouser-clad legs with boots beneath dangled above Dusty's nose. The horse bolted forward, making Laura's horse snort and shy.

Will tightened the reins and brought the startled horse to a stop. "Laura. Calm your horse, then get off."

He waited until the girl obeyed; then he swung Dusty around and heeled him forward, halting him directly under the small boots. Definitely a youngster, but one who needed to be more careful. "Hey you. Boy. Come down here."

A gasp and then a titter sounded above him, but no one answered.

"This isn't funny. You can't go around swinging from trees and spooking horses. My niece nearly got hurt."

Even the birds that had been scolding from branches high up in the neigh-boring tree had stilled their chatter, but the boy didn't respond. In fact, one leg slowly withdrew until the top of the boot began to disappear into the foliage. "Oh no you don't." Will stood in his stirrups and grasped the other dangl-ing leg just above the boot. "You aren't going to get off that easy." He kept a tight grip on the boy and released his reins. He grabbed the other leg at the knee and yanked.

∞

Gracie felt the strong grip on her leg and gasped once again as she almost lost her grip on the tree. This was most definitely not Jerold Carnegie. She had no idea who it might be, as she'd never heard his voice before, but the man seemed determined to dislodge her from her perch. She held on to the branch above her with all her might.

How humiliating—and a bit frightening—to be yanked from a tree by a stranger—or by anyone, for that matter. Gracie's cheeks burned. And he thought her a boy who'd purposely spooked his horse. She'd been daydreaming and hadn't even realized the man had stopped under her tree, or she'd not have allowed her feet to dangle.

It had been a foolish whim to try to shock Mr. Carnegie and scare him off from wanting to court her, and she'd changed her mind minutes ago. She'd climbed to the lowest branch possible with the intention of jumping down and heading home. Maybe her father was right, and it was time she gave up such foolishness.

If only she could get a better grip and climb high enough in the dogwood to keep from being found out by this stranger. Her heart thumped hard in her chest. What would he do to her if he caught her?

He yanked on her legs again, and her grasp on the limb loosened. Perspiration slicked her palms. She wanted to demand the man release her, but speaking would give her away. She kicked one boot, trying to loosen his grasp and instead connected with a solid object.

He groaned.

Oh dear. Had she kicked the man's head? Well, it served him right for being rough. "Let go of me, you lout!"

His hold relaxed for a second, and Gracie made one last effort to heave herself higher into the branches. Pink dogwood blossoms drifting from the shivering tree clouded her vision.

"No you don't, you young scamp. First you spook our horses, then you boot me in the noggin. I ought to whip you when I get you down, but I'll satisfy myself with presenting you to your pa and letting him do the honors."

The hands gripping her legs tightened like steel bands. Gracie hadn't known a man could contain such strength. As the horse danced around beneath the tree, a mighty heave from below tore Gracie's fingers from her hold. She plummeted down—right into the arms of the most handsome man she'd ever hoped to see.

Chapter 2

Will tightened his grip to keep from dropping the young woman he'd been certain was a boy, although she didn't weigh as much as a bag of feathers. He gazed into the wide green eyes staring up into his, and took in the passel of red-gold hair that had come out of its binding. One wayward lock blew across his lips, causing a shiver to run down his spine. He reached for the tendril, not sure what he'd do with it when captured but completely enthralled at the touch.

"Uncle Will, who is that?" Laura's high-pitched voice behind him almost made him lose his hold and drop the young woman.

The redhead clutched at his shirt collar, and dark color flooded her face. "Put me down this instant." She swiveled her head, trying to see over his shoulder. "I don't care to be embarrassed in front of your wife and child."

"Wife and child?" Will shifted the woman's weight a bit, and his lips quirked. "My niece, Laura, is the only one with me, and I doubt she cares one way or the other about what happened."

Laura tugged her horse forward and turned her round eyes on the woman. "Why were you in that tree?"

Some of the stiffness went out of the woman, but she glared at him rather than answer Laura's question. "I will not talk to anyone while in this position—not even a child. Let go of me, or I shall make things quite unpleasant for you."

Will chuckled and shook his head. "I doubt a little mite like you could do much harm, but I'll put you down. Swing your feet over to one side, and I'll let you slip to the ground. Don't want you to fall and hurt yourself."

She did as he said, her boots hitting the ground with barely a whisper. She crossed her arms and took a step back. "I do not appreciate being laughed at or manhandled—or taken for a boy. Whatever did you pull me out of that tree for, anyway?"

Laura tugged on her horse's reins and walked closer to the woman. "What's your name?"

"Gracie Addison."

All the stuffing seemed to go out of the woman when she spoke to Laura, leaving her looking more like a vulnerable child than an adult. But that didn't last long. She swung toward him, her fists planted on her hips and eyes narrowed. "I want an answer to my questions, along with your name, mister."

Will grinned, which seemed to make her madder. "Will Montgomery, ma'am, at your service." He swept off his hat and gave a short bow. He probably should climb off his horse and introduce himself proper-like, but from the looks of the little dynamo on the ground, she'd light into him like a wild bull at branding time. No sir, he was safer staying on his horse.

"And like I said, this is my niece, Laura, who is in my care. As to why I pulled you out of that tree, I told you. You spooked my horse then kicked me in the noggin. I thought you were a boy out to pull a prank." He raised his brows and chuckled. "You can't blame a man for making a mistake when you dress like that and climb trees. What are you, all of fifteen or sixteen?"

∞

Gracie clamped her teeth on a cry of frustration. She'd shout at the insufferable man if it wasn't for the wide-eyed child taking in every word that passed between them. Fifteen or sixteen, was she? "I'll have you know, Mr. Montgomery, that I am nineteen, and what I wear or choose to do is no concern of yours. Why should I quit doing something I love?" She crossed her arms and tilted her chin.

He shook his head, but the smile that both irritated and drew her lingered on those finely carved lips. In fact, his entire face was bathed in laugh lines as though he could barely contain himself. He swept off his hat, revealing brown curls that reflected a hint of gold in the sunlight, and the movement caused his shirt to tighten over the broad, well-built shoulders she'd gripped only moments before. "Why, I reckon most women your age are too busy trying to entice a man to marry them to care for such childish things as climbing trees."

Gracie glowered at him—a cowboy if ever she'd seen one—but there were no big cattle ranches in their area, so what was he doing here? She narrowed her eyes. "Climbing trees is far from childish." She directed her attention to the little girl with the long blond braid and dimpled cheeks. "Do you like trees, Miss Laura?"

The girl giggled. "I'm not a miss. My name is just Laura. I've never climbed a tree. Uncle Will won't let me. Maybe you can teach me."

Gracie stifled a gasp so as not to startle the child. "Whyever not?" She stared at the offending uncle. Why would anyone deny a child such a wholesome pastime?

He stiffened, and his face lost the happy light as quickly as if water had been thrown on a candlewick. "Come, Laura. Mr. and Mrs. Warren are probably wondering why we haven't arrived yet. And we certainly don't want to keep Miss Addison from her—activities."

He arched a brow and waited until Laura mounted. "Nice to meet you, ma'am"—he reached out and snagged the reins of her horse—"and I certainly hope you don't kick the wrong man in the head while swinging from your next tree."

The horses trotted down the path at the fork, their riders' backs to Gracie and the man's gruff response still ringing in her ears. The nerve, talking to her like a silly child. She shivered as she rubbed the spot where his hand had clamped on her arm to keep her from falling after she'd landed in his lap, conflicted by the strange emotions that battled for dominance.

Then she remembered Laura's words—her uncle wouldn't let her climb a tree—and irritation won out over the surprising melting sensation she'd experienced while held in his arms. He'd said they were headed to the Warren home. Word was out that Curt Warren had hired a new woodworking apprentice since his business had grown and his wife had given birth to twins. It appeared Will Montgomery might not be a cowpoke after all, although he didn't look or act like any carpenter she'd ever met.

All children needed to experience a full life outdoors, whether it be wading in a creek, riding a horse, catching a fish just for the joy of the battle, or climbing a tree. She'd have to find a way that Laura Montgomery wouldn't miss out on her childhood, and hoped she didn't irritate the child's cranky uncle in the meantime.

∞

Will had done all he could do to quiet Laura's protests as they rode away from the intriguing young woman he'd left standing under the dogwood tree a hundred yards back. He needed to think about what happened—or better yet, to shut out the vision of her tumbled red curls and green eyes so deep and vivid that a man could sink into their depths and never find his way back.

Once, he'd felt the same way with Lucinda. Her charm and beauty had swept him off his feet at first sight, but her beauty didn't penetrate to her core. Still he'd pursued her, ignoring the gentle warning that must have been sent from God, only to have his heart broken a few weeks later as he was fixing to propose. A pretty face didn't mean a thing, and Gracie Addison was more than pretty; she had a sharp tongue, to boot.

A pang of guilt smote him. In all fairness, he *had* yanked her from a tree and laughed at her when he'd thought her a silly girl. He guessed she'd had the right to set him straight. But it didn't mean he would be taken in by another attractive woman—and certainly not one so reckless as to put herself in danger.

An image of his sister's tragic death arose from long ago, and he shuddered, pushing it back into the dark cave of grief where it belonged. He'd meant it when he'd told Laura to stay out of trees, and Miss Daredevil had better not try to influence the girl.

"Laura, do you feel comfortable trotting for a bit? We're later than I expected after running into Miss Addison, and I'm afraid the Warrens will have supper ready."

She rolled her eyes and booted her horse into a slow trot—about the only speed the horse knew, and the reason he'd been purchased. "I'm not a baby, Uncle Will. You don't let me do anything fun. Why can't I wear trousers and have adventures like Miss Addison?"

"Because I said so, that's why." He snapped his lips shut and pressed them together. Laura would be safe and grow up to be a lady, if he had anything to say about it.

Chapter 3

Gracie stepped into the kitchen and eyed the huckleberry cobbler she'd baked yesterday. It was a little lopsided, but her father never seemed to mind. At least Jerold Carnegie had come down with a cold and had sent his regrets last night. It was enough that she'd had to put up with one insufferable man without coming home and being bored senseless by another.

Color rose to her cheeks as she suddenly realized how silly she must have looked to that handsome cowboy. A giggle started deep inside and forced its way out, and she pressed her fingers over her lips. Climbing trees was unusual for a young woman of her age, but she didn't normally care. It relaxed her when life got difficult, as it had of late with Father pressing her to consider marriage—and to Jerold Carnegie, of all people.

She'd been thinking of driving over to see Deborah Warren to help ease her burden—especially since her life had been exceedingly busy after giving birth to twins a little over a year and a half ago. Maybe they would enjoy the cobbler.

Gracie tried to convince herself she didn't care to bump into that bossy man again, but something inside was unsettled at the memory of his saucy grin and his arms around her. She sobered as she reconsidered the wisdom of seeing him again. But surely he'd be in Curt Warren's workshop, so she needn't talk to him. Besides, wasn't it more important to help Deborah if she needed it?

A few minutes later she reined her horse and buggy to a halt in front of the cozy cottage on the outskirts of town. The front door opened and Curt stepped onto the porch, wiping his hands on a dish towel, his brows almost meeting in the middle of his forehead. His face relaxed at the sight of her, and he hurried forward. "Gracie, how good to see you. Was Deborah expecting you?"

She shook her head and plucked the pan of cobbler off the seat beside her. "I thought I'd surprise her. With all the extra work she has since the twins arrived, I hoped she might enjoy a treat, so I baked a berry cobbler and brought it with me." She handed it to Curt then clambered down the one step and onto the ground beside him. "Maybe I can take over a few chores while I'm here if you need to return to your workshop."

Curt gave a short nod. "Thank you, but you might not want to stay once you're inside. I'm afraid things are a bit turbulent at the moment."

He escorted her onto the porch and through the front door, balancing the covered pan on one hand.

Gracie followed him across the tiny entry and halted in the doorway to the kitchen, gazing at the unexpected mess that had descended on what was normally a well-ordered room. Dishes littered the cupboard beside the washbasin, and a pot of hot water bubbled on the woodstove, putting steam into the already warm air. Deborah leaned over a chair trying to spoon food into a wailing girl's mouth while her towheaded brother banged his spoon on the floor where he sat sprawled in a puddle of spilled oatmeal.

Deborah looked up as a tear trickled down her flushed cheek. "Hello, Gracie. Please forgive the mess."

Curt rushed forward to set the cobbler on the table. He scooped the little boy off the floor. "Deb, you should be in bed. I told you I'd care for the children."

"They were crying, and you weren't in the house, so I decided to feed them. I feel a bit shaky, but I'm stronger than I was yesterday. I can help." She plucked a damp rag from the table and wiped the little girl's face.

Gracie held out her arms toward the toddler. "I can take care of Samuel if you want to take Sarah and clean her up. It appears Deborah needs to go back to bed. I'm happy to stay and help." She bounced the boy on her hip. "I can put this room back to rights in no time." The child squealed in delight and reached a sticky hand up to pat Gracie's cheek, depositing a fair amount of the oatmeal.

The thud of boots on the back porch and the squeak of a door hinge swung Gracie around. Laura, the child she'd seen riding with her uncle, stepped into the room, followed by Will Montgomery. Gracie's heart gave a quick lurch. She met his eyes, and her heart rate settled into a rapid beat. He smiled as his gaze rested on her stained cheek, and warmth flooded her face. This man had already seen her in a poor light when they'd met—what must he think of her now?

She dipped her head. "Mr. Montgomery. I hope you've settled in all right?"

Deborah's lips parted as she looked from one to the other. "You've met Will?"

Gracie nodded. She didn't know whether to be pleased that he'd kept their meeting to himself, or disappointed that he hadn't thought enough of her to share with his hosts. "I. . .bumped into him on the road."

His brow raised, and the corner of his mouth quirked. "Yes, I'd say that was accurate."

Laura snickered and tugged at her uncle's sleeve. "You was holding her in your arms, Uncle Will."

His face sobered, and he leaned over to whisper something into her ear. Her grin faded, and she nodded. "I'm sorry, Miss Addison."

Gracie's mortification faded at the sight of the little girl's distress. "Please don't worry about it, Laura. I think I'll clean Samuel up then help Deborah with the dishes. In fact, would you care to dry them for me?" She gave Laura a bright smile and was rewarded to see her expression clear.

Deborah swayed on her feet, and Curt caught her by the shoulders. He swung her into his arms. "That settles it. I'm putting you to bed this instant. You won't mind watching the children until I return, Gracie?"

"Not at all. I'm happy to help."

A knock sounded at the front door as Curt headed for the bedroom with Deborah. Gracie shifted Samuel to her other hip. "I'll get that."

Will stepped forward. "Allow me. You have your hands full." He swung around and strode down the short hall to the entry.

As his footsteps faded, Gracie tuned her hearing toward the front door. Whoever had arrived hadn't come in, but she could hear soft murmurs that sounded decidedly feminine. And where had Laura gotten to?

The little girl appeared in the doorway from the hall, her eyes wide. "My new teacher is talking to Uncle Will, and I think she likes him. She's smiling real big, and she's awful pretty with her cheeks all pink."

Gracie wanted to sink through the floor. Carissa Sanderson was her best friend, as well as being one of the prettiest and sweetest women she knew. She wouldn't blame Will Montgomery a bit if he was already smitten with Laura's new teacher. Then why did her heart hurt thinking about it? She tried to shake off the sensation and forced herself to smile at Laura. "Miss Sanderson is a wonderful teacher, and I'm certain you'll love her."

Laura nodded and took a step closer to Gracie. She hesitated, peeked over her shoulder toward the front room, then lowered her voice: "Would you teach me to climb trees and fish in the stream? That's the kind of teacher I want." She wrinkled her nose. "I don't care for school, not even if Uncle Will does like that teacher."

Gracie didn't know whether to gasp or laugh, but she settled for a smile. "I'll have to see what your uncle thinks. I can't imagine he'd mind you learning to fish, but I do remember him saying something about not wanting you to climb trees. Did you fall out of one and hurt yourself?"

Laura's expectant look faded, and she dropped her gaze to the floor. "No. I think Uncle Will's being mean. He doesn't want me to have any fun at all."

Compassion swept over Gracie, and she reached for the girl and pulled her close. "I'm sure that's not the case, sweetie. Tell you what—I'll do my best to teach you to fish and climb a tree—"

"Don't make promises you can't keep, Miss Addison." Will stood in the doorway to the kitchen, his expression cool. "Laura, why don't you go play outside while I have a word with Miss Addison?"

∽

Will worked to soften his tone and leaned his shoulder against the doorframe. He wanted to stride forward and make sure this stubborn woman listened this time, but he wasn't an ogre and refused to act like one. "You were saying?"

She tilted her chin to the side and narrowed her eyes. "You are certainly quick to jump to conclusions, Mr. Montgomery. If you'd listened another few seconds you might have discovered what I planned to say to your niece, instead of assuming and scolding us both. I'm not a child. I'm as old as Carissa Sanderson and quite able to make my own decisions."

He straightened, all pretense of ease gone. "Not where my niece is concerned. And I'm not sure what Miss Sanderson has to do with anything. She seemed like she had a sensible head on her shoulders and acted every bit the lady. I expect she'll make a fine teacher for Laura."

Will wanted to bite his tongue after the words left his mouth. Why had the teacher been brought into the conversation? Of course, she was a nice enough young woman, and she certainly seemed capable. Gracie Addison, on the other hand—he couldn't even begin to say what he thought of her—a spitfire who appeared to take foolish chances with her life, but who cared enough to offer to help Deborah Warren and the children. Not to mention her fresh beauty, sparkling eyes, and the determined spirit she'd shown from the moment she dropped into his arms under that tree.

Gracie's face paled, and she took a step back. "Miss Sanderson is an excellent teacher, and yes, she's also a fine lady—unlike me. So don't worry, Mr. Montgomery, I won't taint your niece or lead her down a dangerous path. I'd already told her, before you interrupted, that she must have your permission for me to help her. Not that I understand your hesitation, but be that as it may, I'll not interfere."

If Will could kick himself across the kitchen and back, he'd do so. What an idiot he'd been—and now he'd hurt Miss Addison and implied he didn't believe her to be a lady. "I apologize, miss. It appears we've gotten off on the wrong foot. Again. And it's my fault." He extended his hand. "Friends?"

Gracie hesitated. Then she stepped toward him and smiled. "Friends." She placed her hand in his.

A shock of awareness jolted him so hard he almost dropped her hand. "Thank you." He gently squeezed the soft fingers before he released her. "I don't have to start work in the shop for a few days. How about I help you out here? It looks like you've taken on a big job, what with Deborah ill and the babies so fussy. I hope they aren't coming down sick as well."

Gracie's eyes widened. "Aren't you worried about Laura? I think Deborah is mostly worn out and has a cold, but maybe you and Laura should stay somewhere else to be safe."

Will shook his head. "I promised Curt I'd start work sometime late next week. We were going to start sooner, but he wants to stay close to the house. Laura has always been incredibly healthy, and I'm not worried about myself." He grinned. "I meant what I said about helping. In fact, I'm not a bad cook. How about we get these dishes done and whip up some supper so Deborah can rest?"

Surprise registered on Gracie's face before she swiveled toward the sink. "All right, if you insist." She tossed a saucy grin over her shoulder. "I happen to be a terrible cook, so you'd better be able to stand behind your boast. What's your specialty?"

He chuckled and moved up beside her, snagging a dish towel from a hook nearby. "You wash and I'll dry?"

She giggled. "No specialty, huh? Just as I thought."

"Not what I said. I happen to prefer surprises, that's all. You'll have to stick around long enough to find out."

Her brows arched, and her lips opened when a shout from outside sounded through the open kitchen window.

"Uncle Will! Come see! I'm way up in the tree like Miss Gracie, and I can go even higher."

Will froze, his heart in his throat and fear gripping his insides so hard he thought he'd double over and retch. He bolted from the room, his thoughts flashing to his dead, daredevil sister. *"Like Miss Gracie,"* Laura had said. He shouldn't have gotten friendly with Gracie Addison. He should have known better than to let Laura be influenced by her behavior, and now it could be too late.

Chapter 4

Gracie stood rooted to the floor, not comprehending what could possibly be the problem. Laura was climbing a tree, but Will had raced from the room as though some tragedy were about to occur. She knew he didn't want his niece climbing, but children had done so and taken tumbles, but rarely come to harm, for centuries. She wiped her damp hands on a towel and headed for the door. What could make a grown man anxious about something as innocent as climbing a tree?

She stepped outside and looked into the branches of the nearby maple. Will stood at the base looking up through the leaves, and Gracie could barely see Laura about fifteen feet from the ground.

Will gestured toward his niece. "Laura, I said come down this minute. It's not safe to be that high, and you're going to tear your dress."

"No fair, Uncle Will! I'm not near as high as Miss Gracie was, and she didn't get hurt." Her high-pitched voice drifted through the leaves. "Please let me stay. I want to do fun things like she does. Please?"

"Come down this minute, Laura." His voice shook with intensity.

The leaves trembled as the little girl made her way down a few more feet until she was hardly out of his reach. Gracie moved closer, wondering at the tension stiffening Will's body. "Laura honey, I know you're having fun, and you were very brave going so high, but it's time to come down." She raised her brows and smiled at Will but only got a glower in return.

"Don't encourage her." He hissed the words, and his eyes shot sparks. "Laura, come down to the next branch where I can lift you down the rest of the way."

"Nuh-uh." Laura's face peeked through the branches, and she scowled. "Gonna do it myself." She shimmied over to the trunk then wrapped her arms around it and stepped to the branch below. As her foot touched the branch, she released her hold with one hand and reached down to grasp the one below.

Will growled deep in his throat and walked toward a spot beneath her at the exact moment her foot slid off the branch and she pitched headlong toward the ground.

Will darted the last stride, his arms extended and his heart pounding in his chest like a blacksmith swinging a hammer against an anvil. He couldn't let anything happen to Laura. He clenched his jaw and snatched the girl out of the air before she hit the ground. He set her down gently and knelt in front of her. "Are you all right?"

She pulled back, her earlier scowl reappearing and deepening. "Why didn't you let me climb higher? You aren't fair to make me come down when I was having fun. Miss Gracie likes to climb trees, and she understands, don't you?" She swung her gaze to the silent young woman standing nearby.

Gracie stared at Laura then turned her attention on Will, her eyes soft and inquisitive.

A lump formed in Will's throat, but he pushed it down. He would not be influenced by a warm gaze, no matter how beautiful the woman. "I'm sure Miss Addison does understand, as she takes foolish chances herself, but that does not mean you are allowed to do so. You go straight to your room now and stay there until supper. You disobeyed me by climbing that tree, and you need to think about your actions."

"But Uncle Will—"

He placed his hands on her shoulders and gave a gentle shove. "Now, Laura." Hardening his heart against the sniffles coming from his niece as she tromped away, he turned toward Gracie. "This wouldn't have happened if she hadn't seen you in that tree."

She crossed her arms over her chest. "You're blaming me for your niece's misbehavior?" She shook her head. "You don't make a lick of sense, and as far as I can see, you're taking this too far. Laura was doing a very competent job until you demanded she come down and she scrambled to obey. If she'd taken her time, I'm certain she would have been fine."

Will closed his eyes as memories again flooded his mind. When he opened them, Gracie was staring at him with something like compassion shining on her captivating face. "Would you please come back inside so I can explain?"

She hesitated a moment then nodded. "A cup of coffee or tea sounds good. I saw Deborah had a pot on the stove."

He inclined his head but didn't reply. Why had he offered to explain? If only Gracie didn't turn out to be a flirt or untrustworthy like Lucinda—but what was he thinking? It wasn't as if he were planning on marrying Gracie. For some reason he couldn't explain, he wanted to tell her why he wouldn't allow Laura to attempt anything that smacked of danger. He didn't really know her, but something about Gracie Addison drew him at a deeper level than he'd ever felt before.

∞

Gracie settled into a kitchen chair across the beautiful hand-crafted table Curt had built for Deborah and watched Will as he poured two mugs of coffee. The man still mystified her. Laughing and teasing one minute then scolding her for being a bad influence on his niece the next. She'd like to spurn whatever explanation he gave as irrational, after the way he'd acted outside. But being charitable and listening was the godly thing to do, even if it went against her natural inclination.

Will dropped into the chair across from her and took a drink of his coffee. He set the mug on the table. "I don't know what I was thinking to burden you with my problems."

Gracie blinked. This was not at all what she'd expected. Defiance, chastisement, even a bit of condescension, but certainly not humility or sorrow. She sat up straighter and laced her fingers on top of the table. "Please, Will. I'd like to hear whatever you have to say."

His brows arched. "You called me Will."

Warmth blossomed in her cheeks. "I'm sorry. I didn't mean to be forward."

"Not at all." He reached toward her but stopped a few inches short of her hand. "I can't deny I've been thinking of you as Gracie since you arrived today, in spite of my behavior to the contrary." He leaned back and let his hands fall into his lap. "Am I being too presumptuous?"

She waited half a dozen heartbeats, willing herself to breathe slowly. "I think I'd like that. Now please, go ahead. I promise I'll be respectful and listen."

"Thank you." He closed his eyes for a moment, and a flicker of what appeared to be pain contorted his brow. Finally, he opened his eyes and sucked in a long breath. "Laura's mother was my sister. She died a year ago, and it was all my fault. I killed my sister."

Chapter 5

Gracie bit her lip to keep from gasping. He'd killed his sister? Surely she'd heard wrong. "I don't understand...."

"No, I'm sure you don't. Let me back up to our childhood. Karen and I were always close as she was my only sibling. I was a year older and charged with watching out for her as we grew. The problem was, we were both daredevils, and Karen was quite the tomboy. She loved all the same things you do—riding astride, fishing, climbing trees, swimming in water too deep to be safe. She did it all. And I urged her on to take more risks with every new adventure we conquered. My pa would have skinned me alive if he'd known some of the things we attempted." A smile flickered across his lips, softening his strong jawline.

She leaned forward. "So you loved her? You have good memories."

"Yes. She was a wonderful sister, and I was the big brother who could do no wrong in her eyes. Then when she was only fifteen, she met Vernon, a man I didn't care for or trust. He stayed long enough to marry her, but when Laura was born, he disappeared and never returned. Karen was heartbroken, and I didn't think she'd ever come out of her despair. Then one day she was herself again, and more reckless than ever. I think she would have pushed herself too far, but for baby Laura. As the girl grew, Karen began to see she needed to slow down—to be careful and not foolhardy, even if her heart was broken."

The room quieted, and Gracie waited—she wanted to press him, wanted to understand, but she knew he'd continue when he was ready.

He shook himself like a bear coming out of hibernation, needing to shake off the effects of the long sleep. "Laura was at a neighbor's. I'd ridden with Karen to town—a wire had come in and she was fearful. Turns out a sheriff from another town sent word that her no-good husband got shot cheating at cards. She was numb—she went from defiant to despondent in a matter of seconds. All the way home, she could barely move her horse out of a walk. It was coming onto dark, and I urged her to hurry. 'Let's race,' I said, just to shake her out of her doldrums. Like when we were youngsters—I told her I'd beat her home— that she was too slow to beat me—but I planned to let her win.

"All of a sudden, she dug her spurs into her gelding's side and took off across the flat, running like demons were pursuing her—and I suppose in a way, they were." Will sucked in a harsh breath before he continued. "I stayed behind her, whooping and hollering like an idiot, thinking it would give her a chuckle. When all of a sudden—" He shuddered and put his face in his hands.

Gracie reached across the table and touched his fingers, not caring whether it was appropriate or if Curt might come into the room. Will gripped her hand as though it were a lifeline, but kept his eyes cast down at the table.

"All of a sudden, her horse stepped in a hole. Broke his leg and sent her flying. Her head hit a rock." He gave a harsh laugh. "Must have been the only big rock in a hundred yards, and she hit it. She was dead before I could get to her side. My fault. I killed her. If I hadn't pushed. . ."

Gracie could stand it no longer. She shoved her chair back and stood. "Shh. . . It wasn't your fault." She walked around the table and laid her hand on his shoulder. "You were trying to encourage her, but you didn't know what would happen. You were trying to help, to cheer her up. You can't blame yourself."

He raised red-rimmed eyes and met hers. "But that's why I have to protect Laura. I can't allow her to take the chances her mother and I took growing up. That's why I don't want her to be influenced by you."

Gracie gasped and took a step back. She turned and fled from the house as disillusionment and horrible pain tore her apart inside.

∞

Will sat stunned for a moment at the words that had come out of his mouth. Had he really accused Gracie of being a danger to Laura? The front door opened and closed with a dull thud, breaking him out of his stupor. He bolted from the chair and raced for the door. He jerked it open in time to see Gracie walking swiftly across the area between the house and the tree. What an idiot he'd been. "Gracie! Please, wait."

She didn't slow, but her long skirts kept her from running, even though she'd gathered the hem in one hand and held the fabric a few inches above her ankles.

Will cleared the porch in one bound and extended his stride into a full run as he hit the packed dirt. Within a dozen strides he'd caught her. "Gracie, let me explain. I'm sorry." He touched her shoulder but didn't grasp it.

She slowed then stopped, but kept her back turned to him. "There's nothing to explain. I see now why you don't want me around Laura. Don't worry, I'll stay away."

"No, that's not it. I didn't mean to make you feel that way. I was trying to explain why I don't want her climbing trees or doing things where she might get hurt. She doesn't understand, but I was hoping you might."

Gracie pivoted and looked at him. "I do understand. I accept your apology and I'm saddened by your story, but I believe you truly think I'm a bad influence, or the words wouldn't have come out of your mouth."

Will wished he could wipe the anguish off her face—wished he could wrap his arms around her and pull her close—but he had no right. "Let me prove it to you. Go on a picnic with Laura and me tomorrow. Come over in the morning, and we'll do chores for Deborah and Curt, help with the children and fix the family a nice noon meal. Then we can pack something for the three of us and let them rest. How does that sound? We could go to the pond nearby, and Laura can take a fishing pole. She's been badgering me to teach her to fish, and I'm guessing you're good at that." He cocked his head to the side. "Forgiven?"

She bit her lip and simply watched him for several long seconds. She nodded. "All right." An impish grin softened her face. "And I'll beat you at catching fish any day of the week." She sobered. "But just because I'm agreeing to go, it doesn't mean I believe you're right in being so protective—or that you've shed all thoughts of my bad influence. Don't worry, I'll keep my distance and won't do anything that endangers your niece."

Will's spirits sank. When he'd seen Gracie's sparkling smile peek out, he'd hoped she'd understood his explanation and completely forgiven him, if not moved to a place where she might entertain thoughts of being friends—or even something more.

He couldn't blame her for holding back—every time she'd softened toward him, it seemed he'd said something to push her away. Of course, he'd been burned by Lucinda's deceit and that had made him more cautious, but he refused to entertain that thought. Gracie appeared so much more honest and down to earth than Lucinda. She certainly wouldn't break her word or chase off after another man once she'd come to an understanding.

But doubt niggled at him just the same. How well did he know Gracie Addison, after all?

∞

Gracie helped Will with Deborah's chores the next day and wrestled with whether she should have agreed to go fishing. Deborah was better, but the children had developed runny noses and continued to fuss.

Thankfully, Curt had agreed to finish in the workshop early and take over their late-afternoon and evening care, so Will could take Laura fishing. Will protested, and suggested that he help in the workshop for the morning, but Curt had assured him he was doing more good at the moment helping Gracie, as he had no pressing projects. Gracie narrowed her eyes when she heard his offer to Curt. Was he simply trying to help his boss, or had he already regretted his invitation for her to accompany him and Laura?

She cleared her throat to catch Curt's attention. When he looked up, she gave him a steady look. "Maybe I should stay and help. The twins might be too much for you later if they don't go down for a nap soon."

"Nonsense." Curt shot a furtive glance at Will. "I can handle things fine. You've done far more already than you should have. Besides, I think Laura would be very disappointed if you don't accompany them. That's all she's been talking about this morning."

Gracie noticed that Will didn't look up at Curt's reply, but Laura tugged at Gracie's sleeve. "Please, Miss Gracie. I want you to come with us. Uncle Will said you're very good at catching fish, and he's not."

Something halfway between a snort and a laugh broke from Will's mouth before he stifled it. "That's not exactly what I said, Laura, but I would like Miss Gracie to come as well." He arched a brow at her. "You haven't changed your mind, I hope? I borrowed two poles, as I thought we could take turns fishing and helping Laura. We might even bring back a string for supper tonight."

Gracie's tension eased as she looked into his hopeful eyes. "Trout for supper sounds good, and I'd hate to disappoint Laura, if Curt is sure he doesn't need my help."

Curt plucked one of the toddlers into his arms as the little boy made his way into the room and headed toward the hot stove. "I'll put them down for a nap as soon as you leave, and then I'll go sit with Deborah. Her eyes have been tired, and she was wishing I could read to her, so the quiet time together will be nice."

Thirty minutes later Gracie spread her skirt and settled onto a blanket covering a small portion of the grassy bank close to the pond. She loved the setting, although she would have liked it to be a little farther from the main road into town. But the pond was right on the border of Curt and Deborah's farm, so they easily walked the short distance.

Will glanced at the spot beside her with a longing look but ushered Laura to the edge of the pond instead. The next few minutes were spent baiting her hook with a wiggling worm, which made the girl squeal, but she got excited when he cast the line into the water and handed her the pole. "Hold it quiet now. Wait until you feel a tug before you try to bring the fish in."

She nodded, her face aglow, and gripped the bamboo rod with both hands. "Is Miss Gracie going to fish?"

Will glanced at Gracie, brows raised.

"Yes, I am. But let's see if you catch anything first. I want you to have the chance to get the biggest fish in the pond if you can."

Laura beamed and turned her attention back to the water.

Gracie's heart swelled with tenderness at Laura's excitement, and at the gentle way Will helped and encouraged the girl. He was so different from what she'd thought after he'd practically yanked her out of the dogwood tree. She smiled at the memory. Hopefully he'd noticed a bit of difference in her as well. Somehow she hadn't had the urge to climb a tree since meeting this man.

The clop of hooves on the hard-packed road drew her attention. She swiveled and raised her hand against the bright sun. Her best friend, Carissa Sanderson, drew her mare to a halt along the edge of the road and waved a gloved hand. "Gracie! How nice to see you here." Her gaze moved to Will and then on to Laura. Was that a spark of interest Gracie saw? Her heart contracted. She didn't want to hurt or disappoint her friend if Carissa was interested in Will, but the thought sent a shaft of pain into Gracie's chest.

Carissa's violet skirt cascaded over the seat, and her dark curls were covered by a trim and stylish hat. Her olive skin hinted at being sun-kissed, but Gracie knew it was her mother's Italian blood that gave her such an exotic appearance. She was every bit the lady, in dress, manner, and deportment—something Gracie had given up trying to compete with long ago.

Carissa was one person who never made her feel inferior or less of a woman for being a tomboy, but all of a sudden, Gracie realized how she must look in a man's eyes. Her quickly braided red-gold hair, plain calico dress, and boots, stood in stark contrast to Carissa's striking beauty. How could Will even consider looking at her when someone like Carissa was around?

Chapter 6

Will rose to his feet and bowed to the elegant young woman in the buggy, wondering yet again why he felt no attraction to someone so lovely. The feisty redhead on the blanket at his feet might be the reason, but he still wasn't certain that allowing his heart to get entangled with Gracie was the best idea, no matter how much the idea appealed. "Did you need to talk to me, Miss Sanderson?"

She waved him away. "No, Mr. Montgomery. I was visiting one of my students and saw you fishing. It's good to see you, Gracie. What a lovely day to be outside. Laura, have you caught a fish yet?"

Laura grinned. "No ma'am. But I'm going to catch me a whopper."

"That sounds lovely, Laura." She picked up her reins. "I should be going."

Will glanced at Gracie, wondering why she'd been so silent. From what he'd been told, Miss Sanderson was a friend of hers. Perhaps Gracie thought him rude for not inviting her to stay. "Would you care to join us?"

He sensed Gracie stiffen and wondered. Had he waited too long to make the invitation? "I'm sure Laura and Miss Addison would enjoy your company."

Gracie nodded but kept silent.

Miss Sanderson shook her head. "I really must be going, but thank you. Gracie, we need to get together sometime soon, now that school is out." She lifted a hand and waved then clucked to her horse and drove down the road.

Gracie pushed to her feet and walked over to Laura's side. "Any nibbles yet?"

"Nope. But a big one is going to bite, I just know it."

Gracie stroked Laura's hair. "Want me to fish with you?"

Laura cocked her head to the side. "If you want to, but I want to catch the first fish. Is that all right?"

Will moved up beside Gracie and tried not to laugh. "The fish will bite whichever worm they want to, Laura. So maybe Gracie and I won't put a line in until you catch your first one." He shot a quick look at Gracie, hoping she'd understand.

She nodded. "That makes perfect sense. Are you hungry yet, Laura?"

"I'm going to eat the fish I catch, so you and Uncle Will can eat the lunch you brought. You can save me some cookies though." Laura wiggled the tip of the pole and scowled. "Come get the worm, you silly fish."

Will rolled his eyes at Gracie, and she grinned. "Come on, let's dive into that food. Laura might not be hungry, but I certainly am." He held out his hand to Gracie, hoping she could somehow see into his heart.

She hesitated then slipped her fingers into his. Will gave a gentle squeeze. He led her forward to the blanket and seated her. As much as he'd love to continue to hold her hand, it wasn't proper, and she probably wouldn't allow it, but his soul did a little dance that she hadn't totally rejected his gesture.

∞

Gracie tucked the remains of the food into the basket and placed the checkered cloth over the top. If she didn't know better, she'd think her fingers were still tingling from the touch of Will's hand. Strong yet gentle—firm yet tender. She almost hadn't slipped her fingers into his, but something in his eyes had convinced her that he wasn't playing a game.

But where did Carissa fit into this picture—or did she? Gracie had thought she'd seen interest in Will's gaze as he'd looked her direction, and he *had* invited her to stay. Then why be so tender toward her a short time later? None of it made sense—and she was still struggling with his attitude toward her in regard to his niece. They'd had a wonderful visit while eating, but it was all too confusing, and her own growing attraction toward the man certainly didn't help.

Laura plunked down on the blanket and tossed her pole on the grass. "I didn't catch a thing. Dumb fish."

Will squatted next to her. "Keep a good attitude, Laura. Fishing is about having fun as well as catching fish. Maybe next time you'll do better."

"Next time I'm going to swing on that rope over the pond that's hanging from that tree." She pointed along the bank a ways.

Will shaded his eyes and looked then turned his attention to Laura. "No you aren't, young lady. I don't want you going near that tree, do you understand?"

She glowered then pivoted toward Gracie. "You'll help me do it, won't you, Miss Gracie? You wouldn't be afraid of an old rope swing, huh."

Gracie wanted to groan. Right when she felt she'd started earning Will's trust, Laura had to bring up something that upset him. "You must obey your uncle, Laura. It doesn't matter what I've done or might enjoy. Besides, I'm not climbing trees or swinging off ropes anymore. I'm too old for that kind of behavior now." She desperately wanted to see how Will reacted to her statement, but she kept her gaze fixed on Laura.

The little girl crossed her arms. "Huh. You weren't too old for it a few days ago when you were in that tree."

Gracie's cheeks heated. "I was being foolish. I won't be doing it again. Regardless, you listen to what your uncle tells you, all right?"

Will held out his hands to both Laura and Gracie. "Come on, let me help you ladies up, and we'll head home. Then I'd like to drive you back to your house, if you'll allow me to, Gracie."

His hand touched hers, and a jolt of awareness raced through her. Gracie was certain her cheeks flamed as bright as her hair, but she nodded. "Thank you. It *has* been a long day, and walking home doesn't sound too appealing." She detected a flicker of something that looked like disappointment in his eyes.

Had he hoped she might throw herself at him in gratitude for the ride? She liked Will Montgomery, but she couldn't possibly be in love with him. Besides, she didn't care to give him the wrong impression—no matter how warm or tingly she got when he touched her or how much she ached to have it continue.

∞

Will took Gracie's arm and helped her into Curt's buggy. He still wasn't sure what to make of this woman. He'd thought she was interested in him after the time they'd spent together working side by side in Deborah and Curt's home and then on the picnic beside the pond. She'd been less than enthusiastic in her acceptance of his offer to take her home when he was hoping she'd see it as the first step toward something more serious. Maybe he should declare his interest, but would she reject him the way Lucinda had done?

And then there was Laura. Even though Gracie said she'd given up her tomboy ways, it had only been a matter of days since she'd proven otherwise. Did he want a sweetheart who might be a poor influence on his niece—even to the point of her getting hurt? He ran his hands over his hair then picked up the reins and shook them. "Get on, Charlie."

Gracie swayed on the seat beside him as the wheels went into a rut, her shoulder touching his. She gripped the handrail beside her. "I'm sorry for jostling you. Is everything all right? You've been very quiet since we left the house."

He pulled himself out of his musing, annoyed that he'd not saved his thoughts for later. As much as he worried about Laura, he couldn't deny the growing attraction he felt for this delightful young woman beside him. "Everything is fine. I enjoyed our time together today, and I think Laura did as well."

"So did I. She's a precocious child with a strong spirit, but she's also refreshing and delightful."

A warm glow suffused Will at the compliment. "Thank you. If I can only keep her safe as she grows up, I'll be grateful and feel I've done my job as her guardian." He turned toward her and grinned. "But she can be a handful, I'll freely admit that."

They passed the next few minutes until they reached Gracie's home in comfortable conversation. Will drew up at the front gate, set the brake, and jumped down. He walked around to Gracie's side to help her, and the front door opened.

A young man stood there. He walked to the edge of the porch and lifted a hand in greeting, but a frown gave him a decidedly sour appearance. "Gracie. I've come to take you to supper at the restaurant. Your father told me you were to be home by now. You have kept me waiting for over half an hour."

Will stared at the man. Clean shaven, dressed in a finer suit than Will could afford, and holding a top hat that would typically be seen in a city. All in all, the man was a dandy, and a supercilious one at that. "I apologize for making Miss Addison late for her appointment."

He reached up and helped Gracie down without meeting her eyes. She appeared struck dumb by the man, although she made choking noises and kept a tight grip on his arm.

"I hope you have a fine evening with your beau, Miss Addison." He vaulted into the seat and slapped the horse with the reins, sending the animal into a startled trot.

Chapter 7

Gracie found her voice and let out a startled cry of dismay as Will's buggy disappeared around a corner. How dare Jerold show up at her door and act as though they had an understanding. She hadn't agreed to go anywhere with this man, nor would she. Ever. She hiked up her skirt and almost bolted after the buggy.

She halted. She'd never catch it at the rate it was moving. "What is the meaning of this?" She pivoted slowly to glare at Jerold. "Why did you imply that we had an agreement to meet for supper?" She grabbed the gate and swung it open then stalked toward the porch.

Jerold hunched one shoulder without seeming to notice her distress. "Your father told me you'd be home soon, and since I was unable to come the evening you invited me, I thought I'd make it up to you now."

"Did my father suggest this?"

He hesitated a moment. "Well, not exactly." The corners of his mouth ticked up. "But I'm sure he'd approve."

She shook her head. "I'm truly sorry, Jerold. You're a nice man, but I'm not interested. Please forgive me, but I'm going up to my room."

He drew back as though she'd slapped him. "I'd think, at your age, you'd be happy to have a suitor." His shock dropped away, and a superior smile took its place. "Especially one who can point you down the right path for your life."

Gracie gave a mocking laugh. "You make nineteen—almost twenty—years of age sound like quite a spinster. And believe me when I tell you that I know exactly where my path lies and how I intend to get there—and it is not with you." She flounced past him, yanked open the door, and hurried inside. She slammed the door behind her.

"Father? Papa? Are you home?" She was thankful he hadn't suggested this meeting, but he'd probably hoped she'd be too polite to spurn Jerold's advances. He might have even hoped she'd accompany the man to supper and fall for his charms, if he had any.

She stomped up the stairs to her room and threw herself on the bed. What about Will? He'd gotten the wrong idea from Jerold and thought the man was her beau. She shivered at the thought of the life she'd have if she married Jerold. How arrogant to assume she'd be thrilled at his company and to think she couldn't attract anyone else.

Gracie tucked a pillow behind her shoulders. What should she do about Will? Should she ask him what he thought of Carissa then ease into her opinion of Jerold? No, that would be forward and would give away her concern that he might be interested in her best friend. What then?

She rolled over and punched the pillow, hating the situation she found herself in. Will had sparked more interest in her than any man she'd ever met, and she had just started to think he might find her intriguing as well. Now this.

Something her father had often said came back full force. *"When in doubt, pray."* He had a solid faith that God loved us no matter what the circumstances might show. But he also said that our emotions aren't a good test of whether God is at work in our lives or not—only the Bible and prayer could show us the truth.

She plucked the Bible off her nightstand and settled into her pillows once more. "Father, show me Your truth. Give me Your wisdom." She flipped the pages and started to read, assured that her heavenly Father had heard, just as her earthly father had promised.

∞

Five days dragged by without Will getting so much as a glimpse of Gracie. She hadn't shown up at Curt and Deborah's on Sunday, the day after their picnic, and he started to work the following day. He should have gone to services with Curt and Deborah, but now that she was feeling a little better, Will offered to watch the children so the couple could attend on their own. Both of the toddlers were still fighting sniffles, and their parents were concerned about taking them out.

Will had wanted to go, certain that Gracie would be there, but he'd also hated the thought of seeing her sitting with that man who'd waited at her house. From what the man had said, he could only surmise they were headed toward courtship, and he'd rather not watch it play out.

He enjoyed his job in Curt's shop, but he had a hard time keeping his mind on some of the more intricate details.

Curt walked in as Will gazed out the window toward town. "Something bothering you, Will?"

He jumped like a jackrabbit spooked by a hawk. "I'm sorry. I guess I was gathering wool. It won't happen again."

Curt nodded, but he didn't seem convinced. "Thanks for all the help you've been in the house. That's not what I hired you for, but I'll admit it came at the right time."

Will relaxed at the change in subject, happy Curt hadn't pushed to find out what might be wrong. "Glad to. You and Deborah didn't have to take me and Laura in. You could have insisted we find our own place. I'll be doing that soon, of course, but it's been a blessing to get my feet under me first."

The brisk sound of footfalls in the office leading to the workroom turned Will and Curt around. Will moved forward. "Want me to see who it is?"

Curt shook his head. "I've been expecting a customer. You go ahead and keep working on this headboard. Mrs. Williams is anxious to get it next week, and it still needs sanding and another coat of varnish." He strode across the room then stepped through the open door into the small office area tucked into a corner of the building.

Will reached for the sanding block, thankful he didn't have to concentrate on anything more detailed.

"Uncle Will?" Laura's breathless voice took him by surprise, and he jerked his head up.

"Where did you come from, pumpkin?"

She grinned. "Pumpkins are for pie, silly. May I go fishing?"

"Maybe later, when I get off work."

She bounced from one foot to the other. "How about wading in the edge of the pond? Can I do that alone? Please? You'll be working all day, and I'm hot and bored."

He set his brush down. "Not without an adult."

"Miss Gracie is here. May I go if she'll take me?"

"Here? Where?" He stepped to the window and peered out toward the house, his heart picking up its pace.

"She's visiting Miss Deborah and the babies."

"Did she come alone?"

Laura scrunched up her face. "Yes. She always comes alone, doesn't she?"

He shrugged, feeling foolish that his first thought was of the arrogant man who'd been on Gracie's porch. "I don't want you to bother Miss Gracie while she's visiting. I told you I'd take you later. All right?"

She gave him a mutinous look that he couldn't quite decipher, then slowly nodded. "Yes sir. I won't bother her while she's visiting." She swung around and marched out the door without looking back.

Over an hour passed, but Gracie didn't go home and Curt didn't return—nor did Laura come back to pester him. A feeling of niggling doubt tore at him.

Would Laura disobey him and ask Gracie to take her fishing?

He set the sanding block aside and wiped his hands on a rag. He'd clean up later. Right now he'd better check on his niece.

⚭

Gracie stood with hands planted on her hips, wishing she'd checked with Will first, but she'd hated to trouble him at work—and she'd dreaded seeing accusation in his eyes after what happened last week. She took a step closer to Laura, where the girl waded ankle deep in the water. "Are you certain your uncle said you could come?"

Laura raised innocent eyes. "He said I could if I had a big person with me. That's why I came and asked you. I knew Miss Deborah wouldn't want to leave the children, with them coming down sick, and you're so nice." She dimpled and walked out a little deeper into the pond, the water covering her ankles as she lifted the hem of her short skirt. "I'm having lots of fun. May I go deeper and get all wet? It's hot today, and it would feel awfully good."

Gracie hesitated. Should she take Laura back and ask Will to be certain? The child was already here, so maybe a few minutes of fun wouldn't hurt. After all, Will kept Laura on such a tight rein that she felt sorry for the girl. "I suppose you can sit down there, but no deeper. Understood?"

Laura nodded. "I'll be good." She sank into the water, which only came up a few inches.

Gracie sighed. "I'm going to sit against that tree and rest for a minute. I'll still be able to see you, but I'm holding you to your promise to be good." She traipsed to the tree a few yards away and sank down on the grass at the base of the trunk then leaned her head against it and closed her eyes for a few seconds. She thought she heard something and looked toward Laura, but the child was still playing in the same spot, leaning forward and dribbling handfuls of water over her bare toes. She didn't have a swimsuit, so she'd worn an old dress that was too short for her, and removed her stockings and shoes.

Gracie shut her eyes again. It felt good after so little sleep the last few nights, worrying about Will and what he might think. This was ridiculous. She needed to simply tell him she had no interest in Jerold. She opened her eyes again to check on Laura and gasped. The girl wasn't in her place at the edge of the pond. She'd closed her eyes for ten seconds, if that. Gracie jumped to her feet and dashed toward the water. "Laura? Where are you? Answer me this instant!"

"I'm up here. Look at how good I climbed this tree, Miss Gracie, just like you! Now I'm going to swing on this rope. I'm a daredevil, too. Aren't you proud of me?" Laura stood on a low branch in a nearby maple, clutching a rope suspended from a higher branch.

Gracie sucked in a breath, her hand going to her mouth. She dashed for the tree. "No!" If she could get there before Laura swung out over the water—

Something crashed through the brush not far behind her, but Gracie didn't take time to look. "Laura. Get down before you get hurt!" Gracie felt as though she hollered the words, but they seemed to come out on a whisper instead.

Laura squealed in glee and pushed off from the branch, gripping the rope. She swung out over the pond. The rope reached the full arc and stopped then slowly began to return. Laura's shouts of delight suddenly turned to a cry of alarm. "My hands are slipping! I can't hold on!"

She shrieked again as her grip loosened, and she fell into the water. Gracie watched in horror as the child disappeared. She tore at the buttons holding her skirts. She was a good swimmer—surely she could reach Laura and bring her back to the surface.

Chapter 8

Will shot past Gracie, his feet thundering against the sod. "Laura, I'm almost there."

Laura's head popped to the surface just as Will plunged into the pond. In three hard strides through the deepening water, he'd reached Laura's side and plucked her into his arms. She coughed and spluttered, but she didn't appear any worse for her adventure. He hugged her tight against his chest and waded toward the shore. When he got there, he set Laura on the grassy bank and knelt in front of her, shaking with fear. "First, are you all right?"

"Uh-huh." She nodded, her streaming hair hanging loose around her face. "That was fun. And when you picked me up, my feet touched the bottom. Can I do it again, Uncle Will?"

His fear dissolved into anger, and it was all he could do not to shake the little imp. "What were you thinking coming here? I said I'd take you after work."

She shook her head. "Nuh-uh. You said I couldn't come without a big person, so I asked Miss Gracie, and she said she'd come. So I didn't disobey you."

He ground his teeth in frustration at the child's reasoning. "You could have drowned, or hit your head on a rock, or fallen out of that tree and been killed. Besides, I told you not to bother Miss Gracie. Remember that?"

She tilted her head to the side. "Yes, but I didn't ask her until she was done visiting with Mrs. Warren. I didn't mean to be bad. I was so hot and sticky, and I wanted to play in the water. And it was fun! You should try it."

He groaned then reached down and wrung out her skirt. "Go sit on the grass up by that tree where Miss Gracie was earlier. I need to talk to her alone. And do not move until I get there, or you'll go without supper."

Laura stuck out her lower lip, but she obeyed, trudging up the gently sloping bank to the tree.

He rounded on Gracie who stood clasping her hands in a tight grip, her entire body shaking. Pity engulfed him, but he pushed it away as the memory of the little girl going under the water returned. "I asked Laura, but I'll ask you as well. What were you thinking, allowing her to climb a tree and swing out over that water? Couldn't you see it was dangerous?"

∞

Gracie's stomach roiled, and she thought she might be sick. She didn't blame Will for being angry. This was her fault. No matter what Laura had said, she should have checked with Will. "I'm so sorry. She said it was all right with you, but I should have asked."

"That isn't what I'm upset about. I know Laura can be very persuasive. But why did you allow her in that tree when you know how I feel about it? And to let her swing on that rope—" He closed his eyes for a brief moment.

"I'd checked on her a couple of times, and she was just sitting in a few inches of water nearby. She promised she'd be good. I only closed my eyes for a few seconds. I don't see how she could have gotten to the tree and climbed it in that amount of time." She placed her fingertips over her lips to stifle a sob. "She was my responsibility. I was wrong to not keep my eyes on her every second."

He gave a curt nod. "And from what I heard her say before she swung over the pond, she was mimicking you. There's only one thing I can do so this never happens again. I'll have to ask you to stay away from Laura." He pivoted and stalked toward the little girl sitting quietly under the tree.

Gracie wanted to sink to the ground and cry, but she stood erect, holding her head high. She'd been remiss in closing her eyes for those few seconds, but it wasn't her fault Laura hadn't obeyed Will, nor was it her responsibility that the girl wanted to be like her. So be it. If he didn't want her to see Laura again, she wouldn't see him either. She plucked up her skirts and headed for home. She was done with this man, no matter how much the decision hurt.

∞

Will didn't look back as he gripped Laura's hand and led her across the meadow toward the Warren home. His anger was fading, and sadness took its place. He was thankful his niece was safe, but had he been completely fair in placing the blame on Gracie? Laura could be very persuasive and was prone to disobey. Had Gracie really done anything so wrong? It hurt his heart to even think about not seeing her again.

"Uncle Will, you're holding my hand too tight." Laura tugged at him.

"I'm not letting go of you until we reach the house. You're to go straight to your room, change your clothes, and lie down until supper. With no arguments, young lady."

She gave a huge sigh. "Yes sir. But you were mean to Miss Gracie. It wasn't her fault I went on the swing. I sneaked up there when her eyes were shut."

He ignored her as he battled his own conscience. They arrived at the house, and he waited until Laura scurried up the steps to her room, then he made his way back to the workshop.

Curt stood in the doorway, his eyes filled with concern. "Where's Gracie? And why is Laura dripping wet?"

Will waved him back inside and sank into a chair. "It's not a pretty story, but if you have a few minutes. . ."

Curt nodded and took a seat. "I have all the time you need."

Over the next few minutes, Will poured out the story, including his history and the loss of his sister. All the pain and guilt spewed out in a jumble of words that he couldn't seem to stem. Finally, he wiped his hand across his sweaty brow and gave a feeble smile. "Probably way more than you cared to hear, but I'll admit, it feels good to get it off my chest."

"I imagine it does. I'm sorry to hear about Laura's mother. I understand now why you're so protective of Laura."

Something in Curt's tone caught Will's attention, and he lifted his head. "You think I'm *too* protective."

Curt gave a half shrug. "It's not my concern. You're her uncle, not me."

Will tensed. "I want to know what you think."

Curt hesitated. "All right." He gave a short nod. "I believe your guilt over your sister's death has influenced you more than you realize."

"How so?" Will wasn't sure he wanted to hear this, but somehow he knew he needed to listen. He'd been praying long and hard lately that he'd make wise decisions where Laura, and even Gracie, were concerned, and after the past hour, he was second-guessing everything he'd done and said.

Curt leaned forward, his hands on his knees, and met Will's gaze. "Let's take my children as an example. They're sick right now and even have a low fever. I could race to the doctor—worry over them until I make myself sick with fear. Or, I can choose to trust God with my twins, knowing He loves them more than I do. Of course, if they get worse, I'll be sensible and call the doctor. But their health and the length of their lives is ultimately God's decision, not mine, no matter how much I try to protect them."

"So you think I'm wrong to protect Laura?" Frustration put a sharp edge to his question, and Will tried to soften it. "I don't want something to happen to her like it did to her mother."

"But your guilt over the belief that you caused your sister's death is what fuels that desire." He held up his hands. "I'm not saying you don't love your niece. I'm saying it's not normal to force a little girl with a sense of adventure to never climb a tree or swing on a rope or anything else that might contain a hint of danger."

Will leaned back and crossed his arms. "So you would have let her go on that rope swing? Even if she could have drowned?"

"Did you pay attention to how deep it was where she landed? I've been on that swing, and at the deepest point where you could let go, the water comes up to my neck, and Laura isn't heavy enough to have swung that far. There's not a rock on the bottom of that pond that I've ever found.

"Should she have done it without proper supervision? Of course not. Should she be denied ever having new experiences that other children have? I don't think so. And certainly not to satisfy your sense of guilt over an event that probably would have happened, regardless."

Will winced as he tried to take in all that Curt said. He bowed his head and pondered. "And Gracie?" He finally raised his head. "How about her part in this?"

Curt arched one brow. "I think you're falling in love with her and don't want to admit it, out of fear that Laura will want to be like her. Gracie Addison is a fine young woman, and one I'd be happy to have my daughter emulate when she gets older. She shouldn't have closed her eyes for those few seconds, but are you going to blame her for that forever and cut off any chance of happiness for both of you?"

Curt shook his head when Will stayed silent. "It doesn't sound sensible to me." He slapped his hands on his knees and stood. "I'm going to check on Deborah and the children. The afternoon is pretty much gone. Go see to your niece." He gave Will a sly look. "And anything else that might need to be taken care of, before it's too late."

∞

Gracie had never been much of a crier, but right now she wanted to beat on her pillow and wail the loss of Laura and Will. Especially Will. When had she allowed the man to burrow himself so deeply into her heart? Jerold Carnegie might be boring, but at least marrying him wouldn't have brought this kind of pain. She snorted. No, but she'd warrant she'd have another whole set of problems to deal with, married to that man.

She was thankful her father was at work when she got home, so she'd been able to slip into her room without being seen—or questioned. Papa knew she'd been helping Deborah and Curt, and he'd started questioning her lately about the new man working there. Her blushes had given him all the information he'd needed, and he'd informed her he intended to meet Will and see if he passed muster. She'd cringed at the thought, but now it didn't matter. Will didn't care to see her again.

A knock at the door reverberated through the house, then it came again. She swung her legs over the edge of the bed and pushed to her feet. If it was Jerold, she'd send him packing with no doubt to her feelings this time. She was in no mood to be trifled with after losing Will and Laura.

Gracie threw open the door, her lips wide to get in the first word before Jerold could speak, but they closed as soon as she saw Will, hat in his hands. Stunned, she stood with her heart thudding a dull beat in her ears.

He gestured toward the parlor through the open door. "May I come in and speak to you?"

She nodded and stepped aside. Papa would be home any moment, and they probably should sit on the porch until he arrived, but right now she didn't care about propriety. She simply wanted to get this over—there was nothing romantic about his request. Will had come to make sure she'd understood his demand at the pond about Laura.

"Would you care for coffee?"

"No, thank you. May I sit?" He stood uneasily before an overstuffed chair.

"Please." She perched on one across the room. "I know why you're here, and I'll honor your request not to see Laura again."

He bolted from the chair and stood, towering over her. "That's not why I'm here." He clutched his hat so hard the brim crinkled. "I owe you an apology, Gracie."

"What?" She met his gaze for the first time. "No you don't."

"Yes. I was harsh to you at the pond, and I had no right." He sucked in a sharp breath and plunged on. "Curt gave me a good talking to when I got back, and he's right. I've been letting guilt over my sister's death color everything I do with Laura—and with how I've been treating you."

She listened, not sure she understood. "Could you explain, please?"

He nodded and settled onto the edge of the sofa nearby, only an arm's length from her. "You are so similar to my sister that it scared me. The same bright, sunny personality—the same sense of adventure and fun. You've been trying to disguise it these past few days, I think maybe to show me you aren't a danger to Laura, but it's who you are.

"Part of me has been worried for Laura, but I realized today that the other part has been terrified to allow myself to fall in love with you, on the chance you might get hurt. Or worse, do something foolish and die. I couldn't face that possibility, so I pushed you away."

Gracie sat still, trying to take it all in. Only one thing he'd said stood out. "Terrified to allow yourself to fall in love with me? Is that what you said?" Joy tried to sing through her heart, but fear that she'd heard wrong tamped it back down.

He nodded then reached out his hand and clasped hers. "I know it's too soon to say this—we haven't known each other long—but I care for you, Gracie, more than I've ever cared for any woman. I want a chance to get to know you better. To court you as a woman like you deserves to be courted and, I hope, win your love in return." He paused and sucked in another breath. "That is, unless that fellow who was here the other day has beat me to it."

She giggled and shook her head. "Jerold Carnegie? I think not. I sent him packing a few minutes after you left. I had nothing to do with him appearing on my doorstep, nor did I care to have him stay." She sobered as another thought smote her. "But what about Carissa?"

"Who?" His face was a total blank.

Gracie relaxed. "Miss Sanderson, Laura's teacher. I thought you might be interested in her."

His eyes widened. "She's a very nice lady, but she seems a bit tame. Definitely nothing like a fiery redhead I know." He raised the back of her hand to his lips and pressed a kiss there, long and slow. "Would you allow me to court you, Gracie? With the hope that one day I might win you as my bride?"

A step sounded in the open doorway and Gracie looked up. Her father stood there, a bemused look on his face. "So what do you have to say to this young man's question, my girl? I've been talking to Curt Warren about Will, and it seems he's a good worker and an honest man." He turned his attention to Will. "And while I'd have preferred he ask my permission to court you first, I'll allow it if it's what you want."

Will pushed to his feet and drew Gracie with him, nodding his thanks to her father. He waited, both of her hands held in his.

She raised her face and smiled. "I'd like that very much. I've known since the day you pulled me out of that tree and I landed in your lap that I cared for you." Warmth flowed into her cheeks, but she kept her gaze steady on his. "I'm a bit forward, but you'll have to take me as I am. Although I'll promise not to climb any more trees if that makes you happy."

Will drew Gracie closer. "I don't care how many trees you climb, or teach Laura to climb. I'll even build you both a tree house if you'd like that. I've decided to trust both of you to God's loving care and quit worrying. As long as you'll be careful and promise me one thing."

Her heart skittering like a filly bounding through a meadow in the springtime, she nodded. "Anything."

"I know I said we'd court, but since you said you care, I hope you won't make me wait too long." He leaned down and pressed a tender kiss to her lips.

"I'm praying you'll consider becoming my summertime bride—that you might marry me in a couple months, before fall sets in, under the dogwood tree where we first met. There's nothing that would make me happier."

Gracie looked at her father and saw his happy expression. She laid her cheek against Will's chest to feel his own racing heartbeat and sighed. "Nor me. A summertime bride sounds about as perfect as anything can be."

The Lumberjack's Bride

by Pam Hillman

Chapter 1

L ucy Denson wove her way among the towering pines, her attention focused on the steady buzz of a crosscut saw up ahead.

She hefted the basket, filled with lunch for the lumberjacks, and huffed out a breath, blowing a wispy strand of hair off her face. Why Papa had insisted on returning to Mississippi was beyond her. Of course when her cousin Jack's logging business had taken off and he'd asked for help, Papa had felt obliged to leave Chicago and use his bookkeeping skills to manage the books for Jack and his partner. She wrinkled her brow as the tip of her boot scattered the remains of a rotten log and black beetles scampered out. Seemed like Jack could have found someone else to keep the books.

His own sister, Annabelle, had been a schoolteacher. She was perfectly capable of tallying a column of numbers. But no, tradition dictated the books had to be managed by a man, so her father had packed up the entire family and moved them all back to Mississippi, and no amount of begging could induce him to let her stay in Chicago.

Tears smarted her eyes.

And just when Deotis Reichart had started to take notice of her. Her father's impetuous midlife crisis had ruined the chance for the life she dreamed of. She pushed thoughts of what she'd left behind in Chicago to the back of her mind, hiked her skirt, and navigated a steep incline. Right now she'd promised her cousin Annabelle she'd deliver thick slabs of roast beef sandwiches and roasted potatoes to the men working on the ridge up ahead. She might not be able to cook, but she was willing to help out in any way she could. She paused and cocked her head, listening for the saws.

And that's when she spotted the spiderweb stretched between two trees. She stopped and stared, the intricate design eye-catching in its simplicity. She stood transfixed, trying to memorize the pattern so she could repeat it with her crochet needles. She regretted not having anything to sketch the web. After all, she hadn't expected to run into such beauty when she'd ventured into the woods.

The web quivered, and her gaze snapped upward where she spotted a large yellow-and-black spider. She shuddered and stepped back. The web design was fascinating, but she could do without the spider. The spell broken, she veered around the web, left the spider to its business, and started off again. The sooner she delivered the men's lunch, the sooner she could head back to the cook shack, where the smoke from the stove kept the spiders, mosquitoes, and bugs at bay.

And maybe there she could scrounge up a scrap of paper to sketch the web.

∞

"Keep sawing." Eli Everett's muscles ached with fatigue as he pushed the crosscut saw toward his little brother, Josiah.

An amused grunt rumbled through his chest. He'd have to amend his thinking. Josiah had shot up like a green sapling in the last year, and no one would dare call him little anymore. Hard work behind a crosscut saw had honed his muscles until Eli wouldn't want to be caught on his bad side. Not that that was likely to happen. Josiah was as easygoing as a lazy dog in the shade.

A creaking noise interrupted his musing, and his attention focused sharply on the job at hand. He could feel Josiah letting up on his end of the saw, a sure sign his brother thought it was time to make a run for it. Eli gripped the handles and thrust the saw back toward his brother, an unspoken order that they needed to stay with the tree a few minutes longer.

Suddenly the creak turned into a full-fledged groan that didn't let up. They paused, easing the saw out to protect it from damage. His head tilted back. He lifted his gaze upward, skimming the tall, long length of the loblolly pine. The top swayed, and he nodded at Josiah.

"Timber!" Josiah took off at a run.

Eli turned, and that's when he saw her.

Right in the path of the severed pine tree.

Head down, she picked her way toward him, a wide-brimmed straw hat shading her features, pink gauzy ribbons tied under her chin swaying gently in the breeze. Her gaze lifted and met his. In a split second, Eli took in everything about her, from the brilliant blue of her eyes, hair as pale as fresh-cut lumber, the light-colored sprigged skirt cinched about her narrow waist, to the white shirtwaist and crocheted shawl draped across her shoulders, even the basket looped over her arm.

Then he was moving, running toward her.

The large, brawny man charged at Lucy like a raging bull. She froze.

Before she could think or move, her gaze shifted up and over his head to the tree, big enough to flatten half a dozen cable cars on the streets of Chicago. The tree swayed then, almost in slow motion, began to fall—directly toward her. A scream bubbled up from her chest, only to cut off abruptly as the lumberjack slammed into her. The impact knocked the breath from her, but she felt them rolling, everything a hazy blur as her straw hat was ripped away, and twigs jerked pins from her hair.

Her crazy, tilting world stopped, and she found herself on the forest floor, the lumberjack's broad frame hunched over her, sheltering her. She reached to push him away, but froze, when over his shoulder, she caught a glimpse of the monster tree hurtling toward earth. She whimpered, squeezed her eyes shut, and tucked her face against the roughness of the man's work shirt.

Please, God, don't let me die.

A mighty shudder shook the ground.

Lucy didn't move; she barely even let herself breathe. Everything slammed into her stunned brain at once. The fact that she was alive. The utter stillness of the man who'd protected her with his life. The quiet of the forest. No sound. Nothing. Not a leaf stirred, no birds chirped, not even a cricket could be heard.

Then she felt it, or heard it. She wasn't sure.

The rapid staccato beat of the lumberjack's heart where her ear pressed against his broad chest. She listened as the rhythm slowed, keeping time with her own heartbeat's gradual return to normal. She pulled in a shuddering breath as the truth of what had almost happened struck her full force. Her rescuer stirred, pushed himself up, and gazed down at her. Shadow-filled dark eyes probed hers, then swept her face.

"Ma'am?" His voice rolled over her, breathless and jagged like the teeth of the crosscut saw he'd tossed aside as he rushed to her rescue. "Are you all right?"

"I—" Lucy stammered, trying to control the trembling that set in. "I—I think so."

Chapter 2

When tears pooled in her liquid-blue eyes, Eli panicked. He pushed himself up from the ground, reached for the woman—not much more than a slip of a girl—and stood her on her feet. She swayed, trembling.

"What in heaven's name were you thinking?" He growled, hands anchored on his hips to keep from reaching out to steady her again. If he did, he was afraid she'd dissolve into a puddle of tears at his feet, and then he'd be in a logjam for sure.

"Annabelle sent me—"

"You could have been killed." The more he thought about how close she'd come to getting flattened by that tree, the madder he got. He grabbed her dainty little straw hat off the ground and shoved it at her. "Don't ever do that again."

Her blue eyes flashed fire, and bright pink rushed back into her face which had been pale only moments before. She plopped the hat on her head and shoved her mass of golden curls up under it before crossing her arms and glaring down her pert little nose at him. Or at least it felt like she glared down at him, which was ridiculous since she was a good eight inches shorter than he was. "Rest assured, Mr. Everett, I won't do it again. I'll just leave your lunch on the ground and you can fight the ants for it."

She whirled, lifted her skirts, and marched away.

"Eli?" He glanced over his shoulder. Josiah stood near, looking worried, the basket dangling from one hand. "Is she all right?"

"Yeah. She's fine." Eli jerked his slouch hat off, slapped it against his leg, and huffed out a breath. "Maybe that little scare will teach her to be more careful in the woods."

"Must be Jack's cousin from Chicago." Josiah let out a shrill whistle to call their brothers in for lunch then plopped down on a stump. He dug into the basket, unearthing a thick, juicy-looking roast beef sandwich. "Wasn't Jack's uncle supposed to arrive this week and take over as ink slinger?"

"That's what they said." Eli stared after the young woman as she picked her way through the woods, her pink flower-sprigged dress held clear of the forest floor. Nobody had told him Mr. Denson's daughter was so pretty or that she'd be helping out at the camp kitchen.

Josiah swallowed a bite of his sandwich and nodded in the direction Miss Denson had gone. "You gonna eat your lunch or go tell her she's headed in the wrong direction?"

Eli scowled, slapped his hat on his head, and stomped off after her. The sooner he got her out of the woods and back with Annabelle and Maggie, the sooner he could get his mind back on his work.

As he drew near, she turned, her brow wrinkled in confusion. "I seem to be. . ."

"Lost?" he growled.

"Not exactly lost. Just turned around a bit." A pale pink blush swept over her cheeks, like the gentle sweep of a summer breeze. "If you could just point me in the right direction."

"I'll do better than that. The skid road's this way." Eli gestured toward the road and let her precede him. She hadn't gone three steps before she stumbled over an exposed root. Grabbing her elbow, he kept her upright.

She threw him a grateful glance. "Thank you, Mr. Everett."

"Name's Eli. We don't stand on ceremony around here." Eli didn't bother to ask how she knew who he was. He figured Annabelle had filled her in on every man who worked for Sipsey Creek Lumber and Logging. "You're Miss Denson, aren't you?"

She nodded. "I didn't realize you and your brother were so far away when I volunteered to deliver your lunch. It sounded as if you were right over the ridge from the road."

"Sound carries out here in the woods."

"I realize that now."

Finally, they arrived at the log road, a long swath weaving its way through the pine forest toward base camp. Miss Denson glanced right then left, her brow puckered in a frown. "Which way—"

Eli motioned left and started that way.

∽

Lucy hurried to keep up with Eli Everett's long-legged stride. "I'm sorry for taking you away from your work."

"It's all right." He shrugged.

She *was* sorry, but glad he'd taken it upon himself to show her the way back. She'd been so focused on following the sound of the saw she hadn't really paid attention to her surroundings, and one tree looked much the same as another.

The sound of jingling harnesses reached them, and just around the next bend, she spotted Maggie and Annabelle headed toward them in the wagon they'd driven out to the woods to feed the men. Maggie waved and pulled the wagon to a halt, a look of relief on her face. "Oh there you are, Lucy. We were getting worried."

Annabelle's gaze swept her from head to toe then shifted to Eli, one eyebrow lifted in question. Lucy glanced at her dirt-smudged dress, *tsking* at a rip in the hem. If her clothes were any indication, she must look a sight. She lifted one hand and made sure her hair was still restrained under her hat. Unless she missed her guess, she'd lost some of her pins, but she couldn't very well repin her hair in front of Mr. Everett.

"I had a bit of an accident. I arrived just as the Everetts—Eli and his brother—finished cutting down a tree."

Annabelle and Maggie gasped in unison. "Are you hurt?"

"I'm fine. Really."

"She almost got killed," Eli growled.

Lucy sighed. "But I didn't. You made sure of that."

"Thank goodness you weren't hurt." Maggie shook her head, looking at Lucy like she should've had more sense than to walk up on two men felling a tree. Well, she'd learned her lesson. She wouldn't do it again. Ever. She eyed her ruined dress, confident she'd avoid the woods completely in the future.

Maggie scooted over on the wagon seat. "Well, we'd better get back to the kitchen. Supper will be here before you know it. And Annabelle isn't feeling well."

For the first time, Lucy noticed how pale her cousin looked. "Annabelle?"

Her cousin smiled wanly and pressed a hand to her midriff. "I'm fine. Just a little nauseated."

Eli handed Lucy into the wagon and tipped his hat. A faint grin played with the edges of his mouth. "Miss Denson, my ma used to ring a cowbell when she brought meals to the woods. We'd all come running like a herd of cattle when we heard Ma's bell. Worked like a charm every time."

"Thank you, Mr. Everett." Lucy inclined her head and smoothed her skirt. "A herd of cattle. I'll keep that in mind."

∽

Long strides took Eli back to where Josiah, Caleb, and Gideon were just finishing up their lunch. Josiah waved him over and handed him a sandwich. "Here. I saved you some. Did you get little Miss Priss back to safety?"

Eli chuckled at Josiah's description of the prim and proper Miss Denson.

At least she'd been prim and proper before a tree had almost pinned her to the ground. But even the ripped and torn dress, her smudged face, and disheveled hair hadn't robbed her of her cultured look. "Don't be too hard on her. She's from the city. She couldn't have known how dangerous it could be out here."

"Is she pretty?" Caleb wiped his mouth on his sleeve and grinned.

Gideon snorted. "Even if she was, she wouldn't look twice at you, you big lug."

"Better me than you, that's for sure."

Eli ignored their banter and dug around in the basket Lucy—Miss Denson—had left with them. He frowned when he unearthed a pinecone. Must have fallen in the basket when the tree toppled from the sky. He tossed it to the side, then grabbed a sandwich and took a bite of the savory roast beef sandwiched between two thick slices of bread.

Good, almost as tender as his mother's. He wondered if she'd had a hand in cooking today's meal. His ma missed being able to cook for the lumber crews, but after arthritis set in, her fingers were too drawn and stiff to do much cooking, other than for herself. All she'd ever known was cooking. They'd travelled all over the south, from lumber camp to lumber camp, his pa logging, his ma working in more camp kitchens than a body could count. He and his brothers had cut their teeth on saw blades and loblolly pines.

"So, what do you think, big brother?" Caleb pressed.

"About what?"

"About Miss Denson. Is she pretty?"

Eli scowled. Oh, she was pretty all right, but she didn't seem to be the type to be interested in a lumberjack. "I don't think we'll be seeing much more of Miss Denson. She's a city girl through and through."

Josiah stabbed a finger at the remaining sandwich. "You gonna eat that?"

"Naw. Go ahead. But you'd better be quick. We've got work to do."

Within minutes, they finished their meal and packed up the basket, set it aside and went back to work. The crew set about stripping the limbs on one side of the tree from top to bottom, then used log rollers to roll the heavy tree over to get to the other side.

Eli grabbed his axe and started swinging at the smaller limbs, and that's when he saw it; a soft, gauzy crocheted shawl nestled on the forest floor. Blue. Like her eyes. He reached for the flimsy material and a vision of Lucy Denson crushed beneath the tree slammed into him. How close she'd come to death. How close they'd both come when he rushed to save her.

He tucked the shawl inside his shirt, the cotton warm against his skin. As he picked up his axe, he took a deep breath and released it slowly, closed his eyes, bowed his head, and offered up a prayer of thankfulness that they'd both been spared.

Chapter 3

But I can't."

"Oh, I'm sorry, Lucy." Jack's wife rushed about the outdoor summer kitchen, her brow wrinkled. "With Annabelle sick, I wasn't thinking about your accident. Are you feeling all right?"

"I'm fine. Really." Lucy ducked her head, wishing Maggie would just forget about her near accident. "It's just that I don't know how to fry chicken."

Maggie shoved a bowl of potatoes into her hands. "Well, just peel these potatoes, and I'll take care of the rest."

Lucy set to work, glad of something to do to help. The creak of Mrs. Everett's rocking chair set a frenetic pace as she rocked Maggie's baby, along with the clatter of pots and pans as Maggie prepared supper for the logging crews.

"I'm sorry, child, I should have warned you to be careful." Mrs. Everett's lined face filled with worry. "The woods can be dangerous when the fallers are around."

"It's not your fault, Mrs. Everett." Lucy dipped her head, face flaming. "Any idiot should have known better."

The rocking chair stopped, and a storm cloud gathered on the elderly woman's brow. "Did my son say that?"

"No ma'am." Eli Everett hadn't called her an idiot, but he might as well have. She'd seen the look in his eyes, the one that told her he thought she was a brainless twit who wouldn't know how to get out of the rain—or out of the way of a falling tree.

Mrs. Everett hefted Maggie's colicky baby higher on her shoulder and started rocking again, her foot tilting the rocker back and forth with dizzying speed. "He'd better be glad. I might be old and decrepit, but I'd take a stick to that boy if he said such a thing to a lady."

Lucy ducked her head, hiding a smile. The idea of the tiny, white-haired woman taking a switch to her grown son seemed ludicrous, but the fierce glare in her eyes left no doubt she knew how to give all four of her boys a tongue-lashing they'd never forget if they disobeyed her.

Maggie rushed to the stove and opened the damper. "Oh no, look at the time. The men will be here soon, and I haven't even cut up the chickens yet. It'll take forever to fry it all."

"Maggie, why don't you make chicken stew or dumplings? It would be faster and would fill those men up in a hurry."

Maggie scrunched up her nose. "Frying chicken for fifteen men was not my idea. But it's Samuel's favorite, and today's their anniversary, so Annabelle wanted fried chicken tonight."

Mrs. Everett grunted. "Just wait until she has two hundred to cook for. She'll change her tune right quick."

Two hundred men? The very thought made Lucy queasy. She peeled faster, wishing she could do more to help, but the sight of raw chicken turned her stomach. She finished the potatoes, wiped her hands, and took a deep breath. Poor Maggie looked as flustered as a swarm of bees after a honeysuckle vine. "Maggie, what else can I do?"

Maggie spared her a glance as she cut up a chicken. "Mix up a batch of cornbread. Use that washtub over there, and triple whatever you're used to making. Hopefully, it'll be enough."

Cornbread. It couldn't be that hard, could it? Lucy grabbed the washtub and searched for the cornmeal. That much she knew.

Mama had always shooed her out whenever she'd ventured into the kitchen, saying her daughter's presence made her nervous. Instead, Lucy had turned her talents toward keeping the house spotless and volunteering on various committees at church. She had a knack for decorating, so she'd been quite busy since she'd finished school. At least until her father had plucked them up and moved them to the backwoods of Mississippi. From the looks of the rough housing the lumberjacks lived in and the simple clapboard church, she didn't expect to find many opportunities to pretty things up around here. She plopped the cornmeal beside the washtub and glanced around. What now?

Her panicked gaze met Mrs. Everett's, and without missing a beat, the elderly woman nodded at a tub on the shelf above her head. "Lucy, there's the lard, right up there. Maggie, where are the eggs?"

And just like that, Mrs. Everett gently guided Lucy through the ingredients needed to mix up the cornbread. Lucy shared a smile with the elderly woman and stirred the grainy mixture, pleased with her efforts. Maybe she could learn to cook after all.

The baby started fussing then let out a howl. Maggie groaned. "Not now, Aaron. Mama's busy."

Mrs. Everett rocked harder, trying to appease the crying child. But to no avail. He just cried harder. "It's no use, Maggie. You might as well go feed him. He's not going to hush until you do."

Maggie looked around the disaster of a kitchen. "But—"

"Go on. Lucy and I can finish up here."

"I'll be right back." Maggie clutched her baby and headed toward the cabin Jack had built at the edge of the clearing, when he'd been courting Maggie almost two years ago.

Lucy stared at the mound of raw chicken, wondering how she'd manage. Gingerly, she reached for a piece of chicken, knowing it wasn't going to cook itself.

"Never you mind about frying chicken, Lucy. Boil it and make dumplings."

Relieved to have someone else in charge, Lucy did as she was told. Soon the chicken was boiling in the water meant for the potatoes. "Now what?"

Mrs. Everett nodded toward the stove. "Turn the damper down and let that grease cool a bit. Fried potatoes go a long way toward filling up a bunch of hungry men." She flexed her arthritic fingers. "I wish I could help, but these stiff hands can barely hold a knife anymore. It's a pitiful thing to be old and useless."

"That's all right, Mrs. Everett. You've been more help than you know."

"Might as well call me Ma. Everybody does." Mrs. Everett rocked and kept Lucy busy for the next hour.

"Check on the cornbread."

"How's the chicken?"

"Stir those peas."

"Don't forget the potatoes."

"Oh no, the potatoes." Lucy grabbed a spatula and a dishcloth. She moaned. "They're sticking."

"They'll be fine. Close that damper. Yes, that one. Put a little water in the pan and put a lid on. In a few minutes, they'll be fine. And on the next batch, toss 'em with a little flour. That'll keep 'em from sticking."

By the time Maggie returned with Aaron, Lucy had made headway into the mound of fried potatoes, three pones of cornbread sat in the warming oven, and chicken and dumplings simmered over the reservoir on the back of the stove. And per Mrs. Everett's instructions, Lucy had just fished her first batch of doughnut holes out of the grease and sprinkled them with cinnamon and sugar.

Maggie stopped and stared at the kitchen. "I thought you said you couldn't cook."

Lucy grinned, reached over, and hugged Mrs. Everett, leaving a streak of flour on her weathered cheek. "I can't. But Ma Everett can. So between the two of us, we managed to get the job done."

Chapter 4

At the end of the day, Eli and Josiah took a dip in Sipsey Creek, washing off the grime and sweat from a hard day's work. He tossed his knapsack on the bed, and Lucy Denson's crocheted shawl spilled out across the patchwork quilt.

"You coming?" Josiah called out as he hurried out the door and bounded down the steps, toward the tables set up under the lean-to in the shade of the pines.

"Yeah, be right there." Eli walked to the door, fingering the shawl even as he spotted Lucy flitting about the summer kitchen. He shoved the shawl back in his pack. She wouldn't want him flaunting her mishap in front of the other men. He'd give it back to her later.

Minutes later, he stood in line, plate in hand. Maggie and Lucy ladled chicken and dumplings, fried potatoes, peas, and thick slabs of cornbread on each plate. His stomach rumbled.

"How'd it go today, Everett?" Samuel Frazier slapped him on the back. "Your crew do okay?"

Eli nodded. "We felled a dozen trees and snaked 'em out to the log road. A couple of real good punkins. Couldn't ask for better."

"Any problems?"

Eli's gaze met Lucy's across the makeshift sideboard, and a becoming blush stole over her cheeks. She lowered her gaze and ladled a helping of dumplings onto Josiah's plate. "Nope. Everything went fine."

"Good to hear."

Eli and Samuel moved up in line. Samuel frowned and looked around. "Where's Annabelle?"

"She wasn't feeling well earlier and went home." Maggie took Samuel's plate, heaped it full of potatoes and peas, then held it out to Lucy for a generous serving of chicken and dumplings. Maggie pushed the plate back at her brother-in-law, a smile playing on her lips. "And here's your supper. You can share with Annabelle, but I doubt she'll be able to eat anything."

Samuel blanched. "What's the matter with her?"

"Maybe you should ask your wife that."

The man hurried away, and Maggie and Lucy filled Eli's plate. At the end of the table, a huge pan of cinnamon and sugarcoated bear sign made his mouth water. He popped one of the doughnuts in his mouth and groaned at the sugary sweetness.

As good as his own mother's.

"Maggie-girl, you and Annabelle outdid yourselves today."

Maggie shrugged. "Wasn't us. With Annabelle sick and Aaron being so fussy, Lucy did most of the cooking today."

"Really?" Eli's gaze snapped to Lucy.

She lifted a pale eyebrow.

Oops, he'd offended her. He grabbed a handful of bear sign and nodded in appreciation. "Tastes a lot like Ma's."

As he searched for a place to sit, he caught the glance Lucy shared with his mother. His mother smiled and nodded, looking happier than he'd seen her in a long time.

☙

Lucy frowned at Eli, who sat hunched over at one of the rough-hewn tables, his attention focused on his plate. He shoveled food into his mouth like he hadn't eaten all week.

She wrinkled her nose. No table manners there. But the other men were eating with just as much gusto, laughing, talking, and devouring their food at an alarming rate. She bit her lip, the sheer abandon they exhibited while eating making her nervous. Where were their table manners? Why, Deotis would never make such a spectacle of himself.

But regardless of the way they were eating, she couldn't help but be pleased they seemed to like her cooking—or Mrs. Everett's, anyway. She'd cooked a meal and nobody pushed their plates away. But could she do it again? The last few hours had passed in a blur, with Mrs. Everett not giving her a minute's rest. "*Close the damper.*" Open the damper. "*Remove the doughnuts, no, the—bear sign, from the grease.*" Hurry! Set those dumplings to the side before they scorch. Scorched dumplings weren't fit for a cat to eat," she'd said.

And on and on. Lucy's head was spinning from the instructions, and she'd never wanted to set foot in a kitchen again.

Until the ravenous logging crew devoured what she'd cooked, scooted back the rough-hewn benches, and lined up for seconds. Even Eli, one of the last to arrive, pushed back from the table, made an end-run around the other men, grabbed a handful of bear sign, and taking his mother's arm, led her away toward a two-room shanty nestled among the trees. As the men wandered away, Maggie scraped the last of the potatoes into a battered metal pan. "Well, that went over well. We'll get things cleaned up and get ready for breakfast."

"Breakfast?"

"Oh, it's nothing like this. Flapjacks and ham, mostly. Sorghum molasses and butter. The men will want to be through eating and in the woods by daylight though, so we have to get cracking mighty early. And if Annabelle is still not feeling well—"

"Daylight?" Lucy squeaked.

What had she gotten herself into?

Chapter 5

A clatter jerked Eli awake and he lay in the darkness, wondering what had stirred him from slumber before the gut-hammer sounded.

His brothers snored in their bunks in the shanty they'd built when they first arrived in Sipsey. They'd added a separate room for their mother, so she could have some privacy. Had his mother gotten out of bed? Fallen, maybe?

He swung his legs out of bed and padded on sock feet toward her room. She was still sleeping soundly. As he turned, he spotted the lantern on in the cook shack. Banging and a softly uttered exclamation drifted across the clearing.

Pulling on his trousers, he stomped into his boots and headed toward the kitchen. He'd grab a cup of coffee and watch the sunrise, then bring his mother a cup back so she could enjoy it in peace while the crews wolfed down breakfast before heading to the woods.

The sight that greeted him at the kitchen brought him up short. Lucy Denson stood in the middle of the shack, a cloud of flour hovering around her. "Lucy?"

She whirled, her blue eyes wide. "Oh Eli, what am I going to do?"

"What's the matter? Where's Maggie and Annabelle?"

"Annabelle's still not feeling well and Aaron has got the croup. Jack said Maggie would be here as soon as she could, but for me to go ahead and get started."

Eli glanced around the kitchen at the cold stove and the fixings for flapjacks. He rubbed his neck and squinted at Lucy. "Uh, Lucy, have you ever fixed flapjacks before?"

Her eyes filled with tears. "I've never fixed any meal before last night."

"Never?"

She shook her head. "If it hadn't been for your mother's help, I don't know what I would have done."

"I see." And he did see. Those dumplings and the bear sign had tasted just like his mother's cooking. He rubbed his hands together. "Well, the crew will be here anytime, so let's get started."

She held out both hands, warding him off. "Oh, but you can't. It's not your job."

"Doesn't matter. It's got to be done and looks like it's you and me this morning." Eli hunkered down and opened the firebox on the stove and stirred up the ashes. At least Maggie had banked the fire real good last night. "Do you know how to work the stove?"

"No. Mama wouldn't let me near the kitchen." Even in the dim light cast from the lantern, the misery on Lucy's face was evident. She leaned in close, a look of fierce determination on her face. "I know I'm next to useless in the kitchen, but I'm willing to learn if you'll just show me."

Eli jostled her shoulder. "Hey, don't say that. Anybody who can cook as fine a meal as you did last night, just from Ma's instructions, can learn how to get the stove going in the mornings and whip up a batch of flapjacks."

"You think so?" She sniffed and blinked, her eyelashes fluttered against her cheeks, then swept up to reveal eyes as blue as a clear summer sky. Eli froze, lost in the bottomless pools of her sky blue eyes.

He cleared his throat and jerked open the damper on the stove. "I do. Now, listen carefully."

∞

Lucy watched every move Eli made. His large work-roughened hands got the stove going, sliced ham, started frying it, then showed her how to mix up a batch of pancakes.

"Flapjacks are about the easiest things in the world to make. As long as they're not raw or burnt, the men won't care." He plopped some lard on the large griddle and used a spatula to spread it out. He sprinkled water on the flat surface, and it sizzled and splattered. Lucy jumped, but he snagged her around the waist and pulled her back.

"It's not going to hurt you. See, when the water sizzles and dances across the griddle, the stove's just the right temperature. Now, pour your batter. Not much, about the size of a saucer."

Lucy smiled as the circular rounds of batter formed perfectly on the griddle. But the bowl grew heavy, and on her third attempt, she poured way too much. Eli grabbed the bowl and tipped it up, laughing. "Enough. You won't be able to flip that monster over!"

"I'm sorry." One arm wrapped securely around the large bowl, the other clutching the spatula, Lucy rubbed her face against her sleeve, trying to push a wisp of hair off her face. "It's heavy."

Eli reached out and tucked her hair behind her ear. His brown eyes crinkled at the corners, and his gaze shifted and moved lazily across her face. His thumb rubbed softly against her cheek, and she shivered at his touch.

"You've got flour on your face."

"I'm—I'm not surprised." Lucy whispered past the lump in her throat. She needed to move away, to put some space between them, but there wasn't much room between the stove and the long sideboard, where they served the meals. She took a shuddering breath, willing her lungs to breathe.

Eli's eyelids fell to half-mast and his gaze dropped to her lips. For a wild moment, Lucy wondered if this big, brawny man who towered over her was going to kiss her. Her heart pounded. He wasn't. . .she didn't. . .

An incessant clanging rent the air and Lucy jumped, nearly losing her grip on the bowl of batter. The men's wake-up call had her turning toward the griddle. "Well," she said, her voice high-pitched from sheer nerves—"the men will be here any minute. What next?"

Eli leaned around her, plucked the spatula from her nerveless fingers and flipped a flapjack over, the batter perfectly browned. "You just flip 'em when they're brown, and that's it. All right?"

Lucy nodded, taking the spatula from him.

Maggie came rushing in, grabbed an apron, and tied it on. "Oh Lucy, bless you."

"It wasn't—"

Eli touched his fingers to her lips. *"Shh."*

Then winking, he grabbed a cup, poured himself a cup of coffee he'd made, and settled onto one of the benches. "Morning, Maggie."

Chapter 6

Eli sipped his coffee as one by one the men crowded under the lean-to. They jostled for position near the stove and the coffee he'd set to boiling earlier. He frowned. Or were they just getting closer to Lucy? Even Caleb, who didn't even like coffee, stood near the stove.

Every single one of them dwarfed her slender frame as she focused on making flapjacks. Where Maggie rushed about the open area flipping ham and frying potatoes, Lucy stood firmly in front of the griddle, watching the flapjacks as if her life depended on getting them just right.

She eased up a flapjack and peered underneath. Seemingly satisfied they were brown enough, she scooped the cakes up one at a time and piled them on a platter, then carried them to Maggie. Maggie grabbed the huge platter and placed it on the table. "We'll need more."

His lips twitched when Lucy's eyes grew wide. "More?"

Maggie darted away, forking up ham and whipping around so fast it made his head spin. As the men dug into their breakfast, Lucy turned back to the stove and carefully poured out another batch of flapjacks.

Eli shook his head at the precise way she attempted to make each pancake the exact same size, all of them perfectly round, perfectly browned. She'd learn the men didn't care what the food looked like as long as it was reasonably tasty and kept their bellies full until their next meal.

∞

Lucy felt Eli's gaze on her, but kept her attention firmly on the task at hand. She knew she needed to help Maggie with the rest of the meal, but she was afraid she'd burn the flapjacks if she left them unattended. Better to stay at her station than to show how utterly incompetent she was in the kitchen.

Maggie single-handedly kept the men supplied with fried potatoes, ham, coffee, butter, and syrup, while all Lucy could do was cook flapjacks. Her face heated; she pressed her lips together and peeked to see if this latest batch was done. Satisfied they were, she flipped them over. She eyed the pale yellow orbs. They didn't look done enough. Maybe she should flip them back over. Frowning, she studied the pancakes, trying to decide what to do. Was the stove hot enough? Did she need to open the damper? Or add more wood?

Maggie hurried to the stove, the empty platter in her hand. "Those ready?"

Lucy poked at the flapjacks. "I'm not sure."

Maggie grabbed the spatula and deftly flipped one over. "They'll do."

Within seconds, she'd stacked all the flapjacks on the platter and tossed it on the table. Forks stabbed at the golden cakes, ripping them apart as the men grabbed pieces off the platter. They slathered the flapjacks with globs of butter and sorghum molasses and hunkered over them, shoveling the food into their mouths.

Lucy shook her head at the free-for-all as the men devoured the flapjacks, the rest of Maggie's ham, and six pots of coffee. A man with shoulders like an ox stood, reached across the table and picked up the leftover potatoes, dumped them on his plate and poured half a jar of tomato relish on top. He then picked up a fork and started eating without missing a beat.

Someone clanged on the gut-hammer and just as suddenly as they appeared, the men gulped down the last of their coffee and stood, moving away from the kitchen all as one unit. One bench fell over with a thud as they all trooped out. Lucy stared at the mess they'd left. She'd never seen anybody eat like that. Not even last night had been as chaotic. Eli tipped the bench upright and pushed it under the table, and her gaze met his.

He tipped his slouch hat toward her and Maggie then loped away, hoisting himself on the back of one of the log wagons headed toward the woods.

Chapter 7

By the time Uncle Hiram dismissed church Sunday morning and the congregation filed out to enjoy dinner on the ground, Lucy's smile felt frozen in place. They'd moved away eight years ago and, other than Uncle Hiram, her aunts, and her cousins Annabelle and Jack, she didn't remember any of the people who insisted they'd known her from the day she was born.

While her mother carried food from the wagon to the long tables spread out beneath the towering pines, Lucy enlisted her younger cousins to gather wildflowers. As the ladies laid old quilts and sheets on the tables, Lucy placed canning jars filled with flowers on top. The bright-colored flowers brought out the reds, yellows, and blues in the quilts. She stepped back, admiring her handiwork. She eyed the flowers on one of the tables, grabbed a couple out of a jar that was overflowing, and poked them in a skimpy one.

Aunt Eugenia smiled at her from the other side of the table. "I declare, Lucy, you sure do have a way with flowers. Sunday dinner has never looked so inviting. Would you be willing to help decorate for the Independence Day celebration?"

"Of course. What did you have in mind?" Lucy helped her aunt arrange the food on the table around the flowers.

"Well, flowers for starters. And the men will build a speaker's platform, so we'll need bunting for that."

"What about fireworks?" Lucy loved the annual fireworks display in Chicago. Another thing she'd miss this summer.

"Oh, none of that." Aunt Eugenia frowned. "Too noisy and scares the animals."

A pity about the fireworks. She loved the patterns and stunning colors they made against the night sky. If she could just transfer all of that sparkle to a crochet pattern. She pictured the explosion in her head. Maybe she could come up with a pattern that would look like fireworks. Red-white-and-blue pinwheels, with a bit of a spiral. Stars, maybe. . .

Aunt Eugenia continued to discuss the July Fourth celebration and with an effort Lucy pushed thoughts of crocheting and fireworks to the back of her mind. "Could you make place ribbons for the contests: pies, watermelon eating, canning? That sort of thing. And the men have all kinds of events planned. I'll have to ask Samuel how many so we have enough ribbons."

"Yes ma'am, I'm sure I can come up with something."

"That's settled, then." Aunt Eugenia smiled at someone behind her. "Ah Mrs. Everett, good to see you looking so well today."

Lucy turned to find Eli and his mother behind her. The elderly woman reached out to pat her on the arm, a secretive smile playing about her lips. "Been doing more cooking?"

"A little." Lucy's gaze lifted and met Eli's, and a blush stole over her cheeks. Had he told his mother about their early morning cooking class? From the look on his face, she guessed not. She turned back to Mrs. Everett. "How are you feeling, ma'am? I missed seeing you yesterday."

"I'm fine." She flexed her fingers. "My arthritis has been acting up and I think I overdid it the other day. But I do have a recipe I want to share with you. Eli wrote it down for me." She fumbled with the drawstrings on her purse. "Oh, drat it."

Eli plucked the black bag from his mother's fingers and pulled open the drawstring, his work-roughened hands large against the small bag. He extracted a crumpled piece of paper and handed it to Lucy. Their fingers brushed, and she lowered her gaze. "Thank you."

"It's *kolache*. Such sweet little pastries you've never tasted. I'll be glad to show you how to make them."

"Oh, wonderful." Aunt Eugenia clapped her hands. "You could make these for Independence Day, Lucy. It's always nice to have a new dish or two on the table."

Mrs. Everett leaned close and whispered, "Apricot is Eli's favorite."

Lucy blushed and refused to look at Eli. Had he heard what his mother had said? Instead, she glanced at the piece of paper. Scribbling filled the entire first page and spilled over onto the back. Oh my! "Thank you, ma'am, but I hate to put you to so much trouble."

"It's no trouble, dear. Just let me know if you decide to make them." Mrs. Everett's smile faded, and she patted Lucy on the arm. "Eli, can you help me to my rocker? My legs are getting a mite tired."

Lucy bit her lip in consternation. Had she offended Mrs. Everett by not being more enthusiastic about the recipe? But it looked so complicated! Worry furrowed her brow. She'd have to do something to make it right, starting with making sure she had all the ingredients on hand to try her hand at making kolaches.

૭

Eli leaned against the trunk of a pine tree along the creek bank, watching the children play in the water. Even some of the older folks had removed their shoes and waded along the edges, cooling off as the day grew hotter.

He grinned as Jack dipped little Aaron's bare feet in the water. Lucy and Maggie laughed as the boy squealed and kicked, splashing water all over Jack. When Maggie and Jack headed back to the wagon with a thoroughly wet child, Lucy's attention focused on the wild roses growing on the bank. She plucked one of the blooms and studied it carefully as she walked toward him, her attention totally captured by the pink bud.

She glanced up and her gaze met his. Her cheeks pinkened to the shade of the flower in her hand. "Oh, I didn't know you were there."

"Hope I didn't startle you." He gestured toward the flower. "What's so fascinating about a wild rose?"

She smiled, a shy, teasing smile, and holding the flower up, twirled it around. "I'm studying it so I can figure out how to crochet flowers that look like this."

"Hmm. I see."

Her brow arched. "Do you?"

He squinted and shook his head. "Not really."

She lifted the edges of her shawl, much like the one he'd found in the woods, except this one was white. He meant to return her other one, but every time he'd reach for it, he'd found an excuse to keep it longer. "See this pattern? Do you know what this is?"

He shook his head. "I can't say that I do."

"Pinecones."

He peered at the shawl and nodded. "Well, I'll be. That does look like pinecones."

She laughed, the soft tilt of her lips doing funny things to his insides. "I've been studying the way the cones look and finally got the hang of it a couple of days ago. I just finished this last night."

"It's pretty." He snapped his fingers. "Is that why I found a pinecone in our lunch the other day?"

"Probably." She smirked and held out the rest of the shawl. "See this? It's a spiderweb pattern."

Eli nodded. Even he could see the resemblance. He quirked an eyebrow at her. "Have you ever seen hoarfrost or the early morning dew on a spiderweb? It sparkles and shines in the sunlight. Like—" He shrugged. He didn't have words to describe it, but he knew she'd like it. He shifted and looked down at his dusty boots. "There's nothing like it."

"I'd love to see it sometime, but—" she squished up her nose in distaste. "I'm not fond of traipsing around in the woods, looking for spiderwebs."

"There's really not that much to be afraid of in the woods." He glanced at her and grinned. "Other than having a tree fall on you."

Chapter 8

L ucy placed the last jar of wildflowers on one of the tables and eyed her handiwork. She smiled, wondering if the loggers would notice the sprig of pine needles she'd stuck in the jars for added greenery, or the red-and-white-checked gingham strips she'd tied around the jars for more color.

"What are you doing?"

Lucy turned at the sound of Annabelle's voice. She hurried to her cousin's side and hugged her. "Are you feeling better? I've been worried."

"Much better. Until tomorrow morning, I expect."

"Oh." Lucy held her at arm's length. "Morning sickness?"

Annabelle laughed, a secretive smile on her face, a hand to her middle. "Yes. I think; I hope."

"Oh Annabelle." Lucy hugged her again. "Have you told Samuel?"

"Yes, last night. It's too early to know for sure, but Mama thinks so, too." She glanced around. "So, what are you doing with all these wildflowers?"

Lucy shrugged. "I thought I'd try to spruce things up a bit. The flowers are pretty, and I thought the men might enjoy them."

Annabelle shook her head as she tied on an apron. "Well, don't be surprised if they don't even notice."

The men lined up for supper as calm as could be. No pushing and shoving. They even removed their caps. They took their places at the tables, eating quietly and without their usual rowdy behavior. Annabelle leaned close to Lucy and whispered, "I wouldn't have believed it if I hadn't seen it. Even Ox is showing some table manners. Amazing."

Lucy stood at the sideboard, watching the men eat. Some of them talked among themselves, while the others ate silently, not even glancing up from their plates. She caught Eli's gaze and he gave her a tiny smile. A few of the men came back for seconds, and Lucy ladled hash onto their plates. Ox didn't move, but she noticed him eyeing his empty plate and the tomato relish at the end of the table.

Suddenly, it dawned on Lucy that she'd made a big mistake. The flowers made the men nervous. She tucked the pan of hash under her arm and hurried over to the tables. "More hash, Mr. Ox?"

"Why, thank ye, Miss Lucy." The big man smiled up at her and held out his plate.

She gave him two big helpings then continued to make the rounds, ladling hash on empty plates. The hum of conversation grew but didn't get to the deafening level it had been during previous meals. As soon as the men finished eating, they got up from her pretty table, careful not to jostle anything or overturn the mason jars. They didn't linger over coffee and dessert as they usually did. Respectfully, they thanked her, Maggie, and Annabelle for the meal before walking away.

But something was lacking.

And Lucy knew exactly what it was.

She'd tried to bring a bit of cheer to the table with her girly decorations but had only succeeded in tamping down the men's jovial spirit. Supper was a time for them to relax and enjoy each other's company after a hard day in the woods.

And she'd ruined it for them.

∽

Eli nursed his coffee and watched the men wander away.

Lucy slid onto the bench across from him with a plate of hash, but she didn't eat. Instead, she caught his gaze, looking miserable. "Looks like I messed up again."

Eli smiled at her through the gathering twilight. "How so?"

She reached out and flicked the tips of her fingers at the wildflowers. "I thought the men would appreciate the flowers, but they just made them uncomfortable. I should have left well enough alone."

Eli leaned forward and rested his elbows on the table. "Ah Lucy, they did appreciate them. And it wasn't the flowers, but the thought of messing up your pretty table that made them nervous. And, I imagine it made some of them think of home, of their mama's table, of family."

She stabbed her fork at her hash, her lip turned down in a mulish pout. "Well, I liked the men better the way they were."

He chuckled. "And how's that?"

"When they came rushing in here, pushing and shoving to be first in line, demanding seconds, and—"

"Licking their plates clean?"

"Well, maybe not that." She winced then shook her head.

"Does the fact that they don't have good table manners bother you?"

"Well, yes. No." She took a dainty bite of hash and wiped her mouth with a clean napkin. "But they proved they could act civilized if they wanted to."

Eli dipped his head and stared down at his coffee cup. He seriously doubted today's display of manners from the men would be good enough for polite society. Crumbling cornbread into your soup with your fingers and reaching across the table to grab whatever you needed wouldn't endear them to any woman's sense of propriety. "Civilized enough for Chicago's crusty upper class?"

A small laugh escaped her. "I wouldn't know how the upper class lives."

He motioned at the open-air summer kitchen, the rough-cut boards resting on saw horses, the hard-packed dirt floor. "I imagine this is a long way from what you're used to, regardless."

"Some." She shrugged. "In Chicago, Mama had dinner on the table promptly at six. And Papa better not be late or she was not happy."

"At least your pa gets home on time, now that he's working for Jack and Samuel."

"Last Christmas, I was invited to a Christmas ball by a..." Was that a blush that stole over her cheeks? "...a friend, and I felt a bit uncomfortable. Crystal chandeliers and silver spoons. I'd never seen so much food. And it was served in courses. Soup first, then fish, then—oh, I don't remember what came next, but it was wonderful. I sat across from one of the curators from the Newberry Library, and he talked about his travels abroad to secure books for the library. He'd been to Rome, London, and *Paris*. And there were flowers everywhere. The centerpiece was so big I couldn't even see over it. Can you imagine?"

Her gaze met his, shining from the memory of her fancy feast and even fancier dinner conversation. He wouldn't know a polite conversation if it hit him over the head, and he was still in the woods at six.

"Nope. I can't even picture such a thing." He glanced at the rough tables and Lucy's attempts to pretty the place up. A far cry from silver and crystal. "But it couldn't be any prettier than the wildflowers you picked for the men. Even if they didn't say anything, they appreciated your thoughtfulness."

"Why, thank you, Eli. What a sweet thing to say." She fingered the jar of wildflowers between them. "But it doesn't matter. There aren't going to be any more flowers, not here at least. The men should be able to enjoy their meal without worrying about toppling over a jar of flowers."

Her gaze lifted and captured his as she pushed the jar of flowers toward him. "Would you take these to your mother? I think she'd enjoy them, and I would hate to throw them out."

Eli reached out, his hand capturing hers against the coolness of the jar. He knew he should pull back, but he didn't want to let go, not yet. Slowly, he rubbed his thumb across the knuckles on the back of her hand. Her smile slipped and she lowered her gaze, but she didn't pull away.

"Lucy, got a letter for you today." Samuel strode into the circle of light cast by the lanterns. Lucy slipped her hand away, and Eli slid the jar of flowers toward him as if nothing had happened. But his heart thudded inside his chest like a runaway mule, just from touching her hand. Samuel handed Lucy her letter. "From some feller up in Chicago, named Deotis Reichart."

Eli took a sip of his cold coffee and scowled behind the rim of his cup. Was Deotis Reichart the friend who'd invited her to the fancy dinner party? He'd bet his best crosscut saw on it.

Chapter 9

"C ome on, I want to show you something."

Lucy looked up from the flapjack batter she'd just mixed up. The gut-hammer hadn't even sounded, and Eli stood in the early morning light, his dark eyes shining with excitement. Lucy eyed the big bowl of batter, frowning. "I can't right now. Can't it wait until later?"

"Nope. It'll be gone."

Annabelle took the bowl and shooed her away even as Lucy spotted Maggie hurrying across the yard toward the kitchen. "Go on. I think Maggie and I can handle everything for a while."

Eli grabbed her hand and led her away from the cook shack, down the road, past the sawmill toward Sipsey. A slight misty rain had fallen during the night, just enough to settle the dust on the roads. Lucy hurried to keep up with Eli. "Where are we going?"

"You'll see."

The sun rose behind them, bathing the grass and trees in early morning light. A half mile down the road, Eli paused and walked into a field of wildflowers, still damp with dew. He pointed. "Look."

Lucy stood on the log road, her gaze following his line of sight. There, suspended between two trees, was a spiderweb, the silky strands covered with millions of tiny raindrops. They watched in silence as the sun rose, shining its bright light on the web. The water droplets sparkled and shone in the light, like row upon row of delicate pearls. Lucy gasped in delight and pressed her hands together. "Oh Eli, it's spectacular."

"There's more." He squatted and pointed at the wildflowers. Lucy moved, her skirts swishing through the damp grass, but she barely noticed. She crouched by Eli's side, her attention focused on the beauty in front of her. Small cobwebs connected the flowers, tatting them together much like she tatted lace. Dew clung to the webs, the flowers, the green leaves. As her gaze took in the ethereal beauty, something miraculous happened. The sunlight hit one of the drops of dew at the perfect angle and reflected the flowers in the droplet.

Lucy clutched Eli's arm and whispered, "Look at that."

As the sun rose higher, the magical moment slipped away. The spiderweb no longer sparkled, the drops of dew started to dissipate. The flowers no longer sparkled like jewels, but Lucy still felt the awe of what she'd seen.

Eli stood, pulling her with him. Lucy shaded her eyes and looked up at him. "Thank you. That was one of the most beautiful sights I've ever seen."

His eyes met and held hers, a crooked smile twisting his mouth. "Prettier than the chandeliers in Chicago?"

She glanced around the meadow, God's handiwork still fresh and clear in her mind's eye. She nodded. "Yes, even prettier than that."

Chapter 10

"I learned how to make kolaches from a Czech immigrant in one of the lumber camps over in Louisiana," Mrs. Everett said.

Lucy bit her lip and concentrated on mixing the dough for the pastry, just as she'd been instructed. They made cream cheese, apricot, and blueberry, even though Mrs. Everett lamented not having any poppy seeds, a common staple in the ones the Czech cook had made. Lucy slid the pastries into the oven just as Maggie appeared with Aaron in tow.

"Hand me that sweet baby." Mrs. Everett snuggled Aaron against her and kissed his cheek as she rocked him back and forth.

Maggie sniffed appreciatively. "Hmmm, something smells good."

"Kolaches. They taste like doughnuts, but much better." Mrs. Everett smiled at Lucy. "It's Lucy's contribution to the Independence Day celebration."

"I'm not sure how they're going to turn out. I had a bit of trouble with the dough." Lucy turned at the sound of a wagon lumbering down the road toward them. "Oh, there's Papa with the decorations. But the kolaches—"

"They'll be fine." Maggie tied on an apron. "You go on ahead and take care of making everything look pretty. That is one chore I have no talent for."

"Are you sure?"

"Definitely. Now shoo. I've got a chicken potpie to make, and Mrs. Everett is going to help me. You're not the only one who's taking lessons from her."

Mrs. Everett chuckled.

Lucy took off her apron and fluffed her skirt. She'd worn her prettiest dress for today's festivities. She smoothed her hair back, grabbed her bonnet, and kissed Mrs. Everett on the cheek. "Thank you," she whispered.

"No. Thank you. It makes me happy that you young ones are learning how to cook these dishes." She smiled, her eyes twinkling. "You know good victuals are the way to a man's heart, don't you?"

Lucy's face flamed. "So they say."

❧

Once Eugenia got it into her head that it was going to rain on Independence Day, what started out as a simple speaker's platform ended up being a major project.

Eli pounded in a nail then wiped his brow. "I sure hope she's right about that rain, because it's going to be a scorcher."

"Aunt Eugenia's never wrong." Samuel laughed and slapped him on the back. "Stick around and you'll find out soon enough."

Eli, with Samuel's and Josiah's help, put the finishing touches on the roof just as Lucy and her father pulled up in the wagon.

Mr. Denson waved him over. "Eli, help me out with all this froufrou Lucy's got here. There's enough red-white-and-blue bunting to drape the entire town of Union, let alone Sipsey."

"Oh hush, Papa!" Lucy laughed and let Eli lift her to the ground. A jolt of awareness shot through him at the feel of her soft fingers resting against his arm. Such a simple touch, and so brief, but one he couldn't ignore.

Pulling his attention to the job at hand, Eli helped unload boxes of bunting, wildflowers, and fruit jars, wondering what she intended to do with it all, but knowing she had a plan. As soon as the wagon was unloaded, Mr. Denson pulled himself back into the seat. "I'd better get back to the house. I've got orders from Mrs. Denson to help her load up all her food. You think Lucy has a pile of decorations. Wait until you see all the food my wife's cooked."

"Josiah, get over here and help with this stuff." Eli picked up a box of bunting. "Where do you want this?"

"The bunting goes to the speaker's platform. The tablecloths and flowers on the tables of course."

Josiah hefted a box, and he and Lucy headed toward the tables. Eli frowned at the colorful bunting in his hands, trying to figure out where Lucy wanted it. He tried to remember how it was hung in years past, but he'd never helped decorate before. What did women want with all these notions anyway?

A few good speeches, a horse race or two, pole climbing, shooting anvils, and all the fried chicken a man could want made the day plenty exciting.

"Not that way." Lucy took the bunting from him and shook it out, the vibrant colors fluttering as she snapped them in the air. "Like this."

She held one end of the bunting while he secured the other end. Then he took hers, but before he could attach it, she stopped him. "No, wait. It needs to be little higher."

Eli bit back a grin and moved the bunting. "Here?"

"Too high. Down a bit." She tipped her head sideways, considering. "There. Perfect."

She fluffed out the bunting, making sure the folds fell just so, then stepped back and sighed. "Doesn't it look pretty?"

Pretty described the happy glow on her face. "Yes ma'am. It looks real nice."

A commotion from the other side of the clearing drew his gaze. Josiah and the lumberjacks hoisted a ninety-foot pole into the air and let it drop with a resounding thud into a hole in the ground. A red bandana fluttered from the top.

Lucy eyed the pole that rose to a dizzying height. "What's that for?"

"Pole-climbing event."

"Pole climbing?" Her mouth fell open and she turned her gaze on him. "You climb that pole—all the way to the top?"

Eli laughed. "Yes ma'am."

"It looks dangerous."

"It is. But we do it all the time, so we're good at it." Eli moved closer, his gaze devouring hers. "Are you worried?"

"Of course." She gave him a nervous smile and flicked her gaze away. "Who wouldn't be?"

∞

Lucy couldn't remember even one point from the rousing political speeches. She barely tasted the picnic lunch and accepted congratulations on her kolaches without really registering any of it.

She was too worried about those two poles towering at the edge of the clearing. Her heart pounded at the very thought of anyone attempting to climb such a thing. What was Eli thinking? All too soon, the speeches were over and the crowd hurried to witness the friendly games between the lumberjacks.

The men lined up and threw axes at a wooden target that spanned at least four foot across. The axes whirred through the air, end over end, to embed with solid thuds in the target. She watched nervously as Eli stepped up and toed the line, his gaze intent on the target. Her heart thumped in her chest as he hefted the axe over his head with both hands, set his stance, and tossed it. The crowd cheered as the axe stuck true. Samuel stepped up to the line and tossed, also hitting the target. Back and forth, they competed, the scores tied. Lucy couldn't really tell how Jack could keep score, but somehow he did. And she knew enough about competition to know if one of them hit a bull's-eye, he'd win.

Samuel made a throw and hit the target a bit off center. Jack called out the score. "Come on, Eli, you can do this. You need a bull's-eye to win."

Eli stepped up. He threw the axe and it landed in the middle of the target. The crowd erupted in cheers. Lucy couldn't hold back her grin; she clapped along with everyone else.

Annabelle leaned over. "Well, I can see where your loyalties are."

Lucy's cheeks flamed, and she laughed to cover her embarrassment. "What do you mean?"

"Oh, it's quite obvious." She nodded toward Eli. "He's quite handsome. A bit rough around the edges, maybe. Nothing like your Mr. Reichart back in Chicago, from what you've said."

"He's not my Mr. Reichart." Lucy squirmed.

Josiah and another man stepped up to try their hand with the axe, drawing Annabelle's gaze back to the games. "But you'd like him to be. Has he written to you?"

"Yes." Lucy caught a glimpse of Eli's broad shoulders as he stood among the men, his brawny arms crossed as he watched the competition. When Josiah's axe hit the target, a wide grin split his face, and he whistled and clapped for his brother.

"And. . ." Annabelle jostled her shoulder, letting her words trail off.

Lucy blinked, turning her full attention on her cousin. "And what?"

Annabelle laughed. "And what did Mr. Reichart say in his letter?"

"He told me about the summer walks in the park, the church picnics, and the latest collection of books on display at the Newberry." Lucy took a deep breath. "And he mentioned that he would like to keep up our correspondence if I was willing."

"And are you? Willing, I mean?"

Lucy's gaze sought out Eli, who took his place with Josiah for the final round. Deotis and Eli were worlds apart. Deotis spent his days clerking in his uncle's warehouse, working his way up through the ranks with plans to take over some day. He dressed in a suit, and at the end of the day, took a stroll through the park before joining his family for dinner, promptly at six. When he'd invited her to the Christmas ball, Lucy had felt like Cinderella at the palace, amid all the glitz and glitter.

Eli threw his axe and hit the bull's-eye. He lifted a fist high in victory and turned, his dark brown gaze catching hers. A smile wreathed his rugged face, and her heart tipped as dangerously as one of those axes flipping through the air, straight toward its target.

She'd thought Deotis and the world he lived in was what she wanted, but now she wasn't so sure. Without taking her gaze off Eli, she whispered, "I don't know."

Chapter 11

E li gripped the rope and anchored his calked boot into the sides of the pole, ready for the signal to start. He spotted Lucy standing at the edge of the crowd, her fist pressed to her mouth, looking worried.

Before he even realized what he'd done, he winked at her. Her eyes widened, and she looked away, looking flustered. Like an overheated steam engine, Eli's chest nearly exploded from the adrenaline rush her reaction gave him. Maybe that Deotis feller didn't mean anything to her after all.

"Ready?" Samuel called out. "On the count of three. One, two, three!"

Eli pushed off the ground and slapped his left boot into the pole, feeling the spikes grip the trunk. Left foot, right foot, upward, and onward. As he flicked the rope higher on the pole and concentrated on his rhythm all the way to the top, he couldn't help but think about Lucy. He wanted to make her proud, but would the life of a lumberjack, moving from logging camp to logging camp be enough for her? He'd seen the toll that kind of life had taken on his mother. After his pa had died, he and his brothers had taken care of her. They'd still drug her from camp to camp, and she'd never had a place to call her own, but she never complained. Maybe it was time she settled down.

By the time he reached the top of the pole and grabbed the red bandana off the top, he'd made up his mind. He'd talk to his brothers about finding a plot of land for their mother. They'd build her a sturdy cabin, and even if they had to go far afield to provide for her, their mother would have a home. They could come back here, back to Sipsey.

Close to Lucy.

He headed down, lowering the rope, dropping to the ground as fast as he could. The prize money for today's event would go a long way toward helping fulfill his dream for his mother and a family of his own some day.

No more than ten feet off the ground, his gaze caught Lucy's, and he faltered. Next thing he knew, he'd lost his grip and felt himself falling. Somehow he managed to jerk his spiked boots out of the pole and pinwheel his arms to slow his descent. He tucked his knees and hit the ground in a roll, hoping to lessen the impact. It didn't help. He hit the ground with a thud, rolled over onto his back, the wind knocked out of him. So much for an impressive finish.

"Eli?"

He opened his eyes. Lucy hovered over him, her face as white as her starched shirtwaist. Her trembling hand rested against his flannel shirt, her warm palm covered his heart. He squeezed her hand and winked.

∞

Everyone crowded around, and Lucy eased out of the way as Eli's brothers brushed past her to help him to his feet. Her gaze met Annabelle's and her cousin grinned. Heat swooshed over Lucy—everyone in Sipsey Creek had seen her unladylike rush to Eli's side.

Annabelle, apparently taking pity on her, snagged her arm and led her toward the tables. "Are there any of those pastries left? I've been hankering for some all afternoon. You're going to have to share the recipe with me."

"It's. . ." Lucy couldn't tear her gaze from Eli as he limped away. "It's Mrs. Everett's recipe. I'm sure she'd be glad to give it to you."

Annabelle bit into a blueberry-topped kolache, closed her eyes, and groaned. "That is so good." Grinning, she reached for a second pastry. "And since I'm eating for two, I'll have another one."

The threat of rain became a reality as the clouds rolled in and women started gathering pots and pans, baskets and blankets. They corralled their husbands and children to carry everything to the waiting wagons. Good-byes and hugs were passed around, and everyone hurried to beat the rain. Even though the festivities had been cut short, the promise of rain was welcome in the hot, dry season.

Lucy grabbed her basket of kolaches and headed toward the speaker's platform. She needed to remove all the bunting before the rain set in. As she untied the first piece, Eli limped toward her. She winced at the look of pain on his face.

"Are you hurt?"

"Mostly my pride." He nodded at the bunting fluttering in the wind. "Need some help?"

"If you don't mind. I don't want the bunting to get wet. We can use it next year."

A funny look crossed his face, but he didn't say anything.

Lucy folded the red-white-and-blue cloth. "What did I say?"

He removed another section of bunting and handed it to her. "I wasn't sure if you planned to be here next year."

"Papa seems determined to stay." She folded the cloth without looking at him then tucked it into the box. The sky darkened and a few drops of rain splattered against her cheeks. "We'd better hurry."

Eli and Lucy jerked the last of the bunting off the railings and bounded up the steps as the storm clouds bore down on them. The downpour cocooned them in their own little world while everyone else sought shelter in the church.

Eli leaned against one of the rough posts, his gaze heavy lidded as he watched her. "I wasn't asking about your pa."

"I know."

He straightened and stepped closer, his dark eyes searching hers. Lucy clutched an armful of bunting, her heart pounding at his nearness. The small platform was just big enough for one speaker to engage the crowd; certainly not big enough for the two of them, especially when she was so aware of Eli's presence.

He tucked a strand of hair behind her ear and his fingers slid down the shell of her ear, his palm cupping her jaw. The rain slapping against the roof picked up its tempo, keeping time with her runaway heart.

Without another word, Eli leaned in and captured her lips with his, his kiss sending shivers of delight racing through her veins, exploding in her heart. She only *thought* she'd missed the annual fireworks display in Chicago.

Funny, she hadn't missed a thing.

Chapter 12

The gut-hammer gonged, but it didn't matter. Eli hadn't slept enough to amount to anything. He sat on his bed and fingered Lucy's shawl, the soft, gauzy material sliding through his fingers like silk.

Soft, dainty, and pretty, like her.

How could he expect her to choose him over that man in Chicago? What woman would pick an itinerant lumberjack who didn't even own a home over an educated man set to inherit his uncle's business?

He scowled. And did he want her to choose him?

Well, if the fact that the taste of her lips had broadsided him with the force of a widow-maker had anything to do with it, he did. He'd tossed and turned all night, worrying what he was going to do about his feelings for Lucy. He loved her. He knew that, without a doubt, and he could barely stand the thought of her heading back to Chicago and marrying another man. But all he had to offer was a lifetime of hardship, picking up and moving all the time, never knowing where they'd be from one year to the next. He'd be sentencing her to the very life his mother had lived; one of constant toil and moving and nothing to show for it in the end. He tossed the shawl on the rumpled quilt beside him and dropped his head into his hands. His heart told him one thing, but his head another.

He froze at the sound of the soft, gentle rustle of his mother's slippers as she shuffled into the room. She paused next to him, one hand on his shoulder.

"That's a mighty pretty shawl, son." She sat on the bed beside him and picked it up. "I'm guessing this is Lucy's. I won't even begin to speculate how you ended up with it."

Eli lifted his head and blew out a long, slow breath. "She lost it the day the tree almost fell on her."

"Ah, I see. And yet, you still have it."

He shrugged. "The time hasn't been right to give it back."

"And now you're not sure you want to."

He clenched his hands together and stared at the wall. "I'm no good for her, Ma. She deserves better than to be dragged all over the country from lumber camp to lumber camp, from shanty to shanty with no place to call home. That's no kind of life for a woman."

His mother grasped his chin, turned him to face her. Fire burned in her dark eyes. "It isn't?"

Eli knew better than to answer, and he also knew his mother was about to give him a piece of her mind.

"Eli, when you boys were coming along, I spent winters with your grandmother in Alabama, but after the babies stopped coming, I told your father I'd rather be with him year-round, and that was that. I spent my life following your father from camp to camp. It was a good life for all of us, and it was what I wanted, not just your pa. We never had much, but we had each other, and we were happy. If I had it to do over again, I'd do it."

"It was fine when you were younger, but now you need a place to live out your life, not worry about where you're going to lay your head next month, next year."

"Oh, I don't worry about the future. I know you and your brothers will take care of me."

"But have you thought about settling down? Would you, if—if we found you a place?"

"I would if it was somewhere you and your brothers could visit often." Her eyes twinkled. "Maybe Sipsey is just the right place."

He shook his head, his gaze on the shawl in her hands. "I don't know, Ma. I'd thought it might be, but I just don't know anymore."

The gut-hammer gonged the second time, and Eli heaved himself off the bed.

His mother frowned up at him. "You missed breakfast."

"I'm not hungry." He patted her shoulder and kissed her on the forehead. He fingered the shawl. "Would you see that Lucy gets this?"

∞

Eli trudged from the shanty to the log wagon that would take him into the woods. Was he still limping? Lucy wasn't sure, but it looked like he might be.

He'd hurt himself yesterday. She knew it. That's why he hadn't come to breakfast this morning. She wanted to run to him and ask how he was feeling, but there was no time. The wagon was already in motion. He lifted his head, his gaze meeting and holding hers as the wagon trundled past. He looked plumb sick.

Lucy frowned, worry filling her thoughts. She wiped her hands on her apron and called over her shoulder to Annabelle and Maggie, "I'll be right back."

She hurried across the yard to the shanty and knocked on the door. Ma Everett opened it on the first knock, a look of surprise on her face. "Oh, good morning, Lucy. I didn't expect to see you so early."

"Yes ma'am. Uh, no ma'am." Lucy glanced in the direction the wagon had gone. "Um, it's Eli. He missed breakfast, and I was worried about him. He did hurt himself yesterday, didn't he? Don't you think he needs to go see a doctor?"

Ma Everett shook her head. "No, child, he's fine. Probably a tad stiff and sore, but he'll be all right."

Lucy frowned. "Then why did he skip breakfast?"

Ma Everett walked onto the porch and sat in one of the rockers, patted the other one. "Sit."

Confused at the odd request, Lucy did as she asked, noticing for the first time the material bundled in Ma Everett's lap. It looked like—Ma Everett held out the shawl.

Lucy took it and shook it out. "Where did you find my shawl?"

"I didn't. Eli did. The day the tree almost fell on you."

Remembering the day Eli had rescued her, Lucy wasn't surprised to see the multitude of snags in the yarn. She should have known better than to wear such a delicate shawl in the woods. And Eli had kept it. But why? She shook her head. "I don't understand."

Ma Everett set her rocker in motion, the gentle movement settling Lucy's thoughts. "There's more than one kind of sick. There's sick in the body, sick in the head, and then there's heartsick." She leaned over and tapped the shawl. "Eli is heartsick."

Lucy's heart pounded against her ribcage. What did Ma Everett mean? She wanted to ask, but couldn't speak past the lump of fear in her throat. She bit her lip and waited.

"Eli's got it in his head that he's not good enough for you." Mrs. Everett's eyes twinkled. "And if you care for him, you'll just have to convince him he's wrong."

Chapter 13

Snaking logs kept Eli busy, and staying busy kept his mind off Lucy. Or at least it should have. But it didn't. He'd worked in logging long enough he didn't have to think about it too much, even though he knew the dangers of not having his mind on his work.

He walked to the side of the log and slapped the reins against the mules' backs, urging them forward across the ground, slick from yesterday's rain. Josiah had gone on ahead with a log of his own.

As soon as the ground leveled out and the hauling got easier, his thoughts eased right back to yesterday and Lucy. He'd give anything to go back to the hard day's work of two days ago and erase Independence Day from his mind. Erase the taste of Lucy's kiss, the feel of her in his arms. But it was too late. Her touch was branded into his brain and there was no erasing it.

No, he couldn't undo yesterday, but he could make sure it didn't happen again. He'd pick up his pay tonight and be gone by morning. With him out of the way, Lucy would see that Reichart was the man for her, the man who could offer her the kind of life she'd always dreamed of. The kind he never could.

The mules dipped into an incline and started dragging the log downhill, around a bend. But when they turned to follow the bend, the log began to roll. Eli sidestepped but his boot caught on an exposed root. Even as he fell, he knew he wasn't going to get out of the way in time. The log slammed into him, rolled on top of his legs, and pinned him in place.

He gritted his teeth against the log's weight, praying his legs weren't crushed.

Maybe Josiah was still within hearing range. He yelled for help, but the mules jumped and jerked the log, grinding against his leg even more. Groaning, he lay back against the ground, silent. Somebody would come along shortly. They had to.

Nothing to do, but wait. And pray.

Chapter 14

Fighting back tears of frustration, Lucy concentrated on scrubbing the mound of pots and pans. Around her, Maggie and Annabelle tidied up the cook shack, chatting and laughing.

Eli thought he wasn't good enough for her? She scrubbed harder. He'd probably weighed her, and found *her* wanting instead. She could barely cook, other than what his mother had taught her. And, unlike Maggie and Annabelle, living in Chicago hadn't prepared her for life as a lumberjack's wife. All she seemed good at was decorating, flower arranging, crocheting, and tatting lace.

None of her skills were important around a logging camp, where the work was hard, the hours long, and the men worked from sunup to sundown. . .and the women even longer. Where dainty shawls and pretty flowers were reserved for Sunday dinners. . .if at all.

She sniffed. In his last letter, Deotis had hinted he might like to visit, come Christmas. A man didn't travel all the way from Chicago to Mississippi just to see the scenery. If she expressed interest, she'd be giving him permission to take their correspondence a step further.

A month ago, she would have been overjoyed. Now, she was just plain-out miserable. Her gaze fell on the blue shawl draped across the back of a chair. Why had Eli kept her shawl but given it to his mother to return to her, the very day after he'd kissed her?

Oh, Eli.

She'd given her heart to a lumberjack, and he'd tossed it back with the same precision he'd toss an axe at a target. And from the pain in her chest, he'd hit the bull's-eye.

Annabelle handed her a stack of plates, a frown of concern on her face. "Are you all right?"

Lucy nodded, her heart too battered to talk about it. "I'm fine—"

Pounding hooves shattered the morning stillness. The women rushed to the edge of the summer kitchen's yard just as one of the draft horses raced into view; Josiah rode on the animal's bare back. He barely slacked up. "There's been

318

an accident. I'm going for the doctor."

"Who?" Annabelle yelled after him as he flew past.

"Eli."

Chapter 15

Lucy ran down the log road, still muddy from yesterday's rain, fear threatening to overwhelm her.

Eli was hurt, maybe dying.

No, he couldn't die. She loved him. She wanted to spend the rest of her life with him. She'd learn to cook. She'd learn to love the woods. She'd learn to not be afraid of snakes and spiders, and dirt and decaying leaves in the forest. She'd learn to endure the gnats and the mosquitoes. Whatever it took, she'd do it.

Mud clung to her shoes, the hem of her skirt, but she ignored the mud and the limbs that reached out and snatched at her hair and her shirtwaist as she searched for the logging crew. She came to a fork. What direction had they taken this morning? Log roads crisscrossed the pine forest, and the men could have gone in any direction.

Please, Lord, show me the way.

She heard the jingle of harnesses deep in the woods to her right, and left the road, running toward the sound, her skirts held high. She stumbled over a root and went flying, landing on the ground with a soft *oomph*. Biting back a sob, she scrambled to her feet and kept going. She had to get to Eli.

In the distance, she spotted the wagon, easing down the rutted log road, Samuel on the seat, more men in the back, several walking behind, quiet as death. Her heart lurched.

She saw her cousin Jack and called out to him. Jack turned and hurried to her side.

"Lucy? What are doing here?"

"Josiah said Eli's been hurt." She clutched his arm. "Is he— Is he—"

"He's going to be fine. His leg might be broke though. The doctor—"

Lucy wilted against him, and Jack patted her arm. Samuel pulled back on the reins at Jack's whistle. Jack led her to the wagon, and she barely noticed when he motioned for the other men to hop out. She had eyes only for Eli.

Jack helped her into the wagon, and she scrambled to where Eli lay against its hard-planked bed, his dark hair sweat-stained in the summer heat, his clothes dirty and coated with mud. Lucy cradled his head in her lap. Fingers shaking, she pushed his hair back from his face and smoothed his furrowed brow. "Eli?"

His eyes opened. He gave her a lopsided smile, the most beautiful sight she'd ever seen. "Lucy."

He groaned when the wagon started up again, tossing him from side to side.

"*Shh*. We'll be out of the woods soon." She leaned down and clutched him to her, trying to ease the jolting, but it was no use. "Where does it hurt?"

He grimaced, but didn't answer. Instead he stared at her so long that her cheeks burned. Then a grin tilted up one side of his mouth, and he captured her hand against his chest, right above his heart. "Here."

Her own heart thudded against her chest at the way his dark gaze caught and held hers. "Did the tree fall on your chest?" she whispered.

"The tree fell on my leg, but it's nothing to the pain in here if"—he grimaced and took a deep breath—"if you decide to go back to Chicago."

"I'm not going anywhere." She brushed his hair away from his forehead, her gaze caressing his face. "Eli Everett, will you marry me?"

"What about your city boy, crystal chandeliers, pretty flowers, and dinner at six?" But even as he questioned her, he caressed her face with the tips of his fingers.

"Who needs hothouse flowers when God clothes the lilies of the field in all His glory, or chandeliers when He uses the morning dew to string pearls on a spiderweb, and"—Lucy leaned in and whispered against his lips—"who needs a city boy when I've got a lumberjack?"

The Summer Harvest Bride

by Maureen Lang

Dedication

For Neil, always my hero.

Chapter 1

Morning, Sally," greeted Mrs. Gibbons as Sally Hobson stepped into the dry goods store. "You just missed Willis. He came in for a packet of pipe tobacco for the mayor not ten minutes ago."

Sally held up the basket of eggs she'd brought to sell, suppressing an inward groan. But why shouldn't Mrs. Gibbons assume she wanted to see Willis at every opportunity? The entire town began linking them together since last year's harvest celebration when Willis had claimed her for nearly every dance. Catching the eye of the mayor's son was considered quite a coup among the young ladies Sally's age.

"I brought our eggs, Mrs. Gibbons."

The storekeeper's wife welcomed the basket at the counter, pulling her cashbox from a shelf underneath. "Did you hear about the newcomers?"

Sally shook her head then waited as Mrs. Gibbons counted the two dozen eggs.

"Heard tell there's a gang of 'em, all in one family. Boys as big as David's Goliath, every last one of them, all fresh from some town back East."

Sally looked toward the window, glad she hadn't seen them and hoping to avoid such a sight on her way back home, just outside of town. Having lived in Chicago, she'd learned to avoid bullies and didn't welcome a pack of them here in the peaceful, quiet town of Finchville.

"They were spotted down by the spring this morning, measuring and counting off steps to who-knows-what. Now they're here in town. One of 'em came in here and invited everyone out to the town pump to hear some kind of idea that's supposed to benefit everybody. Imagine that! Don't even live here, and they're snooping around; then inviting all of us out."

"What sort of benefit?"

"Didn't say." Mrs. Gibbons handed Sally a few coins for the eggs. "Why don't you run on over and see what it's all about? Mr. Gibbons is already there, and you'll probably see Willis, too."

Sally pocketed the money and nodded, although she wasn't sure about following Mrs. Gibbons's suggestion. No one in her family had been gladder than Sally to leave the ever-growing swarm of people in Chicago. She'd rejoiced when Father announced his intention to take up farming on the Illinois prairie in Finchville. The little town sat on the main road between Chicago and Iowa, in the middle of one of the few areas that included a forest, river, and rolling hills on the otherwise flat but fertile prairie.

Still, it did stir curiosity for a group of strangers to gather the entire town together. Wasting everybody's time wasn't likely to inspire many friendships, if they planned to stay. The farmers around town had only one thing on their mind this time of year: planting. The fields were too wet after a late snowmelt and early spring rains, but the land would soon be ready to enfold the seeds of this year's crops.

She stepped outside, wondering if her sister was in town yet. Alice and her husband, Arthur, farmed on the opposite side of town, but Sally and Alice coordinated their days to drop off eggs and butter in town. If Alice had heard about the newcomers, she was probably already at the town pump.

Slipping her empty egg basket onto her arm, Sally joined a few others already headed in that direction. Mr. Granger, the baker, tipped his hat her way as he walked along without a word.

The pump was on the east side, near a grove of trees that beckoned travelers to take respite on their way through the wide, open prairie. The oak and beech trees were just beginning to bud, and today's warm sunshine seemed to hurry the process.

Two unfamiliar wagons rested in the shadow of the Finchville Arms, the only hotel in town. Finchville bustled just two seasons a year, planting and harvest. But it appeared anyone in town today, with the exception of Mrs. Gibbons, was at the pump now.

Her gaze fell on the newcomers themselves and her heart unexpectedly fluttered. Perhaps they weren't quite as large as Goliath, but each one tall, broad shouldered, sturdy and hard as the strongest oak. Five. . .six if she counted the patriarch in this family, judging by the thatch of thick gray hair above a still handsome but leathery face.

For a moment she wondered if this was some sort of ploy to get the townsfolk together and rob them all at once. Who would stop them? Sheriff Tilney wasn't the only one absent—she didn't see Willis or his father, the mayor, either. Had some other member of their so-called family diverted the town's only officials so they could be about their crime?

Telling herself she should have waited for Alice at the store, she started to turn back when one of the men stepped out from his pack.

"People! People!" rang his voice as he jumped on the iron bench near the pump. He waved onlookers closer. "Thank you for the warm welcome to your fair town!"

He was definitely not like the pictures she'd seen of the cruel warrior Goliath, always portrayed with a fierce scowl before meeting his unlikely death. If anything, this man was a matured David—someone who'd inspired more than one heroic story.

"Permit me to introduce myself and my family," he said as he crossed his chest with one palm and gave a quick bow. "I am Lukas Daughton and these"—now sweeping that strong palm to the men behind him—"are my brothers." Each one saluted as Lukas called a name: "Bran. Fergus. Nolan. Owny. And finally"—he leaned down to hold up one of the older man's hands—"may I present the best of us all, our father, Nathaniel Daughton, the finest engineer west of Baltimore."

He turned his attention back to the crowd, perhaps counting how many were present. When his gaze roamed he stopped at Sally before going on, but looked at her again—only to let his glance linger with a smile.

She looked away, hiding her face with the brim of her bonnet for fear he would see evidence of the blush his notice had ignited.

"Now why, you might be thinking," he went on, "does this family of burly men want to steal a few minutes of your day? Let me tell you we've heard of this little hamlet, with its sparkling creek and fertile farmland, and the forests to block the harshest weather the prairie offers. So we came out here to see for ourselves if this might be the place for us to do what we do best: Build a gristmill that will serve not only your farms but those from this entire county."

Whispers erupted here and there, but Sally couldn't tell if her neighbors were interested or skeptical. While there were a number of small mills connected to towns between Chicago and Iowa, there weren't many and all were a considerable distance away. How her father would delight in being able to grind corn meal or flour right here in town!

And yet. . .she reined in her interest. That would certainly change things around here. "What's this all about?"

The call came from a familiar voice not far behind Sally. Mayor Silas Pollit, Willis's father, possessed a voice that fairly whistled, like a bullet before hitting its mark. Although he'd already been mayor when Sally and her family moved to Finchville three years ago, she'd always wondered if his voice was one of the reasons he'd been elected. No one could ignore such a grating, if commanding, sound.

"Ah!" The newcomer's voice carried, it had to be said, much sweeter on the ear. "I can tell by the cut of your coat you're a man of some renown." Yes, Lukas Daughton's voice was definitely easier to enjoy. Loud enough to be heard, yet smooth and easy as it slipped inside and coated the inner workings of her ear with pleasing tones. She wondered how he would sound in church, singing a hymn. If he went to church at all.

Willis Pollit had arrived with his father and took a step closer to Sally, greeting her with a silent, familiar smile. He touched her elbow, too, and she crossed her arms to let her basket dangle between them. Why had she never noticed how possessive Willis's touch must appear?

The surprising question filling Sally's mind was why such a motion from Willis should suddenly feel more annoying than it had only yesterday?

Chapter 2

Lukas Daughton believed a face was made for smiling, because it took so much more effort to frown. Usually sooner than later, most people proved him right. Smiling was contagious.

It didn't take long to guess the newcomer, the mayor, someone had called him, looked like he didn't find much to smile about. The comfortable creases in his forehead gave him away.

Undeterred, Lukas included the crowd in their conversation as he made his way closer to the man he no doubt had to convince, if he truly was the mayor.

"I commend you, sir, for guarding the best interests of these fine town folk." Lukas glanced around, starting in the direction of the young woman he'd spotted earlier. Edging closer to the mayor had brought him closer to her. She was even prettier than he thought, with her creamy skin and wide blue eyes. How many shades of blue had God created? The shade in her eyes was surely the prettiest. And her skin looked softer than those kidskin gloves his father gave Lukas's mother on her last Christmas this side of Heaven.

Lukas started his familiar speech, knowing it so well he could let his eyes return often to the girl without losing his place. "My father was born in Ireland, the son of a miller. From his youngest days, he saw the workings of a mill, from the gears under the millstone to the buckets on the waterwheel. Before long his father heard of another miller who wanted to build a new grist wheel in the next county, and so he sent his oldest son—my father—at just fourteen years old, to help with the construction and be an apprentice. That began my father's education of how the best mills work. Something that has benefited others already and will do the same for you. If you let us."

With a wave to remind everyone of his brothers, he added, "Together we have built four mills under our father's direction. Before that, my father worked on or repaired more than a half dozen mills in Ireland. Here in America our four mills serve farming communities that are now centers of commerce and success."

"And how is it you aim to build such a thing?" the mayor asked, looking him over with an eye that didn't miss their humble clothing. "Newcomers around here bring their own investments, and I imagine this will be quite costly. How do you propose to fund such an ambitious endeavor if you don't intend to earn a living from it after it's built?"

Lukas patted the man's ample shoulder with just enough assurance and confidence to avoid any hint of condescension. "We supply the labor, as well as the most important element of all: the know-how. The rest—and by that I mean the cost of material—we humbly submit would be shared by the town that will reap the benefits."

"Ridiculous," the mayor grumbled, shaking his head so that his double chin wobbled. "Do you expect us to entrust our resources or hard-earned money to strangers?"

"We're happy to earn that trust." Lukas looped his thumbs through his suspenders, all the while keeping the girl within the periphery of his vision. He pulled out the newspaper clippings he carried in his pocket, and handed them to the mayor. Several stories recounted the names and successes associated with mills they'd left behind, complete with the Daughton name as builders.

"What makes you think we believe you didn't have these articles printed yourself, just to fool unsuspecting towns like ours?"

"We can show you letters of recommendation from our past customers. But you might think we wrote them ourselves." He winked at the mayor. "The articles name the towns pleased with our work, all four, and you can send for verification. In the meantime"—he smiled again in the general vicinity of the girl rather than straight at her, because he sensed shyness in her refusal to meet his gaze—"we can get to work on first things first. The friendship."

A young man standing between him and the girl took another step closer to Lukas, fairly putting her behind him. Lukas had noticed how close he'd chosen to stand beside her, but Lukas wasn't yet ready to believe the man's claim on her. He was likely related to the town official, unless the similarity in the curve of their frowning brows was coincidence. Why would such a pretty girl want to be part of a family so unaccustomed to something as easy as smiling?

"What's to make us believe the person you recommend we contact isn't some crony of yours, paid to say whatever you want us to hear? You might not even be the Daughton builders you claim to be, but frauds using their name and reputation."

"I can tell this is a town filled with clever people!" Lukas spoke with gusto. "I like that. Why not simply address it to the name of the town, in care of the sheriff, or the mayor, or some other official as you please? A postmaster? An innkeeper? A storekeeper? We couldn't possibly know where the letter would land, could we? But I guarantee everyone in each town we left will know our names and can tell you about the success with our mills. And you can ask for descriptions of us. Six such handsome men as ourselves are hard to forget," he added with another wink.

"Got to admit," said another from the crowd, "if we had our own mill the price of flour would go down. So would the price of bread at my bakery."

There were a few other interested comments, enough to make the mayor lift one hand while at the same time taking Lukas's arm with his other. Lukas tossed a glance to his father so he would follow as he allowed himself to be led away, expecting the interrogation at hand. He knew enough to cooperate if they wanted a chance at another job without a reference already among the town's residents.

Following the mayor, Lukas couldn't remember the last time he was so eager for a job to work out.

Chapter 3

S ally watched as the mayor led two of the newcomers away. Lukas Daughton certainly knew how to stir the interest of a farming community.

"I'm going to join my father."

Willis's voice startled Sally; she'd been watching the trio ahead of them. Of course Willis would be part of the meeting. What surprised her was her immediate interest in going along, too. She detained him with a touch to his arm. "It certainly sounds like a good opportunity for the town, doesn't it?"

"Don't be so easily taken in," he said quietly, glancing at the remaining Daughton brothers not far behind them, who were mingling with others.

Sally's heart thrummed in anticipation of the meeting. Her father was out in the field, her mother at home with countless tasks, and her sister—where was Alice? If any one of them were here right now, they would want the *townspeople* to make the best possible decision, not the mayor alone.

"You don't mind if I come along, do you?"

One of Willis's brows lifted, those brows that were thick and bold just like his father's. Happy or bored or fascinated, his mood was easy to read. Just now they said he was surprised but skeptical. "I can't think of a bigger waste of time."

"But. . . How often does such an opportunity come along? It's worth investigating, isn't it?"

He scowled. "These men likely offer nothing but flimflam. I'm sure my father will see the sheriff escorts them quickly out of town."

"But what if they really could build a mill? Wouldn't the farmers want to know about something like this?"

Willis didn't have the ample stomach his father carried, but he did have a certain softness about him. He was much better suited to the legal work he did for his father than for farming or other manual labor. Right now he stopped, crossing his arms in front of him the way his father did, and regarded her with interest.

"Do you mean to say you really do wish to attend a meeting in my father's office? Not just accompany me?"

"I want to tell my father about it, and if I sat in I'd have more information

332

for him, wouldn't I?"

Willis's surprise gave way to amusement, the way he often looked at her when she raised a question. He'd told her more than once she should have been a schoolteacher, with all the questions she asked.

"If not me," she persisted, "perhaps you could bring Mr. Granger, or Mr. Gibbons, or one of the farmers. Someone who might benefit more directly from a mill—" She cut herself off, realizing she'd been about to infer his father might not be the most qualified person to make such a decision.

Before Willis could disagree—she could see one of his brows pulling downward, just as it always did when he was about to state the opposite opinion of anyone around him—Mr. Granger stepped between them.

"She's right, Willis," said the baker, revealing he hadn't a hint of compunction about having listened in on their conversation. "Your father may think he's protecting the community but he oughtn't make this decision alone. Why don't you lead the way?"

"I don't think—"

But Willis didn't finish, seeing Mr. Granger beckon Mr. Gibbons and two other farmers.

Emboldened that their interest reflected her own, Sally grinned and held out an elbow to Willis as if to escort him, if need be. He managed a smile then took her arm to loop it properly through his.

The mayor's office was on the second floor of the post office, since he was also the postmaster as the town had yet to afford a salaried mayor. Tall windows let in the summer breeze while offering a view of the prairie and farms surrounding the town. His office wasn't a large room, being a converted parlor designed for the private quarters of any postmaster. A large desk took up the center, and along one wall stood an impressive bookcase filled with volumes he'd brought from the East. English law books, he'd claimed them to be, as if possessing them added to his authority as mayor.

Just now he looked none too pleased to see his son and the entourage behind him. The telltale brows revealed annoyance, even when he let his glance fall momentarily on Sally. He was usually happy to see her, at least whenever she was with Willis.

"This is bound to be boring," Willis said in her ear. "Why don't you wait down in the post office and I'll see you home afterward?"

"That's all right," she said gently, as if grateful for his consideration. "I don't mind in the least."

He might have been right about the engineering features of a gristmill being boring, since that was how the discussion resumed once the mayor realized their visitors were there to stay. But as the older man spoke with quiet confidence how he would design such a structure, using the power of the river that ran alongside the town, Sally could see she wasn't the only one impressed by Mr. Daughton's proposal. Or at least by his calm poise and depth of knowledge so obvious in his answers to every question.

"We could be finished by harvest time of this year," he finished, "sooner if some of the young men in your town could volunteer to help out with the digging and lend an ox or two to remove some of the earth we'll be shifting. My boys are strong and hardworking, but can't work faster than they're able."

"You'll have to buy a spot on the river, and most of the parcels are already owned by various farmers," the mayor said. "That'll be expensive."

"We plan to build the mill right here in town, Mayor," said Lukas, in a voice so calmly assured perhaps he didn't expect the gasp that greeted his words.

"In town? But the river will power the mill, your father said it himself."

"And so we build a canal to capture the water for a millpond." The immediate doubt spreading across the room didn't dampen the man's confidence. "We've already measured the distance from the springhead. All we need is the plot at the end of town, where our wagons now stand, and permission to dig between the spring and there."

Sally studied the faces around her, seeing the man's cool certainty impacted a few others as it did her. Perhaps they really could perform such a miracle as putting a mill right where it would most conveniently serve.

She was also more convinced than ever that her father needed to hear about this proposal. Their cornfield stood between the springhead and town.

She looked again at the man called Lukas, hoping to ask if he might talk directly to her father. He happened to be looking at her, and despite her inquiry she dropped her gaze. She wouldn't ask in front of everyone; it would be hard enough just to have his attention, let alone everyone else's. When she looked at him again she noticed he included Willis in his glance this time, with a question in his eyes. She looked at Willis, too, who hadn't seemed to notice the exchange.

Surely she imagined that. Why should he care who Willis was to her?

As the discussion shifted to cost and supplies, Sally tried to listen more intently. Her father would be interested in such details, but for some reason she had a hard time concentrating; she, who was always so good with numbers. She handled all of her father's accounts, with livestock and feed and seed, a job gratefully relinquished by her mother the moment Sally expressed her interest. Sally delighted in contributing to the family in a way they appreciated. Numbers never failed her. There was always a right and wrong answer to make sense of the books. Unlike life, which wasn't always so clear.

To her annoyance, her thoughts were muddled more than once. Surely the young Mr. Daughton couldn't have such a quick effect on her. Willis never flustered her this way.

When the meeting ended, Mayor Pollit agreed to let Mr. Daughton speak to the farmers and businessmen after church on Sunday, in the church itself, since it was large enough to accommodate everyone who might want to attend. Sally moved toward the door, but Willis touched her elbow again.

"I'd like to stay and talk to my father about this," he said. "If you'd like to stay, I can see you home afterward."

She shook her head. "No, Willis. I must find Alice. We were supposed to meet at Gibbons' store and I'm sure she must be looking for me."

He gave her a distracted half-smile. "All right." Reaching up, he stroked one of her cheeks. "I'll call on you later this afternoon?"

She nodded, catching sight of the two Daughtons who seemed to be waiting for her to exit the room before they did. Smiling at them politely, she led the way back outside.

Chapter 4

Watching that young man stroke this girl's cheek flared equal parts envy and desire for Lukas to gain the right to do the same thing. This wasn't likely the first time the man had touched her in such a familiar, friendly way. Perhaps he was her husband—in which case, Lukas's envy was entirely inappropriate.

There was only one thing to do, and that was to find out who this man was to her. Once they were outside the post office, he left his father two steps behind. To his delight the girl appeared to be waiting for them.

"Thank you for your interest in our proposal, miss," he said, using his friendliest smile. "And I'm sorry to be so bold by introducing myself, but since I don't know anyone in town yet, I guess I haven't much choice if I'm going to know your name. You already know mine."

"I wonder if you might speak to my father about your proposal?" she asked without answering his question. "He owns some of the land you might be interested—"

"There you are! Sally Hobson, I've been looking all over town for you."

Lukas couldn't help but welcome the exasperated woman interrupting them, if only for providing the information he'd been seeking. Sally Hobson. As sweet a name as she deserved.

The other woman was perhaps a half dozen years older than the pretty girl at his side—she was a friend or sister, too young to be her mother, though she did wear motherly concern, especially when she glanced from Sally to him.

"This is Lukas Daughton," said Sally. She held her palm toward Lukas's father. "And Mr. Daughton. They've come to build a gristmill."

The woman's brows shot up with interest. "Have you? My husband will be glad to hear that, I'm sure."

Lukas decided to like this woman, even if he did sense she wasn't prepared to return the feeling. Yet. "Perhaps you might have your husband speak to the mayor. The project will need local support if we're to succeed." He turned back to Sally, where his gaze was so eager to go. "And we'll be happy to speak to your father. Perhaps we can schedule to meet back here this afternoon, or in the evening?"

"That could be arranged, I think," Sally said. "Where shall we look for you?"

"At the rooming house dining room. We've already learned the food is good."

Lukas held out his hand to shake the older girl's hand first, not because it was expected but because he could follow with the same gesture toward Sally. He'd already spied the woman's left hand, looking for a wedding band and finding none. Besides, if she were married, wouldn't she have included her husband in a discussion about the gristmill, like this other woman?

He shook her hand gently, finding her hand small, warm, and just as soft as he'd expected. But there was strength there, too, and one tiny blister at the base of her forefinger betraying that she worked at something other than just keeping her skin smooth. He held her hand too long, but he wanted her to notice, to return his gaze, and she did.

He tipped his hat again, watched his father do the same without having spoken a word, and they walked down the street in the opposite direction of the girls.

"You ought not break another heart, Lukas," said his father, low, but thankfully they were well out of earshot from Sally or anyone else.

He patted his father's strong shoulder as if he were the wiser of the two. "I won't, Pap."

∞

Sally let Alice loop their arms together as they walked along the sidewalk. The sidewalk itself was new, built by Willis's school friend who came to town just last year. It was a vast improvement over the street's dirt, so eager to go muddy at the slightest hint of rain, but many of the nails had popped and some of the boards were uneven.

"So you think Arthur and Pa will be interested in supporting a gristmill right here in town?" Sally asked Alice.

"I do," Alice said, but she looked distracted, as if her thoughts were elsewhere. When she threw a glance over her shoulder, Sally guessed where her thoughts had lingered. "You know that man was flirting with you, don't you?"

Sally felt the heat of blood rush to her cheeks. "He barely said a word to me!"

"The way he held your hand like that, waiting for you to look at him." She sighed. "I can't say that I'd blame you if you were flattered. He's fine looking."

"Alice! He's a stranger!"

Her sister nodded, evidently back to her senses. "Exactly. So you better be careful around him until you know him. He's got his sights on you, though, there's no doubt about that."

"Even if he does, it wouldn't matter a bit to me." The words flowed off of her tongue with such assurance Sally impressed even herself.

"Oh?" Alice nudged Sally's side with her elbow. "I didn't think Willis made you blind to anyone else. In fact, I thought you found him annoying."

"Of course I don't!" Now she, too, glanced around, just to be sure no one could hear such a private conversation. "I do find Mr. Daughton. . .well, appealing. But in his speech to the townspeople, he said they've built four grist-mills already—"

"Really? How wonderful! They must have all the experience in the world."

"So that's what they do, Alice. They build a grist-mill, then they move on to the next town and build another. I have no intention of getting caught up with someone for a summer romance only to be left behind when his job is finished."

Alice stopped their perambulation, smiling gently at Sally. "You've always been the sensible one in the family. And of course you're right." She led on again, giving Sally's forearm a squeeze with her free hand. "Maybe that shy streak in you is more protection than I imagined. It's given you the strength to control your heart better than I ever could. Once Arthur looked at me the way that man looked at you just now, I was entirely at his mercy. Yes, you have far more sense than I ever had!"

Sally walked along, telling herself her sister was right.

Of course she was.

Chapter 5

The Arms, as the rooming house was called, boasted a dining room where the owners shared their love of food with everyone who came through their threshold, luring people to stay with heavenly scents from their kitchen or free biscuits when they were hot from the oven. Rumor had it Mayor Pollit had been as slim as Willis before The Arms opened in Finchville some twenty years ago.

Despite the fine taste of roasted chicken, Sally had trouble finishing her meal. It was hard to eat with uninvited butterflies getting in the way. She was never quite at ease eating with people she didn't know, and more than once she'd caught Lukas Daughton smile her way. It was his attention that created those butterflies, she was sure of it.

"We may never leave here even if we don't stay to build the grist-mill," said Lukas as he scraped the last remnant of chicken from his own empty plate. "I haven't had such a fine meal since my mother died, and that's almost five years ago now."

"I'm sorry to hear about such a loss," said Alice, her voice reflecting the same sympathy filling Sally. She'd have voiced her own condolences if she'd been quicker with words, but as usual Alice beat her to it.

She regarded Lukas, as she'd already begun calling him in her mind. How hard it must have been for such a large family to do without the one figure who could play every role from mediator to nurturer, as Sally's mother did.

Mr. Daughton and Sally's father had already spoken at some length about the prospect of building a gristmill and running a canal through his cornfield. That the town needed a mill suddenly seemed obvious. Whether or not the Daughtons were the ones to build it, and if the town could afford for them to do so, were other matters entirely.

But before anyone had finished eating, Father and Arthur had already agreed to support the Daughtons when they presented their plan at the town meeting on Sunday.

Sally couldn't help but be pleased with the development, although she was afraid to dwell on why. After Chicago, the thought of all the new people and traffic it would draw made her shudder, but having their own gristmill would be good for Finchville. Surely that was why she was pleased.

If Lukas Daughton would be staying, she knew already she must guard her thoughts. He was undoubtedly a flirt; he smiled at her in a way he hadn't toward either her mother or Alice. His smiles were slow, as if to extend how long he might politely look at her. And even though she reminded herself he likely chose a favorite girl to spend time with during the building of each grist-mill, she couldn't help but recognize the growing warmth around her heart with each passing moment in his company.

She was only half surprised but entirely pleased when he detained her as the others walked from the dining room after their meal ended.

"I'd be pleased to escort you to church on Sunday morning, Miss Sally," he whispered.

Welcome as that sounded, she knew it was impossible. For the past month, Willis and his father shared the same pew with her family, right up front for all to see. It had been Willis's idea.

"I'm afraid I couldn't, Mr. Daughton. But I will certainly look forward to seeing you and your family there."

His smile went a little crooked, but despite her refusal, the pleasure on his face didn't disappear. "All right, no escort needed. Mind if I save a seat for you?"

Lukas Daughton was definitely easy to look at, and difficult to resist. Yet she knew any change in seating would require some kind of discussion between her and Willis. Besides, she ought not even consider sitting anywhere else. What would Willis think? She was not as eager to get married as Willis seemed to be, and as the entire town seemed to expect, but she knew she could grow fond of him if only because of his persistence. Most importantly, like Sally herself, Willis had no intention of leaving Finchville.

"I'm sorry, Mr. Daughton—"

"Lukas."

She couldn't help but grin, though she refused to be swept up so easily in his flirtation. "I'm sorry, but my family and I have been sitting with the Pollits for some time now, and I'm sure they would be disappointed in any change. And there isn't really room. . ."

"Ah," he said slowly. "The mayor and his son. So I should squash my wishes to shower you with my undivided attention?" His tone was light, even with the disappointment still lingering in that little furrow.

She glanced at her departing family. Only Alice seemed to have noticed that she hung back with Mr. Daughton, but she threw her a grin. Of everyone in town, only Alice supported Sally's unhurried pace toward the altar with Willis. Even her parents seemed convinced it was only a matter of time before she and Willis made an announcement.

"I thought your undivided attention would be devoted to the gristmill, Mr. Daughton."

"Lukas isn't such a hard name to say, is it? I'd love to hear you say it."

She couldn't stop the corner of her mouth from rising, but she refused to answer his wish. Instead, she squared her shoulders and listened to the sensible words forming on her own tongue.

"This is a small town, Mr. Daughton. One I will likely live in for the rest of my life. I can offer the same sort of friendship to you that the town will be prepared to offer to someone bringing the benefit of a gristmill. But that's all."

She turned, proud of herself for having issued such a speech without a hint of the shy nervousness that often plagued her when speaking to strangers. Somehow he already seemed less than a stranger, despite only having met him earlier that day.

She would have walked on, but he spoke again. "Let me ask one more question. Should I withhold my special attention toward you because your heart is already elsewhere, or because you don't trust how easily *you* might enjoy my special attention?"

Sally felt her eyes widen at his boldness, but no answer came to mind. Not a reproach for his diligence after she'd hinted her connection to the mayor's son, nor even a whisper to defend what so many people in town already believed about her and Willis.

Chapter 6

Change was coming, people said, and Sally didn't doubt it was true. For the first few days after the official vote was won, all anyone in Finchville talked about was erecting the mill. While no transformation could happen overnight, a gristmill to be built in a matter of months seemed to present swift change indeed.

She told herself she would grow with the town. She wanted her family and friends to prosper. She just hoped Finchville would stay the kind of town it was now, one where inhabitants either knew everyone firsthand or knew with whom they belonged. She wanted Finchville to stay a town that cared about its neighbors.

After two weeks of little change, life slipped back into what it used to be and Sally breathed easier. She rarely saw the Daughtons except at church, where Lukas Daughton chose to sit directly behind her. She learned he was polite, and had the kind of singing voice she'd suspected the first time she heard him speak. His presence, she had to admit, was a distraction she struggled to hide.

They began felling trees for the mill from wherever they were given permission, while the elder Mr. Daughton marked land that was to be dug. To her own consternation, she found herself eager for the day they would begin digging through her father's field. An eagerness she could only ascribe to seeing Lukas on a regular basis, a fact that tugged at her spirits each and every time she saw Willis.

Today, as she delivered her butter and eggs, she saw several townspeople gathered outside the store, and Willis in the center of the group. As Sally approached, Willis raised a hand in supplication to the two men he'd obviously been arguing with. "All I'm saying is that the location of the mill seems strange to me. Mills are powered by the flow of water. I still don't see how that will work with a building so far from the river's edge. It seems to me the Daughtons might be what my father and I feared: at best incompetent, at worst deceivers, here just to take advantage of our pocketbooks. They've admitted they haven't yet built a mill so far from the actual source of water."

"How are they profiting from this? We haven't paid them a dime." It was well known Mr. Granger had allowed them to remove more trees from his land than anyone else.

"I just wanted to remind you that neither my father nor I have supported this, not from the beginning, and if it proves as foolhardy as we fear, we hope you know we'll still do all we can to right the matter when it falls apart."

Mr. Granger shook his head, but didn't say anything as he walked back in the direction of his bakery. The others soon dispersed, leaving Willis now smiling at Sally, as if nothing unpleasant had just taken place.

"Can I talk you into an early lunch?" he asked Sally. "I passed by The Arms' dining room today, and they're baking a meat pie I promise will be delicious."

"I'm sure it will be," she said, "but my father is expecting me out in the field, and I'll have just enough time to drop off my eggs and get back."

He shrugged, taking her elbow to direct her inside the store.

"I wonder, Willis," she said, "what the Daughtons must do to convince you that they know what they're doing?"

"I have my man out there watching them every day," Willis said. "This trench they're planning on digging isn't coming from the nearest section of the river behind town. They're digging a longer trench than necessary."

His man, Sally knew, was Cyrus, an older man who'd been with the Pollit family from childhood, Willis had once told her.

"Perhaps you could speak to Mr. Daughton if you have some concerns."

"Oh, we intend to, believe me. They may not officially report to my father, but you can be assured we'll keep a close eye on them every step of the way."

"Willis," she said, low, "I hope you're only doing this out of concern for the town."

Willis patted her hand. "Of course. Why else would I spend so much time thinking about this? Or spare Cyrus from his other duties?"

His smile, as always, was so sincere, his gaze so guileless, that Sally couldn't doubt him. Still, she wondered if the Daughtons might appreciate knowing they were being watched nearly every moment of the day.

Chapter 7

Lukas was the first to wake the morning he was to start digging the trench. They'd already dug a preliminary pit, butting up to what was to be the cellar of the mill—a cellar Fergus and Nolan were lining with limestone. The collection pond to hold water for running the mill's wheel would connect with the millrace he would dig, deep enough to tap into water flowing beneath the ice in the winter, allowing the mill to run year-round.

Today he would begin digging from the source of the spring, and be joined tomorrow by Bran, who would follow him and deepen the initial cut. The flow, according to Pap, was more important than digging the shorter distance from the portion of the river that ran closer to town. Their canal would divert some of the water exactly where they needed it to be, while leaving the rest of the river untouched.

He had to admit this was the portion of work he'd anticipated ever since learning who owned the land they needed to use nearest the fountainhead. Mr. Hobson had easily agreed, for a portion of the mill's future income, to let them take the back end of his cornfield for part of the canal. All day Lukas kept one eye on the horse-drawn slip scoops digging into the ground, and another eye on the Hobson house in the distance.

Though he'd gone out of his way to catch Sally Hobson's eye if he happened to see her in town or at church, Lukas had already learned quite a bit about her, in spite of spending so little time alone with her. He knew she blushed easily, chose her words carefully, prayed with her eyes closed, and looked at friends and family alike with open but quiet affection. He wanted her to look at him in such a way. . .but first he needed to figure out her relationship with the mayor's son. So far, he had reason to believe Sally wasn't exactly smitten with the young man, even if he was with her. Lukas wasn't in the habit of stealing other men's girls—unless, of course, they wanted to be stolen.

"Ho, there!" Lukas called to the horse hitched to the scoops that dug into the earth ahead of them. "Ho, Leonidis!"

There, coming from the house in the distance, across the new sprouts of corn, he spotted the very silhouette he'd hoped all morning to see. There was no

344

mistaking that graceful, bonneted form—and she was coming his way.

Taking off his hat, swiping a forearm across his forehead to catch whatever sweat his hat left behind, he pulled off the leather shoulder straps he'd used to direct Leonidis, and stepped around the equipment. He wanted nothing between him and what he hoped was his own special visitor.

"Nice to see you, Miss Hobson," he said. "In fact, you're about the prettiest sight I could imagine."

Without meeting his gaze, she pulled something from the basket on her arm—a corked stone pitcher with a tin cup strung to its handle. She handed it to him and took out another item wrapped in a checked napkin. "I'm in the habit of bringing refreshment to my father when he works this field," she said. "He usually comes home looking like Adam before God's polish: all earthen as if he'd just been created."

Laughter burst from Lukas. "I guess I look like that already, and it's not even noon."

He welcomed her offering, seeing the napkin fall open to reveal a treat of bread, cheese, and a slice of cake. But most of all he was pleased with her company, and not only because she was so unexpected.

"My father enjoys two light lunches while he works, one before noon and one mid-afternoon. I thought you might not mind an interruption."

"Pardon me for saying so, but you couldn't be farther from an interruption."

It was her turn to laugh now, and it made him marvel. It wasn't just her ready cheerfulness. It was how easily he enjoyed her company. Lukas had been on the receiving end of enough smiles and winks to be confident around women, but somehow this was different. He'd sensed intelligence in Sally from the first day she'd followed them to the meeting with the mayor. Lukas imagined he could talk to her about anything, and she would have something to say.

The sandwich and cake melted in his mouth, the cider—last year's batch, she confessed—sweetly chased down every crumb. But even as she waited while he enjoyed the treat, he saw something else on her brow as she scanned the clearing. She almost looked worried.

He might be a new student to reading her face, but he was certain he'd read her clearly. "Anything wrong, Miss Sally?"

"There *is* another reason for my visit. I wonder, Mr. Daughton—"

"Lukas," he said.

"—if you're aware of those who've been watching your progress? Not here, perhaps, but cutting trees, or digging at the mill site."

"Oh sure," he said. "Boys, mostly. Not that I blame them. When I was a kid we always prowled around looking for something of interest to see. Just wait until we raise the water-wheel. That'll give them something to watch!"

"Local boys aren't the only ones watching," she said quietly, but not looking at him, as if she felt the town and everyone in it guilty of not believing in the quality of their work.

He finished the cider, handed the cup back for her to reattach to the jug. "I know. I've seen them."

"Then you should also know they're talking about calling another meeting. Evidently they're concerned about the placement of the mill, so far from the water."

"Let them. We know what we're doing."

She held his gaze steady for the first time, inadvertently giving him the opportunity to admire the blue flecks in her eyes. Various shades mixed together to create the color of the sky. *My, she's pretty.* He was surprised how comfortable he was in her presence. More than one girl had brought up the topic of marriage before he even knew a girl's temperament. Some girls didn't need much more encouragement than he'd already given Sally to start such thinking. But somehow he knew Sally Hobson wouldn't try nabbing anyone who didn't present the idea first, and whoever did would be lucky to win her.

"I believe you do know what you're doing," she whispered, and hurried away.

But her words were all he wanted to hear.

∞

For the next four days, Sally delivered refreshment to Lukas—and to Bran, when he was there—as they worked behind her father's field. She refused to show her disappointment on the days his brother was there, or acknowledge the cause of her disappointment at not finding him alone. She brought larger meals when she saw more than one Daughton at the trench, but her real enjoyment was watching Lukas savor the food, listening as he told her about the other mills they'd built, the towns they'd left in their wake. She'd always enjoyed listening more than talking, and Lukas didn't seem to mind.

On the fifth day when she headed back home after her visit with Lukas alone, she was surprised to see Willis's carriage waiting at the hitching post.

Entering through the back of the house, she paused to drop off the empty jug and basket, and left her bonnet on a chair beside the kitchen table.

"Is that you, dear?" her mother called from the parlor. "You have company."

She walked through the small dining room that separated the kitchen from the parlor, and greeted Willis with a smile that was in sharp contrast to the frown she saw immediately on his face.

"I came to speak to you, Sally."

"Then I'll leave the two of you to talk—"

But Willis was shaking his head before Sally's mother had finished. "You ought to stay, Mrs. Hobson. You'll want to know what I came to say."

"Goodness," her mother said, "that sounds serious. And here I thought you'd just stopped by because you haven't seen Sally since Sunday."

"That's right, I haven't. But my man Cyrus has seen you, Sally. Hasn't he?"

"Has he?"

"Yes. Quite a few times, in fact. Delivering refreshment to those Daughton men. Is that where you've been just now?"

"That's right," Sally admitted. She ought to be indignant that Willis sounded as if this was something to be ashamed of, but knew she couldn't be. If her visits had only been neighborly, perhaps she could have returned his attitude with a righteousness of her own.

Sally's mother was still smiling amiably, looping one arm through Sally's and the other with Willis. She led them to the sofa, as if a comfortable seat would forestall the possibility of disagreement. But no one sat. "Sally always delivers food to her father when he's out on our field. Seeing the Daugtons working so hard in the sun reminded us how much her father appreciates the refreshment."

"And it's been no trouble," Sally added.

Willis made an effort to lift his frowning brows, but Sally saw it was too much for him to conceal the exasperation he no doubt felt. "Don't you see how it might look, dear? It's one thing to be naturally kind to your own father, but to deliver repast to a family you barely know—"

"The Daughtons have been here for weeks now, Willis. They've proven hardworking, and they all attend church and sing with the best of us. How can it be wrong to be neighborly?"

"But they're not neighbors and will never be," Willis insisted. "You must know they're only passing through."

"All the more reason to show them Christian kindness."

Willis's frown was in full view again, and he looked from Sally to her mother as if expecting her support. But she dropped her contact with him instead.

"I'm afraid I agree with Sally, Willis. I've helped put the refreshment together each and every day."

If he cared to extend the argument, he seemed to change his mind after neither one of them agreed with him. He smoothed his brow, with better results this time, and looked at Sally.

"I only brought it up because I thought you shouldn't go alone to carry out such a friendly duty. You are, after all, an unmarried woman, and the Daughtons are all men."

"I'm sure no one would think it odd to treat such hard workers with kindness in the openness of our very own field."

Willis didn't look placated, but he did manage a smile. "Will you come out to the porch with me for a few minutes, Sally? Just so we could visit?"

She followed him dutifully out to the porch, where Willis sat a bit closer on the swing than she expected from someone so obviously concerned about what others thought. He smelled slightly of his midday meal, onions perhaps, mixed with peppermint that hadn't quite conquered the other odor.

"I think we ought to spend more time together than just sitting next to one another at church, don't you, Sally?"

"What do you have in mind?"

Willis looked at her, his eyes now warm, brows smooth. "I see no reason why we shouldn't announce a wedding date."

She let her gaze flutter away, knowing her usual shyness wasn't the culprit for her confusion over what to say now. "There is one good reason we haven't announced anything, Willis. We haven't really spent much time together. And besides that, you've never asked me to marry you."

His laughter sounded unexpectedly high, as if nervous. "I thought my intentions were understood."

"Did you?"

"Everyone expects us to marry, Sally." He inched a bit closer, slipping an arm around her shoulders. At least the peppermint seemed stronger now, with each word he spoke. "Haven't you noticed? Even your parents expect it."

"Is that a reason to marry?"

He laughed a peppermint laugh. "It certainly is. They're wise, and they support something that makes perfect sense."

"But why should it make more sense for you to marry me than for you to marry any other young lady in town?"

"You silly goose! You're egging me on, aren't you? Well, I'll succumb. I'll say it. I don't want any other girl in town. How could I? All my dreams are about you."

This was the first time Willis had spoken so directly of his feelings. As to seeing her in his dreams, she wondered what that had to do with love. Her own dreams rarely made sense, and had little to do with reality.

"Those are pretty words, Willis. But I'm not sure we know each other well enough to announce a wedding day. Besides, my parents depend upon me. I do all of the family accounting; did you know that? I'm not sure I'd have the time to run my own household and continue to help here as well."

"Surely your parents want you to have your own life, not to be shut away taking care of them."

"No, of course not. But until I figure out a way to do it all. . .living in town with you is a bit farther than I expected. I always pictured myself on a farm nearby, not all the way in town."

"Live out here in the middle of the cornfields?"

"Of course. The days go quickly running a farm. And it's lovely out here."

"You mean lonely, don't you?"

"You're proving my point, Willis. We hardly know one another. You would know I'm more comfortable with family and fewer visitors than socializing every day if I lived in town."

"It's only that you're not used to it yet. Once you're my wife and we're entertaining people who need my services as a lawyer, or those we'll know through my father, you'll soon learn to love all kinds of people passing through our door."

Sally pushed away immediate disappointment that he so quickly and easily dismissed her worries. Worse, the image of countless dinner parties left her dreading such a prospect.

Still, she must consider his words carefully. After all, Alice had been telling her for years that she needed to spread her wings, test herself in more social situations. Perhaps she really did have a gracious hostess inside of her. How would she know? She preferred spending time by herself, it was true, but that didn't mean she couldn't learn to enjoy the company of others. There were people at church she genuinely enjoyed and could easily imagine socializing with.

However, rather than a picture of Willis as the host and she, his hostess, a sudden, unbidden image filled her mind. What would it be like to entertain with such a friendly counterpart as Lukas Daughton at her table?

Chapter 8

Spring planting ended as it always did, followed by plenty of chores, fretting over crops, neighbors exchanging goods rather than dollar bills. In addition to the eggs and butter that Sally sold or bartered through the year, she collected honey from the hives on their land to trade along with jams and berry pies she made with her mother. Their creations seldom sat long on the Gibbons' store shelves.

Although it would have been easy to do so, Sally didn't allow herself to deliver afternoon repasts to the Daughtons once their work returned to the mill site in town. As her mother reminded her, Willis was a dependable, popular citizen of their town. It wouldn't do any good to offend him. Besides, both she and her mother were so busy with berries and honey that the sunny days, as always, flew by.

But, as usual, when she visited town at an early time of day, she looked around for Lukas Daughton's familiar face. He seemed as privy to her butter and egg schedule as she was herself.

"Hold up there, Leonidis. Ho!"

Sally's heart skipped, recognizing not only the name of the horse but the voice bidding its halt. She turned, seeing Lukas pulling up in a wagon beside the store she'd just exited.

"Morning, Miss Sally," he called as he hopped from the rig. "It's a glorious day!" Tipping his hat, he stood close, towering over her.

"And what makes this day so good?"

"It's bound to be a good day when I see you."

Warmth flooded her cheeks in spite of herself. "Good morning, Mr. Daughton."

"It's Lukas," he said, and bent closer to whisper in her ear, "but you already know that, don't you? Now if only I can convince you to use that name instead of my father's, this day will be all the brighter."

She had no intention of admitting it was a struggle not to call him Lukas, since his name came so easily to mind. Lukas's charm was as consistent as his attention, but each passing day of progress on the mill brought his departure that much closer. That was enough to help her resist him—at least with her actions, even if her mind had already surrendered.

"I thought you should know your brother-in-law will be joining us next week, after he returns from his visit to Chicago with his most recent load of livestock. He's volunteered to work with us a few hours a day for the next two weeks."

"Yes, so my sister told me. My father hopes to help as well, now that you're raising the walls of the mill."

"We'll welcome whatever help we can get," Lukas said.

She began to turn away, thinking their conversation was at its logical end, but he detained her. "Your brother-in-law invited us to dinner tomorrow night. Will you be there, Sally?"

She knew about the dinner because Alice had slyly invited Sally, too. Sally saw right through her sister's intention to put her together with Lukas. Like it or not, Alice was a romantic. Sally being left with a broken heart at the end of the summer didn't seem to frighten her sister at all.

But the way Lukas had lowered his tone, the same invitation her sister had tried so casually to extend sounded downright intimate. Dropping the polite "Miss" before her name hadn't escaped her either. That must be why she had such a difficult time tearing her gaze from his.

She knew what she must say, despite every silent objection demanding she say something else. "I–I'm afraid I can't be there, Mr. Daughton."

"Why?"

She knew it was wiser to keep her thoughts to herself, especially those having to do with him. But she must make it clear she had no intention of welcoming his attention. "For the same reason I won't call you Lukas."

She tried to leave it at that, to walk on and let him draw his own conclusion, but he stepped in her path. It was a bold move, impolite even, but not unexpected.

His smile, though, erased every bit of his former surprise, as if whatever conclusion he *had* drawn bolstered his confidence instead of the other way around. "Most people," he said, his tone still far too captivating, "might think someone who is avoiding them doesn't like them. But do you know what I think?"

She lifted one brow, not daring to ask but not moving away either.

"I think in some cases, avoidance means just the opposite. It's like someone who loves the taste of candy, but knows they'll eat too much and end up with a toothache. So they won't even look at candy. But it isn't because they don't like it."

"And you, Mr. Daughton, are like candy?"

His grin went lopsided as he nodded. "I just have to convince you I won't leave you with a toothache."

Perhaps not a toothache, but almost certainly a heartache. She bit back the words and walked around him.

"You realize the only way to prove me wrong is to show up?" he called after her. "Prove you can be indifferent to my company. I dare you to be there, Sally."

She didn't look back, just let her gaze dart away with the hope that no one else had heard him.

Chapter 9

Of course, she knew all along she would accept Lukas's dare. Not just to prove something to him, but to prove to herself she was every bit as sensible as she knew herself to be.

As she would have done for *any* dinner party, she wore her newest dress and took special care with her hair. She wished her parents were going, but the table in Alice's kitchen would barely seat the entire Daughton clan without adding two more places.

She arrived on foot at Alice's only a few minutes after six, and the door was already open to let in the breeze. Seeing the two Daughton wagons, she knew her arrival would draw everyone's attention and so rather than going in the front door she circled around to the kitchen entrance, where she found Alice.

"Oh! You've arrived just in time to stir the soup," Alice said, handing her a spoon.

Grateful that her sister was too occupied with dinner preparation to scold her for sneaking in, Sally set to work—knowing she couldn't avoid the rest of the evening for long.

Still, she put it off until dinner was served. She carried in a tray of bowls filled with soup, stealing a glance at the guests until her gaze stopped at Lukas. He hadn't noticed her yet; he was staring out the open door, as if looking for the latecomer. Her.

His gaze didn't find hers until Arthur invited everyone to sit at the table.

Proud of herself for having escaped any before-dinner awkwardness, she took her seat at last. She ignored Lukas's lingering gaze of appreciation, saying nothing as he claimed the seat next to hers. She thanked him politely when he played the servant and filled her glass from the pitcher of lemonade. And when their fingers grazed after they both reached for the bread, she pulled away as if burned, because that was how his touch felt. Like a lightning bolt that tingled throughout her body.

No one who knew her would think her quietness odd. Only she knew it wasn't just her shyness holding her tongue tonight. It was the sinking realization that if Lukas Daughton ever wanted to kiss her, she would be powerless to stop him.

And that was hardly what a woman, who might yet one day become engaged to another man, should be thinking.

⌒

At the evening's end Sally was both relieved and disappointed. Relieved she'd done nothing to encourage Lukas's attention—surely she'd won the dare—but disappointed because, inside, she knew she'd lost. Thoroughly and completely.

Eager to return home, to be alone to conquer her thoughts of him, she was the first to the door after helping Alice to clean up.

"You'll allow me to see you home, won't you?"

Sally shot a panicked gaze to Alice, avoiding Lukas's, who had stolen up behind her to ask the question.

"That's a fine idea," said Alice, much to Sally's dismay.

"But. . ." Sally's heart thrummed. "The stars offer plenty of light, and the road is wide between here and home. I'm sure I'll be fine on my own—"

"I wouldn't let you go off alone. It'll be dark soon," said Arthur, stepping toward the door as well. "Your father would have my hide."

Alice handed her the flour sack she'd filled with leftover cake, an offering to their father for having to miss the meal. The smile on her face was decidedly knowing. "Don't forget to give this to Pa."

"I'll carry it," Lukas offered. For the second time that evening, his touch grazed Sally's and the same fire ignited, reminding her just how eager she was to be alone with him.

How was she to avoid this man when everyone else wanted just the opposite?

The rest of the Daughtons crowded into one wagon while Lukas helped Sally into the other. His father went ahead, and without a word, Lukas directed his horses to follow at a leisurely pace.

If she were less suspicious she might not have noticed the widening distance between the wagons. It was as if Lukas wanted no one overhearing them in the still night air.

"So?"

The single word might have confused someone else, but she knew instantly what he meant. She kept silent, pretending not to know what she fully understood the topic to be.

"If you can't deny it, I'll assume this evening proved you aren't indifferent to me."

"Mr. Daughton—"

"Are you going to call me that forever? Right up to the altar?"

She laughed at his words. Marriage was such a ridiculously unexpected idea, especially coming from him. "The altar, indeed."

He scratched his ear, laughing along with her. "I admit those words came as a surprise to me, too. But I've got to say"—he slid her a smile—"it's easy to see why they slipped out. It's nice having the prettiest girl in town believe in us."

She stared ahead. "I'm sure you've easily convinced a number of girls that you know what you're doing. And will no doubt do the same in the next town you visit."

His grip tightened on the reins; she saw the tension ripple across his knuckles. "This mill is going to be the best we've ever built. I've been thinking about staying to see it work."

"For how long?" Sally asked, heart thudding anew.

She followed his gaze to the nearby undulating land, the row of trees in the distance, and the setting sun still shimmering at the edge of the flat horizon beyond. The fertile ground would produce an unending source of grain to keep any mill working far into the future.

Though he didn't answer her question, he turned his gaze on her. "Sally, I've been patiently watching you in Willis's company since I came to town. Do you know what I see?"

She dared not speak, or even spare him a glance.

He went on anyway. "You look at him the same way you look at any other nice enough fella. You're comfortable around him, and if that's enough for you, maybe you'll be happy. But you don't look at me that way, and I'd like you to admit—to yourself if not to me—there could be more in life than just being comfortable."

A rush of warmth spread through Sally, this time without a single touch. She told herself she should be mortified, to be read so easily by a man she had no intention of encouraging. But even though she knew he was right, she still couldn't look at him for fear of what he would see in her eyes.

"Being comfortable is better than being heartbroken," she whispered. "So if you would please take me the rest of the way home, Mr. Daughton, I would appreciate it."

Chapter 10

Lukas had a good view of the horizon from a beam on the second floor of the mill. Already the landscape of Finchville had been redrawn, now that the second story was nearly complete. Though he scanned the view of town and beyond, Sally was nowhere in sight. He could use some of her sweetened, cool tea.

The thought of her made him smile, despite his growing fatigue. He'd enjoyed working with her father and brother-in-law whenever they could help out, but they weren't there today, with other farm chores demanding their time. Not that their presence guaranteed she would visit.

His hammer rejoined the chorus of his brothers, all perched on corners of the second story. For the past month he'd been hoping she would visit, but so far she'd stayed away. His hopes of seeing her today were about as parched as his tongue just now.

"Bran! Lukas!"

Owny had left them earlier for the shed they'd built on the other side of the millpond, where he was finishing his work on the millstones they would soon place inside the mill.

"Come quick!"

Lukas beat his brothers to the ground, alarmed at his brother's tone. Owny could jest with anyone, but never with a hue and cry.

Inside the shed, Lukas saw remnants of the millstone Owny had been grooving. Mined from local granite, it would have been hard to break, but it now lay in pieces in the center of the wooden floor. Their own sledgehammer was left nearby.

Horror filled Lukas at such a deliberate act, but no sooner had the realization hit him than his father, the last to arrive and closest to the shed door, turned on his heel. Lukas raced past, beating him to the small patch of bushes and weeds, an inconspicuous spot they'd chosen not long after receiving the town's approval to build the mill.

"They're all right," he called to his father, who had lagged behind Lukas and all three of his brothers. They'd placed the French millstone—the best

356

stone to grind the finest flour—in the copse just to be out of the way, freeing their wagon of the ballast their horses had dragged all the way from Baltimore. These two stones were the last of the five pairs they'd purchased, having used the others in former mills they'd built between Finchville and Baltimore.

His father took a look for himself, and with a pat to Lukas's shoulder, directed them away from the spot.

"Who do you suppose did such a thing?" Owny asked.

Lukas was so eager to cast the name Willis Pollit that he barely caught himself in time. Who else in town didn't want their mill to succeed? It was no secret his father had hinted he could have hired someone from Chicago for the job, but it was Willis himself who most wanted the Daughtons to leave. Or at least Lukas. That much was obvious whenever Lukas smiled Sally's way—something Lukas had no intention of stopping.

"I'll go see the sheriff," Lukas said. "Owny, you'll need to scout another piece of granite. We promised a working mill before the first snow, and a working mill it'll be."

∞

"What do you think of the idea, Mrs. Gibbons?"

The older woman's smile bounced between Sally and her sister. "Like it or not, that mill is here to stay. I say your celebration is the finest idea I've heard all summer."

Alice, who had met Sally at the store, fairly squealed with delight. Having the storekeeper spread the word about Sally's idea for their "First-Fruits Festival" was a vital part of their plan. "And we'll have music, too! Think of all the harvest songs we know!"

As they chatted on about a celebration to honor the mill's opening, Sally's enthusiasm suddenly seemed more than just that. She felt hopeful, too. Enough people had doubted the placement of the mill that this celebration would go a long way to bringing the entire town together again.

Willis never hid his doubts about the mill. When he realized they could collect enough water to run the mill exactly where they'd placed it, he claimed the redistributed water would flood the town. But even Sally could see the center of the town stood on higher ground, and with the newly dug millpond and penstock directing the water toward the mill's giant wheel, it would take a great deal of water indeed to threaten even the deepest cellar on main street.

Her confidence in the mill seemed to deepen Willis's resentment, making his sullenness harder to bear his company. She refused to dwell on comparisons to Lukas, but somehow her heart did anyway.

However, believing in the permanence of the mill didn't mean she should trust the permanence of the Daughtons. Lukas may have hinted he would stay after the mill opened, but he'd never said for how long.

Alice looped her arm with Sally's, each with her own thoughts about the festival as they left the store. But shouting from the vicinity of the sheriff's office caught Sally's attention the minute they stepped outside. Sheriff Tilney stood in heated discussion with none other than Lukas Daughton.

"I just don't know what you expect me to do about it, that's all," the sheriff was saying.

"You can ask around, starting with anyone you know who doesn't want the mill."

While the sheriff claimed he'd do all he could about whatever concerned Lukas, Sally caught Lukas's eye. He left the sheriff without another word and came to her.

"What happened?" she asked.

"Someone took a sledgehammer to one of the grinding stones," he said.

Sally's gasp matched her sister's.

"It didn't do more than send a message that somebody wants trouble," Lukas said. "We can make a replacement."

"But what a horrid message," Sally said softly. "Who among us could have done such a thing?"

Lukas's eyes narrowed nearly imperceptibly. But the quick gesture was enough to reveal his suspicions. Who didn't want the mill to succeed? Surely *Willis* wouldn't have done such a thing!

She stiffened, automatically defending the unspoken name—while at the same time determining to speak to Willis the first chance that presented itself.

Chapter 11

As usual on Sunday morning, Willis escorted Sally home from church. All morning she barely kept her mind on anything but talking to him—except she had no idea what to say.

It didn't help that Lukas sat nearby during the service. His silence dared her to confront Willis about the grinding stone, but his obvious suspicion made the impending conversation that much more serious.

At her father's wagon, Sally held back. "Willis," she said, "it's cooler today. Would you mind walking rather than riding?"

He looked delighted at the idea of walking back to her family home alone with her, which would take some time indeed, and her parents went off without another word.

"I certainly enjoy our Sundays," Willis said. "And you know why, don't you, Sally?"

"Willis," she began slowly. Many thoughts collided in her mind, no longer only about the grindstone, but other thoughts she'd been unable to conquer ever since Lukas had brought it up. Lukas was right; she was far too comfortable around Willis. She'd told herself that couldn't possibly be a bad thing, except she couldn't remember her heart ever fluttering at the sight of him, even when she'd first met him. She couldn't remember wishing for just the right words around him, fretting over her appearance, wondering if he thought of her as easily as she thought of him. Because the truth was she rarely thought of Willis unless she knew she would be seeing him. If she were as honest with herself as Lukas had dared her to be, she would admit even if she did feel occasional affection for Willis, it wasn't enough to consider marrying him. It wasn't fair not to tell him the truth.

"Yes, Sally?"

Forcing calm to her jarring thoughts, she stole a glance at him. "I thought you should know I can't consider marrying you." The words had nothing to do with what she'd planned to say, but she couldn't call them back and felt only the utmost relief that they were out.

"What?"

His shock nearly matched her own, but having a suspicion that Willis might have crushed that stone was enough to convince her of what she'd just said. It didn't matter if she accused him or not; it wouldn't change anything, and she doubted he would simply admit it even if he had done such a thing. Right now, all she knew was that she wanted more to marriage than what she felt for Willis. That was true whether or not Lukas Daughton left town.

"I'm sorry, Willis," she said softly.

The initial hurt on his face turned to anger when a brow curved inward. "I was good enough for you before those mill builders came to town. That Lukas, anyway."

"No, Willis. I was wrong to encourage you, when I knew from the start I wasn't ready."

Now one of those brows lifted. "If I'm hurrying you, I can wait longer. I've already waited—"

She shook her head again. "My idea of marriage is. . .different from what I think yours might be."

"Why? Marriage is marriage. Faithful to each other, raising children together. How could your idea of marriage be different from that?"

"I just don't love you the way a girl should," she said at last, and the hurt in his eyes reappeared. "I didn't want to say that, Willis. But I don't know how else to explain how I feel."

He sucked in a breath as if she'd robbed him of air. "Well," he said slowly, stopping altogether. He looked at her, away, then back again. "I suppose you can see yourself home."

An overwhelming rush of guilt swept Sally. Perhaps she'd been too hasty; perhaps once Lukas was gone she truly would regret this decision. But those fleeting doubts weren't enough to stop the sensible words already forming on her lips. "Isn't it better to know I would be so hard to make happy, Willis? Now, rather than later? You would be unhappy, too, then, and it would be my fault."

He nodded, not looking at her, then walked back toward the main street where he lived.

Chapter 12

Rainclouds threatened to dampen the festival, so Mr. Daughton invited the women providing the food to set up refreshments in the wide, open second floor of the brand-new mill.

Sally walked up the stairs, the scent of fresh wood and varnish mingling with the chicken and pies she carried on a large tray. As usual, she kept her eye out for Lukas, who had been especially polite but surprisingly distant since Willis no longer sat beside her and her family at church. But even if he had swooped in on her, she would have refused his company. She might have failed to keep her heart in check, but she would not encourage her growing love for him by spending more time with him before he left town. She spent enough time with him in her imagination.

Especially since it was no secret that Mr. Daughton was training Mr. and Mrs. Gibbons' oldest son, Charley, to work the mill after they left. That had been enough to seal Sally's resolve against Lukas, even though his face haunted nearly all of her thoughts.

Sally stepped into the large, open upper room, where planks and boards had been set upon trestles to hold all of the food for the party. Wind howled through an open window, rippling the cloths draped over the makeshift tables. Before she could drop off her goods to shut the window, someone beat her to it.

Suddenly the large and empty room was far more intimate. Lukas turned from the window, a welcoming smile on his handsome face.

"When I learned you would be working up here with the food," he said as he walked steadily toward her, "I volunteered to help. I even promise not to taste the goods until you give permission."

She laughed but knew she sounded nervous. And why shouldn't she be? She ought to run right out of this room, demand Alice take over. That's what Sensible Sally would do.

Instead, she stood perfectly still until he stopped, a hands width away.

"I want to talk to you, Sally," he whispered.

But before either could say another word, voices clamored up the stairs along with clomping feet and laughter.

"Before the day is out," he added, and went to greet Mrs. Gibbons to help her with a basket of food.

∞

Two hours later, the town gathered for the opening of the sluice. Water flowing from the spring some half mile away now collected on one side of the mill, to be released along the shaft running toward the huge wooden and iron wheel which turned the stones inside the mill. That same water spilled into the millpond on the other side of the wheel, where Sally now stood in anticipation of the mill's official opening.

She heard whispers from every direction, in one form or another: *"The mill is a marvel of engineering."* Her heart swelled with pride—for the town, for those who, like her, never doubted it would work, for those like Arthur and her father who had worked on it alongside of the Daughtons. For Mr. Daughton who designed it. And for Lukas, because it had been his invitation that convinced others to let them build the mill right here in Finchville.

She knew he was destined to leave soon; she didn't expect anything else. But she would always have the mill, a shining spot of community and success, to remember the handsome young man who had captured her heart. Even if she never told him he'd done so.

No doubt the reason he wanted to talk to her today was to tell her good-bye.

With a wave to the crowd surrounding the mill, Lukas stood on the platform above the millrace, where the turn of a wheel would release the water and start the mill. Just as he did so, Sally heard another voice closer to where she stood.

"Lukas! Owny!"

Mr. Daughton shouted from the mill's cellar window, but the desperate call was drowned by the suddenly rushing water and turning wheel.

"Stop the water!"

Sally knew neither Lukas nor Owny had heard their father. But Lukas looked her way, and she frantically waved her arms, pantomiming to spin the wheel to shut off the source of water. Either he understood her motion or had heard at least the tone if not his father's words. Something was amiss below the wheel. Hurriedly he closed off the portal and Lukas and Owny ran to the cellar door and disappeared inside.

By the time she reached the same door, there was no room for her. Mr. Gibbons was already waving people away, preventing anyone else from squeezing inside the already crowded cellar.

The same whispers that only moments ago had touted the project a pioneering wonder were already abandoning their praise. *"Too big a job." "Some things just aren't meant to be built." "I knew it would never work."*

Sally pressed forward again, determined to find out what had happened. She refused to believe anything had really gone wrong. Surely the mill wasn't a fancy shell of a failure!

Someone called for the sheriff, who was already nearby, and Sally stepped aside only long enough to follow him inside.

In the cellar's darkness, Sally could barely see. She searched for Lukas, but she was too short to see above the heads and shoulders pressing into the cramped quarters. She couldn't even hear what they said to Sheriff Tilney, but before long the whispers started again. *"Intentional damage." "Sabotage."*

The outrage and suspicion in those whispers mirrored her own—but something else grew in Sally, and she stopped looking for Lukas. She slipped back toward the door.

Guilt filled her on waves of nausea.

Accusations made her heart sink. Willis had many reasons for the mill to fail. Damaged pride because no one listened to his distrust of the Daughtons. Avarice that he wasn't able to hire someone of his own choosing for the job, perhaps share in the wealth that was sure to come with such a town-altering improvement. And jealousy that it was Lukas who had changed Sally's mind about possibly marrying him.

It might have been Willis's actions, but the damage was Sally's fault. She could have stopped him, if only she'd confronted him weeks ago about the millstone. Surely he wouldn't have been bold enough to ruin today if she had accused him when she had the chance.

The sheriff ordered people out, and for a moment it felt as if she were in the millrace itself, being carried outside on a current—not with water but with people.

She searched for Willis, someone she hadn't seen all day. She'd thought nothing of his absence until now.

Marching up the path toward Main Street, Sally quickly reached the post office building, where Willis lived with his father. But she barely had a chance to knock before the door swung open. There stood Willis, just straightening a crooked tie.

"Well!" he greeted her. "This is a surprise. I didn't think you'd want me as an escort when today will be the crowning glory for the Daughtons. Or have they left already, now that the project is finished?"

Folding her arms, she glared at him. "How dare you! How could you do such a thing?"

"What?" His brows rose indignantly but faltered ever so slightly—whether in anger or guilt, she couldn't tell.

"Someone tampered with the mill. Just as someone broke one of the grindstones a few weeks ago. Who else but you have hated the idea of this mill from the start?"

He raised both palms, but before he could speak something caught his eye from over her shoulder. She turned, seeing the entire town, led by not only the sheriff but by the Daughtons, coming straight toward them.

Sally caught Lukas's eye, who looked at her curiously. Perhaps he, too, believed if it weren't for her no damage would have been done, if only she had voiced her suspicions. Looking away, she stepped aside; no longer bold enough to make her accusations with the entire town ready to cast their own.

"You have anything to do with tampering with the mill, Willis?"

Willis's eyes rounded at the sheriff's question. Fear crept into his eyes as first one, then another man behind the sheriff demanded he confess.

"I don't know what any of you are talking about!" Willis protested. "I was nowhere near that mill. I'm a lawyer, you know. You'll need evidence if you want to make this kind of accusation."

"Somebody put this on a shaft above the gears," Mr. Daughton said, holding out a small metal object. "It was supposed to fall in and gum up the works. This yours?"

It was a simple shoehorn, something any number of people owned; even Sally's father had one. Willis looked at the object as if he didn't even know what it was. Even his telltale brows didn't give him away.

"Of course it isn't mine! I don't even own such a thing."

A commotion broke out at the side of the post office—shouts, pounding feet, a chase. Everyone turned to look, but when Sally looked again at Willis, his formerly rigid face filled with renewed fear at the sound of Cyrus's voice rising above the others. The servant cried out for all to hear. "I didn't mean it! I didn't even want to do it! But he—he made me do it!"

His finger pointed to none other than Willis Pollit.

Chapter 13

After a thorough inspection of the mill, Mr. Daughton learned several of the pins had been loosened along the millrace, inviting collapse. Rags had been stuffed in the hopper that fed grain onto the stones, and one of the mesh screens to separate grain from chaff was sliced.

The sheriff, however loyal he might have been to the Pollit family, had no choice but to take both Cyrus and Willis to the jail.

But repairs to the mill were completed in less than an hour, and once the mill proved it worked, any sourness toward Willis dissipated as the delayed celebration began.

Lukas searched once again for Sally, but he hadn't seen her since the confrontation with Willis. Looming worry edged closer. Perhaps she thought Willis needed her, now that he hadn't a friend in town. Even his father, ashamed of the damage his son had arranged, or perhaps still eager to hold on to his job, stayed at the festival and openly derided what had been done.

It was already growing dark, and the sound of music carried over the gently spinning mill amid conversations and laughter. Lukas was more eager than ever to find Sally. This festival was her idea, and he'd planned from the moment he heard about it to say all he needed to say to her. Tonight. He was tired of waiting, of giving her time to make sure she didn't regret that she no longer allowed Willis Pollit to sit beside her at church.

If only he could find her.

∞

Sally watched the festivities from the second floor window, in the room now emptied since the weather cleared and the leftover food had been taken outside. The earlier storm had passed through quickly, blessing the rest of the day with fresh air and now with starry skies. She stood at the very window Lukas had closed earlier, enjoying the sounds from below but without a sliver of desire to join the party she herself had suggested.

"Do you know I've been looking for you all evening?"

The deep voice should have startled her, but the sound was far too welcome. She'd spotted him several times while he passed through the crowd below. Now and then he stopped to talk, to Alice and Arthur, to her parents. To his own father and brothers. He'd never lingered long, lending credence to the search he'd just confessed.

"I like watching people enjoying one another's company," she said, warning herself silently to keep the conversation light. No use saying anything silly just before he left.

He stopped at her side. "Only watching?"

The room was lit by moonlight streaming in through the new glass. The quiet room and shadowy light added intimacy to the moment, making it more difficult than ever for Sally to tame her tongue and speak only politely. Her mind filled with the truth she couldn't reveal. She wished he would stay. She would never forget him. And the most secret truth of all: She'd fallen in love with him.

"I like people," she admitted. "But at a distance."

"Me, too."

She laughed. "You, who can talk in front of crowds, who charmed this entire town into letting you build the most ambitious business it's ever known?"

"Just because I can act like a salesman doesn't mean I like it." He leaned against the wall, no longer peering out the window with her. "In fact," his voice softened, slowed, "I think I'm better suited for steady work than essentially being a traveling salesman."

"Oh?" Her heart was beating so painfully it throbbed all the way up to her throat, so that single word nearly choked her.

"Can you hear the wheel still going, turning that grinding stone down there?"

She nodded, grateful for the return to lighter fare.

"There are two sets of stones for spinning, you know. One for coarse and one for fine. The finest flour will come from only one set of stones, and that's the set we brought with us. My father bought them in Baltimore—the only place in the country you can get French grinding stones. That was the last set we owned."

"So. . .I suppose your family will have to go back East again. For more stones."

He shifted to look out the window again, bending closer to her, and pointed toward his father at one of the tables. "He's a brilliant man, my father. He wanted to build the best mill possible, and this"—Lukas raised both palms to take in their surroundings—"is it."

"I'm glad he built it here, then."

Leaning so close to the window had brought his face only inches from hers. "This is the last mill he intends to build, Sally."

She wanted to read into that statement, but refused to jump to the best possible conclusion. "I suppose he's taught you and your brothers all you need to know to carry on, then."

He held her gaze, his lips curling into a smile. "Yes. My brothers could build more mills."

"And. . .you?"

His gaze slipped to her mouth then back to her eyes. "I'm staying right here to run this mill, Sally; with my father."

"But. . . But you hired Charley Gibbons!"

"Yes. So?"

"Isn't he going to run the mill?"

Lukas laughed. "Run the mill? All by himself? A man with one summer of training?"

"You're staying then?" The question seemed needless, but she wasn't convinced. "For a while, just until you're sure it's being run properly?"

"No." He drew out the word. "I'm going from mill builder to miller. I'm finished traveling every summer to a different town. I want a home."

"Do you?"

He stood only inches away, yet he took a tiny step closer. Close enough to feel his breath on her cheek. "Home, Sally. Here. With you."

Then he took her in his arms, kissed her gently, and she did exactly what she'd always done when she'd imagined this moment; she threw her arms around him and kissed him back.

Pulling away at last, she saw his smile illuminated so clearly in the moonlight. But then he put on a frown.

"Your kiss isn't quite convincing enough, Sally. There's only one way you can convince me that you want me to stay. Do you know how?"

She laughed, keeping her arms tight around his neck. "I want you to stay. Stay. . .*Lukas.*"

He swept her up into a spin, kissing her again then whispering, "That's closer, my love. But I need to hear the words I see in your eyes."

She'd imagined saying the words so many times they drained away her shyness. "I love you, Lukas."

"Ah Sally, that's what I've waited to hear. I love you, too."

Then, pressing his lips to hers, he spoke in spite of the kiss. "Will you marry me?"

She let her lips answer for her.

The Wildflower Bride

by Amy Lillard

Chapter 1

Maddie?" Grace Sinclair poked her head through the door of the downstairs guestroom then stepped inside.

Her sister whirled around, cheeks flushed, eyes sparkling. She ran trembling hands down her pale blue wedding gown. The satin fell in beautiful folds, edged with a cream-colored lace that suited her sister so well. It might be all the rage for the bride to wear white these days, but no one ever accused Maddie Sinclair of being like everyone else. Her younger sister was her own person, through and through. "Is it time?"

Grace nodded.

"Is he out there?"

"I haven't looked, but I don't think Prissy would have sent me to get you if he was missing."

Maddie nodded and swallowed hard.

"You're shaking," Grace said, taking her sister's hands into her own. "And cold." It was a beautiful June morning yet Maddie's fingers were like ice.

"I'm nervous." Maddie warbled out a smile.

"Not about his love for you?"

She shook her head. There had been a time when Maddie had worried about Harlan Calhoun's love. Or rather, the honesty of that love. But Grace supposed that's what happened when a young woman plied the man she loved with cookies doctored up with a love potion. Suspected love potion, she corrected. It turned out that the herbs Maddie had traded her second-best dress to Old Lady Farley for were no more than ground nutmeg and vanilla bean, with a little cinnamon thrown in for good measure.

And that Harlan's love for her was real.

"Then what's wrong?"

Tears welled in Maddie's dark green eyes. "Nothing. Everything. I'm sad and happy and nervous and. . ." She shook her head.

"Sad because Mom isn't here with us?"

Maddie nodded.

Grace could only imagine how her sister felt. And it was a feeling that she herself would never get to experience. She wasn't being pessimistic, just realistic. That was her, Pragmatic Grace Sinclair, destined to be an old maid. Though she preferred to think about it as giving her life to the Lord. Her destiny had been revealed long ago. She would stay in Calico Falls, never marry, and continue to help her father with his church.

She pushed those thoughts away and lifted her sister's chin. "Don't cry. It'll make your eyes all red. That's not how you want to spend your wedding day, is it?"

Maddie shook her head, her dark brown curls swaying with the motion. Even with tears in her eyes and her lips red from where she had bit them, Maddie was the prettiest bride Grace had ever seen.

"Then come on now." She passed Maddie a handkerchief. "Dry your eyes. Harlan's waiting. It's time to get married."

At the mention of her beloved's name, the sunshine broke free of the clouds, and Maddie's face lit up with a perfect smile. "Harlan," she repeated, her words a whisper of awe.

She wasn't jealous, Grace told herself. Envy was a sin. She was glad that Maddie had found the happiness that every woman deserves.

Then why can't you have it? That tiny voice inside her asked.

Because I'm fated to something different. A higher calling. At least, she liked to think of it that way.

Maddie took a deep breath and smoothed her skirts once again. "I'm ready." She smiled and held out her arm for Grace to take, and together the two of them made their way out to the back porch.

Birds chirped from above, the light wind rustled the leaves in the trees, and sunshine sparkled on everything it touched. God had spared no beauty on this day.

Across the yard a trellis had been set up, intertwined with colorful wild-flowers and green ivy, the perfect backdrop for the joining of two lives.

And in front of that white-painted trellis stood their father. Pa blinked back tears. Grace understood. She had already shed a few of her own. But he managed to keep them at bay as he waited to marry his youngest daughter to the newest member of the community, Harlan Calhoun, attorney at law.

Harlan shifted from one foot to the other as Maddie and Grace approached. He looked nervous, happy, and a little bit sick. And next to him stood—

Grace stumbled. Beside her, Maddie gasped and clutched her arm a bit tighter as if her grasp alone could keep Grace upright. She recovered quickly, managing to steady her steps, thankful she hadn't fallen flat on her face in front of half the town of Calico Falls. Later she would blame it on the uneven ground and the new shoes she had sent for, just for this occasion, but the truth of the matter was standing right in front of them. Suit-cut jacket and vest, pristine white shirt, wide black tie, and kilt.

The man was wearing a kilt. Somehow on him it was attractive, earthy and real, though she had never seen a man dressed like that before. Their laid-back Arkansas town had everyone dropping the formalities that were often found in the big cities, like such formal dress at a morning wedding. Not that they were lax, but just a little less. . .ceremonial. If there were any Scottish residents in Calico Falls, she couldn't think of even one. And they surely didn't go around dressing like that.

To make matters even worse for her heart, he was the most handsome man she had ever seen. Dark, rusty hair the same color as her father's favorite horse, broad cheeks, thin nose, and eyes that even from this distance she could tell were as blue as the sky above them.

But she already knew his story. His name was Ian Mc-something and he lived back East. He was Harlan's best friend and had only come to Calico Falls for the wedding. He was staying less than a week and then heading back.

Why, oh why, Lord? Why was the only man since grade school who had set her heart to fluttering the one man she could never have?

∞

Ian watched the bride approach. Well, that wasn't exactly true. He was facing the direction from which she was coming. Yet it wasn't the love of his best friend who captured his attention but the woman at her side.

He had only just arrived in Calico Falls the night before and hadn't had a chance to meet all of Maddie's family. But he suspected that the blond-haired dream walking next to Maddie Sinclair was none other than her sister, Grace.

Grace. What a fitting name for such a lovely creature. *Ach,* she was the prettiest thing he had ever seen, or as his grandfather, Athol, would say, "A bonnie lass indeed."

During the actual ceremony, he found himself staring at her instead of paying attention to the service. He missed his prompt to give Harlan the ring and despite his friend's personal excitement on the day, Ian suspected that Harlan knew. He hadn't gotten to be the best attorney in these parts without being sharp enough to see what was straight in front of him.

"I now pronounce you man and wife."

Harlan tugged his bride a little closer and cupped her cheeks in his hands before placing a chaste kiss on her forehead. His hands shook with happiness and what Ian was sure was a bit of groom jitters, but he would have traded places with him for almost anything on God's beautiful earth. Well, if Grace Sinclair could trade places with her sister.

Ian tried not to visibly shake his head. What was wrong with him? He was contemplating marriage and he hadn't even talked to the woman. Never mind that he was leaving in a couple of days. His original plan had been to stay the whole week, but summer rains had delayed his journey from the start, and just before he left, he was approached by the First Church of Albany, the largest and most prestigious church in Albany, New York. It was a progressive church, looking for young leaders to take them into the turn of the century. Well, so that wasn't for another thirty more years, and by then he would be anything but young, but the offer was too good to turn down. They wanted him back by Sunday's service to get started in his position as the assistant pastor there. That meant leaving Monday, Tuesday at the latest, to give him plenty of time for the journey and then to prepare for his sermon.

"Ian."

He startled as Harlan hissed his name. "Oh." It was time to leave. He looked around to find Grace staring at him, a small smile playing at her soft, pink lips. "Oh," he said again, realizing that he probably looked about as idiotic as any one man could.

Grace held out her arm and he took it, helping her back through the carpet of grass and around the side of the parsonage. The preacher's words floated over their heads, stating a noon meal would be served followed by the cutting of the wedding cake.

Ian didn't need to look behind him to know that the crowd who had just witnessed his best friend's wedding was headed their way. The murmur of the men's voices and the rustle of crinoline followed them and grew louder with each step.

"We're sitting at the family table inside," Maddie said, blushing with the words. It wasn't an embarrassed color, more of a delighted flush at the knowledge that she had joined her life with another.

Ian was happy for them, so very happy. He climbed the stairs with Grace at his side. She felt elegant on his arm, complete, as if a piece of himself long missing had finally found its way home again.

The inside of the house invited with warmth and style. The furniture wasn't what he'd expected, but then he clamped down on that thought. That made it seem as if he thought everyone in Arkansas was uncouth; that wasn't the case at all. He was just surprised at the fine things and treasures scattered throughout, and the beautifully crafted furniture that bespoke of an unexpected sophistication.

The dining room table had been set for the family. Three other tables had been placed in the parlor so everyone could be close. The promised wedding cake was set up on a table draped with a white cloth. Candles on beautiful silver holders winked at him, their flames seeming to know his secret.

Harlan had said that Maddie wanted everyone to eat outside and enjoy the beautiful day, but Prissy, the Sinclairs' feisty, cocoa-skinned housekeeper had set her foot down and said she wasn't toting all that food outside.

Reluctantly, Ian let go of Grace's arm and allowed her to move about, searching for her place at the table. With a groan, he realized that in all the time he had been walking right next to her, he hadn't said one word to her. He was worse than a schoolboy with his first crush. But the truth of the matter was he wanted to get her alone, talk to her all night and until the dawn, and find out everything he could about this woman he had fallen in love with. Yes, might as well admit it. He was in love with Grace Sinclair. He had never been one to believe in the nonsense of love at first sight, but his grandmother had always told him that God made someone for everyone, and one day he would meet his true love. He just never thought it would be today.

There was that word again. Love. But he loved Grace as surely as if he had known her his entire life. It was like destiny, or fate, or. . .God's plan for his life.

But he had no idea what God was thinking when He gave him this. *"Trust in the Lord,"* the Bible said. And he was trying.

He surely didn't want the first words out of his mouth to be a declaration of that love. She would think him mad and avoid him for the rest of the evening. Come to think of it, that might not be a bad plan. How was anything supposed to come of this love when he lived hundreds of miles away?

"Do you mind if I sit here?" He pointed to the chair directly in front of him, only then realizing that he had placed himself across from the bride, and Grace was heading for the seat next to his. Easton Sinclair had taken his spot at the head of the table, with Prissy sitting opposite him. If anyone else found it strange they didn't say as much, and Ian suspected that the housekeeper had more than a working relationship with the family.

He was secretly thrilled to be sitting so close to Grace.

Once everyone was settled, Prissy stood and made her way to the kitchen, directing the host of young girls who were serving them. When all the guests had a plate, she returned to her seat. Easton asked for everyone's attention and said a heartfelt blessing over their food.

Light conversation started up all around him, but he kept quiet. It was time he got himself in hand before he said something to embarrass them all.

He forked up a bite of his perfectly fried chicken. It was halfway to his mouth when Maddie spoke. "So Ian, Harlan tells me you're a preacher."

He lowered his fork and smiled at the bride. "That's right."

Up went the fork again.

"That must be fascinating," Maddie added.

Fork down. Ian nodded. "It can be." He raised his fork once again.

Before it touched his lips, Maddie said, "And you've just been accepted at your first church?"

Fork back down. He smiled at Maddie. "That's right. The First Church of Albany."

Something brushed against him under the table. He moved out of the way as best he could before trying for the bite of chicken once again.

"So. . ." Maddie started.

Whack!

What could have only been a swift kick sent pain racing up his leg. The bite of chicken he had managed to finally put in his mouth was sucked back and down his throat without the benefit of chewing. He sputtered and coughed, reaching for his water glass to wash down the ill-fated hunk of chicken.

"Don't just sit there, Grace, do something." Maddie jumped to her feet then sat back down as Grace sprang up.

She patted him between the shoulders, softly at first, then with increasing strength until he didn't know which hurt worse, his throat, his leg, or his back.

Her arm swung back again, but he caught her hand in his own before she could make contact another time. "I'm fine now. Thanks." His voice cracked at the end and his words were more of a croak than English, but Grace seemed to accept it and gently pulled her fingers from his grasp.

That in itself was a good thing. Her skin was soft, and she smelled so sweet he suspected if he spent any more time holding her hand he would assuredly embarrass them both.

Instead, he allowed her to move back to his side and return to her place at the table. Ian ducked his head over his meal and tried to concentrate on getting his food down. Chew, chew, chew, swallow. He could do this. Then after he ate he would figure out what he'd do with this crazy love he had for the woman at his side.

"About your church," Maddie started again.

"He doesn't want to talk about the church," Grace interrupted.

"Oh, I think he does." This from Maddie.

"He doesn't." Grace's tone turned stiff.

"Girls." Easton Sinclair didn't raise his voice at his daughters. Ian couldn't help but wonder if they did this sort of thing often. He was an only child, and the banter and teasing between siblings always fascinated him.

"Maybe we should talk about something else," Maddie said, her voice sweet and compliant.

Ian was ready for her to start gushing about the wedding; instead she turned her attention to him and said, "Doesn't Grace look beautiful today?"

He swallowed before answering even though he didn't have any food in his mouth. The moist chicken had somehow turned dry in the time since this conversation had started.

He glanced toward Grace, barely looking at her as he answered. "Very beautiful." In fact, she looked more beautiful than he had ever seen any woman look in his entire life. Ever. Wait, he had already said that. But she did look. . . beautiful.

"The two of you would make such a good couple," Maddie gushed. "Don't you think so, Harlan dear?"

His best friend shook his head then raised his napkin to his lips. Ian had seen that move too many times to count. It was Harlan's way of hiding his mirth and pretending that everything was fine. "I think it best that I bow out of the conversation."

"Oh no, my friend." It wasn't really the conversation he wanted to have, but Ian was stuck with it all the same. And if he had to participate then Harlan did, too. "What do you say? Would we make a good couple?"

Whack!

Again with the swift kick to the back of his calf, but this time he could tell that it was from Grace and had not been intended for anyone else.

He smiled at his friend and without looking away from him, reached under the table, and clasped Grace's hand in his own.

He wouldn't think about how easy it was for him to find her, as if he had some sort of previous knowledge of where she was. Nor was he going to think about the softness of her skin.

He gently squeezed her fingers. She squeezed back, in warning or affection, he wasn't sure. Maybe a little of both.

Harlan's eyes twinkled as he gave a pointed nod toward Ian and the spot where the table concealed their intertwined fingers. Ian hadn't realized it until that moment but he had leaned in a little to be closer to Grace. And she had done the same.

He straightened quickly and she followed suit, but it was too late. Everyone at the table had seen and they all were forming their own ideas about the matter.

"Oh I think the two of you would make a fine couple," Harlan said with a smile.

∞

The bride and groom stood on the front porch, gazing out at the remaining guests. Maddie had changed into a traveling dress, this one darker blue, but just as beautiful as the one she wore to get married. Harlan looked as handsome as ever. Perhaps that's what happiness did to a person, made them more attractive than they had been before. If that was the case, then Grace had to be glowing with happiness. She was so very aware of every move Ian made the entire time they sat at the dinner table side by side. She had wanted to turn to him, whisper in his ear that maybe later they could go for a walk and talk about . . .things. But all she could see down a road like that was heartache. Maddie had already said that he was going back to New York soon. Despite Grace's immediate feelings for the man, nothing could come of it.

"All the single girls get on one side of the yard together. I'm going to throw my bouquet." It was a fairly new tradition that Maddie had heard about from a traveling salesman. Grace thought it had a certain charm, but seemed a little on the silly side all the same. Yet she went to stand good naturedly with all the other single women.

"One. . .two. . ." Maddie counted down. "Three!" She reared back and threw the bouquet toward Grace.

Instinctively Grace raised her hands and caught the bundle of flowers before they smacked her in the face. From her place on the porch, Maddie jumped up and down and squealed as if she had just received the best news of anyone in the world. "You're getting married next!"

Chapter 2

The next to get married. The words rang in Grace's ears as her sister and Harlan prepared to leave. That was the tale: If a single woman caught the wedding bouquet, then she would be the next to get married, but Grace knew better. She knew everyone in the town, and though the men all seemed nice enough, none of them were for her. None of them sent her heart fluttering like Ian McGruer. Bouquet or not, she would be an old maid. She wasn't happy about it, but that was simply the way it was.

Grace watched her sister go, her heart heavy. She couldn't remember a night without Maddie. They were more than merely siblings. Maddie was her best friend. Now she was off with her husband on a two-day honeymoon. Monday, they would be back, but nothing would ever be the same.

She felt his presence before he spoke. How could she be so in tune with someone that she could know he was there without even seeing him?

"Can we go for a walk?"

"No." She shook her head. That was the last thing she needed to be doing, walking and talking with Ian. Wanting more, for things to change.

"Please, I just want a chance to talk to you."

How could she tell him no? She nodded, and he offered her his arm.

Together they walked down the lane that led toward the field separating the main house from the adjacent land where Harlan was building a house for Maddie.

Colorful wildflowers washed the field in a variety of colors: red, purple, white, and yellow.

"I picked Maddie's flowers from here," Grace told him, needing to break the silence between them. It wasn't necessarily an uncomfortable silence, but she needed to say something to disrupt the intensity. Never before had she been with someone she had just met who she felt like she had known forever. Never before had words not been necessary in getting to know another.

"And you caught the bouquet. . ."

She shook her head. "Silly superstition. Besides, she wasn't supposed to be facing the crowd when she tossed it."

"You think that matters?"

"I think she threw it to me on purpose."

They walked in silence for a bit longer then Ian cleared his throat. "Can you feel it, too?"

"This. . ." she trailed off, unsure what name to give the unlikely miracle that was happening between them.

"I don't know what to call it but. . .I saw you at the wedding, and I just knew." He stopped and turned to face her, taking both of her hands into his.

"What did you know?" she whispered.

He gave a nervous chuckle. "That you were the one God made for me."

She closed her eyes and took a deep shuddering breath. "I know, but—"

He shushed her words, placing one finger over her lips. "You don't have to say anything. I know how impossible this is. And knowing that you feel the same. . ." He gave a bittersweet laugh. "Well, knowing that you feel like I do doesn't help at all. In fact, I think it's worse."

"What do we do about this?"

"I have no idea. I almost feel like God is playing some kind of trick on me."

"God doesn't play tricks on people."

"Really? Tell that to Job."

She gave a small nod. "So now we're back to what to do." She couldn't see any answer. There was none. He was leaving, she was staying, and that's all there was to it.

Maybe God was playing a trick on him. But if the joke was on him, it was on her as well.

"I don't think there's anything for us to do. I'm taking over my church this weekend. People in Albany are depending on me."

"I figured my life would be here, with my father. Helping him with his church."

"That's noble."

"I've just always thought that's what God has planned for me."

"Too bad He doesn't send a burning bush or angels these days. I could sure use a definite idea about what He wants."

She could only nod.

"I love you," he said. "I know that sounds mad, but it's true. And though there's nothing that can come of it, I just wanted you to know."

Grace squeezed his fingers and closed her eyes against the threatening tears. "I love you, too." And there wasn't one thing they could do about it.

∞

Grace left Ian standing in that field of wildflowers and went back into the house. It seemed unnaturally quiet without Maddie underfoot. Or maybe it was the stab of jealousy that had her feeling so down. There. She admitted it. She was jealous of her sister. Jealous, jealous, jealous. Long ago, Grace had settled herself to the fact that she would never marry. But was it Maddie's marriage or Ian McGruer's clear blue eyes that had her wishing things could be different?

"Gracie, is that you?" Her father called from the parlor.

"Yes, Pa." She started for the room, passing through the kitchen to check on the cleanup. Ever efficient, Prissy and the teen girls she had hired for the occasion had everything under control. Prissy waved away her offers of help before Grace could even voice them.

She flashed the woman a grateful smile then made her way to the parlor.

"Well, I guess that's it," Pa said as she came in and settled herself down on the settee. He had his pipe in one hand and yesterday's paper in the other. "I think everything turned out fine. You?"

Grace nodded. "The cake was a big hit." Last Christmas Harlan had promised Maddie a big white wedding cake, like was all the rage these days. But that was because he didn't want his bride to get any ideas about serving gingerbread cookies instead.

"I'm happy for Maddie," Grace said, not realizing until the words were out how melancholy they sounded.

"But you're feeling a little sorry for yourself."

It was hard hearing her father say those words out loud. "Yes," she finally whispered.

"That handsome Scotsman wouldn't have anything to do with it, would he?" Her father raised his glass of lemonade and eyed her carefully over the rim.

"Why—why would he have any part in this?"

Pa smiled and shook his head, then looked down into his lap as if it held all the answers. "A blind man could see what was going on between the two of you."

Grace sighed and shook her head. "There's nothing to see."

He sat up a little straighter in his seat. "It may have been a long time ago, but I remember what love looks like."

"Like it matters."

"What's that mean?"

"He lives in New York, and my place is here."

Her father tapped one hand against his chin in a thoughtful gesture. "That may well be," he said. "Yesterday. But today, I think things are a bit different."

Different didn't even begin to describe it. "But—" She changed her mind about her protests and shook her head instead.

"Where is he now?"

"At the house, I suppose."

"Harlan and Maddie's house?"

Grace nodded. "Where else would he be?"

Pa shook his head. "He can't stay there. The house isn't even finished yet."

"Well he is."

"You need to go get him."

"Go get him?" Grace's heart tripped over itself. She couldn't go get him. "Why?"

"So he can stay here of course."

Stay here?

"Go on now."

Her father couldn't be serious. But he looked serious enough.

Grace reluctantly stood and ran her hands over her skirt. She would never disobey her father. But her heart tumbled in her chest. With anticipation. With excitement. With dread. She cast one last look at her father, trying to make sure he really meant what he said, but he had gone back to his paper.

She let herself out the back way, held up her skirts, and made her way across the field where she had walked with Ian just a short while ago. Except they had walked around the field, not through the multitude of flowers. She should've changed clothes before she left, but she didn't think about her skirts dragging through the plants until she got in the middle of the meadow. She hiked up her skirts a little more and continued on. Best get this over with quickly.

The house that Harlan was building fell somewhere in between modest and ostentatious. A large wraparound porch stretched across the front, disappearing around either side. Garret windows pushed through the roof, their real glass panes twinkling in the sun. Grace dashed up the steps and had only just gotten to the door when it opened.

"Oh!" she exclaimed.

Ian stood framed in the doorway, looking even more handsome than he had at the wedding. He had not forgotten to change clothes, and now wore workaday trousers and a shirt with suspenders, like any of the men in Calico Falls.

That made her both sad and anxious. Sad because she missed the kilt and anxious because she didn't need him looking like any of the men that surrounded her. He was unattainable. Off limits. And despite the feelings of head-over-heels love she experienced the first time her eyes met his, he was not part of God's plan for her.

"Grace." His voice was low and husky.

"Pa sent me. He said you couldn't stay here tonight. The house isn't even done. You'll have to come sleep with me."

Heat filled Grace's face, and she didn't need a mirror to know she had turned an unbecoming shade of red. She was burning up. "I mean, us."

One of Ian's rusty brows shot toward his hairline.

"I mean, stay at our house." She was only making this worse. "I mean you need a decent place to stay—this house isn't done. When Maddie and Harlan get back, they're staying with us. You can't stay here."

He looked pointedly toward her feet then cleared his throat.

Grace glanced down. She still had her skirts hiked up almost to her knees. Scandalous. What had she been thinking? She dropped her skirts and smoothed her hands over them as if somehow to take away the fact that she flashed him more than just her ankles. "Sorry," she murmured. "This situation seems to have brought out the worst in me."

"Think nothing of it."

She shifted from one foot to the other, waiting for him.

He cleared his throat again. "I'll be fine here."

Grace shook her head. "Pa insisted."

Ian seemed to mull it over for a few moments then he gave a quick nod. "Let me get my things."

∞

Ian felt a little like a puppy dog following behind his master, as he walked behind Grace all the way back to the preacher's house. He'd never seen a woman move so fast, like her feet were on fire. It was as if she wanted to spend as little time with him as possible.

As badly as he wanted to spend every waking moment with her, those moments were limited. Still, he loved the way she blushed when she said that he was to come sleep with her, an innocent and honest mistake, but one he enjoyed all the same.

"Wait up," he called, hurrying after her. Somehow his thoughts had taken over and stilled his steps. Now she was yards ahead of him instead of merely feet.

Whether she didn't hear him or she was outright ignoring him, he didn't know. But he quickened his pace again and caught her. He wrapped his hand around her arm and stopped her in her tracks.

"Why are you walking so fast? Is there a fire? Or something you didn't tell me about?"

She shook her head. "It's better this way, don't you think?"

"What way? Sprinting across a meadow?"

"No, not being alone together."

"I think it's too late for that." Ian chuckled.

She whirled on him. "It's not funny!" She spun back around and marched toward home again.

He headed after her, this time catching her in three easy strides. "It's hysterical."

"I beg to differ." She sniffed and raised her chin to a haughty angle.

"What happened to God playing tricks on us? I'm sure He's laughing right about now."

She shook her head. "God has more important things to do than mess with our meager lives."

"Does He have more important things than providing us with love and companionship?"

"I'm not destined to have those things."

"Who told you that?"

"It's something I know. Something I've always known. My mother died when I was five. Since then I've been at my father's side, helping him with the church. That is my calling."

His humor dried up faster than a rain puddle in July. "I have a calling, too."

She seemed to wilt right before his eyes. Her chin dropped and her jade green eyes swam with tears. "What do we do?"

"First thing is not to cry." He couldn't stand to see a woman's tears, especially when there was nothing on earth he could do to stop them. "And the next is to do what we can."

"I don't understand."

He heaved a sigh. "We can only do what we can do."

"Ian, stop talking in riddles." She closed her eyes and twin tears spilled down her cheeks.

"We can only make the best of the situation. We can only spend a little time together and that's all."

"I would love to spend time with you, but—"

"I know." She didn't have to finish. Spending time together would only make the longing worse. "But the time we will spend together, that's all there is. Are you willing to accept that?"

She nodded.

What choice did they have? "Me, too."

Her jade green eyes opened once again, this time clear with understanding. "And come Tuesday, you'll leave."

He nodded.

"Until then?"

"We can be friends. We can do that, right? Just enjoy what time we have."

"And then it's gone."

He swallowed the lump in his throat. "Yes."

She sent a trembling smile his way. "If that's all we have, then we need to take it."

"So we're agreed."

She nodded.

He took her arm in his hand and together they walked across the field, back to the white clapboard house at the edge of town.

The feel of her walking beside him, the building of love, and the knowledge this would be all they could have, stilled his words in his throat. Silently he prayed.

Why now, Lord? Why did I have to find a woman like Grace now, when I can do nothing about it?

Chapter 3

Sunday morning dawned as perfect a day as the one before it. Grace had enjoyed eating dinner with Ian. Of course her father and Prissy were there as well, but it was much easier to relax and enjoy herself when she wasn't looking to the future, but living in the moment as it were. Afterwards, her father had his pipe in the parlor while Grace played church hymns on the piano. All in all, it had been a good evening. She even managed to sleep, knowing that Ian was just down the hall and Maddie wasn't.

"We walk to church," Easton explained. After breakfast the four of them set off down the packed-dirt road that led to Calico Falls and the little white church at the end of the lane.

They got there early as usual, and Grace took the position standing next to her father greeting his flock as they arrived.

This was her job, her calling, as she had told Ian. Her place in the world. She caught him looking at her as she hugged the Widow Barnes and could tell from the sad mist in his eyes that he understood.

But she got to sit next to him when her father took to the pulpit.

She loved to hear him preach, and today was no exception.

"It's simple to understand God's will for your life. All you have to do is answer three simple questions."

Funny, but her father looked straight at her when he said the words.

"Is it in the Bible?" He turned just enough to fix his gaze on Ian. "Is this the desire of your heart? And is there a need?" He turned back to look at Grace. "If you can answer no to any of these, then it may not be God's plan for you." Gaze back on Ian.

Then he turned to his Bible. "The book of Jeremiah tells us in Chapter twenty-nine, verses eleven through thirteen, 'For I know the thoughts that I think toward you, saith the Lord, thoughts of peace, and not of evil, to give you an expected end. Then shall ye call upon me, and ye shall go and pray unto me, and I will hearken unto you. And ye shall seek me, and find me, when ye shall search for me with all your heart.'"

Pray, that's what she needed to do. But for what? For patience? Understanding? None of those would change the facts: Her life was in Calico Falls and Ian's was in New York. No amount of prayer could change that.

∽

There had been many a sermon Ian had listened to that seemed as if the preacher was speaking straight to him, but there was no mistaking that Easton Sinclair had singled him out for his subject today. God's will and knowing what God wants from your life. Yesterday morning he thought he knew, but today, he wasn't so sure.

All morning Grace hugged parishioners and greeted everyone as they came to worship. She was the perfect preacher's daughter, Ian had thought, as she smiled and shook hands. The congregation loved her as well, chatting with her about everything from apple pie recipes to how beautiful the wedding had been. He just stood to one side and watched, just as he was watching now, as she and her father said their farewells.

The perfect preacher's daughter would make the perfect preacher's wife, that little voice inside him whispered.

Why now, Lord? Of all the people in the world he could fall for, why her? It was true what they said, the good Lord did work in mysterious ways, but for the life of him, he couldn't figure out why God would want him to fall for someone he couldn't have.

But the Lord only answered with one word Ian seemed to hear from Him all too often. *"Patience."*

Ian continued to watch as they turned down several offers for a Sunday meal, reminding everyone that they had company. And soon they were walking back to the pastor's house.

After a dinner of wedding leftovers, Easton suggested they all go for a walk.

Everyone agreed. After all, it was a beautiful day and considering all the food he had eaten during the last two days, Ian could use a bit of exercise.

Together the four of them, he, Easton, Grace, and Prissy, headed across the field of wildflowers.

"Is this a good idea?" Grace asked. She and Ian had dropped behind her father and Prissy, allowing the other couple to move farther ahead.

"What? Going for a walk?"

"No, spending this much time together."

"I thought we had settled this. We're friends right?"

She nodded, but he noticed she hesitated before agreeing.

"Friends can go on a walk."

"You're right of course."

He was reaching for reasons, but she had agreed to spend time with him and that's all that mattered.

He wanted to grab her hand so badly, entwine their fingers, but that wasn't friend behavior, so he had to settle for her simply walking at his side.

"The flowers are beautiful." Grace trailed her fingers along the higher petals and Ian remembered her saying this very field was where Maddie's wedding bouquet had been picked.

He stopped, the urge to gather Grace her own flowers taking hold. He picked as many different colors as he could, wishing he had a ribbon to tie them all together for her.

She turned as if she had only then realized he wasn't by her side.

"For you." He used a long stem to tie the bundle together and presented them to her.

Her smile let him know just how much he would miss her when he left. She held the flowers close to her face, breathing in the sweet scent. "Thank you," she murmured. But her joy at the simple gift was more than enough thanks.

They started to walk again. Up ahead of them, Easton had stopped and picked a single wild daisy and presented it to Prissy. She curtsied and tucked the flower behind her ear.

"Are they. . ." Ian nodded toward the couple, leaving the rest of his sentence unsaid. It wasn't really his business, but it was a strange relationship to be sure.

Grace shrugged, and he let the matter drop. It was too beautiful of a day for speculations.

Two more steps and Ian watched as Easton crumpled into a heap.

∽

Grace stifled back a scream as her father fell. She hiked up her skirts and raced to his side.

"I'm all right. I'm all right." Her father chuckled embarrassingly and pushed to his feet. He brushed himself off as he continued to laugh.

But his good-natured grin turned to a grimace when he put weight on his right foot. He nearly crumpled to the ground once again, but managed to catch himself before he actually fell.

"Oh dear." Prissy grabbed one of his arms while Grace caught the other and together, with Ian bracing him from behind, they managed to get him safely back to the house.

"What happened?" Grace asked once they had Pa in his favorite chair, his right foot propped up on a small, cushioned stool.

"Stepped in a hole, I guess."

"Let me take a look, sir."

Grace stepped aside as Ian came forward. He gently pulled up her father's pant leg while she peeked over his shoulder.

"What is it?" she asked.

"I don't know. I'm not exactly a doctor."

"I'll get a cold rag and some ice," Prissy said and hustled toward the kitchen.

"I'll be fine," her pa blustered, pushing his pant leg back in place. "No sense flashing my ankles all over creation."

Grace straightened, and Ian did the same. He caught her eye and she was instantly taken back to the day before, standing on the porch of her sister's new house with her skirts up to her knees.

Her face filled with fire at the light in his eyes, a light that said he was thinking the same thing.

She turned away before she completely burned up, thankful then that Prissy bustled back into the room, carrying a large pan and a hunk of ice, half wrapped in a kitchen towel.

"Move back," she admonished, stirring Grace to action.

She stepped out of the way, and Ian followed suit.

"No sense in you young folks hanging around. Go on out and finish your walk."

"Yes, Pa."

Together they stepped from the room, but the desire to laze about in the bright summer sun was replaced with concern for her father.

"I hope it's nothing serious," she said.

From the tight set of Ian's mouth, she couldn't tell how he felt about the matter. Or maybe he was frowning over her scandalous exhibit yesterday. Surely he knew that she didn't go about like that all the time. Or even often.

"It's hard to say," Ian finally said, his sky blue eyes giving nothing away. "I guess we'll have to wait and see how he is tomorrow."

∞

But Monday dawned with Easton still unable to walk. Frankly, Ian was concerned. There didn't appear to be anything wrong with Easton's ankle. But Ian wasn't a doctor, he was a pastor. How was a man of God supposed to know about invisible injuries?

They ate breakfast, each lost in their own concerns about Easton's mysterious injury. Afterward, they helped him to the parlor, where he took up his spot in the same place as the night before, pipe at the ready, newspaper at hand, foot on the stool, and frown on his face.

"I'll be fine, I tell you." He shot his oldest daughter a pointed look that brooked no argument.

Ian had a feeling the spirited Maddie would have fought her father over the matter, but Grace was more reserved. He could practically see her calming herself, biding her time to make the most of her arguments.

"Very well," she said, but Ian knew the matter was far from over. "I guess I'll get Maddie and Harlan's room ready for their return." She nodded toward Ian as if to excuse herself.

Helplessly he watched her head for the parlor door. He wished he had some reason, any excuse to call her back and have her spend the day with him.

"Oh, I almost forgot."

Ian turned to find Easton's eyes sparkling with something akin to mischief. He wasn't sure the look could be trusted, but it was there, all the same.

Grace turned as well. "Yes, Pa?"

"I almost forgot that Tom Daniels has been sick. His neighbor asked for me to go out there today and pray with the family. And now. . ." He waved a vague hand toward his injured foot. Then he snapped his fingers, the action too deliberate to be anything but planned. "I know. How 'bout the two of you go out there in my stead." It wasn't quite a question.

"But Maddie's room. . ." Grace trailed off as Easton shook his head.

"Prissy can handle that."

"And who will take care of you?" She winced as she said the words, as if she could hear how weak they sounded before they even left her lips.

"Bah, I'm fine, I tell you. I have my pipe and the paper." He patted his Bible sitting on the table next to him. "When I get done with that, then I can work on my next sermon."

Ian could almost see Grace crumble. She really was a delightful soul, willing to help. So beautiful. And so out of his reach. *You've already decided this, McGruer. Get your head right and your priorities straight.* Tomorrow morning he would be on his way back to Albany. And that was that.

But today he was riding out to the Daniels' farm to pray over a sick man. How could he say no to that?

"Of course," Grace said in that elegant way of hers. "I'll hitch up the wagon."

Ian stepped forward. "Allow me."

A stricken look crossed her face, but it vanished almost as fast as it had appeared. She nodded. "Let me get my Bible, and I'll meet you out front."

∽

The last thing—the very last thing—she wanted was to be riding out to the Daniels' farm with Ian McGruer. But there she was, sitting next to him, doing her best not to let their shoulders accidently touch as they swayed along.

He felt the same. She could tell. He was leaning so far left he was almost falling out of the wagon as they ambled down the country lane.

So much for wedding bouquets determining who was getting married next. Just another fantasy built to break girls' hearts when it didn't come true. Thank heavens she didn't let her hopes get too high. Still. . .

The bouquet of wildflowers Ian had presented her worked its way into her thoughts. So sweet and beautiful. Yet, she had dropped them when her father had fallen. It was for the best. That was one less thing she needed: another bouquet with too much meaning behind it and a dead end ahead.

And the flower her father had given Prissy. They might be all God's children, but where could a romance between the preacher and his dark-skinned housekeeper lead?

They were almost to the farm when Ian cleared his throat, rupturing the silence and breaching her thoughts. "Your father is acting sort of strangely, yes?"

"You mean with Prissy?"

He shook his head, and Grace immediately regretted letting her thoughts go so easily. "His ankle."

"It's very unfortunate," she said. "I'm glad he didn't get hurt before the wedding. Maddie would have been crushed if he couldn't have stood up long enough to marry them."

Ian cleared his throat again. "So you don't think he's faking?" His voice dipped on the last word, so low she almost didn't hear it.

"No." She shook her head, pushing away any doubts that had been creeping in. "He can't be faking. My father is a good Christian man. Why would he lie about something like hurting his ankle? Unless. . ." She turned to look at Ian. Was her father trying to push her toward Ian? Pa had certainly managed to get them together in the wagon fast enough. Why would her father want to do that? So she would fall completely in love with the young preacher and move away and be heartbroken for having to leave her family? She could barely stand it now that Maddie was gone. Is that what her father wanted?

The look in Ian's eyes said he understood and was thinking the same thing as she.

But it was just as likely they could both be wrong about her father's injury. It was a small hope, but one she would cling to all the same.

Chapter 4

The Daniels' farm was in worse shape than Grace had imagined. Weeds grew in the garden among the ripening fruits and vegetables, and she could see as soon as they pulled up that the barn needed tending.

Ian set the brake and jumped to the ground. He came round to her side and lifted her down before she could protest. His touch on her waist as he guided her was chaste and necessary, but it still made her wonder about things that could never be.

She pushed those thoughts aside and concentrated on the farm.

"Looks pretty run down," he commented. "How long has Daniels been sick?"

"A couple of weeks." She thought back. "Maybe more." How had they slipped through their thoughts? Her father was dutiful about keeping up with his parishioners.

The wedding, Grace realized, and said a quick prayer of forgiveness for letting her personal life get in the way of her duty to church and community.

"Looks like there's a good bit more to do here than pray."

The door to the house swung open, and a young boy stepped out into the yard. He shifted the slop bucket to one hand and tried to shut the door behind him. But his efforts stilled when he saw them standing there.

"Ma? There's people out here."

Grace searched her brain to remember the boy's name. "Hi, Gordon. Do you remember me? I'm Grace, the preacher's daughter."

His eyes lit with recognition then settled warily on Ian.

"This is my friend," she said. "His name is Mr. McGruer, and he's a preacher, too."

"Gordon, why are you standing here with the door op—" The lady of the house came to a quick stop when she caught sight of her guests. She flung the dishtowel she had been using to dry her hands across one shoulder, her fingers immediately flying to her hair.

Frazzled. That was the best word Grace could think of to describe the woman. Her shoulders slumped, her dress was dirtied, and dark circles lined her weary eyes. Tired, worn, and on her last leg. It seemed Grace had another request for forgiveness to make.

"Mrs. Daniels, I'm so sorry it's taken me so long to come check on you. We missed you at church yesterday."

The woman flashed a quick smile toward them and urged Gordon toward the pig pen. "Go on now, son. The beasts are waiting."

The boy did as he was told, leaving the adults standing at the door.

"This is my friend, Ian McGruer," Grace continued, all too aware of the hand Ian had placed at the small of her back. Was he even aware that he was touching her?

"It's nice to meet you," he said.

Mrs. Daniels stood a little straighter then dipped in a small curtsey toward the man. Her smile was wide and a few of the lines left her face. Grace knew all too well the smile he had bestowed on the lady. "Won't you come in?" She stood to the side to allow them entrance into the cluttered house. "I apologize for the mess. Tom has been sick awhile and well, it's hard for me and Gordon to keep up with everything ourselves. Can I make you some coffee or tea?"

Grace shook her head. "Thank you though. The pastor fell yesterday and is laid up with a twisted ankle." At least that's what she thought was wrong. "He asked us to come out and pray over Mr. Daniels."

But it was obvious more than prayer was needed to help this household. Dishes were stacked near the washtub. The floor needed a good sweeping and, for the most part, the little house sagged under the weeks of neglect.

Tears welled in Mrs. Daniels's eyes, but she blinked them back, managing to hold on to what was left of her dignity and pride. "Please, sit for a spell." She collapsed into one of the wobbly chairs surrounding the small wooden table and gestured for them to do the same.

Grace eased into a chair and laid her hand on top of one of Mrs. Daniels's. Vaguely aware of Ian sitting across from her, she focused her attention on the weary lady in front of her. "Would you like for us to pray for you as well, Mrs. Daniels?"

"Esther," she corrected with a weak smile.

Grace returned the smile and reached for Ian's hand. Together the three of them prayed for health, strength, and healing.

∞

For the remainder of the afternoon, Ian and Grace worked beside Gordon and Esther doing more than just praying. He mucked stalls, cleaned stables, weeded the garden, and groomed horses until he was certain he wouldn't be able to move come the morning.

But he had never spent a more satisfying day. He had prayed, worked the land, and prayed some more. And all with the most beautiful woman he had ever known.

He had watched Grace with Esther and Gordon Daniels. She had laughed with them, empathized with them, and then helped them get back on their feet.

She had prayed with Tom Daniels, swept floors, and didn't think twice about washing clothes in what had to be one of her best Sunday dresses. Never before had he met a woman like her. She was all he could hope for in a life partner, but she was not for him. The longer he watched her, the more apparent it became that she belonged here with this country church and the people who needed their pastor in so many different ways than those who lived in the big cities.

Suddenly he wanted to be a part of that life, to muck stalls and milk cows and pray for the infirm, and the healthy, who were affected by a loved one's illness, all in the same day. But he had made his promise to the First Church of Albany.

Just because he wanted it to be so didn't mean it could truly be that way. God had plans for them both; despite the overwhelming feelings he had for Grace Sinclair.

He helped her into the wagon and after waving good-bye to the very grateful Esther and Gordon, the two of them set off for home.

∞

"Thank you," she said quietly.

"For what?"

"Helping the Daniels."

"I'm a pastor. It's my job to help those in need."

"Praying and counseling. But you didn't have to do all the farmwork. I could tell that you aren't used to such chores."

He chuckled. "That's true. I haven't worked on a farm in many years. Since my family came over to America."

"How old were you then?"

"Eight."

She tried to imagine him then, scrawny and gangly, rusty hair a bit shaggy around the ears, blue eyes with the innocent light only the youth can hold. "But you did before that?"

"Yes. In Scotland; my family had a small farm, sheep and such."

"I bet that was beautiful."

"It was very beautiful. In fact, Arkansas reminds me a lot of East Lothian.

Oh, not the weather. But the fields and the hills, the green grass."

Grace tried to imagine, but Scotland seemed so exotic compared to workaday Arkansas. She couldn't imagine anything the two places had in common, save the man who sat next to her. "Do you still have family there? In East Lothian?"

"My grandparents stayed. As did most of the family. I've got a herd of aunts and uncles still living there, scores of cousins."

"Do you miss them?"

He shrugged. "It's been almost twenty years. I'm from New York now."

Grace fell quiet, allowing his words to wash over her. His life was in New York as much as hers was in Calico Falls, but what she wouldn't give for a common place for the two of them, somewhere in between where they could be together and let their love grow.

∞

"Maddie!" Grace rushed down the steps and greeted her sister with open arms. She may have only been gone for a couple of days, but it had been a very eventful weekend and she needed to connect with her sister again.

Maddie returned her hug, her smile wide and eyes sparkling.

That was what love did to a woman, made her confident and beautiful. Suddenly Grace was more envious of Maddie than she had been their entire lives.

"Come in, come in," Prissy called from the door, waving the returning couple inside. "Supper's almost on the table."

They all washed up and gathered round. Even Pa managed to hobble his way to the table. His limp looked a little different, though Grace couldn't tell if it was better or worse. But, she decided, if he wasn't back to himself in the morning, she would go fetch the doctor.

Their meal was a bright affair. Grace loved listening to Maddie talk about their time in the city, staying in the hotel, and having people bring them food to their room. The thought of lounging about and enjoying the company of the one she loved sounded so sweet; it almost brought tears to her eyes. She had never really thought about it before, that she would have such a relationship with another. Oh, maybe when she had been a young girl, but as an adult, the thought was never allowed to cross her mind. But now that it had. . .

She cast a look at Ian. He was seated next to her, listening as quietly and intently as she had been. But when her gaze fell upon him, he turned as if the touch had been physical. His eyes met hers and she knew their thoughts were the same.

She gave him a sad smile then looked away.

"So," Maddie started, her bright green gaze darting from Grace to Ian then back again. "Anything interesting happen while we were away?" Maddie's eyes settled on Grace, and suddenly she felt like a beetle pinned to a board in a little boy's bug collection.

"Pa fell and twisted his ankle." What else could she say?

"Uh-huh." Maddie's attention was unwavering.

"Oh, I'm fine," he started, then quickly followed it with, "Or I will be. In a day or two. . .maybe a week. But it's okay since I have Ian here to help with the duties."

"Duties?" Harlan looked from Ian to Pa, then he too turned his attention to Grace.

She squirmed in her seat. "Ian and I went out to visit the Daniels' farm. Tom has been sick. His poor wife and son have been working their fingers to the bone trying to keep up."

Maddie smiled as if Grace had confessed that Ian had taken her out in the wagon and kissed her silly. "Really? That is interesting."

Grace frowned. "It is nothing of the sort. It's downright sad."

Maddie forked up a large bite of mashed potatoes. "Mmm-hmmm," she said, the food keeping her from any further answer.

"So as long as Ian stays here until I get back on my feet." Her father chuckled. "Both of them," he clarified, "I think everything will be just fine."

"I thought you were leaving tomorrow." Harlan raised his brows at his friend.

Ian shrugged. "I can't really leave his church in need."

"What about your church?" Harlan asked.

"I'm just one of three pastors. They'll get along fine without me for a day or two."

"Maybe a week," her pa interjected.

"Or a week," Ian conceded.

Grace wasn't sure if she should be happy Ian was staying a few more days or feeling sorry for herself, that she would have more days to fight these feelings she carried for him.

She caught Ian's gaze. Filled with remorse, it brought a lump to her throat. "I'm sorry," she mouthed to him.

He pressed his lips together and gave a small nod. For a moment she was lost in the bottomless blue of his eyes.

Then a nudge under the table.

Maddie grinned at her in a knowing way that sent alarm bells clanging in her head.

Harlan frowned, but Grace couldn't tell if he was upset or concerned.

At the head of the table, Pa's grin was wider than Maddie's. Grace knew then, if the two of them had anything to say about it, Ian would never make it back to New York. The thought was thrilling and infuriating all at the same time.

Chapter 5

After supper, Maddie and Harlan decided to walk over to the house and look around before it got dark.

They invited Grace and Ian, but they turned them down so quickly the couple looked as if they had been slapped.

Pa limped his way to the parlor and set himself up with his pipe while Prissy took care of the supper dishes.

"Do you want to go for a walk?" Ian asked, as Grace tried to decide what to do with the rest of her evening.

"I didn't think you wanted to go for a walk."

He had told Harlan no quickly enough.

"It's not that I don't want to walk."

"You're not tired after all that work you did today?" she asked.

"Not that tired."

Grace gave a small nod. "Do you think it's a good idea? I mean, I thought we weren't going to spend any more time alone."

"We were alone all afternoon, and we managed to get through that just fine."

True, but it had taken all of her self-discipline to endure, and she just didn't have much left where he was concerned. Plus, she wanted to walk with him. If only for one last time. "All right, then. Yes, I'll walk with you."

They headed down the road toward town. Grace was sure Ian started in that direction to keep them well away from Maddie and Harlan's blatant meddling.

She wanted him to reach out and hold her hand, make some sort of contact, but they merely ambled along, side by side, neither one touching.

It's better this way. She knew that in her head, but her heart had started wanting more than her brain knew was right. Could two people in love with each other remain friends? It was the question of the ages.

"Is it mad?" she finally asked. "These feelings we have for each other?"

He shook his head. "I've asked myself that same thing a hundred times since I met you."

"And have you answered yourself, yet?" Grace tried to make light, but her voice held a weary edge.

"I just know what I know." His cryptic words fell between them, confusing her all the more.

"And what is that?"

"My grandmother always said that God made someone special for each of us. When we meet that person we'll know it. My someone is you. Every day I spend with you confirms it time and again."

Grace stopped, shaking her head as she tried to make sense of a love that was beyond reason. "It can't be. I can't leave here."

"I know." He took her hands into his own and squeezed her fingers. His touch was like a piece of heaven on earth, the home she had always dreamed of, the one true love she had always wanted. "That's what makes this so confusing."

"I've spent my entire life trying to live by what God wants from me. All this time I thought I knew what that was."

He nodded and she knew she didn't have to continue. He felt the same as she. *Why now, Lord? Why now?*

"I think your father is trying to get us together."

"But that would mean I'd have to leave." A wife's place was with her husband. It would be her responsibility to follow Ian. Who would help her father? Is that what he wanted for her?

"And that would make you unhappy."

She nodded. Being married to Ian would be the most wonderful thing in the world, but being away from her family just didn't seem right. Was she looking at this all wrong? Was she being unreasonable? She couldn't imagine life outside of Calico Falls. If that's what God intended for her, shouldn't she at least be able to picture it in her head?

But if Ian wasn't the one God intended for her, why did she feel the way she did?

"If things could be different," he started, "and you didn't have to leave here. . . ?"

"Then there would be no question." She blushed. She was being so very forward, but there was something different about Ian McGruer. He wasn't like any man she had ever met. "If things could be different, would you. . . ?"

He nodded.

He wanted to kiss her; she could see it in his eyes. Yet what good would it do? It would only serve to break both their hearts. Right now they were a little bruised, but they would recover.

He released her hands and shoved his into his pockets as if he didn't trust them to be free.

"Is this a test?" she finally asked. "Like God gave to Abraham? Is he testing my faith? Your faith?"

Ian took her elbow and they headed back to the house. "I wish I knew. Oh, how I wish I knew."

∞

"Grace?" Maddie's whisper floated across the darkness. The door to Grace's room swung gently inward as her sister filled the soft light filtering in from the hall. "Are you awake?"

"Maddie?"

Her sister flew across the room and jumped into the bed next to Grace, snuggling under the covers like they did when they were little.

"What are you doing in here?"

"I wanted to talk to you." Maddie pulled the covers up under her arms and grinned at Grace.

"You're supposed to be with your husband," she groused, though secretly glad that her sister was there. Oh, how she was going to miss her when the house was finished.

"I know, but I wanted to see you. Ask you about Ian."

Grace's heart gave a hard pound at the mention of his name. "What about him?"

"Well, you love him, for one."

She sighed, unable to deny it. "It's that obvious?"

"Yes, but I'm in tune with love right now."

They lay there in the darkness, each one captured in her own thoughts until Grace asked, "Do you believe that God made someone out there for each of us?"

"Yes," Maddie said emphatically. "Do you?"

"I would like to believe so. But what happens when your someone turns out to be someone that isn't right for you?"

"What are you talking about? He's perfect for you."

Oh, how she wished that were true. "How can you say that? He lives in New York."

"I had forgotten about *that*. Whatever was I thinking?" Maddie's tone dripped with sarcasm.

"Will you be serious? If I were to marry him, I would have to move away from Calico Falls."

"And?"

"Isn't that enough?"

Maddie pushed herself up onto her elbows, staring hard into Grace's eyes. The look was incredibly intense for whimsical Maddie, and Grace shifted uncomfortably under its weight. "Do you think that if Harlan needed to move away that I would hesitate for a moment? I mean, I would miss you terribly, but I love him."

"But Pa—"

"Doesn't need you as much as you think he does. Without you he would simply do something else."

The thought washed over her, almost stinging with the truth. Was she necessary to her father's church? Or was she only making his life easier? "Are you saying—?"

"I'm saying that if you love him, you shouldn't let anything stand in your way." She stopped, then her tone changed, lightened as she continued. "If you want I could go down and work out a deal with Old Lady Farley."

"Maddie, be serious."

"I am serious." But even in the dark bedroom, Grace could see her sister's eyes twinkling. "There's someone out there for you, Grace. Haven't we always dreamt of getting married and having babies? That dream will come true," she said.

But as confident as her sister sounded, Grace had her doubts.

∞

Tuesday morning, Ian arose to another beautiful day in the Ozarks. Birds chirped, the wind rustled the green leaves, and the blue sky seemed to stretch on forever.

But when he made his way downstairs, he found Easton limping around and Grace frowning.

"I'm going to get Doc Williams," she said, ignoring her father's protests.

Ian glanced at Easton's ankle, still covered with his pant leg, then looked back to Grace. "Do you think it's that bad?"

She shrugged. "I don't know, but he's been limping around here for days and it's time to get the doctor."

"Just give me a couple more days," Easton grumped from his favorite chair.

Grace propped her hands on her hips, and Ian was convinced she had never looked prettier. "I have. Now it's time to get some professional help."

"Do you want me to walk with you?" Ian asked.

She shook her head. "I'll be fine."

But something in her tone said that she was distancing herself from him. As much as his heart ached at the thought, he knew it was for the best. They had tried ignoring their love. They had tried being friends. Neither had worked. Staying away from each other seemed to be the only solution they truly had.

Grace returned with the doctor in record time, sweeping into the parlor with the gray-haired man trailing in her wake.

Doc Williams had a thick mustache, wire-rimmed spectacles, and a string tie that bobbed when he talked. He folded up Easton's pant leg and gave his ankle a thorough examination. Everyone looked on with furrowed brows.

The doctor straightened and shook his head. "Well, Easton, I can't see anything wrong. But if it's hurting you, give it a couple days rest. Maybe stop by the office on Friday."

Easton pulled down his pant leg and crossed his arms as he surveyed his family. "See? Rest. That's what I need."

"And breakfast," Prissy called from the door to the kitchen. "Y'all come and get it."

Sitting around the table with Grace on one side and his best friend across from him, Ian wondered what it would be like to stay here in Calico Falls. Would every day be like this? Or was this just part of the visitors' trip and once he left things would go back to how they normally were? How was he even to know?

"Ian, would you mind going out to the Dursleys' this morning? Grace can go with you." Easton wiped his mouth on his napkin and looked at each of them in turn. Going out to another farm today was not the way to keep his distance from Grace, but how was he supposed to refuse?

"Harlan, why don't you go with Ian?" Grace asked. "Maddie and I have plans to start new dresses today."

"We do?" Maddie asked.

"Yes." Grace said, her jaw tight. "We do."

Ian felt the brush of her skirts against his calf, then watched as across the table Maddie jumped.

"Ow," she mouthed and he knew that Grace had kicked her sister in order to gain compliance.

"I can drive out there with you," Harlan said. "What's needed at the Dursleys'?"

"Mrs. Dursley's twins have been under the weather. They could use some prayers. And probably someone to play with for a while."

Harlan looked back to Ian. "Twins?" he mouthed.

Ian hid his smile. It looked like they were in for an eventful morning.

∞

Eventful was not the best word to describe the morning at the Dursleys' farm. As far as Calico Falls went, the Dursleys had to have been one of the wealthiest families. Fences stretched for miles and livestock dotted the green fields in between. The two-story house was well-kept, white-painted, and stood majestically to one side of the large red barn.

The Dursleys didn't need the same kind of care and attention that the Daniels had, but Ian enjoyed himself all the same. The twins were rough-housing, six-year-old boys just recovering from the chicken pox. Thankfully Ian and Harlan both had already had them. They spent the better part of the morning playing with the boys and generally getting them out of their mother's way for a while.

They ate lunch on the farm then headed back to the pastor's house. All the way there, Ian kept thinking about the church in Albany.

He had visited a couple of times before accepting the position. But now he wondered if he had been a little enchanted, maybe even overwhelmed with the thought that they wanted him, Ian McGruer, to be a pastor there. What in his humble training had made him worthy of such a large and prestigious church?

It was a big church and everyone dressed to the nines every Sunday. At the time, he had been impressed with all the fancy ties and hats, but thinking back, he realized now that a lot of the members were more concerned with how everyone looked instead of the Good Lord's message.

He needed to be fair, there were a lot of people who came for the Word, but it still wasn't like Calico Falls. The tiny town was filled with people who loved the Lord, their country, and their preacher. They pitched in when something needed to be done. They depended on each other in a way that he had never seen before. And then there was the countryside. It was so beautiful and remarkably reminded him of his beloved Scotland. Of course it had been a great while since he had lived there, but just being near the lush green fields made him nostalgic for something he couldn't even name.

"Got something on your mind?" Harlan asked.

Ian stirred himself from his thoughts and faced his friend. He had been so lost in his own mind that he hadn't realized they were over halfway back to the parsonage. "You could say that."

"Do you need to talk about it?"

It was on the tip of his tongue to say yes, but he realized that talking about it wasn't going to change a thing. He needed to pray and pray hard that the Lord would give him the answer he needed.

Chapter 6

The next morning Pa came limping down the stairs. Grace bit back her sigh and her worry as she watched him slowly make his way across the parlor toward the kitchen. Something wasn't right.

"That's the wrong foot." She turned toward her father, feeling a bit surly as she pointed to him. Lack of sleep could do that to a person. And though she pleaded a headache and retired for the evening early in the afternoon, she hadn't slept much at all.

"What?" Pa stopped.

Ian and Harlan turned to stare at the two of them, and Grace immediately regretted her outburst.

"I—I mean, your limp," she tried again.

"Oh. Oh," her father said, continuing on his way. This time both ankles were stiff, confusing Grace to whether she had been seeing things in his misplaced limp.

"I've hobbled around for so many days, both my legs are giving me fits now."

Surely lack of sleep was starting to play tricks on her mind. After all, she hadn't slept much since the wedding, not just the night before.

Ian and Harlan swung their gazes toward her, and she could do nothing but paste on a concerned look and try to cover up her shrill accusations. "Has anyone seen Maddie?"

"She's in the kitchen helping Prissy with breakfast," Harlan explained.

Grace nodded. "I'll just go check on everything, then." She fled the room to the relative safety of the kitchen.

The interior was warm and smelled spicy and inviting, but Maddie shooed her out, stating that she had everything under control.

Grace had no reason to doubt her, as breakfast was on the table in record time. Soon the blessing had been offered and all that could be heard was the clink of silverware against the plates as everyone devoured their pancakes.

"These pancakes are delicious," Ian said, holding up a bite and examining it a moment before he stuffed it into his mouth.

Grace had to admit they were extra delicious this morning.

"It's a special recipe," Maddie explained, her green eyes sparkling.

"Bravo," Harlan said, shoveling in his own huge bite.

Soon everyone had finished their breakfast. Prissy waved the girls out of the kitchen.

"Grace?"

She closed her eyes at the sound of Ian's voice close behind her. She opened them again and turned to face him. "Yes?"

"Walk with me?"

She shook her head.

"Please," he pleaded. "It's important."

How could she refuse him a second time? "Okay."

Together they walked out into the field of wildflowers between the pastor's house and Harlan's. She had a feeling she knew what this was about. He was leaving. There would be no more speculation on what was the right thing to do.

Maddie's words rattled around inside Grace's head. Was she being unreasonable to think her father needed her? Should she take the chance on Ian and see what adventure might lie in her future? Was that what God wanted from her? Was that what He was trying to tell her?

She turned to Ian, these questions seeking a voice. All she had to do was tell him that she had changed her mind. She had thought about their situation, and if he would still have her, then she was willing to take the chance that God had something different in mind for her than she had originally thought.

But as she turned, he was there. Close. So very close. And then he was closer, cupping her face in his hands, his lips pressed to hers.

Grace's eyes fluttered closed and she swayed toward Ian, loving the feel of his fingers on her face, his lips on hers in the sweetest kiss she could have ever imagined. A kiss much, much better than the one Davey Miller gave her at the spring hoedown when they were thirteen. She had slapped him then, but she couldn't raise her hand against Ian. She was too far gone in love with him. She could admit that now. God really had intended him for her and her for him. Her place was at his side, wherever that might be.

He gave her one more little kiss then dropped to one knee.

She could only stare at him as he pulled a ring from his pocket. "Will you marry me?"

Her mother's ring sparkled in the palm of his hand. The ring her father had saved for her. "You've talked to my father?"

He shook his head.

Something wasn't right.

"How did you get that?" she asked.

"Maddie gave it to me."

Then she knew. Her heart sank in her chest and she bit back her tears as she pulled Ian to his feet.

"What's the matter?" A confused frown pulled at his brow.

"I'm going to kill her," Grace stormed. She whirled on one heel, nearly tripping as the flowers tangled beneath her feet. Such a waste of good wildflowers. Heat filled her cheeks as she started back for the house.

"Killing is a sin," Ian said from somewhere behind her. Poor man. He had no idea what had been done to him. But she couldn't stop to explain now. He wouldn't believe her anyway.

"Then I'll just maim her." Grace marched into the house. "Maddie!" she called. Then louder, "Madeline Joy!"

Maddie pushed through the kitchen door to stand in the foyer, all wide-eyed and innocent. "Yes, sister?"

"What did you trade for this time?"

"I don't believe I know what you're referring to."

Grace opened her mouth to refute the claim, but closed it again as Ian came into the house.

He drew her gaze like a magnet draws metal and her heart broke all over again at the confusion and hurt on his face. "Grace, would you please tell me what's going on?"

"Yes, Grace," Maddie echoed.

Harlan cleared his throat but didn't say anything.

"It's a long story," she started, resisting the urge to pinch back the headache that was starting between her eyes.

"I have time."

She turned toward him then, wanting to explain but not knowing where to begin.

"I thought we had something special," Ian said.

"We do. We did. I mean it might have been special if Maddie hadn't. . ."

"I didn't do anything." Maddie held up both hands in surrender, though her eyes sparkled with that mischievous light Grace knew all too well.

"I don't understand," Ian said.

Harlan intervened, saving Grace from having to come up with a suitable answer. "Maybe we should all go into the parlor."

The last thing she wanted to do was drag this out, but knowing Maddie, she would hold on to her innocence for as long as possible.

For once Pa wasn't sitting there reading the paper or smoking his pipe. For that, Grace was grateful. She didn't need another witness to her sister's shenanigans.

"Now," Harlan started, "what's this all about?"

"I haven't the faintest idea," Maddie said demurely.

"Madeline! It's a sin to lie! You know very well what you did."

"Since you seem to be so confident as to my actions, why don't you share it with us all?"

Grace took a deep breath and reminded herself that she was a lady. No matter how badly she wanted to pull her sister's hair, like she did when they were younger, the coercion wouldn't make her admit her wrongdoings any more now than it had then. "You went down to Old Lady Farley's and got a love potion to put in the pancakes."

"I thought you didn't believe in such things. Isn't that what you told me last Christmas?"

Grace faltered. "Well, maybe this time it really did work." Why else would Ian kiss her, like there was no tomorrow, and propose marriage after all they had discussed?

Maddie shot her husband a knowing look.

Harlan chuckled.

"Will someone tell me what's going on here?" Ian looked from one of them to the other. Grace couldn't blame the man. After everything he had been through. And he was just about to leave all the madness behind, when Maddie had to go and do something like this.

"Will you, darling?" Maddie asked, with a smile to her husband.

Harlan explained about the gingerbread cookies from the Christmas before. How Maddie, in her desperate attempts to get him to fall in love with her, had traded her second-best dress for a pouch of herbs guaranteed to make Harlan fall madly in love. "What she didn't know was that I was already crazy about her." He tapped one finger against her cheek. Maddie blushed and returned his smile. Somehow Grace felt like she had just witnessed an intimate moment between the two of them.

"Why haven't I heard this story before now?" Ian looked from Maddie to Harlan and back again, while Grace twisted her fingers in her lap. Why did everything have to turn out so complicated?

Harlan shrugged his big shoulders. "I don't know. It just never came up."

"And this love potion," Ian asked, "Did it work?"

Maddie smiled. "No, it was nothing more than nutmeg and vanilla."

"It did make for some tasty cookies," Harlan added, patting his trim waist in memory.

Grace squirmed in her seat as Ian turned and pinned her with a stare. "Do you really doubt me that much?"

She hadn't looked at it that way. "It's not that." She shook her head, gathering her thoughts. "The pancakes this morning—"

"Were tasty," Harlan interjected.

Maddie shushed him.

"You think they had a love potion in them and that's why I proposed?"

"I'm completely innocent," Maddie said.

This time Harlan shushed her.

"But the kiss. And the ring." That was no sort of explanation, but she hadn't the words. "It wasn't doubt," she finally added. She had jumped to conclusions and had forgotten to trust God.

Now, the man she loved most in the world, the man God had created just for her, was slipping right through her fingers and she was helpless to stop it.

She closed her eyes. *Lord, if he's the one for me, help me. Help me find the words. Help me explain. Help me show him that I believe him. Show him how much I love him in return.*

"What's all the ruckus in here?" Pa strode into the room, taking in each of their expressions in turn. Grace could only imagine what he thought.

Wait. There was no limp in her father's steady gait. "You're healed?" she asked. Anything was better than dwelling on the prayer she sent up and the lack of answer she had received. *"Sometimes God says no,"* her father often said. Was this one of those times?

Pa pulled himself up a little straighter. "I, uh—I mean. . ." he blustered.

"You've been faking this whole time?" Grace asked.

"Well, I, I. . ."

Grace could almost see him coming up with excuses and then tossing them aside. "I needed to find a way to get Ian to stay," he finally said.

Now Grace was well and truly confused. "Can we go back and start at the beginning?"

"Like when I proposed?" Ian asked.

Grace pinched the bridge of her nose. "Ian, I'm—"

"Afraid to take a chance on me?"

She shook her head. "I had already decided that my place is right by your side wherever your side happens to be."

"And if I decide to go back to New York and take over the church there?"

She took a steadying breath, but said without hesitation or heartbreak, "Then I'll go with you. If you'll have me."

"Have you? I'm never going to let you go." He fell to his knees then practically crawled across the floor to be in front of her. As if he was afraid that she would change her mind at any second, he slipped the ring onto her finger and pressed a sweet kiss to her fingertips. "I'll do anything and everything to keep you by my side."

Maddie squealed and clapped her hands as Grace basked in the glory of knowing that Ian loved her, and would always be there for her.

"What about the church?" Pa asked.

Ian released her hands, but didn't take his gaze from her. Grace felt the heat of that look as surely as his touch when he had trailed his fingers down her cheek. "What about the church?"

"This has been sort of a test, you see."

All eyes swung to him. Pa shrugged. "I've been talking to the deacons. I'm retiring, and I want you to take over for me, Ian."

"Me?" he asked. "You're serious?"

"I am. The Lord has called me to do some work a little closer to my heart. Prissy and I are going to be traveling for a while. So, do you want my church or not?"

"More than anything." He stood and pulled Grace to her feet. She swayed toward him.

"Well, almost anything," he corrected, looking longingly into her eyes.

"Are you sure?" she whispered.

"That I want to marry you more than I want the church? Absolutely."

Grace shook her head. "About taking over a country church when you could have the big fancy cathedral in Albany."

"I prayed about it all night. God said this is where I need to be."

Maddie jumped to her feet. "You could have a fall wedding."

Autumn was beautiful in the Ozarks.

"Now, about this love potion," Ian asked. "Does it really work? Because I have this cousin. . ."

Grace laughed. "There might not be anything to Old Lady Farley's love herbs, but Maddie's wildflower wedding bouquet? I'm keeping that forever."

"As long as I'm there at your side," Ian said. "Right where I belong."

The County Fair Bride

by Vickie McDonough

Chapter 1

The slowing train screeched like Aunt Louise did whenever she encountered a mouse. Prudence Willard smiled at the image her thought provoked, but as she stared at the Bakerstown Depot, growing bigger with each yard she traveled, all humor fled. Her stomach churned faster while the train decreased its speed. Would her mother be waiting? In light of the illness Prudy's father was experiencing, more than likely her mother would not. Dare she hope some of her friends would be there to greet her? Did they even know she was returning?

Prudy sat back in the seat. She dreaded facing the townsfolk after her shameless pursuit of Clay Parsons, the town's only pastor. And to think she'd attempted to get Clay's fiancée—Karen Briggs, who was now his wife—to leave town. And she almost did. She'd treated the kind woman horribly, and it would serve her right if not a soul showed up to welcome her home.

The train shuddered to a stop, like a beast of burden exhausted from a long journey. Several people picked up their satchels and headed for the door. A part of Prudy wished she could keep on riding down the track, but she needed to see her father. They'd never been close, but he was gravely ill, and she hoped she might be able to cheer him during his remaining days on earth. Heaving a sigh, she rose, picked up her travel bag, and headed for the door.

As she disembarked the train and searched the platform, her hopes of a cheerful welcome plummeted. She didn't see a soul she knew. With a sigh, she walked down the platform and handed the porter the baggage claim ticket for her trunk. A few minutes later, after making arrangements for her belongings to be delivered to her parents' home, she picked up her satchel and headed for the stairs. Just as she reached the top, a man dressed in a gray sack coat and trousers rushed up the stairs, his gaze directed toward the train. Since he was obviously in a hurry and hadn't spotted her, she stepped back, lest he run her down.

The man buzzed past her as he reached the platform. Suddenly he halted and spun around. A pair of deep blue eyes, set in a handsome face, turned her way and widened. He yanked off his straw hat, releasing his thick, dark hair, which tumbled onto his forehead. He moved forward, forking his hair across his head. "Miss Willard?"

More than a little intrigued, Prudy nodded. "Yes. And who might you be?"

His cheeks flushed a bright red as he replaced his hat. "I'm Adam Merrick. Your mother asked me to see you home since she didn't want to leave Mr. Willard. . .uh. . .your. . .uh. . .father alone."

Prudy bit back a smile at the flustered man, who looked to be only a few years older than herself. She couldn't resist teasing the befuddled man. "I do know who Mr. Willard is."

"Uh. . .of course." He offered his elbow. "Shall we?"

"Yes, thank you. I'm quite anxious to see how my father is faring." She looped her arm around his and glanced up. "Do you know how he is doing?"

The man's lips firmed as he pressed them together. "You should probably consult your mother concerning that."

She nodded. Turning to the stairs, she released his arm and shifted her satchel to her other hand so that she could hold onto the railing as she descended. The last thing she wanted to do was fall flat on her face in front of her shy but charming escort.

"Do allow me to carry that." He suddenly snatched the bag from her. "I'm sorry for not offering in the first place."

Thrown off balance, Prudy hovered on the top step, toes hanging over, and flapping her arms. Like a duck stuck in the mud, her efforts availed her little. Mr. Merrick dropped her satchel onto the edge of her skirt and yanked her toward him, away from the drop-off. Her foot hit the bag, and she fell hard against his chest, taking them both to the ground. A woman behind them gasped. Prudy pushed against his solid chest, wrestling her tangled skirts, and struggled to sit.

Less encumbered, Mr. Merrick hopped up. "I'm terribly sorry, Miss Willard. I really don't know how that happened."

Prudy refrained from fussing at him. Even flustered, the man certainly was comely, but she wasn't attracted to his bumbling manner in the least. "I don't suppose you could help me up."

"Oh! Um. . .certainly." He shoved his hand in front of her face, and she took it. He proved quite capable, hoisting her back onto her feet. She avoided looking at him and straightened her skirts. Peeking around the depot, cheeks blazing, she was relieved to note they were the only ones left. Thank goodness only a few people witnessed her humiliating stumble.

She was of a mind to give him a good tongue-lashing, but she was trying to change her ways. Better to pretend the embarrassing deed never happened. Needing distance, Prudy bypassed her satchel, grabbed hold of the railing, and safely descended the stairs. At least she hadn't fallen down them. The last thing her mother needed was for her to show up in need of care. The year and a half with Aunt Louise had helped her grow up and see how selfish she once was. She shivered at the thought of how rudely she'd treated others.

Though glad to be home, she couldn't deny she had many reservations. Would the townsfolk give her a chance to prove she was different? Or would they assume her to be the same sometimes-cruel woman she had once been?

Mr. Merrick hurried to catch up with her quick steps.

"I assume by the quick pace you're keeping you weren't injured." He shifted her bag to his other hand and reached for her elbow, tugging her to a stop when she'd have trotted across the street in front of a nearby wagon. "What's the rush, Miss Willard?"

To get away from you before some other reprehensible event occurs. "I'm anxious to see my parents of course."

"Well, it won't do for you to get run down by a buckboard before you see them."

She jerked free of his hold and lifted her chin. "I didn't plan on getting run over."

Instead of being taken aback, he had the audacity to grin. He pushed his hat back on his head. "And I bet you didn't plan to fall at my feet the first time we met."

Prudy sucked in a breath. The bumbling fool had been replaced by a rogue—and she didn't know which one she liked the least. She attempted to snatch her bag from his hold, but he refused to let go. She glared at him, but inside she secretly admired the vivid blue of his eyes, only a few shades darker than her own. Who was Adam Merrick? And how did he know her parents?

She blinked. She was staring too long.

Spinning, she picked up her skirts and made a beeline for her house. The sooner she was away from this intriguing, insufferable man, the better.

☙

Adam watched the princess sashay toward her castle for a moment then rushed once again to catch up with the feisty woman. Mr. Willard had warned him his daughter could be as blunt as the hot end of a branding iron—her fiery tongue stung as much. He smiled at the remembered comment. Prudy Willard was feisty, that was for sure, but she hadn't been rude or cruel—not even when he'd caused her to fall down and create a spectacle. He suspected her father was exaggerating a tad bit.

He blew out a loud sigh. Being late to greet her certainly wasn't the way to impress the lady, not that he wanted to. Still, since he'd taken over her father's job as mayor of the town, he was sure to see her on a regular basis and would like to be on friendly terms. But as she hurried to get away from him, he doubted she would be eager to see him again.

Her father should have warned him of her beauty. He'd been so taken off guard when he first saw her that he'd been tongue-tied—and he had never been accused of that before. She must think him a bumbling fool.

Ah well. What did it matter? He had a job to focus on—guiding this town and preparing it to ease into the twentieth century. He had no business worrying what a blond-haired, blue-eyed beauty thought of him.

His head was full of ideas for improving the town's business structure and bringing more money to Bakerstown, and he'd love to see electricity brought to the town by the turn of the century. He even had an idea for bricking the streets so that the townsfolk no longer had to walk through a quagmire after a heavy rainfall. Surely the women would appreciate such a gesture. But Bakerstown was a small town, and as such, his annual budget was minuscule.

Adam dodged a pile of fresh manure and caught up with Miss Willard. A pair of lovely blue eyes flicked his direction then quickly away. He wasn't sure what he'd expected in Prudence Willard, but her name had him imagining a book lover in a drab dress with glasses and a bun so tight it pulled her eyes into slits. Instead, her pretty hair, the color of cornsilk, poofed around her face in a very feminine manner. Behind her, thick locks hung in dangling ringlets. His foot hit a rock. Adam took several quick steps and righted himself as heat marched up his neck. Miss Willard stopped in front of the gate to her parents' yard and eyed him like he was three-day-old trout. He picked up her satchel and dusted it off, then cleared his throat and motioned to the gate. "Allow me."

She stepped back with a loud sigh. Adam opened the gate and held it for her to pass through, never having felt so inept. No one would know he'd graduated from Briar Glen College at the top of his class with a business degree. It's what had allowed him to get the job as the mayor's assistant in the first place.

As he helped Miss Willard up the porch steps, he shook his head. What had started out as a beautiful day had ended up as one of the worst of his life.

Chapter 2

Prudy rushed into her mother's arms, glad to finally be home. She'd wanted to return around Easter, but the town had been dealing with an influenza outbreak, and her mother wouldn't hear of her coming back until it was over. Then her father came down with that awful illness, and Mother had postponed her return once again.

"How is Papa? Any better?"

Her mother stepped back, shaking her head. "I'm afraid not." She looked past her daughter, and her gaze lit up. She slipped around Prudy. "Mr. Merrick, I can't thank you enough for seeing Prudence home."

"It was my pleasure, Mrs. Willard." His gaze shot to Prudy and back to her mother. "Where would you like me to put your daughter's satchel?"

"Just set it on the hall tree bench. I'll have Clarence take it upstairs."

Mr. Merrick did as ordered then stood in the foyer holding his hat. "Forgive me, but did I hear you say Emmett—uh. . .Mr. Willard is no better?"

Helen Willard nodded. "He had a rough night—trouble sleeping."

"Then I won't ask to see him." He looked at Prudy. "It was a pleasure to meet you, Miss Willard. I look forward to seeing you again." He donned his hat and gave a slight bow toward her mother. "Good day, Mrs. Willard."

"Thank you again for bringing Prudence home, and if Emmett is doing well on Friday, I'll expect you and your sister for dinner."

Mr. Merrick smiled. "Thank you, ma'am, but I don't want to be a bother."

Prudy watched in surprise as her mother touched Mr. Merrick's arm. "No bother. You know Emmett enjoys your visits and hearing about your week."

"Jenny always enjoys the time, too." He shot a quick glance toward Prudy, touched the end of his hat, and spun toward the stairs. Helen closed the door then turned and stared at Prudy. "You're a bit taller, I believe—and you've lost some weight. Did Louise not feed you properly?"

"Of course she fed me well." Prudy hated the rivalry between her mother and Aunt Louise. Though sisters, the two were completely different. Why couldn't her mother be as sweet and gracious as Louise? "What's this about Mr. Merrick and his sister coming for dinner?"

"When your father had the stroke after his severe sickness, Mr. Merrick was elected interim mayor, and he's tried hard to keep Emmett informed of all he's doing, even though it's not required of him."

"Does he need Papa's guidance in order to do the job properly? I have to say he seemed quite a bumbling fool today."

Her mother cocked her head, looking perplexed, and then she smiled. "Adam must have been disarmed by your beauty. I've always found him to be quite capable."

Prudy decided her mother must be enamored with Mr. Merrick's comeliness. It wasn't like her shrewd mother to admire the very person who'd taken over her husband's job. That must be it.

She glanced up the stairs. "Is Papa awake? I'm anxious to see him."

Her mother pursed her lips and gave a brief shake of her head. "No, I'm afraid he was sleeping a few moments ago, just before I came downstairs." Helen looped her arm through Prudy's. "I have tea ready in the parlor. Come."

She hadn't been home two minutes, and her mother was already telling her what to do. She forced herself to relax, knowing her mother had missed her. And tea would taste good, especially if it were cold. Though it was only late May, the temperature was already quite warm. "Tea sounds wonderful. Thank you, Mother."

Helen beamed as she guided Prudy into the parlor. "So tell me, how is that sister of mine?"

"Aunt Louise is well. She wanted to accompany me, but with Papa still ill, she thought it best to wait. She may come this fall and stay with Aunt Loraine."

"That was thoughtful of her to wait."

Thoughtful was a good word to describe her kindhearted aunt. Her mother was a busybody, always trying to tell people what to do or how to act, but Aunt Louise was quiet and preferred baking a pie to intruding in someone else's business. Prudy sighed.

While her mother filled her in on the town's activities, Prudy's thoughts turned to Adam Merrick. As interim mayor, he was to oversee the town until her father could return to work. He hardly seemed capable of such a task. Maybe she should talk with her father and then visit Mr. Merrick at the office to make sure he wasn't overstepping his authority.

"Prudence, you're not listening."

She blinked, sorry she had gotten caught lost in her thoughts. "I'm sorry, you said someone was with child?"

Her mother nodded, smiling wide. "Pastor Clay's wife is in the family way."

"That's. . .uh. . .nice." Prudy sat back in her chair. The man she'd once hoped to marry would be a father soon. And the woman who'd ruined her dreams would hold his child in her arms. She sighed. Aunt Louise told her she needed to put aside her disappointment of not marrying Clay Parsons and look to the future. Prudy had been able to do that at her aunt's home, but now that she was back and would surely face the two who had broken her heart, it was much harder. "So, is there still only one church in town?"

"Yes, I'm afraid so." Her mother reached across the table and laid her hand on Prudy's arm in an uncharacteristic show of emotion. "I realize it may be hard for you to face Pastor Parsons and Karen, but it's best to just do it and get it over with. I've found they are both kind, forgiving people."

"Perhaps I'll sit with Papa while you attend church."

"No, that won't work. Dr. Blaylock comes to play chess with Emmett every Sunday morning—at least they play when Emmett is able."

There would be no escaping her fate. Suddenly, Prudy felt as wrung out as a mop. "So, tell me about Papa. Is he getting any better?"

Her mother's lips tightened into a straight line. "I wish I could say yes, but the truth is, he's worse, if anything. He hasn't been able to regain his strength. His severe case of influenza would have been fatal to a weaker man, and then he had the stroke before he had a chance to fully recover." Helen batted her lashes and stared out the parlor window. "I don't know how I'll go on if—"

Prudy rose and hurried around the table, bending down to hug her mother. "Don't think of that now. We'll pray and do what we can each day to help Papa and try not to worry about the future."

A few minutes later, Prudy stepped into her frilly, pink bedroom. It looked like something that belonged to a young girl. She took a slow spin, studying the pink-and-white-striped draperies with rows of ruffles, the matching quilt, and the striped sofa and pink side chair. She felt as if she had walked into a peppermint stick factory. Before she left town, she had loved the bright room, but now it left her nauseated. Had she really changed so much?

Perhaps her mother would allow her to paint and make some other changes. It would give her something to do—besides overseeing Mr. Merrick.

∞

The next morning, Prudy strode into the mayor's office. The door made a familiar click as she closed it. Most of her teen years, her father had been mayor, and she'd visited him here many times after school before heading home. Even though she knew Adam Merrick was more than likely using her father's desk as his own, seeing him sitting there still rattled her.

He glanced up from perusing a stack of papers and popped to his feet so fast, the papers went flying. Mr. Merrick made a comical sight as he grabbed for several pages in midair and slapped them on the desk, ignoring those that fluttered to the floor. He snatched up his frock coat, which had been lying across one end of his desk, and shoved his arms into it. "Miss Willard, how nice to see you again. Might I inquire after your father?"

Prudy looked around the office, attempting to regain her composure. She hadn't counted on noticing how nicely Adam Merrick filled out the crisp white shirt he wore. Shifting her gaze away from him, she noticed a college diploma hung where her father had nailed up an award he'd received from the town. There were other subtle changes. Was Mr. Merrick taking over when his job was temporary? Turning her thoughts to her father instantly sobered her. "I fear he's worse off than I expected, but I'm hoping he will rally now that I'm home and can take some pressure off his shoulders."

He picked up a paper, set it on the desk, and moved toward her, compassion filling his eyes. "I'm sorry you couldn't have received better news, Miss Willard." He gestured at a chair sitting in front of his desk. "Would you care to sit?"

"Yes. Thank you." He held on to the back of her chair as she lowered herself onto it, then he returned to his seat on the far side of the large desk. "To what do I owe the pleasure of your visit?"

Prudy stared at her lap, irritated that she'd noticed the intriguing dimple that winked at her when Mr. Merrick smiled. His kindness would only make her task more difficult. She drew in a breath then lifted her head. "I'll be honest. I was stunned to find my father so wasted away. He is a shell of the man he was when I left town, a year and a half ago."

He pursed his lips. "I truly admire your father and enjoyed the year we worked together. He's quite intelligent and has a heart for this town. It's been hard to watch such a vibrant man go downhill." He tugged at his collar, his ears turning red. "Uh. . .pardon me, Miss Willard. I probably shouldn't have said that."

Prudy stared at him, watching him squirm. "Well, it is true. That's why I've come today. Instead of visiting with my father in the future, you may talk to me, and I'll relay the information to him that I feel is warranted."

He blinked, looking confused. "I was under the impression your father enjoyed my visits."

"I'm sure he does, but I believe they are overtaxing him. I think he will improve quicker if I act as mediator."

He cleared his throat. "Things have been going fine without your interference."

Prudy stiffened, taken off guard by his harsh tone. "I disagree."

He rose and tugged on the bottom of his coat. "Regardless, you are not the mayor."

She hiked her chin. "Need I remind you that you are only the *interim* mayor?"

He rounded his desk. "Appointed by the town council. And might I add that your father wholeheartedly endorsed my taking over for him."

Prudy rose, struggling for a comeback. "Well he was ill at the time."

Mr. Merrick's nostrils flared. "Thank you for taking the time to visit, but as you can see, I have work to do."

She glanced at several papers still on the floor and lifted a brow. "Indeed."

He glared at her for a long moment then blew out a loud breath. "I'm not trying to replace your father, Miss Willard, so you can relax your ruffled feathers. I do, however, plan to do the best job that I can until he returns."

She hadn't expected his acquiescence, and it momentarily disarmed her. Maybe he didn't realize he wanted to take over, but he was having the same effect. She was certain he was part of the reason her father was still ill. The man was doing too good of a job, and her father felt he no longer had anything to live for. And she couldn't tolerate that. "I plan to return tomorrow to help you."

His mouth dropped open. "I don't need your assistance. My sister does the filing and serves as my typist."

"Nonetheless, I will see you tomorrow." Prudy rushed toward the door, her heart pounding. She hadn't planned on becoming Adam Merrick's partner when she left home. What had gotten into her?

∽

Adam stared at the closed door, unable to move. Talk about a whirlwind. Emmett had warned him that his daughter could be headstrong, but never once had he considered she'd resent him for stepping up as mayor when no one else wanted the position. The salary was so minimal he had to supplement his income by keeping books for several businesses and auditing the bank quarterly. And the town's annual budget was so puny, he barely had the funds to replace the nails that came loose from the boardwalk.

He sighed and walked to the window. This job certainly didn't pay enough if he had to work with Prudence Willard on a daily basis, no matter if the fire in her eyes stirred him in a way he didn't like.

But he promised Emmett he'd keep the town running smoothly until the man recovered. Although, from the look of things, that might not happen for a long while. They'd discussed ways to improve the town's coffers, but the only viable solution Adam could come up with was to hold a county fair. So far, no town in the county had one, and if Bakerstown could be the first, the town stood to earn a lot of badly needed income.

Adam rubbed the back of his neck and looked out the window, gazing up at the sky. "I could use some help here, Lord. What am I supposed to do with Emmett's daughter?"

The door rattled, and Adam stiffened, fully expecting Prudence Willard to return and give him another tongue-lashing.

"Who was that woman I saw leaving?"

Jenny—not Prudence. Adam blew out a breath and relaxed. He smiled at his sister. "That was Emmett's daughter, Prudence."

Jenny's brown eyes widened as she lifted her hand to cover her lips. "So she has returned. I hate to admit it, but I've heard some dreadful things about her. What did she want?"

He shrugged. "I think she believes I'm trying to take over her father's job, and she resents that." He didn't want to confess she also blamed him for her father not recovering. Could there be a thread of truth in that idea? If Emmett thought he didn't have a job to return to, it might affect his recovery. The first chance he got, he needed to reassure the man. Although Adam enjoyed serving as mayor, there were other things he could do to earn an income.

Jenny removed her hat and gloves. "She's much prettier than I expected."

Adam nodded. "You should see how her eyes blaze when she's angry."

His sister cocked her head, eyebrows lifted.

He knew that look and waved his hands in the air. "Don't go getting any ideas about matchmaking. She is a pretty woman, and I'd not be a man if I didn't notice. That doesn't mean I'm attracted to her."

"Hmm. . ." A smile graced his sister's lips as she set her gloves on the small table that served as her desk.

"Don't *hmm* me, Jenny. And might I remind you that your job is filing, not finding me a wife."

She didn't respond but rather thumbed through the papers he'd left for her, that ornery smile still on her lips.

He grabbed the last of the papers that had flown from his hands when Prudy first stormed in. He didn't have enough tasks to keep Jenny busy. How was he going to manage to find work for Prudy, too?

And how was he going to get anything done with her lavender scent filling his office?

He wouldn't.

He'd just have to find a way to get rid of her.

Fast.

Chapter 3

Prudence Willard arrived promptly at ten o'clock, and an hour later, Adam was ready to resign as mayor. He heaved a sigh. "Miss Willard, surely you're wise enough to realize that Bakerstown is too small to support an opera house."

"I'm well aware of the town's size, Mr. Merrick. I have lived here most of my life, unlike you." She smirked as if thinking she'd landed a killing blow with her last comment. "An opera house would bring in money our town desperately needs."

He took a step toward her. "Only if people are willing to travel a great distance to get here. And once they are here, where would they stay? We don't even have a hotel." He blew out a sigh. "Where are we supposed to get the money to build such a facility?"

Prudy blinked several times, and he could almost see the wheels spinning in her mind. She snapped her fingers. "If we built a hotel with a restaurant, we could earn even more income."

Adam pinched the bridge of his nose and glanced at his wide-eyed sister. Jenny had hardly uttered a word since Emmett's daughter arrived. "Jenny, please tell Miss Willard how much money is in the town treasury."

"After we pay Mr. Michaels for repairing the boardwalk where the wood rotted, we'll have one hundred and three dollars and sixty-two cents."

Prudy's eyes widened. "How can there be such a trivial amount? Surely there's more." She stepped close to Adam, glaring at him. "What have you spent it all on?"

He resisted rubbing his forehead where an ache was building. "Did your father share with you how much was in the bank account when he was mayor?"

"Um. . .well. . .no. But there certainly had to be much more than that."

"There wasn't, I'm sorry to say. That's why I'm trying so hard to come up with an idea to bring in additional funds."

"I don't understand. Surely my father made a decent salary. Otherwise, how could my parents have afforded such a nice home?"

Did she not know about her father's inheritance from his uncle? Emmett had once confided that was how he kept his two women happy and living far above their current means. He never could have afforded such a nice home on his mayoral salary. But that wasn't his news to share. "You'll have to ask your father about that, I'm afraid."

"Believe me. I will." She lifted her chin. "So, back to raising money. What wonderful ideas have you come up with?"

Adam stuck his finger in his collar and tugged. Why did it feel as if it were choking the life from him? "I think we need to concentrate on getting new businesses to come to town, which will generate more money in taxes. Then we should focus on improving the streets and maybe even bring electricity to Bakerstown."

Prudy crossed her arms. "Just how do you plan to entice those businesses to come to town? I've been gone a year and a half, and as far as I can tell, there are no new ones."

Jenny rose and cautiously approached them. "You have to understand, Miss Willard, Adam has only been the interim mayor for half that time, and a good chunk of it was spent learning his duties and getting to know most of the townsfolk so that he could understand how to best serve them. And he does have his other jobs to attend to."

He cut a sharp glare at his sister as Prudy's head jerked toward him. He hadn't wanted her to know about his other places of employment.

"You work somewhere else, besides fulfilling your mayoral duties? How can you expect to prosper the town when you don't devote your full attention to it?"

"Oh dear. I'm sorry, Adam." Jenny turned and fled to her small desk. "I . . .uh. . .need to. . .uh. . .run an errand." She snatched up her reticule and rushed out the door.

He felt like a lily-livered cad for making her feel bad. He owed her an apology. But first he had to deal with Miss Willard, who was quickly becoming as bothersome as a splinter underneath a fingernail. He straightened, taking advantage of his height to force her to look up. "The truth is, this job doesn't pay enough to support my sister and me, so I have no choice but to work other places."

"What kind of places?"

He lifted a brow. "That, Miss Willard, is none of your concern. I can assure you, though, that my other duties do not affect my performance as mayor."

"Interim mayor."

He pursed his lips to keep from saying something he'd regret. He'd devoted many hours to this town for a pittance of a salary, and he didn't appreciate her attitude. He'd never met a woman so obstinate—so interesting. Adam swallowed, appalled by that last thought. Yes, he admired her ardent desire to protect her father's job, even if her efforts were heavy-handed. And she was quite pretty, but he would not allow himself to become attracted to Prudence Willard—not even if she smelled better than a hot apple pie or the fact that he enjoyed seeing her cornflower blue eyes spark. A trickle of sweat ran down his temple as he continued to stare at her. All manner of expressions crossed her face, and she finally ducked her head, breaking his stare.

"I'm sorry if I said something to upset your sister. It wasn't my intention. I'm far too outspoken—too much like my mother, I'm afraid."

Adam couldn't deny the truth of her comment, but he wouldn't have her believing she'd upset Jenny. "I'm afraid it was the glare I turned on Jenny that sent her running. She's a gentle soul and can't stand thinking she angered or disappointed me."

Prudy cocked her head and looked at him with a placid expression. "Might I ask why she lives with you? She is young and quite pretty. In fact, you two greatly favor one another."

Adam cocked his mouth in an amused grin. "Why, Miss Willard, are you insinuating I'm pretty?"

Her mouth dropped open, and her cheeks flamed. "I. . .uh. . .well. . .You are very handsome, but I wouldn't say you're pretty."

She thought he was handsome? He'd hoped to take some delight in seeing her at a loss for words for once, but she'd shocked *him* speechless. In truth, she was one of the prettiest women he'd ever encountered. Too bad her tongue was as sharp as a new knife. He blinked, trying to regain control of his senses.

"I asked about your sister."

"Yes, well Jenny can tell you her story if she wants, but suffice it to say, she had a bad experience with her intended." He held up his hand when she opened her mouth. "Please don't ask me to share more."

Her lips pinched. "I was only going to say I'm sorry. I believe I can understand a little bit of what she feels."

Adam had heard the story from Prudy's father how she shamelessly chased after Pastor Parsons before he married Karen. He'd thought it awful how she'd treated Clay's bride-to-be, but he'd never before considered her side of the story. Had Prudy truly loved Clay? Did his marrying Karen hurt her like Jenny had been wounded?

He rubbed the back of his neck. "I would appreciate if you'd not mention to Jenny that I told you about her misfortune. If you two become friends, I'm sure she'll tell you herself."

She smiled and held up her palm. "I promise. I have no desire to hurt her."

"Thank you." Adam glanced at the door. "I would really like to make sure Jenny is all right. Would you mind postponing our discussion?"

Prudy glanced at the clock on the fireplace mantel. "I should be returning home anyway. Mother likes luncheon to be served precisely at noontime." She flashed him a grin. "I will see you tomorrow morning, Mr. Merrick."

Adam's heart sank. Would he have to endure her challenging his every move on a daily basis? "Really, Miss Willard. There's no need for you to be here. I'm perfectly capable of doing the job myself."

"Regardless, I need to protect my father's interests, and that includes this office."

If he hadn't promised Emmett he'd keep things running until he could return to work, Adam might consider walking out and leaving the job to Miss Willard. She sorely tempted him to forget he was a Christian man who believed in turning the other cheek. He sure hoped he wouldn't have to do it every day.

∞

Prudy exited the office with Adam and waited while he locked the door. He bid her good-day and walked away. She watched him go—tall, confident, and handsome. Her heart had nearly burst from her chest when he'd stood close and stared at her for so long. She was used to men staring, so why did it affect her so when he had? He was her adversary, after all.

Spinning on her toes, she headed home, reminding herself what a stubborn, single-minded man Adam Merrick was. She didn't want to like him. She really should stay far away from him, for she feared she could like him much too easily. She hadn't expected him to be so passionate about his duties, and even though she'd treated him harshly, which she could see irritated him, he never lost control of his temper.

With his dark brown hair, deep blue eyes, and tanned skin, he was delightful to look at. She even enjoyed the way his mouth cocked to one side when he had teased her about thinking he was pretty.

Ugh!

She had to stop dwelling on his comeliness and focus on the fact that he could steal her father's job if she wasn't careful. She needed to talk to Papa if he felt up to it after lunch. He had to understand how comfortably Adam Merrick had settled into his job. Maybe Adam's ideas for making money for the town weren't the best, but he certainly seemed dedicated to the task. She feared he might succeed where her father hadn't—and then the townsfolk might not want her father to return to his job. Her papa had always been so proud to be mayor, and her mother relished the clout of being the town's first lady. If Papa lost his job permanently they would both be devastated, and she couldn't let that happen.

Chapter 4

After lunch, Prudy carried a tray of hot tea into the parlor of her family home. She'd promised to sit with her papa while her mother ran some errands. Every time she saw him, her heart broke a little more. He'd always been so strong and robust. She remembered delighting in how he would toss her in the air when she was small.

He turned from gazing out the front window and smiled at her. "It's so good to have you home again, princess."

"I wish I had returned months ago, but. . ." She bit back the words *mother wouldn't let me* and set the tray on a drum table. "It's good to be home."

"I know my sickliness upsets you, but I wish it didn't."

"Really, Papa, how could it not? I want you to regain your health."

He looked toward the window again. "I would like that, too, but I fear it's not meant to be. Still, I've made my peace with God, and it's in His hands now."

Prudy hated that he sounded so resigned. "Don't give up. Please."

He smiled. "There's a big difference in losing hope and resting in the arms of the Savior."

"I do believe I understand that. Aunt Louise helped me to see my need for God." She nibbled her lip and dropped a spoonful of sugar in his tea as she considered the question that had been bothering her for days. There really was no easy way to ask but to just do so. "How will we get by if you're unable to work again?"

He accepted the teacup she held out and took a slow sip. "Sit down, Prudy. There's something I should have told you years ago."

Curious, she plopped onto the edge of a side chair.

With a shaky hand, her father placed the teacup and saucer on the table beside his chair. For a moment, he rested his index fingers against his chin and returned his gaze to her. "We're not as destitute as you may think. Some years ago, I received a substantial inheritance from my uncle Max."

Prudy's eyes widened as she considered the news. "Why have you never told me?"

He grinned. "Because I was afraid you'd want more clothing and froufrous than you already had. You were only nine when he died, and I didn't feel you were old enough to know about financial issues then. I've managed to save the majority of the money so that when I'm gone, you and your mother will have plenty to live on."

There was a huge relief in knowing he'd planned for the future. "I remember Uncle Max. He lived in a mansion in Boston—a very large mansion. Just how well off are we, if I might ask?"

"Well enough that you have no reason to worry about us becoming destitute. And I don't want you pestering Adam about my old job. He's doing a fine job as mayor."

"Interim mayor."

He shook his head, a sad look darkening his gaze. "You have to face the truth, princess. It's highly unlikely that I will be able to resume that job." He blew out a loud sigh. "I'm not even sure I want to."

"But how can you say that? You lived for that job. I know how important being mayor was to you."

He lifted a brow. "My job was not what I lived for. You and your mother always came first. My job was important because I was able to help the town I grew up in, not because of the prestige."

Things were so different than she'd thought. "But what about Mother? She loves being the matriarch of the town."

"True, but she will be fine as long as she can continue to live in the manner she is accustomed to."

She hated how haughty her mother sounded, but in truth, Helen Willard did see herself as better than others because of their financial status—and to think, it was all because of an inheritance. Prudy's heart clenched. The same could be said about her. She winced as she thought of how horribly she'd treated Karen Parsons when the pastor's fiancée first came to town. She had wanted Clay for herself and had tried to chase Karen away. She needed to apologize, but she was afraid. Bakerstown still had only one church, and all decent women were expected to go to Sunday services. If Karen snubbed her, attending church could be terribly uncomfortable.

A knock at the front door pulled her from her troubling thoughts. "I'll get it. Are you feeling up to having visitors if it's someone to see you, Papa?"

"Yes, but don't let them linger overly long."

She nodded and rushed to answer the door, hoping one of her friends had come to visit. As she pulled it open and saw Pastor Parsons and his wife standing there, she felt the blood drain from her face. Prudy forced a smile.

"How nice to see you both again."

Oh dear, she'd just told a falsehood to the preacher.

Pastor Parsons smiled, as did his wife. "We wanted to welcome you back to town and also see how your father is doing."

"I'm sure he's delighted to have you home again, as is your mother," Karen said.

Prudy dared to glance at her and was shamed by the woman's friendly smile. "Thank you. Papa is in the parlor and said he would welcome a short visit."

Pastor Clay removed his hat and escorted his wife inside. Prudy closed the door then led them to the parlor. "Please have a seat. Papa and I were just enjoying some tea. I'll go reheat the water while you visit with him."

"Could I help you?" Karen offered.

Prudy's pulse raced. Did Karen want to get her alone so she could gloat about winning Clay's hand when Prudy had so desperately wanted to marry him at one time? "Uh. . .it really isn't necessary."

Karen's kind smile sparkled in her eyes. "I really don't mind. Now that you're back, I'd like to get to know you better, if you're agreeable to that."

Prudy didn't know what to say. Could the woman be as guileless as she seemed? She glanced at Papa, and he nodded for her to go on. Perhaps he wanted to speak to Pastor Clay alone. "Of course. Just let me get the tray."

In the kitchen, she placed the tray on the table, refilled the teapot, and set it on the stove to heat. With nothing else to do, she forced herself to face Karen. "So, how are you and Pastor getting along?"

"Wonderful!" She beamed and leaned in as if to share a secret. "You probably can't tell yet, but we're expecting our first child."

Prudy blinked, trying to be happy for the couple, but she couldn't help thinking that if she had married Clay, she might now be the one who was carrying his child. A pair of deep blue eyes intruded on her thoughts—Adam Merrick's eyes—but she pushed the troubling thought away. "Oh my, that's. . . um. . .exciting news. Congratulations to you both."

"Thank you." Karen's smile dimmed a little. "I know you and I had a bit of a rough start when we first met, but I'm hoping we can put it behind us and be friends."

How could she be so forgiving? "I have to admit that you've surprised me. It would well be within your rights to despise me for the deplorable way I treated you."

"I understand that a woman will do almost anything for the man she loves. I'm sorry you were unaware of my relationship with Clay before you fell for him. No one can blame you for something you didn't know about."

Disarmed by the woman's kindness, Prudy leaned back against the counter. "Um. . .I'd like to be friends, too. Thank you. That's very kind of you."

"Don't give it another thought." Karen swatted her hand in the air. "Now that you're home, I hope you'll consider coming to the sewing circle again. I suppose your mother told you that we're meeting at the Spencers' home now."

Prudy nodded. "Mother wrote and told me how she felt it best that she no longer host it, in light of Papa's illness."

"How is he doing, if I might ask?"

Prudy shrugged. "Not nearly as well as I'd hoped."

Karen laid her hand on Prudy's arm. "Your father is a good man. Clay and I have been praying for him."

Tears filled Prudy's eyes. Her mother wouldn't hear of her father not recovering and in some ways seemed oblivious to how ill he actually was. She'd not been able to talk with anyone about her fears, other than crying out to God. A sob slipped out, and Karen wrapped her arms around Prudy. She wept as all her worries gushed to the surface like an overflowing rain barrel. After a long minute, she stepped back. "I'm sorry. I got your lovely dress wet."

Karen smiled and patted her shoulder. "It will dry." She tucked a strand of Prudy's hair behind her ear. "Please know that if you ever want to talk, you're always welcome at my home."

Fresh tears blurred her vision. "Thank you. I don't deserve your kindness."

"None of us deserves the sacrifice that Jesus made for us in giving His life to set us free from the chains of sin, but He went to the cross anyway. He commands us to love one another. How can I not obey?"

As she lay in bed that night, Prudy wrestled with all that had happened that day. Karen's kindness still astounded her. How could she be so forgiving? She flipped onto her side and stared out the open window. A gentle breeze wafted in, cooling her, and the repetitive chirp of crickets lulled her to a relaxed state. Karen made her want to be a better person. To be more forgiving and less demanding. More like Karen and Aunt Louise and less like her mother. She'd become a Christian while living with Aunt Louise and had grown in her faith, but since she returned to Bakerstown, she had reverted to her old, blustery self.

She yawned. She'd treated Adam Merrick almost as bad as she had Karen. Tomorrow, she needed to apologize.

Chapter 5

Prudy's mother glided into the kitchen. "What's that delicious smell, Betsy?"

Glancing over her shoulder, Prudy smiled. "Good morning, Mother. I talked Betsy into allowing me to bake some dried-apple bread."

Her mother shot a scowl at the cook. "It's Betsy's duty to prepare any treats you want, not yours."

Prudy rolled her eyes. "Don't fuss at Betsy, Mother. It was my idea. Besides, how could you be so proud of those awful rhubarb pies I used to make and then fuss at me if I want to do some baking? I learned to cook many things while staying with Aunt Louise."

Her mother motioned for Prudy to follow her. Prudy checked the clock on the shelf—fifteen minutes more before the bread would be finished. She followed her mother to the library, where Helen closed the door.

Crossing her arms, Mother stared at her for a long moment, making Prudy feel the need to squirm. Had she done something wrong? One thing she hadn't missed while she was gone was being scolded for minor mistakes. "What's wrong?"

"I pay Betsy good money to cook for us. You'll only confuse her if you start assisting her."

"I wasn't helping her. I was making the bread as a gift for someone."

Helen lifted one brow. "For whom?"

Prudy shifted her feet, hoping her mother wouldn't make a mountain out of a molehill. "I was rather rude to Mr. Merrick yesterday, so I'm taking him the bread as part of my apology."

Her mother's gray eyes widened. "You can't do that. Why, he'll think you have designs on him."

"Oh for heaven's sake. He'll think no such thing."

"If you were hard on that man, I'm sure he deserved it."

"You don't like him? Papa seems quite pleased with his efforts."

Helen pointed a finger in her face. "Mark my word, that man is trying to steal your father's job while he is too ill to be aware of the fact."

Prudy scratched her temple. "Why did you invite him and his sister for supper on Friday if you don't like him?"

"I like him fine, but I don't care that he's doing such a good job replacing your father."

"Would you rather he did a bad job?"

Several emotions crossed her mother's face before she narrowed her eyes. "You're trying to trick me, aren't you?"

"No, Mother, I'm not. At first, I was also annoyed that Mr. Merrick was filling Papa's shoes—and his office—but after talking with Papa, I've come to realize he puts his faith in the man doing a decent job and is able to relax, knowing the town is in good hands. If Mr. Merrick fails at his task, then Papa will be sorely disappointed and distressed, so it would be in our best interest to want Mr. Merrick to succeed, don't you think?" Prudy could hardly believe she was defending the man, but she'd realized the truth yesterday afternoon.

After blowing out a loud sigh, her mother relaxed her posture. "I suppose what you say is true." Her hand quivered as she brushed several hairs from her face. "I've almost given up hope that Emmett will ever be able to work again."

Prudy clasped her mother's hand. "Don't give up. Somehow I'll find a way to help Papa get better." But even as she said the words, she knew there was little she could do.

Helen smiled. "Maybe having you home again is just what he needs to rally."

Prudy truly hoped that was the case, but deep down she doubted it.

∞

Adam stood facing his desk, studying a bid to repair the fences at the stockyard. They'd been standing since the railroad came through town nearly two decades ago and were sorely in need of replacing. But doing so would require using up nearly one-third of the town's remaining funds. On the other hand, not repairing them could cause cattle to break free and stampede the town, injuring its citizens and damaging property. Maybe he could ask for bids from other towns, although he hated not giving business to a local carpenter.

A woman glided past his window, and he frowned. It looked like Prudy was going to arrive early today. Lucky him.

As he watched her through another window, she suddenly halted. A man stood directly in front of her. He bent over and smelled something she carried. She took a step backward, and the man followed. Adam rushed to the door. He might not care for Prudy's overpowering ways, but he wouldn't stand by and watch her be harassed by an ill-mannered man. Still, he opened the door and listened to make sure he wasn't jumping to conclusions.

"You sure are pretty, miss. And whatever you're carryin' sure smells toothsome."

"I. . .uh. . . Thank you, but I must be on my way. Please let me pass."

He stepped closer. "What say you and me go somewheres quiet-like and share that delicacy?"

"No. It's a gift for someone. I insist that you let me pass."

Adam had to give Prudy credit for not cowering. The man barely seemed to rattle her. He stepped around the stranger and glanced at Prudy, noticing instant relief when her gaze met his. "Are you all right, Miss Willard?"

"Yes, I believe so. But thank you for coming to check on me."

The dusty cowboy glared at Adam, but he met him gaze for gaze. "We don't like our womenfolk to be pestered on our streets. You'd best tend to your business and be on your way."

"Who are you? The marshal?"

"No, the mayor—and the boxing champion of Briar Glen College for three years running." He stepped in front of Prudy and lifted a brow at the man, issuing a silent challenge.

After a moment, the stranger dropped his gaze to Adam's fist then shrugged. "I didn't mean no harm. Just wanted to yammer with a purty gal."

"That's fine, as long as the gal in question wishes to talk with you. This one doesn't."

The stranger nodded then shuffled back the way he'd come. Adam faced Prudy, whose eyes were wider than normal and emphasized the blue of her irises.

"Is that true?" Her head cocked, eyebrows puckered. "Were you a boxing champion?"

Adam nodded. His manly pride at coming to her rescue wilted a bit, confronted with her disbelief. "I don't need to resort to lying to defend your honor, Miss Willard."

She smiled. "I didn't mean to insult you. I was merely curious. And do you suppose we could use our Christian names since we'll be seeing each other frequently?"

Adam stared at her. What happened to the snippety harpy who'd barged into his office yesterday demanding all manner of information? He searched his mind. Was it possible Prudence Willard had a twin sister?

Her smile drooped. "Would that be such a difficult thing?"

Baffled, he cleared his throat and took a chance this was the same woman. "Uh. . .not at all, uh. . .Prudence. Would you like for me to carry that for you?"

Her smile returned, lifting his spirits with it, and she handed him a plate covered by an embroidered towel. "Thank you, Adam. Now, do you suppose we could go inside? I have something to say that I don't want aired in public."

Down went Adam's spirits. She was putting on an act—being nice while on the street in case anyone was watching. He sighed and stepped back, allowing her to enter first. While her back was turned, he took a whiff of whatever it was he carried, and his stomach gurgled at the delicious aroma.

Prudy removed her hat and gloves, setting them on the corner of Jenny's desk, and then she took the plate from him and also set it down. He'd hoped she'd brought something to share, but perhaps it was for a friend, something he certainly wasn't.

He waited for her to lash out, but this morning she seemed different, less sure of herself. She looked up at him, nibbling her lip, then glanced at the window and back at him. She sucked in a breath and spewed out, "I owe you an apology."

If she'd grown feathers and started squawking, he wouldn't have been more surprised. The woman who left here yesterday didn't seem like someone who'd ever be so contrite. "For what?"

She threw out her hands. "For everything I've said and done since we first met. I was a nasty shrew yesterday, and for that, I'm sorry."

Dumbfounded, he stood there staring at her. "Are you sure you don't have a twin sister?"

She laughed. "Would you want me to?"

"To be truthful"—he brushed a hand across his cheek—"not if she was like the woman who stormed in here yesterday, but this one, I wouldn't mind so much."

She cocked her head and studied him, probably wondering if he was teasing. "I brought a peace offering." She lifted the towel, folded it, and set it down; then she picked up the plate and held it out to him. A sweet cinnamon scent filled the air, making his mouth water. "I hope you like apple bread."

He grinned. "I hope we argue every week and you feel the need to bring more peace offerings."

Her soft laughter warmed him, making him want to hear that delightful sound over and over. Suddenly she frowned. "Oh bother. I forgot to bring any plates or forks."

"I can help with that. Jenny and I sometimes eat lunch here, so I believe there are a couple we forgot to take home." He opened a cabinet on the wall, removed a pair of plates, and held them out to her. "There are no forks, but these will help a little."

"I apologize for using my fingers. Next time I'll prepare better." She slid a fat slice of apple bread onto one plate then handed it back to him and placed another piece on the other plate. "Is Jenny not coming in today?"

"No, a friend of hers, Patsy Mullins, recently had a baby, and she's helping her."

Prudy gasped. "Patsy is a mother? That's wonderful. So many things change when you're gone for a year and a half."

Adam bit into the bread and closed his eyes, savoring the tantalizing flavors. "Mmm. . . This is amazing, Prudence."

"Prudy, please. Prudence is what my mother calls me, especially when she's angry."

He imagined living with stuffy Helen Willard wasn't easy. The woman reigned over the town, and it had taken him months to get her to leave him alone and let him do things his way. Much like the Prudy who'd been here yesterday, she had tried to run the mayor's office.

"So, have you thought up any new ways to make money for the town?" she asked.

He licked the crumbs from his lips. "As a matter of fact, we may have. What do you think of the idea of a county fair?" Adam took another bite as he watched her mull over the idea.

A slow grin pulled at her lips. "I think that's a wonderful idea. Do you know if any other towns in this county have had one?"

He shook his head. "They haven't. A few host Founder's Day celebrations, but they are small events."

"Are you thinking of something large scale?"

Adam shrugged. "I don't know how big it could be considering the budget. I'm thinking we could have a horse race or two—maybe one for adults and another for older youths. A livestock show and sale. Calf roping and sheep riding for the children."

Prudy frowned. "That sounds more like a rodeo than a fair. What about events for the women?"

He helped himself to a second slice while pondering her question. "What do you have in mind that wouldn't cost much?"

Her eyes brightened as she set her plate down. "The women of Bakerstown pride themselves on their sewing and baking skills." She started pacing. "We could have a quilt show and offer ribbons to the best ones, girls could enter their samplers or sewing projects if we have an event for youth, and we could hold contests for the best pies, jellies, and various canned foods."

"Whoa there. Where do you think we could hold such an event? No place in town is big enough."

She tapped her finger on her lips, drawing his gaze to them. His gut tightened. This Prudy intrigued him—interested him—but what if she turned back into yesterday's shrew? What could have prompted such a drastic change so quickly?

"You're not listening." She whacked his arm, making him jump.

He rubbed the spot. "What did I miss? I was thinking." *About you.*

"I said we could rent a big tent. My Aunt Louise and I went to a circus held in one last year. I think it's just what we need."

He pursed his lips. "I don't know. . . . I'm afraid we'd have to spend too much money. And we'd need lots of judges."

"Leave the judges to me. As for the money, we could charge a nominal entry fee for each contest with the winner getting a blue ribbon and a small percentage of the total money collected for each event. I'm sure I can get the ladies of the sewing circle to help make ribbons if we need to."

"We'd need tables for most of those events. That would be an expense."

"True." She walked to a window and stared out then pivoted around again, eyes twinkling. "What about asking Pastor Clay if we could use the benches from the church? They would be low, but they just might work."

Adam nodded, catching her vision. "You're right, but we'd have to be mighty careful. Can't you imagine the ruffled feathers if someone bumped into a bench and knocked over a bunch of pies?"

Prudy giggled. "That would be dreadful. Perhaps we need to rethink that plan."

"I agree."

She clapped her hands, her excitement obvious. "This could really work, Adam. With all those events, we could add a lot to the town coffers. We'll have to advertise it though. That's another expense."

"I wonder if we could offer free room and board during the fair for reporters. Say a town's newspaper gives us free advertising, and we put their reporter up in the boardinghouse so they can attend the fair and cover it. That will give us even more exposure and make their readers want to attend next year." He couldn't remember when he'd been so excited.

Prudy laid her hand on his forearm. "That's a brilliant idea."

He glanced down, enjoying her gentle touch, then looked up, capturing her gaze and holding it. His insides simmered, his senses on alert. He hadn't wanted to be attracted to Prudence Willard yesterday, but today, everything had changed. She had changed.

She lowered her eyes and stepped back, a becoming blush staining her cheeks. "It seems we can work together, doesn't it?"

"Indeed." He smiled.

"So, where do we start?"

Chapter 6

Prudy rushed into the mayor's office the next morning, her head swimming with ideas for the county fair. Adam rose from his chair behind the desk when she closed the door.

"Good morning." His deep voice rumbled through the office sending delicious chills up her arms.

She smiled. "Yes, it is." After removing her hat and gloves, she hurried to one of the chairs in front of the desk and sat down. "I told Papa about your idea for a county fair, and he thought it was brilliant. He and I chatted about it all evening, and he gave me some wonderful ideas." Prudy glanced up from scanning the list in her portfolio to see a perplexed expression on Adam's face. "Is something wrong?"

His lips twittered, as if a humorous thought had crossed his mind. "I wasn't sure which Prudy to expect this morning—the sweet, helpful one or the. . .other one."

She lifted a brow. "I do believe I told you that I'm trying to change my ways. Being around my mother again has made me realize how much I had started acting like her; and I have to say, I don't want to become that woman."

"I'm very relieved to hear that."

She cocked her head, wondering what he really thought of her—and why it mattered. "Was I truly so awful?"

His eyes lifted to the ceiling for a moment. "Maybe unexpected is a better description."

She fought a grin. "I suppose that is fair. I did rather barge in and take over. Again, I apologize for that."

He sat back in his chair. "So, let's hear your ideas."

The door rattled, and Prudy peeked over her shoulder to see Jenny entering. Adam's sister soon joined them, casting Prudy an apprehensive glance. Prudy smiled, hoping to relieve the young woman's concerns.

"We were about to go over the list of ideas that Prudy and her father came up with last night." He looked at her. "Please proceed."

"Concerning the tent, Papa thought we might use the church benches to create a sitting area. We could have a stage at one end of the tent with all of the items to be judged there. People can sit and rest while they view the judging events for the women."

He nodded. "I like that, but we still have the issue of needing tables we don't have."

"There's a sawmill in Sweetgum. I wonder if we could get them to donate the lumber in exchange for some type of free advertising or possibly a complimentary booth?"

"What if we had flyers made announcing the various events and times they will be held?" Jenny said. "Then we could offer free ads to people who help us with donations."

Adam stared at his sister for a long moment then shifted his gaze to Prudy. "I think both ideas are brilliant."

Excitement filled Prudy. "So do I."

"Good. Jenny, do you think you could be in charge of the brochures?"

Her eyes widened but she nodded.

Adam rubbed his jaw. "I'll see about getting the tent and talk to the sawmill owner and some other businessmen who might be able to help. Prudy, could you work on the schedule of events and create short descriptions so we can advertise them in area newspapers?"

"I'd love to. Have you settled on which events you want for the men?"

The next few hours passed quickly as they tossed around ideas and made decisions. Prudy loved the interaction and camaraderie and felt like she had made two new friends. "We have an excellent start. I'm so excited to see how it all plays out."

Jenny nodded. "I sure hope the townsfolk of Bakerstown and the other towns in the county support the fair. It would be dreadful if we did all this work and spent more of the town's money, only to have it flop."

Adam sat with his elbows on his desk, fingers steepled against his mouth. "It won't," he said with confidence. "People love events that bring them together, give them a chance to see friends and family, and they love to compete. I expect the fair will be a rousing success."

Prudy enjoyed the way his eyes squinted when he smiled. He was so different than she'd first thought. It shamed her that she'd judged Adam Merrick so harshly.

Adam slapped his hands on the desk, making both her and Jenny jump, but his gaze was directed only at her. "What say we go out to lunch and celebrate?"

Prudy nodded. "I'd like that."

∞

Adam was walking in dangerous territory allowing himself to be attracted to Prudy. This sweet, helpful version intrigued him more than a little, and surprisingly, he'd caught himself thinking of her in terms of romance and even marriage. It was crazy since he'd known her less than a week.

If he were honest, he'd have to say the shrewlike Prudence had also caught his interest with her passionate defense of her father's job and insistence on ensuring the town's money and concerns were safe.

He liked that she recognized how she was behaving badly and was working hard to change her ways. So far, he believed she meant what she said. Time would tell though.

He escorted the ladies, one on each arm, down the empty street toward the small café. Jenny had settled in well to life in the small town, and for that, he was grateful to God. As he listened to the women's chatter, he realized that Prudy and his sister were on their way to becoming friends, and nothing could make him happier.

Adam stood a bit straighter, enjoying having two pretty ladies at his side. He'd often wondered why God had sent him to such a small town. His dreams had been for something loftier, but if God brought him here to find the love of a good woman, well. . .he wouldn't fuss about that.

He smiled as he opened the café door, releasing a barrage of tantalizing smells. He'd prayed so hard to find a way to help the town with its financial crisis, and God had sent him help from a most unlikely source—Prudence Willard. Adam bit his lip to keep from smiling as he seated the ladies. Just think, after the stories he'd heard about Prudy, he'd been half afraid to meet her at the depot.

He dropped into his chair and winked at her, drawing a becoming blush to her cheeks. Yes sir, God sure had surprised him.

Chapter 7

A s Adam and Prudy walked away from the stockyard, she checked another item off her list. She looped her arm around his and glanced up at him. "I'm really glad Mr. Hampton decided to build another corral at the livery, and that he's willing to let us use it during the fair."

"Me, too. I've had visions of stampeding cattle, with women and children getting hurt."

Prudy lifted one brow, a bit surprised by his comment. Adam didn't seem the type of man to worry so much that it would affect his dreams. In the past few months they'd worked together, he had always been calm, organized, and self-controlled—well, except for the few times she riled him with her stubbornness. "If it makes you feel better, I still have visions of pies on the church benches and someone plopping down on one end, sending them all flying into the air and landing on my mother."

He chuckled. "That might almost be worth seeing."

"Oh!" She spun and smacked him on the arm. "What an awful thing to say. That would be a waste of good pies."

Adam glanced down, his eyes dancing with humor. He pressed her arm against his side. "I'm going to tell her you said that."

She gasped in mock horror. "You'd better not. I'll quit, and you'll have to tend to all the fair details yourself."

His smile drooped. "That would be a nightmare. I don't think I've told you half enough how amazing a job you and Jenny have done. We wouldn't be having this fair without you, Prudy."

She warmed under his praise. "Remember that first day I stormed into your office. I was so certain you were trying to steal Papa's job from him."

"It felt like a cyclone had blown through."

"I'm sorry for that. I suppose I was in a rather stormy mood." As Adam guided her down Main Street, Prudy watched Mr. Lane, the grocer, tack up a row of patriotic bunting, as many of the other business owners had already done. It was a delight to see how excited the whole town was to be hosting the county fair in Bakerstown. "Did I tell you that Mr. Lane told me he's had to reorder sugar and flour and other baking supplies three times in the past month? It would seem the ladies are planning to do their part."

"I'm glad. I've heard plenty of the local farmers and ranchers bragging about their crops and livestock. Each one thinks he has the winning bull or horse. I'm expecting a large turnout."

Adam opened the door of the café, and Prudy entered and sat at an empty table. She flipped back a few pages in her notepad. "On Friday morning, I've arranged with several women to teach classes in ten-yard rag rug making, log cabin quilts, straw hats with decorations, and chair tidies, while the men will be occupied with the livestock sale. After lunch, in the early afternoon, we'll have the first round of horse races and stock horse pulls as well as some of the children's events. Late afternoon will be the preliminary judging for all of the food items and show stock. Then on Friday night, we'll have a square dance and barbecue." She glanced up, hoping he approved of the schedule since it would be hard to change at this late date. "How does that sound?"

He reached across the table and took her hand. "You're an amazing woman, Prudence Willard."

Cheeks flaming, Prudy tugged her hand from his as the waitress rushed toward them. Adam was like no man she'd ever known. Even kindhearted Pastor Clay paled in her eyes when compared to Adam. He made her heart sing and her body tingle with a simple touch or when they shared a private smile. What had started out as a mission to rescue her father's job had turned into an unexpected romance—at least that's how she felt. Was it possible Adam felt the same?

"Prudy? Did you hear the waitress? She asked what you'd like."

"Oh, my apologies. I was thinking. Too many things muddling my mind these days. I'll have a bowl of ham and beans and some lemonade, if you have it."

The waitress nodded, took Adam's order, and then scurried to another table. The delicious aromas made her stomach grumble. She'd been too engrossed in the fair when they entered to notice her hunger.

Adam shook out his napkin and placed it in his lap. "After we eat, I need to make sure the tent crew doesn't need more help. They're going to start erecting it at two."

Prudy's insides swirled. "I can't wait to see it standing. Until that happens,

I don't think I'll believe the fair will actually happen."

"Oh, it's happening all right." Adam's look of pride, directed at her, made her sit a bit straighter. "I don't know how you managed to get so many businesses from other towns to come and rent space to advertise their products." He shook his head as if astounded. "A candy maker, Simon & Barnes clothier, a wagon company, and have you seen that water tower going up near the stockyard?"

"Of course I saw it. We were just there."

"So, did everyone come through with the donations for prizes?"

"Yes, surprisingly so. Simon & Barnes donated an overcoat valued at fifteen dollars, which is the prize for the best eight-pound pail of butter exhibited at the fair, and an English worsted suit also valued at fifteen dollars is the prize for whoever wins the horse race. A gunsmith from Independence is coming to show his wares, and he donated a rifle for the winner of the shooting competition. And there are the cash prizes the winners will covet. Jenny is collecting money today from the businesses that are sponsors."

Adam sat back. "I'd say we've done it."

Prudy's mind raced. "Done what?"

"Saved the town's treasury. With all the money we've taken in and will still receive on entry fees, especially since you and Jenny had the foresight to get prizes donated, the town fund is at its highest point ever."

She basked in his praise. "It was a lot of work, but we never could have done it without your help and support."

Embarrassed to receive such a loving gaze from Adam in public, Prudy glanced at her notes. "Oh, did I tell you that several ranchers are going to put on an exhibition of riding tricks for the children on Saturday afternoon while the men play baseball?"

The waitress slid their plates in front of them and spun away.

Adam reached across the table for her hand. Prudy glanced around the crowded café then slid hers into his, hoping no one noticed.

"Lord, thank You for all we've accomplished with Your help. I'm most grateful for this wonderful woman You've brought into my life. We ask Your blessing on this meal. In Jesus' name. Amen." He glanced up, capturing her gaze with his.

Prudy's heart stampeded at the promise in his alluring blue eyes. She didn't tell him her real dreams included him—and a future together.

∞

Adam beamed like a boy with his first knife as Prudy approached the site where the tent was being raised. "The crew foreman is going to let me erect one of the two center poles."

"Are you sure that's safe?"

His brow dipped. "These men put tents up all the time. They know what they're doing."

"True, but you're not experienced like they are." The wind whipped her skirts, causing her to sidestep. Adam reached out, steadying her.

He exhaled a loud sigh. "Have you no faith in me? All I'm doing is holding a pole."

Prudy stepped forward, sorry she'd wounded his manly pride, and touched his arm. "Of course I have faith in you, Adam. I guess I'm a little concerned for your safety."

He cocked his head, a sweet grin tugging at his lips. "Are you worried about me?"

"Didn't I just say that?"

He glanced around then stepped closer and ran his finger down her cheek. "If you're worried about my safety that must mean you have feelings for me, Miss Willard."

She fought a smile. "I wouldn't go that far, Mr. Merrick."

He stared at her for a long moment, and Prudy held his gaze. "Me thinks you doth protest too much." The warm words whispered across her cheek.

"Perhaps." Her grin broke loose, and she shrugged. "A woman does need to keep up appearances. I can hardly wail and gnash my teeth and cry out if you enter that tent before it's securely staked up, can I?"

"Honestly, I have no doubt you could do that, but I'm thankful you have enough self-control not to."

"Mr. Merrick! We're ready for your help." The foreman jogged toward them. He spied Prudy and tipped his hat. "Afternoon, Miss Willard."

"Mr. Andrews. How is the tent raising coming?"

"Fine and dandy. We're ready to lift the center supports then we'll put up the side poles and tie them down. Should be done in an hour or two."

"Thank you so much for getting the tent here a few days early. I want to have everything prepared and ready to go before the visitors start arriving."

"My pleasure, ma'am." He touched his cap again then punched Adam's arm. "Let's get at it, Mr. Mayor."

Adam's blue eyes flashed with eager anticipation. He squeezed Prudy's hand, flexed his right arm, revealing his bulging muscle, then spun away. She shook her head, chuckling. Behind her rose the excited buzz of conversation, and she turned to see a growing crowd. The tent raising was something far outside of the ordinary for Bakerstown, and at sixty by one hundred twenty feet, it would be the biggest structure in town.

The pole on the right was lifted, and the tent rose in the air with it. Right away, the second pole created a point in the top of the tent and rose higher and higher until the left side was even with the right side. Releasing the tense breath she held, Prudy glanced down at her clipboard. She needed to check with Pastor Clay to see when the benches could be moved from the church to the tent. Surely there was no reason it couldn't be done right away since there were no church services until Sunday, and the fair would be over by then. She glanced around again and spied Pastor Clay and Karen strolling toward the crowd and started toward them.

A fierce gust of wind whipped at her skirts and blew a strand of hair across her face. The tent snapped and popped like a hundred sheets on a line. Holding down her skirts, she turned as a loud, unified gasp rose from the crowd. Two men fled the entrance. The tent shuddered, listed to the left, and fell.

"Adam!"

Prudy started forward, but someone grabbed her, holding her back. She looked over her shoulder to see Silas Hightower shake his head.

"You'll only get in the way. Let the men handle things. It ain't the first time this has happened."

Although a bit annoyed, she nodded her head, and he released her. Surely the men trapped would be all right. It's not like the canvas was overly heavy, but could they breathe in there? Her heart clenched at the thought of losing Adam. She thought of him trapped, maybe hurt—she closed her eyes—suffocating. And in that moment she knew—she loved Adam Merrick.

Please, heavenly Father, keep him safe. I can't lose him. Please.

The duo who had raced from the tent returned and were struggling to lift the opening. Men from the crowd rushed forward to help. Together, they lifted up the heavy tent enough to find the opening. Several men set up the poles to keep the side standing while others disappeared inside. On the far side of the tent, bumps lifted and dropped under the canvas, reminding her of when she was a child and her cat crawled under her bedcovers.

Two men hurried out, helping Mr. Andrews. He was on his feet and looked to be all right. He started yelling commands immediately. By her count, at least six more men were still inside. The minutes ticked by tormentingly slow. Why was it taking so long to get everyone out?

Another man crawled out from under the canvas then rose and walked out, fanning himself with a crumpled hat. A man with a bucket jogged up to him, sloshing water. He lifted out a ladle and handed it to the worker. Prudy stared at the opening. Where was Adam? If the other men were fine, surely he was.

Time crept by at the pace of a reluctant schoolboy on his way to the first day of classes. Prudy felt someone near her and glanced over to see Karen standing beside her with Pastor Clay next to her. Karen reached out and squeezed Prudy's hand. "They'll get him out. We're praying."

"Thank you."

A man ran out of the tent, looked around, and yelled, "Someone get the doctor!" He spun and rushed back in.

Heart pounding, Prudy glanced at Karen. The woman stepped closer and wrapped her arm around Prudy's waist. She couldn't stop the trembling in her hands and legs. *Please don't take Adam from me.*

A man appeared, backing out of the tent, carrying another man by the shoulders, while Mr. Andrews held his feet. Prudy stared at the wounded man's light blue shirt—the same light blue as Adam's. *No!*

Her feet pushed into motion, and she hurried forward. They laid him under a tree, and several men crowded around him. "Let me pass. Please. Move!"

The crowd parted. She stopped at Adam's side and dropped to her knees, heedless of propriety. A trickle of blood from a cut on one eyebrow ran down toward his ear. Someone had removed his belt, strapped it around Adam's shoulder and tucked his left arm into it. She glanced up at Mr. Andrews.

"I think his arm is broke," he said. "The big pole fell on him."

"It sure hurts like it's broken," Adam grumbled.

Prudy gasped and jerked her gaze back to Adam's. A pitiful smile pulled at one corner of his mouth. "Howdy, princess."

She took hold of the hand lying on the ground. "You scared ten years off me. Are you all right? How's your arm? What about your head?"

Eyes shut, he chuckled. "Careful, Pprincess. You're going to make these good folks think you care for me."

With an air of authority, the doctor forced his way to them and ordered everyone back. Prudy refused to move, even when the man glared at her. She merely glared back. He stooped and examined Adam's head wound and bandaged it, then carefully checked his arm. Adam groaned, and Prudy's heart nearly broke at seeing the man she loved in such pain. In spite of their rocky start, which was mostly her own doing, she'd fallen for Adam Merrick.

Chapter 8

September 10, 1892
County fair, day two

Prudy jumped when the starting gun for the first horse race blasted. The crowd cheered. Riders hooted and kicked their mounts into a quick gallop, stirring up a cloud of dust. She checked the race off her list and looked for Adam. It was time for the final round of the pie judging, for which he'd eagerly volunteered, along with her father, and pie lover Silas Hightower.

Assuming he was already at the tent, she swung in that direction. All around her, people chatted and laughed. Children ran, squealing and playing impromptu games. She relished the sounds of happiness. Yesterday, the first day of the county fair had gone nearly perfect. More people had signed up for events and contests than they'd dreamed possible. The town treasury had more than quadrupled, and they'd been able to raise the amount of prize money for the winners. Except for the disaster with the tent falling and hurting Adam and a bullet at the shooting competition that ricocheted, breaking a nearby store window, everything had gone smoothly.

On the outskirts of town, she paused where a fat hog was being roasted. The delicious aroma taunted her, reminding her that she'd forgotten to eat lunch. "How's the hog coming, Mr. Poteet?"

He tipped his hat. "Slow and steady, ma'am, but it'll be ready in time for tonight's supper."

"Good. Thank you so much for donating the hog and seeing that it got cooked. I know everyone will enjoy it this evening."

She glanced at her list as she continued to the tent. After the final rounds of judging, all but the three winning pies, which would be returned to the ladies who baked them, would be set out on tonight's food tables, as would all the cakes and sweet breads that had been baked. Never in her wildest dreams could she have imagined so many ladies would want to compete.

With his arm in a crisp, white sling, Adam stood at the entrance to the tent, greeting people as they walked in. Her heart leaped at the sight of him.

Who could have dreamed she would find love so quickly upon returning home? Her pulse quickened the closer she got to him. He looked up, sent a special smile directed only to her, then tipped his hat to the man and woman he'd been talking with and walked her way.

"There's my pretty lady."

Blushing like a schoolgirl, she glanced around to see if anyone had overheard. "You're shameless, sir."

"That's not what I'd call it. Overwhelmed by your beauty, amazed with your organizational abilities, and delighted by your sweet demeanor."

Prudy laughed. "I don't know that anyone has referred to me as sweet before, except for maybe my father."

He held out his right arm, and she looped hers through it. "They don't know you as well as I do."

She ducked her head. This man could make her blush faster than the flit of a hummingbird's wing.

He tugged her away from the entrance toward the back of the tent. With no activities in that area, the only people they encountered were a couple of adolescents sparking. The youths stopped suddenly, stared at them wide-eyed, then rushed away in the other direction.

Adam chuckled for a moment then stopped and faced her, all humor fleeing. He studied her face, tucking a strand of hair that had come loose behind her ear. "You're not working too hard, are you?"

She shook her head. "No. I'm having the time of my life. It's so wonderful to see everybody have such fun. What about you? Is your arm hurting?"

"Not too bad. I took a half dose of the powder Doc gave me. It's enough to curb the pain and yet not knock me out." He brushed his knuckles down her cheek. "You're sunburned."

She shrugged. "I took off my straw hat during the three-legged race I ran with Jenny, and then I couldn't find it afterwards."

Adam grinned. "I'll never forget watching that race. You two looked so funny trying to walk with your legs tied together and maneuvering in those long skirts."

Prudy smiled. Seeing him so happy made her happy. "We need to get inside for the pie judging." She cocked her head and sent him a teasing smile. "I know how much you're dreading that."

He straightened and blew out a breath in a self-important manner. "Yes, the things I do for this town. Pure torture."

Prudy giggled.

He sobered and took her hand. "I was going to wait until tonight, but I fear you might be too tired to appreciate the moment."

Her mind swirled. What was he talking about?

His gaze captured hers. "Prudy, this summer has been the best I can remember. Planning the county fair, seeing it all come together, and spending time with you while doing so has been a delight. I almost dread seeing it come to an end."

"There's always next year."

"True. I wish I could hire you as my assistant."

Prudy's hopes dimmed a bit. She'd hoped—prayed that he would soon ask for her hand. But obviously that was not the case. "I'll work for free, Adam. You don't need to hire me."

He stared into her eyes. "What I need, is you at my side—always. Will you marry me, Prudy, and make me the happiest man on earth?"

Prudy gasped. "Do you mean it?"

"With all of my heart." He cupped her cheek, his gaze intense. "I love you and can't stand the thought of being without you. Please, marry me."

Tears blurred her eyes. "Of course I will."

A wide grin split his mouth, and he leaned in, touching his lips to hers. He pulled her close, deepening his kiss and showing her the depth of his love. Far too soon he pulled back and sighed. "I wish I didn't have to judge those pies now."

"Why is that?"

"They'll all taste sour after the sweetness of your lips."

Prudy groaned. "Oh Adam, that's so droll."

"Too much, huh?" His embarrassed grin warmed her heart.

"Yes, but I love you anyway." She tugged on his shirt, pulling him closer.

Joy engulfed his handsome features, and he pulled her in for another kiss.

"Anyone seen the mayor?" Someone shouted from the far side of the tent.

Prudy giggled. "We really have to go."

"Yes, I believe we do. Come along, my love. There are pies to be judged."

The Columbine Bride

by Davalynn Spencer

Thou wilt shew me the path of life.

PSALM 16:11

Chapter 1

Colorado, 1886

Lucy Powell's ears pricked at her children's excited voices. She looked up from the vegetable seed packets to the candy counter where a tall bearded man reached for Elmore's ear. Three quick steps took her past a table before she stopped. The man squatted, and her son's eyes widened at the sight of a copper penny. Cecilia, ever the guardian, stayed her little brother's hand.

"We don't take things from strangers, Elmore."

Lucy clutched the packets she'd already chosen and listened for her son's reply.

"He ain't no stranger, Sissy. That penny come out of my ear."

Cecilia pulled him back with a sharp whisper, eyes narrowed at the man. "It's just a trick. He fooled you."

Elmore's lower lip bulged, and Lucy suppressed an impulse to intervene. Intrigued by her daughter's protective instincts and partially hidden by a display of granite ironware, she inched forward, waiting to see if Cecilia had the pluck she suspected.

"Pardon me saying so, miss, but you've got something in your ear, too."

The man's warm voice touched forgotten places in Lucy's mind and weakened her daughter's defenses as well. He reached toward one dark braid, and six-year-old eyes rounded at a second mysterious penny. Lucy covered her mouth and blinked back a burning sensation as he straightened and laid both coins on the counter.

"I'd thank you kindly if you'd help me out with these since I have other things I need to tend to."

Lucy stepped forward. The man set his hat upon his head, turned on his heel, and strode squarely into her.

"Oh!" Seed packets scattered as she flailed for balance. The man's arm linked around her waist, and he jerked his hat off and mashed it against his leg, dangling her from his arm. "Pardon me, ma'am."

Emboldened by her motherly motives and the ragged beard sweeping her forehead, Lucy gathered her footing, pushed out of the man's grasp, and bent to retrieve her potential garden. He joined her, scooping up most of the packets as she scooped up her breath.

"No harm done." She accepted what he'd gathered and scoured the beard bristling above her before lifting her eyes to meet his. She stilled at their clarity—blue as the sky. And slightly familiar.

"I hope you don't mind them having a sweet." One eye tightened at the corner with an unspoken thought.

She regarded her children, whose hope plastered their faces like a newspaper headline, then returned her attention to the man. "How very kind of you. Thank you."

He nodded and stepped around her toward the hardware. Lucy tried to imagine what he looked like clean-shaven. Clutching the seed packets, she joined her children, who were less concerned with her near-trampling than with how many licorice whips could be bought for a penny. Cecilia's calculating pleased Lucy, though guilt warred with sensibility as she justified not treating her children to this simple pleasure since their father had died. She did not have money for nonessentials, not with saving everything to buy supplies for the summer. And were it not for Mr. Wellington's generosity at the mercantile, they'd have even less. His tally always came out different than what Lucy calculated. He'd best not let Cecilia help him with the order.

May was spent, school out for summer, and Lucy and the children would leave tomorrow for the ranch to salvage what they could from winter's neglect. *Ranch* seemed such a grand term for their two sections and handful of cows, but it had been William's dream, and Lucy determined not to let it die as well. By now their small herd must be scattered to the hills and their hayfield decimated by deer. But she and the children could plow and plant, round up and repair. Rubbing the tightness that lately pulled between her neck and shoulder, she sagged against the counter.

"You all right, Mrs. Powell?" Fred Wellington's squeaky question announced his approach, and she straightened. The man's generous spirit must be what endeared his wife and daughter to him, for Lucy could not imagine living day in and day out with that voice. Though it couldn't be much worse than living with no husband or father's voice at all.

Glancing toward the stranger, she found him looking at coffeepots, of all things. Mr. Wellington's daughter, Priscilla, had come from the back and wore lovely flushed cheeks as she presented a varied selection to the man whose voice could melt ice on a winter pond.

"Mrs. Powell?"

"Oh—yes, Mr. Wellington." She stashed her curiosity and opened her reticule. If only the stranger could work his sleight of hand with her meager savings, then she would not be weighing the value of sugar over sorghum molasses and Arbuckles' over tea. Wellington penciled her items on his notepad, tore off the sheet, and slid it across the counter. Lucy read the figure and drew a deep breath. "I don't know what we—"

He raised a palm to interrupt. "Good Lord takes care of us all, Mrs. Powell. 'Sides, what the Spruce City school board gives you I am sure would not keep a tiger in stripes."

"Fredrick, really." The man's wife swept around the end of the counter and swatted his shoulder with a feathery touch. What a pair they were, one tall and squeaky, the other plump yet elegant. But a pair, two halves of one whole. "It's none of our business what Mrs. Powell receives." Rosemary Wellington's cheeks puffed with a pleasant smile as the children giggled over the sacks her husband handed them with much more than a penny's worth of candy in each.

"Thank you, Mr. Wellington," Cecilia said in her most proper voice.

"Thank you," Elmore parroted.

Rosemary shook her head. "Looks like Mr. Reiter has been at it again."

Reiter. That was it. Buck Reiter, the next rancher over the ridge who ran horses with his widowed sister. Pulling the draw on her reticule, Lucy turned casually toward the hardware and stole another quick glance. The man helped raise his nephew, from what Lucy had heard, though that was years before she and William came to Spruce City. The boy was grown and married now, just last Christmas, if she recalled correctly.

Ducking her head, she fingered the hair knotted at her neck and caught the sweep of her black wool, so dark and hot for the summer's work ahead. Tomorrow she'd pack it away. Cows and coyotes would not notice if she put off her widow's weeds a bit early.

"I'll load your supplies and have you on your way quick as a wink." Wellington hefted a sack of flour on one shoulder and headed out, while his wife shuttled the children through the door to wait on the boardwalk. Then she turned to Lucy.

"I am so glad you're not leaving us, dear, but do you have anyone to help you? There are several strapping boys here in town who could lend a hand."

Indeed there were, but with what would Lucy pay them? Free spelling and arithmetic lessons they'd left behind for the summer? She smiled at Rosemary's kindness. "I want to see what needs doing first. Maybe then I'll have someone help me find the cattle and build up the woodpile."

Lucy shivered, but not with cold. The woodpile had indirectly led to William's death when rogue lightning struck the tree he was cutting. A throat cleared and she looked up to see Mr. Reiter crumpling his hat in his hands again. She squelched the urge to slap his fingers.

"We've wood for three winters at our place, ma'am. I'd be happy to bring over a wagonload."

The man confessed to eavesdropping, yet showed not one shred of embarrassment. She pulled the cord of her already tightened reticule and looked out the storefront windows. "Thank you, but that won't be necessary. We will be fine." Accepting Mr. Wellington's deliberately poor ciphering skills was one thing, but taking charity from a neighbor she could never repay was quite another.

His retreating boots pricked her pride. A part of her wouldn't mind seeing the deep-voiced Buck Reiter drive into their yard with a wagonload of wood. But a bigger part feared letting anyone see how bad things really were.

Chapter 2

L iquid they were, and warm, like hot syrup on biscuits. The Widow Powell's dark eyes sent a shiver up Buck's spine in spite of the sweat collecting at his hatband. She had scrutinized his beard as if it held clues to his breakfast, and he pulled his fingers through it, hearing again his sister's scolding to shave.

Picking up a Gem Food Chopper he didn't need, he nodded at Priscilla Wellington's prattle about the ease of grinding vegetables and meat. Wouldn't he be a dandy with a food mill in his saddlebags, breaking trail through the mountains on the hunt for high pasture—which reminded him why he was in the mercantile to begin with. He'd volunteered to pick up Lilly's supplies so he could lay in his own provisions without causing a stir. He didn't need much, just some ground coffee and dried beef. Beans, salt pork, canned fruit. Come to think of it, he needed a plate and cup, too. Lilly would fuss and fret and try to make him stay, but it was time. He had a string of mares and a fine yearling colt comin' on as his share of the ranch. If his sister looked straight at the situation, she'd see that twelve years were enough. She and her boy had moved on with their lives. It was time he did the same.

He huffed and cranked the chopper's wooden handle. The widow had turned him down flat. Fool woman. Did she expect to chop her own wood and do all the chores herself with two young'uns? He cut a look her way, and like a queen she bid Wellington's wife good-bye, walked out to her buckboard, climbed in, and drove away. Again he combed his fingers through his beard.

Two hours later, he drove beneath the high gate where HORNE RANCH hung across the road on a long flat timber. He'd burned the sign himself when he wasn't much more than a colt. A wedding gift for Lilly and her new husband, Nathaniel Horne. Buck never dreamed that a decade later, the ranch would become his home for the next dozen years—years that most men use to find a place of their own and raise a family. But he couldn't leave his big sister and her boy alone in the Rocky Mountains after Nathaniel died. No more than he could turn a deaf ear to what he heard today at Wellington's.

Lucy Powell didn't want his help, but it wasn't in him to sit by idle when he had what she needed. Besides, his days as substitute father and foreman were near done, and he'd be setting out soon.

When he pulled up at the ranch house, Lilly and Nate's wife, Ara, were wrestling sheets at the line. Ara stopped to press her hands against her arched back, looking like she carried two foals instead of one. Lilly would have his hide if she heard him comparing her daughter-in-law to a mare, but there wasn't that much difference between animals and people when it came to bringing on new ones. Beetle lay in the shade by the open barn door, which meant Nate was inside mucking stalls. A mongrel pup tugged on the dog's ear the same way leaving the ranch tugged on Buck's insides.

He stacked their stores on the wide porch, and Lilly came out the front door with a pitcher and two glasses.

"I don't know what we'd do without you." She handed him a glass and took one of the rockers. He folded into the other and nearly told her exactly what she'd do without him. She'd do just fine.

"Glad to help." He pulled off his hat, sleeved his forehead, and downed half the lemonade. Too early for the evening breeze. Everything but his thoughts stood still and held its breath, waiting for a break in the heat. "You know the Widow Powell?"

Lilly slowly nodded and set the rocker to moving. "The new teacher. Lost her husband late last summer when dry lightning sparked a fire. Searchers found him beneath a charred tree, didn't they?"

"That'd be the one." He finished off his glass and reached for the pitcher on the railing. "Saw her at Wellington's today."

Lilly stilled her chair with a toe. "I thought she was leaving, selling out."

He cut his sister a look. "Like you did?"

She eyed him over her glass and pushed damp hair off her forehead. "I never considered leaving, not for one second. Then you showed up." Her weathered hand patted his on the rocker arm and gave a slight squeeze. "Nate and I would not have survived here without you."

An old conversation, played out more times than Buck cared to count. "Good Lord had more to do with it than me." The good Lord would do right by Lucy Powell, too, but somehow Buck wanted to be in on it. "She was laying in stores, and Wellington's wife tried to talk her into hiring help. She's got two babies at her skirt, can't be more than five or six. I figure she doesn't have much money because not much crossed the counter." He downed the last of his drink. "Other than my two cents."

Palming the lemonade from his mustache, he caught Lilly's look, her thoughts as plain as a pencil mark on a tally sheet. "Remember that trick Pa used to pull when we wanted candy?"

Lilly resumed her rocking. "I could never manage it without dropping the coin. But if I recall, you were quite good. Even fooled Nate a time or two."

He huffed at the memory, a clear reminder of just how long he'd been there. "Gave each young'un a penny and waited around till Wellington loaded her order. From what I could tell, she's set on getting the place in shape by herself. I offered her a load of firewood, but she turned me down flat." Another huff and he shoved his hat on, handed Lilly the glass with his thanks. He returned to the wagon.

She picked up the empty pitcher and paused at the door.

"So when will you be taking the wood to her?"

"Tomorrow morning."

∞

Lucy stopped the wagon behind the schoolhouse and the children clambered down, candy sacks in hand. She unhitched the horse to graze and slowly mounted the steps into what had been their home for the last nine months. Parting the curtain that hung across the front of the narrow room, she passed through from their meager quarters to the schoolroom proper. In spite of a good scrubbing, chalk dust lingered. The school board's need of a teacher had met her need of a livelihood, and they had been more than generous to let her live there. A form of charity, yet one she felt she had worked off. She straightened the inkwell and blotter on her desk, and resolve rippled up her spine on a sudden wash of memories.

Her mother had struggled alone after Pa left, taking in sewing and nearly blinding herself working long hours by lamplight. Lucy's good grades had spawned hopes of a better life. And when her classmate William Powell said he wanted to leave Chicago's swelter and go west, she accepted his proposal and went with him. One less mouth for her mother to feed. Now she faced near the same challenge.

In what remained of the day, Lucy started beans on the woodstove and loaded most of their belongings in the wagon. She set aside extra quilts for tomorrow's early departure. Cecilia and Elmore could sleep between the sacks and stores. Compared to the pallet on the floor they'd all shared, the wagon ride might be a luxury.

After a meal of biscuits and canned peaches, she put Cecilia and Elmore to bed early and sat outside on the small back stoop. Dusk dropped down with a sigh, and shadows tucked themselves beneath rocks and roots as she surveyed the small meadow. Crickets took up their chorus, doves joined with their melancholy song, and Mr. Wellington's words rolled over the grass. The Lord surely had taken care of her and the children through the long winter. And it had taken most of those months to loosen her grip on resentment.

God had not chosen to keep William alive—a fact with which Lucy was weary of wrestling. Death was not an uncommon visitor in this rugged land, but she'd not expected its sudden and brutal call at her home. Hugging her waist, she closed her eyes and let the evening breeze tug loosened hair and familiar words across her shoulders. *"Thou wilt shew me the path of life."* William had often repeated those words in their evening prayers, and for nine long months she had clung to them in his absence. Had he uttered them with his last breath—perhaps not for himself, but for her and the children? Was it his dying prayer she felt cooling her cheek?

Her job was to live, and to do so, she must accept that God knew what He was doing. She did not have to like it or agree with it. She just had to trust His love. If her children learned nothing else from her, they must learn that.

"Oh Lord, I am willing, but I need Your help." The breeze freshened, and she turned at the familiar caress. William had often touched her just as gently, and habit pulled her heart into her throat. She clenched her jaw. Too easily she could melt into a pool of self-pity. But such indulgence drained her strength and left her weak, and she dare not risk weakness if she and the children were to survive.

Chapter 3

Fumbling in the dark, Lucy buttoned an old housedress, tied on her bonnet, and pulled William's shotgun from beneath the pallet's edge. The change of clothing increased her excitement as she bundled her sleepy children into their makeshift bed. She stashed a fragrant pot of warm beans beneath the seat and took the road out of town.

Was she doing the right thing? Was it fair to Cecilia and Elmore to return to the mountain meadow William had so loved and try to make a go of it? Nearly every night she'd fallen asleep to the same question and wakened the next day with the same answer: *"Trust Me."* She hurled the whispered words into the darkness and listened as her doubts splintered beneath them.

The wagon stole past outlying houses and farms and barking dogs, but her old mare paid no mind and plodded on, memory tugging her home. Dawn spilled over the hills as they climbed toward the higher ranges, and it warmed Lucy's back once they reached the little valley. A lacy green ribbon of bright aspen rimmed the meadow at the forest's edge, and knee-high grass skirted the barn and cabin, a silent invitation to snakes and other unwelcome guests. She shuddered.

Across the yard the barn door hung askew on a crooked hinge, loosened by winter storms. William's tools were in the tack room if no one had wandered through and taken them. She could fix the door. And chop the grass. And gather the cows. Her shoulders dipped. Oh Lord, how would she do it all? A light breeze fluttered around the wagon and ruffled the grass as she reined in near the cabin. Cecilia climbed over the bench seat, scrubbing her sleepy eyes.

"We're home, Mama."

Home. Lucy kissed the top of her daughter's mussed hair then stilled at a dull thump coming from behind the cabin. Cecilia's eyes widened.

"What is it, Mama?"

"Shush." Lucy hurried her daughter back over the seat. "Cover your head and Elmore's, and don't make a sound," she whispered.

"But, Mama—"

"Hush. Do as I say."

Thump. . .thump.

With tingling arms she reached beneath the seat for the shotgun and climbed down. Gripping the gun in both hands, she cocked the hammer, pointed it ahead of her, and crept toward the building. She could shoot a bear if she had to, or a deer, but would a shotgun bring them down? That had to be what was making the noise—just an animal poking around. Her hands grew slick, and she wiped one on her skirt and then the other. No honey trees grew nearby, and it wasn't the time of year for bucks to be raking their antlers. She pushed her bonnet off, back pressed against the wall, and edged toward the corner. Sucking in a deep breath, she raised the gun to her shoulder. Lucy stepped into the open and drew a bead on. . .Buck Reiter.

The bearded bear of a man stood in his wagon and stared at her, firewood in each hand. "You're not gonna shoot me, are you?" He tossed the pieces on a pile between himself and the cabin, a dare burning in his eyes.

Lucy lowered the gun, fit to fly into him for ignoring her refusal and scaring her half to death. But he wasn't a real bear, or an outlaw, and for that she was grudgingly grateful. He bent for another log and tossed it on the pile. *Thump.*

"Mama, don't shoot!"

Lucy's trigger finger flinched at the high-pitched squeal, and she quickly aimed skyward. Whirling on her daughter, she bit back a fiery retort at the sight of the child's frightened expression. Elmore stood behind his sister, chewing on a suspender, his dark eyes shifting between Lucy and the man in the wagon.

Lucy let go her breath and dropped her arms. The gun's muzzle hit the ground and the world exploded.

Dirt flew up around them, and the children's screams tore the air as they rushed her. Clutching them close, Lucy fell to her knees. The wagon creaked, and pounding boots brought Buck Reiter to her side with a hand on her shoulder, warm and strong. She nearly melted beneath his touch.

∞

Buck scanned the huddled bodies, looking for blood. "Are you all right?"

Two heads with dark saucer eyes answered with sober nods. Gently squeezing their mother's shoulder, he stuffed down the fear that had jerked him from the wagon. "And you, Mrs. Powell? Are you hurt?"

She shook her head and drew herself up. "I'm all right. J–just shaken."

He straightened and pulled his hat off to wipe the cold sweat from his forehead. Lord, have mercy, he thought she'd shot 'em all. The boy craned his neck back and squinted up at him, the first to recover. "Where'd you find all that wood, mister?"

Buck blew out a heavy breath and set his hat on. "Can you stack stove wood for your ma?" He pointed at the wall by the back porch. "Like I started there?"

The youngster shed his mother's clutches and ran for the woodpile. "Sure can."

Mrs. Powell made to stand, and Buck helped with a hand to her elbow. Her face was white as a headstone, and her arm quivered beneath his fingers.

"Cecilia and I will unload our wagon." Sounding tougher than she looked, she brushed Buck with a wary glance and pulled her daughter closer.

He took a step back. "I can help if you need—"

"No." Sharp. Certain. "You've done more than enough already." Tugging at her bonnet ribbons, she pulled them from her neck.

He'd helped all right. Nearly got himself and the children shot. He picked up the gun, cracked it open, and kicked out the empty casing. "You have more shells?"

She stared at the weapon. "Yes. . . Yes, I have." Fumbling in her skirt, she withdrew another shell and handed it to him. "I'm sorry. I didn't expect to see you here and I heard the noise and I didn't know what to make of it and I. . ."

"No harm, ma'am." Her eyes simmered like black coffee. Strong and brave, in spite of the fright that shook her hands. He reloaded. "I'll set this inside the front door where it'll be handy in case you need it."

With a tight arm around her daughter's shoulder, she turned and walked around the end of the cabin as if she hadn't heard him.

Not exactly the way he'd hoped things would go.

Chapter 4

Still trembling, Lucy pulled the dutch oven from beneath the wagon seat and found the lid secure. How dare that man go against her expressed wishes that he not bring them firewood. He nearly got himself and her precious children buckshot. Shaking off the fear and anger, she wadded her skirt in her hands and grabbed the pot. "Open the door for me, and I'll set this on the table."

Cecilia pulled the latch, and the door squeaked open.

"Move over, honey. This is heavy." Lucy squeezed by and into the musty cabin, raising dust swirls with her boots. "Open the windows, and let's get some air in here, shall we?"

Setting the heavy cast iron on the table, she glanced back at her daughter who stood like a stone in the doorway. "Cecilia?"

The child blinked then ran to hide in Lucy's skirts. Lucy pulled her to the rocker and onto her lap, holding her as tightly as she held her own breath.

"I miss Papa." The thin voice pierced Lucy's heart, and she dipped her head against Cecilia's.

"I do, too." Closing her eyes, she searched for a comforting word to ease her daughter's sorrow and calm her own frayed nerves. Wood thumped against the cabin. "We are going to be just fine, sweetie. Help me get the things from the wagon. You can hang the quilts over the porch railing while I bring in our supplies."

Cecilia slid off her lap with a sniffle. "I want to be like you, Mama."

Lucy's throat tightened. "How?"

"I want to not cry."

"Oh baby, I cry." She framed her daughter's face between her hands and thumbed the tear trails. "Crying is part of healing. It waters the dry places in our soul." She kissed the pert little nose. "Don't you be ashamed of your tears. Even Jesus cried."

"He did?"

Lucy nodded. "He knows what it feels like to miss someone we love."

Cecilia swiped at her cheeks and returned to the wagon, and Lucy tucked her words into her own heart. The Lord knew.

Soon they had the cabin dusted and swept, the rope bed in the corner made up, and their extra things stored in the loft. Lucy sent Cecilia to the creek with a tin pitcher as Elmore scuttled inside with an armload of sticks. Mr. Reiter waited in the back doorway, hat in hand.

"Stack it neat. Don't want your ma tripping over anything while she's cooking."

Elmore piled the odd pieces and clapped dust from his hands.

"Good job, Button." The man's whiskers twitched.

Elmore frowned. "I ain't no button."

Her son's pout drew a chuckle from Mr. Reiter. Lucy went to the stove. "Elmore, you should say, 'I am not a button.'"

"I did." He locked his arms across his chest and scowled.

"That's what my pa called me when I was your age," Mr. Reiter said. "Button."

Elmore considered it then nodded once and turned to her. "Can we eat now?"

Oh, that all life's issues were solved so simply. She lifted the lid on the beans and stirred the contents, certain that Elmore's *we* included the stubborn man. Uninvited, but not unappreciated, he could eat in exchange for his labor. "The two of you need to wash up first, but I haven't primed the pump." She took a bucket from the corner and handed it to her son. "Rinse this out at the creek, then Mr. Reiter can help you fill it and bring it back. Cecilia's there now with a pitcher."

She looked the man's way and caught his smile as Elmore ran out the door. At least she thought he smiled. It was hard to tell with that buffalo robe he wore on his face.

She busied herself at the stove, feeding in the smallest pieces of wood and reaching to a high shelf where she felt for the matches. She hadn't thought about matches. What if there were none?

A footfall behind her, and Mr. Reiter's long arm produced the matchbox. This time she saw a smile for certain, with him standing so close she could smell the sunshine and sweat from his shirt. "Thank you." More words came before he stepped outside. "You are welcome to eat with us."

He paused with a hand on the doorframe and looked over his shoulder. "Thank you kindly."

Relief trilled through her at his acceptance, surprising her as it doused her earlier resentment. Uninvited or not, Mr. Reiter's presence delayed the inevitable. Her fatherless family would soon be alone, far from town tonight and for many more nights to come.

Baked beans and biscuits greeted Buck on his return with the children. Cecilia managed to get a half-filled pitcher back and a pocketful of wild strawberries. Elmore's mouth was red with what she couldn't reach first, and Buck helped the boy haul the bucket inside and set it in the sink.

Four plates topped the plank table, with spoons and cups at each. A bowl of canned peaches sat in the center with a plate of golden biscuits and a pot of beans. Feeling as handy as a leash on a polecat, Buck held his hat against his stomach and waited by the hearth on the opposite side of the room.

Mrs. Powell poured creek water in the tin cups then took her seat. The children settled in with ease, leaving empty the chair at the end. Three pairs of eyes looked his way.

"Ma makes the best beans. Don't you want none?"

"Don't you want *any*, Elmore."

"Yes, Ma, I sure do."

Cecilia giggled, and her ma appeared to choke back a laugh. Welcoming the lighter mood, Buck took the remaining chair. Cecilia slipped from her seat, delicately lifted his hat, and hung it on a row of hooks by the front door. "Pa always hung his hat there," she said on her return. "I s'pose you can do the same."

Grateful for the beard that hid his discomfort, Buck cleared his throat. "Thank you."

The children bowed their heads, and he did the same.

"For this food we give Thee thanks. Amen." Three voices recited the brief prayer, one with a tight edge. Buck raised his head and kept his eyes on the peaches, away from the determined woman to his left.

After dinner Lucy and the children cleared the table. Buck primed the pump with a ladleful of water from the bucket, and soon well water pulled up clear and sweet.

"Thank you, Mr. Reiter." Lucy stood by the table, her hands resting on a chair back. The set of her jaw and shoulders had eased a bit, and she looked downright weary.

"My pleasure, ma'am, but I'd like to ask you a favor."

Her schoolmarm brows snapped together then smoothed as she caught herself. "You may."

He took his hat from the peg. "Please, call me Buck, ma'am. Mr. Reiter was my pa, and I feel old when you and the children call me that."

Elmore stepped close and cocked his head back for a better look. "But you got an old beard."

"Elmore!" Lucy's face flushed, and she drew the boy to her. "That is not polite."

Buck grinned and stroked the bushy mass. " 'Out of the mouths of babes,' they say." Babes and his sister. He chucked the boy's chin and headed outside to finish stacking wood.

Pausing on the porch, he drank in the forested sweep that rose above them to the west. Sweet pinion and juniper perfumed the air, and he pulled in a deep draught. Behind him water gushed into the sink, Cecilia giggled, and chairs scraped their way under the table. Sounds of home. A home that wasn't his. An empty spot in his chest tore a little wider, and he rubbed the ache. Time to be heading out.

Elmore bounded through the door and bowled into him. "Come on, Mr. Buck. I wanna show you the barn." Small fingers clasped his hand and pulled him toward the neglected structure. He hefted the boy up and onto his shoulders.

Inside, a flattened pile of musty hay littered one dark corner. Stall doors gaped, and dried-out tack hung from one wall. A small room held a workbench and tools that waited for their owner to put them to task. "Duck your head," he said as he tucked down to step through the door.

"Them's Pa's tools." Two chubby arms clamped around Buck's neck as he smoothed the long handle of a hammer. "Ma says he's gone and not coming back. Said he died in the woods."

Buck lifted the boy off his shoulders and set him on the ground then squatted before him, eye to eye in the slatted light. "It's hard not getting to see the people you love." He straightened a sagging suspender over one small shoulder. "I know someone else who lost his pa, too, but he grew up to be a fine, strong man. So will you."

Elmore stared at the dirt floor and shoved his hands in his pockets.

Buck stood and reached for the hammer. "If you remember where your pa kept the nails, we can fix the big door."

Elmore cocked his head and looked up at him. "Pa was good at fixin' things, too." Then he stepped up on an overturned box and reached for a tin at the back of the workbench. "He used these long ones for the doors."

Buck gathered a handful and dropped them in his vest pocket. "Bring that box you're standing on and you can help drive the nails."

Shadows licked across the yard as Buck and Elmore patched the barn, and cooler air pulled through the open doors on each end. Soon the evening breeze signaled a ride over the near ridge and back to Horne Ranch. As Buck returned the tools and took a final look around, a slender silhouette marked the entry.

"Would you like to stay to supper?"

Weariness rippled through her voice like a dying stream, and one hand rubbed her shoulder at the base of her neck. He'd like to stay forever.

"I expect they'll be watching for me at the ranch." He'd not take more of her food. "But thank you just the same."

She closed the door after him, and with Elmore in hand, followed as Buck climbed in the wagon and gathered the reins. The boy broke away and ran to the wheel.

"You comin' back tomorrow?"

Buck's insides knotted, and he glanced at the young widow. Her jaw held firm as did her stance, but no resistance filled her eyes.

"If it's all right with your ma."

Elmore whirled around. "It's all right with you, ain't it, Ma?"

A near smile broke, and she nodded. Cecilia joined her and stood close, their skirts touching.

Buck slapped Rose ahead and tugged his hat brim. Lucy Powell stood with a hand pressing each child against her, watching him as if he'd tied up the daylight itself and was dragging it out of her world.

Chapter 5

Lucy lay awake between her children, their shallow breath rising together as one. She rubbed calloused hands over her face, her muscles aching from the unaccustomed work. But these moments of predawn peace were priceless, for in them she heard the Lord's soft whisper again: "*Trust Me.*"

The storms made it difficult.

Every afternoon for a week they had rolled in over the mountains, each thunderclap and lightning strike reminding her of what she'd lost and how. She could bear the hard work, her dried and cracked hands, even the pain in her neck. But the storms mocked her, delivering again the blow of losing William.

Slipping from the bed, she checked each angelic face before padding to the stove and stoking the fire for coffee. Water flowed freely into the pot, and Buck came to mind, his bulk filling the kitchen corner as he primed the pump. As he sat at the table's head. As he chucked Elmore under the chin and tugged Cecilia's braids. If a body were to judge by outward appearances, one would think Buck Reiter liked being around her family. If a body were to judge by hidden feelings, one would think Lucy liked having him around. Somehow his presence lessened the drudgery.

Thin light seeped above the eastern ridge, and she quickly dressed and pulled on her boots. As she tied off the end of her braid, a wagon rolled into the yard and stopped at the barn. Elmore would be thrilled.

After returning the second and third day as Elmore had requested, Buck had since been gone for four. Each morning the child hung from the porch railing, dangling his feet off the edge, waiting for the familiar wagon to drive up the road. And each morning it did not come he'd gone about his chores like a lost pup. Yes, Elmore would be happy. So would Cecilia.

Lucy's insides fluttered as she ground the coffee and added it to the pot. Glancing at her sleeping children, she slipped out the back door, surprised that she hadn't yet adjusted to the altitude. She couldn't quite get her wind.

The horse stood tied to the hitching rail at the barn, and Buck pulled long planks from the wagon and stacked them against the outer wall. Even in the new light, Lucy could make out posts and crates and covered baskets in the bed. Grumbling hens clucked their displeasure at being caged, and she bristled. *Charity.*

She marched to the wagon, ready to tell him to take everything back. But he turned at her approach and his eyes brightened like the dawning sky. Her pride melted into a pool of warm butter.

"Mornin'." His beard puffed out on each side in what she'd learned was a smile.

"Good morning." She gripped the edges of her apron. "This really is too much." His eyes disarmed her, bore right through her, until a scratching whimper drew her aside. From a crate at the end of the wagon, a pink tongue licked between the slats. Buck lowered the board and pulled the crate to the edge. "I figured your young'uns needed a young'un of their own." He gave her a sidelong look. "Hope you don't mind. We don't need two dogs at our place."

Mind? How could she mind? In fact, where *was* her mind? Holding her fingers against the slats, she sniffed a laugh at the quick washing. "Seems a happy fellow." Next to her, Buck released a tight breath. Did he really seek her approval?

He opened the crate and a black-and-white puppy wriggled over the top and into Lucy's arms before she could refuse it. Climbing her body, it stretched to lick her chin and draw her laughter. "What a rascal you are!"

Buck retrieved the squirming bundle and set it on the ground. "That's as good a name as any. Rascal." He skewered the pup with a blue glare. "You mind your manners."

The puppy skittered around the wagon, sniffing and pawing. What a delight for the children! Lucy brushed her bodice and apron and caught Buck appraising her reaction. Preparing to voice her concerns, she straightened her shoulders.

"I can never repay you for your kindness—for all you've done for us."

"I'm not lookin' for repayment, ma'am. Just lookin' to help a neighbor."

Dare she believe him? "Why?" The hard word felt heavy on her tongue, but she needed to know before he did more. Before she imagined the wrong motivation. Few men did anything without thought of recompense.

He pulled his hat off and ran a hand over his wheat-colored hair. "Good Book says to help widows and orphans"—he looked her straight in the eye—"and the way I see it, you qualify."

His words pressed a bitter barb in her wounded heart. What had she expected? Affection? Enjoyment of her company? She drew a deep breath and raised her chin. At least he wouldn't be forcing himself on her. She made to turn away, and he stopped her with a light touch on her arm.

"I like helping you, ma'am. You and those babies of yours. I enjoy doing what I can for you. But if I make you uncomfortable, just tell me and I'll move on."

His eyes clouded, and a crease formed between his brows. At such a contrast from his greeting, she felt near guilty for stealing what joy she'd seen earlier. A sudden decision fell from her lips before she could reconsider. "Call me Lucy. 'Ma'am' is so formal."

His whiskers bulged, and his brow smoothed. "Lucy, then." He shoved his hat on and looked at the pup scratching around his feet. "Rascal here shouldn't be too much extra work for you. He'll do on table scraps and help keep the critters from your cabin."

The man thought of everything, like a good friend. Her shoulders relaxed. "Let me help you." He could handle three times or more the weight she could carry, but still she reached for a pole. Together they dragged it out and started a second pile next to the barn. "What are your plans for all of this?"

"The chicken coop needs repair—looks likes coyotes dug in." He turned to face the garden she'd worked to resurrect. "Deer fence needs work." He grazed her with a quick glance. "I brought a bag of seed spuds." He paused and looked away. "And I see you've got some pie plants coming on—"

His gaze jerked to the wagon. "I almost forgot." Two long strides took him to the front where he lifted a handled basket and presented it like a gift. "Lemons. Lilly said she had plenty."

Lucy took the basket and peeked beneath the checkered cloth, stalling to stuff her emotions back in place. Lemonade. How appropriate. Her mouth watered with the bitterness of endless work and the sweetness of this man's kindness. Pulling a rare smile from her heart, she looked into his sky-filled eyes.

"Do you like hotcakes?"

Chapter 6

Hotcakes. Cold cakes. Any kind of cake Lucy Powell offered, he'd take. Just thinking her name left Buck feeling as spur-tangled as his nephew last fall after bringing Ara home in a snowstorm. Buck just never thought the same thing would happen to an old bronc like him.

He pulled his fingers through his beard. Wasn't white, but it *looked* old, according to Button. It hadn't mattered till Buck ran into the boy's mother at the mercantile. She had to be ten years younger than him, but if she worked this place by herself, she wouldn't look it for long. Wasn't right for a woman to use herself up on hard work—man's work. And if he had any say in it, she wouldn't.

Elmore nearly bowled him over in the yard, and Buck snagged him and dangled him upside down. Didn't know a boy could laugh so hard or hug so tight. And when he and his sister saw Rascal, Buck thought they'd squeal themselves silly. Made his throat tight, and he walked into the barn for a spell to check the hinges on the stall doors.

Not long after, a sweet ribbon of fried bacon drew him to the cabin, and it was hard to say which was better—the hot coffee Lucy poured or the warm smile that accompanied it. Her braid hung over her shoulder, and he wanted to run it through his fingers like a horse's mane. She might not think kindly of the comparison, but that was the closest he'd come to long fine hair such as hers.

By midmorning he and Elmore had the chicken yard repaired, and he carried a slatted crate inside the small henhouse. "She's setting," he told the boy, "so you best not be reaching under her for eggs."

Elmore peered beneath the nest. "When will they hatch?"

Buck eased the crate into a corner. "Maybe not at all if she leaves off setting after being moved like this. But you keep an eye on her, and let me know how things go."

He brought the other cage from the wagon, set it on the ground, and released a trio of pullets and a young rooster. "If she doesn't hatch that clutch, she'll get another chance with this fella here."

Elmore eyed the small comb and red wattle. "Ma says roosters don't lay eggs."

Buck backed away from that prickly pear and hurried to the wagon with the empty cage. He'd not be getting into such things with Elmore. His ma was a teacher. She could educate him on the ways of hens and roosters.

Flushed at his close escape and talk of nature's ways, he reset his hat and pulled on his thick work gloves. Elmore joined him as he grabbed a roll of barbed wire. "Can you step off your ma's garden and show me the boundaries?"

The boy's whole face grinned, and he picked up the napping puppy and ran off around the cabin.

Lucy brought a water crock and ladle to the back porch, tied on her bonnet, and with Cecilia set to work weeding the garden. Later, when she straightened to rub her neck and shoulder, Buck's pulse hitched at the sight, and he made for the porch and the dipper. A new thirst was burning its way through his chest, but it had nothing to do with water and everything to do with brave, beautiful Lucy Powell. His plans to leave began to lose their luster, and he could hardly imagine the rumble of horses' hooves across distant pastures any longer.

After dinner, Elmore held posts while Buck tamped them in, and by supper time they had the garden fenced and a few hills of potatoes. While Lucy watched from the porch, he showed Cecilia and Elmore how to plant them. "Might take three weeks for the fuzzy leaves to appear, but don't be digging them up to peek."

Cecilia giggled, and Elmore threw her an irritated look. Reminded Buck of him and Lilly when they were sprouts. He stood and brushed the dirt from his knees. The children ran off to play with Rascal, and Buck dropped a wire loop from the gate around the end post. More-determined critters would make it through, but at least the deer wouldn't ravage all their work.

Lucy waited on the porch, and he could feel her eyes runnin' over him like cool water on a hot day. Lord, help him. What had he expected when he set out to help a widow and her young'uns? It for sure wasn't what churned through him every time he thought of her.

"Stay for supper?"

Her quiet invitation nearly pulled his heart up through his gullet, and he approached slowly, deliberately, until he met her eye to eye where she stood on the porch. He longed to touch her, but instead drank in every feature of her face, hoping to slake his thirst.

"I best be getting back before dark to help Nate with chores." Nate didn't need help, but Buck needed to leave. Needed to keep things right between him and Lucy Powell, even if it drove him loco. She tipped her head and smiled that sweet-water way she had that closed up his throat and made him sweat. It'd be so easy to lean in and taste her lips.

"Thank you for all your help." She touched his arm. "Be careful going home."

Home. He could find it right here if she'd have him. He swallowed hard. "Just got one ridge to cross." And one porch rail and one decade. He swallowed again. "Tell Button and Sissy to make sure Rascal has plenty of water." Like she wouldn't know that herself. But what else was he going to say—*I love you, Lucy Powell*?

He stepped back with a brief nod and worked at not running for the wagon. But he rode hard through all the advice he'd given Nate last fall. "*Tell Ara how you feel,*" he'd said, all bold and brassy when it wasn't his own heart at the snubbin' post.

By the time Buck pulled onto the Horne Ranch road, coyote chatter had chased daylight over the hills. His sweaty shirt had cooled, and he pulled at his beard and scratched his cheek. Nate was waiting for him in the front porch rocker, feet up on the rail and wearing a grin to rival Elmore's.

Buck knew what was coming. He just didn't know what to say to it.

Chapter 7

Lucy scorched the coffee, burned the hotcakes, and nearly wore a hole in her apron rubbing her hands on it. Her heart beat like a running rabbit when she closed her eyes and saw him again—standing so close she could smell his scent and the toil he'd spent on her and the children. She longed to hold her hand against his face, beard and all, and kiss his sweaty brow. Oh Lord, how could she have such feelings?

"Mama, are you all right?"

Lucy's eyes flew open with a guilty start. She owed her children more than to swoon at the table over a man she had no business even thinking about. "Yes, Sissy, just resting my eyes." Her mother's weary words so often repeated spilled from her lips without thought. Resting her heart was more like it. Resting it in daydreams of a kind man's tenderness and help. She picked up her coffee, tepid and bitter. *Oh Buck. Why did you leave us alone?*

She yanked back the unspoken words. No—not Buck, William. Her hand trembled as she set down her cup.

Cecilia poked her blackened cakes, and Elmore picked up his and tore off a chunk. Neither complained, but Lucy knew what dampened their childish hearts. Buck had not been back for a week. She pushed her plate aside and added another spoon of sugar to the thick coffee. At least the chickens would eat the burned cakes. Chickens Buck had brought, thriving in a henhouse Buck had repaired. Everywhere she looked and everything she did brought him to mind. His bushy face had pushed William's countenance from her memory, and guilt weighed as heavy as her responsibilities. But William wasn't there to laugh and play with the children and work beside her and hold her in a blue gaze until she thought she would melt with longing.

Now, neither was Buck.

She missed him desperately. Not just his helpful labor, but him. The way his eyes twinkled when he teased the children. The way they warmed when he looked at her. The touch of his rough hand on her shoulder and the heat it sent clear through to her bones.

Rascal rumbled into her thoughts with a fierce puppy growl. The children looked at each other and then at Lucy. She scooted back and went for the shotgun. Cracking the door, she scanned the yard between the cabin and barn then saw the lone rider coming across the pasture. Rascal joined her, ears cocked as he sniffed at the door. His sharp yap made her flinch, and she signaled Cecilia, who scurried to the door and took the pup to the loft.

"Lord, protect us," she whispered as Elmore followed his sister up the ladder.

The stranger neared the cabin, and Lucy gripped the gun with both hands. Still blistered from the incident on their first day, she held it steady as she eased her foot in front of the door, aiming just shy of the rider. He didn't slow his pace but steadily walked his horse until it reached the hitching rail and stopped as if it belonged there.

The broad shoulders. The hat shading his eyes.

"It's Mr. Buck! It's Mr. Buck!"

Lucy jerked at the sharp squeal from above but managed to lower the muzzle without blowing a hole in the man. Twice she'd had him at the wrong end of a shotgun. The children clambered down the ladder and stormed past her, jumping up and down on the wood-plank porch.

"You're back. You're back," Elmore chanted. "I knew you'd come back."

A grin split the man's face in two, and his blue eyes locked on to Lucy, drawing the very breath from her lungs.

"You cut off your beard," Cecilia said. "Can I feel?"

"Sissy!" Mortified, Lucy stepped outside.

Buck swung from the saddle and took a knee on the bottom step. "You sure can."

The children launched into his arms, and he tossed his head back with a warm laugh. Lucy shivered. Elmore pressed his hand against the smooth face, and Buck's eyes closed, his firm mouth lifting in delight.

Lucy leaned the gun against the house and hid her own hands in her skirts to keep from doing what her heart wanted. If she touched that dear face, she would likely kiss it, and then what would her children think?

"Do you like it?" Buck's question refocused her.

Cecilia tilted her head. "You got younger."

Elmore stepped back and thumbed his suspenders like a little man. "It's fine by me."

Buck stood and removed his hat, mauling it in his rough grip. "And you, Lucy?" His deep voice resonated through her. "Is it fine by you?"

Her thudding heart drew her fingers to her throat. "Yes. . .but I didn't know you. I mean. . ."

"I'd hoped you'd like it." His mouth tipped. "At least enough not to shoot me off my horse."

His teasing loosened her nerves and drained away her anxiety. Elmore grasped Buck's fingers and tugged him down, cupping a hand against his mouth with a loud whisper. "Did you cut off your beard so Ma would kiss ya?"

∞

Buck choked at Lucy's horrified look, but he refused to laugh at her expense. For once, she had no teacherly words to come to her aid. He stepped up on the porch and chucked the boy's chin. Both children giggled, and Lucy flushed. Pretty as a filly in a flower bed, she was, standing there with rosy cheeks and her apron knotted in her hands. She looked everywhere but at him.

"I, uh. . .would you like some coffee?" she asked his horse.

"Don't know about Charlie, but I'd be obliged."

Her head jerked around. "Charlie?"

"My horse."

"Ma, you know horses don't drink coffee." Elmore grabbed her hand and pulled.

"Oh, shush, you." She tousled his hair and pushed him ahead of her into the cabin.

Sissy lingered. "Whatcha got in your poke?"

The girl didn't miss a lick. "Flowers for your ma." He untied the saddle strings holding the bag.

"That's a funny way to carry flowers."

Dropping to one knee, he opened the bag and carefully folded the edges down around the rich dark soil and a cluster of blue-and-white flowers. "They're columbines. Do you think she'll like them?"

"Oh yes, Mr. Buck. I *know* she will."

"Where should we plant them?"

Brightening at his *we*, she smoothed her skirt like her mother. "I know just the place." She dashed off the end of the porch and around the corner, and he found her by a sheltered spot near the back door.

"Good choice."

"I'll get the shovel." She sprinted for the barn.

When the task was completed, Sissy stood back with her hands on her waist like a little Lucy. Then she rushed through the back door.

"Mama, come see what Mr. Buck brought you."

Through the open doorway, Buck saw Lucy dry her hands on her apron and push at her hair. She followed Sissy outside to the end of the porch, and again a hand fussed at her throat and her cheeks pinked the moment she saw the flowers.

"They're lovely, Buck."

Hope sparked at the softness of her voice.

"I helped plant them." Sissy beamed. Lucy hugged the girl and cut a glance his way that fanned the spark. Spotting that bunch of blue at the edge of the meadow was sure enough worth having to dig it up with his knife.

"Coffee's almost ready. And I have biscuits, too, if you're hungry."

Hunger didn't begin to describe what swirled through his middle. "Thank you kindly."

Elmore scooted by with a can of scraps, and Buck stepped inside and took a seat in the rocking chair. The smell of charred coffee gave way to fresh beans that Lucy ground. His hands itched for a willow branch, and he looked around the cabin as if he'd find a peeled piece just waiting to be whittled. A curtain draped back from a bed, and a braided rug covered the floor beside it. Fancy plates leaned against a hutch back, and a large trunk sat beneath the front window with a shelf full of books close by.

Lucy didn't chatter as she worked, and he watched her the same way he watched cottontails scatter at sunup or deer drinking at a stream. A small hand touched his arm. Sissy stood close with a yellow-haired doll. "Pa used to set me on his knee and rock my baby to sleep."

A tight gasp flitted across the small room, and Lucy turned with startled eyes. Buck lifted the child to his lap. "Like this?" He pushed against the floor and the chair tipped slowly back and forth. She leaned against his chest and stroked her doll's golden curls, so unlike her own dark braids. Then she sighed and nodded her head in silent assent. He curled his arm around her and his gaze met Lucy's. Did she resent him? Was he stepping into her husband's place, disregarding his memory? He held her eyes and saw a yearning there that burned clean through him. He had half a mind to hope it might have something to do with him.

While Lucy set plates, butter, and biscuits on the table and poured the coffee, Cecilia fell into a deep sleep. Lucy came softly, bending down, her eyes grazing his lips as she slipped her arms beneath the child. Then she regarded him steadily and mouthed the words, *Thank you*.

Fighting for a solid breath, Buck made his way to the table and took a seat. Elmore climbed into the closest chair, and Rascal curled in a ball beneath him.

"Rascal let us know you was here."

"*Were* here," Lucy whispered as she passed behind her son and on to her chair. This time she held her hands out, one across the table for Elmore and one for Buck. Accustomed to the practice at his sister's table, he grasped Button's tiny hand in his, and with the other, Lucy's slender fingers. Her touch sent his thoughts as far from table grace as snow is from summer.

"For this food we give Thee thanks," she said quietly. "And thank You for bringing Buck safely to us this morning. Amen."

He waited, head bowed, not willing to let go. Lucy withdrew her hand and reached for the platter. She dropped a golden round onto her son's plate and turned to Buck. "Two or three?"

Chapter 8

Lucy's fluttering emotions spread to her serving hand, and she prayed Buck didn't notice. What would she tell him? That the columbines matched his eyes? That he made her achingly mindful of a strong and thoughtful man in her home again? Heat crept up her neck, and she left the table on pretense of warming the already hot coffee.

Upon her return, she found Buck had eaten the three biscuits she'd given him and was reaching for another.

"Lilly invited you and the children to the ranch next Saturday. With Ara in the family way, we're not driving into town for the Fourth of July festivities, so Lilly's making pies and chocolate cake for our own celebration."

"Whatcha mean 'family way'?" Elmore asked.

Buck choked on his biscuit.

"Elmore." Lucy stifled her laughter at Buck's discomfort. "Shush, and eat your breakfast."

"But Ma—"

"Now." She eyed her son into submission, dabbed her mouth with a napkin, and turned to Buck. "What can I bring?"

A bit ruddier without his beard, he busied himself with his coffee then cleared his throat. "Yourself and the children."

Pinning him with a long look, she folded her arms. Truth was, she appreciated the opportunity to stare. "We will not go unless we can contribute to the celebration." Perplexity made him even more attractive. He didn't take his eyes from hers, but they searched deep, as if trying to find a breach in a rocked-up canyon. Finally, he huffed in resignation.

"Baked beans."

The duel ended when she laughed, and his handsome face pulled a worried frown. "Something wrong with baked beans?"

She laughed again and reached for his hand resting on the table, as if such a move were as natural as taking a breath. "Baked beans it is."

He caught her fingers, and his warmth and strength seeped into all her cold and empty places. "I'll come for you early, and you can spend the day."

Scrabbling for self-sufficiency, she withdrew her hand. "We have a wagon, you know. Just tell us how to find your place."

His mouth opened then clamped shut, and his jaw tightened. Lucy balled her apron in her lap but held her head steady. Buck glanced at Elmore, the biscuits, and then settled his blue gaze on her with another huff. "Take your road to the ridge, then turn north and follow the trail about three miles. I'll wait for you at the top."

A compromise, but it suited her. She exhaled and smiled. "We'll leave at sunup."

By early afternoon, Lucy had sent the children to the creek to hunt strawberries. She still had the lemons, and wild-berry lemonade would be perfect for the Fourth of July if the berries lasted another week. Buck worked on the steps leading into the root cellar, and Lucy joined him with a bucket of water, lye soap, and a rag to give the shelves a good cleaning. A distant rumble froze her feet. She turned to scan the range sweeping north of the wide valley, where steel gray clouds bellied over the ridge. A sudden wind whipped across the meadow and tugged at her hair and skirts. Buck set his hat and cut her a look. She dropped the bucket and ran for the creek.

∞

Buck closed the cellar door and took Lucy's bucket and soap to the back porch. He then secured the barn and henhouse. Her sudden dash hinted at more than caution, and he ached to see a common squall upset her so. But it hadn't quite been a year, according to Lilly, since lightning had taken her husband.

By the time he returned from the barn, the children were on the porch and Lucy had planted herself in the middle of the garden. Her hands balled into fists, and she lifted her head to the storm as if she could hold it off by sheer will—one woman against all of nature's thunderous power. If he'd learned anything about Lucy Powell in four short weeks, that was exactly her intention.

The fast-moving storm rolled down the wooded slopes and dropped into the valley. Lightning fired a warning shot, but Lucy stood fast. Buck gripped the porch railing and glanced at Sissy and Button standing stock-still near the doorway. He loved this family more than he thought possible—Lucy with her fight and fire, and those two young'uns who worshipped the light she walked in. He had hoped to cut their hay this summer, but from the looks of the white wall coming at them, he might not get the chance.

The clouds unfolded, banked against the opposite mountains and packed down like a feather mattress. Rain came gentle at first, errant drops, plump and singular. Lucy stood like a ship's mast, wind whipping her skirt through her legs. Buck screwed his hat down and strode to the gate but waited, holding himself back from her private war. Gorged to its limit, the sky broke open, and within minutes water ran like a river. The meager garden floated in a dark lake that licked at Lucy's skirts. When the hail came, her hands went slack and her shoulders slumped. She dropped to her knees.

Lucy Powell didn't want to be coddled, but he'd not stand by and watch her drown in defeat. Splashing into the running current, he scooped her into his arms and offered his back to the stinging fury. Ice the size of checker pieces pelted into every living plant, beating them into the muddy water.

Wide-eyed and white as sheets, Sissy and Button followed him inside where he fell into the rocker with their mother. Her great wracking sobs gouged his heart like Mexican spurs, and he jerked off his dripping hat and leaned back, pulling her closer. She pressed into him, trembling, he suspected, with more than the cold and wet. Her hair was smooth against his lips, and he murmured low, aiming to calm her as he would a frightened colt.

The children stood mute by the table, staring at their strong, independent mother curled up in Buck's arms. Thunder cracked, and the windows flashed a blinding blue. They ran and flung themselves against him, and he drew them close like a covey of rain-soaked quail. Huddled together in the sturdy cabin, they waited, and Buck thanked God for seeing fit to lead him there.

As quick as it had come, the storm tucked tail and ran. Lucy had soaked him through, but she no longer shivered or sobbed. Outside, blue sky peeked through running clouds and sunlight winked in the water dripping from the roof.

"Button," he whispered, "can you build a fire for your ma?"

The boy peeled himself from the rocker and shoved out his thin chest with a nod. "Yes sir, I can."

Buck returned the nod, man-to-man. "Then be about it."

Sissy laid a small hand on her mother's back. "You need to get out of those wet clothes, Mama." The girl's brow pulled with motherly concern. "I'll help you."

Lucy uncurled but didn't fly from his lap. Instead, she cupped her daughter's cheek in her hand. "Thank you, honey. Lay out my black dress, and I'll be right there."

Then she turned her eyes on Buck, and the aching, brimming pools stopped his heart.

"I can't do this anymore," she whispered.

He caught her hand in his and turned it over. Blistered, red, and cracking, the palm bore testimony to her determined spirit. He raised it to his lips fearing only one thing—seeing her break.

"Not by yourself, you can't." His voice felt thick and unfamiliar. "But *we* can."

A heavy sigh shuddered through her. "You are a kind man, Buck Reiter."

He locked on her eyes, refusing to let her slip into despair. "Two are better than one, the Lord says." A current surged between them, swift as the water through the garden. Did she feel it?

Standing, he set her feet to the floor then curled his fingers against her cheek. She tilted her head into his touch, and he would have kissed her had Cecilia not returned to lead her to the curtained-off bedroom. As daughter and mother crossed the room, Buck's jaw set like a sulled-up bronc. He'd stay and see them through the summer, find their cows and brand the calves. Salvage what he could of the hay and the garden, and wait for Lucy Powell's heart to heal.

Then he'd ask her to be his wife.

Chapter 9

The pale pink muslin hid near the bottom of Lucy's trunk, beneath baby clothes and linens she had saved against a better day. She'd not worn the dress since last summer, before she'd donned her mourning black. Pressing the cool fabric to her face, she squeezed her eyes shut to hold the tears.

Last week's hail had shredded not only the garden but had torn deeply into her resolve. Already July, and what little progress she'd made lay pounded into the mud. At least the outbuildings stood undamaged, thanks to Buck, upon whom she could not depend indefinitely. Someday he would not return. She had no right to wish otherwise.

She draped the muslin across her arm and pulled out Cecilia's church dress and Elmore's good trousers then gathered a handful of pins and headed outside to air the garments.

A pungent sweetness swept down from the mountains, kissing the meadow. Her skin prickled in the cool air as she took in her surroundings with new eyes. How many horses could graze here and in her higher acreage? Buck had once mentioned his intent to take his band of mares and find his own mountain, as he'd put it. Would he be interested in leasing her land? And if he did, where would she and the children go? But why would he want to settle so near the Horne Ranch when he said he wanted new country? Her heart hollowed out at the thought of his leaving.

If she could sell off some of her cattle in the fall, she might make a go of it this year. But she had to find them first. Buck had set out early to locate the small herd, and suggested she ride with him after the Fourth to bring them back. The children could stay with his sister who, he insisted, would jump at the opportunity. What a temptation—a day riding the hills with no cares other than trailing a few cows. She'd promised to give it some thought, and when she'd mentioned it to Cecilia and Elmore, they had stormed her with pleas.

Before the hail, she had looked forward to the Fourth of July, celebrating not only the nation's independence but her own. She wanted to visit with Buck's sister and learn her secret of surviving as a widowed mother in this harsh land. But Lucy already knew the answer.

A heavy sigh slid over Cecilia's dress as Lucy pinned it to the garden wire Buck had raised. He'd raised the woodpile, too, and she'd allowed him to raise her hopes of success and more. But she wasn't his sister. She wasn't his anything. His "two are better than one" remark referred to how they had worked—side by side as two individuals. Not two parts of one whole.

The only thing Lucy knew with certainty was the way she'd felt in Buck's arms after the storm. Safe. Protected. A bitter taste hit the back of her tongue.

"Oh Mama—do I get to wear my Sunday dress to Mr. Buck's house?" Cecilia's hopeful voice pinched Lucy's heart.

"You must promise not to ruin it. No grass stains or rips, please."

Cecilia clasped her hands beneath her chin. "I promise."

Lucy turned to scan the sky then placed a hand on her daughter's shoulder. "Remember those strawberries?"

Delight sparked in the child's eyes, and she nodded.

"Take Elmore with you and pick what you can. But pay attention to what you hear. If it thunders, come home immediately. Understand?"

Cecilia nodded fiercely then hugged Lucy's legs and dashed to the house for a basket and her brother. Lucy's gaze fell to the columbine cluster at the end of the porch, so fragile and lovely, untouched by the hail in its sheltered corner.

"The path of life, Lord," she whispered. "I need to know the path of life."

Again the words came, whispering across the meadow and dancing around her shoulders. *"Trust Me."*

∞

The aroma of sweet beans drew Lucy from bed before dawn. She set the iron pot on the sideboard, punched down the bread dough she'd left to rise, and pinched off rounds to bake while she hitched up the horse. The children stirred and excitement rimmed their faces as they hurried to dress in their sun-kissed clothes. Even her pink muslin smelled fresh and clean from its airing out. Hope stirred. With shaking fingers she twisted her hair, dropping more pins than usual. Elmore picked up each one, and with the last coil in place, she chucked his chin.

"Thank you, Button." *Buck's gesture. Buck's nickname.* "You are a big help."

"I never seen you drop so many pins before, Ma."

Her heart would break for love. "Saw. You never *saw*." She leaned down to kiss his sweet head and swatted him toward the sink. "Take the scrap can to the chickens, but don't get dirty, and hurry back. We want to leave before the sun peeks over the ridge."

Cecilia took the rolls from the oven, carefully shielding her small hands with toweling, and set them on the sideboard. "You sure look pretty, Ma." She lined a basket with a napkin and arranged the rolls just so. "Did you dress up for Mr. Buck?"

Lucy's breath caught. "I dressed up for the occasion. Just like you." Reaching for another piece of toweling, she lifted the cast-iron pot.

"But you do like Mr. Buck, don't you?"

What had he said? "Out of the mouths of babes?" Her throat ached. "Yes, I like Mr. Buck."

"Is he going to be our pa?"

The dutch oven landed on the table with a thud. Now was not the time to discuss such things, but a six-year-old did not have a keenly developed sense of timing. Lucy swallowed a scolding and instead chose truth. Stooping to meet her daughter face-to-face, she looked into William's eyes, and sorrow tightened like a drawstring.

"A lady waits until a man asks to marry her. You will do that someday— wait for a young man to ask for your hand." Taking that small hand, she smoothed it with her own. "Mr. Buck is very special to us all." Warmth bloomed in Lucy's chest, pressing to expose more than she cared to admit. "I believe God sent him to help us, but whether he wants to be part of our family is up to him. And neither you nor I will ask him about it."

Cecilia blinked. "But would you say yes if Mr. Buck asked?"

Lucy closed her eyes, attempting to close off her heart from her daughter's keen perception. Squeezing the small hand, she opened them again with purpose. "Do you want to be late for the party?"

Instantly refocused, Cecilia gathered her basket and hurried to the wagon. Lucy followed with the beans then returned to the cabin for her wildberry lemonade. Two contrasting halves made one delicious whole—berries and lemons. And Buck had provided one of those halves. Was there anything in her life he had not touched?

As they drove from the yard, a sharp, golden light cut across the mountains, and Lucy tugged her bonnet forward. Elmore held Rascal on his lap and Cecilia cradled the basket. Not one word of complaint came from either of them, not with Independence Day breaking clear and bright with the promise of pie and cake and maybe games. Lucy shook her head. How little they knew of true independence—of leaning only on one's self and not another for everything. Aside from where it pertained to armies and kings and governments, independence was overrated. For without God's help, where would she be? She depended on Him for everything. And perhaps a little too much on Buck Reiter.

At the base of the ridge, she stopped at a path little more than a deer trail cutting through the cottonwoods. A strip of flattened grass on either side bore witness to Buck's many wagon trips to the cabin. She tightened her grip on the reins and turned north. Her wagon was not as large and sturdy as his, but she trusted him not to set her on an impossible journey. Lifting her scrutiny from the road to the horizon, her pulse quickened at the silhouette of a lone horseman against the brightening sky.

Chapter 10

The Powell place lay southwest of the ridge, and Buck watched Lucy drive from the yard and along the meadow's edge. At the juncture, she hesitated then slapped the horse on. Her hearty "yah" carried up through the trees and spread a warm spot in his chest.

A month ago, he was set to take his string of mares and move on. Then he ran into Lucy Powell and her children at the mercantile and delayed his leaving. A week later, he thought to give her a few more days, help her get on her feet, then set out. The week after that, he shaved off his beard and reckoned one more week would do. And last week he held her in his arms and gave up on leaving her at all.

The creak of her wagon sounded beyond an aspen cluster, and he nudged Charlie from the brush and onto the trail. Lucy drove round the trees and pulled up in front of him, her bonnet hiding her face and her young'uns grinning like opossums.

"Right on time." He leaned on his saddle horn and winked at Elmore. Lucy wore a fancy dress, not the same one she'd worn for so long. "You ladies look mighty fine this morning." Cecilia beamed, and Elmore pointed at his britches.

"You, too, Button." He reined Charlie around. "Follow me."

That morning before Buck left the ranch, he'd helped Nate carry the kitchen table out to the yard. As he approached now, a checkered cloth waved from it like a red-and-white flag. He tied Charlie at the house rail and helped the children from the wagon. When he reached for Lucy, she placed both hands on his shoulders and he swung her down. His heart raced ahead and he pulled his hat off and rolled the brim, waiting for words to catch up. She smelled fresh as the meadow after a rainstorm, and he swallowed hard. "You look. . .*mighty* fine, Lucy."

Her cheeks pinked to the color of her dress. "I thought you might be tired of seeing us in our everyday work clothes."

"I never tire of seeing you." The words were closer than he thought and fell out of his mouth without his say-so. A full flush rose on her face, and she turned to the wagon and reached for the bean pot beneath the seat.

"You made it!" His sister strode across the porch, down the steps, and around to Lucy with a hearty hug. "I'm Lilly and I'm so glad you came."

Lucy clutched the beans and flicked her eyes over Lilly's trousers. "It's nice to meet you, Lilly." She looked around with concern. "The children—they were right here."

Lilly waved off the worry. "Button and Sissy introduced themselves quite properly and they're in the kitchen helping Ara get things together. Darlings, they are. What a delight to have them here. It's been too long since I had a little one around."

Button and Sissy? Buck tucked away his pride as his sister took the beans and a basket over her arm and charged up the porch steps. "Come inside and we'll put these in the oven to keep. My, but they smell good. Buck said you make the best beans."

Lucy retrieved a Mason jar from beneath the seat but couldn't leave because he blocked her way. He longed to pull her close and ask her right then and there to marry him, but wouldn't that set the bees to buzzing. "I'll unhitch the mare."

She smiled, nervous, and nothing like the fiery, shotgun-wielding woman he'd startled a month ago. He touched her shoulder. Ran his hand down her arm and wrapped her fingers in his own. "I'm glad you came."

∞

Lucy's arm still burned from Buck's touch, but she hugged her middle and bit her cheek while he regaled the children with the story of his nephew's courtship. Cecilia and Elmore laughed outright at Buck's tale, but they were children. Lucy merely *felt* like a child.

Everyone lounged back from the large table covered with the remains of cakes and pies and beans and beef. Lucy had eaten so much she felt as stuffed as poor Ara looked. Never had Lucy seen such a large and handsome young man as Nate Horne blush in utter silence, and never such a becoming bride as Ara, who was not only in the family way, but could be carrying the entire family all at once for the size of her.

"You really hid in the buckboard?" Cecilia turned wide, innocent eyes on Ara. "But Mama says—"

A quick swat to her leg and Cecilia's mouth clapped shut like a cellar door.

"What does your mama say, dear?" Ara rested her arms across her swollen belly.

"Her mama says she must mind her manners." Lucy's recent conversation with Cecilia burned about her neck and ears, but she smiled to assure Ara that all was well. And indeed, it felt so. The Hornes had welcomed her and the children like family, raved over her wild-berry lemonade, and cleaned up every last bean in her kettle. And Buck showed a playful side she'd not seen before.

Not that he'd had opportunity to play or relax when he was busy stacking wood, building fences, or doing the other hundred things he did to help her. Here, in the comfort of his family, if he wasn't teasing his nephew, he was touching the children. A pat here, a hug there. And Button and Sissy, it was as if they were his own.

The thought snagged in Lucy's throat, and she covered her mouth with her napkin. Buck's hand found her back, gentle and warm.

"Are you all right?" His deep whisper fired chills up her arms and stole her breath, and she feigned a coughing fit. He refilled her glass with lemonade then handed it to her with concern tugging his brow.

With little more than a squeak, Lucy thanked him and envisioned Mr. Wellington trying to comfort his wife. Stifling a moan, she choked even further, bringing Buck's hand down firmly. She coughed in earnest, the wind nearly knocked from her. Holding up a hand, she shook her head. "I am fine. Truly."

His eyes darkened as he smoothed circles on her back and lit rings of fire inside her. "That you are."

If she didn't put distance between herself and this man, she was liable to beg him to marry her and show Cecilia what it meant to be two-faced and brazen all at the same time. "Let me help you clear the table, Lilly."

Ara also stood, and Buck's sister fired a warning look. "Sit."

As obedient as a pup, the girl fell back to her chair with a chuckle. "Yes ma'am!" But the way she rubbed her rounded self—even in front of the men— told Lucy the expectant mother needed rest. The baby might be early. Or the *babies.*

"Button." Buck jerked a thumb over his shoulder. "Got something in the barn for you." Elmore jogged away beside Buck's long strides as they made for the stables.

"And I have something for you." Lilly motioned for Lucy to follow her inside. The sprawling log house enclosed her in a welcoming embrace, and at once Lucy felt at home. But when Lilly handed her a pair of folded denim pants, Lucy stared.

"Buck said the two of you are riding out tomorrow to drive the herd down. These will make the chore a lot easier on you." Lucy blushed beneath the woman's bold appraisal. "They'll be loose on your slight frame, but they'll do. I'll find a belt for you, and one of my old shirts."

Lucy took the denims and shook them out. A puff of laughter bounced out when she held them against her. She looked up at Buck's sister, as tall and generous as he. "I will be the talk of the mountain in these."

Lilly laughed and hugged her around the shoulders. "You won't be the first, dear. You won't be the first."

That night Buck retired to the barn with Rascal, leaving his room for Lucy and the children. Delighted with such a large bed, Elmore crawled in first, a hand-carved willow soldier from Buck clutched in his fist. Cecilia snuggled in next, and Lucy followed. The children's excitement helped ease her discomfort at sleeping in Buck's bed.

Surprised that anticipation hadn't kept her up most of the night, she awoke the next morning to the children giggling and dressing before they dashed outside. Nervous beyond anything she'd ever felt, Lucy pulled on the denims and shirt, belting them as tightly as she could. She found Lilly in the kitchen pouring coffee into two china teacups. Apparently sensing Lucy's need to discuss weighty matters, the woman volunteered her story.

Lucy was right: Buck had made all the difference.

Chapter 11

Every muscle in Lucy's body ached as if she'd run down the mountain herself and not trailed the herd on horseback. But the animals seemed to know their way home, and she and Buck had merely encouraged them on through the woods and scrub brush and into the valley. Oh, that her pathway were as easily found.

Buck had ridden back to the Hornes' and brought Cecilia and Elmore home in the wagon with his horse tethered behind. He promised to return soon, in a day or so, after he found the fallen tree they'd come across. It'd make good firewood, he said. Lucy's heart lurched at his intentions, but she bit her tongue.

The children fell quickly to sleep that evening, their cheeks ablaze with sun and happiness, and Lucy welcomed her own exhaustion, praying it would silence her churning thoughts. Easing the front door open, she slipped out to breathe in the night. The corral creaked with an unfamiliar cadence as the cattle shifted and settled against the boards. Stars spilled across the moonless sky, and Lucy pressed a hand against her heart, imagining Buck atop the ridge. He was a good man. He would be a good father and husband. But she could not bear to be anything to him other than the woman he loved. She saw it in his eyes, felt it in his touch, but he made no mention of affection. What if her longing led her to believe what was not true? "Oh Lord," she whispered, "show me Your path."

The next day she fretted over Buck's insistence to drag out the fallen tree, and countless times she searched the pasture's edge for a rider breaking clear of the forest. When he did not return by sunset, fear snaked in and coiled around her insides. She couldn't breathe. Was he hurt as William had been? Trapped, unable to ride? Or had he simply decided not to return? To leave in search of new country and a mountain of his own.

Weary in heart and body, she tugged off her stockings that evening and combed out her braid. She hauled the rocker out to the porch. Huddling in a quilt, she strained to hear an approaching horse, a rider's hail, the scrape of a long pine dragging through the dark, colorless grass. Rascal curled at her feet with a puppy groan as if he carried the weight of her worries on his thin shoulders. What a ludicrous thought. As ludicrous as hoarding her troubles when the Lord waited to lift them from her. "I am no wiser than this poor dog, Lord." Her whispered prayer winged across the night and lit among the quaking aspen. She pulled the quilt tighter. *Bring him back to me, Lord.*

The meadow curled beneath its starry blanket, and still she remained, as fixed in her place as a cedar on the ridge. Crickets and coyotes lifted their voices, and she sank into the quilt, succumbing to the mountain song.

Waking at Rascal's yap, Lucy pushed against the stiffness in her limbs. The pup stood alert, nose pointing toward the wooded slopes, a whimper beneath its ribs in the pearly predawn. She bent to stroke the soft coat then scanned the dim meadow, dull and gray. There—at the tree line, something small and brown broke through, a rider cutting into the grass. Tossing aside the quilt, she bounded off the porch before the cry escaped her throat.

∞

Buck scrubbed his face and looked again. Were the shadows playing tricks on him, or was Lucy running across the pasture?

His heart slammed into his chest. It *was* Lucy. He jerked the reins and hit the ground before Charlie stopped. Was something wrong at the cabin? Was Sissy hurt? Button?

At fifty yards he slowed and drank in the site of her—skirts hiked above her bare legs, her loose hair a dark and flying mane. And then she was in his arms, gripping him so tight around the neck he felt her hammering heart. The scent of her overcame him, the feel of her warmth against him, her breath on his neck. Her heartbeat slowed and her arms loosened their hold. As he set her feet on the ground, her hands slid around to frame his face.

"I—I was afraid"—she struggled for breath—"afraid you wouldn't come back."

He clutched her to him again and buried his face and hands in her unbound hair. "It took longer than I thought, but I'll always come back to you, Lucy. I love you more than life. You and those babies of yours."

She pulled back and swept his face with a yearning that burned clean through him. "Then marry us." The words struck lightning in her eyes and she clapped her hands over her mouth, a look of horror swimming above them.

Joy sprang deep in his gut, and he hauled her up and swung her around, his laughter drowning out the meadowlarks. "Marry you? You'd have this old cowboy with nothing to offer but a string of near-wild horses? No land, no money?" The sun broke over the ridge and lit a halo around her, and he set her down and pulled her hands from her lips.

"I'm so embarrassed," she whispered. Her eyes glistened, and her chin trembled as much as his heart.

Lifting both of her hands to his lips, he kissed her fingers. "You've read my soul, Lucy darlin'. Are you truly willing to be my wife and share a home and life with me?"

She smiled, and the dawn dimmed at her beauty. He dipped his head to catch her lips, and the taste of her was like honey in the comb, sweet and soft and full of God's promise he thought he'd missed. He scooped her up and carried her to his horse, set her in the saddle, and turned for the little cabin he called home.

Epilogue

A ra Horne's babies came early—halfway through August—a boy and a girl as fair-haired as their handsome father and dashing uncle who stood straight as pines at the head of the church.

Lucy had only one regret: that it was too late in the year for a columbine bouquet. But her wedding dress bore the color of her dear love's eyes, thanks to the insistence of Rosemary Wellington and Lilly's skills as a seamstress.

"It itches." Elmore ran his finger inside the collar of his new blue shirt.

"Shush, now. You don't want to upset Mama on her wedding day, do you?" Cecilia flounced her matching skirt.

Lucy bent to plant a kiss on each dear head then took their hands to await the pastor's signal. She had asked for a private ceremony, with only Buck's family, but she couldn't refuse the school board members, or her students' parents, or the Wellingtons who must have spread the word through town. Slowly, one smile at a time, people trickled into the sanctuary until the pews, and Lucy's heart, were overflowing.

At last the pastor joined Buck and Nate at the front of the church, and his brief nod told Lucy it was time. The path that lay before her and the children led to the man who had won their hearts and hers.

"Thank You, Lord," she whispered as she took her first step. "Thank You for helping me trust You to show me the pathway of life."

The Sunbonnet Bride

by Michelle Ule

Dedication

My favorite businessman and my favorite teacher:
Glenn and Charles Duval

Along with their families:
Bettina, Lynda, Bennett, Elizabeth, Anne,
Catherine, Christopher, and Christina

Chapter 1

Malcolm MacDougall shook the reigns and peered at the sky late Saturday afternoon. The big draft horses were dancing down the familiar road between Sterling and his hometown of Fairhope, but that was highly unusual. After a long day delivering cargo, they usually plodded home slow, steady, and boring. Today, though, they were in a hurry.

The soggy July heat weighed down on the countryside, and the clouds swirling above looked like fluffy bruises with an odd green tinting the gray. He swallowed a few times, uneasy.

The big Nebraska sky stretched from horizon to horizon, stopping to peek between rustling healthy cornfields of rich emerald green. Gusts of wind shook the tops, waving gold tassels at him. Malcolm frowned. Shouldn't birds have been flying through the corn? Shouldn't he have seen varmints like rabbits and gophers scuttling through the stalks? What had happened to the hum of cicadas?

All he heard was the relatively quick stepping plop of his horses. Something was up and nature and God knew. He whistled for his dog.

Sport burst from the cornfield ahead, startling the mahogany horses to a halt. He yipped three times and leaped onto the box seat beside Malcolm, jarring the wagon and nearly knocking Malcolm over.

"Here, there, old boy." Malcolm scratched Sport's ears and tried to calm the shaggy mutt who often looked more like a bedraggled sheep than a dog.

Sport's scratchy pink tongue slurped Malcolm's cheek before he sat. He threw back his head and howled—a long drawn out sound that raised the hair on Malcolm's forearms and set the horses to shuffling.

"Git on, girls," Malcolm called. The clouds scudded way too fast and the light kept shifting from dark to clear. He wrinkled his forehead. Unpredictable weather always bothered him.

Too big to really fear much, Malcolm decided to think on good things rather than those he could not control. Reverend Cummings liked to quote a verse from the Good Book that summed it up well: *"Whatsoever things are true, whatsoever things are honest, whatsoever things are just, whatsoever things are pure, whatsoever things are lovely, whatsoever things are of good report; if there be any virtue, and if there be any praise, think on these things."*

Problem was that one verse summed up Sally Martin, and her unpredictability unnerved him, too.

Malcolm sighed. The pretty new seamstress in town slipped through life as light as a feather. He could still feel his big hands on her narrow waist as she flew through the air at the last dance. Ewan's fiddle had sung up a fever into Malcolm's bones and made his heart soar. When he danced, his feet moved with a grace he never felt in real life, especially when he partnered with Sally.

Wide brown eyes, silky blond hair, trim little figure, and a wit to match. He knew he was heartsick, but had no idea what to do about it. How did Ewan win his sister Kate's hand?

Music.

Malcolm pursed his lips together and blew a high whistle. Sport sprang to his feet and howled.

He'd have to try something else. Sport's tail shook and he quivered. He barked his alert but happy cry. The horses' ears twitched and up ahead, coming out of the corn at the end of the field, he saw a kid in patched overalls and his smaller sister. They waved; Malcolm stopped the horses.

"Wind's blowing up fierce, Mr. MacDougall. Can you ride us into town? Pa's sending us to his brother."

Malcolm jerked his head at Sport, who jumped into the back of the empty wagon, tongue out, rear end wagging, joyfully inviting the children to climb in. "No problem, Joe." He reached down to grasp Anna's hand.

Her sunbonnet flapped in a gust of wind, and she folded to fear on the seat beside him. "We'll be there soon," he said. She trembled.

Her twelve-year-old brother pushed back his straw hat. "Looking mighty wild. You thinkin' something might happen?"

Malcolm mopped the back of his neck with his kerchief. "You always got to think funnel cloud on a day like this, but look up ahead. Blue skies over Fairhope."

"Anna don't like the weather. But she does like your Miss Sally."

A warm glow filled Malcolm's gut, but he had to speak the truth. "She's not mine."

"Then why does she smile after you?" Anna asked in a tiny voice.

He cleared his throat over a spurt of pride. "She's friendly; she likes everyone in town."

Anna pulled a handkerchief from her pocket. "She made this for me." The girl traced an embroidered blue letter *A* in the corner. "She's right good with her needle."

"That's why Mrs. Sinclair hired her."

He wondered how long Sally would stay in the small shop on Main Street across from the MacDougall Mercantile. Kate said Sally dreamed of having her own shop. With her skills and cheery disposition, Sally was bound to succeed. She just needed time and capital, but Malcolm couldn't help her there.

"Wind blew down part of our cornfields," Joe said. "Pa thought he saw a twister touch down."

Malcolm urged the horses faster. "Where's he now?"

"Hunkering down near the house. Not enough room in the shelter for all of us, so he said to go to town."

Putting the children into possible danger? Malcolm stared. Thin and wearing patched clothing, Joe and Anna were the oldest of eight children of a sharecropping farmer. If they'd lost corn, the winter could be lean for this family. He frowned. They'd need help.

"You know any songs?" he asked. "I like to sing when I'm afraid."

"You git scared?" Anna whispered.

Only when a pretty girl holds my heart in her hands, he thought, but answered with a nod. "I like to remember God's always with me and I can trust Him. Look, the storm is moving east. We'll be safe in Fairhope."

"Three times three is nine; three times four is twelve; three times five is fifteen." Joe shouted into the blowing wind. Malcolm and Anna echoed his chant.

Ewan had taught him that understanding math meant seeing the pattern. Singing the times tables had helped him. He'd learned to cipher real fine, even multiply and divide; his business thrived now that he could figure the invoices himself.

Learning was a matter of turning your mind to solve a problem. Winning Sally could be like learning math.

Malcolm merely had to figure out the solution to make her love someone. Someone like him.

∽

Sally Martin knew her latest hat was the envy of all the women in church Sunday morning. Oh, no one said anything, of course; they were all too refined to countenance the sin of envy, but she saw it in their eyes.

Up front her dear friend Kate played a reed flute, accompanying her fiddler husband on "Blest Be the Tie That Binds." "The favorite hymn of a seamstress," Kate had laughed. "You know, tying off the thread?"

Of course she knew. Sally spent her days in front of a newfangled sewing machine or with a needle in hand. She tied knots all day long.

Sally stifled an urge to reach up and knead the base of her neck. After bending over her work all week, she yearned to loosen those muscles, but she couldn't do so here, not in the plain wooden church that brought such comforting worship each Sunday.

She loved her move to Fairhope in May for many reasons, but being able to go to church made her the happiest. She could worship God in an actual church now that she lived in town. Out on the farm a mile from Sterling, her father read the Sscriptures on Sunday mornings; they rarely visited with anyone.

But here in Fairhope—Sally glanced about—were far more interesting possibilities of interaction. Pa had sent her to make a future for herself—and her younger sister. They'd never find husbands on the isolated farm, and he knew it. He was counting on her.

Josiah Finch, the youngest banker in town, tipped his straw hat in her direction.

Sally immediately faced forward. Why wasn't he paying attention to the music?

She looked out of the corner of her eye across the aisle. Malcolm smiled at her then turned red.

"Our hearts in Christian love," sang the congregation. Sally dropped her eyes and tried to hide her answering smile.

Afterward, she hurried outside to join the other women setting up the church potluck. A puff of wind tried to lift her hat. She scanned the horizon. The weather had been unsettled the last couple of days; storms this time of year always worried her.

"Appreciate the prayers, Pastor," said a weathered farmer in his Sunday best. Sally wondered if she should volunteer to let out the straining seams in his cotton shirt.

"Last night's rain should be the last before harvest," Reverend Cummings said. "I just hope it doesn't stir up tornadoes."

"Bad weather went east." He pushed back his hat. "Blue sky's coming our way."

East. Sally looked in the direction of home. Surely they'd hear if a tornado had set down near Sterling?

"Let me help you." Josiah Finch took the white bowl from her hands. A tall man with piercing blue eyes, he wore a thin goatee under a sharp mustache. Folks thought he looked down his nose at people, but that was only because of his height. His fingernails were always clean, and he smelled of soap. Even on the hot summer day, Josiah tied a ruby cravat under his gray linen suit.

"I'm looking forward to sharing a meal with you today," Josiah said.

Sally nodded, flustered as always at his attention.

"Did you make these pickles yourself?"

She found her tongue. "Kate and I put them up last month. They've been pickling ever since."

"Sweet or dill? Not that it matters; anything you've made will be sweet on my tongue."

"Dill," she said, unsure his remark was proper, especially on Sunday. "Did your mother send a dish?"

His mother seldom left her home, an invalid whom Kate's mother said needed all the sympathy and social contact she could get.

"I brought sarsaparilla. It's what they call a 'soft' drink in Clarkesville."

Josiah had recently returned to Fairhope to help his father with the bank, bringing with him a number of new items from the county seat. He'd showed her *The Ladies Home Journal* and *Women's Home Companion* magazines for his mother, and a surprisingly light bar of hand soap that floated on water.

"What's sarsaparilla taste like?" She stumbled over the name.

He tapped her nose. "You'll have to try it and tell me."

Blushing, Sally hurried to help Mrs. MacDougall, the mercantile owner's wife, with her famous light biscuits. "Have you seen Malcolm?" his mother asked. "I need him to bring the fried chicken from the stove."

"I'll get it." A chore away from Josiah's intimacy could only be good for her.

She pushed open the door to the MacDougall kitchen, only to hear a muffled, "Oomph!"

Sally's fingers went to her lips. She had shoved the door into Malcolm. "I'm sorry. I didn't realize you were here."

He held the platter of fried chicken. "My mother asked me to help."

"She asked me, too." Sally couldn't contain her worry any longer. "What do you think of the weather?"

"Should be fine here. Not so sure about Sterling. How far out of town do your folks live?"

"My father and sister are on the farm, couple miles this side of town. I'm afraid something might have happened to them."

If anyone could help, it would be Malcolm. Big, comfortable, slow-talking Malcolm would have an answer. Not quick like his brother-in-law the schoolteacher, but solid and reliable. When Malcolm said something, you knew it was true.

He gazed at her. Malcolm couldn't always find words, but he danced beau-- tifully. He moved like a hawk in flight, smoothly riding the air currents, but then swooping down at the right moment to spirit away his prey into a heartfelt swing or do-si-do.

Prey? What a silly idea. She felt as safe with Malcolm as she did with his sister Kate. All the MacDougalls were trustworthy folk, willing to help even at inconvenience to themselves. Of course when he looked at her, Sally often felt breathless—and not simply because they danced well together.

"Would you like me to go out and check for you?" Standing there with the chicken platter in hand, Malcolm scarcely looked like a knight in shining armor, but she knew his well-meaning heart, always favorably disposed toward her.

"Thank you, but I expect we'd hear if a tornado touched down."

Malcolm nodded. "Neighbors would send for us. Most tornadoes happen late in the afternoon or early evening anyway."

"No one has come since last night? They're probably fine."

"Will you open the door for me?"

Relief made her giddy. "I'd do anything for you, you know it."

Malcolm stumbled. "Maybe you better carry the chicken. I'm likely to drop it given half a chance."

She laughed and waltzed out the door with him trudging after. She'd just reached the tables when a boy rode up on wild-eyed black stallion lathering at the mouth. "Funnel cloud hit outside of Sterling in the middle of the night," he cried. "We need help. Now!"

Sally turned to Malcolm with stricken eyes.

"I'll take you." Malcolm plunked the platter onto the table. "We'll get Ewan to come, too."

Chapter 2

Debris littered the road and landscape as far as they could see. Crops had been uprooted, tattered leaves lay everywhere, and halfway to Sterling they came upon a wide swath of cropland gashed to the dirt. Ewan veered his horse off the road to follow the tornado-churned field south.

The petite woman beside him shivered. "What do you think?" he asked.

Sally clutched Sport's neck so hard, the dog whimpered. "It headed straight toward home. I hope they're still alive."

He urged his horses forward. "We'll find out."

Bessie and Daisy stepped gingerly off the hard road into the soft field where the wagon wheels turned more slowly. The healthy cornstalks of yesterday were beaten down on either side, the smell of broken corn husks heavy in the air. Sally moaned. "This is the Hulls' field. The crop is lost. What will they do?"

"They're farmers. They'll make do as best they can."

The tornado had destroyed acres of fields. A windmill spun its flag in the distance and Malcolm spied a pile of rubble. "The barn?"

Tears dripped down Sally's cheeks, and she nodded. "What about my family?" Sport licked her cheek.

He put his big hand on her small one and squeezed. She shut her eyes and wept. Malcolm didn't know what to do beyond urge the horses faster and hold her hand. Any other occasion it would have thrilled him, but on that sultry afternoon he meant only comfort.

Folks had already arrived at the Hulls' place. The house had been knocked sideways and they'd have to replace the barn, but the family survived, shaken but unhurt.

Sally rubbed her hands together. "Thank God." She blinked rapidly and stared in the direction of home.

Malcolm prayed they'd find no worse at the Martin farm.

Ewan joined them. "Plenty of helpers here." He met Malcolm's eyes. "I'll ride ahead and meet you at Martin's." He kneed his horse into a gallop.

Malcolm chirruped Bessie and Daisy through the devastated fields.

When they reached the Martin wheat field everything had been turned to straw. Parts of wagons and random tools stuck out of the ground. A rag doll lay face down in a pile of tree branches. Sally whimpered.

"Looked like a good yield," Malcolm observed, then cringed and shut his mouth.

"Pa had big hopes for the crop," Sally said. A windbreak divided the fields from the homestead. Tall trees had been snapped off halfway up with the bark stripped off the north side. When they entered what had been the barnyard, Sally moaned.

The house lay in splintered ruins. A busted wagon rested against the base of the barn—now leaning to its side. Nothing stood upright. Ewan walked among the ruins, scuffing now and then to peer closer at an object.

Bessie and Daisy halted, and Sally jumped from the wagon. Malcolm dismounted and tied off the horses to one of the trees. By the time he turned around, she and Ewan were tossing wood from the house remains.

"We need your strength," Ewan shouted. "There's a beam over the door."

Sally scrubbed at her face but stood back when Malcolm joined them. Sport pawed at the wood. "Storm cellar?" Malcolm asked.

She nodded.

The two men levered the beam off the battered wood cover using a stout branch. They pounded on the door and stood back as it slowly opened out of the earth. The top of a ladder poked up, and Angus Martin followed. He grinned and scrambled out when he saw Sally. "You're alive!" Sally flung her arms around her father's neck.

Her younger sister climbed out behind him and the three clung together.

Malcolm heard a whimper and looked into the shallow hole. A yellow mutt barked and leaped. He reached down and pulled out the family dog.

Angus Martin brushed at his eyes as he surveyed his acreage. "It came on at night, a roar like I never heard before. Filled my ears and near stopped my heart. Didn't think we'd live through it."

Sixteen year-old Lena wept. "What'll we do?"

Martin stepped about his yard looking in all directions. He paused and pointed east. "Some corn is still standing. We're going to be thankful we had stores in the cellar and the land is still here." He turned a bleak face to Malcolm. "You see much damage on your way over?"

"Crops mostly down, but this is only the second place we've come."

"The Hulls are all right, but their barn was destroyed and their house damaged." Sally held Lena and rocked. "I'm so glad you're alive."

"Yep," her father agreed. "Now we'll have to figure out how to rebuild."

∞

Sally stepped among the scattered remains of the family's home. The clock Ma had brought from back east was shattered. The curtains made from gunnysacks were shredded and tossed about the yard. Here and there she spied an unexpected item: an English bone china teacup nestled in a soft pillow; one of her father's boots, Lena's cross-stitch. Little seemed salvageable. She couldn't imagine how they'd manage.

Malcolm found a wooden bucket and filled it at the well. Sally dipped the china cup in the cool water and handed it to her sister—who gulped it down. Her father drank straight from the bucket. "I might as well get used to it. Any sign of my cows?"

Ewan pointed south. "I see something moving."

Ewan climbed onto his horse and with Sport running alongside, trotted off to inspect. Malcolm retrieved the basket of food his mother had pressed on them. He carried blankets and medical supplies in the back, too, along with an axe and other tools. "You hungry?"

They sat in the wagon and munched on the picnic leftovers from Fairhope's church social. "It was dark," Mr. Martin said. "Sky looked like trouble all day. I told Lena we needed to sleep down cellar. We took our bedding and candles and lay among the canned food. When the roaring barreled down and things started flying, I closed the hatch. The wind screeched till we were fair deaf. Worst night I've lived through. It scared me half to death."

"I'm sorry I wasn't here," Sally said.

"Weren't nothing you could have done. I was glad you were safe in Fairhope. You'll stay there."

"I'll come home and help."

"No. Take Lena back with you. You've got a place to stay in town. This farm'll need rebuilding afore womenfolk can live here again. Lena can sew with you."

Sally gathered up the food remains while her father and Malcolm unhitched the horses. The two men planned to ride the countryside looking to help. She and Lena would sort through the ruins.

"When will you be back?" she asked.

Malcolm squinted at the sky. "It'll be nightfall in a couple hours; we'll be back by then. I figure we'll spend the night and see what else needs doing."

"You'll help?"

"You can count on me."

Chapter 3

Bessie and Daisy preferred to work as a team, but could be ridden single. Their broad backs without saddles made riding painful, but in the face of the destruction, Malcolm couldn't complain. They traveled south, following the line of the tornado until they came upon Ewan and Sport staring at the ground.

"Do goats usually give birth in July?" Ewan asked.

Mr. Martin kneeled down. "Old Nanny. Let me help you."

They'd just gotten the tiny kid on his feet to nurse when five horsemen rode up. Reverend Cummings led them, with Malcolm's father, Josiah Finch, and two other men from church. All the men looked tired and drawn, though Josiah hardly had a speck of dirt on him.

Malcolm passed a grubby palm across his forehead. The same could not be said of him.

"What have you got?" Da asked.

Malcolm pointed. "New life springs from the rubble."

Reverend Cummings grinned. "Glad one good gift has come of this weather. Other than livestock missing here and there, everyone's accounted for. Plenty of damage, but no loss of life."

"Thank God," Malcolm said.

"Always. Folks will need help to rebuild though."

"The bank can be of service," Josiah said. "We can loan money against the land."

Malcolm looked at his father. They both knew many of the local farmers relied on credit with the mercantile to get through the year until harvest. Storm damage like this could force many off their land.

"More loans aren't going to help us," Mr. Martin muttered. "Have you seen all my neighbors, then?"

"Looks like the twister gave up about here," Da said. "I reckon one more farmstead and we'll have finished searching this area."

They rode to another farmhouse destroyed by the winds. Malcolm dismounted and joined the men to lift rubble and wood out of the way. Just as at the Martin house, they found another battered storm cellar with the Hulburt family grateful for their release. As the sky cleared toward sunset, the men turned back to the Martin property.

"You're a strong one, aren't you?" Mr. Martin said as he rode Bessie alongside Malcolm on Daisy.

Malcolm shrugged.

"I saw how you got in there and worked. That pretty boy never got his hands dirty."

Josiah traveled at the front of the group, talking earnestly to Reverend Cummings. When the breeze turned the right way, Malcolm could hear the words: "*compound interest rates,*" "*security.*" The pastor didn't seem impressed.

"Malcolm is good with his hands," Da said. "He can cipher and run his business, valuable skills for Nebraska farmlands."

"My girl speaks well of you. Take care of 'em both for me. I don't know how long it'll take me to make the farm livable."

Malcolm outlined Mr. Martin's plan for his father, who nodded. "A sensible strategy. My wife could use a strong girl to help around the house if Lena needs a job. I'm sure Sally's boardinghouse will make room for the girl in this situation."

"That's what I figure." Mr. Martin shielded the sunset's rays with his hat. "I hope I don't lose it all."

Malcolm patted the kid draped across his horse; the bleating nanny goat trailed behind. "You got a good start to rebuild, and your land's still here."

Mr. Martin stared after Josiah. "Maybe."

⟳

Pa said to make Lena sew, to take her mind off what happened, and that's exactly what Sally did when they returned to Fairhope. Welcomed as a refugee by Sally's landlord, Lena was embraced by Fairhope residents, and several brought her clothing and other necessary items. On Tuesday morning at the dressmaker's shop, Sally provided Lena a piece of fresh linen and her box of threads while she got her day's work organized.

The two sat in front of the large window that looked across the dirt street at MacDougall's Mercantile. Sunlight shone in, making the delicate stitching on Mrs. Campbell's new dress easier to see. While Sally hemmed, she tried to find a way to talk to Lena about what had happened. Last night the girl had cried herself to sleep, even though she was thrilled to be in town. While Sterling had a schoolhouse, a blacksmith's shop, and a cramped general store, Fairhope boasted three whole blocks of businesses.

The sweet scent of honeysuckle wafted through the open window. "What was it like?" Sally asked.

Lena shrugged. "The sky looked scary. The wind blew hard. Pa figured we were in for a severe storm, so we took shelter." A ghost of a smile crossed her face. "You should have seen the chickens trying to stand upright. They kept blowing away, so we put them in the hen house."

"Good thinking; it made them easier to find," Sally said. Malcolm had discovered the battered chicken coop a half mile away from the farm; the disgruntled chickens squawking and clucking, but alive.

"My sunbonnet kept trying to blow away, but I tied it tight. It's so clever, the way you shape the brim with reed. You should make more and tell ladies they're twister proof!"

Sally watched her sister playing with the gray silk thread she'd found in the thread box. Lena whipped her hand in a circular fashion, trying to produce a triangular shape. She frowned, shook her head and picked it apart, only to start over.

"What are you doing?" Sally asked.

"Trying to picture what it looked like. Don't funnel clouds start small at the bottom, twisting and turning into a triangular shape?"

"Are you embroidering a tornado?" Sally reached for the linen cloth.

Lena had captured the swirling motion of a funnel cloud with her deft stitches. Sally turned the cloth, marveling at how the threads caught the shimmering light from the window. "You should embroider one of these on your sunbonnet to remember how it stayed put."

Lena picked up her bonnet. "Where should I embroider it?"

This was Sally's specialty: hats. Where would Lena's clever thread picture look best? On the cloth-covered brim, or perhaps on the side where the tie strings attached to the body of the bonnet?

The bell above the door jingled, and Kate entered. She carried soft gauze and wore a shy smile. "Can I hire you to run your machine and hem these?"

Sally raised her eyebrows. "Why?"

Kate giggled. "You're among the first to know. We'll use them as diapers come winter."

The girls squealed together and chattered about the baby to come. After a glance at the clock, Sally set the cloth aside. "I'd be pleased to. The work will be my gift to you."

"Will Mrs. Sinclair allow it?" Kate whispered.

"I'm welcome to use the machine on my own time. Yes."

Lena showed Kate her thread funnel cloud and asked where she thought it belonged on the bonnet.

"What a charming idea. I'd embroider it above the left tie ribbon. It will hide the back of your stitching better there."

Sally turned over the embroidered linen and handed it to Kate. Lena's stitching was so fine, she didn't need to hide the backside.

"It's charming in either spot. I must get back to the mercantile. Thanks!"

They watched her cross the street and pause to talk with a tall man in a pristine jacket.

"Josiah's sure a handsome dandy," Lena said.

He looked in their direction and raised his hand in greeting. Lena waved. Sally felt her face redden and picked up her needle. "Back to work."

They sewed in silence for twenty minutes before Lena held up her olive sunbonnet. "Done."

The clean silver-gray embroidery gleamed against the tired dusty bonnet. Sally bit her lip, trying to figure out why the little funnel shape dressed it up so much.

"This is to show I survived," Lena announced.

The door opened, and Josiah entered. "Welcome to Fairhope, Miss Lena. I extend my condolences on the difficult occasion of your relocation."

Lena ducked her head.

"I trust your father is managing?"

"Yes," Lena murmured.

"Malcolm and Ewan are helping the folks in Sterling. There's a lot of work to do to find their possessions, much less rebuild." Sally looked at the sky out the window. "They hope to bring in what remains of the harvest, too, before another bad storm."

Josiah's brows contracted. "Does your Pa think he'll have a crop to sell this year?"

Sally darted a look at her sister. "He hopes he's got enough food to last until spring planting. The farmers who lost their fields are in a bad way."

"One man's loss is another's opportunity. I hope he fares well. I must return to work. Good day." Josiah tipped his hat and exited. They watched him step carefully down the boardwalk to the bank on the corner.

Lena stared after him. "He doesn't look like he's ever walked behind a plow."

"No. But then, he's never needed to." Sally poked her needle through the cloth and pricked her finger. She stuck it in her mouth.

Financial security was the reward for hard work and often the result of creative activity. Josiah had told her so at the dance, and she meant to prove it in her own life. Sally had plans, and they involved owning a dress shop of her own.

She looked at her sister's newly embroidered bonnet and wondered if it might hold a key to her future.

Maybe.

Chapter 4

Malcolm filled Bessie and Daisy's trough with oats and curried the dust out of their coats as they ate. His muscles ached, and he felt dog-tired—Sport had already curled up in a ball near the stall door—but his horses were the key to his livelihood as a teamster for the family mercantile, and they needed care first.

Daisy huffed, and he smiled at her pleasure. The oats even smelled good to him.

The last three days had been exhausting as he'd toiled with Reverend Cummings and others to aid the Sterling farmers. The damage would set back many, including Mr. Martin, by years. He didn't know how they would survive the winter.

Malcolm tightened his jaw. Josiah had been out talking to the farmers, discussing their assets and liabilities. He cringed whenever he saw the polished banker arrive on the scene and while Reverend Cummings had explained the man meant well, Malcolm wasn't so sure.

He was a businessman himself; he understood about profit and loss, but in the midst of catastrophe? Jesus told people to "weep with those who weep." Did they have to lose so much to a tornado and then forfeit whatever they had left to the bank?

Folks needed time to mourn. Later, they could calculate and make the best decision for their families.

Malcolm brushed harder.

He stepped out of the stall as the sun dipped toward the horizon and headed toward Mrs. Sinclair's shop, hoping Sally would be finishing up. Her father had sent him with an assignment.

Sally met him on the boardwalk out front. "Any news? How is Pa?"

"Working hard. He wanted me to give you this." Malcolm handed her a small blue-and-white cameo.

Her pretty red lips opened in a gasp of joy. "It's not lost! My mother's most precious possession." She showed it to Lena, who clapped her hands.

"When are you going back? Can you take me with you?" Sally asked.

Malcolm hesitated. "I think your pa wants you to stay in town. It's tough living out there without shelter. Once we get all the boards separated out, he'll build a lean-to with what he's got, but it's not a place for womenfolk right now."

"Don't be silly. We lived in a lean-to when we first proved up the land. I should be helping him. I could cook, if nothing else."

Malcolm lowered his voice. "You need to stay on your job so you'll have income. He's worried about eating this winter."

Sally went still and closed her eyes. Her lips trembled, and Malcolm ached to put his arms around her. But he watched and waited while she processed his words.

"We'll make more sunbonnets," Lena declared. "We can earn money to help Pa that way. See what we've got."

She handed him a green-and-white-checked sunbonnet, cleverly made with a reed frame to keep the sun out of the wearer's eyes. Malcolm had admired the style before—both his mother and sister had bonnets made like this and he'd once cut the thin reeds for Sally. Based on his family's experience making reed flutes, he'd shown her how to keep the reed flexible by soaking it in water until she could form it into any shape she wanted.

That had been a good day in the spring sunshine, with the scent of early wildflowers and the shrill calls of fledglings learning to fly. With the dust caked to his clothes and hot skin, Malcolm had a sudden yearning for the cleansing creek waters.

He took a deep breath and attended to the bonnet in his hand. "What's this?" He traced a triangular shape on the brim, realized how filthy his hands were, and stopped.

"Lena thought it would be memorable to mark the sunbonnet even a tornado couldn't blow off her head. Go ahead and inspect it," she smiled. "It washes."

He turned the creation over, and even his uninformed eye recognized skilled embroidery. "It looks nearly the same on top as on the bottom."

Sally nodded. "My sister is talented."

"You both are. This is real nice. A badge of honor the sunbonnet survived the storm."

"We made two more last night. Perhaps we should give them to women in Sterling whose bonnets did blow away." Sally's shoulders drooped. "How bad is it? I feel so guilty living comfortably in town."

"It's no worse than pioneers deal with everywhere," Malcolm said. "It gives your pa peace of mind knowing you're both safe here."

"I get off on Saturday; will you take me out?" Sally touched his arm, and Malcolm struggled not to react.

"I'll let you know. I scarce know my own business these days."

"Of course." Sally's eyes fell. "I shouldn't presume. We'll see you at the church meeting tonight."

Malcolm watched them walk to their boardinghouse. What meeting?

His mother had filled the hip tub with warm water by the time he entered the house. "Dinner will be in half an hour. I roasted a chicken."

Malcolm could hardly wait.

Scrubbed for the first time in days, Malcolm sat at the loaded table and stared at the potatoes, greens, and applesauce from last fall. His stomach turned. The good folks of Sterling weren't eating so well and probably wouldn't for months.

He pushed the food around his plate and told his parents what he and Ewan had seen and done.

"Reverend Cummings called a meeting tonight at the church to discuss what more Fairhope can do," his father said. "Are you going back to Sterling tomorrow?"

"Any hauling work needed?"

"A small load when you can get to it out at Brush Creek. Matthew Boden said you should concentrate on those who need help first, but he'd like the goods by the end of the week."

"I'll tell you after the meeting."

Most of the church members were in attendance when they entered the plain wooden building. Kate entertained them before the meeting began by playing her bagpipes—a sound growing on Malcolm, though he knew Ewan still cringed when she played out of tune. Of course, playing out of tune was practically a given with the instrument, but Ewan bore it all cheerfully.

Must be the power of love, Malcolm thought. His eyes drifted across the aisle to where Sally and her sister sat with Josiah and Mr. Finch.

After an opening prayer, Reverend Cummings got straight to the point. "Our brothers and sisters in Sterling are in great need. Several men worked hard this week to help them sort through the ruins. Next week we'll need men to help bring in the harvest. But long term, this winter in particular, will be tough. What can we do?"

Reverend Cummings liked to challenge them, Malcolm mused. He presented a spiritual problem and waited to see how his congregation responded.

"I've been listening to my husband's and brother's stories," Kate said. "We need to raise money to feed them through the winter and buy more seed for next spring. How about a dance? I'm sure Ewan would play and my bagpipes, of course, are always at your disposal."

A good natured groan from Kate's husband and a smattering of laughter ran through the congregation. Reverend Cummings looked about the church. "Ewan? You game to play?"

Ewan stood and bowed. "I'm at my wife's service." He looked at her with loving eyes. "Always."

"We could have a pie auction," Kate continued. "All proceeds for the townsfolk of Sterling."

Malcolm figured the congregation would like the idea; most of their social life involved eating.

"My sister can make more of these to sell." Lena jumped to her feet and waved her embroidered sunbonnet. The sharp-eyed deacon's wife behind her leaned in for a closer look.

"Very nice, Sally. I'll take one."

Sally's mouth dropped open and she nodded. "I'd be honored."

Josiah Finch examined the sunbonnet. "I believe this would be of interest to women in Clarkesville. I'll take a sample to town on Tuesday. Perhaps folks from all around, including our county seat, would come for the dance."

The crowd got to work forming committees. Malcolm watched Sally's excited face and thought only one thing.

He wished it had been him, not Josiah, who had volunteered to take one of Sally's sunbonnets to Clarkesville for sale—so the sparkle in her eyes would be aimed at him.

∞

Sally and Lena worked every spare minute to create new sunbonnets. Sewing late into the evenings after work, they devised a system: both cut the fabric from a pattern Sally devised, Sally ran the machine while Lena embroidered. On nights Ewan stayed to help in Sterling, Kate joined them to hem and finish off.

Kate's visits cheered Sally, especially hearing Lena's laughter and enthusiasm when Kate played one of her reed flutes. During the day working alongside Sally, Lena hardly spoke a word. If Sally dropped the heavy shears or a wagon rumbled past the window, the girl startled and her eyes grew round with fear.

Sally's heart ached with tenderness for her baby sister reliving those awful moments in the dark cellar when the tornado tore apart the only home she knew.

Sally herself trembled if she thought about it too much.

Mrs. Sinclair provided shirts for Lena to hem and other odd jobs while Sally attended her sewing. Spare time previously used to fashion clever hats for the women of Fairhope, she now spent working on the more practical sunbonnets, but the women who stopped in all claimed they'd be purchasing a new one.

"So clever with the framing," Mrs. Fitzgerald said one day. "I don't know how you thought of it."

She passed it to her bosom friend, Mrs. Downdall, who nodded. "Could you make me one in my favorite color: sky blue?"

"A nice color with the dark gray funnel cloud embroidery," Sally said. "And it would look lovely with your features. Do you mind if I sew them after the dance?"

The women agreed and took their leave. They'd purchased a copy of *The Ladies Home Journal* and wanted to read the story together. Sally watched them stroll away arm in arm. She loved Fairhope's friendliness.

Malcolm entered the shop, his large presence filling the room with the smell of horses and sweat. "I'm headed out to see your Pa tomorrow. Do you have anything for him?"

"I'll gather a few things together. When can I go with you?"

He turned his hat in his hands. "I'll ask him. Anything you need?"

She dropped her eyes to the bucket at her feet. "I'm almost out of the reeds I use on the sunbonnet brim. Perhaps if I could go with you on Saturday, we could cut more reeds at Pa's creek?"

His nervous face lighted into a broad grin. "I'd like to take you. But what about Lena?"

Sally bit her lip. "Do you want to come, Lena?"

The girl shook. "Yes. But. . .but not yet." She rubbed her hand across her face and turned away.

"Kate would probably welcome a visit from you, Lena. Why don't we ask her?"

Sally closed her eyes in relief. She knew Malcolm would fix everything.

The two young women returned to the boardinghouse after work. They ate a small meal and gathered foodstuffs and a fresh blanket for Malcolm to take with him the next morning. Afterward, they sat on the front porch drinking lemonade and stitching.

Josiah stopped at the gate and tipped his hat. Sally invited him to join them.

"I'll get another glass." Lena hastened into the house.

Josiah nestled into her vacated chair, and they sat together in companionable silence. From the pond behind the house, peepers tuned up for a night of song. A lark trilled, and in the distance a dog barked. The neighbor's chickens settled into their coop, and on the table in the window behind Sally, her landlady Mrs. Campbell set a kerosene lamp for light.

"How goes the sewing?" Josiah asked.

She held up the apple-green bonnet made from scraps she'd scavenged from Mrs. Sinclair's shop. "We've made seven and received orders for four more. I'm pleased."

"You got any here tonight? I'm headed to Clarkesville tomorrow and will show them around town. Kate gave me a poster to put up at the post office in town."

How kind everyone was! Sally dropped her hands into her lap and beamed at Josiah. "I'll send Lena to fetch them and you can choose the best. Perhaps you could take two?"

He stretched out his long legs. He wore a crisp cotton shirt, neatly pressed. His boots were polished and the buckles on his suspenders gleamed. She felt proud sitting next to him where all the townspeople could see.

"I'll take all you've got. They're a good example of your ability and will impress the seamstress over in Clarkesville. It's always good for people to get a sense of your skill when you're in business. You said you want to own a shop one day. What do you like about sewing?" Josiah asked.

"I love the feel of the material and the creativity in putting it together into a garment or hat. I enjoy seeing women walking down the street wearing items I created with my own hands. It gives me satisfaction knowing I made a woman's life prettier and better. Don't you feel the same way about helping people at the bank?"

He shrugged. "You need to make a living with a business. People need clothes, you provide; just make sure you turn a profit so you can stay in business. Most people are undercapitalized and don't always pay attention to where their money goes."

"What do you mean, undercapitalized?"

"I assume you're not in business yet because you don't have enough money to begin."

Sally nodded. "I've been saving, but haven't made much money, so far."

"Do you have an account with our bank? We pay interest on money invested with us." Josiah hooked his thumbs under his suspenders. "If not, come in and

I'll open an account for you."

Sally thought of the fifty-seven cents stored in a glass jar under her bed. She knew she'd need much more to begin a business. Calico cost seven cents a yard and cashmere for winter clothing thirty-three cents. A spool of thread could be had for a dime. While she had enough money to make the sunbonnets, nothing else was affordable yet.

"Thank you, but I'm content with my system right now," she said, embarrassed to have him know how little money she had.

Lena returned with a fresh glass of lemonade and promptly retrieved the sunbonnets at Sally's request.

Josiah examined the stitching. "My mother said you can tell the quality of work by how messy the backside is. I can scarce tell the difference."

"Ma taught me how to make invisible knots," Lena said.

"I can see you do excellent work. Which two do you think are your best ones?"

Lena indicated a red-checked sunbonnet and a blue calico. Sally wished she didn't have a pang of misgiving about giving away the bonnets now she knew the cost to make them.

She shook her head. She'd do the right thing even if it cost all the money she had.

Josiah set the bonnets aside and sipped the lemonade. "How's your Pa? Things look mighty difficult out in Sterling."

"He's building a lean-to; Malcolm's helping him."

"I saw MacDougall out there the other day with his grasshopper brother-in-law. He looked as disheveled as ever."

The way he referred to Malcolm and Ewan bothered Sally. "They've given up their time for others."

"Some work with their hands and brawn, others use their brains." Josiah fanned himself with his immaculate straw hat. They sat in a circle of light spilling from the window. The peepers were in full chorus now, and a full moon rose. "He's been building a shack for himself over by his sister and brother-in-law. Imagine, he constructed a barn first for those horses of his."

"Farmers always build the barn first." Sally didn't mean to be short. "They need to take care of the stock. Pa's been searching the countryside for his lost cows."

Josiah sniffed above his precise moustache. "I bet you're happy to be in town. It's much more comfortable here."

"I'll say," Lena agreed.

Sally knew the answer this man expected, but she couldn't bring herself to speak disloyally about either her father or Malcolm. She looked at her hands. "The people of Fairhope have been very generous. We're excited about the dance. It's good when church people reach out to help others."

"Of course. That's what they're there for." He pulled out a gold pocket watch and frowned. "I must be on my way. I've got to leave early tomorrow for Clarkesville. I hope to have good news for you when I return." He picked up the bonnets. "Good night."

They bade him the same. As he went into the moonlit night, Sally rubbed her hands together and wondered if she really understood townspeople after all.

Chapter 5

Malcolm helped Sally onto the bench seat and set her picnic basket into his wagon amid the building supplies, rope, hardware, and four cases of canned goods his father sent from the mercantile. Sport leaped in with a yelp.

"Don't you worry about Lena," his mother called, her arm circling the girl's waist. "We'll enjoy our time together. She's going to help me bake before we visit Kate."

Lena waved good-bye as Malcolm climbed onto the seat and called to his horses.

The early morning dawn felt cool as they traveled the well-worn road east. Blackbirds soared through the grasses and into the cornfields on the outskirts of town. One farmer burst through his field waving his hat and shouting at the persnickety birds. Sport agreed with him and barked in greeting.

"Does Pa know I'm coming?" Sally asked.

"He's looking forward to seeing you, but worried about how rough life is on the farm these days, especially after you've grown used to town."

"I'm coming to help, not visit."

Malcolm shrugged. "There's plenty to do. If it weren't for the tornado, where would you prefer to live?"

"I'm better suited for life in town, which is why Pa arranged for me to work for Mrs. Sinclair."

"What do you like about it?"

"You see so few people when you live on a farm. It's one long round of tending the livestock, praying for rain at the right time, and preparing for winter. I want to do more with my life."

"Like what?"

Sally sat up straighter. "Don't you think God created us with unique gifts we should use for His work?"

His shoulders were still stiff from all the hauling he'd been doing the last week. "Yes."

"I like to create with fabric and needle. A town has more folks who can use my talent than a little farm in the country. It's a friendlier place with more people to visit with than on a farm."

"Growing up in the mercantile, I had my fill of seeing people. Driving a rig means I talk with folks all the time. I never thought much about how lonely it might be on a farm, especially for a girl as lively as you," Malcolm said.

She glanced up at him, coloring. "I don't mean to complain. I'll always keep chickens and horses, but I like to make things with my hands rather than grow food. That's all."

Her eyes went dreamy, and Malcolm deliberately turned his head away to watch the road. The angel beside him distracted him too much. He tried to think of another conversation topic.

"Where do you see yourself in the future?" Sally asked.

"Working with Ewan and the mercantile when Da gets too old or Ewan decides not to teach anymore. We're saving our money, and I'm going to buy another team. We'll then do business hauling to the outlying small towns, the places the train will never go, like Sterling."

Malcolm snuck a look at her. "I'd like a wife and family, hopefully a pretty church-going woman who likes town life."

Sally went still. "All you want is beauty, church going, and a woman who likes town living?"

He tugged his hat low over his eyes against the rising sun as they crossed a low hill. "I think marriage is a partnership, a couple working together to make a life. Each is necessary for comfort, encouragement, and entertainment. You're not going to agree on everything, but part of the fun is learning to live together in spite of your differences. You get the basics right, the rest will fall into line."

Sport thrust his head between them, and Sally absently scratched his ears. They traveled in silence.

At a flattened field near where Malcolm had picked up Joe and Anna, he turned off the road toward the ramshackle sod hovel the family called home. The rutted passage bumped him sideways into Sally. "Sorry."

She laughed. "Maybe we should have walked."

A pack of mutts streamed from the fields barking and yipping. Malcolm ordered Sport to stay. The flimsy door opened, and Archibald Owens stepped out, pulling up his dirty suspenders and yawning. "Yer out early, Malcolm."

Joe and several smaller children spilled out from behind him.

"I've brought supplies today. Do you need anything?"

"No way to pay you."

Malcolm had expected his answer. "I've got a case of food to help. How'd your house fare?"

"We'll get by. Unless you got a sack of nails in your wagon and a piece of stovepipe."

Malcolm handed him a three-foot piece of stovepipe and a handful of nails. Owens squinted at him. "I can't pay anything."

"Make sure the children get to school in the fall so Ewan can teach them a new song. Sounds like they know the times tables."

"That right?" He looked at his oldest son.

Joe began to sing the multiplication song.

"He learned them a lot younger than I did." Malcolm shook Owens's hand and climbed up beside Sally.

"I'll do my best to get 'em to school. Pretty odd courting buggy you got there, but I suppose it will do the job." Owens slapped his knee and laughed as they drove out of the yard. The children and dogs ran after the wagon shouting and barking.

Malcolm swallowed and hoped Sally, who had been leaning over her side of the wagon to hand something to Anna, hadn't heard.

Sally bounced against him and grabbed his arm for balance. "Kate told me about you learning math by singing."

He stiffened.

"I'm impressed you stuck with it and learned mathematics well enough to run your own business."

Malcolm could only nod, his tongue too twisted to explain the pleasure he got from turning numbers over in his head now. Ewan had set him to studying geometry, and the straightforward logic of figuring out proofs and angles made long hours on the road go faster. "It pleases me Joe and his brothers and sisters won't learn mathematics as late as I did."

Even as he spoke, he winced. He should be talking to Sally about more romantic things, but maybe it was too early in the morning.

They stopped at the Hull farm where Malcolm off-loaded two cases of food and building supplies. "Thank your father for me," Mr. Hull said. "I'll pass cans along to the neighbors west of here. They're scrambling like the rest of us. Due east, the farms weren't even touched."

"Why would God allow a tornado to destroy one farm and not another?" Sally asked as they drove away.

Malcolm shrugged. "Hard to know why God does the things He does."

Like fixate Malcolm's heart on this pretty girl.

∞

Her father was hoeing the remains of the garden plot when they reached the farm. Sally hugged him and tugged the picnic basket from the wagon. "I've brought you biscuits and a loaf of bread with Mrs. MacDougall's butter and jam."

"A real treat. I've been living on eggs boiled over the fire. Good thing the chickens are still laying."

The men spent the day strengthening and fixing the barn. "I'll live with the animals this winter, but we need to make sure the whole thing won't collapse on me," Pa said.

Sally scrubbed clothes and stretched them over bushes to dry. She inspected her father's food supply and put together a list of items to send out. He'd found the iron stove in the rubble, and she cooked a hot meal.

"Smells mighty fine." Pa rubbed his hands together. "Thank you."

He looked thinner and worry lines crossed his forehead. Sally kissed his cheek. "Maybe you should move to town with us, Pa."

"Who would look after the livestock?" He smacked his lips and forked a piece of fried ham onto his plate.

Sally's heart sank. "I'm sure we could think of something."

"I might have room in my barn, Mr. Martin," Malcolm said.

"I can manage out here for now." Pa waved him off. "You're a good worker, Malcolm. I appreciate all you've done for me and the other folks around here. Not sure I'd be as well off as I am without your help."

"It's about loving your neighbor as yourself." Malcolm's face turned red.

Pa elbowed her. "He doesn't live on the next farm over, but he calls me neighbor."

"Sally works across the street from the mercantile," Malcolm said.

"She's your neighbor, then, not me." Pa laughed.

Pa lay down in the shade for a rest after dinner, but Sally had another need. She led Malcolm down a well-worn path to the creek not far from the homestead, carrying a wooden bucket and a sharp knife.

He rolled up his pant legs and Sally tucked her skirt between her legs and tied it high around her waist. They waded into the slow-moving creek to the green reeds growing along the water's edge, and he filled the bucket with water. "Watch for leeches," she called.

Malcolm grimaced and shuffled in the water to discourage their latching onto his skin.

A friendly breeze blew up, flapping the ends of Sally's bonnet as she scrutinized the green reeds. She called him over, indicating the pliable narrow reeds she wanted.

He fingered them. "How many should I cut?"

"Let's fill the bucket. I don't know when I'll get back out here."

"Are you giving away all the money you make on these sunbonnets to the tornado fund?" Malcolm asked.

"Yes."

"After you pay for the supplies?"

Sally stopped, and the creek water eddied around her knees. "What supplies?"

"Reed is free, but what about the cloth and thread? You can give the cost of supplies to the cause, but no one expects you to go into debt to make them. What would be the point?"

She hadn't considered it that way. Mrs. Sinclair had donated fabric scraps and she'd used her own, but she only had enough free fabric for about a dozen bonnets. "What should I do?"

"Once they sell, pay yourself back the amount you spend on making them and put the rest in the donation box. No one would quarrel with you."

Sally stared at him and licked her lips. Trust Malcolm to see the right answer to a problem she hadn't even anticipated. She took a step closer to him and plunged into an unexpected hole.

Malcolm grabbed for Sally and then tumbled into the water on top of her. They floundered, the heavy skirts tripping Sally, while Malcolm gulped a mouthful of the creek.

When they finally spluttered to shore, Sally laughed at the water streaming down Malcolm's face. "Look how well my reed brim kept its shape." Her clothes were a soggy mess, but the brim shielded the water from dripping into her eyes. "Thank you for saving me."

"That's a might clever bonnet you got there." Malcolm took a deep breath, leaned in, and kissed her, sweet and gentle.

"Where are you?" Pa shouted from the knoll above.

Malcolm spun away, slipped, and floundered in the current.

Pa climbed down the path, reached the creek bank, and put his hands on his hips. "You may be a man of action and few words, Malcolm, but surely you know better than to fall in." He reached for Sally with a frown. "You better stay away from him until your clothes dry off."

Sally put her fingers to her lips and watched Malcolm float around a bend in the creek. Despite the clingy wet clothes her cheeks flared hot, and she wondered what else Malcolm knew that she had not anticipated.

A man of action and few words, indeed!

Chapter 6

Helping Sally cut reeds reminded Malcolm of his childhood and the reed flutes he'd made with Kate and Ewan. Ewan had taught the Fairhope school children how to make and play reed flutes last Christmas; you could still hear them piping around town.

But the Sterling children didn't know about reed flutes and the joy of making music.

He'd watched Lena shake when asked about the tornado, but he'd also seen her face light up when Kate blew her ridiculous bagpipes. Music might help calm Lena's jittery soul.

Malcolm decided to find out.

He visited the Martin sisters sitting on the front porch after supper Monday night.

Dusk came, and the first bats flitted in the dying light. Children at play shouted down the street, and the heavy scent of honeysuckle hung in the air. Mrs. Campbell waved at him after she set the kerosene lamp in the window.

"What's in the bag?" Lena craned her neck and sat taller on her chair.

"A present for you." He brought out two reed flutes. The teenager's eyes grew wide, and she set aside her embroidery. "One for you and one for me."

He looked at Sally. "Did you want one, too?"

Her eyes gleamed, and she shook her head. "Thank you for thinking of Lena."

Malcolm demonstrated how to cover the holes with his fingers and blew. He played up the scale, nowhere near as clearly as his sister, but good enough to satisfy.

He'd already taught Lena to play "Twinkle, Twinkle, Little Star" when Kate and Ewan joined them.

"Sweet piping!" Kate called. She took the flute from her brother and blew. "It's new, but has a nice tone. What are you up to?"

He looked at Ewan, who clapped him on the back. "He's seen the kids out in Sterling who've lost everything and thought he'd make them a gift, right?"

Malcolm nodded.

"I'm proud to call you my brother. Your heart is good, like the preacher says, and you let those little children come to you."

"Thinking about their needs, that's all."

Kate hugged him. "God often reveals himself best in the little things. We're going to Ma and Da's house for ice cream. They've got one of those new crank machines and a little bit left of last winter's ice. Would you like to join us?" She extended the invitation to all.

Lena jumped up. "I would."

"Your embroidery?" Sally asked.

"I'll take it with me—Mrs. MacDougall won't mind."

"I'll be there in a bit," Malcolm said.

The three strolled away while Sally bent her head over the latest sunbonnet, this one in navy blue with red strings.

"The reeds work all right?" Malcolm asked.

She nodded and licked her lips, seemingly intent on what she was doing. "How did you know she needed a flute to cheer her up?"

"It seemed like the right thing to do," Malcolm finally said, desperate to say something about his feelings, but unsure of her reaction. He scratched at a mark on the porch. "I'd do anything for you, Sally."

She opened her mouth to reply when Josiah's voice rang out. "I've found you! I've got great news from Clarkesville."

"I'll be on my way, then," Malcolm said. "Ice cream."

⁓

Sally's heart sank as Malcolm shuffled down the street, but she put a pert smile on her face and indicated the empty chair opposite. Josiah removed his jacket and sat. "Pleasant out here, isn't it?"

Actually, the mosquitoes were buzzing, and the humidity meant she dripped sweat. The MacDougall ice cream sounded refreshing, but she'd missed her chance. Sally pushed back her hair. "How was your day?"

"Very profitable for you. The shop owner I saw in Clarkesville fell in love with your bonnets. She sold one while I stood there and asked me to bring more."

Sally rubbed her hands on the cotton fabric in her lap. "They're just bonnets."

"Apparently the woman who bought one appreciated that the brim didn't droop. She loved the idea of helping victims by purchasing one. You could easily sell a dozen." He pulled six bits from his pocket. "Here's your pay for two bonnets."

"Thirty-seven cents. It's a good start."

"Would you like to open a bank account with this?" Josiah tapped his index finger on the coins.

"No. I'm going to turn it over to Reverend Cummings. It doesn't belong to me."

"You should deduct the costs. You shouldn't go into debt trying to help people."

Malcolm had said the same thing. Sally shifted in her cane-back chair. She understood the reason now, but it still didn't seem quite right to her.

"There's nothing wrong with turning a small profit," Josiah said. "If this gets you started with the Clarkesville ladies, you could sew other clever hats and the like. This could be your foot in the door. Why not sell there?"

"We'll see how many I have left after the dance on Saturday. You could take those to Clarkesville next time you go."

He stretched his hands behind his head. "You may sell out in Fairhope. Then what will you do?"

Light spilled from the house across the street, and she heard friendly laughter. "I'll be thankful God heard our prayers for those in need, which includes my father."

His eyes danced. "Are you thinking like a businesswoman or a do-gooder?"

She knew the answer he sought, but she felt uncomfortable holding back some of the money received for the bonnets. There was so much Sally needed to learn about business before she could open her own shop. A banker could advise and help her. He knew all about money and interest rates.

Josiah spoke slowly. "Profits are one thing; if you don't feel comfortable keeping the profit, don't. But the material costs are something else. Good business sense isn't greed. By managing your resources you'll ensure you can keep on making sunbonnets and thus help those in need."

Sally bit her lip, trying to think of a good response. "Why can't I be both a seamstress who turns out quality work and provides for those in need; you know like the Proverbs 31 woman?"

Josiah closed his eyes. "Is she the one known for being worth more than rubies and pearls?"

"Yes, 'she reacheth forth her hands to the needy' and 'she maketh herself coverings of tapestry, her clothing is silk and purple.' She's very resourceful."

"As are you. I work hard for the same reason," Josiah said. "I want to make a life for my family and clothe my wife in silk and purple. How's that sound?"

Sally thought of the way cool silk slipped through her fingers when she'd had opportunity to stitch it. "Any woman married to you would have a comfortable life."

"My father gave me a parcel of land outside of town where I'm going to build a house. The bank will be mine one day. I'm thinking an elegant two-story with a wraparound porch and scrollwork. It'll include four bedrooms upstairs and a deep cellar beneath. Would a house like that appeal to you?"

Her father's lean-to flashed in Sally's mind, along with gratitude for the cellar that sheltered him and Lena during the tornado. "In this area a storm cellar is a good idea. It saved Pa and Lena's lives."

"I drove out there to survey the damage before I went to Clarkesville. Many of those folks are pressed to the wall. We're offering them reduced interest on any loans they take out against their land, but some farmers may go under."

Josiah looked at her and stopped. Sally couldn't keep the horror off her face. "You would take advantage of people in this situation?"

"Not at all. We're offering lower rates. A small loan could help them keep their land until they get a good crop or they can sell."

She rubbed her face and thought of Malcolm's hands dirty from working for her father and his neighbors. He had asked for nothing in return. Sally glared at Josiah. "Did you ride your horse or buggy?"

"I took my horse; the roads are chewed up and hard on the buggy."

"So you took no provisions with you? No extra food? No building supplies? Did you even get your hands dirty?"

He frowned. "No need. I carried paperwork in my saddlebags. It takes all kinds of people to help. The Good Book reminds us the body is made up of many members. Some are teachers, some are workers, and some are leaders."

Josiah scratched the back of his head, frustrated. "What good would it do for me to build a barn if I don't know how? I'd be in the way. We've been busy at the bank making sure we have the funds to help. My skills lie in using my brains, not my brawn."

Josiah could add up a column of numbers faster than anyone she knew. He understood how the world outside of Fairhope worked and wanted to do the right thing. She doubted he could pound a nail straight. Drumming up sales for her bonnets and seeking ways to reduce the financial burden on farmers was important.

Sally took a deep breath of the warm evening air and thought of Malcolm's cheerful and strong helpfulness. She wished Josiah's clean hands and suit didn't feel like shirking to her.

Chapter 7

Malcolm woke early the morning of the fund-raising dance. The heat had moderated and he had work of his own to do. He started with the most important task: finishing a dozen reed flutes for the children of Sterling.

Kate thought they'd make these flutes different from their normal ones. She'd painted them red and then decorated the front with a twister shape. "Sort of like what Lena did with the bonnets."

Once they dried, Malcolm sanded the bottoms and carved finger holes. He tested each one in turn to make sure it wasn't difficult to blow. They looked pretty and should cheer up the children.

Afterward, he cleaned his wagon and harness, brushed Bessie and Daisy, threw sticks for Sport to chase, and sat on a bench to think. He even prayed for wisdom and was still resting in the shade when Ewan came looking for him.

"It's a big day today." Ewan leaned against the ash tree beside the Mac-Dougall house. "What are you going to do?"

Malcolm frowned. "I'll go to the prayer meeting at three o'clock, then attend the auction and bid on a pie. I expect I'll dance while you play." He sighed. "I'll enjoy dancing again. Feels like I've done nothing but work since the tornado came through."

"What are you going to do about Sally? While you've been tongue-tied and quiet, Josiah's been courting her. He's been describing a big house he's going to build and the fine clothes he'll buy for his wife and family."

The peace Malcolm thought he'd found evaporated and his gut clenched.

Overhead a mockingbird called, its trilling voice starting high and sweet and descending into a noise that sounded like a whining dog. Both men looked up, and Sport ran into the yard, barking to match, spinning around looking for the strange animal, and finally collapsing against Malcolm's leg in confusion.

"While he explored the neighborhood," Ewan said, "a nosy bird landed in his yard and stole his voice."

"What's your point?" Malcolm had to push the words past a tight throat.

"Josiah's not a bad guy. He's lonely and is attracted to a pretty girl. He's a smooth talker and has a lot to offer." Ewan picked up a stick and threw it for

Sport to chase. "I'm saying I think Sally has more in common with you than Josiah, and you could make her happier. Don't let her fly off with a wealthy bird."

Malcolm could feel his ears turning red. He'd never been as quick of tongue or clever as his sister or Ewan. What he knew to do was work, and to work hard. Surely Sally had recognized his affection for her through his actions?

Ewan watched him through steady eyes. "Put your mouth in front of your muscle. Offer your heart to her. I'd pray, too. In fact, I will pray."

Malcolm had been praying about what to say to her, and then his brother-in-law came over warning him to speak up. His heart sank.

"Maybe she'd be better off with Josiah. He can give her all the things she wants, a beautiful home and clothes."

Ewan tossed the stick again. "I told myself the same thing when he tried to court Kate. But what kind of man throws away the love of a good woman because he's afraid of being rejected? Give her the choice, Malcolm. Right now, all she sees is one man interested, and he's dangling security."

Malcolm squeezed his big hands together trying not to shake at Ewan's forcefulness. He meant well. He'd taught Malcolm how to solve seemingly insurmountable math problems.

But music and singing couldn't help him past this problem. This required more action than words, Malcolm knew. If only they could dance or work together. How could he demonstrate his feelings to Sally and his hope for a future with her?

Dance?

Pie auction?

"They were baking pies when I went by the boardinghouse," Ewan said. "Lena was pitting cherries on the front porch."

Sport returned with his stick, and Malcolm scratched the dog's ears. "Thanks."

∞

Prayer comforted and encouraged her every time, Sally thought as she exited the church with the dozens of folks who had gathered. Pa had come in early from Sterling. He nudged her. "Proud to be here in my new shirt to ask God for mercy and help."

She'd stayed up late the night before finishing it, along with completing the last of the dozen sunbonnets. Up since dawn, Sally felt lethargic on the warm day. She'd need to muster energy for tonight's dance. The auction's excitement should help.

Pa shook hands with Josiah, who tipped his hat in her direction. "Will you give me a hint?" Josiah asked.

"Gingham ribbon," Lena said.

Sally whirled on her. "You're not supposed to give hints of what pie is yours."

"Thank you, kindly. I'll be watching for it. How goes the rebuilding, sir?"

Pa eyed him. "I'll be able to winter over. I'm thankful my girls have a place in town."

"Your family will always be welcome here."

"Will your mother join us today?" Sally asked. She'd never laid eyes on his mother, though his father would be conducting the auction in a short time.

"Alas, no. She never goes out." He touched her cheek. "I'll see you soon." He hustled out of the church.

"He's mighty forward," Pa said. "He courtin' you without my permission?"

"Pa."

"He likes her, but she likes Malcolm better," Lena said.

"Shh."

"Better choice," Pa grunted.

Sally glanced about to see if anyone heard. Her chest felt tight and her stomach roiled. She wanted to rub Josiah's touch off her cheek and lean against someone strong and immovable, a man to hold her up and encourage her. She had felt reassured when Malcolm's deep voice had prayed not twenty minutes before. Where was he now?

"What kind of pie did you make for me?" Pa asked Lena.

She batted her lashes. "You'll find your favorite on the table."

Outside the church, people hurried to finish organizing tables of goods and pies for auction. Mr. Finch shouted for their attention.

People must have come from all around the county, including well-dressed folks Sally suspected journeyed from Clarkesville. The livery stable was full of extra horses and buggies. Josiah greeted several and motioned for her to join him. Sally shook her head and hurried to assist Kate whose arms were full of plates.

"Quite a turnout. Did you see that Clarkesville woman's hat?" Kate ducked her head in the direction of an elegant woman in a fine poke bonnet.

Sally told herself not to stare, but she wanted to inspect how the hat had been constructed. A hatter had woven reeds to create the shape and adorned it with silk flowers. She'd try to create a similar style when she got a chance.

Her landlady joined them, shaking her fine skirts and spinning with pleasure. The hoops she wore belled out the new dress beautifully, and Mrs. Campbell preened with rosy cheeks and a spring in her step. "I'm going to try for one of your bonnets, Sally. I've enjoyed watching you and Lena make them on my front porch."

"Thank you for providing the lamp for us to work."

Rev. Cummings joined Mr. Finch and called the excited crowd to order. They bent their heads and prayed for God's blessings on their day, reminding Him the purpose was to provide relief to their brothers and sisters in Sterling.

"Amen," Sally whispered, as a curious thrumming grew inside her heart. This day could change her family's fortunes from grim to hopeful. She had to trust God to provide the means to deliver them, even though Pa thought he could winter over successfully in the barn with his animals.

Sally hoped for better options.

She looked around the churchyard. Where was Malcolm?

Mr. MacDougall handed Mr. Finch an auctioneer's gavel and he hammered it onto the podium brought from the church. "Let the auction begin!"

Chapter 8

Malcolm stood in the back of the crowd, watching as Mr. Finch auctioned off livestock. A cheer went up from the crowd when the livery agent passed the hearty banker a note. "Charlie Grech from the north side of Fairhope announces he's got more laying hens than he knows what to do with. He'll give one layer to each of the first ten Sterling families who find him."

A spirited bidding broke out when five jars of his mother's wild blackberry preserves went up on the auction block. They sold for two bits each. Ma blushed until she saw the winner: his father. "I'm not letting these preserves out of my house if I can help it!" Da shouted.

Laughter.

The spirited crowd obviously enjoyed themselves, but Malcolm couldn't join in. He kept his eyes on Sally, who scanned the crowd and twisted her handkerchief. He couldn't make sense of it; Josiah stood nearby and obviously sought her attention. Still she looked, and he scanned the crowd with her, for what, he didn't know.

Children ran about with a freedom Malcolm envied. Even Joe and Anna, along with their siblings, seemed lighthearted. A mockingbird in a nearby tree, maybe the same one from earlier, coughed a sound similar to the auctioneer's gavel. It felt like the whole world was making fun of him.

"Miss Sally Martin needs to come forward to model this fine bonnet," Mr. Finch called. "A beautiful girl wearing a beautiful hat. Who can resist?"

Not Malcolm. He paced. Perhaps he could buy one for Kate or his mother? He still hadn't come up with an idea yet as to how to win Sally's hand, but this seemed to be the day.

Kate needed a green hat with her hair color, so he let the first two bonnets go by. On the third choice, however, he realized a murmur had begun as the price, once more, went to five bits. It seemed a reasonable price to Malcolm. He didn't understand the restlessness.

The fourth choice, a sky blue model; the fifth and sixth, both made of blue calico; all went for five bits, though the seventh yellow bonnet went for seven.

Ewan appeared at his elbow. "What do you think he's up to?"

"Who?"

"Haven't you noticed? Josiah's bought them all. He hasn't got seven heads to wear a bonnet on, and everyone knows his mother never goes outdoors. Who's he buying them for?"

Sally didn't look so merry anymore as she modeled a green-checked bonnet. Malcolm raised his hand to bid. "Eight bits," he shouted.

People turned in his direction.

Josiah went to ten.

While Malcolm fumbled in his pockets checking his money, the gavel came down hard. Sold.

And so it went. Josiah bought all twelve bonnets.

Sally climbed down from the chair, her face downcast and red. She nodded at Josiah and then hurried into the mercantile with Kate following close behind.

∞

"What is he thinking?" Sally burst into tears. "Why would he buy all those bonnets? It's presumptuous and humiliating and"—her eyes widened—"what will people think?" *What will Malcolm think?*

Kate stretched out her arms. Sally went to her, and they hugged each other. "I'm sure he's got a clever reason; he never acts impulsively. Let's be thankful for how much money your bonnets raised for the fund."

"I can't go out there. People will think I put him up to it. They'll think. . . I don't even know." Sally looked into Kate's sympathetic eyes. "They'll think he's courting me, won't they?"

"Isn't he?"

"I don't know," she wailed. "I just wish someone else had bought a sunbonnet."

The bell jingled above the door, and Malcolm entered. "Is Sally okay?"

She buried her face into Kate's shoulder. She couldn't look at him.

"I'll take care of her," Kate said. Sally felt Kate motion to shoo him away.

"Would you like me to punch him in the nose, Sally?"

Trust Malcolm to make her feel better. "No!" She laughed in spite of herself. "But thank you."

"They'll be bidding on the pies soon," he said. "I'll see you then." He shut the door with a click, and the mercantile went silent.

Kate rubbed Sally's arm. "What do you want to do?"

She felt wrung out. "Find out who's won my pie. It's wrapped in a plain white pillow slip with a sunflower on top."

They returned to the auction, where Mr. Finch had just announced Rev. Cummings as the winner of the suckling pig. "Raise him up and you could have bacon next year."

The reverend's daughter Grace began to cry. "I don't want to kill the piggy."

A murmur of sympathy moved through the crowd. Grace carried the pink creature to her spinster aunt who frowned at her brother and took her niece and the piglet home.

"Here's a novel item you don't see very often." Mr. Finch fumbled with a collapsing pile of sticks and bellows.

"Hey," Kate cried. "What are you doing with my bagpipes?"

He pretended innocence. "These are yours? They came from an anonymous donor."

Kate put her hands on her hips and looked about the people gathered around him. "All I can say is the donor better be bidding."

Ewan sheepishly handed Mr. Finch a silver dollar. "We need to keep harmony in the family, whether this instrument will provide it or not."

The congregation roared. "Won't you play a little song, Mrs. Murray, to entertain us while we get the pie auction organized?"

"Thank you, Mr. Finch. I'd be glad to." Kate stepped up, adjusted her instrument, blew hard into the bellows to engage the low drone, and played a fair representation of "Amazing Grace."

"She sounds much improved." Sally said to Mrs. MacDougall. The woman had proud tears in her eyes.

"She's been practicing. My Kate's a determined young woman, as you know." Mrs. MacDougall darted a look at Sally. "And my Malcolm is a fine and honorable man."

"I know," Sally whispered. "He's a problem solver and so steady and helpful. I feel safe when I bring a concern to him."

"Mark my words. When Malcolm loves, he loves deeply. Don't break his heart." Mrs. MacDougall hurried to help with the pies.

Sally's mouth dropped open in surprise, while the thrumming grew stronger in her chest. Could Mrs. MacDougall be right? She surveyed the crowd, suddenly anxious. What had become of Malcolm?

Chapter 9

Malcolm returned to the back of the crowd after helping Grace Cummings find a spot in the family barn for her piglet, which she had named Hamlet.

His mother held aloft the first item as Mr. Finch extolled the virtues of a cherry pie with a red gingham bow. The young man who ran the livery stable started things hopping when he shouted "four bits."

Josiah jumped in with five while a man in a white hat from Clarkesville bellowed six. "I haven't tasted a good cherry pie in years."

Mr. Martin bid seven, but Josiah's ten silenced him. Malcolm pulled the coins from his pocket. He had two silver dollars to spare. He shouted them out.

The crowd silenced, and then Josiah raised him. No one said a word, the gavel came down, and the fine cherry pie went to the young banker.

Malcolm set his jaw and blinked several times, tightening his fists and wishing he'd saved more than two dollars. He heard children playing by the creek and picked up his bag of flutes. Time to swallow his own disappointment and pass them out to those who needed encouragement.

Eight children swarmed him when he reached the creek. Two knew exactly what to do and began piping immediately. The rest needed help to spread their fingers across the holes and a demonstration on how to play. Their excitement made Malcolm's sore heart lighten.

One boy attended Ewan's class and tried to teach them how to play the school's signature tune, "Joy to the World." Malcolm sat on a rock watching until his sister Kate hustled up.

"What are you doing? Get up there. Her pie is nearly the last one to be auctioned."

"Who's pie? I only wanted Sally's."

"Exactly. Sally's pie is in a white cloth with a sunflower on top."

"I thought she made a cherry pie with a gingham ribbon."

Kate laughed. "No. You should have seen Josiah's face when Lena took his arm. She made the cherry pie, not Sally."

Malcolm ran back to the church, just as Mr. Finch raised his gavel on two bits.

"A silver dollar," Malcolm shouted.

Josiah glowered at him, Sally stood tall and smiled, and Mr. Finch brought down the gavel. "Eight bits. You've won yourself a wild blackberry pie, Mr. MacDougall."

Behind him, Ewan pretended to faint in relief.

Sally's rosy face beamed as she approached him. "Thank you for not letting me be embarrassed," she whispered. "Old Man Reynolds was the only bidder."

Malcolm looked to where the crippled farmer slumped against a cottonwood tree. "Let's share a piece with him."

So giddy at winning the pie, Malcolm gave half of it to the eighty-year-old bachelor.

"Thank you, Malcolm," he said. "You've always been a generous young man."

They joined Lena and Josiah at a table. His teeth were red from the cherry juice, and he growled a greeting.

Lena cut him another piece, her face a wreath of happiness.

"Why did you buy all my bonnets?" Sally asked.

"Purely a business proposition. The Clarkesville haberdasher asked me to buy them. The Sterling fund makes money, and I'll turn a little profit selling them to him. He obviously expects to do the same. I told you, these bonnets can be a foot in the door for selling your creations in Clarkesville."

Sally picked up her wild blackberry pie pan. "How dare you?"

"What do you mean? I've marketed your creation. All sorts of women will want you to sew for them after this. These bonnets can be a good start to the business you said you wanted."

Sally put one fist on her hip and leaned toward him. "Are you going to put your 'profit' into the funds box?"

Josiah put up his hands. "I've already contributed plenty by buying them in the first place."

Malcolm stirred. He didn't like how she balanced the remains of his pie on her fingertips. "Let me take the rest of the pie. I haven't had a slice yet."

Joe, Anna, and their younger siblings burst into the area before the church, piping shrill whistles on their flutes. Several Fairhope children ran off to get their flutes, and before long "Joy to the World" rang in the square.

Kate stepped forward to shout over the noise. "The dance is about to start. Finish your pie!"

Malcolm lunged for his.

☙

"I didn't mean for it to slip like that." Sally stared at the blackberry mess in Josiah's lap.

He sputtered and shoved back his chair, nearly upending it. Lena ran for a cloth.

"I'm so sorry, Josiah," Sally began.

Malcolm's dog Sport lapped at the juice.

Malcolm slumped. "My pie."

"I would have given you everything you ever wanted," Josiah sputtered. "Beautiful silk clothing, a house, a buggy. With my business savvy and your creativity, we could have built your business together. But you never appreciated my efforts. Every time I tried to get close, Malcolm was there, worming his way into your affections. What type of man do you really want?"

She looked between them. Wild blackberry pie juice stained Josiah's once-pristine clothes.

Malcolm sat clean and neat, an empty plate waiting beside him for a slice of pie he'd never get. Which did she prefer, a quiet man with workman's hands, or a fine gentleman with clean fingernails? She saw Pa heading toward them.

"I appreciate the qualities both of you have," Sally said slowly. "You're both businessmen who care for those in need in your own ways. I realize you're offering me a beautiful life, Josiah, with plenty of fashionable hats, but I've decided I'm really a sunbonnet girl. There's no question in my mind."

Malcolm slowly lifted his head as understanding dawned, and his well-loved face split into a grin. Ewan's sweet fiddle began the Virginia Reel. Children ran among them piping their flutes; the dog lifted his now-purple muzzle to howl.

"Choose your partners," Ewan called from the church steps.

Malcolm rose and bowed. "A hard-working sunbonnet girl you are."

Sally curtseyed.

"May I have your hand?" He colored. "I mean, may I have this dance?"

She laughed, joy filling her soul, and she placed her hand in his. "The answer to both is yes."

He led Sally to the dance area and looked deep into her eyes. "I would like to work with and for you always. Will you marry me?"

Sally tilted her head. "You're not so tongue-tied now."

"No. Will you?"

"Yes."

Ewan's fiddle set their feet, and hearts, a dancing.

And not once did Sally's sunbonnet slip off her head.

About the Authors

Christian author Diana Lesire Brandmeyer writes historical and contemporary romances about women choosing to challenge their fears to become the strong women God intends. Author of *A Mind of Her Own, A Bride's Dilemma in Friendship, Tennessee* and *We're Not Blended We're Pureed, a Survivor's Guide to Blended Families.* Sign up for her newsletter and get free stuff. www.dianabrandmeyer.com

Bestselling author Margaret Brownley has penned more than forty historical novels and novellas. Her books have won numerous awards, including Readers' Choice Award of Excellence. She's a former *Romance Writers of American* RITA® finalist and has written for a TV soap. She is currently working on a new series. Not bad for someone who flunked eighth grade English. Just don't ask her to diagram a sentence. www.margaret-brownley.com

Amanda Cabot is the bestselling author of more than thirty novels and half a dozen novellas, including Jeremy and Esther's story, *The Christmas Star Bride*, and *Waiting for Spring*, which tells Madame Charlotte's story. Although she grew up in the East, a few years ago Amanda and her high school sweetheart husband fulfilled a lifelong dream and are now living in Cheyenne. In addition to writing, Amanda enjoys traveling and sharing parts of her adopted home with readers in her Wednesday in Wyoming blog. One of Amanda's greatest pleasures is hearing from readers, and so she invites you to find her online at www.amandacabot.com.

Mary Connealy writes romantic comedy with cowboys. She is a Carol Award winner, and a RITA®, Christy, and Inspirational Reader's Choice finalist. She is the bestselling author of the Wild at Heart series, Trouble in Texas series, Kincaid Bride series, Lassoed in Texas trilogy, Montana Marriages trilogy, Sophie's Daughters trilogy, and many other books. Mary is married to a Nebraska cattleman and has four grown daughters and a little bevy of spectacular grandchildren. Find Mary online at www.maryconnealy.com.

Susan Page Davis is the author of more than sixty Christian novels and novellas, which have sold more than 1.5 million copies. Her historical novels have won numerous awards, including the Carol Award, the Will Rogers Medallion for Western Fiction, and the Inspirational Readers' Choice Contest. She has also been a finalist in the More than Magic Contest and Willa Literary Awards. She lives in western Kentucky with her husband. She's the mother of six and grandmother of ten. Visit her website at: www.susanpagedavis.com.

Miralee Ferrell is an award-winning, bestselling author with eighteen books, as well as numerous articles, short stories, and novellas in print. She and her husband, Allen, live on eleven acres in Washington State. Miralee loves interacting with people, ministering at her church, (she is a certified Lay Counselor with the AACC), and riding her horse. Miralee speaks at various women's functions and has taught at writers' conferences. Since 2007, she's had eighteen books release, both in women's contemporary fiction and historical romance. Miralee recently started a newsletter, and you can sign up for it on her website/blog www.miraleeferrell.com.

CBA Bestselling author Pam Hillman was born and raised on a dairy farm in Mississippi and spent her teenage years perched on the seat of a tractor raking hay. In those days, her daddy couldn't afford two cab tractors with air conditioning and a radio, so Pam drove an Allis Chalmers 110. Even when her daddy asked her if she wanted to bale hay, she told him she didn't mind raking. Raking hay doesn't take much thought so Pam spent her time working on her tan and making up stories in her head. Now, that's the kind of life every girl should dream of. www.pamhillman.com

Maureen Lang writes stories inspired by a love of history and romance. An avid reader herself, she's figured out a way to write the stories she feels like reading. Maureen's inspirationals have earned various writing distinctions including the Inspirational Reader's Choice Contest, a HOLT Medallion, and the Selah Award, as well as being a finalist for the RITA®, Christy, and Carol Awards. In addition to investigating various eras in history (such as Victorian England, First World War, and America's Gilded Age), Maureen loves taking research trips to get a feel for the settings of her novels. She lives in the Chicago area with her family and has been blessed to be the primary caregiver to her adult disabled son.

Amy Lillard loves nothing more than a good book. Except for her family. . .and maybe homemade tacos. . .and nail polish. But reading and writing are definitely high on the list. Born and bred in Mississippi, Amy is a transplanted Southern Belle who now lives in Oklahoma with her deputy husband, their genius son, three spoiled cats, and one very lazy beagle. When she's not creating quirky characters and happy endings, she's chauffeuring her prodigy to guitar lessons, orchestra concerts, and baseball practice. She has a variety of hobbies, but her favorite is whatever gets her out of housework. An award-winning author, Amy is a member of RWA and ACFW. She loves to hear from readers. You can find her on Facebook, Instagram, Google+, Twitter, Goodreads, and Pinterest. For links to the various sites, check her website: www.amylillardbooks.com.

Bestselling author Vickie McDonough grew up wanting to marry a rancher, but instead married a computer geek who is scared of horses. She now lives out her dreams in her fictional stories about ranchers, cowboys, lawmen, and others living in the Old West. Vickie is the award-winning author of more than forty published books and novellas. Her novels include the fun and feisty Texas Boardinghouse Brides series and the Land Rush Dreams series. Vickie has been married forty-one years to Robert. They have four grown sons, one of whom is married, and a precocious ten-year-old granddaughter. When she's not writing, Vickie enjoys reading, antiquing, watching movies, and traveling. To learn more about Vickie's books or to sign up for her newsletter, visit her website: www.vickiemcdonough.com

Multi-published author Davalynn Spencer writes inspirational Western romance complete with rugged cowboys, their challenges, and their loves. She is the 2015 recipient of the Will Rogers Gold Medallion for Western Inspirational Fiction, second place winner in the 2014 Inspirational Reader's Choice Award, and a 2014 finalist for the Holt Medallion and Selah Awards. As a former rodeo-market and newspaper reporter, she has won several journalistic awards and has over 100 articles, interviews, and devotionals published in national periodicals. She teaches Creative Writing at Pueblo Community College and pens a popular slice-of-life column for a mid-size daily newspaper. Davalynn makes her home on Colorado's Front Range with a Queensland heeler named Blue and two mouse detectors, Annie and Oakley. Connect with her online at: www.davalynnspencer.com

Michelle Ule is a musician, historian, and Bible study leader who lives in Northern California. She's the author of six published works, including *The Sunbonnet Bride*'s prequel, *The Yuletide Bride*. Michelle's next project is a biography of Mrs. Oswald Chambers due out in fall 2017. You can learn more about her at www.michelleule.com